SKELMERSDALE

D1492021

THE HILL OF DOVES

The Hill of Doves is an historical novel set in the Transvaal during the war of 1880. Its central character is Lena du Toit, whose marriage to Dirk van der Berg is the closing scene of the book. It is a sequel to *Watch for the Dawn*.

This is an extrovert, picturesque novel — packed full of action and colourful people with a good deal of the South African background painted in vivid detail. It has an exhilarating sense of freshness and adventure about it, and captures admirably the excitement in the minds of the people and the broad horizons that they found before their eyes.

The
Hill of Doves

STUART CLOETE

CEDRIC CHIVERS LTD
PORTWAY
BATH

First published 1942
by
William Collins Sons & Company Ltd
This edition published
by
Cedric Chivers Ltd
by arrangement with the copyright holder
at the request of
The London & Home Counties Branch
of
The Library Association
1972

SBN 85594 712 8

Printed in Great Britain by
Redwood Press Limited, Trowbridge, Wiltshire
Bound by Cedric Chivers Ltd, Bath

CONTENTS

5

CONTENTS

THE HILL OF DOVES

CHAPTER I

THE CANDLE

I

LENA's heart was beating fast. It was like a bird in her breast. It was hard to breathe quietly. She wondered if all girls felt like this. Dirk was sitting opposite to her. The candle on the table between them made a little circle of light that held them enclosed. We are in the light, she thought, everything else is dark. Outside in the kraal a cow lowed for her calf. She let her mind drift on the sound, following it out into the night. The calf answered. The cow lowed again. It went on: cow, calf, cow, calf. A draught ruffled the flame of the candle and the shadows of the horns nailed to the wall swung to and fro; the barrels of the guns that hung by their slings twinkled. Then the flame burnt steadily again. It was yellow on the outside, bluish in the middle, but there was no colour round the wick. It stuck up, black out of the melted grease, surrounded by nothing. It was funny that there should be nothing in the middle. That was where it should have been brightest. Suddenly it was very still: the cow and the calf had stopped calling to each other.

It was a wonderful silence. Lena concentrated on the empty space in the middle of the candle flame. Soon, when Dirk proposed, they would get married. They would have a home of their own and kraals full of their own beasts. He had already spoken of it, but not directly. He was still making up his mind. Sometimes, a man came courting a girl, coming once a week for many months, and then never came again. But Dirk was not like that. Their minds were made up. It was just that he did not know what to say. It was harder for a man. He had to make a speech of some kind. All a woman need do was to say yes to what he said. The fact that she was there at all showed her willing, and all she could do was to choose longer and longer candles, if they could be found, and wear her best clothes. She was always uncomfortable in her best clothes. And it seemed strange to be wearing a silk dress on a weekday even if it was getting small for her and would soon have to be discarded. She moved her feet uneasily. She had stockings on. She hated them, but one could not wear one's Sunday clothes without stockings.

It was a long time since Dirk had spoken: or had moved. The last time had been to get up and go to the dresser for a pinch of salt to put round the wick of the candle to make it burn longer. When it burnt out, he would go. That was the custom and it was right that he should go then, but to-night

9

he was going to speak. Something told her that he would speak to-night. She did not want him to stay after the candle had gone out. That would be wrong. All she wanted was for the candle to go on burning for ever : for it to go on holding them in the narrow circle of its light. She thought of making Dirk more coffee, but that would mean leaving him and going into the kitchen. She wanted never to leave him. He was wonderful to her. Ja, she thought, Dirk is wonderful because I love him.

She clasped her hands tighter on her lap and stared at the second button of his dark-blue coat. It was strained, pulling on the threads that held it. It should be moved forward nearer to the buttonhole. One day she would be able to do it for him. It was his best coat. She wondered if he was comfortable. He looked very hot and the coat was tight across his chest. We are both still growing, she thought. A man went on growing till he was thirty years of age. At least it was said that men did not attain their full strength till then.

The calf was crying again now from the calf-hok. It was bawling plaintively, like a baby. Lena felt Dirk's eyes on her face, but she did not dare look up. If her eyes met his, he would look down at her bodice. She did not want him to do that now, it made her feel funny, almost sick; but sometimes she did it on purpose so as to make him look down, and then, when she was sure it was safe, she could examine his face. It was a fine face, she thought, wide and flat with a small golden beard like a frill running round it. He wore no moustache.

The dog lying by the door got up and came over to her, putting his head on her knee. Then he left her and went to Dirk. She saw his arm moving as he pulled the dog's ears. She played with the edge of the tablecloth, feeling the crocheted pattern with the tips of her fingers. The little balls fastened to the fringe moved against her hand. She began to count them, one, two, three . . . she could count up to ten without moving her arm. She counted up to ten again. It seemed important to be able to do this. The candle was burning down. No matter what one did, the candles always burnt down.

She planned a new dress in her mind. This one was too tight. It was getting much too small. She wondered if she would have dared to wear it if it had not been. A Sunday dress belonged to Sunday—belonged to God. But Dirk liked it. Next time she went into the dorp, she would get the material. It was two years since she had had a new best dress. To-morrow she would talk to Grandmother about it. Yes, first thing in the morning she would speak to her.

She heard the back door open. That was Oupa going out. He was very old and often went out in the night. She wondered if he was all right. He was like a child to her. He was a very good old man. But he got angry if you said that. " Magtig, Lena," he would say, " I am only good because I am old. When you are old you have to be good, but when I was young, I was not good. Nee, I was bad. Very bad." It was hard to think of Oupa being bad and harder still to think of him as young; as young as Dirk, for instance. He had had four wives, and got them muddled sometimes. But usually he was not muddled at all and his mind was very clear.

Dirk moved his chair. "I am worried," he said.

Lena waited. Why was he worried? What was the matter?

"There will be trouble soon," he said. "It cannot go on as it is. You will see that it cannot, and when are we going to have peace in this land?"

"What is it, Dirk?" she asked. "Not the English?"

"Yes, the English," he said. "Do you think we will go on like this? What has happened to Shepstone's promises? Where is our independence? Three years ago those promises were made and not one kept." He leant forward. "I come night after night to court you, Lena. We both know what is in our hearts, but I want peace. I want a home-place and a farm. If there is war, I must go, and my father must go. We must leave my mother and the baby and Boetie, who is blind. And how much will we have left when we get back? Who can tell in a war? There will be stealing. Our horses and goats and cattle may be run off. I may come back and have nothing. Yet it must come, Lena. We must make an end. Three times we have run from them. Three times have they come after us. Now there is no place to go and we must fight."

Lena had never heard Dirk say so much at one time before. He was a silent young man resembling Groot Dirk, his father, after whom he had been named.

He banged the table. "Next month there is to be a big meeting at Paardekraal. All the world will be there, and we are going armed. We are tired," he said. "We want to live in peace, but we are going to have to fight. Before God, my heart, I think we are going to have to fight before we get our freedom."

He pushed back his chair and came to her side. She had never seen him so moved. Without warning he put his arm round her and swept her up to him, lifting her from the ground, with his forearm against her back. He was kissing her. Murmuring in her ear . . . My heart . . . My love. She heard his words above the hammering of the blood in her ears. He loves me . . . he is telling me he loves me. She repeated each thing he said to her to herself. My love—my heart. They were going to get married as soon as things were settled . . . after the meeting it would be known.

It had taken the threat of war to break through his silence. Or was it the threat that had made him silent? Had the uncertainty of the future, and his fear of it, prevented him from speaking sooner? But nothing mattered now. He loved her. There would be no war. She was sure there would not. It was just one of those things men spoke of. When he saw that her people were serious, Lanyon would agree to their demands. They asked no more than had been promised. Dirk still held her. He still kissed her mouth, her eyes, her hair, his lips moved over her face and neck. She felt as if she would fall to pieces in his arms, as if she would flow out of them like water. If he had not held her, she would have fallen. There was no strength in her legs. She felt for the chair behind her and sat down. Dirk towered above her. The candle was still burning, but it was low, a guttering stump with ribbons of melted fat along its side. When I was little, she thought, I used to play with the fat on the edge of a candle, making it into little balls and figures . . . pinching out the arms and legs. They were always black with finger dirt; even if one's hands were clean, the figures were dirty. They were dirty, too, if one made them of bread, so it could not be the fat. But why should she be thinking of these things now? Dirk bent over her. She felt his hand on her hair and neck. It rested for a moment on her left breast, he had passed his arm under hers . . . and then he was gone. The candle burnt up suddenly, flickering in the little breeze that came in between the shutters. The familiar things—the big brass-bound Bible on the dresser, the tinware, the guns, the horns, the table and the chairs—all seemed different. Each thing seemed to speak of its past; to represent something other than what it was. All were links with the past : the past huntings, fightings, and journeyings of her people.

As she undressed, she kept thinking of Dirk and what he had said. She tried to remember his words, but though he had said so little she could not. Not the exact words. He had called her his love, his heart, but which had he said first? And what had she said? Had she spoken at all, did he understand what was in her heart? It was not that it had been over-sudden, but that, expected as it had been, she had felt herself unable to speak her mind. All I could do, she thought, was to let him kiss me, and to kiss him back. She had thought that it would be different—better, once things between them were really settled. But it was worse. There was none of the ease she had expected, none of the certainty. There was only an added anxiety. She could not get comfortable on the bed. Her body no longer seemed to fit her skin. It was like her best dress, too large for it. He said they would be married when things were more settled. But when would they be more settled? Politics, which had been something apart and very distant from her, were now near.

Lena had never before understood her grandmother's bitterness against the English or seen how public matters could affect your own life. Now everything depended on politics. If there was war, Dirk would go. He might get hurt, killed. She thought of Tanta Johanna, Dirk's mother; of Klein Johanna, his baby sister; of blind Boetie, his brother. They were her cousins. Tanta Johanna was her father's sister.

She must get a new dress at once now, and perhaps some shoes. She had never had shoes from the store. Her father had made her shoes when she was little and since his death Oupa made them. It would be wonderful to have real shoes from the winkel. She wondered when Dirk would be back. He had not said when he would come. She wanted him to come terribly, so that she could just be with him. She was so afraid alone. I will always be alone now, she thought, unless he is with me, no matter how many people there are about. Her mind went back to the dress she wanted and then the cocks began to crow. First one and then another. The kraaled beasts were restless. She separated each sound in her mind . . . the low roar of the bull, the lowing of the cows and calves, the bleating of the sheep and goats. Soon she would get up, and after they had eaten she would talk to her grandmother. Generally, she was afraid of her, but Oupa would help her. He would be on her side and, when he wanted it, her great-grandfather got his way.

Anna was lighting the fire in the kitchen. Lena thought of all the mornings that she had got up in this room. Outside there was a heavy dew on the grass. She wanted to walk in it with bare feet while she had the world to herself.

She opened the door quietly. It was wonderful to be alone in the cool of the morning with the silver dew on her feet. Looking back from the orchard gate she saw her spoor, green on the kweekgras that surrounded the house. The orchard wall was backed by a thick hedge of kaalblad, whose big leaves were like flat, dull-green hands. Some of the leaves had yellow flowers on their edges, and by the gate, from a leaf on one side to a leaf on the other, a spider had spun its web. The whole of its silken wheel was as thick as string with moisture and jewelled at each joint with drops of shining dew. To go into the orchard she would have to break it. It was too beautiful to break.

The smell of coffee came from the house. She saw Oupa on the stoep with a beaker in his hand. His servant Reuter was beside him holding the pot waiting to refill the cup. She went back stepping carefully in her own spoor. The world was fresh and clean. Everything was going to come right. There would be no war. There could be no war.

Old Philippus Jacobus looked at the sky first. He saw Lena near the orchard gate, but it was the sky that interested him. The sky was a man's business. When you were old and had seen a great number of skies, you could read it like a book. Seeing the words that clouds spelt out by day and reading the pattern of the stars by night. There would be no rain to-day. There would be none till the moon changed, but it was no use explaining these things to the young. The moon, as any but a fool could see, was like a cup. There could only be rain when the cup turned over and began to empty itself, and then only if it had been full at the time of the change. But like most simple and logical explanations, few were ready to accept it. Still there was this advantage, even in their refusal, for he knew when it would rain and they did not, which gave him a superiority over them.

He took a sip of coffee. No doubt Dirk had spoken last night. That was why Lena was out there. She was puzzled, poor child. She was like a young mare that first feels a riem on her neck. And from now till the day she got married, they would have a fine time with her. She would be as sweet as honey. She would forget everything and sit in a dream. She would be suddenly bad-tempered, snapping and biting at every one near her. But Dirk was a good boy, inclined to argue with those older and wiser than himself, yet one who would make her a good husband, and the sooner he was her husband the better it would be for them all. If it went on long, there would be no comfort in the home for anybody. A girl being courted was one thing, but a girl betrothed and all but married was another.

He got out his pipe. He would be glad to see her married. It would round off his life very neatly, and it was not every one who lived to see his great-great-grandchildren born. He thought of the birth of his eldest son. That had been over seventy years ago. Before God, Martinus had been dead twenty years and he still lived.

Lena came up to him.

" Good-morning, Oupa," she said.

" Good-morning, my heart."

He took his pipe out of his mouth and stared at the bowl. It was burning well. He looked at the sky again. " There will be no rain till the moon changes," he said.

What did it matter if there was rain or no rain? Lena thought. Of course, they needed rain. One always needed rain, but it must be strange to be old and spend hours, whole days, looking at the skies and waiting. Oupa had looked so much that he was always right. He always knew when it would rain.

" It is two years since I had a new dress, Oupa," she said. She made a pattern on the smeared clay floor of the stoep with her toe. First she drew a little circle and then put a line through it. Then she made another little circle. Because her feet were wet from the dew the red dust she raised stuck to her big toe. She watched it accumulating with interest.

" Two years, is it, Lena? That was the blue dress with white stripes?"

" Yes, Oupa. And I have grown out of it."

" Then you must have grown in the night, Lena, for last evening you had it on."

She felt herself getting hot. " You see too much, Oupa," she said. Then she laughed. " Perhaps things have changed since last night. Perhaps you are right. Perhaps I have grown." She stamped her foot suddenly. " And I am going to have a new frock. I am, no matter what any one says. I am." Her mouth began to quiver. Philippus put his hand on her wrist, but she flung it off and ran into the house.

So it had begun. It had begun even sooner than he had thought it would. He was always right about everything. It would not rain till the new moon,

and Lena was in a state. The day was warming up nicely. He closed his
eyes and lay back in his chair.

2

"A dress, Lena?" Tanta Katarina looked up from her sewing. She
always had some work on her knee that she sewed with small tight stitches.
She moved the glasses on her nose and looked down again. Lena watched
her put the needle into the black linen. She saw its point disappear,
reappear, and disappear again. Then her grandmother pushed it home
and pulled it out. The thread made a little hissing noise as it followed the
needle. Tanta Katarina was making another kappie. While she waited,
Lena wondered how many kappies she had seen her grandmother
make . . . and would she let her have the dress? Perhaps she should have
led up to it. She had thought of several ways of asking and then had forgotten them all. But now that she was going to marry Dirk, she was no
longer much afraid.

"Yes, you can have it," her grandmother said suddenly. "Since you
are getting married, you must have a dress."

"And you are glad I am getting married, Ouma?" Lena knelt beside
her. "And how did you know?"

"Yes, Lena, I am glad. You are grown up now and should be married.
I was married when I was younger than you are . . . And how did I
know? By your face and by the fact that it has been expected by every one."

"When can I go, Ouma? When can I go and get it?"

"Next time you go to the dorp. That will be Wednesday."

"But that is nearly a week!" A week, now that she could have it,
seemed an endless time. A week before she got the material and then it
would still have to be made up. With her other work it would take a fortnight to make.

"Yes, it is nearly a week," Tanta Katarina said.

The needle began to move again. There was nothing more to be said.
Going to the dorp was a monthly occurrence and nothing would change
it. Anything that was really wanted could be waited for, her grandmother
said. It was good to have to wait for things; such waiting inculcated fore-
thought and thrift. And often the things you wanted, the things that at
the time you felt you could not do without, lost their appeal and were,
even after the lapse of a few days, no longer attractive.

And why were they no longer attractive? Would her grandmother never
know the truth? That while you waited, you thought and hoped; you
rubbed your desire in your mind till it had lost its bloom; you bruised it
till it became unrecognizable and then you hated it. Surely, now that she
was seventeen and going to be married, she should not have to wait. But

it was no good talking. You could not explain to Ouma that, as she was really going to get the dress, it was even harder to wait. Each day, each hour mattered. She had chosen the material long ago. That is, she had seen it in the store and thought : I should like to have a dress made of that stuff. It was a dark-bronze silk, shot with green, a lovely changeable taffeta that almost seemed alive. It was cool and slippery, and when you held it the green sprang out of it like the bright lights on the flank of a horse as it breathed. And at this moment, while she waited, someone might be buying it. Mr. Brenner had said there was only enough for one dress.

'In her mind she saw it made up. As soon as she got it, she would take it to Tanta Martha, who would help her cut it out. Tanta Martha was very good at cutting out, and all the time while she worked she would talk of the old times—she had wonderful stories—and tell her about illnesses and how to cure them. Those were things every good Boer wife should know— the history of her people and the use of the medicines which God had seen fit to let grow upon the veld. Then she would bring the dress home and sew it. She longed to be sewing it; tacking, basting, fitting, and finally sewing it permanently.

Outside the sun shone brilliantly, as it had shone for weeks. The sky was cloudless, a pale summer blue that threatened still further heat. Now there was no dew. It had gone long ago, and everything was colourless, black and white in the glare. Lena looked at the orchard. By now some- one was certain to have broken the web that had been so lovely this morning. Beyond the lines of fruit trees were the lands and then came the open veld of the farm. She was angry with her grandmother. She was angry with herself for being so impatient. But you were born like that, either patient or impatient, and she could not imagine life—not her life, at any rate—without this burning anxiety about everything. She wanted to do things, to know them, to feel and hear them.

Curiosity, another of her defects that she had tried to curb, was a different part of this same urgency. Ouma said she would get over it with age, but her great-grandfather, who was over ninety, had not got over it. She began to laugh. He said that he had never waited for anything—that it was stupid to wait. He questioned even the wisdom of Jacob's waiting for Rachel, saying he had never understood it. " If I had waited as long as that, Lena, I should only have had two or three wives," he had said. His arguments seemed good, too. Certainly as good as Ouma's. The Rachel Jacob had waited and worked seven years for could hardly have been as beautiful as the Rachel he had first seen at the well. Seven years was a long time. Seven years ago she had been a child of ten. In seven years, she thought, I shall be old. I shall be twenty-four. I shall be married with many children. Her grandmother had been angry at Oupa's blasphemy when he had called Jacob a fool for waiting so long, and the girl a fool too, to remain a maid so long, if she had, which he doubted, since nature in or

out of the Scriptures was bound to take its course. " At my age, I know,"
he had shouted.

No, patience was something you were born with, and she was like Oupa,
impatient, and would remain so even if she lived to be his age. One was
either urgent or not urgent. One either cared greatly for things and wanted
them at once—at once—or one did not.

That was why her great-grandfather and her grandmother did not get
on. The old man had no patience with her grandmother's patience. No
confidence in its unplacid acceptance. He said it was not real. If you were
patient, he said, then you should be really so and not sit with folded hands
while your heart burns up within you. And she felt he was right. Her
grandmother's acceptance was without resignation. It was, at best, an
angry acceptance of the worst. A kind of armour against the ills of Providence; almost a despair that killed each hope stillborn rather than suffer
disappointment.

Lena thought of the dress again. Then she made herself stop thinking
of it. What was the good? It would be better to put it out of her head
for a week. She thought of Dirk, but thinking of him brought the dress
back to her mind. She would make it secretly and surprise him. When
it was all done, she would come into the room wearing it. She thought of
the stiff silk rustling against her knees. She must be careful making it and
see that no snippets of material were left on the floor when he came. If
there were, he would see them and ask what they were. He was like that.
He would notice a single tiny piece of stuff on the floor, and yet might
easily not see that she was wearing something new if she sat in her accustomed place and did not call his attention to it. But he would hear her
walking in it. That was why she wanted to come in like that, quickly, from
her room the first time she wore it for him.

She suddenly felt nervous. The dress, Dirk, marriage, the war. Oh,
there could not be a war, not now. Or it might be that a storm was coming.
There was thunder in the air, and that always made her nervous. If only
there would be a good rain, I should feel better, she thought. Then she
hoped there would not be rain. If it rained hard, the roads would be bad
and she would have to put four horses into the Cape cart. This would
mean another argument. Her grandmother would suggest more waiting.
But it would not rain. Oupa had said it would not, and if it did, there was
plenty of time for the spruits to run down and the roads to dry. Plenty of
time. Had the days never mattered to Ouma? Had she never counted
them? Had she never wondered when her husband was coming? Leaving
her work every few minutes to stare out of the window? Or even going
out of the house so that she could see farther? It was so hard to tell what
went on in the minds of older people; to tell what they thought.

Lena looked at the oaks near the stable. It was hard to think of those
trees being small, of their being planted, of the whole farm having once

been bare veld; of her grandfather's coming here and making the place, laying it down stone by stone, tree by tree; of his casting his mind forward into the future and seeing everything as it now was. Hard to think of his being here all those years in the intervals between his wars and hunting trips and explorations, of his watching his children grow, and their children's children, while he stood still like an old rock and let the flood of his paternity rush by him.

And with all this, with all these matings and births that he had witnessed, and deaths that he had survived, he remained sharp. Undulled by time, he was worn smoother by it. Worn thinner and thinner like an old knife that is worn, but still the sharpest of them all : the old one that is called for when the new ones have failed. Yes, she thought, that is what he is like; an old worn knife. And as for his not remembering things, she knew that he could if he wished. It was just that he often did not wish to remember and also that his forgetfulness annoyed her grandmother. Oupa was as mischievous as a baby. He liked to be bad and see them all impotent to correct him. He said it was good to be so old and to know so much, for then you need know nothing and could have many jokes that no one understood except yourself.

A peahen screamed. A peacock flying down from the wall of the kraal landed in front of the house and spread his fan. Enormous, metallic green and blue, it blotted the gate of the orchard from her sight. His wings were stiff. He held them firmly down, dragging them so that their tips rustled against the ground. How stupid people were to speak of a peacock's tail! As he turned, you could see clearly that the long feathers came from his back and that under them was his real tail of short strong feathers that supported them.

The peacocks—there were a lot of them—had been obtained by her great-grandfather in the early days. They were one of the things that endeared him to her. She never heard of another farm with peacocks, but they fitted into Mooiplaas. Perhaps she only felt they fitted because they had been there long before she was born, or even before her mother was born. She remembered their cries, heralding rain or giving notice of a stranger's arrival, when she was a baby in her cradle. They were part of the farm, part of her life, of the setting into which she had been born, like the fruit trees, the weeping willows by the dam, the oaks, the blue gums, the white poplars along the spruit, the sheep and goats, the cattle and the horses; like the dogs, the chickens, the Muscovy ducks, the geese, and the turkeys; like the wagon that always stood in the shade of the mulberry trees; like the forge with its big leather bellows and sacks of wood charcoal; like the sheds and the kraals. It even seemed to her sometimes that the peacocks made Mooiplaas one, made it what it was, by the thread of brilliance they wove through it. You never knew where you would find one, crouching in the shade of a bush, sunning his wing on an outstretched leg, exposing the glories of his plumage from a dunghill, or crying wildly, eerily, into the coming storm from his high perch in the trees.

But that they should belong to old Oom Philippus never ceased to astonish every one. It was still a subject of conversation. And yet was it so strange? Was it not like a vein of gold running through a bult of quartz? And was it not this streak—the peacock streak in him, she called it—that had led him North and sent him trading and adventuring in the old days and that later had sent his son, her grandfather, up to the same region? It was there that he had met her grandmother, Tanta Katarina, the daughter of Rudolf de Wet and Maria Bezuidenhout. And his blood had flowed on through her father Pretorious into her own veins. The blood of all these people was in her, but most of all, it seemed to her, that of the old man. The blood that loved adventure, that cared for things of beauty like peacocks with spread tails and for sights and sounds and smells; things that though they were without practical value remained, for such as her, the very core of life. She had more in common with her great-grandfather than with her brothers, Stoffel and Louis. The hot strain of his blood seemed to have passed on to her alone, and because they shared it, she loved to talk with him.

Talk was perhaps the wrong word; listen to him was better, for when he was in the mood he would, for hours together, tell her of the past; tell her of the history of their people and how it had been made; tell her of Louis Tricharts; of Hendrick van der Berg, her own ancestor, the famous voortrekker, whose name and deeds had been deleted from the records on account of his immorality and looseness; of Piet Retief, of Coenraad Buys, of Christiaan van Ek, and the others he had known. Best of all, she liked to hear of Sannie van Reenan, who had been killed fighting to the last at her lover's side. The Lily of the North she had come to be called, her beauty a legend, and her daughter, Jacoba, was Lena's own mother.

That was the strangest thing of all. That she should have two grandmothers as diversified as Tanta Katarina and Sannie van Reenan. It was all long ago. It was forty-four years since the Great Trek, and things had changed. Men had changed, too, for the worse, Oupa said, and big things could not happen now, in eighteen-seventy-nine, for in this modern world there could be no exploit or excitement. Everything was circumscribed and with the world so full and all land taken up there was hardly room to move. But somehow, because her great-grandfather had seen so much and because her grandmother had, though she spoke of it seldom, more seldom and more bitterly than he, those old events they spoke of seemed near and more easily understood than the present trouble and unrest. The old stories were clear to her. What could be clearer than the old Kaffir wars, or the love of a man like Swart Piet for her grandmother?

The peacock closed his tail and came up to the stoep. His long snakelike neck was extended; the little plume-tipped feathers on his crest, set rather sideways, nodded at her as he stood looking from side to side. He wanted bread, but she was in no mood to fetch it for him. He had made her think of the new dress again. Soon it would be to-morrow. And then there would be more to-morrows till at last Wednesday came and she could go and get it. So much seemed to depend on the dress. It was part of her love for Dirk, part of the future, almost a guarantee against war and disaster.

It was all so new. Her love, her fears. The peacock had spread his tail again. The material for the dress was shot with colour, it was as iridescent as the peacock's tail, and the eyes that ended each plume were like the candle that had burnt last night holding them enclosed in its light. The eye of a candle, the eye of a peacock's tail, the miracle of a dew-jewelled spider's web, were all a part of her love, of the new world that had just begun.

CHAPTER II

NO SALE TO-DAY

I

As THE CART moved off, Lena memorized the things she had to get. Tobacco for Oupa, some black linen thread and needles, a bag of Boer meal, and a gallon of paraffin for her grandmother; and she was not to put the paraffin near the Boer meal. I'll put it between my feet, she thought, and the meal at the back. Five pounds of six-inch nails—they went seventeen to the pound, and she was to be sure she counted them—for Stoffel. Also a new ploughshare, some farm oil, and two hundred rounds of ammunition for his Mauser. And her grandmother said she was to tell Mr. Brenner that next month there would be ten pounds of goose-down for him. The geese were plucked every two months or so and always looked half naked.

They were all plucked but one, an old gander, and that one Oupa would not have touched. He was, he said, an historical goose. No one knew how old he was, but very old, fifty, perhaps. He had been brought up from the Colony to Natal in thirty-six and had survived the massacre of Uy's laager by the Zulus. Someone had picked him up afterwards swimming casually in a pan, his white breast streaked with bloodstained water. He was as wise as an old man and a terror to every dog and child that came on to the farm. Lena had been frightened of him for years. Only two things did that old gander love : his wife, a grey-and-white goose, whose wing feathers grew in reversed, and a red roan mare that was almost white with age. These three, the old mare and the two old geese, grazed continually side by side.

The horses trotted slowly down the road. They would be on their own farm for half an hour. After that, when they got on to the main road, it would be a full hour before she could see the blue gums of the dorp. Lena was excited. She was going to get her dress and shoes. The day had come at last, as all days did, nagmaals, festivals, Christmas, and birthdays that one thought would never come. But she was always excited at going to the dorp. She loved, as she drove along the road, to think of the people she would see and talk to. There were no young people near, only her brothers and Dirk and little Boetie.

She often wondered what other girls did and thought about. Were their thoughts the same as hers? At nagmaal, her only chance of meeting them, except when she went shopping like this, they were generally too busy to talk properly. Besides, one could not talk openly to girls one saw so

21

seldom. It might be that all her thoughts were foolishness. Thoughts were so strange. One did not know where they came from. It might be that when she was married and older, she would laugh at the ideas that she had now; at the hopes, fears, and aspirations that filled her life : at the conclusions that, without logic or experience, she had reached through the daily reading of the Bible, the conversations she had listened to, the cryptic utterances of her great-grandfather and the gentle words of her dead father. Her mother she had never really known. She remembered her as beautiful, though less so, it was said, than Sannie, by those who had known them both.

Sometimes Stoffel went in to do the shopping, but he went seldom and preferred to ride. On horseback, his club foot was less apparent; at least, if it was not, his deformity was counterbalanced by his horsemanship. In a cart he felt that people considered him a cripple : on a horse he was a man.

And sometimes her grandmother went in, dressed in stiff black cloth with a black silk apron and black linen, pleated kappie. Louis often went to the dorp, but refused to do any shopping, so it was usually left to her. She liked to do it and her grandmother said she was easily spared : pretty but useless, she called her. Whether she was pretty or not Lena did not know. Certainly men stared after her and pulled up their horses for a word with her. But Ouma said this meant nothing, only that they detected a latent looseness in her. Looseness was also strange to Lena. She thought, as she drove, of the loose women she knew about, Delilah, Jezebel, Mary Magdalene, and could find no common ground between them and herself. Yet her grandmother must be right. She was right in all things.

Lena stared ahead. Soon she would see the trees. She was always glad to see the gums : first, as a blue-green mass at the bottom of the hill, and then slowly, as she dropped towards them, they took shape, towering over the houses, their trunks white and grey, festooned with ribbons of hanging bark. One tree, the third on the right as you came in, had a branch that could be reached from the cart. Every time she passed it she plucked some leaves and rubbed them in her hand to smell. Eucalyptus oil was made from trees like these, she had been told, and she loved them. They were so straight and beautiful, calm with their years of life in the village.

Brennersdorp was not like Canaan and so many other places. Nothing had ever happened here. There was no tragic history of massacre, or laagered camps. From its small beginnings it had been peaceful, a place embowered by trees : the wild bush trees . . . thorns, karree booms, willows and wild olives, and then later by the wattles and blue gums and orchards of peach and apricot that men had planted in the rich red soil. When Lena had been a little girl, held between her father's knees to keep her from falling out of the cart, he had always picked gum leaves for her, crushed them, and put them into her hand. She remembered how she had wondered if she would ever be tall enough to stand holding on to the dashboard rail as he did, and grasp them for herself. When I can do that, she had thought, I shall be grown up. But now that she could do it, she did not feel at all grown up. She felt, as she had always felt, very small and helpless.

Lena always thought of her father on this road. He had died ten winters ago, in July, when the wattle was out. At that time whole patches of the veld were a blaze of yellow, sweet-scented bloom. She had brought in an armful of branches, the yellow balls nodding and covering her with pollen, for him just before he died. But her grandmother had not let her go in to him, and afterwards, when they buried him in the koppie behind the house, she had got more wattle to put on his grave. How he had loved flowers and all living things!

She let the horses trot with slack reins. They knew the road as well as she. The blue gums always reminded her of her father. He had been like them, big, straight, and untroubled. She had never seen him angry. She wondered if anger was necessary for success. Certainly since his death the farm had prospered. Stoffel and her grandmother were often angry and the servants worked for them as they had never worked for her father. Only her other brother, Louis, never got angry. He was big and quiet.

But the farm was different now, or perhaps it was because she was older that it seemed less benign; that the servants talked less and hardly ever sang; that the horses were thinner and the geese perpetually mangy from their pluckings. Her father had refused to have them plucked alive. He said it was shameful and indecent and made them look ugly as well. Nor would he allow the finks that ate so much fruit in the orchard to be destroyed. He had liked to see them flying. Now there were no more finks. There was no doubt that her father had not been a good farmer, but he had been a good man and she missed him. There was no one who could explain things as he had done or show her the reasons for things. It was he who had shown her how even in the smallest of His creatures the Almighty manifested the perfection of His creation.

There was the dorp. This was the last hill. The pole went down on the neck-straps snapping against the bar. She sat back and it rose again. The horses trotted easily, their unshod hoofs muffled in the dust. She was near the trees now. She pulled into the side and stopped the horses. She could not think of herself passing the trees without stopping for some leaves. She had always done it.

The first house belonged to Meneer Erasmus. He was a wheelwright and a blacksmith. There were always carts and wagons outside his house jacked up on packing cases and logs, and great wheels leaning against the wall. She heard his hammer beating against iron in the forge.

As she passed, he came out. "How goes it, Lena, and what is the news?"

"There is no news, meneer."

"You will hear some soon enough," he said: "news which keeps me working safely at home."

He waved his hand and she went on, wondering what he meant. He
always came out when any one passed. Oom Jan was a great one for news.
He knew all that went on and what he did not know he invented. After
Erasmus's house there was some waste land, covered with bush, that had
not been built on, though it was said that the English were going to put
a church there. Then came more houses, the Marais, the Bothas, the van
Neikerks—some with trees and gardens in front of them, others built right
up to the road. Then came Hutting's Hotel where the coach stopped. It
was on the corner of the outspan place. The store was on the opposite
corner.

The town seemed to be empty, but there was a crowd in the distance at
the far end of the outspan near the slaughter poles. She wondered what
they were doing. Selling something, perhaps, some oxen or a horse; or
it might be a meeting of some kind. There had been so many meetings
lately. She laughed at how angry Jan Erasmus would be if it was anything
important. It must have been sudden or he would have heard of it. Or
had he heard of it? Was it this that had kept him at home? She was
suddenly afraid.

2

After the bright light of the outer world the store was dark. It was like
going into a church. But the material was there, her eyes went to it at
once. No one had bought it, which seemed extraordinary to her, it was
so beautiful.

For years nothing had changed in Brenner's store. When things were
sold they were replaced exactly. Outside, on the stoep, were the single-
furrow American ploughs, a pile of yokes, trek gear, and three-legged
Kaffir pots of various sizes, chained together by their handles. Inside, at
the back, were the piled sacks of mealie meal. These were arranged like
bricks, headers and stretchers in alternate rows. First a double line, raised
on blocks of wood from the floor, going longways; then a line going cross-
ways; then another double line going longways again, till they reached the
cross-beams of the roof. There was no ceiling and the heat drove through
the corrugated iron turning the store into an oven. Here and there a sun-
beam, a thin blade of light, came through an old nail hole.

A long counter ran down the right-hand side of the store. Behind it were
shelves of goods, groceries in packets, bolts of material, bright blankets for
the Kaffir trade, and Boer meal, rice, and sugar in sacks. On the other
side were tools of all kinds : picks, shovels, hoes, axes, cross-cut saws, nails
and screws in boxes, ploughshares, bolts; and on the floor, three ten-gallon
barrels with little brass cocks, full of paraffin, turpentine, and creosote.
Over the whole hung a smell of foodstuffs—cheese, bacon—and of paint

and skins and offal from the butcher's shop behind the store, the animal smell of Kaffirs, and the smell of stale tobacco smoke. It had always been like this, enthralling and wonderful.

As a small girl it had been the sweets in the bottles that stood along the counter that Lena wanted. The green and pink ones, the orange and white acid drops, and the big bull's-eyes, striped black and white like zebras, that tasted of peppermint. Then it had been the toys, the dolls and little cups and saucers. Now it was the dress materials, the bright Indian silks, the muslins, ginghams, linens and cottons, and the bronze shot silk. It was still there. It had not been sold.

Lena stood with her hand on the counter, her eyes fixed on the brass yard measure let into it on the far side. It was shiny on the edge, its markings partly obliterated by countless measurings. The material for every dress she had ever had had been measured there and cut by the scissors that hung from a cord beside it. She wondered now why no one came; why there was no one in the shop : no Kaffirs staring and fingering, talking endlessly before they bought, no women with fat babies strapped to their backs. That was why it had seemed churchlike when she came in.

Lena went to the door and looked out. The far side of the outspan was even fuller than it had been and more people were going; men, women, and children moved quickly through the dust towards the crowd. She looked back into the store. The shopping could wait. It would have to, since there was no one to serve her. She must know what was happening. She must go and see. She suddenly felt ill. Perhaps the storm which had been brewing was about to break. Perhaps Dirk was right and the patience of the people exhausted. She began to run.

The heat of the day, the empty store, the dust, the people all moving in one direction, were ominous. She felt afraid. For weeks there had been talk of the mass meeting to be held at Paardekraal on December the eighteenth. This might have something to do with it : might be a prelude to it. She knew every argument; she had heard it discussed so often : the taxes, the impositions, the English excuse that they had only annexed the country because the Boers, despite the Sand River Convention, continued to raid slaves and trade them. As if the orphaned Kaffir children that were apprenticed could be called slaves! Would the English have troubled if gold had not been discovered in the Lydenburg? And every one knew that where the Boers went the English followed.

All her life Lena had heard these things spoken of—the murders of Slagtersnek, the Great Trek, and the other wrongs done to her people.

The crowd was growing. Someone seemed to be speaking : another injured burger speaking of their forfeited rights, their land, their heritage. Soon she would know what it was : nothing new, perhaps, but another straw blowing in the wind of Boer indignation. No single promise that Shepstone made had been kept. Once again the hand of the English was stretched out over them, its shadow darkening the land, and the country was tired of it, irked after years of freedom to find itself yoked once more.

Lena began to recognize people. All the townspeople were here and many from the country beyond. She saw Mr. Brenner. His coloured boy, Jacob, who no doubt had been left in charge of the store, was hiding behind him. She saw her cousin Frikkie van der Berg standing near Tanta Martha's cart; his father had been her mother's brother, but she saw him seldom. She saw the Nels with some of their ten children, the Bothas, Pierre de Wet, Hans Schoeman, Hendrik Marais, old Oom Albert Erasmus, the father of the blacksmith, who had just married Tanta Maria Stegman. He was eighty years of age and she was said to be seventy-six. They had had a hundred and forty direct descendants at their wedding. Everybody was here. The whole world was gathered round a wagon, pressing round it, sullen and angry. The anger and sweat of the people seemed to make it hotter.

Lena forced her way into the crowd. She felt men pushing against her. She knew they were men. She felt herself pressed into women. Someone trod on her foot. A child screamed and started others screaming. She was near now. Piet Bezuidenhout stood with his foot on the disselboom of a wagon staring down at the crowd that milled round him. It was quiet here, like the centre of a whirlpool.

Piet was a big man and towered over them. Taking his pipe from his mouth he spat, wiped his mouth with his hand, and said : " There will be no sale to-day . . . nee, kerels, there will be no sale."

The crowd took up his words : " There will be no sale . . . there will be no sale . . ."

What was it about? What did it mean? Why was every one so angry? What was going to be sold or not sold? And why was Groot Piet there?

3

Piet Bezuidenhout moved back and leaned against the big rear wheel of his wagon. The people made way for him, leaving a space of trampled ground between them.

It was strange to be here with his wagon on the outspan talking to his friends. It was the first time the wagon had ever moved without him. He ran his hand along the buck rail. It looked funny standing without trek-gear, unloaded, bare even of the jack that should hang from the hook on its side. A Boer's wagon was as much a part of him as his bed : more, for he slept in it, or near it, as often as he did in his house. Piet had come back from a visit and found it gone. " They have attached your wagon, Piet," his wife had said. " It is to be sold against the cost of the judgment and for taxes owing."

He had gone into the house for his gun, changed his saddle from one horse to another, and ridden into the dorp. That had been the day before yesterday. Yesterday he had sent messengers out and the answer was in his pocket. He patted his hip.

When he had got into the town, he had galloped across the outspan to his wagon. It had stood as it did now in the blazing sunshine, stark and bare over its own shadow : a big eighteen-foot wagon looking no larger than a child's toy in the middle of that bare space. His father had built it and they had dared to come and draw it away : dared to come and take it from his father's son. It had travelled thousands of miles. It had come up from the Great Fish River in the early days. It had carted stone for his house and beams and thatch. It had carted skins and wood. It had carried dead men and women. Children had been born in it. He lived in it while he hunted each year in the bushveld. His children had played under it. Before God, he had played in it himself as a child, cracking a small whip and calling to an imaginary span of oxen in a small, shrill voice. His wagon was more than property : it was a home on wheels.

He spat. The spittle landed at the feet of the sheriff who was here to see it sold. He was a small man and Piet was almost sorry for him. It was not his fault. He was only trying to do his duty, but he looked like a small dog surrounded by oxen. The oxen had their heads down and menaced him with their long horns. Yes, his people were like their own oxen, slow and strong : patient, but with a limit to their patience. They were getting ready to turn, to stop, they had come far enough.

One of the younger men jostled the sheriff.

" Leave him," Piet said. " It is not his fault. But listen, meneer "—he leant towards the sheriff—" I want to ask you something. How are you going to have a sale if there are no buyers ? "

" There will be buyers," the sheriff said. " I have posted notices and it is a good wagon."

" Are you telling me my wagon is good ? " Piet shouted. " Ja, magtig, it is good. It is the finest wagon in these parts. But where are the buyers ? Can you see one here ? Can you see any one who would buy Piet Bezuidenhout's wagon from under him ? "

A man took hold of the spokes of the back wheel and shook it.

" It is a fine strong wagon," he said.

" It is a strong wagon. I have loaded it with four tons before now," Piet said. " That was with a full span of sixteen, of course," he added.

" It would take sixteen good oxen to pull four tons," the man said.

" Well, my oxen are good," Piet said. " They are the best you can get. I bred them."

" Who built it ? " Hans Schoeman asked.

" My father built it," Piet said. " It came up from the Great Fish River in thirty-seven, and now "—he laughed—" they say it is for sale. By God, they seem to think a voortrekker's wagon can be sold on the open market to pay his son's taxes to the English."

Every one knew this. Every one knew Piet, and that his father had built the wagon. Hans had just asked his question in order to get things started. Lena understood the ways of her people : at the way they would listen to the oratory of any one. It was as if they knew their own slowness and used each other to whip up their indignation. She could feel it mounting like a tide all round her. Her fears deepened. Dick was right. Why had she not noticed it before. The men's faces were different. The women's breasts were rising and falling fast.

" We will pay no taxes!" Oom Erasmus shouted from the back of the crowd.

" I still do not see why you did not pay, Piet," Hans said. " It would have been less trouble and you have the money."

There it was again. Hans Schoeman giving Piet a new lead.

" I have the money, but why should I pay for what is my own? Did the English give me my farm? And someone has got to begin. Someone has got to start not paying taxes to the Uitlanders."

" That is good, Piet," someone said. " You are like your Uncle Frederik."

" Ja, I am like him. All Bezuidenhouts are like that. My family has never cared to pay taxes. My old Uncle Frederik died sooner than pay. Why should we pay? And to whom? And for what? Are our taxes to pay the expenses of Shepstone, the promise-breaker? Or of Landon, the soldier? No, I say. They have taken enough. This is the end. Is it our land, our country."

The sheriff pressed forward again.

" I have my orders," he said. " I will sell the wagon." He took out his watch. " In five minutes I will begin."

" Who is preventing you from selling my wagon?" Piet asked. " Has any one stopped you in the performance of your duty? Has Meneer Fourie? Has Mevrou Kleinhouse? Has Lena du Toit?" He looked at Lena. " Or Meneer van der Byl? Begin at once, I say, and see if you can sell it. But it is in my heart that wagon will stand here till it rots before you can sell it. There will be no buyers for my wagon while there are free burgers in the dorp."

" If it was my wagon, I would not let him sell it," Tanta Martha shouted. She laid the lash on her horses so that they sprang forward and nearly overthrew the sheriff. " Why did you not take my cart?" she asked. " I have paid no taxes to the English and I will never pay them. Nor to our own government either. Taxes are nonsense," she said. Her horses were plunging. " I will tell you why you did not take my cart," she said. " It is because you did not dare : because you are afraid of an old widow woman and only take from children. Magtig," she said, " Piet Bezuidenhout is a child that I have held naked on my knee. Do you think I will let you take a wagon from a child that I have held naked on my knee?"

The crowd laughed at Piet's red face.

"Take him naked on your knee now, Tanta Martha," someone cried. It was a good joke. Tanta Martha had no knees. When she sat she went straight down.

Piet ran his hand through his beard. "Tanta Martha," he said, "they took from me what they did not dare take from you, and they were right. It would be safer to take a barrel of dop from a wedding than a single mealie cob from you. And it is not every man who has sat naked on your lap. . . ." He stopped speaking and jumped on to the wagon-bed.

"They come!" he shouted. "Look, friends, they come!" He pointed to across the outspan. Lena turned. Every one turned. "For my uncle they came too late, but for me they come in time," Piet said.

"Who is coming?" the sheriff asked, trying to see over the crowd.

"Our folk, the burgers," Piet said. "I sent for them."

Lena climbed on to the wagon beside him. A cloud of dust was sweeping towards them. She could see horses and the glitter of rifle barrels. They were quite near now. She could distinguish the bearded faces of the men above the dust and the colours of the leading horses—reds, browns, bays, blacks, greys, roans, their manes and long tails flying. The men were shouting.

"Cronje is at their head!" Piet cried. "It is our Cronje!"

At the outskirts of the crowd the horse pulled up, drawn back in full gallop on to their haunches. The men's rifles swung into the air as they leaned back in their saddles. Lena was stifled by the dust they raised. For a moment she could see nothing, then it passed and all was clear : the men with their rifles in their hands, and the sweating, champing horses that plunged under them, fighting for their heads.

"This is rebellion," the sheriff said. "They have come armed."

"Ja, they are armed," Piet said. "They come mounted, with rifles in their hands. You can choose your own name for it."

Rebellion. . . . War . . . that word again. How determined they looked with their weapons, their rolled coats and blankets! The horses had head-collars on under their bridles and riems knotted about their necks or under their throats. There were bags of food and water-bottles tied to the saddles and some men wore two bandoliers across their breasts. They were ready. They could stay weeks or months in the field, equipped like this, living on the farms and shooting game.

Piet got off the wagon and went to take Piet Cronje's hand.

"You came in time, Oom Piet," he said. "There will be no sale to-day."

"No," Cronje said. Standing up in his stirrups, he shouted : "There will be no sale to-day, friends. Nee, vragtag, there will be no more sales of Boer property. It is over. We are in arms."

The Boers slipped from their saddles and stood leaning against their horses. Most began to smoke. Fourie came forward and with the tail of his coat wiped the chalked " For sale " from the wagon side. The sheriff slipped off. No one tried to stop him. A dark boy Lena did not know said he would go and get some oxen. One of the men who had come with Cronje's commando climbed on to the wagon. His face, except for his eyes, was covered with dark brown hair and his beard came down to his belt.

Lena, putting her foot on the brake handle, got down. The hairy man was going to speak.

" So it has come again," he said. " Wherever we go the Rooineks follow like dogs on our spoor." He was breathing hard and his eyes blazed. " Listen well," he said. " As a calf comes out of a cow so does day spring from day, event from event. To-day is the child of yesterday. It is born of the past—of Slagtersnek, the Trek, the rape of Natal, the disaster of Boomplatz, and the perpetual overrunning of our land. Are we to sit while the Egyptians despoil us? Our Volksraad is gone, our independence as burgers is gone, our land is gone, and again the women call to us. On every farm mothers call to their sons to saddle up and ride. Wives call to their husbands, young women to their betrothed, children to their brothers."

Why am I not like that? Lena wondered. Am I different from all women? Again she wished she knew more girls. Her grandmother felt like that, but were more women like Ouma than herself?

" All cry to their men," he shouted; " all call upon them to save the land of their father. The predikants, in the name of God, tell us to get our guns down from the walls and defend the land that is being ravished from us."

He paused to wipe the sweat from his eyes, and went on :

" You know what happened when Frere came to Pretoria. He was met by our men : I was among them. He argued with us, but gave us nothing. Still he promised us our rights and our flag. He was even ready to forward our petition to the Queen, asking that the annexation should be repealed. Frere was not to our liking, but he was honest for an Englishman. Then came Lanyon with his soldiers and his taxes. Frere had been too gentle. And now Wolseley, in Pretoria, says that as long as the sun shines the Queen's sovereignty will be upheld. Taxes!" he cried, " for roads and schools and police. Taxes for things that no good Boer needs or requires. Before the Uitlanders came we had no police. The roads are good enough for us who live in a godly manner and make no haste. And schools—is not the Bible-reading in our homes to which we are accustomed school enough? For a while we waited. Ja, we waited peacefully enough to see if those early promises would be fulfilled. But they have not been held : not one of them; and to-day we are a nation in arms. To-day is the beginning. God is with us, for our cause is just. To-day we have rifles in our hands : good German guns, and we will not put them down."

He stopped again and rubbed his eyes with a red rag.

"We are to be feared," he went on, "for though we are few, we have seen visions. Ja, brothers, there are some who dream in the watches of the night, as they sleep, but their dreams are without significance. They vanish with the dawn. But we are the day-dreamers and dangerous. For years we have dreamed as we rode about our separate farms. No sun was too strong for our dreams : no light too bright. Our dreams are built solidly with the mortar of our toil and blood; they are built upon the rock of our fathers' dreams, who dreamed them before us, and handed their dreams on to us, together with their farms and guns and horned stock and cattle and sheep, when they died.

"This land our fathers made and they left it to us. They left us, too, the open spaces, the wide veld, the soft breezes, and the hope of their dreams. To this end they worked, and this end we will achieve now that the day is done.

"And what do they want of us, these others, these English, but the gold and diamonds of our lands?—the dross, the ornaments of it, to clothe their harlots. Our land they do not love. They would milk it as a cow is milked and leave it dry and empty, desecrated with the abrasions of their mines. If we had the gold loose, we would give it to them and let them go, for all the gold of Mammon is not worth one dead burger. But the gold is not loose, it is spread on the rocks and under the rocks. The riches that they want are beneath our sacred soil. To get it they must stay. To stay they must have us in bondage. To get the riches they must take our rights, our freedoms, and before we submit to that, we are ready, to the last old man, to the last young boy, to die."

He took off his hat and stood with his head bowed. The people below him were silent, many took off their hats. Lena heard some of them praying. Others cursed beneath their breaths.

In the middle of the stillness, the dark boy who had gone for the oxen came back. He was leading six yoked oxen. The chain was undone from the last yoke and they were put in. The dark boy took up the riems of the leaders again. He said they were his father's oxen. Someone lent Piet a whip. He clapped it, the oxen got into draught, bending their backs to let the chains rasp over them. Piet sprang on to the disselboom, sitting sideways across it. Cronje's burgers mounted and surrounded the moving wagon, riding before and behind it. The crowd cheered and shouted : "There has been no sale! . . . Our Piet was right when he said there would be no sale to-day!"

His wagon was going home in style with a white voorloper and a commando about it. The red dust rose again in a long, low-drifting cloud. The crowd closed up to watch the wagon go, clung together, eddied, covering the space where it had stood, and then, solemnly, with serious faces, broke up into smaller bodies. Waiting a minute, hesitant, still sur-

prised at the suddenness of it all, Lena watched them. There was going
to be war. She felt it in her heart. Dirk would go and his father and her
brothers. That must be why he had not come back to see her. Soon only
the women and children would be left, and the helpless, like Boetie.

Tanta Martha called to her. "Are you going back to the store, Lena?"
She pointed across the outspan with her whip.

Going to the store? Of course she was going to the store. That was what
she had come in for, to get the material for her dress, Boer meal, paraffin,
cartridges, and five pounds of nails that were seventeen to the pound. I
must remember to count them, she thought. She tried to straighten out
her mind : the wagon, Piet Bezuidenhout, the commando, Dirk, her
marriage. . . . Tanta Martha would be pleased to hear of that. She was
pleased at all marriages. They meant births and she enjoyed births. There
was nothing like a baby, Tanta Martha always said. But there was going
to be a war. The crowd was thinning out. There was no one between her
and Tanta Martha's cart.

"Yes, I am going to the store," she said. "I am going to get . . ."
She did not finish, having just thought of the things she was to buy. She
could not remember them. But it would all come back when she was
calmer. "What does it mean, Tanta Marha? What has happened?" she
asked.

They were both looking at the people. Scattered now, they were wandering in two streams, one in the direction of the store, the other towards
Hutting's Hotel.

"Come, get in with me," Tanta Martha said.

Lena put her foot on the step and climbed into the cart. Her own cart
was standing at the store. She could se it from here with the picannin,
Willem, squatting in the dust beside it.

Tanta Martha let the horses go. They sprang forward at a gallop.

"It is like old times," she said. "It is like the days you do not remember
when things used to happen. Magtig, it makes me wish I was a girl again
and not so old and fat." She looked at her black horses with satisfaction.
"I weigh two hundred and fifty pounds, but I still get about," she said.

The rocking cart swung past a group of men. Some of them cursed, but
when they saw who it was they laughed.

"Is it Tanta Martha. There is no one who drives like Tanta Martha."

Tanta Martha looked back and shouted : "There is no one who feeds
his horses as I do. It is the mealies in my horses' bellies that put wings upon
their feet."

Turning to Lena, she steadied the horses. "Drive fast, indeed! They
should have seen old Tanta Anna de Jong drive. You ask the Old Baas
how she drove. Like Jehu," she said. "And now those men will get
drunk. Ja, they will go to Hutting's and drink dop. Men are like that, my

little heart. When anything happens, they seek courage and wisdom in the bottle." She pulled up.

" Are you coming in?" Lena asked.

" If I got out of my cart, how should I get back?" Tanta Martha said. " I will sit here and watch. All my life I have been a great one for watching. I am well known for it. Go in," she said. " I will wait. When you have done, we can go to my house and talk. You can tell me what they say in the store and I will tell you if there is any sense in it."

What did it matter what they said? Lena thought. In her heart she knew what had happened. Dirk had been right. The people had turned openly against the English.

The first overt act had taken place. The war, without a shot fired, was begun.

CHAPTER III

I

TANTA MARTHA sat staring over her horses' heads. There was a pattern in life and a new design was just begun. She saw it like this. Design after design, apparently irrelevant and meaningless, that in the end all fitted into each other to form the immense tapestry of life. Thus, the continual coming and going of people; their loves and hates, their births and deaths, their tragedies and joys, which seemed so personal to them, were really not only personal, but at the same time a part of some greater thing. A man in a moment of idleness sent a flat stone skipping across a dam, a frog was disturbed and moved, a heron speared the frog. That was how things worked. Precisely, like a clock; significantly, but with a significance that was beyond the comprehension of man. Man could only follow in the wake of events. He started things moving and then was caught up in the repercussions of the movement. He mounted an act as if it were a horse, found himself unable to control it, and was carried on whether he would or no. It was destiny, Providence, the will of God.

Tanta Martha thought of the troubles she had seen in her own life, the wars, the schisms among her own people; the quarrels, the dangers, the never-ending threat of Africa. She thought of the other old people in the district : of old Erasmus, old Philippus Jacobus du Toit, of Tanta Aletta, who had married Kaspar van der Berg. They would all be involved in this one way or another. War, and there would be war, was not a thing that could be kept isolated. Good men would be killed; bad, clever ones would manage to save their hides. Homes would be broken up, women left widows and children fatherless because of Piet Bezuidenhout's wagon. A Bezuidenhout again as it had been at Slagtersnek. A coincidence . . . why should it be? Why not the strain of their blood passed on from father to son?

And if it had not been his wagon, it would have been something else; the country was bubbling like a pot and ready to boil over. She knew her folk. Once they began something, they went on with it. It was their nature and could not be changed : the English, on the one hand, with their desire for riches, gold, and diamonds and what they called progress : the Dutch, on the other, with their farms and cattle, their lack of interest in riches, and their hatred of all development. One, a people who liked change; the other, a race who hated it. A great man might have been able

34

to reconcile these contrary interests, to find a middle way, but there had been no great man, and now it was too late. It made her sad to think of it; even the fat backs of her horses gave her no pleasure to-day.

2

The store was full when Lena went in. Mr. Brenner was behind the long counter in his shirt-sleeves, serving the people who clamoured round him. Every one was talking of the commando and the rescue of Piet's wagon. Every one was speculating about what would happen next. This was something that could not be ignored. The English would have to act. Women pushed past arguing men to reach the counter. Lena heard the name of Paul Kruger mentioned several times. He seemed to be the man they counted on in this crisis—he, and Joubert, and Pretorious. But Kruger most of all.

Mr. Brenner greeted her. " So you were there," he said. " You saw it all. That will be something to tell your grandmother when you get home. And how is the Old Baas?"

If there was war, things might be difficult for Mr. Brenner. He was not Dutch and, though he had come to the country as a child, many still regarded him as an Uitlander. People like her grandmother said an Englishman like an Ethiopian cannot change his skin any more than a leopard can cast off his spots. He pulled out a bag of Boer meal, reached for a spool of linen thread, gave her a card from which to choose a big needle, and called to Jacob to bring paraffin, farm oil, and a ploughshare from the other side of the store.

" And I want the cartridges for my brother," Lena said.

Old Erasums, who was beside her, said : " Stoffel is a fine shot. Perhaps he will shoot Rooineks instead of rooibok now."

Every one laughed at his joke. Already there was an atmosphere of war, of blood, of excitement. The women were looking at the young men with pride. They were going to retrieve the honour of their land.

" I was there when they took down our flag," Erasmus said. " Ja, magtig, I was there in Pretoria when they dragged the Vierkleur in the dust." There were tears in his eyes. " Our flag," he said again.

" It will fly once more," Hans van Neikerk said. " Blue, yellow, white, and green, our country's flag will fly again."

A woman upset a parcel of rice. The little grains spread over the floor and every one walked on them.

" I will give you some more," Mr. Brenner said. " I will give you more for nothing."

Men pressed forward to buy ammunition—Mauser cartridges, Steyr cartridges. " We may need them," they said.

Lena felt that by buying ammunition for her brothers she had started the others buying. There was something terrible about those packets that were handled so carelessly on the counter. Van Neikerk broke his and put the cartridges loose into his pocket. The greasy blue wrappings he threw on to the floor.

A man going out turned and shouted: " Tot siens, jong. . . . We will take our guns to Paardekraal; we will make an end this time."

It was all astonishing. Till to-day she had not known the temper of her race: the slow patience that flared into sudden anger. These men, and she knew them nearly all, were changed. They were no longer farmers, fathers of families, but a people getting ready to fight. The leaders would no longer be able to hold them: they had taken the bit between their teeth. The Secocoeni War was just over. The Zulu War, which the English had won after incredible early defeats, was just over. But these wars had been far away. This one was going to be here, in the Transvaal, in Brennersdorp, perhaps. The men who were going to fight were her friends. Her brothers would go and Dirk and Dirk's father. All quarrels, all personal and political differences were already forgotten. Within a few hours, as the news spread, men would get out their saddles and their guns to be ready. Women would bake rusks, mend coats, and prepare blankets. Biltong and tobacco would be packed into saddlebags, spare riems greased and prepared. Kaffirs would be sent running from farm to farm. All Africa north of the Vaal would be seething and it would spread across the Vaal into the Free State: it would spread south and the burgers of Cape Colony would get ready to ride. The fuel of Boer wrongs, added to day by day for more than eighty years, was aflame, kindled by the spark of Piet Bezuidenhout's resistance to authority.

There was no longer any doubt in Lena's mind about the war. It would happen. Nothing could stop it, and Dirk like the others would be caught up in it and swept away from her. There was nothing she or any woman could do except to help them prepare and then sit down to wait and pray. The wide veld would be filled with bodies of mounted burgers. The farm homes would be empty of men till it was over.

Her mind was suddenly very clear. She thought of the shopping. Yes, she had everything. There was only the dress material now. She had saved that till last, like the cherry on the top of a cake, because she wanted it most. But the savour had gone out of it. She handled the silk, letting it ripple through her fingers, and wondered how it was that a piece of stuff could be two colours at once—brown that changed to green as you moved it. A pigeon's breast did that, too, shining purple and green. She thought of pigeons; of how the young ones had long yellow hairs on their breasts and soft pointed beaks. A young pigeon's eyes were brown, and then, as it got older, they changed to orange. She wondered why she had thought of pigeons.

Now she had everything: the nails—she had counted them—the thread, the Boer meal, the ploughshare, the cartridges, the paraffin. They were all packed in her cart. Tanta Martha was still there waiting, the reins slack in her hands, her horses resting on three legs with drooping heads.

The dress material, carefully done up in paper, she held under her arm. As she drove, she would keep it on the seat beside her. She was very tired, hot and untidy—she hated to be untidy; her clothes were sticking to her. Why hadn't she driven across the square instead of running like a fool? That's because I am impatient, she thought, and really it would have been quicker to take the horses. With the meat at the back she would have to move the seat farther forward.

Tanta Martha turned her head as she got into the cart.

"Are you ready, Lena?"

"Yes, I am ready."

She looked back; the store was almost empty; the talk of war had driven them home to spread the news; only some Kaffirs were watching her from the stoep. One of them had a sheep's entrails in his hand.

"Then we will go," Tanta Martha said.

Lena let her go, waited till the dust behind her cart had settled, and followed her.

She liked to go to Tanta Martha's. Her house was on the outskirts of the village. It was made of sun-baked mud bricks, had a thick thatch roof, and was set well back from the road. It had four rooms and a storeroom full of the preserves, konfyt, and medicines she liked to make. Tanta Martha was never happy unless she was making something, stirring something in a copper pan over the fire, simmering a concoction of herbs, or straining the juice from steeped roots. She had remedies and simples of every sort in bottles, jars, and pots, in little bags, in paper parcels neatly tied with string and labelled, or hanging in great clusters from the roof-beams—veld medicines for every ill. She said there was nothing that could not be cured by some plant or root. Bark, branches, dried flowers, bulbs were all collected and saved.

Many herbs she had growing in her garden. They had been put in as she got them, planted here and there without order among the orange trees, hibiscus, and poinsettias. It was she who had brought these shrubs from the low veld and now every one had them, all grown from her cuttings. There were always sugar birds and great numbers of bees, butterflies, humming and swift-darting haw moths in the garden, so that wherever you looked there was brightness and movement. Oupa had his peacocks and Tanta Martha her bees and butterflies. She had three round straw hives of bees and used their honey in many of her salves and draughts. The honey tasted as orange flowers smelled, very sweet and good unless you had too much of it. When Lena's father had taken her there, Tanta

Martha had always given her bread spread thick with white honey; and mebos, dried apricots cured with salt and sugar, to take away with her.

3

Tanta Martha drove slowly. Was this land never to know peace or security? She thought of the old Kaffir wars, the Trek, the recent trouble with Secocoeni and the Zulus, and now this one that was on them.

She thought of her first husband, Jan Coetzee, a fine carpenter and musician. How they had sung together! She thought of his son that she had been nursing when Gert Kleinhouse came to try and verneuk her out of a pig. Poor Gert, he had been a good husband and the father of six children, but he had not come up to her expectations, nor been in any way comparable to Jan. Perhaps no husband was like one's first. Now all her children were grandparents. That was extraordinary when you came to think of it, the way they grew up while you remained the same. Sometimes it made her laugh to think of the way one minute you held a pink, naked baby in your lap, and the next, that baby came back with a beard on his face and put his child on to your kness. Even Louisa's bastard by Jappie de Jong was a grandfather : she saw him sometimes. And Louisa, the mother of many others, by other men, still worked for her : an old shrivelled woman with no trace of beauty except for her great black eyes. She thought of Hendrik van der Berg's children; of Jacoba, Lena's mother, and of Frikkie, who had remained, inexplicably, unmarried. It was strange to have seen him on the outspan to-day, for he hardly ever left his farm. She thought of old Tanta Anna de Jong who had come to live with them in Lemansdorp, bringing the children, Frikkie and Jacoba, and the old witch doctor Rinkals with her. He had gone off later, no one knew where, leaving Louisa with child : a miracle, indeed, from so old a man. He had sold much medicine for potency before going among the servants and perhaps he had intended to return after this proof of its effect.

How she had quarrelled with Tanta Anna at first! It had gone on till she bore Gert's first child and then they had become friends. The old woman had taught her all she knew about herbs and simples and the relieving of pain. It was as if the mantle of Anna de Jong had fallen upon her. But when she had died she had sold up in Lemansdorp having no further heart for the place, and come here to rest in peace, to sit on the stoep, drink coffee, gossip with her friends, and to help her neighbours if she could.

She let her mind go back over the past, over the well-worn road of her life—so much misery and war, so much happiness, so many dead. She had seen them dead by massacre, by mutilation, by accident, by illness, and to many she had brought help. With age came peace : not a restful peace, but one of understanding : a peace of heart because men meant nothing now, and a peace of mind because you could no longer be surprised. With age, too, came the habit of living in one's memories. The things that happened to-day served only as reminders of those that had happened yesterday and made those of yesterday more fresh, more vivid than the present which was actually taking place. Young people were less real than their parents and grandparents. You found yourself looking for their ancestral traits and recognizing them with pleasure as though the trait itself was the friend. This boy had his grandfather's nose, that girl her grandmother's eyes. It was comforting; it gave life length and strength, a continuity that reached past the individual back into the distant past, and forward, into the unknown future.

She wondered what had happened to her old friend Tom Tryolla. It was a long time since she had seen him. He was a Cornish miner, a prospector, and she had learnt much from him : old remedies of amazing excellence; for ague, six pills of cobwebs, or the application of soot and treacle to each wrist; for baldness, the head should be rubbed with onions till it was red and then soothed with honey; for gout, the part must be rubbed in warm treacle and bound in flannel; for the inflammation of the eyes, powdered alum, very completely mixed with white of egg and applied with a linen dipped in water; for a sty, a bag of boiled tea leaves; for toothache, the parings of a turnip laid on very hot behind the ear; for a whitlow, a piece of salted butter worked into the part affected; and for strains, an embrocation of egg, vinegar, and turpentine.

A strange man, Tom Tryolla. She had nursed him once when he was sick and he had told her these things; told her also about his land that was full of fairies, pixies, goblins, and little people that he called Knockers. They were, he said, quite friendly unless crossed. This seemed very reasonable to her and made them much like other folk. They were withered creatures about the size of a yearling child with big ugly heads and the faces of old men. Formerly they had been much bigger, but they were growing smaller, and in time would be no bigger than an ant. He had been looking for them in Africa among the old mines of the north and asked her if she had ever heard of any. He said they lived in abandoned mines and sang carols at Christmas. They were the spirits of the Jews who had crucified our Lord. Not good enough for heaven nor bad enough for hell, they remained on the face of the earth and their presence indicated rich ore. He had told her, too, of a little white animal like a hare that gave warning of disaster. These animals were the spirits of maidens who had died when forsaken by their lovers and often caused the death of the seducer.

Mr. Tryolla was a very well-educated man and had seen many interesting things. It was a pleasure to talk to him. She wondered when she would

see him again and what he would do if there was war. If he was up in the
mountains he might never hear of it.

The horses turned in at the gates. A boy came with a chair for her to
step down on. Louisa came to the door to watch her descent, and a dog
ran out.

She was glad to be back. One could think better at home among familiar
things and to-day there was so much to think of.

4

When Lena came in, Tanta Martha called for coffee. She was sitting
by the window with her feet on a footstool. Lena knew the stool well :
she had often sat on it when she was a child. It was hollow, with a little
drawer that in the winter was filled with glowing charcoal. It had been
wonderful to sit on it in cold weather. She held her parcel on her knee
as she looked round the room. She knew it so well. She had been so
happy here; as a child with her father, and as she grew up; sometimes she
had stayed the night.

She watched Tanta Martha settle herself, wriggling slowly to get comfortable. She watched Louisa come in with coffee—the brass tray, the
coffee-pot, the cups with a blue-and white design, the jug and the bowl of
sugar. Louisa knelt down in front of Tanta Martha and took off her shoes.
A young girl, nearly white, one of Louisa's grandchildren, came in with
a whisk of ostrich plumes set on a stick and began to wave it to keep the
flies from settling. There was a steady hum as they flew round and round.
Did flies never get tired? And how did they walk upside down? The hot
silence, except for the slow brushing of the whisk through the air, the flies
buzzing, and Tanta Martha's heavy breathing, was brittle as glass. Lena
did not dare to break it. From outside came the noise of her horses being
outspanned, the voice of her picannin talking to someone. She heard her
horses being led away—they were going to be watered and fed—and the
sound of the harness being slung on to the dashboard.

She looked at Tanta Martha again. Her eyes were half-closed. Tight
and enormous, her black linen bodice rose and fell. Louisa went out silently
as a cat, her bare feet making no sound on the smeared-clay floor. The girl,
Netta, stood behind Tanta Martha. Each time she waved her whisk, her
high pointed breasts moved up and down. Her dark eyes were expressionless in her magnolia face. She must be about my own age, Lena thought.
Netta changed her weight from one foot to the other and looked at her as
though to include her in something.

Lena thought of her dress again, she had almost forgotten it, and of
Dirk. Tanta Martha would be glad she was going to marry him : she
liked him. The skirt must be cut in six panels. That was simple, but the

bodice would be difficult. It must fit closely, be tight, and supported with whalebones. She had them ready at home, pale grey, springy, and bored with holes at either end. She had taken them out of an old dress of her mother's that Ouma had thrown away. It must cling to her figure neatly without bulges, smoothly, like the breast of a bird. From having been of no importance, the dress had become very important again. She felt that it was significant, that it would have something to do with her life. It was going to be her wedding dress. She would never part with it. The coffee, whose fragrance filled the room, would soon be cold. The scent of orange blossom and herbs came in from the garden and there was an undefinable scent from Netta : a sweet acrid scent that disturbed her. The black and white plumes moved slowly. The flies still circled, rising and falling in a kind of dance that centred on the feathers.

Tanta Martha opened her eyes. " There will be war," she said.

" Ja, Tanta Martha, from what I saw in the store, there will be war."

" But what have you on your knee, my heart? Is it a dress?"

Lena laughed. " Yes, it is a dress for you to cut out. But how did you know?"

" From your face and the way you held it. By the shape of the parcel and the fact," she pointed with a fat stubby finger, " that it is torn at the end where you have picked at it with your nail."

" I am going to be married, Tanta Martha."

Netta looked at her again. Her heavy lips—they looked as if they had been put on from outside—smiled.

" To whom? To Dirk?"

" Yes, to Dirk."

" I am glad," Tanta Martha said. " He is a fine young man. Come, give me the stuff and let us see what we can make of it. A wedding dress. . . ." She began to chuckle. " Ja, Netta," she said, " if you had waited for a wedding, perhaps I would have given you a dress."

So that was it. Lena spread the material on the table. It felt cool and slippery. The brown looked almost black in the shuttered room, but the green sprang to life as she moved it.

" It is beautiful," Tanta Martha said, taking hold of a corner and rubbing it between her finger and thumb. " It is beautiful and strong and will wear for ever. Get the scissors, the big ones, and the pins, Netta. We will have our coffee and then begin."

5

Lena drove back fast, trotting and cantering her horses. The dress, cut out and partly pinned together, was in a basket at her side. She could manage it for herself now if her grandmother would help her with the fitting. But then would she wear it? If there was war, Dirk would have to go—would want to go. She thought of the way he had banged the table the other night, of the way he had talked. I ought to want him to go, she thought, but I don't. When he came he would make her tell him everything. She wondered when he would come—to-night, to-morrow night? It would be soon, she knew. He would want to know what she thought. He always wanted to know what she thought. He did not seem to understand how little she thought of anything except how beautiful the mountains were in the evening, or how strange it was that a hen took only twenty-one days to hatch her eggs and a duck took twenty-eight.

She thought, too, of being a wife, of having children and a home of her own, but these were not things to discuss with a man, not even one's betrothed. When they had been little, it had been Dirk who led, but now he kept asking her things, asking her what he should do, and she always answered the way she thought he would like. When she guessed right, he took her advice and said she advised him well. Now he would expect her to want him to go and fight. She did not want him to go, She loved him. She wanted to marry him, to cook for him, to move that button on his best coat and to bear his children.

She slowed her horses. They pulled against her hand; they were excited with the nearness of home. She turned off the main road. She was back on Mooiplaas. Driving was more difficult here. There were deep ruts and outcrops of rock that had to be avoided. On each side of her cattle grazed. A herder squatting on an antheap raised his tattered hat. She waved her whip to him.

She steadied the horses to cross the drift. She liked to hear their feet in the water and to see it run off the wheels. When they got out, the horses' black legs shone bright with water that lasted till they began to trot in the dust again, then it stuck to them and their black points were red. The water in the spruit was very low : lower, Stoffel had said yesterday, than he ever remembered it. The traces were slack as the cart ran down. They tightened as the horses began to pull again. The iron tyres banged on the stony bottom. A hammerkop stood brown and still on a rock. He did not even move his head as she passed. She knew his nest. It was higher up in a willow. What big nests they made—more than a yard across, of sticks and rubbish, bits of rag, of anything they could find. The horses bent their hocks and lowered their heads as they got into their breastplates. They were up and trotting again.

In the distance the hillside was dotted with sheep and goats. She could see the house now, half-hidden by the oaks her great-grandfather had planted and by the belt of bush that ran along the rankie. Boers always built their houses like this, hard to find, nestling against a hill, and near the water. There were the white poplars. They were always being cut for roof-poles—the white ants did not eat them—and always growing again, suckering from the bottom. She loved to see the young trees in a wind when they turned the skirts of their white leaves upward into the sun till they shimmered and glinted like silver.

And there was the patch of Spanish reed that her father had planted. People came to beg for roots and reeds to plant. If you laid a reed down in moist soil and covered it, it grew from every joint. The geese some-times made nest among the reeds and so did the finks, hanging their nests from the reed tops, tying two or three together in a wonderful fashion to give them strength; and behind the reeds and the white poplars were the willows that drooped their branches into the dark water of the dam. As a very little girl she thought them like women, like sad women, bending over the water to wash their long streaming hair. There was a wild bees' nest in one of them that was hollow near the top.

She drove over the grass in front of the house. It was kept very short and neat by the geese and hand-raised lambs that grazed it. The dogs got up. Bismarck and Wolf were always glad to see her. Their mouths were open and their tails wagging. They seemed to be laughing at her.

Her grandmother was sitting on the stoep with Oupa. She sat watching. Her hands were folded on her lap. Oupa waved his pipe at her.

"You have come fast," her grandmother said, looking at the horses.

"Yes, I have come fast. . . . I have news. . . ."

"I hope you have not spilt the paraffin on the Boer meal."

Lena looked down. The paraffin was not spilt, which was lucky, since she had forgotten it. Oupa said nothing, but he was smiling and stroking his beard. It was stained with yellow streaks of tobacco. Once she had asked him why he did not wash it off. He had said that he did not like to get soap in his mouth.

Below the stoep was a fenced-off flower-bed. In the spring it was gay, scarlet with Natal lilies. They were over now. But the purple salvia was out and alive with hawk moths. There must have been fifty of them or a hundred. They hung suspended, wingless like sugar birds, flitting arrow-quick from flower to flower. Even from the cart she could hear the whirr of their wings. It happened like this sometimes that there were a great number of them together. She had seen it twice before. Pa would have liked to see them, she thought. She wondered if her grandmother had noticed them; probably not. She only noticed things that were useful. Beautiful things, she said, were generally bad. So were the things you wanted to do. Duty always ran contrary to desire. Willem, who had clung to the back of the cart, got down and went to the horses' heads. A farm boy carrying a hoe put it down and came to help him unharness. Rosina came out of the house to fetch the parcels.

Lena stood watching the horses trot off. Her grandmother was right. They were hot, black with sweat, and curded with lather on the chest and flanks where the harness had rubbed them. They lay down to roll and went towards the water. How different it would have been in her father's time! He would have wanted to hear the news at once. He would not have minded the horses being hot. When he had been in the mood he had driven wildly himself, inspanning a young unbroken horse beside a steady one and galloping them over the veld till the young horse was tame. She looked at her grandmother again. She had not moved. Oupa watched her with twinkling eyes. He knew what she was thinking. Then he pointed the stem of his pipe to the moths. She was glad he had noticed them.

" And what is the news, Lena?" her grandmother asked.

" The news, Ouma? This is the news. It's Piet Bezuidenhout. The English took his wagon for taxes and were going to sell it on the outspan. All the world was there, and then Cronje came with a commando and took it back. It's home on Piet's farm now. I saw it go with the commando all round it. It is said that they will camp on his farm and fight if they try to take him. The dorp is in an uproar . . . every one shouting and the men buying ammunition. . . ."

Her grandmother nodded her head. " So it has come! It was bound to come."

There was no change in her position except that her hands were no longer folded over her sewing. The left hand still rested on her lap, but the right one was raised over it and she rubbed the nail of her thumb against the ball of her second finger. Her face was composed, as cold as stone. Her eyes, which had been on Lena while she spoke, now looked past her towards the north.

Then she stiffened, sitting very upright in her chair and throwing her shoulders back.

" Fetch your brothers," she said. " Stoffel is in the big kraal and Louis on the lands. This will take men. My husband and your father died too soon. If they had lived they could all have ridden out together. My husband, and my son, and my son's sons——"

CHAPTER IV

THEY SOWED THE WIND

I

STOFFEL DU TOIT stood in the kraal with two boys looking at four young oxen he had just bought. Two were black, one was a clear cherry red, and the other, the biggest of them all, was dark red with a white speckled face and a white line down his back; a Bechuana ox—many of their beasts were marked like this.

His branding iron was heating in a fire of sticks and dry cow-dung. The oxen stood bunched, their tails to the rails of the kraal, their heads low and turned towards him. Only Yukman, the tame ox that had led them in, was unconcerned. He chewed his cud, rolling it from side to side in his mouth.

"Come," Stoffel said to the boys, "get the vangstok."

One of the Kaffirs picked up a stick. Making a wide loop with the slip knot of a riem, he put it round the stick and went towards the oxen. The riem, which was very long, dragged like a snake behind him.

"Take the black ones first," Stoffel said.

The oxen moved away from the boy, leaning outward against the rails. They began to trot. He ran beside them and held the loop in front of the hind legs of the second black ox, which put his foot into the loop. The boy dropped the catching-stick and lay back on the riem. The other Kaffir joined him and they pulled together. Terrified, the ox jumped forward dragging them after him. His hind leg was stretched out behind him and he fell. He got up, turned, and tried to charge. They kept the riem tight and swung him to the side. The ox lost his balance and went down.

"He is a good one," Stoffel shouted. "He shows fight."

Hobbling forward, he slipped the noose of another riem over his horns pulling it tight behind them. He went on pulling. As he pulled, the boys gave a little. Gradually, sweating and panting, with the ox plunging forward and pulling back, they worked him towards the tree that stood in the centre of the kraal. There was a loose loop of heavy, twisted wire round its trunk. Stoffel put the end of his riem over the loop, gave it a double turn, and shouted to the boys to slack. As they let go, the ox jumped forward and Stoffel tightened his riem, bringing him up short against the wire loop. Then as he snubbed it, the ox fell on his back.

"Make fast!" he cried.

One of the boys pulled a riem from his belt and tied the ox's hind legs

45

below the hocks. He got up on his forelegs. The other boy, seizing a horn, pulled him over on his side. The boy who had held the stick took the head riem from Stoffel's hand and tied it. He went back to the hind legs and, taking the ox's tail, pilled it up under his thigh on to his back.

Stoffel went over to the fire for his iron. He turned it over to look at it. It was just right : hot without being red. He put it on the ox's quarter, high up near the root of the tail. A brand there was easy to see from a horse. He held the hot iron down, pressing it. There was a smell of burning hair and skin. He felt the iron bite. At first it did nothing, and then, as it took hold, as he felt it go in, he withdrew it. It must not break through the skin and produce a wound. Stoffel liked to brand cattle. It made them his beyond all argument.

He put the branding iron back, took out his knife, and bent over the boy who was holding the ox's tail. The knife cut through the pointed hairs of the tip, squaring them off : an extra mark of identification. Now he could be picked out fifty yards away if he got lost or mixed up with a neighbour's beasts. By the time the tail had grown again, he would be used to the farm.

New cattle were a nuisance. Sometimes they went home, many miles, to the place where they had been born. Cows were worse than oxen, and horses worse than cows. You never knew when a horse would take it into his head to go back, and they went fast, sometimes a hundred miles or more in a day.

" Let him up," he said, " and catch the other one."

The ox got to his feet, tried to break away, fell, and got up again. He was tied very short and the wire ring rose as he raised his head. He walked round the tree pulling and roaring. Then he gave up and stood still. The second ox was caught, branded, and tied beside the first. Two riems were passed round their necks, several times, like dog collars. Each time they went round, they were passed through the links of the iron swivel that joined them. They were pulled so tight that their horns overlapped and yet were loose about their necks. They could neither choke nor gore each other; nor could they, because of the swivel, succeed in strangling themselves. The rails were pulled from the gate of the kraal. The red-and-white ox and the plain red ox dashed out. Yukman followed at a slow, lumbering walk.

The riems were now withdrawn from the heads of the shackled couple. They stood still for a moment. Then they sprang away, galloped round the kraal, jumped the fallen gate bars, and were out, bounding across the veld. The off ox changed direction suddenly and, checked by his mate, fell, turning head over heels. As he got up, the other fell. The two stood milling, getting up, falling down, trying to escape in different directions, bringing each other to their knees, till finally they found themselves facing one way and were able to gallop off.

Stoffel and Kaffirs watched them, laughing. In an hour they would tire themselves. In a day, except for an occasional effort to break apart, they would be calm. In two days they would have settled down and be moving peacefully about together : grazing or lying down in company. From this hour till one or both of them died they were matched, mated, to labour in the same yoke.

"We will call them Dingaan and T'Chaka," Stoffel said.

"They are good names, Baas, and they will make good oxen when they are tame."

Before he had thought of the iron swivels, he had lost oxen by strangulation. Joined only by riems, in their first wild endeavours to escape, they sometimes turned complete somersaults and twisted their collars tight. But this way there was no great danger, even if they galloped into a tree and tried to pass one on either side of it. To-morrow he would brand and couple the other pair, and in three or four days, when they had all settled down, he would loosen them and put on new collars to which a heavy chain was tied. This would tire them and get them used to its touching their flanks and backs. When first they felt the chain they bolted, the chain jumping behind them. But after a few days they got used to it too. Then they would be coupled again, yoked and inspanned to a loaded wagon between two pairs of steady beasts. Once inspanned, by the use of the whip they would learn their names and their life of work could begin.

Ever since he had been a small boy Stoffel had trained oxen and watched them trained. The wilder and more difficult they were at first, the better they were in the end. An ox that could be inspanned at once, without resistance, had no heart and was no good. All animals had to be broken, and there was always, between man and beast, whether it was a horse, a dog, or an ox, a contest of wills, an effort in which the one had to prove its mastery over the other. Stoffel liked to train animals : to train horses to the cart, to teach them to stay still when the reins were thrown over their heads and to stand rifle fire; to train his dogs so that he could take meat from their mouths; his oxen so that at a cry from him, and in fear of him, they would bend themselves double in their yokes. No one trained beasts better than he. No one used the whip more to begin with and less when they were broken.

"Break them first," he said, "and then they are yours."

"Stoffel . . . Stoffel . . ." Lena was calling him.

She must have just got back from the dorp. He wondered if she had his cartridges.

"Ja," he shouted. "I am here. I am in the kraal."

"Ouma wants you," Lena said. "She sent me for you and Louis."

"What does she want?"

"There will be war," Lena said. "She wants you at the house."

"War! Who said there would be war?"

"Ouma says so and Tanta Martha . . . all the world says so and in the dorp men are getting ready."

"Then you brought the news?"

"Yes, I brought the news."

"What happened? Tell me what you saw."

Lena had turned from him.

"Go to the house. You will hear there," she said.

"Aren't you coming?"

"No, I am not coming."

She was some distance away from him now and going fast towards the spruit.

Lena hurried. She had done what she was told : she had called Louis and Stoffel; but she would not go back herself; not go back to the house and listen to it all. She did not want to hear her grandmother's bitterness, her tongue flaying the English and those who would not fight them alike. She wanted to be alone; to sit on a flat stone by the water and think of Dirk. She felt he would come to-night. War . . . From now on there would be no other talk. Her wedding, which should have been a big thing, was now a little one and without importance except to her. Even Dirk would talk of war. She knew already how he would act and what he would say. He would go with the others. He would say, As soon as I get back we will marry.

As soon as he got back! Suppose he did not get back? Every one did not come back from a war. And he would suffer even if he was not killed or wounded; sleeping out on the veld for weeks, half-starved, sometimes short of water, or soaked with the rain of thunder-showers and without a change of clothes. He was mad. All men were mad. Kaffirs, one had to fight. One had to kill them before they killed you, but war between white men was stupid. She wanted Dirk to come, to stay with her, to hold her in his arms and make love to her. She had not really thought about that before. At least, she had only thought about it vaguely, as she supposed all girls thought of it. It was one of those things which would come and she had been content to wait. But now that she was betrothed and her man was going, she thought about it passionately so that it hurt her. She wanted Dirk's arms about her, his hands, all of him. She wanted Dirk.

She began to cry. It was easy for the one who went away. It was easy to go on an adventure with other men. They would all be together riding, fighting, talking, helping each other. But she would be alone without news, waiting all the time. She would be in the places that they had known together; the places where everything cried out his name to her. She knew about it from older women. They had talked about that waiting, that knowing nothing, with everything about them reminding them of their men : everything crying out—"He is gone . . . he is gone." She knew she would think of him all the time and remember where he had stood, where he had walked, what he had looked like when he was tired and at a loss; of the expression on his face when he was·unhappy and when he was happy. The whole farm would remind her of him.

The hammerkop she had seen in the afternoon passed overhead. He was flying home to the nest where his wife was sitting on her eggs. The birds had no wars to disturb them. She was suddenly very envious of the birds and the wild things that lived out their lives so simply. It would be nice to be a bird and sit on your eggs thinking about nothing, just waiting for your husband, who had spent his day catching frogs in the water, to come back.

2

Dirk came as she had known he would. He dismounted to kiss her.
" You expected me? " he said.
" Yes. I knew you would come."
" That is wonderful," he said, " that you should know. I did not decide till an hour ago."
" It was an hour ago that I knew you were coming."

They walked hand in hand towards the house, his horse following behind him. She said nothing of what she had seen. He would hear in good time. This might be the last time they would walk along the spruit together. She wanted to notice everything so that afterwards she could hurt herself with this memory too.

She looked at a stick he picked up and threw out of the path—it was a branch of Kaffir boom. She had an impulse to pick it up, to keep it : it was a stick he had thrown; but that would mean explanations. It would be better to get it later—after he had gone. She felt ill, as if she would faint. She came closer to him and he put his arm right round her so that his hand was on her breast. It hurt her. She wished it would hurt more. The horse walked quietly behind him—Swartkie, his favourite horse. He was the one Dirk would ride when he went. She put all thought of his going from her. I must live now, in these minutes, while I have him, she thought.

How could it all have happened so quickly? She had known him all her life; she had wanted him to ask her to marry him for weeks; she had loved him for a long time. At least, she thought she had. But everything was changed. He had never made her feel ill before. She had never wanted him as she wanted him now, before. She felt herself blush and looked down. She was much smaller than he and he could not see her face. But suppose he knew her thoughts. Then she found she did not care if he did. She wanted him to know what was in her mind. If he knew he might do something . . . she could take it no further than that even to herself.

She stopped and swung into him. The horse stopped abruptly, banging his nose into Dirk's back as he picked her up. She pushed closer to him, clinging to him with all her body. Her arms were round his neck. She was holding him with all her strength. His left arm was under her knees, his right round her shoulders.

He kissed her mouth. He bent back her head and kissed her throat.

" You are crying, Lena," he said.

" I am not crying," she said. " Why should I cry? I have a cold."

" You must not cry," he said. " I cannot bear to have you cry."

He was so gentle that she cried harder. It was no good. She must cry.

" Yes, I am crying," she said.

And she had not meant to waste to-night. She had meant to be brave and loving, to encourage him. That was why she had gone so far up the spruit to meet him.

" You will come back," she said. " Promise to come back."

Somehow, if he promised, it would be better. It would be a kind of charm against his death or hurt.

" Come back? Where am I going?"

" To the war, Dirk. There is going to be war. Already men are riding. You know it, so why pretend?"

" Stop now and wipe your face," he said.

They were near the house. He dropped his reins and went to the spruit to wet his handkerchief. He gave it to her. She wiped her eyes and nose and dried her face with a corner that was not wet. It smelt of him, of tobacco and Dirk. She had never thought before of how people smelt; that they all smelt different.

" Yes, Lena," Dirk said, " I am going, but it is not certain that there will be war."

She could see Stoffel and Louis outside the house.

They called to Dirk. " You'll have to stop your courting," Stoffel said, " till this is over. Word has come in that the meeting at Paardekraal is to be earlier. They have put it forward and we ride to-morrow. Are you coming with us? We are to take rifles and bring food for a week."

Lena had never seen Stoffel so pleased.

It had come quickly. There must have been more news while she sat waiting for Dirk. Things moved fast when they were bad. She held Dirk's hand tighter. This was the last night. To-morrow he would go with the others.

3

They went in to eat. Oupa sat in his accustomed chair. Stoffel and Louis sat on one side of the table. Dirk sat opposite them. Ouma was in and out of the kitchen. Between waiting on them, Lena sat beside Dirk, her knee touching his.

Dirk and her great-grandfather argued as they always did. Nothing was said about the war. But it was there, a shadow over them all while they talked of lions.

Oupa said that there were no lions now. Dirk said that there were plenty of lions, but perhaps not quite as many as there used to be.

"When I was a young man I once saw thirty-one lions together, and who sees such things to-day?" Oupa asked. "Why, if a man see a klompie of seventeen or so he comes back with a long story about it."

"I have never seen more than twenty together and that only once on the Koodoos Rand," Dirk said.

They went on to speak of cubs, Dirk saying that they were born with their eyes closed like kittens, Oupa swearing that their eyes were open; that he had once found a nest of young lions, quite new, in a krans and their eyes had been blue and open. "There were three of them, and how the mother charged!—like lightning. Only when a lioness has cubs does she charge like that."

"Some say it is the lioness who charges more than the lion," Dirk said.

"Nee, it is the lion who charges, not his wife, unless she has cubs or is hit. But there is no yes or no with lions: there is no always. They are as different as men in their natures. Black-maned, yellow-maned, or mane-less, male or female, there is no rule. Do you know how long a lioness carries her cubs?" he asked.

"I do not," Dirk said. "Nor does any man."

"I know," Oupa said, "for with the cubs I spoke of, I saw the mother served. Ja, she was served like a cat with roars and cries and much rolling over. I made a note of the day, for it was a wonderful thing to see. It was four months later that she cubbed, to the very day; in summer, just before Christmas."

"Ja, that is so," Dirk said. "They drop their young in summer; not before November and not after March."

"I have had many lion cubs," Oupa said. "I like them. They are beautiful with their pale spotted backs and tame as dogs once they know you. Ja, I like lions," he said again, "and I miss them. I like to hear them roar in a storm. People complain about them, but I never had trouble with a lion. I always know what they will do.

"Your grandmother Sannie had a fine tame lion," he said to Lena.

" Since you are not a lion, Oupa, I do not see how you know so much about how a lion thinks," Dirk said.

" No, Dirk, and since you are not me, you cannot know how much I know about lions."

Then they talked of dogs. Louis said that the way to find a lost dog was to go to the place where you saw him last and leave your coat there. He would come back to that place and when he found your coat he would stay by it. Stoffel said : " If I had such a dog I would shoot him. A good dog does not get lost."

How puzzling men were! Lena thought. It had not occurred to her before. She wondered why it had not. She knew they were all thinking of the war, but refusing to speak of it. A man was different from a woman in this. When a woman had something in her heart, it had to come out. These men were making a play with words, avoiding the issue and waiting for the good Lord only knew what, before they spoke. When they began, they would go on, but they could not make up their minds to begin and must talk of wild beasts, crops, and cattle.

She took away the coffee-cups. Her grandmother got out the Bible. They all sat with their heads bowed while she read. As though it was a picture, Lena studied their faces through her open fingers. Her grandmother's face and Stoffel's looked hard. Stoffel's lips were drawn in, a little vein on his forehead was throbbing. She knew what he was thinking. She knew that, though the Bible was being read, he was consumed with hatred. He had always hated the English and he wanted war. It would prove he was as good as other men. He was praying for war. She could not understand why he hated so much. It was very hard for her to hate any one. Her grandmother was different : she had cause. Her hatred was that of an old hawk that will not bear restriction. It was because the English had kept pressing on the Boers that she hated them. And because, when they came, they brought their blasphemous customs and wicked ways of life with them, corrupting all who came near to them, or so she said.

Louis was big and solemn. Nothing showed on his face. He would go to war because the others went and there was no option. He would fight, not for pleasure like Stoffel, but because there seemed nothing else to do. Oupa, she felt, was an observer only, but interested and curious. He had fought so much ever since his childhood that there was nothing strange to him in a new war.

Dirk she could not see, but she knew what was in his heart. He wanted to fight for freedom. He wanted it over so that they could marry and live in peace. Her grandmother's voice went on. It was all meaningless to-night. Try as she would, Lena could not tie the words together as she heard them. To-morrow these men, except for Oupa, would be gone, their chairs empty. There was the dress to make. She thought of how the material changed colour. It was like a brown pigeon's breast.

She thought of the hammerkop. He must be home, his head sunk into his shoulders as he sat on the big willow beside his wife . . . The horses had been hot when she came in . . . What would the Brenners do if there was war? The dorp had been built up round the store. Old Brenner, Mr. Brenner's father, had set it up on the trekpad many years ago to trade with Kaffirs and hunters from the North.

Above her head a swallow moved. There were two swallows' nests, made of little dabs of mud, in the room. They were set high up where the walls met the roof. All day the swallows darted in and out of the half-door, bringing insects tirelessly to their young. Under each nest Louis had nailed a little plank to catch their droppings. They went away with their young ones each autumn and came back in the spring—always the same ones coming to the same place. In the autumn they collected into great flocks and sat twittering. The flocks were like commandos, they had leaders who told them where to go. She wondered what would happen between now and April when they left. So much could happen. . . . When would it be over? When would she be married to Dirk? She wanted to put out her hand to touch him, but you could not do that while the Bible was being read. Would her grandmother never stop? She moved her elbow nearer to Dirk's.

Her grandmother went on reading. The names and words made a rhythm, like the beating of wings in her mind. They sounded meaningless and yet important, divorced from life, but in some way an expression of it, symbolical of something one knew, but did not understand. She thought of the white stone cross that had come from Pretoria and stood over her father's grave. It was just like the one on her mother's. They lay there side by side in death beneath their marble crosses.

Moths fluttered round the hanging lamp, casting shadows on the table. There were no flies, only moths: the flies were asleep: they dotted the walls and ceiling with a thick black pattern like the markings on a flea-bitten horse. Lena thought of the flies at Tanta Martha's and of Netta waving her ostrich-feather whisk. That was only this morning, only a few hours ago! She thought of Netta's face and the expression in her eyes. Sometimes a moth would bang into the lamp glass. One fell suddenly with its scorched wing crumpled. It could not rise, but spun round and round in circles beating its good wing on the table, marking it with fluff till it fell on the floor. Stoffel put out his foot; she heard him crush it. It was a hawk moth, one of those that had been humming, poised over the flowers, when she drove in: so beautiful and so suddenly ended. Netta was different because she was going to have a child. By that she had been changed—not only her expression, but her life. The look she had given her was part of her new life: part of the direction it had taken. . . .

Ouma's voice went on. Beyond the table it was nearly dark. By the doorless kitchen the servants stood, moving their feet. Very reverent they looked as they stood with bowed heads, but in a minute, when it was over, they would be giggling and squealing as the men pinched them. No one knew what went on in a Kaffir's mind . . . "Begotten" . . . It was strange to think that her grandmother had ever been begotten; that she had ever been a little girl and had gone North in the early days as a child, with Tanta Aletta and Kaspar van der Berg; that she had been young, lovely, beloved; that her son was Lena's own father: strange that one day a man would beget children of her . . . that Dirk would. He was beside her now. She could feel him there, wanting to touch her. She listened to his heavy breathing.

Her grandmother closed the Book. They all leaned forward, their elbows on the table, in prayer. She prayed for Dirk, for his safety and return unharmed. Their arms were touching now. There was a scraping of chairs.

"I do not believe in war," Oupa said.

So it had begun. Now they were going to talk, but talking would change nothing. There would be war . . . they would all have to go. She was thankful Oupa was too old. She would get some comfort from him, when Dirk had gone.

"Strange words from you, Oupa, who have spent half your life fighting," her grandmother said. "And it is they who sowed the wind and they who will reap the whirlwind now that the day is at hand."

"Yes, I have spent my life fighting and what have I got for it?"

Pulling open his shirt he exposed a slash across his chest. He showed another on his arm.

"That is what I got," he said. "Wounds and more wounds: wounds and my friends killed: my sons killed. They would have looked after me properly if they had not been killed. Magtig, it is because of war that I am so alone."

"It is because you are so old," Ouma said.

"Too old, you think. Ja, you think it's time the Old Baas died: you and your precious grandson." He looked at Stoffel. "But I shall not die to please you. I shall not die to please any one. In this, at least, I will please myself. Before God, I swear I will only die to please myself."

Lena went up to him and put her arm round his neck.

"We will drive the English into the sea," Stoffel said. "We will drive them out and then it will be our land again."

"You will drive them out? You and the likes of you?" the old man said looking at him contemptuously. "And then what will you do?—that is, if you do it. Not that I love the English; I have no reason to; but I dislike war. It spoils the land. Ja, magtig, I know I stand alone among the old men in this. It is very easy for the old men to send the young men to fight, but I see nothing in it. Win or lose, it is disaster for white to fight white in a black country."

Stoffel jumped up. "Are we then to become like the Colony?" he shouted—" where an honest man dare not offer himself as a parliamentary candidate because he speaks no English : where if he be summoned to court, his case is taken in a language he does not understand and he sees acting between himself and his judges an interpreter who is a coloured Bastaard : a coloured man, who looks down upon him because he understands two languages to his one; where if called upon to serve on a commando, he must serve under a man he has not elected, in whom he has no confidence, of whom he has no knowledge, one who does not know his speech and despises him? . . . Are we to wait to see these things here? Are we to stand idle while the net is thrown about us and the cords drawn tight about our freedom? Our flag is gone. Our language, the speech of our fathers, is threatened. Our ways and religion are laughed at by strangers. Our country is desecrated."

He sat down.

"Ja," Dirk said. "That is true. All you have said is true, but I wish it could be some other way."

"That is because you want to marry Lena. You would rather lie with her than fight. But I love nothing but my land. It is in my heart to fight, to drive them from our sacred soil . . ."

All this must have been going on in the mind of her brother for years. It was all part of Ouma's teaching. She should have known it, but had not. She had paid small attention to what her grandmother said except when it dealt with the romances of her people, their loves and deeds of daring, their fights with the Kaffirs, hardships and struggles in the early days.

"We will fight if they want us to," Louis said. "I am ready to fight. It has been in my mind for a long time that we must."

So Louis, too, had been thinking of it while he went about his work. Every one seemed to have been thinking about it except her. She had been too busy, too happy with the little things that made her life, to think about the great things, and now the great had overtaken her and were pressing the goodness out of her.

Her great-grandfather sat with his chin upon his chest. His eyes were closed. Her grandmother had opened the Bible again and was reading it to herself. Stoffel went for his gun and began to clean it. It was spotless, but still he cleaned it, and filled the magazine with cartridges. Louis got up and left them. He was going round the dorp, he said, to see if there was more news.

Dirk came over to her and took her hand.

"Come out, my heart," he said. "The moon is nearly full and bright."

4

Old Philippus was not asleep : he was thinking. A man to his mind never got old. He remained what he had always been. Moulded by experience, he stayed the same, and experience was no more than an over-lay, a lacquer, upon his real self. When a boy grew old enough, women came into his life. At first supremely important, they later became accepted as normal, then they became unimportant and passed out of his life, as women. He thought of his first wife, of Helena and their love together, of its hot passion, of their partings, and finally, of her death. Since then he had had other wives, other passions, other partings, other deaths. With Helena he had thought nothing has been like this before, nothing will be like it again, but things had been like it. Things, emotions, were so alike that you recognized them when they came and remembered the previous occasions when you had felt them. Women were the same, different in degree, but not different in actuality. Each thing was a recapitulation. The reason death was feared was because no man could twice experience it. Everything, as you got older, lost value. Achievement, even, lost value as it was found valueless and a means only to an end. Possessions were respon-sibilities and too many destroyed the pleasure of possessing. Life from being urgent became a routine where things were done so often that they were no longer acts consciously conceived of the mind and executed. Even words, spoken and written, were reproduced continually and lost signifi-cance. The first time a man said I love you to a woman, it meant some-thing. It turned his heart over. But when he had said it to many women, and knew how they looked as he spoke, it meant very little. Touching a woman, feeling her heart in her breast, was the same, only the first time counted or the first few times.

Out there in the moonlight his little Lena was being made love to, was making love, for a woman made love as much as a man. She did not know yet that love brought no happiness, only pain. The more you loved, the greater the suffering. Many men never loved. They married and had children, but still knew nothing of it. It's our French blood that does it, he thought. Men and women with that blood are different, hotter, like horses with a racing strain. They smash themselves against the obstacles of circumstance.

Thinking back, he remembered clearly the discomfort of love, the pain, the difficulty of settling down to anything. the urge, ever present, to get against the woman, just to be near her. That is what you thought when you were parted from her, at least that is what you thought you thought, but when you were near her you wanted more, always more. More even when you took her because what you wanted was in your mind and unattainable by the body that you used. Yes, that was so, when you had her you lost her, getting all women in her stead. She, the woman you loved, disappeared into the emptiness of the hungry earth. Woman was the earth, everlasting as the earth, and man a random sower without precision. A woman's children were her own, a veritable part of her that was broken off like the branch of a tree. A woman's world; her life was entirely apart from that of a man. She lived in a different world, seeing it differently and interpreting the things she saw in a different manner.

To love and to hunt were in a way the same. A man liked to hunt, to put up his gun and fire. But did he? Was there not some strange compulsion that made him do this? There was the buck, a separate thing, standing detached in its own world, the world of bucks. There was the man armed, and the will to kill that went with the bullet. At these times, as one fired, one was certain. There was the triumph of seeing the beast fall, and then, after that, there was nothing. Only an emptiness, a feeling that something was over.

Now that he was old and no longer troubled by such things, it interested him to think of them. As a young man, he had heard old Christiaan van Ek talk much. It was he who had taught him to think and to see the wonders of the world. And in his life he had cared for so many things, women, children, dogs, horses, cattle : cared greatly and the things he had cared for were gone. The companionship of men and beasts had been his : also the companionship of places; of green trees and flowers; of nesting swallows like those in this room that came back yearly and were watched for; of fields of growing things—mealies, wheat, oats, and barley that came up out of the ground and grew, caressed by the wind into long waves of shadowed sunlight; of orchards bride-flowered in the spring, mantled with blossom; and of vineyards, the gnarled vines bent beneath the purple splendour of their grapes.

So many men had been his friends—hunters, farmers, traders, fighting men who were dead of fighting, dying as they had lived. He had seen them die to his left and his right, before him and behind. His life had been charmed. He had survived them all and was left behind, singularly alone, with young men about him—boys. That was why he now dwelt in the past, in his memories, in his lost vigour among the dead companions who had known it—an old man getting ready to die. But he was not afraid. Sometimes he thought he would be glad when it was over. Still, he wanted to see his little Lena with a baby at her breast and to annoy her grandmother by living on.

Often he wondered how his son could have married Kattie. Even the scarcity of women in those times was no excuse, and it was sad to think of the time he had wasted begetting fools. But the blood was out again with Lena. In that little maid he saw himself. She was out in the moonlight with a young man who was going to war. That was the way he had courted

Helena before he rode away to fight and it was good. Such situations were the enemies of delay. He sighed happily. His head slid lower and he slept.

5

The night was warm, almost palpably soft, black-shadowed and brilliantly moonlit, alternately, patches of velvety darkness cut with patches of velvety light. We are enclosed, Lena thought, in this night of darkness, as last week we were enclosed in the circle of candlelight. But the darkness of the moon shadows would not change : there was no candle to watch : there was no door that might open on this warm privacy. She was alone with Dirk in the warm night with scent of the orange blossoms from the orchard in her nostrils, and his arm was about her, his thigh against her thigh. To-night was at once the beginning of something and the end of something. The end of their courtship, the beginning of their love . . . at once the coming together and the parting . . . at once the birth and the death.

She did not want to speak : she was content to be. She felt herself ripening, as fruit ripens, suddenly. One day it is hard and the next it is warm and soft, sun-ripe. Perhaps women were like that, too : coming to fruition suddenly; one day girls and the next women, like Netta. It was not just the night, the moonlight, the perfume of the orange blossoms and the blue gums. Such things were beautiful, but they were not new. She was used to them all. Only what she felt was new . . . only the change that had taken place in her heart and body. She felt tense as a drawn string and yet soft, incredibly tender, as fluid as water. Her feet, when she put them down, felt different, as if they trod a different world. She was walking lightly as a buck.

A nightjar screamed. She saw it turn in the air, black against the night-blue sky as it caught a moth. How strange it was that when the moon was big you saw no stars ! At least, you saw them, but they were faint, killed by the moonlight. The nightjar swooped again coming close to them, its wings cracking against the air as it swept upward. She hid her face in Dirk's shoulder. He pressed her into his chest. She could feel his heart beating. Why had she turned to him? She was not afraid of nightjars. I turned because I wanted to, she thought. I turned because the nightjar gave me the chance. I wanted my head against him. She slid her hand into his shirt. She wanted to feel his heart under her hand. She wanted to feel his skin with her hand . . . the smooth hardness of his ribs that were heaving as the sides of a horse heave when it has been galloped and is nearly spent. Her own breath was coming in gasps. She could hear nothing for the hammering of the blood in her ears. Dirk's arm was still pressing her, not relaxing : just holding her.

Then he began to tremble like a frightened horse. Why should he tremble? Why should she think of horses? She felt him throw back his head as if he was plunging. She had seen horses do that, too, pausing as if frightened before they leaped. Now . . . now, she thought. The instant was interminable, and then it came. He pulled her to him. He bent over her and forced her back. If it had not been for his arm, she would have fallen. He was kissing her, but in a new way—without gentleness. She was kissing him, clinging to him with her lips. She had not known that kisses could be like this . . . that you could be carried away and cease to be.

His arm slipped down nearly to her hips . . . lower. She was in his arms now. He was carrying her. She was holding on to him. She would never let him go. He was taking her into the deepest shadow of the gums. She closed her eyes. He was kissing her again as he lay beside her. She opened her eyes. His face was black against the sky. She could see the outline of his head cut by the branches of the trees above her, and the line of his neck. She closed her eyes again. He was touching her; touching her breasts; touching her . . . touching her; holding her. She felt his hands. He must stop. She wanted to tell him to stop. But she did not want him to stop. She was pressed as a flower is pressed in a book. Her life was running out of her : she was nothing : she had ceased to exist . . . ceased to be.

She remembered everything : all her life : everything that had ever been said to her. Everything she had ever done and thought was in her mind, but it had nothing to do with her. It was all irrelevant. From now on she had ceased to be Lena. Now she was Dirk's . . . Dirk's . . . Dirk's. She was lost to herself in Dirk. Possessed of him . . . by him . . . she was a part of him.

She felt herself sinking through warm water. She no longer lay on the ground under the blue gums. She was going down . . . down. She was drowning. She must fight against it . . . against death. She felt herself struggle. She thought how stupid of me to fight when I do not want to, and then she found she was not fighting, but clinging to Dirk, burrowing into him. She saw the gums again and the stars gleaming faintly in the sky. She thought how strange it is that when there is a full moon they burn so weakly! She remembered having had that thought before. I thought that long ago. But it was not long ago . . . it was just a few minutes ago. But it was long ago : it was a whole life ago. She was a woman now. The world was wonderfully beautiful, perfumed with the scent of orange blossoms, soft with the night breeze that stirred the leaves on the trees, shimmering them in the moonlight. And she was at ease : never had she known such ease before.

Dirk was kissing her again and caressing her, but gently : as gently as the wind caressed the leaves, and she was turning to him as the leaves turned to the night breeze. The storm was over : the tempest done. This was love that they had between them . . . the accomplishment, the fulfilment of life . . . its consummation . . . its end and its beginning. In an hour, half an hour, perhaps, everything had changed. She belonged to Dirk. Time and space had ceased to exist.

She found she had no idea of how long they had been out, but while they had been together the war had come nearer. She had forgotten the war, but it was coming nearer every minute. How could she have forgotten that? Had she forgotten it or, knowing it, had she turned into him? Knowing it, had she used a nightjar to demand that which she had had of him? She did not know : she would never know.

She tried to think back as she ran her hand through Dirk's hair and over his face. How soft his young beard was! It was like the yellow hairs on a young pigeon's breast. Her new dress was shot with green as a pigeon's breast was shot with green and purple. How big the moon was to-night! Like a great orange in the sky flaming as it rose. How sweet the night scents! How beautiful the stars that twinkled so faintly in the heavens! They were like tender, watching eyes. How wonderful the nightjars swooping and diving, crying eerily as they stooped on the insects that they were able to see in the darkness. And the bats . . . Some people could hear bats squeak as they flew. She must ask Dirk if he could hear bats squeaking. She was sure he could.

" Can you hear bats squeaking when they fly, Dirk?" she asked.

He seemed surprised. " Yes, I can hear them, Lena."

So she had been right : he was more than other men : only very few people could hear them. He was the world to her. She felt suddenly practical, maternal towards him.

" We must go back now," she said.

" Yes, we must go back."

He gave her his hand and pulled her up.

She smoothed her dress and tidied her hair. She felt she was wonderful to be able to think of such things at this time. And she was glad it was dark. No one must see her eyes till she had had time to calm them. Dirk put his arm round her shoulders. They walked slowly towards the lighted window. They were all in there : all thinking their own thoughts.

She looked in. Oupa was half asleep, probably dreaming of the past. Her grandmother sitting still with folded hands, brooding and hating. Stoffel was still polishing and repolishing his Mauser : loading the magazine and unloading it again, rattling the bolt while Oupa looked at him contemptuously through lowered eyelids. His lids were those of an old eagle—veiled, veined, wrinkled. He did not think anything of repeating rifles. There was no skill in their use; there was no risk, he said. It was something else to face a charging elephant or a lion with a single shot in your muzzle-loading roer. And Louis had gone. She had often wondered what Louis thought about. He seldom spoke of his thoughts, but she loved him. He was big and gentle. To-morrow the house would be empty of them all. Only Oupa would be left, and Ouma. In a few minutes Dirk would say good-bye: say, "Tot siens, my heart . . . till I see you . . ." Till she saw him! . . .

Dirk would be gone to-night. Her brothers to-morrow. Then there would only be waiting, and empty chairs, and memories . . .

She must kiss Dirk again, he must hold her. What did her hair matter . . . her eyes? It was war. What did anything matter in a world so soon to be empty—empty of Dirk?

"Kiss me," she said. "Kiss me, Dirk; kiss me."

She drew him back. Without knowing how it happened, without ever thinking of it, she found herself under the trees again. Something stronger than us has drawn us here, she thought. This time she had needed no nightjar. This time nothing was needed to draw them together. Nothing could have kept them apart.

CHAPTER V

. . . A BLIND BOY . . .

I

DIRK rode home slowly. The reins lay loose on Swartkie's neck. He loved
Lena and there was going to be war. Lena . . . war . . . Lena . . .
war—and both had come suddenly, within the last few days, within the
last few hours. He had loved Lena for a long time. He had felt that there
would be war for a long time. But neither feeling had been clear, definite.
Neither had cut into his life. Rather had they been a part of the atmosphere
in which he lived. He had been continuously conscious of them, but only
as you were conscious of the weather . . . a fine day or a storm rising. His
love for Lena had been like a fine day. He had lived in it, aware of it as he
worked and lived his life. The threat of war was the cloud on the horizon.
Last week he had seen it growing, to-night it had come. It was no use
pretending it had not.

He patted his horse's shoulder. To-morrow they would be away : he and
Swartkie on the road to the meeting : riding as hundreds, as thousands of
others would be riding from all round, coming in, as bees came in, to the
hive of their national assembly at Paardekraal.

And Lena. Till to-night he had not known how much he loved her. He
had known it in his heart, but it had not come forward. Till to-night he
had been able to manage his love, to restrain it, to guide it. He had been
able to until Lena . . . Why had she done that? It would have been better
to have waited.

He picked up his reins again. He was in two minds : to gallop away
from her . . . to turn and gallop back. What had she done that he was
now ground between the upper millstone of his desire and the nether millstone of his citizenship as a burger of the Transvaal Republic? He wanted
her as he had never thought it was possible to want any one. He wanted
to touch the crisp darkness of her hair where it curled away from her neck :
to look into her eyes. When she was pleased or excited, the right one went
out of focus. It seemed incredibly beautiful to him that it should do this.

No, till to-night I did not know what I felt for her, he thought. All I
knew was that I was unhappy away from her and that when I was with her
I felt ill. Now he no longer felt ill. He felt strong and well. She was his :
as much his as a woman could be. She was the whole world and the rest of
it nothing set in the scale against her.

He thought of his father; he would have to go, too; of his mother and the baby, and of Boetie. Why should a boy, for no fault of his own, be born blind? Boetie was so gentle, so helpless, so brave, making nothing of his disability. "It is not as if I ever had seen, Dirk," he said. "I have lost nothing and I am very happy." It was this happiness of his that tore the heart out of your body. No one seeing him would have guessed that he was blind. His eyes were brilliant blue—flower blue, the colour of a bright blue sky. What would become of him? Of them all? Of the country? As soon as things began to go well, something happened : a war, a drought, a flood, political disturbance after political disturbance.

This moon-wet land that he rode through—opalescent, black, and shining silver, vast, silent, empty—was his land, the home, for two hundred years, of his people : his people and Lena's : his land—her land—the land of their children. He had been very near to her under the trees to-night, holding her, touching her, loving her. Lena was Africa : Lena was all the world. And South Africa was their country. He thought of its mountains, its bushveld, its wide plains, its watercourses and fountains, its thick matted kloofs. He was riding through some Kaffir lands now; the mealies were shoulder high and rustled in the breeze. The season had been a good one: the orchard trees on every farm were borne down, bowed, under their fruit.

It was midsummer, and he loved Lena and he must leave her. He loved her. What she wanted she must have : he would get it for her. Before God, he would shake the golden fruits from the very tree of life and drop them into her lap. If she wanted a new home, he would build her one. He would hew it out of the wilderness and give it to her on a platter of wrought silver. That was what he felt—an immense desire to give, a wild surge of possible achievement for her : achievement only made possible by his love for her : achievement for her alone. On her he wanted to shower the gifts of his hands, his brain. To her he was ready to give everything that was in him, eager to give both his body and his soul into her hands to do with what she willed. He would reach for the songs of the birds on the trees, for the blue lightning of the kingfisher's flight, for the flowers of his love, whole armfuls of them, fragrant and lit with butterflies. He would reach for all the beauty in the world and give it to her.

He remembered how foolish he had thought young men in love. Abstracted and ridiculous, able only to talk of the girls to whom they were betrothed. He wondered how foolish he must appear now, and did not care. He saw suddenly how the facts that, at the beginning of his ride, had seemed utterly irreconcilable were now reconcilable, coming together till they made one thing. Because he was young, he loved, and because he was young and loved, he must fight for the freedom of his country, for Lena and their unborn sons. Their children must be born free. It was for their heritage that he would fight. He began to canter.

It was enough that he loved Lena. She filled his world. War or no war, now his life had a reason and a purpose.

He had said a last good-bye to her in the thick darkness of the trees. She had made him take her back there before he left. They would meet again when he came back. To-morrow he must say good-bye to his mother and Boetie and Little Johanna. This was the last time he would ride home from Mooiplaas for many days . . . perhaps the last time. But he was not the only one. It was no use his being sorry for himself. All over the country the farms would be empty of men. All over the country men would be riding in to the meeting.

Ardent politicians, Boers loved to talk and to argue, to go to meetings, to protest, to censure, to say, We want this and that, we must have our freedom and no taxes. But how could a country be run without taxes? The Secocoeni War had been disastrous. The Boers had got tired and had refused to fight any longer under President Burgers. They had said to fight under François Thomas Burgers, the President they had elected, was to court failure. They wanted Kruger to lead them. Dirk was curious to see this Paul Kruger of whom all men were speaking. Kruger, the Dopper, considered Burgers impious and wicked. When asked if he would lead the troops, he had replied : " I cannot come with you, for with your merry evenings in laager, and your Sunday dances, the enemy will shoot me even behind a wall. And God's blessing cannot rest upon such an expedition."

Kruger was bigoted, but was said to be the finest leader that they had. The sky of Africa was black with storms; from all sides the Republic was menaced. Broken by the internal dissension of rival parties, everything seemed uncertain. Not a man who had ridden home after the Secocoeni War had been satisfied : not one had failed to see more trouble ahead.

Hendrik Mostert, his friend, who lived near Paul Kruger in the Rustenburg, called him their only hope. " In that man lies the hope of our nation's freedom," he had said. Kruger and he were close friends, farming side by side, hunting together and meeting often. It was Hendrik who had told him of how, at the annexation, Shepstone's carriage had had its horses outspanned and had been dragged into Pretoria by the Uitlanders. Of how a little later the Vierkleur had gone down and the flag of England gone up in its place.

" That day, jong," he said, " I shall never forget. That day, the twelfth of April, eighteen hundred and seventy-seven, is one we must all remember."

But he was prejudiced. And he was not in love with Lena. To be in love changed everything. He had told him how Kruger had asked the English Queen to reconsider her decision, of how he had gone to Holland, to Germany, and France for help. All the world knew of these matters, but, because Hendrik was Kruger's friend, he spoke with greater feeling and more authority. No one knew what would happen now : no one knew anything save that something was in the air, something that had never really ended was about to begin again. That business in Brennersdorp last week looked like the new beginning.

And there were many like Stoffel who wanted war; who thought that things could be decided by rifles. As far as he could see, nothing was ever decided this way. The only way to decide things was by talking and yet they had talked so long without result. At Paardekraal there would be more talk, but talk backed by armed force. Dirk wanted no war; all he wanted was to work on his farm, to marry Lena and make a home-place where he could live with her and their children, grow crops and breed sheep and cattle and horses.

His horse was walking along a narrow path, snatching at mouthfuls of grass as he passed. Once he stopped and snorted as a porcupine, its quills rattling and shining in the moonlight, shuffled across the road.

There was life everywhere, all round him on the veld : invisible life : aardvarks digging up ants' nests with their strong claws and catching the ants with their long, sticky tongues; jackals and meerkats hunting; snakes crawling on their bellies in search of frogs and mice; and the night birds— the jars, the owls, and plovers—were on the wing. He thought of old Oom Philippus and his talk of lions. He liked to talk to the old man : he knew so much and had seen so much. There was nothing he did not know of wild beasts and their ways.

He pulled up and looked about him. It came to him that the veld had two populations, that there were two worlds of animals, birds, and insects : one of the day and one of the night. He seemed to understand everything. to-night : to see the tremendous pattern and significance of life : his own and Lena's—all life; that of men and women, of beasts and birds. It is because this is the end of a period I see it, he thought : to-morrow is a new beginning. If there is to be war let it come soon so that it would soon be over. To-morrow they would be off. He saw himself going : his father on Galant, the sire of Swartkie—two fathers and two sons, two generations of man and horse. He touched Swartkie with his heels.

2

Boetie was not asleep when his brother came back. He was lying awake, waiting and thinking of the day he had spent in the mountain. He called it his mountain : the Kaffirs called it Duifkop, the Hill of Doves. A good name, for when you were up there, there were many doves cooing from the trees and passing with swift, whistling wings. Dirk was courting Cousin Lena. It would be a fine thing when they were married. It would make Dirk happy, and he had promised to keep him with them.

Lena was good to him. She had played with him when he was small and it was she who had shown him how to make little oxen out of clay, fit them with horns of thorn, and bake them in the sun. It did not matter if you were blind, for you could make them without seeing, once you had felt what they should be like. After that, once he had known how, he had made many hundreds of clay oxen for the children of his father's friends and for relations. They had all been very pleased with them and had come to say thank you, or had sent messages, if they lived too far away. Yes, he had made oxen for many children that he did not know and they had gone to all parts.

He began to play a game. He had played it since he was quite small, when he wanted to stay awake. It was an interesting game. You lay still and imagined yourself getting smaller. You let your arms and legs get smaller and smaller, shortening them till they disappeared. Then your body got smaller, as small as a baby's, you could feel it going, and finally, only your head was left. You made that get smaller, too. You went on till it was about the size of a nut, and then you got frightened because, if you went on any longer you would disappear entirely. There was another game in which you made your head grow and grow, but that was not so interesting. It had neither the charm nor the variety of the first game, and it gave you a headache.

He was glad when he heard Dirk come. He felt uneasy when he was away, even when he knew where he was. Suppose something should happen to him? He never knew what could happen, but always feared that something might. Now that he was home, he could go to sleep.

It had been a lovely day on the mountain. To-morrow would also be lovely. He would be able to sit there and think of all that Dirk would tell him when he came in. Dirk would tell him what he had seen and heard, and talk about Lena. He loved to hear him talk about Lena. His voice was so soft when he spoke of her.

There he was coming now. He had turned Swartkie loose. He was opening the door. That was the clink of his stirrups as he carried in his saddle. He came into the room and lit the candle.

" What is the news, Dirk?" Boetie asked.

" No news, Boetie: at least, nothing much."

" Tell me the news."

" I will tell you in the morning," Dirk said. " You must go to sleep."

Sometimes it was like that. It all depended on Dirk's mood. To-night he was sad. Boetie knew he was sad from the way he moved. He is worrying about something. If only he would tell me. Day and night . . . What did night or day matter to him? But his mother had said that Dirk was not to talk at night because it excited him and he could not sleep. He could not make her understand that it was better to sleep in the day. That was when all wild things slept, lying down in the warmth of the sun. Whether Dirk spoke to him or not he was often awake at night. There was so much to listen to; at night the world of beasts he loved was awake, hunting, being hunted, and quite often he crept out of the house to enjoy it. They had never been able to stop his doing this. He heard Dirk blow out the light.

"Good-night, Dirk, and you will tell me in the morning."

"Ja, Boetie, in the morning. Good-night."

In the distance, at the stad, where their Kaffirs lived, a cock crowed half heartedly. You could tell the hour by the way cocks crowed. In the morning, they were sharp and challenging, calling to each other with flapping wings. It was at night. Dirk was back, lying near him. He listened to his breathing, then he turned on his side. He did not like to sleep till Dirk did.

In the morning when he woke Dirk was gone. He dressed quickly. Something was wrong. There was too much movement in the house.

"Dirk!" he shouted . . . "Pa . . . Ma!"

"Ja, what is it?" It was his mother. She had been crying.

"What is it, Ma? What is the matter? Something is not right?"

"Nee, Boetie, something is not right when the men must go from their homes."

"Men go . . . go where?" What did it mean? Then it came to him: that was why Dirk had been uneasy last night. "It is war," he said. "Dirk and my father are going."

"Yes, we are going, my son. We are leaving you to take care of your mother."

"If I was not blind, I could go too, Pa. I am old enough. I am fourteen. Many no older than I will be there."

His father put his arm round him. "You will look after your mother and sister till we come back," he said. "And there may not be war. We are only going to the meeting. We were always going to the meeting, but it has been put forward."

"Ja, Pa, and you are taking rifles to the meeting." He had felt the gun lying on the table.

Dirk came in. "The horses are ready," he said.

Horses . . . then they were going at once.

"Are you going now?" Boetie asked. "At once, before you have eaten?"

"We are going now and we have eaten. We ate while you slept. We are meeting Stoffel and Louis at the crossroads," Dirk said.

"And Lena?" Boetie asked. "Are you seeing her again? When are you going to marry her?"

They were moving round him. He heard his father pick up his bandolier. He could tell by the sound that it was full, heavy with cartridges. His mother put a package on the table. That was veld kost—food for the journey.

"Yes, I am going to marry Lena, when it is over," Dirk said. "We will be married and you will be there and play on your flute. It will be fine."

"I have no more room in my saddle-bag, Johanna," his father said.

"I can take it," Dirk said.

Everything was changed. They loved him, but paid no attention to him. He was blind. This was the outside world which he had always feared. It had come into Doornkloof while he slept.

Dirk and his father moved about aimlessly. Boetie knew they were taking a last look at the room : touching familiar things, looking, looking. I could not look, he thought. If I was going, I could only touch.

"Come, Dirk," his father said. He heard him kiss his mother. Then he went into the other room to kiss Klein Johanna. Johanna was lucky. She would not know what it meant. Dirk kissed his mother; then he kissed him. He felt the hairs of Dirk's bare forearm on his neck. Then Dirk went in to kiss his sister. His father kissed him. "Take good care of everything, Boetie," he said. "You are the man on Doornkloof. Ja," he said, "the Klein Baas is now the Groot Baas."

He was the man, but if he had not wakened, they might have left him sleeping. In this new world he was no more important and of no more use than his little sister.

His father and brother moved heavily with creaks of leather. They were loaded, strung with bandoliers, water bottles, and slung rifles. The gun butts touched the furniture as they moved. His mother was very brave. She was not crying any more. She had gone to get Johanna, who was asking for her food, from her bed.

"I am hungry," she said. "I want breakfast. I want to eat. Where is Pa going? Why has he got his gun? Is he going hunting? I want to go hunting."

His mother stopped her talking with kisses. She must be holding her very tight. Johanna hated to be held tight and he heard her struggle out of her arms.

"I want to go with Dirk and Pa," she said, and ran towards them. She would be holding on to their trousers now with little soft hands and trying to drag them back. His mother picked her up again and she began to scream.

"Come, Dirk," his father said again.

They went out, their accoutrements rattling and creaking. He followed them. He could hear the horses moving, throwing their heads so that their bits rattled, and stamping their feet at the flies. It was all unreal. There had been talk before and he had been afraid, but he had not thought it would be like this. He had thought there would be more talk and warning. It had come like a storm. The wind of war had swept his home away in the night. It had taken his father and his brother, his dream of security, while he slept.

They felt their girths and tightened them : the horses grunted. They kissed him again. They kissed his mother and Johanna. She was quiet now. When they kissed him good-bye their bandoliers had pressed into his chest.

He stood very still as they mounted. He listened to their movements, to the scuffle of the unshod hoofs on the ground, the creak of leather, the rattle of bits and stirrup irons as the horses turned. He must remember all this. It was the sound of his father's and his brother's going.

"Tot siens," they shouted. "Tot siens, Johanna . . . Ma . . . Boetie . . . Johanna."

He could feel the horses buckle under their riders as they raised their reins. They broke from the stand into a canter. Though they ran together, he could distinguish them apart. Dirk's horse, Swartkie, was faster and lighter than his father's. It struck the ground harder, with quick little beats of its hoofs, as if it was eager to get on and hated to have them on the ground. Swartkie was a hot little horse, urgent and strong. His father's was more solid and slower. Dirk would be having to hold his horse: Swartkie would be shaking his head and spilling foam over his chest and knees. He knew how they would ride side by side, his father only leading when they came to a narrow path, with Dirk's horse snatching at his bit and pulling to get up as soon as the ground opened.

He stood mouse-still, listening as the sound of hoofs faded into the distance. He stood frozen by the silence and the emptiness of their going. A cock, standing on the wall of the kraal, crowed. He thought of last night when he had heard a cock at the stad crow. They would go on crowing all the time they were away, every morning, and on moonlight nights. It was nothing to them that Dirk and his father were gone. There was no sound now, they were far away. Now, there was nothing to do but strain his ears for their return. Among a thousand hoofbeats he would know those horses.

He felt his mother beside him. She held him to her. She was crying bitterly, sobbing great sobs that shook her. He felt his lips tremble. His sister pulled at his legs, whimpering. They were gone. Their places were empty. He was the Baas of Doornkloof. Tears ran down his face. They were salt in his mouth. He hid his face in his mother's breast. He was the Baas. He must remember that. He must not cry.

"What shall we do, Ma," he asked, "now that they are gone?"

"We are going to stand by the place as is our custom. Before God, Boetie, this is hard, but it is nothing new in the history of our people. Always the men have gone, and when we could not go with them we have stayed behind and farmed till they came back. But we must be ready, Boetie. We must have horses always ready in the kraal, and food for any of our people who are in need. If there is war, and it is in my heart that it is come, we must be ready, for if there is fighting nearby, our men count on the farms to supply them."

"We will be ready when they need us, Ma. Everything will be ready on Doornkloof."

He would see to it. But the work must go on. He was a man. His father had gone, but he must take out his father's goats.

3

Up in the mountain, Boetie sat leaning against a rock. His hat was tilted over his eyes. His head and body were in the shade of a rock, but the sun was on his bare feet. He could feel it on his ankles, feet, and toes as he wriggled them, opening them a little, the one from the other, and then closing them over the balls of his feet like fists. He could pick things up with his toes. His toes and the soles of his feet told him where he was. They knew the feel of the sand and the stones and the different kinds of grass.

To-day he felt utterly lost. He had come up with his goats because he always did. That was his work and the mountain had become a part of him. Happy or unhappy he climbed it. But what was life going to be like now? How was he to look after his mother and Klein Johanna? Where were his father and brother? They must have met Stoffel and Louis and be riding on together. Perhaps they had met others. All the world of men and boys, who were not crippled, were riding in from the veld, all armed, running in like the spokes of a wheel towards the hub.

War with the English. . . . He had met an Englishman once. He had spent the night at his father's house and on going had given him a knife with several blades, a pair of scissors, a corkscrew, tweezers and a pointed pin to get thorns from your hands, and a big hook for removing stones from the feet of a horse. No one in those parts had seen such a knife before. He had it in a box at home. It was too good to use and he had kept it safely, his most treasured possession. I will give it to Dirk on his wedding, he thought. Dirk should have it. It was the finest knife in the world.

Why should Dirk and his father be going to fight men like that Englishman? He had been a nice man, who spoke their language in a soft voice, and his horse had a neck like warm silk. It was said that they brushed their horses daily which would account for its sleekness. It had felt red, and when he had asked what colour it was, they had told him he was right. It was a red horse, but how had he known? "I did not know," he said. "It felt red, that is all."

He tried not to think of war, of killing. It was wrong. It was wicked to hurt other men. It was beyond his understanding. It had something to do with a flag, but he could not understand flags. The Volksraad he understood and the English should have given it back to his people as had been promised. When would it be over? When would Dirk and his

father be back? He must be brave. Since he could not go with others
he must be brave at home, but it was hard to be brave alone.

To his right, a fink twittered. It seemed to him that he knew what it
was saying. It was talking of the beautiful new nest it was going to make.
It was saying : " It will be a beautiful nest, Boetie, softly woven of grass
and torn reeds. It will hang with others like a great pear among the
swinging willows of the drift."

It seemed to him that he knew what all the birds and beasts said to each
other. Because he was blind, they let him into their world, made him,
because he was helpless, a party to it. He never spoke of this except to his
brother, Dirk, and old Oom Philippus. They never laughed at him for his
fancies. But it puzzled him that great hunters and killers of beasts should
also love them. Perhaps you had to have great sight—Oom Philippus in
his youth had been able to see a buck at a thousand paces and kill one at
six hundred—or no sight at all, to be one with the wild.

Dirk, too, was a great hunter. But Dirk was wonderful and above all
other men. Perhaps now that Dirk was gone, he would be able to talk of
these things to Cousin Lena. She was gentle and not much older than he.
He wished Mooiplaas were nearer. But if she did not come, he might get
one of the boys to drive him over or his mother might, and they they could
take Johanna.

Boetie knew people were sorry for him. It made him draw back from
them into his own world. If only they could guess how beautiful it was,
they would envy him. Every one was kind to him. Nothing distracted
him, and till to-day he had not known real unhappiness. There had been
little things that had seemed great. But he had something that no one else
had—time to himself : time in which to think, and wait, and listen, and
feel. Most people heard nothing. They did not know about the little
rustlings in the grass, or the sounds of wings in the evening when the doves
went down to water. They did not know the warm feel of a tarentaal's
nest filled with eggs. They missed so much in not knowing the feel of
things—round things, eggs, water-worn stones; the rough surfaces of rock,
hot beneath their fingers, or leather, or of skin. And they knew nothing of
smells. They went through life with blind noses. They might be sorry for
him, but he was happy because he had so much.

Only to-day when his father and brother had been taken from him did
he know how happy he had been, how complete and perfect his life, the
life that he spent herding his father's goats upon the mountain. He knew
the goats apart by the sound of their cloven hoofs on the stones, by the feel
of their horns and hair, by their smell—the rank smell of the billies, the
sweet smell of the nannies, the milky smell and soft hides of the unweaned
kids. Their colours he did not know. How could he, since colour was
only a word to him? He could see no colour, yet he had a feeling for it.
Sometimes it seemed to him that a thing felt red, or white, or black, beneath

his hands, which was strange, as he did not know red, or black, or white. But this was only with living things, and then only sometimes.

The leader of his father's goats was Witbooi, a big white goat, they said. He had never been able to feel his colour. But he knew Witbooi by his height, by the rasp of his long hair under his hand, by his smell, which was very strong, and by the nicks in the rings of his horns that he had got by fighting.

Sometimes, as he lay in the sun, a goat would come up and nuzzle him. Their noses were not wet, smooth and cold like a cow's; they were not feather-soft like a horse's; they were not hard like a donkey's. A goat's nose was smooth as leather, with little stiff hairs on it and lips immune to thorns. A kid nibbled at his ear; then he butted at him, rearing and charging with little leaps. He put out his hand to feel the scurfy bulbs where the horns were growing : they were coming, small thick needles. He was a billy, bold and playful as a puppy.

It was easy to herd the goats. When he called them, they came to him. When he piped, they followed. He had a pipe made of soft wood; old Reuter, Oom Philippus' Zulu servant, had shown him how to make it. Together they burnt the little holes that made the notes and hollowed it. It was worn smooth with carrying and was good to touch. He knew many tunes. Dirk often took him to dances, leading his horse beside his own. He would sit there till the dance was over, listening to the dancing, and make every tune his own. He liked to hear people dance, to hear the music and rhythm of their feet, to smell the dust and the people as they got hot and happy. He sometimes thought that you could smell if people were unhappy or frightened, and also if they were happy. You could not explain this to any one, but animals knew. That was why dogs came and pushed their heads against you when you were sad, and horses, once they knew you were afraid, became unmanageable.

He knew other tunes, too, ones that he had heard here and there; and there were still others that he had made up. These last were very beautiful to him. They were like grasshoppers climbing in the grass stems, like chameleons on trees, walking slowly with one eye turned forward and one back. They were like running water, like rain falling on a canopy of leaves; and some were like the things you felt with your hands, like the silk of a tasselled mealie, like the warm udder of a cow, or a dog's wet nose, pushing.

No one cared for this kind of music : they said there was no tune in it. But he never thought of it as tunes : only he and goats liked it : the goats followed it. And his father said : Let Boetie play what he likes, since the goats follow. But the predikant, who had heard him once, said such music was sinful and wicked : not the dance tunes and the songs, though these he did not seem to like, but the mountain music that told of secret things. He was often puzzled by what the predikant had said. He had spoken of fauns and satyrs and a god called Pan. He had never heard of such a god in the Bible and no one he asked had ever heard of him. After that, he gave up worrying and played his music, and the goats followed him over his father's veld and the mountain—a long stream that pattered on small sharp hoofs behind him.

There was less heat in the sun now : it was only reaching his toes : the shadows were lengthening : it was time to go. He was in no hurry to go. The house would be empty of Dirk and Pa. He did not know how to meet his mother or comfort her. He got out his pipe and smoothed it with his hand. He would play it in a minute. In a minute he would go down the mountain, playing, the goats spilling down beside him, jumping from rock to rock, playing as they came. The mountain-side was steep, but he knew it. His feet knew the path.

He raised the pipe to his lips. He blew a note softly. He could feel a movement about him. The goats had raised their heads and were looking towards him. He blew again. The same note, but louder; and louder still, till his cheeks were blown out like apples and his eyes were closed. The goats were running. They were all round him. He put down his hand to feel them. He sought head after head, horned heads and hornless. He felt the cuts in their ears by which they were marked till he found the head he sought. Witbooi was there to lead them. Now they could go.

He turned and began to play. He would play them down the mountain, play them home, play them into the kraal, and to-morrow, when Ma had given him breakfast and food and water for the day, he would lead them out again. Since he began doing this, four years ago, each day had been the same : all happy, beautiful, with sounds and smells and touching beyond compare. Only now was it changed—his happiness broken like a cup.

The notes came oddly. I am making something new, he thought. It is coming from my heart into my fingers, neither my ears nor my mind know it. He listened carefully to what he was playing. It was so sad that the tears ran down his cheeks. It was a lament. It was the song of a boy who had lost his father and his brother. It was a little like a Kaffir chant, the one of the returning warriors defeated and with many dead. He had cried twice to-day. But this time it was not so bad. There was no one to see him. Only the goats, and before the goats he had no shame. The goats and he were one.

He piped higher, the music climbed the mountain-side, echoing into the kranses till it died. He stopped playing and shook the water from his pipe. He felt better now that he had played. It was as though he had emptied some of the sadness from his heart into the hills. They were as ready to take sorrow as to take joy. The hills were everlasting.

There were some who said Boetie was simple. His brother Dirk had struck a man once who had said he was simple. " If all the world was as

simple as our Boetie," his Dirk had said, "it would be a better place."
There had been a great scuffle and a chair had got broken. He had run
away into the kraal and hidden under the bellies of his goats. They had
covered him like a cloak. He wondered if he was simple. Perhaps it was
simple to love things as he did, and to be afraid sometimes for no reason.

But he must not be frightened of things any more. He was a man and
must protect his mother and Klein Johanna. They must not know what
was in his heart or how frightened he was. He thought of Dirk's return
and his father's. When they came back, he could be frightened again.

He got out his pipe. He was near the house. His mother must hear him.
He began to play *Sarie Maré* . . . a cheerful song, one of the great songs
of his people.

All round him, like water, the goats flowed, brushing their bodies against
his knees.

CHAPTER VI

OUPA

I

Oom Philippus had been thinking about death for twenty-five years. He had thought about it ever since he had reached the span of years allotted to man by God.

Only two desires were left to him : he wanted to see Lena's baby : he also wanted to live to be a hundred. If he lived to be a hundred, men would talk of him when he was gone. There was also the hope that he would outlive Kattie. That girl had always annoyed him. She was sixty-seven now and subject to attacks that he considered brought about by temper, but still attacks that might prove fatal. He was never going to lose his temper again. Last year he had lost his temper, decided that life was dull, and gone to end it under the oak trees that he had planted. It had been in his heart just to go there, sit under them, and die. Few people understood how simple it would be. He had only stayed alive so long because he wanted to, and because a man like him did not die easily in bed. He wanted the stars and the wind in the trees when he was dying, or the sunshine. He wanted to be outside. At that time, he had felt like a pond drying up in a drought and had got ready for his end. Nobody wanted him. He would leave them.

It was Lena who had found him lying there, and he had never quite forgiven her. It was the one thing he held against her, apart from the fact that she was allied to her grandmother, that Kattie, in seeing that he was not properly fed, given only slops, pap and milk, like a baby, and no brandy in it except as a treat.

And what had she said when she found him? She had talked without sense, like a woman, when he told her what he was doing.

She had said : " What will the neighbours say when they find you died out on the veld like an ox?"

He had never cared what the neighbours thought—that was why he had had such a fine life—and he was not going to begin now.

" I want to die here in peace," he had said, " without a crowd of human vultures and jackals watching round my bed while they wait for my carcass."

In addition, he had thought that his dying in this fashion would be a scandal and be attributed to his daughter-in-law's neglect of him. They would say : " Tanta Katarina did it. She never took good care of him."

To do such a thing would be a final thumbing of his nose at convention, a final gesture that would offset any pain that dying might entail.

But Lena had been clever. That little one had been slim, she had fooled him. She had said : " What, Oupa? Would you die and please them?"

" By God," he said, " you're right. It would please them. Since they want me dead, I will not die. I will live to have your baby on my knee."

She had blushed then because she pretended never to think of such things. Ja, magtig, she was so foolish as to pretend that even to him. But she had been right about them wanting him to die. They were like aasvoels, that Kattie and her grandson Stoffel. Louis was all right. He took life as it came and would not have minded either way. But those two . . . you could see it in their eyes when they looked at him.

He thought of that afternoon again when he had prepared himself for death. It must have been Reuter, his servant, who had fetched Lena. He had denied it, but it could have been no one else. And in a way it was his own fault. He should have taken Reuter with him. Instead, he had left him at the house and had gone to the oaks by himself, and Reuter had betrayed him out of jealousy. That damned boy had to have his hand in everything.

Well, if it had not been for Lena, it would all have been over; but he bore her no grudge, for it was probable that Kattie's shame at what was said of her would have been overbalanced by her pleasure at his death. And Lena was a good girl, if too tidy. She carried his blood, but it was badly diluted; some of the entrails of his race had been bred out of her. She was good, and pretty in a small way, though she was not what would have been called a woman in his day; she was too flat and soft. She was too small and had no bone. When he was young there had been women in the land, women big as houses with arms as thick as his thigh, and thighs like elephants—fine, fighting women who could have ten, fifteen,- and twenty children without dying, and rear them all.

He thought about his age again. It struck him as in no way remarkable that he should have gone on living as he had. On the contrary, knowing himself exceptional, he had expected to live till seventy. After that there had been some surprise that he should go on, but he had got used to it. At seventy-five, he had more or less retired from active life and had given up hunting big game alone. He had become an observer, a thinker, spending hours in his chair, turning over his memories as though they were pages in a book, thumbing them with the wetted finger of his leisure as he sat smoking and watching the mistakes that others made.

No one was willing to take advice. They always knew best and were always wrong. It was strange that now, threatened by age alone, he was farther from death than he had been in his youth. Young, death had always been round the corner. From day to day, almost from hour to hour, death and he had played a game with life, tossing it about, like dice in a leather cup; gambling his skill with a gun, his agility of mind and body, the speed of his horse, against the wild beasts, savages, and fevers that death had thrown against him. Then, at any moment, he might have died fortuitously. Now, he reflected, it would take him a week, or a month, or a year to die.

Death would approach stealthily, coming in the chill of a south wind, in a fall from a fruit rind set before his feet. It would come the way it came to a woman. Unless he took the matter into his own hands, he would die in bed without his shoes on his feet or his gun at his side. Before God, he despised a death that could do no more than this; a death by attrition, by the slow undermining of his strength. He laughed at it, a death that came so warily, while he fought it off, in a rearguard action that would last while he had the will to live.

One day he knew that will to love would lose its urgency, and then, when he chose, he would fold his hands on his shrunken belly, close his eyes, tired from having seen too much, and consign his world-weary spirit to his God. At that moment, when it came, death would not have conquered him. Death only conquered by violence; in age or illness, if a man died, it was because he preferred death to life; because he was tired; because, having seen so much, each thing was a repetition of what he had so often seen before; because he found life of no further interest and welcomed death as a change, a rest, a final holiday.

Men talked of pain, but age defeated pain. The old had suffered too much. They were no longer angry and surprised when their bodies failed them. They were used to this, too, and knew that real pain could only live in a man's heart, in his unhappiness. It was the young who fought against pain : the young, whose nerves and sinews were full and strong, whose capacity for pain was enhanced by the vitality which lit their frames. A man felt pain in a direct proportion to the amount of life that there was in him. It was the leaping blood that could not bear the restraint of sickness, not the old, tired fluid that passed for blood in ancient bodies. The old felt pain less and were well accustomed to it. It had been their companion for so long. The old were less surprised at the failure of their limbs than pleased at such activity as was left to them. Before God, an old man was as pleased at still being able to button up his trousers as a small boy who did it for the first time. Truly, the very old and the very young had much in common.

He looked at his hands, veined, knotted, crippled, tied like the claws of a crab by enlarged and frozen joints. They interested him. He examined their scars, their calluses, their intricate network of raised blue veins through which his thin blood flowed, and thought of what those hands had done; of how they had used gun against man and beast, of how they had throttled. It was strange to look at them and think of them as once being as strong as bands of brass against the throat of a man, or silk-soft and urgent on a woman's body. Before God, he had killed with them alone and made love with them. Almost it seemed to him that he had made his children with those hands, potting them like clay. Certainly he had protected them with his hand and fed them, putting pieces of meat from the bucks he had shot, and vegetables from the ground that he had grown, into their small red mouths. Little children were like young birds in a nest chirping and opening their bills. He had flayed game with those hands—had pulled the skin from hundreds, perhaps thousands, of beasts. Once he had used them to wrestle with a wounded buffalo, holding it by its horns and half-drowning it in the muddy water of the pan where they fought, as it tried to gore him.

And now they were almost helpless, as fumbling with buttons as the chubby fingers of a child—old claws, no longer hands with fingers pliable and strong as snakes, supple to shoot, to skin, to plait, to cook, to sew, to climb, to swim, and to soothe, by the power that flowed out of them, the wildest horse. With them he had caressed dogs, horses, cattle, children, women. With them he had eaten thousands of meals. He wondered suddenly how many meals he had eaten, how many wagonloads of food they had conveyed into his mouth; how many bucks they had killed; how many thousands of pounds of ivory he had sold. . . .

A very old man did not feel old. He felt like a small boy again. He had gone round the circle of his life, and the past, his maturity, with its worries, its loves and hates, was no more than a dream. He knew now that he had never felt a man even when he was one; that throughout his life it had been a surprise that men should fear him. He thought again of the old and young : the young whose life was a dream set in the future; the old whose life was a memory set in the past.

With his potency, his maturity, a man's troubles came upon him, born of his desire. Then man was a flame that consumed itself and knew no peace. For peace was in dreams and not in living, and only the very old and the very young had dreams. What you thought was life was not life at all. It was an urging forward, like that of a spurred horse. Sometimes you could not get forward. That was like a horse both spurred and held, that reared himself up and cast himself in despair. A spurred horse must have room to move. You could spur and whip any horse, however hot, if he had room to go forward at speed. And in their maturity, in the height of their powers, men and women were whipped hard.

These last weeks had been very peaceful with the boys away. Kattie was kept busy seeing to everything and she left him alone. It was strange how peaceful it was with a war going on : not that it had begun yet, but it would. And it was good to be so old that you did not bother with such things. Suppose it happened a few years ago when I was younger, he thought. Suppose I had been only eighty and could still eat hard food.

He moved his chair into the sun. How things changed! It was cold even in the summer now. His pipe slipped from his hand.

2

In the house Lena was sewing. The dress was nearly done, every seam finished, every tuck made : there was only the hem to finish. Her grandmother had helped her with the fitting, with the length of the skirt, the back, the fullness of the arms and the tight-boned bodice that clung to her breasts. To-morrow she was going to take it to Tanta Martha's to show it to her.

A month had passed. Such a month as she had never conceived possible, a month of aching want for Dirk, of loneliness, of empty chairs in the sitkamer, of bitter remarks from Ouma, of odd philosophical comfort from her great-grandfather, and of pathetic efforts on the part of the dogs, who, sensing her misery, tried to console her. There had been no news. No one knew if it would be peace or war. Perhaps she would hear something in the dorp. The meeting would be over now, just over, and surely something would have been decided : surely they would hear soon. Even war was better than this uncertainty.

No, it wasn't. She hoped suddenly that the uncertainty would go on. She wanted it to go on till she heard there would be no war. She felt herself suspended in time, dangling at the end of a rope of events over which she had no control. It was no use wishing. It was no use hoping or crying. She had cried enough already, sobbing her loneliness into her pillow. Sometimes she felt across the bed for Dirk. She was ashamed of this, of her dreams, for she was still a girl, and, except in her heart and her dreams, unmarried. That night she had put from her. She could remember so little of it, only its unbearable pain and its unbearable pleasure. She was ill from these secret, shameful longings, desires that melted her beyond tears, beyond sleep, into tortured, writhing agony. Oupa was right in one thing—love hurt. It tore the heart from your body and stopped you eating. If only it had come sooner. If only they had been married and she had his child, something of him to hold or nurse, or lying heavy under her heart when she moved. She felt cheated of something by time, for that was all it was. If only Dirk had spoken sooner, or the war had come later! But it was not war . . . not yet. It might all be nothing. That is what you wish, she said to herself, not what will be. What will be, will be, and will have nothing to do with you or your hopes and wants.

At first she had thought she was going to have a child. That might have accounted for her sickness. But last week had proved this half hope and half fear wrong. Yet she was still ill : ill from wanting. A child could have been conceived under the trees that night, and had it been she knew now that she would not have been ill. On the contrary, she thought, I should have been very well, since to bear his child is my heart's desire. It would have stamped her as wicked, as sinful, but perhaps it was better to be bad and well than less bad and sick. She threaded her needle again, wetting the silk and pulling it between her fingers into a point.

She had tried every way she could think of to comfort herself, reading the Bible, working harder than ever, even churning the butter alone without a maid to help her, polishing the pewterware, sewing, and walking out on the veld. She had driven over to Doornkloof once to see Tanta Johanna and Boetie. Boetie had been so brave that it made her ashamed. But Boetie was not in love.

He had said : " You are going to marry my brother "

She had said : " Yes, Boetie, I am going to marry him when he comes back."

" Then you will be my sister and cousin too."

He had put out his hands. She had stood quite still while he felt her. His hands were like butterflies on her, flitting over her. He only touched her with the tips of his fingers. He ran them over her hair, her face, her neck, her breasts, her waist, her thighs. He touched her legs, her calves, her ankles, her feet, going down on one knee to do it. Then he stood up and looked at her with his bright blue, unchanging eyes.

" You are very beautiful," he said. " I had forgotten how beautiful you were."

His eyes were so bright that it was hard to believe he saw nothing. They were so clear, so very bright, like stars, yet flat and expressionless as stones. She knew he saw nothing, though each time she had to persuade herself anew. He only saw with the long fingers of his hands. She wondered what he had been thinking. Because of those eyes, one never knew what he thought. And seeing nothing, he knew so much.

" I will miss my brother when you take him," he said. " But he says I can come with you, if you are still willing. Will you be willing, Lena?"

Of course she would be willing. She loved him. She was sorry for him and he was blind.

" All my life my brother has helped me," he said. " And a man who will help a small blind brother is a good man. Ja, my brother Dirk is a good man, the best man in all the world, and I am happy that you should have him."

Then he had straightened his shoulders and left her. He had walked very erectly and firmly. She had sat still. A little later, she had heard the sound of his flute from the kraal. She knew where he would be sitting; she had often seen him there, in the corner, propped up against the walls, with his knees up and his hat over his eyes. As he played, sometimes, he had little Johanna with him, crouched on the powdered goat-dung at his feet. It was strange to see him walking with her hand in his among the beasts. His mother said it was dangerous, but she could do nothing. As soon as Johanna saw her brother, she would run to him, and he was not happy away from the stock. But Boetie was safe with them; nothing would hurt him except perhaps a snake curled up in his path, but Johanna knew about snakes. Together they were safe enough and in the hills the goats protected him.

In a few minutes the dress would be finished. She had nearly reached the end of the hem. That was like your thoughts; they went round in a circle, and when you hoped you had settled something in your mind, you were back where you began.

It was done. She shook it out and put it on the table. She picked up some scraps of material from the floor. There was no need to worry about Dirk seeing them. Tears came into her eyes at the thoughts she had had about making her dress—at how she had been going to surprise him. She put the dress over her arm and took the scissors and skein silk she had used to sew it into her room. Tanta Martha had said if she did it well, she would give her a lace collar and cuffs. To-morrow Tanta Martha would see how well she had sewn it.

She sat on the bed and thought of Dirk. As soon as she sat down, as soon as she stopped doing things actively, her thoughts began again. Dirk. . . . Dirk . . . where was he? That seemed terribly important. What was he doing? When would he come back to her? I must not go on thinking of him, she thought; it makes me ill. It had made her ill. She felt faint and leaned forward, clasping her forehead with her hands. Her thimble rolled off the bed on to the floor. She would go for a walk. There was still time before it got dark. She heard her grandmother scolding someone: one of the maids or a boy. What did it matter? It was always the same. The house was empty, and bitter with anger.

The heartbreaking stillness of evening struck at her. Such beauty hurt. From horizon to horizon the world stood still, bathed in roseate mauve: illuminated like a missal, like a very old Bible she had once been shown; each tree, each bush, each rock punctuated the wilderness, a proof of its immensity. Long, iron shadows supported trees whose every leaf was sculptured. Distance was killed by this sudden clarity. Far hills and mountains revealed their folds, crevices, and kloofs, flaunted them shamelessly, flawlessly; so clear were they that she felt that by stretching out her hand she could touch them. But it was an illusion. The hills were many miles away. Dirk's home was under that one. An hour's drive away, but it looked like a toy hill, furnished with toy trees and rocks. The mountains looked like something that could be picked up and carried off, something unreal, but beautiful as a painted picture against an egg-green sky. Everything was without thickness, sharp and flat; each object, oddly menacing, in this world of soft, diffused light. It was as though the world and the atmosphere that enclosed it were divorced from each other. As though nature, rebelling against loveliness, thrust its stark reality, spearlike, against the coming night.

This was Africa. It was for this land, this peace, these breathless moments, that Dirk and her people fought. She was sure they did not know it, many of them, but she knew it. And deep inside them somewhere, they knew it too: not as a conscious thought, but as a feeling: knew that nowhere else was there such a place; nowhere else such vast stillness, such endless morgen, uninhabited and open, untouched save by the hand of God.

A korhaan, its white breast red in the sunset, flung chattering into the sky. Another answered it. It grew darker. Already, before the birds had reached the ground, things lost their shape; softened, they merged into a mauve greyness tipped with fire. The scarlet had changed to crimson, turned slowly to black purple, and another night had nearly come. The mountains, ink-blue, spread their blackness over the intervening plain. The darkness, approaching, became palpable, something alive that crept towards her.

Dirk was out in it somewhere. Perhaps he had been watching the sunset, too, and now was standing with his friends about a fire while they cooked their meal. She looked towards the house. The lamp was lit.

When she went in, her grandmother would ask her where she had been. If she said she had been out to sit staring over the veld, Ouma would not understand: only Oupa would understand. She would say she had been out and had not noticed how late it was. That was the truth, the smallest part of it, but to speak of some things was to destroy them.

CHAPTER VII

"PAARDEKRAAL"

I

As soon as they were clear of the farm, Dirk reined Swartkie, checking him to a tripple. It was strange to be riding over the land you knew so well with a rifle on your back, a bandolier slung over your shoulder, and your saddle-bags filled with food. There was a folded blanket under his saddle, another rolled and strapped behind it. His overcoat was in front of him. For weeks perhaps this was all he would have with him. He had carried nearly as much sometimes hunting, on a two or three days' trip when the hunters did not take the wagon, or hunted away from it, but it had all felt different. Then your heart was high as you searched the bush for game.

Swartkie knew it was different, too. Dick could feel it through his hands on his horse's mouth and through his legs as they gripped him. When they went hunting, Swartkie was gay. He would flick his long tail and cock his ears this way and that. A good shooting-pony knew what you were looking for; would stop if he saw a buck and break from a stand into a gallop the moment you had fired. Swartkie would follow a wounded buck like a hound, dodging through the trees, jumping low bushes that were in its way. But to-day the little stallion was serious. He was tossing his head and flicking his tail, but he was angry—snorting and showing the whites of his eyes.

Swartkie knows it is war, Dirk thought. There was a bond between a horseman and his horse. He wondered which way it went. Did the horse tell you what he was feeling or did you tell the horse? But the horses knew : all horses knew; so did dogs. If a man lived much with his beasts, they grew to understand each other in a very particular fashion. You did not have to tell them anything : they knew it.

But there might not be war; perhaps he would soon be riding home again. He thought of Lena. She was with him in his mind. He held her in front of his saddle as he had held Boetie when he was smaller. The scent of her hair was in his nostrils : the feel of her waist under his hand. What was the good of thinking? I must put her out of my head till this is over, he thought. Yes, that would be easy . . . as easy as pulling your arm from your body. . . .

Dirk looked at his father's back as he swayed over his saddle. There were thousands of Boer fathers riding with their sons to-day. They were on every little Kaffir path, on every road. They were riding in from all sides—from the north, the south, the east, and the west. Men in their prime like Pa with wives and families; young men like himself; boys, and old men coming slowly on old horses scarred with other battles and huntings. Horses as wise to gunfire and stratagem as their masters.

Soon they would pick up Stoffel and Louis. They would all ride together through Brennersdorp, picking up others as they went. They might meet Cronje and his commando there. That was the custom in war—near neighbours meeting at crossroads, riding on to meet other groups of neighbours and joining them. When a hundred or so were gathered together, they would elect their leader, if he was not already chosen. Every man was responsible for his own horse, rifle, ammunition, and food. Over these no man had jurisdiction. Each man was complete, a law unto himself : his only duty to accept the fighting orders of his leader. That was the way they had always fought : loosely knit as they moved, but combining for action.

There they were. Stoffel was sitting his roan horse, his rifle held by the barrel, its butt resting on his knee. Louis had dismounted and was leaning against his horse's shoulder. They waved. Dirk and his father waved back and began to canter.

" Good-morning, kerels."

" Good-morning."

" Ja, it is a good morning," Stoffel said. " We are going to fight."

" Who says we are going to fight?" Groot Dirk asked.

Dirk looked at his father. Did he really think there would be no war or was he just angered at Stoffel's pleasure?

" There will be war," Stoffel said. " We want it. All the young burgers want it."

" Young men with nothing but their lives to lose may want it, but they are not the nation. We ride to Paardekraal to see what the nation wants. Before God," he said, " though we are armed, this is not war, it is a demonstration."

" That we shall see," Stoffel said.

Dirk dropped back to ride with Louis.

" What do you think of it all?" he asked.

" How should I know, Dirk? I have no desire to fight. It is in my heart that few desire to fight : neither Boer nor English; and if all men would dare to speak their minds there would be no wars."

" And Stoffel?"

" Stoffel is different," Louis said.

There was no more talk. They lit their pipes, filling them with loose tobacco from their pockets and clapping on the metal tops that kept it in.

That this meeting had been put forward a month meant something. If it was not war, war at least seemed likely. Dirk took off his hat to wipe the sweat from his forehead. It was very hot. The air was heavy with storm, laden with heat. They were riding through a small land now. The mealies stood with hanging ribbon leaves as though exhausted. The ground between them was parched and cracked for want of rain. On other farms the crops were doing well; it was funny how the rains could miss one place and strike another only a few miles away.

Stoffel was talking to Dirk's father again. He was telling of a conversation he had had with Gerrit Labuschagne about Paul Kruger. It seemed that at the meeting at Wonderfontein, Gerrit had asked Oom Paul when they were going to begin to shoot. He had said: " We have been talking long enough, you must let us shoot them now," and Kruger had answered, " Before I say ' sah ' to my hunting dog I must be certain that he will hold on."

" That was last year," Stoffel said, " and much has happened since last year. Now we are ready to bite and will hold on."

" Ja, Stoffel, we will hold on if we must. But I do not want to begin."

" Yet we are ready to begin. Every one is going to the meeting, all are riding armed, the young and old together. It will be something to see that meeting. The greatest gathering of our folk! "

Yes, it would be something to see, Dirk thought. And no one would dare to interfere. That it was illegal, that such mass meetings had been called high treason, meant nothing. There would be too many of them. They were banded like brothers. A small people, but all of one blood: a free people. He moved the rifle on his back. It is for the freedom of our children that we will fight, he thought: my father for my mother and Boetie and Klein Johanna. And I will fight for Lena and the home-place we will make when it is over . . . for the children we will have.

He saw the trees of Brennersdorp in front of him. Soon they would be in and meet the others. There might be more news; something might have happened since yesterday.

The outspan was filled with mounted men, with men on foot, with men leading horses, with knee-haltered horses, with Kaffirs, with wagons, with the women and children who had come to see the last of their men, with dogs of all kinds, with draught oxen. It was like a hive of bees. Every one was coming and going, every one moving, drifting, leaving one group to join another, shouting to friends, to native servants, cursing the dogs that got under their feet, calling for the children they had lost; and everywhere smoke rose from the cooking-fires—thin plumes feathering the sky, rising into it and fading into nothing.

Except for the rifles the men carried on their backs or in their hands, it might have been a nagmaal instead of a gathering of their people for war, or for peace if they could come by it on their own terms, without war.

Before they reached the crowd they fell in, dropping behind Dirk's father. Louis rode on his left and Stoffel on his right. Stoffel was making his horse prance. His rifle was on hip again. His head was high. But

Louis rode quietly. A boy dived almost under their horses for some dry cow-dung. He had an armful of it. Wood was scarce on the outspan.

Dirk did not know the two men standing beside a dead springbok that hung from a wagon, and who greeted his father.

" So you are here, Lirk," they said. One of them shouted : " Groot Dirk van der Berg is here from Doornkloof with his son."

" Ja, we are here, Servaas," Groot Dirk said. " Where are you camped?"

" Over there." He pointed towards the slaughter poles.

That was where Lena said they had tried to sell Piet's wagon.

" You will join us?" he asked.

" We will join you," Groot Dirk said. ' It is good to see you again after so long."

The other man came up to Groot Dirk's horse and put out his hand.

" Johannes du Plessis," he said; " I am from the Magalaqueen."

Groot Dirk took his hand, bending forward over his horse's neck. " I am Dirk van der Berg," he said. " I have heard of you, Meneer du Plessis. You are one of Kruger's men."

" Ja, I am one of Oom Paul's friends."

" He is well served by his friends."

" And ill by his enemies."

" Tot siens, then," Groot Dirk said, ". . . till to-night."

" Till to-night, meneer. We ride to-morrow."

So they were riding to-morrow. Groot Dirk turned in his saddle.

" Is Cronje here?" he asked.

" Ja, he is here. It is under him we ride."

" I will find him. I have fought under him before."

Fight : so that was what his father really thought. They would fight. When they had found their friend's camp Dirk would go and see Tanta Martha.

" W ᵥ will stop here," his father said when they reached the poles. " That is Servaas's boy."

A coloured man ran forward. He was leading a fine bay horse.

" Baas, Baas!" he shouted. " Baas Dirk, it is I. Do you not remember Shilling, the boy of Meneer Servaas Espach?"

" Yes, I remember you. Is this where the Baas is camped?"

" This is his camp."

Groot Dirk dismounted and began to offsaddle.

" Shall I water the Baas's horse?" Shilling asked.

" I will water him myself."

Dirk dismounted. What a number of things there were about his father that he did not know. It came to him how separated men's lives were. These friends of his father's—this Cape boy, Servaas Espach, and the others who had greeted him—they were all old comrades of his father's :

they had served together in Kaffir wars, had hunted together as young men, played together as children, perhaps.

.Stoffel and Louis had dismounted. Stoffel looked very different when he got down.

" I am going to Tanta Martha's, Pa," Dirk said.

" Well, you know where to find us."

" Yes, I know." Dirk mounted again.

Tanta Martha was his godmother and he was very fond of her, but it was not just that. There were things he wanted to say to her : to ask her. He would think them out as he rode. She was a wise woman, but he must be careful to see that she did not load him down with gifts and medicines. That was her habit, and few left her house without medicine enough to last a household a year. She was liable to give a hunter remedies for child-birth fever if she happened to have a lot of it in stock, and tell him to give it to some farm wife on his road. That to do so might be embarrassing never entered her head. But she was a good woman, a friend to all, and he would be able to talk to her about Lena.

Brennersdorp looked very different to-day. There was nobody about, roads were empty. They were all at the camp—the men riding themselves, the women seeing the men off, going to look for friends or to gather news. Perhaps he would miss Tanta Martha, but somehow he did not think so. She would be at home. She never walked, and the outspan was too full to drive through easily.

There was smoke coming from her chimney, which was a good sign. He increased his pace. Swartkie cocked his ears towards the house and pulled up at the gate. Dirk leaned down from the saddle to open it : rode through and closed it again.

" Tanta Martha, Tanta Martha," he shouted. " Are you there? I have come to say good-bye."

" Who has come to say good-bye? Magtig, I get no peace in war with every one coming to say good-bye."

She came to the door. " So it is you, Dirk, who come to bid me good-bye from the back of your horse. If I were a young girl you would get down. But because I am not young you sit there. If you had come fifty years ago, you would have dismounted and your horse would only have been one of many tied to my father's stoep." She set her hands on her hips and laughed as he dismounted. " I am not the kind of cook who praises her own sassaties, yet I would say this : I would tell you that the old fiddle plays as good a tune as the new, and that if the little pot is soon hot the big one stays hot longer."

He took her in his arms. " Tanta Martha, I love you. Are you not my peetanta?"

" Yes, I am your godmother and a sore burden it has been to keep you in the narrow path of virtue. It will be a great relief to me when you are married to Lena."

" Then she told you." He looked into her face.

" Ja, she told me and I am glad. Now come in. You must have coffee. And I have meat and roasted pumpkin. Frans! Frans!" she shouted. " Where is that boy?"

He came running.

" Where were you, Frans?" she said.

" In the kitchen. I was working in the kitchen."

" Ja, you were working with Netta. That kind of work you can do at night. Not that I approve, but if it was not you it would be another, and at night I have no need of you. Now take the Baas's horse. Give him water and oat forage. Give him plenty. It will be many days before Swartkie gets his belly full of oat forage again, peetkind. In my heart I feel it will be many days."

" Then you, too, think there will be war?"

" Where there are bees there is honey, and where there is smoke there is fire. Netta! Netta, bring coffee . . . bring meat and the roasted pumpkin and the orange konfyt."

While he ate she said nothing. She sat opposite to him smiling and watching each mouthful he took, filling his cup with coffee and giving him more sugar than he wanted as a sign of her love for him. He was hungry. He had been unhappy thinking of Lena, but as his belly tightened against his belt, as it filled with Tanta Martha's food, his unhappiness became less, which disturbed him on two counts : first, that his love should be related to his stomach at all, and secondly, that he should find himself able to eat so heartily. It did not seem right.

" Now a sopie of French," Tanta Martha said, getting out a bottle of brandy : " a klein sopie." She nearly filled a glass. " And then smoke. Ja, Dirk, it is in my heart that it will be a long time before you eat like this again." She laughed. " It is a trick to make you think of me whenever you are hungry, which will be often. You will say : ' What a meal that was that old Tanta Martha gave me!' and water will come into your mouth. You will be surprised at how much you think of me . . . more than you think of Lena, perhaps, for men are made that way. They only think of love when their bellies are full. They have no room in their hearts when their stomachs are empty and crying to them."

" You would seduce me from Lena with food, Godmother?" Dirk said. And certainly he was less unhappy now, though he loved Lena just as much, which was confusing.

" How else could I seduce you now? Once, Dirk, when I put food before men they could not eat it. The sight of my great beauty spoilt the food for them unless they were very hungry. But now the smell of my food reconciles them to the sight of my body. Why, after I was first married, my husband, my first one, Jan, could not eat for six months. I thought he would die. He just stared at me and sang. Ja, we sang together. Kleinhouse was different. He wanted my pigs and my cattle. Though he could sing too. And he sang bass as a true man should."

Tanta Martha was trying to take Dirk's mind off things, to make him laugh, but it was no good. His unhappiness was back again. He wanted to go to Lena.

"There will be war?" he said again. He had known it must come for a year or more, but still could not believe it.

"You cannot tell the size of a cock from its crow, Dirk."

"Do not talk to me in parables, Tanta. What do you think?"

"I think that death is in the pot, jong. Feather by feather they have plucked the goose and our people are tired. So little would have satisfied them once, but that little, the Volksraad and their flag, has been denied them."

"That is what my father thinks."

"Your father is a good sensible man, Dirk, but do not worry too much. It does no good, and when it is over you will marry your Lena and I will be godmother to your first child if you ask me. I have sixty godchildren," she said. "Every one asks me to be godmother to those that I bring into the world. Thirty-two little burgers and twenty-eight maids have I delivered since I have been here. There were others before, but I lost count of them then."

She got up and left him. In a minute she was back with a parcel.

"Now you must take these with you." She began to spread things on the table. "Here is Baviaan's ooren." She picked up a root. "That is for cuts and sores And here is a pot of buck-fat with fried blue-gum leaves and turpentine. That is for colds in the chest and hoarseness. These are genesblaren for boils and abscesses; you put the leaf on the sore and bind it there. And this is dassiepis "—she held up a small lump of something that looked like gum or bitumen. "It is hard to get," she said, "and comes from the mountains where the dassies live. It is their urine which they make always in one place on the rocks. It is good for hysterics, epilepsy, and convulsions of all kinds." She put it down and began to wrap the parcel, each thing separately, and then put them in a little breyed buckskin bag.

"Now kiss your Tanta Martha," she said, "and get back to the commando. Give my love to your father. Tell him that Tanta Martha has not forgotten the day that he stole a duck from her."

"My father stole a duck?"

"Ja, he stole a duck. It was a beautiful knob-nosed duck. It is in my heart that he fell in love with it. It was black and white, with red warts on its beak and round its eyes."

"But why did he steal it? Why did he not buy it from you?"

"He had no money, Dirk. Nee, he had nothing then, poor man."

"Nothing?"

"No, nothing, nephew, he was only five." Tanta Martha began to laugh again, chuckling so that the fat on her body rippled, her breasts, stomach, and thighs all wobbling with laughter as she thought of the way she had verneuked him about his father. "Now saddle up and take your rifle from my fire corner. I have seen too many of those things in my life. Ach sis, we spend our time breeding children to men and then they ride out to kill each other."

Dirk put his arms about her.

"I will take care of Lena for you," she said. "I can manage Kattie, though she is sour as bad cream—too sour and too old to churn into good butter; but she can do nothing to me. So ride in peace."

She went out on to the stoep to watch him saddle. Swartkie, fresh with oat forage, snapped as he was girthed up. Dirk mounted and waved his hat.

"Mind you shut my gate!" Martha shouted. "Shut it good or I shall have Fourie's pole oxen in here again."

"Tot siens, Tanta Martha."

"Tot siens, my Dirkie."

He swung Swartkie up on his hind legs and raised his hat again. As Swartkie's forefeet touched the ground, he slacked his reins and leaned forward. It was good to be galloping on a good horse. His heart was light. Tanta Martha would see to Lena. That was what he had come to see her about. And the bag of medicines she had given him was not too big. He had been lucky. If she was right and the English wanted war, they should have it. The Vierkleur, Lena, the Volksraad, Africa, and the unborn children he would have in his unmade home were all mixed in his mind— mixed into the cake of his indignation. I am like the others now, he thought. We are slow to move, but it has begun. It is for Lena. But he wished he was riding to her instead of to war.

2

Every one was cooking when Dirk got back. Where there had been one fire there were now a hundred, each with a group of men round it: bearded men and boys; men with frying-pans in their hands, with pots; old men roasting small bits of meat threaded on their ramrods while their dogs sat beside them watching and waiting for their share. His father was seated with Servaas Espach and du Plessis. Louis was lying on his back with his head on a saddle, smoking. Stoffel was cleaning his rifle; the bolt was on the ground beside him.

"And how was Tanta Martha, Dirk?" his father said.

"She was well. She sent you her love, Pa."

"I hope you gave her mine, and what medicine did she give you?"

Dirk laughed. "Enough for all of us, Pa." He began to off-saddle. He loosened the rein round Swartkie's neck and tied his head to his near foreleg just below the knee. Then he slapped his flank and watched him hobble off, his head bobbing up and down as he walked. He watched him roll and go towards the river. He would drink and then graze, if he was still hungry after Tanta Martha's forage. Dirk spread his saddle-blanket and sat down.

"There is springbok," his father said. "We were in luck to fall in with Servaas, his friend gave him two legs and half the back."

Dirk took his knife out of its sheath and began to eat. It was good to eat meat with the smell of wood smoke in your nostrils and the sting of it in your eyes. How often had he eaten like this when they were out hunting! Despite what he had had at Tanta Martha's, he was still hungry, and in these times one must eat what one could get and when one could get it.

"Springbok is good," du Plessis said. Turning to Groot Dirk he said: "Do you know what is wrong with a sheep, Meneer van der Berg?"

"What is wrong with a sheep?"

"Well, meneer, a sheep is too much for one man and not enough for two."

Everybody laughed. Stoffel put the bolt back into his rifle and got out his pipe. Dirk cut more buck.

"Is Cronje here, Pa?" he asked. "Have you seen him?"

"He is here with fifty men," his father said. "Groot Piet Bezuidenhout among them."

"And what about Piet's wagon?" Servaas asked. "Will they not take it now that he and the commando have left?"

"No, they cannot. Piet told me himself. The wagon-bed is jacked up on logs and the wheels have been sent to Erasmus to store. The beasts have gone, too. They are distributed among the neighbours. All that is left on the farm is an old horse, three milk cows, and some hens and a pig. If they come they will find nothing." Groot Dirk knocked out his pipe and refilled it. He lit it from a burning ember, holding it between finger and thumb.

It was dark now. All round the fires lit up the faces of the men grouped about them. The tented wagons stood out like the backs of elephants against the sky. Dirk heard a girl laugh nervously. He heard a woman crying: in a nearby wagon she was sobbing as if her heart would break. In the distance a man was singing and a dog howled.

Last night, Dirk thought, I was with Lena: only last night. And riding home he had thought about the animals on the veld: those of the day

and those of the night. To-night he was one of them : a man of the night.
From now on, till it was over, they would live like this, sleeping in the
open, sharing the darkness with the beasts.

His father was talking about courage. " I do not know what courage
is," he said.

" Nor does any man, Dirk," Servaas said. " One day a man can be
brave and the next a coward. It depends on how he feels—on who is
watching him : on the state of his mind and his heart. Young men are
very brave because they do not know, or underestimate their danger.
Also they are afraid of being afraid. The really brave man knows fear and
conquers it."

" That is true," du Plessis said. " I had a dog like that once. He was
a young dog and I was hunting a lion. He had had no experience of
lions. Magtig, how lions frightened that dog, even the smell of a lion,
but he followed the spoor with the others. That was twenty years ago,
but I remember it like yesterday. There were many lions up there then."

He pointed to the north with the stem of his pipe and went on.

" He was a big lion and had killed two of my oxen. I had spoored him
all day since early morning and then the dogs ran into him. They were
all round him baying, running in and running out, bewildering him, as
good lion dogs should do. But the young dog—he was a big brindle-and-
white hound—would not go in nor would he run away. He stood midway between me and the other dogs that were round the lion. His hackles
were up, he was growling, but he kept looking from me to the lion and
back again. He was very frightened. His tail was between his legs, he
wetted the ground, but, magtig, he stood fast.

" Then the lion charged, smashing through the dogs about him, and
the dogs all ran away as he came, all but the young dog that was afraid.
He crouched down, and as the lion passed him, sprang after him. I shot
that lion as he was in the air. The bullet passed through his lower jaw,
his chest, and took him in the heart. But when he fell, the pup was clinging to his tail; as he leapt, so had my young dog jumped at him.

" That is what I call courage, meneer, and loyalty. That dog knew fear.
He knew the danger and still was ready to die, not without thought, but
after he had thought. Do not let any one tell you that the beasts do not
think. They consider matters. Ja, they consider all matters, not as men
do, but as beasts, and act, each according to his kind."

" Yes, animals think," Groot Dirk said. " They think, they love, they
hate. I once saw a horse, with his teeth, pick up a man that he hated, and
shake him as a dog shakes a rat. Then he chopped him with both front
feet together. That man I found out afterwards had injured the horse
many years ago, and the horse killed him. I knew the horse well. He
belonged to a friend whose children used to ride him. He was a small
grey horse with a twist in his tail."

"That comes with Arab blood," du Plessis said. "They always have it. And they have dish-faces, beautiful wide eyes, and flaring nostrils."

"They have faces like women," Espach said. "That blood is in many of our horses. It is that which gives them their fire and their gentleness."

"Like women," Dirk's father said. He was smiling.

"Ja, meneer, like our women. Our woman are like our horses, they are beautiful and they do not forget."

"We had better sleep now," du Plessis said.

"Yes, let us sleep."

They spread their blankets more comfortably, arranged their saddles for pillows, and spread their coats. Louis was already sleeping.

Dirk lay, his head supported on his hands, watching his father. He was still smoking. "Are you going to sleep, Pa?" he asked.

"Not yet. I wish to smoke and think for a while. My mind is not at rest. I miss your mother, Dirk, and Boetie and the baby and my dogs. I am lonely for them—for my home, my children, and my beasts. I would think of them and pray a little. But go to sleep, Dirk. Alles sal reg kom."

"Yes, Pa, all will come right." But when would it come right? he wondered. When would it be over, since it had not yet begun? Soon they would know more. To-morrow they would ride on Paardekraal.

The next few days were like a dream. Riding, offsaddling to rest their horses and let them roll, halting to cook, camping and riding again, the commando moved along the road. Each day was the same to Dirk. Each hour . . . each minute . . . nothing seemed to change. There was always red dust and the smell of horse sweat and men's sweat; the glint of the sun on rifle barrels, bits, and stirrup irons; tossing manes, switching tails, and an occasional scurry of dust as a courier passed them at a gallop, riding God knew where or on what mission.

As they got nearer to Paardekraal, they saw other columns of dust made by other commandos riding in as they were themselves. Men from all round were riding in. The men of all the nation were in the saddle, their horses' heads all pointing inward towards the centre. Paardekraal was suddenly the middle of South Africa, its heart and its head. Undecided, all these men were riding in to decide. Personally afraid—for many must be, even as Dirk was, doubtful of their courage—they would become collectively bold.

The commando kept changing shape, opening and closing like a concertina. Sometimes it was an almost circular klompie of men and horses; at others it was strung out thinly, a mile long, as they rode down some narrow, stony path. Then all you saw was a line of dust ahead and the tail and back of the man and horse in front of you. They did not keep to the road, but sometimes were on it and sometimes off it, as they took short cuts across the open veld.

On commando you stopped being a man. You became a part of a whole. And when they got to Paardekraal, the commandos would stop being commandos and become part of the great gathering. As more and more men joined together, so each man became less, till eventually he was nothing. You were caught up in this. You went on. If you lived, it would be something to have seen it. If you lived . . .

3

There were six thousand men at Paardekraal. Armed burgers with their horses, wagons, and some from nearby with women and children. The farm was a tremendous camp. It had been chosen as the best place for a mass meeting because of its central position. Men were camped everywhere in commandos, with their friends and relations, under their chosen leaders. Grazing horses covered the hills, and as the days passed they had to feed farther and farther off. The near hills were bare.

The men of Brennersdorp were lucky. They were by the water, and had a good supply of wood near them. But the wood was getting smaller, each day it was going up in the flames and smoke of the cooking-fires. In the evening it was beautiful to see those fires and look at the valleys filled like vessels with thin blue smoke—a mist that smelt of cooking between the hills.

There was nothing to do except talk and walk about from group to group, but sometimes Dirk got Swartkie and rode off alone. He could not think of Lena among a crowd of men. He had never seen so many gathered together before, and was astonished at the differences between them. Some prayed and read the Bible continually, others sang and drank the dop they had brought with them till it was gone. Then they were morose and wished they had given less away. Some told stories of their own exploits all the time. Some were voluble, some silent.

Many of the young men, lovers and husbands, were like himself, he thought, thinking of some woman and unhappy at being parted from her. They were the silent ones and the absent-minded. Their bodies were here, but their minds were not. They were passionate like himself about the freedom of the land, but their hearts were elsewhere. Their thoughts were of some woman and her softness that was theirs. Or of their children, the little ones who could just walk, and those who still sucked at their mothers' breasts. It was for them they were ready to fight and die. Yet because of them they were miserable, missing their chatter, their cries, the general nuisance and anxiety that they caused.

It was good to get beyond the camp and its noises, its perpetual coming and going, and to see the veld empty of men and horses. Only when you were alone could you think clearly. Or was that not true? Did he really

ride away in order to think things out or merely to build pictures in his
mind as he stared over the rolling hills : pictures of Lena walking and
talking, of her laughter, of her getting up and sitting down, of her fingers
as they moved on her sewing, of her hand as it raised a cup to her lips, of
the look in her eyes that he had just come to know. Did he come out here
to think of her urgent gentleness that promised everything, mutely and
without words, with only looks and the touchings of her hands on his
body? Did he come to long, to think, or to hope?

He would ride out, think, and make pictures in his mind till he could
bear it no more, and gallop back. What was the good of thinking, plan-
ning, hoping, when the world was like this?—when there was no security,
when at any moment you might find yourself at war and in danger of
being killed. All you could do was to wait and try to live from hour to
hour : endeavour by some trick to keep yourself afloat in this strange new
element of uncertainty.

But whatever happened, whatever a man was constrained to do by his
public duty, his mind remained concerned with his personal affairs. Dirk
could see that clearly. In a battle he thought he would still be able to think
of Lena. He thought again of the idea that had come to him about the
beasts of the day and the night. A man's mind was like that, too, filled
with the population of two sets of thoughts—public and private—day and
night. You lived the day for the night that was to come.

The English were strong, they had many soldiers; but they were un-
prepared, and his people not only knew the land, but were wonderful
horsemen and shots. They were very mobile and would be able to operate
at great speed against the English foot-soldiers.

He thought of Lena again, and then of the men in camp. They were
ready for anything. The whole nation was up, for if they had waited to
be called, many would not be there. The first call was for men from
eighteen to forty, the second for men of thirty-four to fifty, and the third
for boys between sixteen and eighteen and men over fifty. But they had
not waited. They had picked up their guns, their veld kost, mounted
their horses, and come. At Paardekraal there were boys of thirteen who
had no vote riding beside their fathers, with guns in their hands, and men
of over sixty with their sons and grandsons. If Boetie had not been blind,
he would have been here. Dirk thanked God that Boetie was blind, and
then was astonished at himself. What a time to live in, when you could
solemnly thank God that your brother was blind! But it was true to-day,
and many mothers must be thankful for their crippled and damaged boys
and men. So that what had, a short while before, seemed a disaster to
them was now a matter of thankfulness.

If only it would begin. If only something would happen. He thought
of riding back to see Lena if only for an hour. But what good would that
do? It would only hurt them both, only be difficult for them both. As

hard for her as for him. He knew this now. They must get married. He knew that in their own hearts and thoughts they had been one many times. It would do no good to go back. It would only do harm.

When Dirk returned to the camp, Jan van Niekerk was talking. Before God, every one was talking now, making speeches, shouting, ranting. But Jan was a good man. He dismounted to listen.

"We have suffered as much as we can bear," Jan said. "We cannot move again. This land is full, we are hemmed in and must fight. Now at last we are ready and the leaders are ready. They have only been waiting for us to decide. They had to wait till we were of one mind and of one heart."

"We are no longer of two opinions," someone shouted.

Dick turned loose his horse and took his saddle to his place. That was strange, too, that this place, rubbed bare of grass by his sleeping, with a hole in the ground that he had dug for his hip, should now be his home. That was all the room a man took up in the world, some six feet by two, whether he was alive or dead.

There had been some method then in keeping them waiting, in getting them angry so that they wanted to force an issue. Now they would bite. Those had been Paul Kruger's words. Yes, men were like that, like dogs if you kept them tied. They became savage. Now they would follow Cronje, and old Joubert, the commandant general. They were hot to be led, to be off the chain of their indecision, and be committed. Like dogs again. Though they might hesitate to attack dangerous wounded game, once they began they would continue. And their women were behind them.

Jan was right. Before, they always had been able to trek, the world had been open, but now they were trapped, encircled, and surrounded. There was no more free land, no more room. They were without option. And when it came to this—that they must fight for their freedom to live as they wished, or give up their freedom—they would fight. A Boer would die rather than live in bondage. They were the freest people in the world. They had the habit of it. It had become their nature. The Uitlanders that had flooded the land had no love of Africa. They were landless, lawless, worshipping only the golden calf of Mammon. Where there was gold was their land while there was gold. After that, when it was done, when nothing more could be squeezed out of it, they would go.

They were the sweepings of all countries: Jews, Englishmen, Americans, Australians, Frenchmen, Swiss—but renegades of these lands and races without ties in them or stakes. And with them had come the women of their kind: the whores of Babylon, the harlots, the dancing girls, the daughters of the horse leech: women who got on to tables in the diggings and auctioned themselves off nightly. Dirk spat and slapped Swartkie, who was picking in the dry grass at his side.

To-morrow he would ride out again. He would go farther and stay longer. To be out alone on the veld, to feel the movement of his horse under him and watch the swaying of the long grass in the breeze, was the only peace he knew. The trees and the grass and the distant mountains were soothing to him. They were not explicit. They denied nothing and affirmed nothing except the glory of God and the majesty of His creation. Out there he looked back; away from the camp, he could dream of Lena: dream loose, impalpable dreams of her in which little images came to him, little memories that fluttered like birds in his mind. He let them flutter, never putting out a hand to grasp them. Between the horizons of Africa; set between the mountains, above the rolling veld where he sat alone on his horse, she seemed more near to him than whn he was enclosed between the four walls of a house, or in camp where, surrounded by other men, it was impossible to think. Among the birds and buck and creeping things she was his—bone of his bone, flesh of his flesh. He had possessed her. That memory no man could take from him. A man lived by his body, but with his mind; in a sense, mind and body were forever parted. The lust of the mind was in the body, but in the lust of the body there was no mind.

That was why he could know what had happened at their parting, but could not remember it. He could only remember what he knew: that Lena had become his under the trees. That was what his mind knew. That was his memory. But of the possession he knew nothing. It came to him that he could never know: that no man could remember what it felt like to touch the woman he loved: that he could only remember his desire to touch and that it had been good. The body was the annihilation of all dreams. It was actuality. It was of further fulfilment that he dreamed continually. But in creating, a man all but died, was ready to die, was—for an instant, in the height of his consummation—dead. Then afterwards he came slowly back to life, slowly out of the valley of creation, and this was what man sought all his days—to lose himself in the death that would make new life. A new anxiety beset Dirk. Was Lena with child? But the trees and the rivers knew nothing of this, nor did the waving grass. And because they knew nothing there was peace among them. Peace in communion with the earth; peace and unutterable loneliness in the wide spaces.

4

When it comes, Dirk thought, it will come suddenly. The brooding unquiet of the Boers, the festering sore of their wrongs would break out like a fire. Their thoughts, hopes, angers, and regrets became more and more palpable day by day, as real as the smoke that hung in a low cloud over the camp. They knew what they were here for : why the meeting had been set forward. It was to decide whether they were going to protect Piet Bezuidenhout from English justice. Were they going to endorse his action, countersign it with their blood, or give him up? But this was only the symbol and all knew it. You could feel the change taking place. You could feel the fever rising.

Paul Kruger was everywhere, walking, talking, and sitting by his wagon, available to them all. Limping, thick-set, and heavy, dressed in a black frockcoat and battered top hat, he dominated the camp. It seemed to Dirk that he was taking the pulse of the burgers. Would they fight? Would they bite if he said " sah "? He asked questions. He answered them. He asked men about their farms, their wives and children, he conducted religious services, he listened continually, his little eyes savage with resentment. He was a fighter and ready to fight again, as he had fought all his life, but he could not fight alone. He was like an old bull with his head lowered. In this man Dirk could see his people : their life and what it stood for; a steadfast adherence to their customs and an unswerving faith in God and in the laws of God.

Day followed day. Day fanned day; night fanned night, urgently. There was still nothing to do but talk, and smoke, and think. Nothing to do but wait in this immense concourse of men. But the English were making a mistake in keeping them waiting for the Commission that was coming to examine their wrongs. The crystals of the salt that had been rubbed into their backs for a century were forming. No, the English did not understand his people, who were so slow to decide and so swift to act when they had reached their decision. Simple farmers, Boers. Ja, we are Boers, Dirk thought. We are South African Boers. Men who live on the veld in the little homes we have made in the wilderness; but we are also men who live on our horses with guns in our hands. This is what the English do not understand.

Then it came as he had thought it would. One night a rumour : The Colonial Secretary is coming at last; he had been unavoidably delayed, it was said. Next day as a fact : Mr. Hudson had come. He had told Kruger that it was " no longer an affair of individuals but of nations."

Piet Bezuidenhout, the symbol, was now excluded. The small affair of his wagon was now the great affair of all men, of, in Meneer Hudson's words, the nation. Was Piet Bezuidenhout to be given up? Were the others who had refused to pay taxes to be prosecuted? Were they going to abandon their habit of mass armed meetings whenever something happened of which they disapproved? Were they going to submit to the annexation when the promises that had been made to them, and agreed to at that time, had not been kept . . . when after three years of protest they were no nearer to a final settlement than they had been at the beginning? If they agreed to all this—for such was Mr. Hudson's message to them from England—they were to disperse and go home. If they did not agree and stayed in the field, then it was treason, it was rebellion, and they would be dispersed by armed force. They had the choice: submission or war . . . peace or war . . . freedom or war. . . .

As the men stood talking in groups, Dirk could feel the answer. It was palpable in the air. He could see it in Paul Kruger's savage eyes as he went about them refusing to advise, but saying: " It is your choice, it is for you to decide; but if you wish to fight, then I will lead you."

The vote was to be taken. The young men and boys went with their fathers. Not yet of an age to vote, Dirk went with Pa. Pa had said nothing, but he knew how he would cast his vote. The votes were to be taken by the captains. Then each leader would take his totals to Paul Kruger. Cronje was now a general, and they were under Joubert, a cousin of the commandant general.

" And how do you vote, Groot Dirk?" Joubert asked.

" I vote for war. I am against it, but there is no choice. God help us, Joubert, it is war."

Joubert's quill made a little tick against his father's name. Dirk looked over his shoulder at the list. There were ten ticks to one cross. It would be war. You could see it in the faces of the men you passed, in the way they carried their shoulders, in the way they tied the riems under their horses' necks. You could see it, or thought you could, in the horses themselves.

" Then we will fight them, Pa," he said.

" Not yet, Dirk. Not yet. There is still a chance. We are forming a government at Heidelberg under Paul Kruger, Joubert, and Pretorious. Cronje is riding with his commando to Potchefstroom to get the proclamation printed. He has orders not to fire unless he is attacked."

" And we," Dirk said—" where are we going?"

" Back towards Brennersdorp. There are troops coming from the north to Pretoria. We are to intercept them."

" Will they stop, Pa?"

" How do I know if they will stop? If they do not, we shall engage them. Magtig, Dirk, this is something I have thought of, but always believed could never happen—that white men should turn their guns upon each other."

Even as they went back to their camping place, the meeting was breaking up. Commandos were forming. Men were shouting: "Now we are riding. . . . Now the Rooineks will see the Boer nation in the field." Horses were being driven in at a gallop. Herds of cattle were being broken up, each commando taking meat on the hoof according to its strength.

Dirk looked up and saw Joubert sitting on his horse near them. He was smoking his pipe and watching all that went on.

"When do we ride?" his father asked.

"At once. As soon as all are saddled." He leaned forward. "I would take your hand," he said. "It is good to have you with me. And you, jong." He held out his hand to Dirk. "With such men, such fathers and sons, and the Almighty God on our side, what have we to fear?"

CHAPTER VIII

THERE WILL BE DANCING

I

As LENA drove to town, she thought of the last time she had been on this road. She had been happy then. It seemed wonderful that she had been so happy and had not noticed it till afterwards. Was it always like that? she wondered. Did you never know you were happy till you became unhappy, and could look back upon your happiness as something you had lost? How was it that you could lose happiness as you lost a button from a dress? You looked down and it had gone.

Those days were so clear, so complete. She had thought she was unhappy because Dirk had not spoken, but in her heart she had known all the time that he loved her and that she need only wait. Now he had spoken. They were betrothed and he was gone. He was somewhere out on the veld. She looked round feeling that he might be near, that she might see him riding towards her on his black horse. It was terrible to think of him, of all those men, her brothers, Dirk's father, and the others, homeless, riding over the emptiness of Africa and sleeping under the stars. And everywhere their women must be thinking her thoughts. Wondering, wishing, trying to answer their children when they asked about their fathers: lying to them: telling them that they would come back soon, that they had gone hunting, that they had gone to visit, and trying to disguise their tears as they lied. The old days had been better when the women had gone too. The days of the Trek, of the Kaffir wars, when they had fought and died beside their men. That was a woman's place—beside her man. In health, in sickness, in peace, in war. . . .

Suppose Dirk were wounded: who would take care of him? Men could bind up a wound, but they were not skilled like women in the field medicines, the herbs and simples that cured wounds and illness. She supposed the wounded men would be taken to farms and left there. She wondered if there were any doctors with Dirk's commando. There were some, she knew, but how many? Were there enough? Her mind was filled with questions to which no one knew the answers. Time was the only answer. In time they would know everything, and time became an enemy, as much to her as Oupa. Time was killing him. No faster than it killed any one, since each day brought every one, even a baby, nearer to its end, but more obviously. And time was draining the life out of her already, and the war was only just begun. In fact, it had not yet begun. As far as she knew no shot had been fired, and, until it was, there was still a chance. It was said that all England was not for the annexation : that many were against it. Would they be strong enough to make the Queen give her people their freedom without war?

Lena whipped her horses up. She was urgent to get into the dorp. Tanta Martha might have heard something. She had so many friends who came to talk to her. Lena tried to reason with herself, to explain things, but could not. She had not the experience. Only old people like Oupa could do this, for they had the measuring-stick of their years, the vast store of their knowledge to draw upon. When she talked to him, he tried to calm her as if she were a horse. She could feel it in his manner, hear it in his words, see it in the questioning glances he gave her. He could see into her, but she did not care. He was so old that it was like God seeing into her. He knew very well that it was not the war that tore her, but Dirk, his absence and her desire for him, that had been held in check when he was there, but that now in his absence ravished her nights and blurred her days. It was natural, he said. It was not even new or different in any way from what other girls in her position felt.

That was Oupa's idea of comfort. But Lena could not believe this. It hurt too much. No one else could feel as she did : this craving, this emptiness : this feeling of waste and aloneness. She wanted Dirk, not to possess him, but to give to him. Without him and this giving of herself there could be no life. The days she was living now were something else; they were not days, they were hours which had to be got through somehow while she waited for the future that last month had seemed so golden with promise.

Lena found herself in Brennersdorp. For the first time she had driven past the blue gums without reaching for a leaf. She swung the horses towards Tanta Martha's. She would see her first and then go to the store. Tanta Martha would be pleased at the way she had made the dress. She would try it on for her to see and then put on the lace collar and cuffs that Tanta Martha had promised her if she made it well. She was looking forward to putting them on. It seemed wrong in a way to care about such things now, but on the other hand, only by making oneself care about little things could life be tolerated. And Tanta Martha would talk. In a minute she would be enveloped in words.

Only now did she realise how silent every one had been since the men had gone. Her grandmother rarely spoke and Oupa's conversation was a monologue, a recital of his past experiences, of his views, of his conclusions on life and love mixed up with habits of lions and buck, the death of his children, the beauty of his first wife—none of the others had been like her—and demands for meat and brandy. Talk—how she wanted to talk and fling herself into that big breast again and feel those arms thick round her, those fat strong hands patting her back!

She turned into the yard. Lucina called shrilly for one of her grandsons to come for the horses, and ran into the house.

" Magtig, what is it, Lena?" Tanta Martha said. " What is the matter, my heart?"

" Matter? Tanta Martha, nothing is the matter, only I think I am going to die." As she said this she felt it. She was laughing and crying : crying at her unhappiness, laughing at her sudden tears.

" Coffee!" Tanta Martha shouted. " Bring coffee, Lucina, the child is sick."

" I am not sick," Lena said.

" If I say you are sick, you are sick, my baby. Ja, you are young and in love and your man has gone to war. That is enough to make a maid sick. So I will give you a good purge. Before God, you have not even been seduced and that is what makes you sick, though you must not tell your grandmother I said so. She is a fool and knows nothing."

Tanta Martha was trying to make her laugh. She must be brave. She calmed herself a little, pulling herself in like a horse. Yes, it was like that. You could do that with yourself, drive yourself, and hold yourself like a horse. What was it Oupa had said? You could do anything to a horse if he had room to run in. That was what she lacked. She had no room. Perhaps women were like horses after all, or like cows. There were women like cows. It was better to be like a horse than a cow. She began to laugh and cry again. She knew she was like a horse, but not very like a horse. She gave it up, and settled down to cry again. Did Tanta Martha really think she had let Dirk go without making love to her? Or did she put her assertion in the form of a denial to put her at her ease?

" Are women like horses, Tanta Martha?" she asked.

" Ja, Lena, they are very like : more like than they will acknowledge. Now tell me what it is? What is the matter? Is the dress done? See," she said, " I expected you. I have the collar and cuffs ready." She poured out a cup of coffee. " Now drink it, my child," she said. " It is good and I have half-filled the cup with sugar because I love you. Drink, my dove, and do not worry. Magtig, when you have seen as many men ride out as I have . . ." She sighed. " But I have been lucky; both my husbands died in bed. It gives me great satisfaction to think of it."

Lena began to cry again. What did she want to talk about death for? Suppose Dirk was killed . . . suppose he never came back . . . that she had seen him for the last time . . . that just as it was beginning it ended.

" That was stupid of me," Tanta Martha said. " I always forget how young you are. It was such a long time ago and they were happy. I ministered to them, giving them draughts of boiled leaves and roots that eased their ends.

" Come," she went on, " I am tired of it now. You are a good Boer girl and to cry is a fine thing. It does you good, but to go on crying is not good; nothing comes of it except swollen eyes and a red nose. Women who cry after men are fools. To get what you want from a man, put on your best dress, or take off your dress if you are married to him, and sit on his knee. Do that and you will get your way with any man while you are young. Men are simple like babies," she said. "However big and strong they are, they are just like babies, so forget their beards and remember what I tell you while I am here to advise. I will not always be here." She folded her hands and looked up at the ceiling. "Ja, one day, Lena, I will go to join them. Both loved me well. It was wonderful how they loved their little Martha." Tears began to roll down her cheeks; she became angry. "You have spoilt my day, Lena. You have made me cry also. Men are like children, but they are also like the devil and it is hard to live without a devil in the house. It is dull when everything goes too right."

She wiped her eyes on her apron and called for brandy. "There is nothing like brandy wine," she said, "when you are sad." She made Lena drink some. It burnt her mouth and throat. It was like fire in her belly. She got up.

"You see, it makes you better," Tanta Martha said.

"Yes, it makes me better." She did not know if she was better, but it had made her get up. She wiped her eyes.

"Here is more coffee," Tanta Martha said, "and where is the dress?"

"It is in the cart."

"Then Lucina can get it. Get the dress, Lucina. Bring it in and you can help to put it on."

Lena took off her dress and put on the new one. It felt nice. It rustled when she walked, but it did not fit as well as it should have done. She was getting thinner all the time. She touched the breast where it was loose.

"You will fill up there," Tanta Martha said, "when you are married. Look at me. I was smaller than you once, though better made, with stronger bones. You are slim like a buck now, but wait and see what marriage will do to you. Marriage to a woman is like mealies to a horse, it is the contentment of it that fattens them." She handed her the collar. "Now put it round your neck and I will give you something else." From her pocket she brought a big gold brooch. It was glass-fronted and contained a flower design beautifully wrought in golden and black hair.

"It's lovely, Tanta Martha," she said. "Whose hair is it?"

"I do not know," Tanta Martha said. "Meneer Tryolla gave it to me after his sickness. But it is human hair. Perhaps it is his mother's."

"It is of two kinds," Lena said.

"That makes it more rare," Tanta Martha said. "But put it on, I want to see it."

Lena fastened the collar with the brooch.

"It looks very fine, Lena, and now you had better take off the dress, for it is too good to wear. Then we can sew on the cuffs. After that it will be time to eat. As you get older you will find eating a great pleasure. It is almost the only one to which a widow is entitled, without reproach."

As they ate, Tanta Martha watched Lena. The girl only picked at her food, pushing it about on her plate, putting pieces of meat into her mouth and having difficulty in swallowing them. That was the way war took women. She had often marvelled at the way it took men—most men : at the eagerness with which they went forward, especially the very young, those who had seen no war, because they wanted to be men. But the young were over-eager for all things and perpetually looking forward; saying : When I grow up, when I get married, when I have children, when I have a new farm; and with all the changes nothing was changed except that they were older. Not till they were really old did they understand life, which in its fullness comprised also death, its last and final achievement. As the first act of man, against his will, was to be born, so was his last, against his will, to die. Thus in coming into the world and in his taking leave of it, was man without free will.

But if it was one thing for the men and boys to ride out on commando, it was another for the women who were left. They had to wait newsless and to content themselves with rumour. Already the land was full of rumours . . . of victory, of defeat, of what the burgers of the Free State and Colony would do, of the strength of the English or their weakness; and all this before a shot had been fired. Every one talked and no one knew anything. It was impossible to sort out the grain of truth from the chaff of rumour. Time and time only would prove what was true and what was false.

Still they had good leaders. Paul Kruger and Joubert were good. Tanta Martha knew them both. She let her confidence rest on the leaders, on the justice of their cause, and the support of God. She put more food on to Lena's plate, more meat, potatoes, and roast pumpkin.

"You must eat," she said. "You must stay strong for Dirk. You cannot let him come back and find you as lean as a Kaffir cow." There was so little she could do for Lena. Nothing she could tell her to make her happy. She thanked God that she had never been like that. It must be Lena's French blood that she got from Old Philippus that burnt her up. It showed in her. Those big dark eyes the colour of brandy wine and that black hair were French. It was hot, unpeaceful blood that would not let her wait.

She heard the gate open and looked out of the window. A boy was coming in. It was Carlus, the young brother of Jacob, Brenner's coloured boy. He had not shut the gate. When he came in, she would tell him about gates. What did he think they were made for? What was the point of a gate? Why bother to hang one if every Kaffir or coloured boy who came in was going to leave it open?

He had gone round to the back. Lucina came in with a letter.

" Send that boy in," she said; " I want to speak to him. Carlus, are you so used to living on the veld that you do not know what a gate is for? That a gate must be shut when you pass through it? Do you think I want every loose beast from the road in my garden?"

The boy stood watching her, his eyes searching her face.

" The letter," he said. " The Baasie is sick. The mevrou will come?"

She tore open the letter. It was from Mrs. Brenner. Their little boy was ill, would she please come.

" I will come," she said. " Run back and tell them that I will, and shut the gate. Frans, Frans!" she shouted. " The horses! The horses and the cart! Finish your dinner, Lena, and we will go. You can do your shopping at the same time."

" I can eat no more, Tanta Martha."

" Then we will go. I can hear the horses being put in."

There were the usual things to get at the store. Each month they were the same and yet a little different this time—more thread, white this time; sugar, coffee, tobacco for Oupa, a bag of salt; and the shoes—she had persuaded her grandmother to let her buy a pair to go with the dress.

Tanta Martha turned the cart sharply, rocking it on one wheel. Lena could see Mrs. Brenner on the stoep, standing by the ploughs with her hand raised to her eyes. The boy must be very ill, since she watched for them so anxiously. But Lena had confidence in Tanta Martha, and the remedies were lying at their feet in the bottom of the cart. Charlie Brenner was not strong. He had been ill for a long time with a curious, intermittent fever that came and went, leaving him white and weak. She wondered if it had returned. Still he had always been cured before and Tanta Martha would be able to make him well again.

" If he was older," Tanta Martha said, " it would be better, but he is only eight and I cannot use strong medicine. With a man I would use something else. With men, you can kill or cure them quickly. With men you can purge the devil out of them. All sickness," she went on, " is from not purging. At least that is the beginning of an illness, but generally they call me too late. When the ox is down, he is likely to die. The time to get him is when he begins to be sick, when his eyes are dull, his ears cold, his nose dry; and it is the same with men. Ja, Lena, the more I see of sickness, the greater resemblance do I find between men and beasts. Four legs or two legs, all living things are much the same in their habits and sicknesses."

They pulled up. Mrs. Brenner ran forward. " I am glad you came so soon, Tanta Martha."

" How is he? Is he worse than usual? Send for some boys and a chair to get me down."

Jacob came out of the store carrying a box.

"That will do," Tanta Martha said; "put it near the wheel. Is it firm?" she asked.

Jacob pressed it down. Lena jumped out of the cart.

"Now let us go and see the child," Tanta Martha said. "I have brought everything, but if more is needed I can go back for it. You have not given him anything?" she asked. "Nothing out of a bottle?" How Tanta Martha suspected those patent medicines in bottles—the oils, the universal cures, the embrocations, the pills that were sold by travellers! No one knew what was in them, and why use things you did not know when good medicines grew all round you on the veld?

Mrs. Brenner led them to her room where Charlie lay in bed. The house was terribly hot, and such air as came in from the window was warm. It was like the air that came from an open oven door. A coloured girl was waving a fan over him, trying to keep him cool and prevent the flies from settling.

He looked very white, his hair was matted with sweat, his lips coated, and his eyes closed. As his mother smoothed his pillow, he looked up.

"Hallo, Tanta Martha . . . Lena," he said. Then he closed his eyes again and turned over.

"Yes, he is sick," Tanta Martha said. "He is too sick to purge, but we will do that later. Now we must make him sweat." She felt his pulse. "It is fast and jumping like a springhaas," she said, "but it is not weak. Do not fear, your little boy will get well if you leave it to Tanta Martha. Alle wereld, I have seen much sickness and I know my business. I know it much better than many doctors who have only learnt from books, and then mostly about illnesses such as they have in the other parts. They know nothing of the sicknesses of this land, which are special. Come, Lena," she said, "we will go and make his medicine."

They went into the kitchen to make an infusion of wood chips, covering them with boiling water. Mrs. Brenner followed them.

"I shall want blankets," Tanta Martha said, "and then you must stay with him to see that he does not throw them off."

"But it's so hot," Mrs. Brenner said. "I have been trying to keep him cool. He keeps saying he is too hot."

"He must sweat. The fever must burn out. It must come out in water from all over his body, then he will sleep quietly and wake up well."

She handed Mrs. Brenner the cup. "Make him drink it," she said, "and then cover him. I will sit on the stoep. Call me if he does not sweat soon."

"You are going to stay?" Mrs. Brenner said.

"I always stay when someone is ill unless I am wanted elsewhere. I want a chair and I want food for myself, my boy, and my horses; also for Lena, who will stay with me. It is time she learnt about sickness. All women should know about it: its cause, and how to cure it with the field herbs

that the good Lord has planted for us. . . . But what is happening here?"
she said as they looked into the store.

Everything was being cleared away from the middle of the room and
stacked along the walls.

"Where?" Mrs. Brenner asked. "Oh, in the store. Some troops are
expected to-day and Mr. Brenner thought it would be nice to give the
officers a dance. This was before Charlie was taken sick and it is too
late to change the plans now."

"There will be war," Tanta Martha said. "It is not right to dance when
there is going to be war."

"I do not believe there will be war," Mrs. Brenner said. "What would
be the good of fighting? Who is to gain by it? The English are too strong."

"There will be war," Tanta Martha said again. "But it would interest
me to see the Rooibaadjies. I have never seen a regiment of redcoats. Where
are they going?"

"They are going south, to Pretoria," Mrs. Brenner said. She was giving
Charlie his medicine. She had him raised against her, propped in her arms.
"Drink it, Charlie, it will make you well."

"To Pretoria," Charlie said. "Can I see them? I want to see them; I
want to see the soldiers."

"If you drink your medicine you can see them."

"Then I'll drink it." He gave her the empty cup. "Can I have something, Mother?" he asked.

"What is it?"

"Can I have my birds brought in here? I would like to watch my birds."

"Bring in the birds, Jacob," Mrs. Brenner said.

He came in with a cage of wild birds. It was a big cage and full of
finches of all kinds—little blue-breasted finks, king finks, rooibekkies, that
chirped and hopped from perch to perch.

"They are lovely, Charlie," Lena said.

"Jacob, put a chair for me on the stoep," Tanta Martha said.

"I will bring you coffee, Tanta Martha," Mrs. Brenner said.

"Coffee would be good, but cover up that boy and don't leave him. He
must sweat."

"I will stay with him," Lena said.

"I would like you to stay." Charlie put his hand into hers. "And I am
glad you like my birds. My father got them for me from a man who catches
them with birdlime. He makes it of berries and spreads it on the trees."

Lena pulled the blankets over him. "Now be good," she said, "and
keep them on."

"I am so hot, Lena."

"You have got to be hot, Charlie, and then you will get well."

He dozed off. The hand she held was getting hotter and hotter, and
then suddenly it was wet. She slipped her hand under the blankets on to

his body, the water was running off him and breathing was easier. He lay quite still. He was really sleeping now. Tanta Martha's medicine had worked.

Lena contined to sit beside him. What had Mrs. Brenner said? Soldiers were coming—English soldiers. A dance . . . but who would dance with them? Mrs. Brenner had gone to lie down for a few minutes, she needed a rest, she had been up all night. How dreadful it must be to have a child ill and be able to do nothing for it! She waved the fan the coloured girl had left. When Mrs. Brenner came back, she must do her shopping and get back home. If only she could get some real news. The meeting at Paardekraal must be over now. Where was Dirk? She thought of her dress with the new lace collar and cuffs and the hair brooch. He had never seen it. Would he like it? Perhaps he would not even notice it : he would be so glad to see her. But whether he saw it or not she wanted to put it on for him so that she should come to him in her best. These things meant a lot to women afterwards. They remembered the things that had happened in the different clothes they wore. There could be happy and unhappy dresses. Suppose anything happened to Dirk, then the brown would be an unhappy dress, for though he had never seen her in it, it was part of him. It had been made for him.

She looked at the birds and wondered what it was like to be caged. In a way she was caged too, caged by the war, enclosed by it so that she could not move. But there would be no war; whatever any one said, there would not be war. Perhaps Dirk was even now on his way home. She thought of him on Swartkie and almost got up to see if he was coming. She was getting sleepy. It was so hot, so quiet. She wondered if birds felt the heat. They did not seem to, they still hopped about, drank from a little cup fastened to the bars and cracked seed in their beaks. The seeds made funny sharp little noises as they broke them, and many of the husks fell on to the floor.

Mrs. Brenner came back.

" Will you stay with him?" Lena asked. " I have some things to get."

" Yes, I'll stay. Some things . . . things, you mean in the store?"

" Yes. Is Meneer Brenner there?" How dazed she seemed! Nothing, neither the store, nor the dance, nor the war mattered to Mrs. Brenner. Her child was ill.

Lena went into the store.

Mr. Brenner came towards her. " How do you think he looks?" he asked.

Looks . . . he was thinking of Charlie. " He looks ill, Mr. Brenner, but Tanta Martha thinks it will soon pass. He is asleep and seems better already."

" Has she given him anything?"

" Yes, she has given him something and is going to stay to watch him."

" Thank God she came . . . and we are having this dance. Perhaps we shouldn't "—he rubbed his hands over his eyes—" but I don't see how to stop it now. . . . Did you want anything, Lena? Is there anything in the store?" He looked round vaguely.

" Yes," she said : " a bag of salt, white thread—the strong linen thread I always have—five pounds of coffee beans, a bag of sugar, and a pound of tobacco for Oupa. And shoes. Mr. Brenner, have you any shoes that would fit me?" She held out her foot.

" A six," he said.

" I do not know the size. I have never had bought shoes before."

" Shoes," he said—" for the new dress." He smiled suddenly. " I have got just the thing. Look "—he pointed to some boxes on a shelf. " Look for yourself while I get your things. It's hard to clear the store and work at the same time." He rubbed his hand over his eyes again. " Have you got your cart here?"

" I came in Tanta Martha's."

" Will it be all right if I put your things in it? Your horses are at her house?"

" Yes, put them in hers," Lena said.

She was reaching for the boxes he had shown her. Six, he had said. The boxes felt wonderful. She pulled three out. There were only three sixes. The first one had black shoes in it : the leather looked good; they had nice steel buckles that were cut in a design. She wondered what was in the other boxes. She opened the next one. Oh . . . oh, it was what she had dreamed of. It was what I would have dreamed of, she thought, if I had known there were such beautiful shoes in the world. They must have been made to go with the brown dress. She thought of it as she had seen it last while they sewed on the cuffs. She had been sewing one wrist while Tanta Martha did the other. The dress had hung, almost standing, between them. Brown shot with the green, and these shoes were bronze, bronze as a turkey's breast.

She put out her hand to touch the leather. It was soft, finely grained. I must try them on, she thought. She wondered if Mr. Brenner would mind her trying them on. It could not spoil them. But she hesitated. She wanted just to look at them. She moved the box where they lay like twins in a bed—twins lying opposite ways, lying head to toe. The light caught them; they shone softly, dark bronze brown, almost green and purple.

She kicked off her shoes, rubbing the heels off with her toes. How clumsy they looked. She took out one shoe. It was the right one. She put out her right foot and slipped it on. Her heel pinched her finger. The other one. She stood up. It was wonderful. They might have been made for her. How could any one have made shoes for her who had never seen her and did not know the size of her feet? Mr. Brenner had said six. How had he known? How did people know?

Mr. Brenner came back with the small parcels, the thread and tobacco.
"So you found them," he said. "And they fit."

"I found them and they fit," Lena said. "They are wonderful, Mr.
Brenner. How much are they?"

"They are nothing at all," he said.

"I must pay," Lena said.

"If you pay, you will not get them. Listen, Lena. Tanta Martha is
here. You came with her. She will never take anything from any one for
what she does. So you can call them her gift to you, since they are mine
to her. I looked in," he said, "when I went to load the cart. Charlie is still
sleeping well."

"I do not know what to do," Lena said.

"You will take them," he said, "or his mother and I will be hurt. I
hope they make you happy, Lena. I hope you will be happy in them."

"They will be for best," she said. "Oh, what are you doing?" He had
taken them out of the box and scratched the lovely new soles with his knife.

"That is to stop you slipping. You can slip on new shoes," he said.
"And now they are spoilt. They are not new. I can no longer sell them.
Look," he said, "I will put the thread in with them and then it won't be
lost."

Lena felt tears come into her eyes. They were so beautiful. And he had
given them to her. She had never had a present from someone who was
not related to her before. She laid her hands on Mr. Brenner's shoulder
and stood on tiptoe to kiss him. "Thank you, meneer," she said, "thank
you. And I am sure Charlie will get well soon."

"Yes, he will get well." Mr. Brenner was spreading out a flag: the
Union Jack. He turned it over. One way up looked very like the other to
Lena. But he seemed to like it better this way. That was the flag of the
English, the one that had replaced the Vierkleur in her country. Those
flags were the symbols for which men fought. The dress . . . Dirk . . .
the shoes . . . her wedding . . . Oupa and his peacocks . . . little
Charlie Brenner so sick that he might die . . . the commandos on the veld
and the English marching. . . . Life—was this life? It suddenly seemed
a great confusion, a great movement of different waves and currents like the
water in a big dam under a high wind. She suddenly remembered the
goose-down Ouma had given her. She put the pillowcase on the counter.

"Here is the goose-down I spoke about last month."

"Thank you, Lena," Mr. Brenner said. "I will weigh it and give you
credit."

2

"And I say you are to stay here with," Tanta Martha said. "You can send your cart back with the Willem and tell your grandmother that I will bring you back to-morrow. I want to come to Mooiplaas. I want to see Oupa."

Lena hesitated. She wanted to stay. She wanted to see the soldiers and hear what was going on. Already she heard something.

The meeting was over. A Republican government had been set up in Heidelberg, and if English troops were moving in one direction, it was likely that the commandos would be moving in the other. She might see Dirk by staying, or she might miss him by staying. Charlie was better. Tanta Martha was a wonderful old woman. It gave her confidence to be near her. Oupa was wonderful, too, and very wise, but so near his end that he was detached from life, held to it only by the thread of his indelicate determination to see her child, his ambition to live to be a hundred, and his pleasure in annoying her grandmother and Stoffel by staying alive.

From where she sat near Tanta Martha on the stoep, she could look into the Brenners' garden. They called it a garden, but it was not really one. It was a patch of fenced ground attached to the house and filled with peach trees. The peaches were ripe; they bent the boughs down under their weight. Some of the branches were even broken. What a year it was for peaches. Everywhere, every tree was covered, laden with pinkish yellow fruit.

"If you think it will be all right, Tanta Martha, I will stay," she said.

"It will be all right. I will tell Tanta Katarina that I made you. Now we will go back to the house and you can send your cart home. There are more things I need for Charlie, and for myself. We are sleeping here and I must have my pillow that is stuffed with goose-down; with that under my head I can sleep anywhere. And I must get my best dress. I will put on my black satin and you will wear your new dress and the shoes you have just bought. Do not worry about your grandmother, my heart. I will tell her that I need you here. When I need any one, they stay."

The dance! Did Tanta Martha mean they were really going to it? That she was to wear the new dress to it . . . Dirk's dress and the shoes. . . .

"Me dance with an Englishman?" Lena said. "That I will never do." She stamped her foot. "I will stay to help nurse Charlie, but I will never dance with an Englishman."

"Ja, I know you will never do it, and the new dress is for Dirk, is it not? Ach, sis, young girls send me mad with their stupidity. Do you think then that I love the English? Do you think I am not a patriot . . . a Boer woman? You are a pretty miss, and do you not know yet that men talk to pretty misses? You understand English. They will talk to you and you may learn something that will be of use to our people. Now will you dance? Magtig, nothing can happen to you. They are not devils, and it would not kill you to be kissed or have your waist squeezed. God knows you have stitched in so much that there is nothing but whalebone that they can feel."

"A spy, Tanta Martha? You want me to speak to them, to dance with them, to let them make love to me for information?"

"A kiss is not making love. You should know that by now. Nor do I suppose you will be kissed unless they are drunk. They are cold-blooded and not like our folk."

Lena looked back into the store. The floor was bare and Jacob was scattering mealie meal on it for the dancing. "Many girls are coming in," Tanta Martha said. "They are curious to see the English, and it is a month since most of them have seen a man; besides, it is not war yet. There is no harm in it, and it may do good. That is why I am coming. Not to dance "— Lena looked at her in astonishment—"not to dance, but to watch and listen. There is always something to be learnt by watching. And if I can go, then you can; and there will be music. I love to hear music—loud music that turns your stomach upside down—and it has no nationality. You should have heard my Jan sing. It was beautiful, Lena—like the roaring of a bull. When he sang, the dust fell from the thatch. Always afterwards I had have the room swept. The maids hated him to sing because of the work it made."

"I do not think it is right, Tanta Martha, but I will come."

"Well, my young miss, if you only do what you think is right you will do little. I have been very happy, and I have done much good in the world, but I have rarely stopped to consider what was right, for what is the good of doing right if no one else does it? Magtig, the righteous man is very alone. Do you think your grandmother Sannie did right?"

"No, she did not do right," Lena said, "and she was punished. She was assegaied."

"Ja, she was speared with her lover, but it is in my heart that she was happy, much happier than she would have been had she lived with that old devil Hendrik. Hendrik was a righteous man till he was seduced by Louisa. But that also is true, the most righteous are the most easily seduced. Mind, Lena, these are my views and I have seen much. But they are not Kattie's views. She is a narrow woman who has no confidence in human failings. She has no understanding of love; that is why she is so thin, and as dry as a book-pressed flower. It is human to love and grow fat, and men like it. They like a woman they can get hold of."

"Dirk does not think I am too thin," Lena said. She did not want to be like Tanta Martha, and anyway there was time enough. Nor did she want to be like her grandmother. She did not want to be soured and bitter. She wanted to be happy, to marry Dirk. And he did not think her too thin.

Mrs. Brenner came out to them. She put her hand on Tanta Martha's arm.

"How can I thank you?" she said. "He is so much better. I thought he was going to die. He has never been so bad before. It frightened me."

"It is nothing," Tanta Martha said. "Where there is sickness I go. It gives me pleasure to relieve pain, and is not Charlie one of my babies? Did I not bring him into the world for you? When I bring a baby into Brennersdorp he stays there," she said.

"He is so excited about the soldiers," Mrs. Brenner said. "I hope it will not hurt him."

"As long as he does not catch cold, it will not hurt him," Tanta Martha said. "It will do him good and give him something to think about. Lena and I are coming back when we have got our clothes."

Jacob came to say the horses were in. They were going back now. Lena clutched the shoe box. Tanta Martha was still sitting. She never got up till everything was ready for her. She was waiting for the box to be put beside the cart.

"I am glad you are both coming and are going to stay the night," Mrs. Brenner said. "But I hope there will be no war. It is too terrible to think of. We have so many friends on both sides, and it would ruin us."

"You are English," Tanta Martha said, "so it is not my place to say what I think, and politics are for men. Ja, politics are for them and children are for us. I have seen more war than you. I have seen many dead, and it is in my heart than men are mad to fight unless they fight the Kaffirs. Still they have a grievance and men are like that, they have no sense. They have not even sense to know that they have no sense."

She looked at Lena and wondered what was in her mind. A young girl's mind was as empty as her womb. That was one of the great mysteries. It had never ceased to interest her. Men were stupid, but by association with them women became intelligent. Perhaps it was because they had to take care of them, and that this responsibility developed their brains and their figures. But marriage was an art. You had to be subtle with men and let them think that it was they who chose their course. But this was something you could not pass on. There was no way that she could teach Lena the management of men. It would come to her as it came to most women, or it would not come.

Before God, a man, if you kept him in love with you, could be led like a bull with a ring in his nose. Ja, man, by his lust and his vanity, was a dumb creature, as easy to deal with as a child, once you understood the simplicity of his nature and were not deceived by the long words he used, his eloquence, or his ideas. Only sometimes did they break away from you and then it was for one of two reasons, another woman or a new idea. Another woman you could understand, an idea you could not. Another woman would employ every device that you employed yourself, but because she was new and strange, men thought that what she did was new and strange. Men were easily seduced by strange women, but they generally came back. An idea was a madness that took them. It was seasonal, periodic, like the breeding fever that overtook beasts in the spring, or the brain worm that sent them mad.

To-night would be interesting. Apart from Mr. Tryolla she had known few Englishmen, and John Tryolla was not really English; he came from the very bottom point of that country and had left it so long ago that he spoke the taal better than his own language. And there would be music : music and strange men. She wished she was a girl again. I would like to see, she thought. Ja, I would like to see if they are different; and Lena is too shy and young, she will waste her chances.

She sighed and turned her hands over on her knees to look at their palms. Some people said you tell the pattern of your life from the lines in your hands. If this were so, it would be very convenient, for then you could get ready. She wondered what the lines in Lena's hands would tell. She thought of a baby's hands with nails no bigger than a mealie pip. There was going to be war. She must prepare more salves and bandages. She thought of her pots and jars and bottles, of her salves upon the shelves. If there was to be pain, she had much there to relieve it. Men would be wounded. They would need her. It came to her that that was all a woman wanted in her life. A woman had to be needed : by a baby for her milk, by a young man for her beauty, by her children for her love, and when old, as she was now, for the wisdom the years had given her. To be wanted, to be loved, desired, to be of use, that was the beginning and the end of a woman's life : the necessity of being necessary, of knowing that without her someone's life, a child's, or a man's, would be empty and of no value.

But it was no good sitting here dreaming. Lena was moving restlessly.

" Come," she said, " we must be off."

She got up, took the reins from the dashrail and stepped on to the box.

At Tanta Martha's house the dress lay on the bed. It was stiff, shining, metallic. There it was, the embodiment of so much thought, so much work, and so much hope. My wedding dress, Lena thought. And I am to wear it to-night. . . . It was strange to have taken all these pains about a dress and then betray it . . . to have wanted bought shoes so much; to have found shoes that exceeded all her imaginings and then to betray them too. She slipped the dress over her head and began to fasten the hooks and eyes. Her fingers fumbled with them. Why did they fumble? They had not before when she tried it on.

She smoothed the bodice. It was cool and lovely to touch. As she ran her hands down her body, the silk changed colour in front of her hands : it went from brown to green, from green to brown . . . like metal . . . like water. The cuffs were lovely. She fastened the collar, put on the

brooch, and sat down on the bed. There were tears in her eyes. Her lip
was trembling as she put on her new shoes. How smooth and supple they
were, and light—they felt like nothing on her feet. I am going to cry, she
thought. I am going to cry because of my beautiful dress and new store
shoes.

Someone was coming. She started up.

" Tanta Martha . . . oh, Tanta Martha."

" Crying, Lena! What are you crying for?" She held her in her arms.
How big her arms were! " You must not cry, my heart. You must not
cry. And, magtig, you must not cry on my black satin, it will mark it.
Come, wash your face and let us go back to Charlie. And don't forget
your other clothes. A best dress, if it is to remain best, must only be worn
for best."

3

When Lena and Tanta Martha drove back to the store the troops had
come. The outspan was filled with soldiers. They were cooking, and
washing stripped to waist in buckets. There were oxen tied to the trek-
tous of the transport wagons that had been hired, and horses made fast
to a rope fastened between two trees. There were pitched tents and straight
lines of piled arms. Line after line of rifles stacked in little triangles. There
were men shouting and singing and small parties moving from place to
place. They marched in orderly little lines, like worms, their feet moving as
one. Lena had never seen such a thing before. They were not like men
at all. " Why do they walk like that?" she asked.

" That is what makes them soldiers," Tanta Martha said. " They do
not think our men soldiers because they cannot do it. No, they cannot
do it, and why should they? They are not so dom as to walk at all if they
can help it. Our men ride horses, and soon they will see if they are soldiers
or not. Soldiers!" she sniffed. " Why, our men were soldiers, veterans
of wars, when these Rooibaadjies were but children. Look at the time these
English had with the Zulus, more than a thousand getting themselves
killed at Isandwhlana. Our Oom Paul said if they would give us our freedom he would finish the Zulus for them. Ja, he said he would take five
hundred picked burgers, experienced men, and drive the Zulus into the
sea. But they would not let him. Oh, no, they must fight the Zulus themselves in their own way."

" Why would Kruger have taken married men?" Lena asked.

" Married men are the best soldiers," Tanta Martha said. " That is well
known. They are the best because they are of two kinds : those that are
very brave because they are glad to be away from their wives, and those
who are very cautious and ready to save themselves because they love their

wives and farms. This combination of bravery and caution makes them irresistible in war. Married men are stronger, too, and more serious. And more virtuous. They have to be."

Lena nodded her head. No doubt Tanta Martha was right that picked men would be mature and married. There was something wrong with a man who did not marry.

Some soldiers walking arm in arm smiled at her. " Nice evening, Miss," they said.

" Good-night," she said, and they laughed. They did not look like soldiers. They were boys in red coats with white helmets whose faces were burnt by the sun nearly as red as their coats. Across their chests and round their waists they wore belts of white leather and at their sides they had small swords that they fitted to the tops of their guns, she had been told.

" Those clothes look too good to fight in, Tanta Martha," she said.

" Red and white," Tanta Martha said. " They can be seen for miles. What do you think our folk will do to them if there is war?—our men who can shoot the eyes out of a buck at two hundred paces."

" There will not be war," Lena said. " I am sure there will not, now that they see we are standing firm. No, Tanta Martha, it is all nothing. There will be more talk and then we shall be made free and our men will come home."

The sound of music came from the store. It must have begun already.

" That may be, Lena. It may well be, and then we will all dance at your wedding. Even I who have not danced for twenty years, I will dance at your wedding." She paused. " I will dance with Oupa to make your grandmother angry. . . ."

She turned her horses between two Cape carts that stood resting on their poles. Many people had arrived while they were away. The music was loud now, it came in gusts. There was laughter . . . the sound of shuffling feet.

" Be careful getting out, Lena," Tanta Martha said; " do not brush the wheel as you turn."

CHAPTER IX

"KISS YOUR DARLING DAUGHTER"

I

THE store was bright with gold and scarlet. Mr. Brenner had decorated the walls with yards of bunting, coloured trade cottons and blankets. The band sat on chairs at the far end, by the bags of mealie meal, now draped with flags, their instruments glittering in the lamplight. There were many girls and women, all dressed in their best, their eyes bright and faces flushed with dancing, and on a long trestle table set below the counter there was food—pots of steaming coffee and wine in bottles; and on the other side a barrel of beer was mounted on two ploughs set sideways.

Lena knew everyone by sight, but it was funny to be here with all these Boer girls and none of their own men, only English officers in short scarlet jackets and tight blue trousers with a red stripe running down them. Some wore spurs, and some had on little medals that clinked on their breasts as they moved. She looked at their faces. They looked nice and gentle. They were very clean, so clean that their faces shone. The older ones had big moustaches, but no beards, which made them look strange.

Mrs. Brenner welcomed them. " I am so glad you came," she said. " The colonel says there will be no war and we are all so pleased; and Charlie is much better, he slept for three hours. The colonel," she went on, " says that this is nothing, and that the burgers will not stand up to regular troops."

Tanta Martha began to laugh. " That is a fine thing to say to a Boer woman," she said. " But I will forgive if you tell your colonel one thing."

" What is that?"

" That he is right, our men will not stand up to fight him. It is not their custom. Tell him they will be behind every bush and tree and rock and anthill, and from there will pick off his little red-cheeked boys like chickens."

Mrs. Brenner flushed. " Tanta Martha, I am so sorry. It is just that——"

" Ja, I know that you do not want war. Do you think that we want war ? We do not want it : only our freedom. Now dance," she said to Lena. She leant towards her. " And listen. Remember what they say, and do not scream if you are kissed." She pushed her towards a man who was near them.

" May I have the pleasure of the next dance?" he said.

" Ja, meneer," Lena said.

He took her in his arms. " You talk English?"

" I talk a little," Lena said, " but I understand it well."

He seemed very polite. She did not think he would kiss her. What shall I say to Dirk if I am kissed? she thought. As they danced she kept wondering how she would explain to Dirk. Her partner danced very well, once she got used to it, and her dress felt lovely. It swirled as he turned her, billowing like a wave. And she was pleased with the lace collar and cuffs and brooch. She was as well dressed as any other girl. She was better dressed than any other girl. But what would she tell Dirk if . . . and how would her absence be taken by her grandmother? She wondered about Oupa. He would miss his dop. She generally managed to put some brandy into his pap at night when no one was looking. She stole it during the day and kept it in a little bottle for him. He would miss his brandy with his supper.

She nodded to Maria van Zael, to Trudi Marais. They smiled back at her. Hester Marais, Trudi's sister, was wearing rose pink. How beautiful she was with her blonde hair and strong, curved figure. She is no older than I, Lena thought, but she is more fully made, more complete, more of a woman. She smiled at Hendrika Bothma, she was in blue; at Cobie Erasmus in yellow; at Elizabet Prinsloo. It was beautiful to see such colour, to watch the bright dresses of the girls mingling with the brighter scarlet of the uniforms. She wished she could tell them about Dirk. But how did one tell those things? Surely one had to wait till one was asked. In her heart she was dancing with Dirk. This is the way it will be at my wedding dance, she thought. It will be like this, only it will be Dirk who holds me. It was good to dance in store shoes. She tried to stick them out so that the other girls would see them. There was only one other girl there with store shoes on and they were not so pretty or so new as hers. Her mind returned to the officer she was dancing with. He danced differently from her people, smoothly when she wanted to hop. There could be no joy in dancing unless you hopped, and he stood very straight. Perhaps his clothes were tight . . . like Dirk's. She thought of Dirk's best coat and the button she wanted to move. But she must say something to her partner.

" Where are you going?" she said suddenly. " You have come from the north, have you not?"

" We are going to Pretoria," he said. " We are concentrating there— till this is over."

" You do not think there will be war, then?" Lena asked.

" Of course not. How can there be? The Boers have no troops."

" I am a Boer girl," Lena said.

" I am sorry," he said, " but it's true, isn't it? You have nothing to compare with our disciplined troops, and it's discipline that counts."

" No." She thought of the little worms of marching men she had seen on the outspan and said : " We have nothing like your soldiers."

" That's just it. But don't think I don't admire your people. We all do. And we think they have a great deal on their side. In fact, Mr. Gladstone never believed in this annexation."

" And if you think we are right, why are you ready to fight?"

" We are soldiers and do not think!" He laughed. " But we like South Africa as a station. Good climate, good shooting, some polo . . . What more can you ask?"

The music stopped.

" Then you go where you are sent?"

" Yes, that's right. South Africa, India, China, Burma . . . I was in India before I came here."

" You liked India?" Lena was not certain where India was—near America, she thought.

" Yes, I liked it," he said. " I had some wonderful shooting in Kashmir."

" And where are your wife and children when you travel like this?" Lena asked. " Is it not very hard for them to trek all the time from land to land and even across the sea? I have never seen the sea," she said. " Tell me what it is like. They say it is salt and that it cannot be used for drinking; that it is even too brak for beasts."

" Let's sit down," he said, leading her to a bench. " Now, can I get you a glass of wine or some cake?"

" Some cake," Lena said, " and coffee." He was a nice man. He had not tried to touch her. There would be nothing to explain to Dirk. When he comes back, she thought, I must ask him again about his wife.

" Where is your wife, meneer?"

" I have no wife. We do not marry till we get a captaincy."

" A captaincy," Lena said; " what is that?"

" That's a captain," he pointed to another officer. He looked about forty.

" You mean you have to be a certain age and serve so long before you can marry?"

" Yes, that's about it."

" Why, that is like the Zulus," Lena said. " Only the warriors when they have fought in many battles can wear rings on their heads and marry. I did not know that was the same with the English. Did you learn it from them?"   •

He laughed. " No, we did not learn it from them. It's a matter of money. Women are expensive."

" Then it is like the Kaffirs," Lena said, and began to laugh. She had no idea the English were so funny. " Do you buy your women with cows, meneer? Do you give your father-in-law ten cows for his daughter?"

" Of course not. But women are expensive, they have to have things— clothes, servants, houses, carriages, horses. They have to have hundreds of things to make them happy, and then half the time they aren't."

" But what is the matter with them? Can't Englishmen make their wives happy?"

The captain that he had pointed out came up to ask her to dance.

" Are you married?" she asked.

He looked surprised. " No," he said. " Why?"

" Well, he "—she nodded towards the man she had just left—" said captains could marry, and he said you were a captain."

" Yes, I am a captain, but I'm not married."

" I do not understand it at all," Lena said. " You are a strange people. With us it is not respectable not to be married."

" I am quite respectable," he said.

She was enjoying herself. After the captain she danced with others, and of them all only one, a major, said he had a wife. She liked the officers, the music, the food and coffee. Someone gave her a glass of wine that bubbled and pricked her mouth. She wished she had been outside so that she could have spat it out. The store was so changed by the flags and bunting that it was unrecognizable and the pleasure her new dress gave her made her happy. It was all wonderful. It was like fairy land. There would be no war. These men would not fight. There was nothing brutal about them. They seemed very good and simple, though odd in many ways. She wondered how Charlie was getting on and decided to go and see. His mother was with him and one of the officers.

" This is the doctor," Mrs. Brenner said as he got up to take her hand.

" Langdon, my name is," he said.

" Captain Langdon," Mrs. Brenner said. " He came in to see Charlie when I told him he was ill, and he has given me some medicine for him."

" And are you married, Captain Langdon?" Lena asked.

" No, I'm not. Not yet, anyway."

" But you are a captain?"

" Yes, I am."

She gave it up. They could and they didn't.

She sat down. The captain sat down. She wished she understood why these men kept getting up and down. They seemed very restless.

" I saw them come in, Lena," Charlie said. " And Mother carried me into the dance. I saw you dancing," he said, " and the store looks beautiful—like Christmas. I wish it was always like that."

His mother smiled at him. He certainly was better.

Mrs. Brenner pointed to some tins on the floor. " Captain Langdon has given us all that food for him, too, as well as the medicines. They are special things from England that we can't get here."

It was all very friendly, the sick boy, his young, smiling mother, the doctor in scarlet and gold, talking and laughing. Charlie's birds were asleep on their perches, huddled, with their heads under their wings.

" And do you know what I've done, Lena?" Charlie said.

" No, what have you done?"

" I have given the doctor my birds. He has promised to take them with him. They will go to Pretoria on his cart. He likes them. You do, don't you?" he said, turning to him.

" Yes, I do. I love birds and make a hobby of them. I am an ornithologist. It's a good hobby when you travel about the world as I do."

" He liked them so I gave them to him," Charlie said again. " He knew all their names, though he is English, and much more about them than I do."

They certainly were a strange people. What was an ornithologist? And why should a grown man care about little birds? She cared about them. She loved them and so did Charlie and Boetie, but she did not think a man would.

" What do you do with birds?" she asked the doctor.

" Well, I make drawings of them, and when I can I skin them and send them home."

" You skin little birds like that?" Lena said. " What do they use them for?"

" They don't use them. They stuff them and mount them so that people can come to see them in the museums!"

" Yes," Lena said. But it was not all clear to her. What was a museum and why would people want to see a lot of little dead birds from a foreign land? Nothing was clear about these people except that they were not dangerous. Not one of them had tried to kiss her. Perhaps it's because they don't think I'm pretty, she thought. And they were quite mad with their little birds and their marriage habits . . . not till you are a captain and then none of the captains she had spoken to were married. It might be that they did not like women. If they did not like women, it was funnier than ever, but it would account for the fact that none of them had . . . anyway, there would be nothing to confess to Dirk.

Tanta Martha came in. " This is Tanta Martha," Mrs. Brenner said. " It was she who made Charlie well."

The doctor got up to take her hand. Up and down again.

" Magtig, I am hot," Tanta Martha said, " and I have been dancing. Not for twenty years have I danced, Lena, and I said I would not till your wedding. But the beautiful music went to my heart. It made me feel quite sick with pleasure, and the men in red—the Rooibaadjies with their pink shining faces like the behinds of babies." She wiped her face. " Ja," she said to the doctor, " I have danced with every one except you. And it is a good thing I am not a spy," she said, " for I know all about you. I know where you came from and where you are going. And how many men you have and how many wagons." She began to laugh. The doctor laughed too.

" Well, there's no secret about it," he said, " and the march will do the men good. They were getting soft. We were not getting enough exercise, and it was too hot for many games. I think we'd better leave him now "— the doctor looked at Charlie. "Seeing too many people is not good for him. Good-night," he said.

"Good-night," Charlie said, "and you won't forget the birds in the morning?"

"I won't forget them. Sleep well . . . and remember, if you're not much better in the morning I won't take them."

"Good-night, Charlie," Lena said.

Tanta Martha and Mrs. Brenner were talking. She was trying to find out what medicine the doctor had prescribed.

The dancing was still going on as the doctor led her out. The colonel came towards her and offered her his arm.

"The prettiest girl in the room," he said, "and I have not danced with her yet."

As they were going to begin, Mr. Brenner came up to them. "I've just had bad news, Colonel," he said. "There is a commando between you and Pretoria. They have come to stop you." He handed him a letter.

"Stop me?" the colonel said. "I have my orders and I am going on."

"You had better stay here, Colonel; they mean business."

"They do, do they? Well, so does the Ninety-Fourth, by God. Come," he said. Lena slipped into his arms. For a moment he was silent. He looked flushed and angry. Then he said : "I am sorry about that, but they won't stop us. It's a lot of fuss about nothing."

Fuss about nothing! It was wonderful how little they seemed to understand. Did he think the burgers left their homes for nothing? If it was true, if there really was a commando out, something would happen. She wondered where Mr. Brenner had got the news. From someone passing, no doubt, a traveller, or a Kaffir. If it was a Kaffir, it was not to be relied on . . . if only it was a Kaffir, and it was nothing! But why had there been a letter? And why had the colonel stuffed it into his pocket without reading it? Surely a letter was important.

"You do not think there will be war?" she asked.

"Of course not. Why should there be?"

"People say there will be."

"'People,'" he said, "always 'people' . . . gossip . . . nonsense. Don't worry, young lady. In a month everything will have settled down. Are you fond of dancing?"

"Yes, I love to dance."

How funny it was to be talking like this! She was surprised at the way she could talk while she was thinking of Dirk and of the waiting commando . . . he might be with it. . . . She went on thinking of all those men out there on the veld, waiting with their horses and guns. If only she knew what was happening! But nobody knew. It was just as the colonel said. Talk . . . people . . . what they said. What someone had said to someone else—rumour passed by word of mouth, stories without confirmation. Only two things were certain—that the Boers were out : her brothers, Dirk, and Dirk's father, and the others; and that the English were here and marching on Pretoria. Both these things she had seen with her own eyes.

The colonel brought her more cake. They sat down; they went on talking. She was not clear what they talked about : shooting, game, hunting, his travels—she had never been anywhere—and then something about elephants. In India, he said, they rode on elephants. She tried to think what riding on an elephant would be like, and why ride on them? Had they no horses?

Then suddenly the band played a different tune. It was not a dance tune. All the men stood up. The women got up, too, looking surprised. The men stood very stiffly. They looked like scarlet-and-blue posts. Their heads were high and their hands held close to their sides. It was the English tune, someone said, *God Save the King*, a thing they played when anything was ended, and they always stood up to hear it. That was a strange experience, that she, a Boer girl, whose lover and brothers were in the field, should be here to listen to it.

She looked round for Tanta Martha, but she was not there. Perhaps she had gone to look at the bedroom they were to have. The dance was over: she had worn her new dress and shoes; she had seen the English, danced with them, and listened to their music. She thought of Boetie. How he would have liked those tunes! He would have remembered them. It was wonderful the way he remembered all the tunes he heard.

Suddenly she was tired of it all. What was happening? Where was Dirk? What had all these soldiers, these red-and-gold-coated officers and men to do with her? Why were they here? The implication of their presence forced itself upon her. Why were they in Africa? While she had been dancing and talking, she had forgotten. It seemed awful to have forgotten that these men were the enemy. That it was because of them that their own men were out.

She went to the back door. Tanta Martha must be cooling off outside. She hesitated, looking about her. Then, as her eyes got used to the darkness, she saw Tanta Martha. She was talking to a man. It was one of their own people. He stood by his horse. Man and horse were black shadows against the sky. She went towards them. She heard Tanta say : " You can remember?"

" Ja, I can remember."

Lena hung back, unwilling to break in. What was he to remember? Why was one of their men here in the dark with his horse? He looked very big, massive, even beside Tanta Martha.

" Repeat it," Tanta Martha said.

"The Ninety-Fourth Regiment. They are marching to Pretoria. Each man has seventy rounds of ammunition. There are nine officers, two hundred and forty-eight men, and thirty-four wagons. They have three women and two children with them."

"That's right," Tanta Martha said. "Now go and tell Joubert that it was I who told you, then he will know it is no lie. Also tell him that they are going to fight if they are stopped."

"They will be stopped, but I wish they would stay here. That was why Joubert sent me to tell Meneer Brenner to warn them that the roads were closed. I brought a letter. Before God," he said, "we do not want to fight, but they force it upon us."

"That is for Joubert and the Almighty to decide," Tanta Martha said. "I have given you the information. Good-night, young man, and good luck."

"Good-night," he said.

Lena felt him look at her. "Who is that?" he asked.

"That is Lena du Toit. She is safe."

"That is good," he said. "Tot siens, Tanta Martha, and thank you."

He mounted, raised his hand, and rode off.

"Now we will go to bed," Tanta Martha said. "I have enjoyed myself and have done good work. I am old, but sometimes brains are better than beauty. They last better, too. Though when I was young I was exceptional, for God endowed me with both."

2

In the morning when Lena and Tanta Martha went in to see Charlie, he was better, to Tanta Martha's annoyance, since she feared Mrs. Brenner might attribute it to the doctor's medicine. Still, whatever his mother thought, it was she who had cured him, the doctor had only come after the crisis. Charlie must be purged now. She saw to it. Then with rest and good food he would soon be well. Once the rains came, he would be better, for the weather would get cooler, and the drying heat that pulled his skin so taut would be gone.

When Lena looked into the store, it was in order again, the flags and bunting were gone. Last night was a dream . . . last night had never been. It was impossible to think of it, the blaze of scarlet and gold, the red-faced officers, the band playing, the women and girls, the man standing with his horse's bridle in his hand as he talked to Tanta Martha in the dark. Tanta Martha had got all the information she needed and had passed it on. How she had laughed at her as they went to bed! She had said: "Now you see an old woman is wiser than a pretty miss: but the old woman was once a pretty miss and the pretty miss will one day be an old woman. And it is a mistake to think that a black hen cannot lay a white egg or that a white egg may not turn into a black hen. Those redcoats never suspected an old Boer vrou like me. They never thought of the beautiful white egg of information that I would lay." Tanta Martha was always dressing her ideas up as proverbs and translating proverbs into action.

Charlie was pleased to see them. "He is coming for my birds," he said. "He is going to take them, and my father will make the cage fast on his cart. He has promised to tie it himself with a strong riem. I hope they will not be frightened."

Outside the wagons were being inspanned. Orderlies led the officers' horses up and down. Non-commissioned officers were shouting orders as the men put on their packs and adjusted their belts. A sergeant was issuing ammunition, passing it out to the corporals from the back of one of the baggage wagons. Mr. Brenner stood beside her watching it all.

"I don't like it, Lena," he said. "They should not go. They will meet the commando and there will be trouble. I can't see why they go when your people sent to stop them, asking them to wait for the negotiators."

How young they are! Lena thought: just boys. And she wondered what the colonel had meant by disciplined troops. Did he really think that these children could stand up to men like Dirk and his father or her brothers? True, some of the Boers were only boys, too, but they were different. They were not boys on the veld; there they were men. She watched the soldiers being herded like cattle—shouted at. Our people would not stand that, she thought. On commando all were equal, even the commandant who, to lead, must persuade. He could not command his men like this.

A soldier came up to Mr. Brenner. "Could we have some peaches, sir?" he asked.

"Peaches? Yes, take all you want."

The peaches were ripe; the trees bent beneath them. The word went round. In a moment the men were swarming over the wall of the orchard, picking the fruit, eating it, and cramming it into the pockets of their jackets and the haversacks at their sides. The green orchard was filled with scarlet uniforms. They were like boys the way they ran from tree to tree. They were boys who wanted fruit, who did not want to fight. Why should they? What quarrel have they with my people or my people with them? Lena thought. What has the freedom of the land to do with these young men? How are they responsible for it? And how would killing them advance the cause of freedom? It was all beyond her.

She saw the band coming carrying their instruments. It was hard to believe that this was the band she had danced to last night. That these white-helmeted men were those who had sat with their backs to the decorated mealie sacks in the store. Why, the drummers were just little pink-faced boys who looked longingly towards the orchard. She hoped someone would give them peaches, and then laughed. They were so little that no doubt the officers were afraid they would make themselves ill if they were allowed to eat as many as they wanted.

They put their drums on the ground and stood staring at the older bandsmen, who were smoking and laughing. The men's rifles were still piled in a long line. Smoke still rose from the cooking-fires, but if there was confusion it was an orderly confusion. It was like a birth that was taking place before her eyes. The officers and non-commissioned officers and men were gradually forming the thing that they called a regiment. By a series of orders, of moves and counter moves, they would compose this thing, this strange anomaly of men, boys, beasts, and wagons, into what they called the Ninety-Fourth.

It had a life of its own, this thing. From what she had been told it seemed that it went back, behind these men, into the past, into the old battles whose names they carried on their colours, and beyond them, into the future. A regiment was everlasting. It was more than the men who composed it. That was what the officers had tried to explain to her last night. They had also tried to explain what they called their duty—to go here and there, wherever they were sent, and to fight any one they were ordered to fight. They did not ask for reasons. They did not have to. It was all very strange.

She pulled her kappie over her eyes and went down among them. They were friendly and smiled at her. Perhaps they had sisters. Some of them must have sisters. It was strange to think of them so far away. Perhaps at this moment they were wondering about them. And they must have sweethearts, mothers, aunts . . . It became terrible to her that these young men should be here, away from their homes.

She went towards the wagons and limbers. Coloured drivers were bringing in oxen, mules, and horses. They were shouting and clapping their whips. It was fun to hear them talking Dutch to each other, while the soldiers looked on. She saw the doctor's cart, with a red cross painted on the canvas tent. Charlie's birds were on it, tied to the tail-board.

A bugle sounded, someone shouted : " Markers . . . markers!"

A man beside her ran forward, there were more shouts : " A Company . . . B . . . B Company . . ." The men were making final adjustments to their equipment. She saw them trooping back from the Brenners' orchard, a red stream, laughing and talking as they clambered over the wall. A bugle rang out again . . . " Fall in! . . . Come on there, get fell in . . . Fall in . . . Fall in . . . Fall in!" It was taken up.

Men from all round ran towards the outspan sorting themselves out as they ran . . . " B Company . . . A . . . A . . . A Company . . ." They formed up in lines by their piled rifles. " Right dress . . ." " Unpile arms." The orders came crisp and sharp. The men moved as one, putting out their hands for their rifles. They were in a double line facing each other. Another order : the front rank turned round . . . " 'Shun " . . .

they stiffened like ramrods. " Slope arms " . . . their rifles moved up—One . . . two . . . three—on to their shoulders.

This was discipline. This was what they meant. But how would it help them? What good was blind obedience like this unless those they fought were also blindly obedient? In the Zulu War they had stood in firm red squares while the impis poured over them, but they had had guns and the Zulus had only spears and courage. If the Zulus had had guns—and what about Isandwhlana . . . a thousand English dead because they would not profit by what Oom Paul had told them. Did they think her folk would fight like Zulus? What did they think? Did they think at all?

She was suddenly very proud of her people—her men, ons volk, farmers and hunters who refused to be intimidated by these Rooibaadjies.

She saw the colonel mount on his white horse. He gave an order. The order was repeated. The leading company began to unwind itself. The band got ready to play. The drum major raised his long stick, the little drummers stood with raised sticks round a man with a big drum fastened to his stomach. He had a tiger skin over him, and a knob kerrie in each hand. They began to play, side drums rattling, the boys throwing up their sticks and catching them, the fifes piping. It began very suddenly. The big drummer banged on the drum on his stomach with his kerries, twirling them. The drum major marched in front, his chest blown out, twirling his long stick. One of the transport guards beside her began to sing to himself accompanying the tune . . . *Kiss me, darling . . . Mother, kiss your darling daughter*. It was funny to hear him. He was an oldish man with a red moustache, but his eyes were misty as he sang. One of the women—Lena thought it was the sergeant-major's wife—took it up. *Kiss me, darling* . . . The line was still uncurling. The first company had gone. The music was thinner. She could no longer see the colonel on his prancing horse . . . The second company was gone . . . the third was moving . . .

The transport officer—she remembered having danced with him last night—galloped down the line of wagons, cursing them : " God damn it, you bloody niggers!" he cried. " Can't you get moving . . . can't you get ready?" The transport sergeant was beside him. "And what are you supposed to be doing?" the officer said. " This is your job, Sergeant Mulligan." " Yes, sir, but I can't do nothing with them cows. If they was 'orses . . . cows!" he said. " Cows in the army!"

Some of the drivers began to laugh. They called to the voorlopers. They shouted at the oxen. The long whips sang through the air, one of them, a little wizened Hottentot, clapped his whip beside the officer's horse. It began to buck. He spurred it and turned back to the head of the column . . . *Kom trek . . . Loo . . . oop . . . Loop, you Dwuivels, loop . . . Springbok . . . Yukman . . . Bosveld . . . Irland . . . Scotland . . . Gentlemaan . . . loop . . . loop* . . . the oxen began to move drawing the trek chains tight. Crack after crack came from the whips. Shouts, laughter, cries, and yells from the drivers as the wagons rocked, dogs barked, the great wheels creaked, groaned, and began to roll.

The last wagon was moving, the whole column was moving—a long snake unwinding itself before her eyes. She could see it fading away into the distance. She could hardly hear the music. Music . . . And all those feet moving to the music, going on and on, not knowing where they were going—just following the music . . . going . . . going . . . where they were led. Hundreds of boys marching south to Pretoria, with guns on their shoulders and their pockets full of peaches. Now she could only see the last wagon and a long, low cloud of drifting dust. The regiment had come yesterday, it had paused, and now it had gone.

She must get back to Tanta Martha, and then get home. Tanta Martha said she would take her back to-day. She wondered if Charlie had seen the soldiers go. She wondered what the birds would think of it. It was odd to think of wild veld birds on the back of a British cart.

CHAPTER X

THE SHOT IS FIRED

I

DIRK lay on his belly with his chin on his hands. He was watching the horses grazing in the distance under their guards. They formed patterns, continually grouping themselves, breaking away, joining up, and moving all the time as they fed. The horses occupied his eyes. It was satisfactory to watch them while he thought. But it was strange to be here with Frans Joubert's commando camped within twenty miles of Brennersdorp . . . within easy riding distance of home. It was always like this, his father said. Whenever possible commandos operated in districts that they knew, which gave them a great advantage.

The English were marching towards them and they expected to meet them in twenty-four hours. Their orders were to halt them : no more than that. There was to be no shooting unless they would not stop. Negotiations were in progress. But still it was strange to be lying waiting with a rifle in one's hand on the veld one had known since childhood. They were on Sterkwater now; beyond that was Elandsfontein, Jan Hoffmeyer's farm, and beyond that was Klipgat. His father sat beside him. He was smoking his pipe. There was nothing to say or do. One could only wait and see how things turned out.

In a way it was all unreal. And yet what could be more real than war? He wondered about fear. He was afraid of being afraid. I have never been shot at, he thought. They would meet the English in twenty-four hours: before this time to-morrow, that was. Pa was very calm; but then he always was, he had seen other wars; he knew about them. Dirk was glad his father was with him. I would not like to be alone in this, he thought.

Then there was Lena. Where was she? What was she doing? He saw Mooiplaas in his mind—the house, the trees, Oupa, Ouma, the peacocks spreading their tails. He saw it very clearly before his eyes; but the vision was thin; through the trees and walls of Mooiplaas he saw the horses grazing. Mooiplaas, and Doornkloof his home. His mother and his wife. He thought of her like that. She was his wife in his mind, but he had better not think of her.

" We could ride home easily from here, Pa," Dirk said.

" Ja, we could ride home, Dirk. And then what would we do? Mount our horses and ride back again. There would be more tears, more unhappi-

130

ness for every one. It is in my heart that when one is in the field it is best to stay there till it is over. Nothing may happen, jong. They may be ready to negotiate now that they see we are in earnest." He knocked out his pipe on a stone and refilled it.

They could go home. In three hours easily he could be there on Swartkie. In three hours I could hold Lena in my arms, he thought. But his father was right. What would be the good of it? It was no good meeting just to part again.

Dirk looked for his horse among those grazing on the hillside, but could not recognize him. They were too far off to distinguish their shapes or colours. Only a few whites and greys stood out; the others all looked black against the yellow grass of the hills. They were moving slowly down, drifting towards the valley. Any horse that tried to separate himself from the herd was driven back. They were grazing eagerly, hungrily, not picking and choosing as horses generally do. If there was rain—Dirk looked at the sky, it was dark with clouds—they would soon grow sleek and fat again. It did not take long, only a few days, for the grass to spring up after a good rain. If I was home, he thought, I could ask Oupa du Toit. That was one of the things the old man did know, almost infallibly. He said he could tell from the sky and the moon, but Dirk thought it was his wounds. They hurt him before rain, though he would never acknowledge it. He was too proud of them to admit that they mattered or interfered in any way with his comfort.

The horses had come much nearer. The sun suddenly pierced the clouds above them. The valley was carpeted with gold and the horses stood out sharply—chestnut, black, brown, and bay; the white ones shone like stars. The rest of the world was dark and menacing. Only the horses and the valley were alive, living with light. A small, moving patch of brilliant colour in a dark and threatening world. If only it would rain! They would be uncomfortable, but there would be good grass.

There was Swartkie. He could see him now. If he came a little nearer, he would whistle. Swartkie was like a dog and came at once to his call. From the camp came the shrill scream of a piquetted stallion. He knew the horse. It was Stoffel's roan. He could not graze with the others because he fought. The wind was blowing from the loose horses towards the camp. He screamed again, a challenge as clear as a trumpet call; and a big cream horse, detaching himself from the herd, went galloping towards him. A herder, leaning forward in his saddle, rode to cut him off. There could be nothing in the world more beautiful than an angry stallion, Dirk thought. The cream's long mane and tail flowed like water. His crest was high, his forelock flung back from his ears. The ground trembled beneath his hoofs. As he passed, Dirk could see the red flare of his wide nostrils, his dark muzzle, and the white flash of his rolling eyes. Pale yellow, almost the colour of a lion, he paused, head high, to challenge again. That gave the herder his chance. He got between him and the camp and turned him back with his heavy whip, cracking it like a pistol in the stallion's face.

The sun was hidden by a cloud. The glory of the evening was gone. It went so suddenly that Dirk wondered if there had been any glory. He was hungry. What would there be to-night? Beef again, and mealie pap, a cup of coffee if they were lucky, and someone might have shot a buck. If only they could capture an English convoy, not only for the rifles and ammunition, but for the food.

He began to think of his mother's cooking, of the meal he had had when he said good-bye to Tanta Martha—and they had only just begun. In fact, they had not yet begun. Later, if it lasted, and there was really war, things would be worse. They might have to count on their captures to refit themselves with clothes, saddles, blankets, horses, and ammunition. The worst of being short of cartridges was that it would mean parting with one's own rifle and using an English one.

Dirk was fond of his gun. He had killed much game with it. And after a while your gun became a part of yourself. It was like a horse or a woman: as much a part of you as a hand or a foot. You could not make a mistake with it. You got to know it so well that you did not have to adjust your sights with every shot, but could tell as you put it up where the bullet would strike. Before God, when you knew your gun you knew it, and could shoot fast, the bolt moving in your hands like a thing alive, the bullets spattering your target, making the dust fly behind, in front, and then upon it. No one could shoot like his people. No one had such speed or accuracy of fire. They had been brought up to it.

He trembled with excitement at the thought of what they could do. They—we, the men of Joubert's commando . . . and then he became afraid and tried to put his thoughts from his mind. If only I was like Pa and could wait, take everything as it came—the good, the bad, the indifferent—all with his confidence in God and right.

He went over the position in his mind. The government was formed in Heidelberg. Cronje had ridden with a strong commando to Potchefstroom to get the proclamation printed. He had orders not to fire unless attacked, just as they had themselves. He carried a letter to Major Clark, the Special Commissioner. Its contents had been made public in order to restrain the more hot-headed. It said: "The government of the South African Republic, now restored, wants a certain document printed. We trust that from your side no measures will be taken to hinder us, as it is pressing, and of the most serious importance to both parties. The publishing of this document all over the world is very likely to prevent bloodshed. Therefore it must be done, and it shall be done. . . ."

No, his people did not want war. And the proclamation might stop it if they let Cronje pass. There was a precedent too. When Shepstone had wanted the annexation proclamation printed, the Republic had allowed the government printer to do it, so why should the British Government be less generous?

To-morrow they should make contact with the Ninety-Fourth Regiment, Joubert said. They were on their way from Lydenburg to Pretoria. A letter had been sent to them too. It had been read out. But would it stop them? God knows it was mild enough. He thought of the wording. It informed the colonel that a new government had been formed, and that pending an answer from the British Government—" we do not know whether we are in a state of war or not; consequently we cannot allow any movement of troops from your side, and wish you to stop where you are. We, not being at war with Her Majesty the Queen, nor with the people of England, but only recovering the independence of our country, do not wish to take up arms, and therefore inform you that any movement of troops from your side will be taken by us as a declaration of war, the responsibility whereof we put upon your shoulders, as we know what we will have to do in self-defence. . . ."

That was how things stood this evening. They were going to stop the Ninety-Fourth. Other commandos were riding to stop other regiments that were moving into concentration. While Cronje rode to Potchefstroom to get his proclamation printed, Englishmen marching . . . Boers riding. At such a time one reckless man firing a shot could start a war. Everything had a beginning. A war must begin. The first shot must be fired, the first spear must be flung by someone. Always there must be someone who began it. It was almost too much to hope there would be no such man, but still Dirk hoped it. It was said that the English themselves were divided about the war: that Gladstone was much against it. But he was not in power now. Dirk wished he understood English politics. Things were very different over there, it was said. Still there was hope. It had not begun.

His father was still smoking, still staring over the veld.

" It is over there, Pa," Dirk said again. " It would not take us long." He could not get it out of his head. They were so near home. It would be so easy.

" Ja, Dirkie, our home is over there and it would not take us long, but it would do no good. It is only good to think of it. To look at the mountains and know that it is over there. To think in your heart of the road—of the mountains, the poorts, the rivers and sluits we would cross as we rode. And then we would see the house. Ja, the house that I built with my hands for my wife and children."

Swartkie was grazing near them now. He had left the klompie. Perhaps he had picked up their scent on the wind.

" Call him, Dirk," his father said. " I like to see him come."

Dirk whistled. The black trotted towards them and stopped at his feet.
" He is a good horse," his father said, " and in war such a trick can be
useful. It is good to have all animals tame, and the taming of them is not
time wasted."

They got up and went back to camp, the black horse following them,
stopping to snatch a mouthful of dry grass and then trotting to catch up.

The smoke of the cow-dung fires hung low, a blue mist above the moving
men. There was a smell of burning meat, and fat, in the air. Someone was
laughing loudly. When Dirk had eaten, if he was not on sentry duty, he
would sleep with his head on his saddle and dream of Lena till the cold of
dawn woke him.

The day was over. To-morrow would bring the English, or so they said,
and there would be no rain. The clouds had gone.

2

" There they are . . ."

The commando had halted. The moment so long feared had come. All
the men sat their horses staring at the line of dust that approached them.
It was very faint. A long thin line that looked like a red smoke, drifting.

That was the English. That was the Ninety-Fourth marching from
Brennersdorp on Pretoria. In an hour or so they might be fighting that line
of dust. It was strange to think of them having slept at Brennersdorp, but
they had had news of it. They knew they had danced there and they knew
the strength of the regiment : the numbers of the officers, non-
commissioned officers, and men : the numbers of their wagons. They knew
everything about them.

Dirk looked at his father. Their knees were touching. Their horses
nuzzled each other. They, too, were father and son. All round them the
Boers had unslung their rifles and were holding them across their saddles
as if they were out hunting. Their faces had changed. They sat low in their
saddles, loosely, with hard, staring eyes.

" Shall we open out a bit, Frans?" Old Joachim asked Joubert.

" Ja, kerels, spread out thinly and we will go on . . . there is a spruit
about a mile from here. They will not cross it. That is the line where we
will stop them," he said.

A spruit a mile from here . . . Of course there was. It ran through
the top of Mooiplaas. They were going to fight on Mooiplaas.

The Boers swung their horses on to the veld in a long, thin line. Looking back, Dirk saw some men driving the slaughter cattle and the spare
horses to the rear. This was a strange feeling to be riding like this, a part

of a line but completely alone. He had never felt so lonely in his life. It is as if we were driving game, he thought; and almost as he thought this, a steenbok got up from under his horse and ran in front of them with little leaps. He watched him appearing and disappearing as he jumped through the high grass. His horns were like black needles: a little ram . . . then a hare got up, running with ears laid back . . . a covey of partridges skimmed the grass tops on his left. A korhaan flung itself into the air, calling out as it rose; its breast flashed white in the sunlight. Then it fell, fluttering its wings. They would put it up again later. To the right a secretary bird was running on long legs. Suddenly it extended its great wings and rose. And the dust cloud in front of them was bigger. He lost it as they breasted a hill. The spruit was on the other side.

"There is time to water the horses," someone said.

"Has Joubert said we can water?" his father asked.

"Water your horses and get back." The order was passed round.

"Pace your distance as you come back . . .

"Leave your horses behind the rankie when you have watered them and take up your positions."

Dirk rode down, converging on the water with his father. Stoffel was beside him as they watered. He had a feather from a guinea fowl's breast stuck on his back between his shoulders. The water was slow-running, and green with watercress, just as he always remembered it, but lower.

"Slack your girths a bit, Dirk, and let him drink his fill; but tighten them again," his father said. "If we must ride, we want no slipping saddles."

The horses drank fussily. This was not the clear water that they liked riffling against their noses. They pawed at it, splashing themselves. Stoffel's roan tried to roll, and he hit him with his fist in the belly. The stallion sprang away from him. He dragged him back. Men began to turn away. As they walked up the hill with long strides, you could hear them counting. Dirk counted. His father counted. Near a little bush his father threw down his hat. Three hundred, he said. Dirk found a bush nearby. Stoffel had left his horse and was already lying behind an antheap. He was sliding the bolt of his rifle, half-opening it and closing it again. As he passed him, Dirk could see the brass cartridge lying in the chamber.

When he had left Swartkie, his reins dragging, he went to his father.

"Have you set your sights, Dirk?" he said.

"Not yet."

"Then set them. Three hundred, and when you fire, shoot slow. Do not get excited."

"Then you think . . ." Dirk said.

"Dirkie, why should they stop? They have their orders to go on; we have ours to stop them. They are brave men. Lie close to the ground, son, and shoot slow if it begins."

Dirk lay down. He moved his bandolier. It hurt him to lie on it. They were still coming. The sound of music came to him. Magtig, it was war, and they played music! He caught the glint of the sun on their rifle barrels and saw the brass of the musical instruments shining as they played. They were marching without advance guards, without flankers, advancing to war with music. Or could it be a trick to verneuk them.

He rolled on to his shoulder and searched the veld. Were there some cavalry coming at them from the rear? There was nothing. Only Joubert on his black horse against the sky. He had some other mounted men with him. He was certainly giving them full warning. Joubert was a good man to serve under : a brave man who was ready to expose himself on the skyline. That should stop them. But they still came on. The music still played. You could see the red of their coats now, the white helmets, the mounted officers. Were they mad, these redcoats? Was every one mad? He knew that from where they were not a Boer would be seen except the mounted group on the brow of the hill.

He looked round again. Joubert's rifle was still slung on his back. He leant forward over his horse, cupping his hands round his pipe to light it. Dirk laughed. The commandant was sitting his horse and smoking while he waited.

He looked back again. Joubert was doing something; he was writing. He handed a letter—it must be a letter—to a man beside him. Someone on foot gave the man who held the letter a white lappie tied to a stick, a white rag on a stick—a flag of truce. As he took it, his horse shied and bucked. Dirk found himself laughing. He was surprised and ashamed that he should laugh. But it was all unreal—the group on the hill; Joubert sitting his horse smoking his pipe with his top hat pushed back on his head; the bucking horse—it was still restless; the men round the commandant looking towards the English . . . And the music was still nearer.

It stopped suddenly. The man with the flag raised it and swung his horse; he reared. The man must have struck his spurs into him, for he set off down the hill in a plunging gallop. He passed quite near Dirk so that the stones he flung up with his heels fell all round him. Dirk watched him splash through the spruit, the flag held high in his rider's hand.

The English were buzzing like bees. They were lining the road and seemed to be trying to laager their wagons. The man with the flag gave his letter to a mounted officer. That must be the commandant of the English— the colonel, Dick thought. He took the letter and turned to another mounted officer. All the time the Boer with the flag sat waiting on his horse. Dirk noticed he had left his rifle. He was there with the English talking to them, unarmed and helpless. His horse was still fidgety, passaging back and forth, and switching his tail. He is nervous, Dirk thought. The man is nervous, no matter how proudly he holds his flag, and the horse knows it.

Then he turned. He must have had his answer, and galloped back leaning low over his saddle, the flag lying against the horse's neck. He did not slow down for the water, but came through it at speed. It splashed up all round him almost hiding him from sight. Now he was up the bank. The horse faced the hill. He was pushing him.

Dirk looked from him to the English. He could see the officers moving among the men. They were standing up and walking about among them. Surely they would lie down . . . surely they must know that they would be shot first. But what was their answer?

The messenger had reached Joubert. He had pulled his horse up from full gallop to his haunches. He saw Joubert raise his hand to his face. He saw him raise his hat. The men round him raised their hats. They are praying, he thought. It is war. They turned their horses suddenly and disappeared over the hilltop. There was a shout of " War!" A voice cried : " They say they will not stop." There was a rustling over the hillside. It was like a gust of mind in a mealie land that rustles the leaves, as the Boers flattened themselves and raised their rifles.

The first shot that he had feared came from beside him. It was Stoffel. He had fired the first shot of the war. An officer staggered. He put his hand to his side, turned slowly, as if he were at a dance, then his legs gave way at the knee and he went down slowly. That is the first man I have seen shot, Dirk thought : the first man. He was astonished at himself, at how little he felt; he felt nothing for the man. But the war was begun as he had known in his heart all along that it must.

There were more shots. They came from all round. More redcoated men were falling, throwing up their hands, or just falling, some spinning on their heels. So a man fell as a buck did, wounded and twisted, or dead in full stride. Dirk felt the butt of his rifle at his cheek. That one, I will have that one, he was saying to himself. At the tip of his rifle, beyond the V of his backsight and the point of his foresight, there was a speck of red. His finger pressed the trigger. The spot of red was no longer there. I have got him, he thought.

A sort of elation filled him. He began to fire fast. It has begun, he thought. It has begun. It is war. This is war. Now we are fighting, I am fighting. I have killed a man . . . two men . . . more men. The ground round him was splattered with bullets, but they had not got the range. Some were shooting short, and others very high. He heard the crack of the English bullets over his head . . .

Time ceased to exist. There was only before. Dirk's mind went back into the past. He tried to think of what he would do after it was over, but could not. That it should ever be over, that he should survive, seemed too much to hope; to think of it was to tempt Providence. When it was over, if he was still alive, it would be enough. He thought of how he would thank

God that he was alive. Because the present was so vivid, so uncertain, there was no present. To-day could not be balanced against a hypothetical to-morrow; and since to-morrow might never come, not for him at any rate, there was no to-day. Nor was there yesterday. By the circumstance of to-day, yesterday was set back infinitely, as far back as the days of his boyhood; set among them, taken out of the context of his life which, because it lacked the promise of continuity, had ceased to be life and was merely a series of isolated moments, each lived as years, under the pall of smoke and the air crack of the bullets.

As he fired he wondered at his previous worries. What absurd things men worried about, and yet he knew when it was over he would be beset by new ones. It was only now, now in the roar of battle, that those worries and the things that caused them seemed nothing. Now all that mattered was to stay alive. He dropped his rifle. In his love of life he clung closer to the ground, gripping it with his fingers, digging his nails into the harsh roots of the grass, flattening his belly into the rock-hard soil. Fear had taken hold of him, and then as suddenly as it had come it went from him.

Someone was shooting the oxen inspanned to their wagons. That was a good idea. To stampede them would create more confusion. Picking up his rifle again, Dirk put a bullet into the oxen. He turned his head to look at Stoffel. He was smiling. His hand was moving up and down on his bolt. As Dirk looked at him, he rolled over to reach for more ammunition. He slid the cartridges into his magazine and began again; he was not like a man at all, he was like a machine. Men continued to fall. Dirk went on firing. Wherever he saw the flash of a red tunic or a white belt or helmet he fired. He had conquered fear. He was happy. "Take your time," his father shouted. "Shoot slowly." He was shooting slowly, but his gun was getting hot. It was a good feeling to have it hot in your hand : to shoot and to know that you were killing. I never knew it would be like this, he thought.

A cart turned over. He watched the horse kicking in the shafts and then lie still. Another horse bolted. The English fire was slowing down. The veld was covered with their dead . . . little red dolls that lay scattered, singly and in heaps. They had been so thick on the road that some of the first bullets must have hit several.

Dirk fired again. Nothing happened. His magazine was empty. He felt for cartridges to refill it and looked for another target. It was hard to find one now. He heard a shout and looked round. God Almighty, what was this? A Boer, a solitary one, charging on the English from the flank. He was riding a chestnut horse at full gallop with loose reins and firing as he came. He was on them. Dirk saw the horse plunge down into the road; he disappeared; he reappeared, was over it, and through the other side. He had gone through them—a madman. Dirk could not take his eyes from the horse as he swung away in a wide arc. And then the rider fell from the saddle. He must have been hit after all. Who was he? What was he doing?

The English bullets were thin now. There was a bugle call; it was followed by another. The firing ceased. He waited for it to begin again. What did that call mean? Could it be over?

"That's the *cease fire*," Stoffel shouted. "It is over. The first battle is over and we have won it."

So it was over. The English were standing up now, moving, bending over their wounded and carrying them in from the veld to the edge of the road. There were women among them. He saw two of them and a child. The Boers were standing up to see better. He saw them rise from every bush, every antheap, every tussock of grass. They were leaning on their rifles. Many were lighting their pipes. Their guns held over the crook of their arms, they stood watching. Some had already got their horses and were preparing to ride down.

"Shall I get the horses, Pa?" Dirk shouted.

"Ja, bring them, Dirk. You are all right?"

"Yes, I am all right . . . are you all right?"

"I am all right, but they have spoilt my hat."

Dirk went towards his father, who held up his hat. There was a hole drilled through it.

"That was near, Pa," he said.

"Ja, it was near, son. But I have had nearer things than that. It was not the will of God that I should die at Bronkerspruit."

That was what the stream that ran through Mooiplaas was called because of the watercress that grew in it. Dirk thought of how often he had picked it lower down. How long ago those days seemed to be!

Frans Joubert came riding down. He was followed by his staff, three Boers that Dirk did not know. One of them was the man who had carried the white flag.

"What have we suffered, Oom Frans?" his father asked.

"Little, Dirk; only five men hit and one killed. It is the will of God, but I am sorry. They should have stopped when I told them. They should have camped on the far side of the spruit and we on this side. It is in my heart that it is we who fired the first shots of the war. Ja, friends, and to think that makes my heart sore." There were tears in the old man's eyes. "War," he said—"war between white men." He rode on. His rifle was on his back, his top hat was in his hand : a good man who rode bareheaded to see the dead and succour the wounded if he could.

Dirk went for the horses. Swartkie had hardly moved and came towards him when he whistled. His father's horse was nearby. Picking up the reins, he led them to the hilltop. The English were busy. They were putting up tents. They were good at this sort of thing, Dirk thought, better at it than fighting. But why have them? Why could they not sleep as the Boers did, out in the open under the stars. He mounted Swartkie and led his father's horse to him.

"I am going down to see, Pa. Are you coming?"

"I will come."

His father mounted and they rode down together. How quick it had all been! It was less than an hour since they had watered the horses. Now they were splashing through the water again. And they were so near home. Two miles away was the house of Mooiplaas, and ten miles from there was home. Lena must have heard the shots. Perhaps he would be able to ride over . . . perhaps. Swartkie stepped sideways to avoid a dead Englishman. The horse was snorting and throwing his head.

"They do not like dead men," his father said.

"No, they do not."

"And they will never walk on a man, Dirk. A horse would never hurt a man unless he hates him."

No, Dirk thought, it is just men who hurt each other. What had these men done to him? He looked at the bodies, and the wounded who were being bandaged. Boys of his own age. What have they done to me? he thought. The elation of battle was gone. So was his joy at the conquest of fear. He knew now that he was a man and able to face death as well as others, but there was no joy or pride in his heart. Rather was there a great sadness, an overwhelming depression at this culmination of his living. He felt that he now knew the ultimate. Suddenly, with blinding clarity, within a period of days, he had known love and war. Beyond these no man could go. To create and to kill. These were ends, seemingly divorced from the means of living, apparently irrelevant to them, since one had little memory or knowledge of either, yet both were irrevocable. A life begun must go on, as a death, created equally in passion, must remain a death, and the spirit of the dead was gone utterly, beyond recall.

He was high on the wings of his manhood, alive to what he had done, certain that no higher point could be reached, astonished at the facility of his reaching and depressed in his heart that all life could only bring repetitions of these things—of loving and killing, of being loved, and perhaps being killed . . . at any rate, of dying finally himself on the veld or in bed; old, the father of many, or young and childless.

A man was strung between the two poles of his birth and his death. He lived thus, too, dealing out life and death to man or beast, birth being as violent as death, a matter of blood and pain, a breaking open of things that previously were whole. When a man died by violence, his spirit escaped from his broken body as a child escaped, in birth, from the torn tenderness of a woman's belly. And against the background of these violences, men lived their lives, thinking, eating, working. Their lives were peaceful as a valley through which a cool river ran among great trees, but it was menaced by the mountains that surrounded it.

You could reflect, you could hope, but you could never know.

Dirk's stirrup brushed his father's, clinking against it. There was comfort in the sound, since there were so many precedents to it. How often had they ridden like this side by side! He looked at his father's face. It was unchanged. It had not changed since the day they had ridden from home together. It was almost as if he had set it in those lines, fixed his eyes in an expression of hurt bitterness he would not alter till it was over.

" It is terrible, Pa," he said.

" It is war. You will grow used to it. To-day it is they who lie here dead and wounded. To-morrow it may be us." He spat over his horse's neck. " It is war, Dirk. Note it well and do not let any one talk to you of glory. There is no glory except in the prosecution of a peaceful life, in the worshipping of God, and in the performance of homely tasks."

" What shall we do now?" Dirk asked.

" We will wait, son. That also is war. Most of it is waiting. Either you have to do more than man can do, suffering incredible hardship and exertion, or else you do nothing, you just wait. Mostly you wait." He pulled up his horse and dismounted.

" We will sit here," he said, " and wait for orders." He undid a bag from the near side of his saddle. " We will eat."

" I do not think I can eat."

" Eat. You will see worse things than this and you must not let your stomach turn."

" It has turned," Dirk said. He felt faint and was sweating.

" Dismount and eat," his father said. He dismounted.

As he sat down, his father got up and picked up some peaches that were lying on the side of the road. One had blood on it and he threw it away. It left his hand like a ball and bounced when it struck. Like a ball, Dirk thought. Once Pa was a child as I was. He played with balls, throwing them and catching them, and now he throws a bloodstained peach. The irrelevance of peaches on a battleground struck him. They had no business here. He wondered where they had come from.

His father was peeling a peach with his knife, taking the skin off it in a long yellow snake.

" How did they get here?" he asked.

" The English must have picked them," he said. He cut the peach through and picked out the clinging stone. " Take it," he said, giving him half.

" Thank you," Dirk said. Absent-mindedly he put it into his mouth, thinking : This is a peach an Englishman plucked; I may have killed him, and now I eat his peach. Other Boers were eating peaches and so were the English prisoners. Parties of English were carrying in wounded. The wounded were very brave. Hardly a sound came from them. Tents were still going up. They were being dragged out of the long sacks in which they had been stored on the wagons. Poles were being fitted into holes dug in the ground. There was the dull thudding of wooden mallets on tent pegs. Guys were being tightened. Everything, amid the wild disorder, was orderly and looked the worse because of it. The tents were in an exact line. The wounded were laid in another line. They were carried into the tents as they went up. A water party marched in step behind the water cart that men, since the horses were dead, were dragging towards the spruit. The Boers stood easily, leaning on their rifles, some with their arms round their horses' necks, and watched with cold, hard eyes. Others were sitting down. A few had let their horses go and lay with their heads on their saddles.

Dirk thought of the charging Boer. Who was he? What was he doing alone?

" Who was that man, Pa," he said, " that charged through the English ?"

" I do not know, but a brave man."

" Perhaps we should look for him," Dirk said. " I saw him fall, but he may not be dead."

" I think someone has gone," his father said. " I saw the commandant send two men over that way."

They both looked at the commandant. Frans Joubert was standing fifty paces away in the middle of the road. He had on his top hat again. His rifle was slung. His head was sunk forward on his chest, his hands were folded behind his back. As they watched him he knelt down to tighten the strap of one of his spurs, then he walked towards the wrecked wagons.

" He is a good man, Dirk," his father said. " He does not like it. No farmer can like destruction, but now that it has begun he will go on. A great leader and a God-fearing man. We are lucky to be with him."

" Ja, we are lucky, Pa."

" Eat, my son. We are also lucky to be alive. We should give thanks to the Almighty God. We are his chosen people. We fight for our rights and liberty. There is no end for us but liberty or death."

Dirk's mind went back again to the charge of the single Boer. " I wonder how he had the courage to ride into battle like that alone," he said.

" I also wonder," his father said. " I have never been like that. I am always afraid in war. Not very afraid, but still afraid and not over-eager."

Fires were being lit. It looked as if they would be here some time.

" I will offsaddle the horses and let them run," Dirk said.

" Yes, offsaddle, Dirk. It is as I said. In war there is much waiting."

Knee-haltered, the two horses drifted off, their heads bobbing. Dirk took out his pipe. He was calmer now, but still in his mind he saw the action again. It kept coming back. He felt his rifle hot in his hand. He saw men falling. He smelt cordite and heard the crack of the high bullets and splash of low ones hitting the ground. And the charge of the solitary Boer. That was something that would stay with him while he had breath. A man alone on a red horse charging a regiment. . . . He wondered who it could have been.

CHAPTER XI

THE SHOUTING OF THE CAPTAINS

I

OUPA was happy. Once again he was master of Mooiplaas. Not that he was not always master: he was, but with the boys away he was master without argument. Now he could say "do this" to the Kaffirs and it was done. There were no counter-orders. Of course there was that girl—Kattie—with her face curled up like a leaf that has been hit by a cold winter wind. And what had happened to her mouth? He often wondered about that. Had she sucked it in so hard and for so long that she had swallowed it? Any one would think that she was the only person in the world who had seen trouble. What about the bothers he had had? And here he was nearly a hundred and sweet as an apple. That was the remarkable thing about him. Not only his great age, but the excellence of his disposition.

He lit his pipe. Yes, I am happy, he thought. But I wish Lena would come back from the dorp. There was some life in her—laughter and tears and anger. She was as fretful as a baby after her Dirk. She was like a horse in a fenced camp when his mate is taken away, running round and round whinnying and kicking up his heels. But it was a pleasant distraction to have Lena bothering him, and to be able to instruct her with his knowledge. It was a great shame that when he died all that he knew must die with him. It was really unbelievable that it should die.

And what could Lena be doing in the dorp? Why should she want to stay the night with that old fool Tanta Martha when she could be with him? A girl's place was at home. A girl's duty was to look after her great-grandfather; to honour him, to give him brandy when he needed it.

He had looked everywhere, even among her clothes, and could not find the little bottle of brandy. It had not been easy to search her room with Kattie prying and spying on him, but he had done it, sending Reuter to distract her while he hunted, and this was his reward—nothing at all. It was a disgrace that a man of his age, in his position, should be denied his small comforts. It was no use asking Kattie. She would simply say that they had no brandy, which was a lie. No doubt the Kaffirs had some hidden away, but you could not ask a Kaffir, though he might tell Reuter to steal some from them. But there would be no certainty in this. Not that Reuter would not get it: he would. But he might also be drunk for days.

When Lena came back he would give her a piece of his mind. What

144

right had she to go gallivanting about the country with that old mountain Martha Kleinhouse? She would just fill her head with nonsense, as if God did not put enough into every girl's head without human help. God made virgins foolish. It said so in the Book, as large as life and in black and white; and only a man could cure them: taking their foolishness with their virginity.

He did not believe in Martha with her purges, but once a woman got an idea she rode it hard, and there was a reason for this too. They had so few ideas, so little ingenuity. Marriage could do a lot for them, but not everything, which was perhaps as well. She nearly purged me to death once, he thought, but I have never given her another chance.

He thought about his life, of the things he had wanted, of the things he had had, of what he wanted now—of brandy, and his anger with Lena. But he would not go back: not through all that again. Why should any one want to? he wondered. Life was like a path, a long one, winding and beset with many dangers. Who but a fool would want to brave those dangers again, suffer that exhaustion again, that pain? Wounds, illnesses, sorrows were all weakened by the passage of time, but still he remembered them, still felt them in retrospect—the heartbreak, the effort—and it was good to sit in the sun and know it was nearly done. The world was now shrunken, its hidden spaces known. Why, as a boy, few had crossed the Limpopo or seen the lakes. There had been no strangers from over the seas in the land, just one's friends: other men and women of one's own race, and Kaffirs. You were with the one and against the other. Before God, life had been simple then with a gun in one's right hand and a Bible in one's left. Sometimes, when it was expedient, one put the Bible down. Sometimes it had taken both hands just to stay alive.

The world when he was young had been full of great people—leaders, hunters, they had towered above the others by the stature of actions, their daring and the wild lives they led. Though later, as he had come to know them well, they had been reduced in size. They had been great still, but less great, and then he had become one of them. This had come as a surprise to him. Ja, it was a surprise when he had heard himself referred to as one of the great ones . . . Philippus Jacobus, the great hunter and fighter, the man who knew the north as other men knew their orchards and their cultivated fields. Then the others, the great ones that he had respected so much, became ordinary, since he was counted among them: just men like himself.

It was strange how as a child one said: "When I am big," then, "When I am married." Then, "When I have this farm . . . this property . . . a thousand head of cattle . . ." It was always something else, something new. A man spent all his life looking ahead and thinking that if he had this or that he would be more content. Then later, as he looked back he seemed to have missed everything, and found that life had flowed past him, a thundering river of events that, somehow, no matter what he did or how he sought it, he always missed. Life was such a disappointment. He thought of what he had done and seen. Certainly it sounded all right when he spoke of it, when he told his tales of war, of huntings and disasters. But what had they really been? Nothing at all, just incidents. He had always been looking and waiting for something big. Something that was really exciting, really wonderful—some woman, some hunt, some battle, some special horse, tusks that ran two hundred pounds apiece—only Helena had been worth while. Always hoping, worrying, fighting.

He thought of all the things he had worried about. Before God, how much time a man spent worrying about things that never happened! By his own fears man cut the glory out of his days, gelding the horse of to-day for fear of the stallion of to-morrow. A man should think more of to-day. Yesterday was gone. To-morrow might never come. Men regretted yesterday, hoped for more to-morrow, and ignored to-day. Why should they hope for more? Why should to-morrow be better than to-day, which was yesterday's to-morrow. And, while you hoped and regretted, life passed.

That was what had happened to him and he had not had the sense to see it. He had let his days slip by unlived, while he speculated, hoped, regretted. A man should live on the instant, riding it like a horse, for instants were fleeting, scarcely perceived before they were gone. Each act was in reality passed before it was finally accomplished. There was no now, for as you spoke the word, it was gone. Yes, as you spoke so was the moment, with its opportunity, gone past. Man lived by thought; and in the realization of thought, in its fruition, the thought became the act. The act was never realized, it was only accomplished, and thought alone remained : the thought from which it was born, and the thought that followed it—the memory. There was only vision before, and memory after. There were no acts.

But it was interesting to look back even if only to think of the things that he had missed. And it was something to have lived so long. The very fact that he was still alive was in a way a feat, an achievement. He had outlived his friends, outwitting them in the final race for life. When you were young, you regretted the death of a friend. You had lost a comrade, a brother, one who would stand at your side in a crisis. But when you were old, it was a triumph to hear that one of your friends was dead. You were a little sad, or said you were. But in your heart you were elated. It showed you were a better man than he. Especially if he was your own age or younger. It proved finally something you had always known, though never boasted about—that you were the best man of them all.

But he had fooled Providence so often that perhaps the Almighty had given up trying to gather him to his fathers. How often had he been nearly killed! Perhaps God thought he would be a nuisance among the heavenly host. He began to chuckle at the thought of all those angels. There must be some very fine plump angels. And then there were his four wives. No, perhaps it was better to stay here. But how beauiful Helena had been! How good! And it was really very nice at home here when Lena was about. He began to wonder where she could have hidden that bottle again. She ought to have given it to me before she left, he thought. Surely I am old enough to take care of my own bottle. Women were all the same, but you had to be old to know it.

He thought of how afraid of them he had been as a boy. As a boy, he thought, I was shy and of an astonishing delicacy. How little he had known then! How little all boys knew of women! Why, any man could have any woman, or nearly any woman, to wife, or not to wife. A woman was as ready to be lain with as a man to lie with her. It was nature that made them both like it, but it was hard for a boy to know this or to believe that women were ready; that though they might pretend it was not so, they demanded little else of life. It did not matter who or what they were—black of white, Dutch or English, dressed in satin and lace or homespun cloth—their bodies and desires were the same, and their chastity something that they put on like a garment, something to be worn during the hours of light. In all women there were two women: the woman of the day ruled her man because of the woman of the night. The woman dressed owed her being to the woman undressed, to her own nakedness, not only of body, but of her desire that kindled man, like a fire, to her bidding, that kindled him into the fulfilment whereby she herself was fulfilled.

It was funny that now, when he no longer had anything to do with women, he thought of them so much. He liked to smoke in the sun and think of women, of men and women. Now that all that was over, he could begin to understand it. The world was divided into two parts, male and female, man and woman; and each part was perpetually aware of the other. Woman created of man was aware of him, and man, born of woman, was aware of her. By this awareness and preoccupation were more men and women made—a slow, invisible process, yet one that continued without ceasing; children being conceived and carried and finally born throughout the seasons—growing, following the same path, the endless chain of increase, and dying, as inconspicuously as they had been born. Coming into the world as shadows, they left it, old, as shadows. The very old withdrawn into the womb of their homes, sitting by their chimneys, unimportant, unnoticed, the caul of their memories about them.

Death, that all men feared and blamed for the ills that went before it, was more of a friend than an enemy. It was the great liberator, the ender of all troubles. By death, and by death only, was the weight of the yoke of life removed, for while men lived they were crushed by the anxieties and complexities of life; by their loves and their hates, by their hopes and their fears: as much by the one as the other, knowing neither peace nor respite in their battle with the circumstances of life. It was thus Old Philippus saw it. For now, at his great age, knowing death was near, he was unappalled by the rustle of its wings.

His body had in its time been very alive, had done all and more than he or any man could expect his body to do. Now it was gone; his juices were dried up, his blood thinned like wine with the water of old age, and only his mind remained. More active than ever, more alert, his mind beat out its thoughts on the anvil of the physical dissolution that held him tied to his chair and bed. Compounded of his thousand memories, his mind, like a bird, beat itself against the frail cage of his frame. By death he would be rejoined to his memories, to his loved ones, to those that he had been warm with in the hot days of his youth. In death, perhaps, an old man's life began again. Sometimes he wished it this way and sometimes he did not. Future life or complete extinction : there was a lot to be said for both.

I am like a bird, he thought, seeing the thoughts that move, like worms, in the minds of little men : seeing their small ambitions, and small betrayals, and the little, ignoble methods of their lives; seeing, too, the ineffectual beauty of their strivings, which it hurts me to watch, for in my heart I know all to be vanity and that the hand stretched forth so purposefully to happiness will grasp only wind. Yet by its grasping, by its effort towards good, is something still achieved. What it was he did not know, but it was something : for in the ultimate end, good was greater than evil; sacrifice greater than selfish security, and humbleness, respect for the creation of God, a prouder thing than arrogance and brutality. With great age came great understanding and great patience.

Since there was so little time, time did not matter. Nothing mattered but life : not his own, not the life of his body, for that already was passed on many times, and no longer fruitful he was, in this sense, no longer alive— an observer only. But life, the thing that no man rightly understood, the power that made the grass grow, that sent the sap coursing savagely through the trees in the spring, causing them to flame with leaves; life that forced a mating and a fruition on all living things before they died, was for ever interesting, for ever beautiful; life was like the tail of a peacock opening to glory and then closing, dropped in the dust.

He thought of his great-grandchildren. He had the greatest objection to the lot of them, except for Lena. Neither children nor anything else were what they had been. Not that his own children had been perfect. They had had their faults. Martinus, the eldest, had drunk a little. And there had been some question about Kristina's daughter, nothing serious, merely a little doubt about its paternity. And there was very little doubt in his mind that Jacobus, named after him, really had killed the Kaffir servant whom he found ill-treating one of his oxen. He remembered the ox well, Bosman he had been called : a red ox with a fine spread of horns.

But the more he thought of the matter, the more certain he was there had been nothing intrinsically wrong with his children : nothing that mattered or could be held against them. His grandchildren, too, were above the average, though not as good as their parents. But their children. . . . Magtig, it was terrible to sit back and see your stock go down like this. Physically, mentally, and morally they were beneath contempt. They could not shoot—not as men used to shoot. They could not ride—after fifty miles they were tired. Even at breeding they were a failure. Loose in their morals and inept in their approach.

He spat reflectively. His great-grandchildren could not even spit. Certainly they could empty their mouths of foreign matter, but they could not send it where they wished. Spitting with them was a matter of chance and not of certainty. And as for manners, as for the respect due to age, of this they were sadly wanting. No, that would have been nothing if they had not gone beyond it, into active rudeness : into thinking him in his dotage and refusing to listen to his tales, or the warnings that he gave them, choice selections culled from the garden of his vast experience. Only Lena was good, and now she had forgotten him Tears came into his eyes, that his little Lena could forget him like this and hide his brandy from him.

But he was wrong in saying none of them could ride or shoot. Stoffel could do both up to a point and Louis was not a bad boy. He was just dull, without vice or virtue. And both annoyed him by their celibacy, if it was celibacy. They were without consideration for him, they never thought of the pleasure a small baby would give him. He would have liked a baby now when he had time to watch it. Before he had always been too busy, but now he had leisure and it would be pleasant to sit with a baby, a great-great-grandson, on a mat on the floor beside him. Babies were nice. They were pleasant and soft to poke with your finger in the middle. No, it was not Stoffel and Louis and Lena that he really complained of, but the others whom he never saw, that were scattered over the face of the land. He had given their grandfathers and grandmothers farms that they had accepted with hardly a thank-you, and they had stayed on them, marrying and breeding like a lot of dumb cattle with never a thought of their illustrous ancestor. Fools, the lot of them, who had bred greater fools.

Still, it was good to sit in the sun with your servant squatting at your feet and watch the peacocks spread their tails : good to watch the ducks and geese, the turkeys and hens : good to listen to a cock crowing and watch the light and shadows play on the wall of outbuildings you had made; good to know that you had many cattle, horses, and sheep, and that they were second to none in all the land.

That business of his descendants worried him again. They were so much less than he. So many had died. They had had no business to die so young. But again would it have been better if they had been his equals or superiors. . . . Though it was hard to think of any one being his superior.

He spat again. No, it was better this way. To be the best of his blood, to be, as it were, one's own ancestor; to be Philippus Jacobus du Toit the hunter, and the greatest of them all.

He stuck his feet out in front of him and pulled his hat over his eyes. " If anything happens, Reuter, you will wake me," he said.

" If anything happens I will wake the Baas."

That was the way it had always been. He would sleep while Reuter watched. How often had that happened! And that fool Kattie said it was not right that he should always be accompanied by a naked Zulu with an assegai in his hand or driven into the ground beside him. Not right—what did she mean, not right? And Reuter was no longer naked. He had made him wear trousers years ago, despite his complaint that they chafed him.

Yes, it was nice in the sun. Good to be alone in your home in your old age; at peace even though others were at war. Fools, as though war did any good. If only he could think of where Lena had hidden the bottle. . . . If only they would let him eat what he wanted—the loin of a rooibok, a stuffed sucking pig. . . . Bread and milk indeed . . . pap for a man of his parts and distinction—and no brandy. If only . . .

2

Oupa woke suddenly. What was that? He sat forward. " Reuter, Reuter, what was that?"

Where was Reuter? Where was that damned boy?

" Reuter!"

Then he saw him. He was standing beside him. His spear was in his hand. He was trembling like a hunting dog that scents game.

" It is guns, Reuter," he said. He cupped his hand to his ear. " It is the firing of guns."

" Ja, Baas, it is firing, guns are being fired."

" How long has it beeen going on? Why did you not wake me? There is firing on Mooiplaas and you do nothing?"

" I thought the Baas . . ."

" You thought, dog! My horse . . . my gun. . . . Run, run quickly."

" The Baas is going? It is six years since the Baas was on a horse, and his horse is old. Bles is too old now."

" Who said Bles? Bring me a young horse. The red stallion that Baas Louis sometimes rides."

" Ja, Baas." Reuter turned to go. He turned back. " What horse shall I take, Baas?"

" No horse. I go alone. This is a white man's war. There will be no Kaffirs in it."

" I am not a Kaffir, Baas; I am a Zulu."

" Ja, you are a Zulu. You are a good boy, but a fool, never satisfied and obstinate as a woman. Go, you skelm . . . go . . . go. . . . Are we to stand arguing about the colour of your hide till the war is over? Get my horse! ride to war."

Reuter ran towards the kraal.

Philippus got up and went to his room. War. That was luck. Too old to go, and the war came to spread itself over the farm like jam on bread. What they needed in war was men like himself who understood it. Why, when he got there, if he liked it, he might never come back. It would be good out there on the veld—to eat what he wanted, to fight and drink brandy and sleep under the stars. He got his gun down from the wall. How good it felt in his hand. He was a boy again. The bullets and powder were in a box under his bed. He bent down slowly, his knees cracking. I was a fool to put it under the bed, he thought. I should have kept it handy. But then Kattie would have found it. She never liked gunpowder in the bedroom, though where else one should keep it only the Almighty knew.

He had it now. The powder-horn . . . now he had everything. Where was Reuter? What was he up to? If Kattie came now and tried to stop him, she would see something.

" Baas . . . Baas, I have the red horse."

He looked out of the window. There was Reuter holding the chestnut. He slung his gun over his shoulder and went out.

" What are you doing with Baas Louis's second horse?"

It was Kattie. Whatever you did she was always there to spoil it.

" The old Baas wants him," Reuter shouted. " It is for the old Baas."

" Old Baas be damned," Philippus shouted. " I am the Groot Baas— the master. That is something that has been forgotten in this place for many years."

" Where are you going like that? What are you doing?" Kattie confronted him. Yes, she had swallowed her mouth, that was certain.

" You have swallowed your mouth," he said. Then he shouted : " Stand away, woman. I ride to the war."

" You to the war, an old dodderer like you! Your place is bed."

" In a coffin, you think. Do you think I do not know what you think? Sour-faced you always were, and that my son married you showed him a fool. Many's the time I told him so. You . . . when there were fine women in the world, sleek and good-tempered as cows. Get out of my way, I say . . . get out! Who are you to come between the master of Mooiplaas and his fighting?"

" Go on, then," she said. " Magtig, you will be flat on your back before you mount that red horse. Horse! . . . a donkey you should have, then it would be a donkey mounted on a donkey."

" That's what I said to my son," Philippus shouted. But doubtless that would be too subtle for her, and it was not easy to find the stirrup iron with the horse jumping under him.

"Hold the horse still, Reuter," he said. "Before God, have you been eating the bread of idleness so long that you can no longer hold a horse?"

Now he had it. His foot was in. His hand was on the pommel. This was the big moment. If he got up. If . . . His back hurt him. Those muscles, as he pulled, were running over sharp stones in his back. The Almighty damn Kattie. If she had not been watching, he might have given up. After all, he was no longer a boy. But she was watching. The horse plunged away. He held on and rose on the swing. He was in the air. If anything happened, it would be her fault. The saddle was under him. He found the other stirrup. Before God, he was on a horse again! Nearly a hundred and on a horse with a gun on his back and riding to war.

"Tot siens, and damn you, Kattie!" he shouted. "Damn you, damn you! Maak los, Reuter. Let him go."

The chestnut went up in the air, pawing at it with great white hoofs. That was a fine feeling: a horse pawing at the skies . . . a saddle under you . . . your gun a hard line across your back. He was young again. It was all nonsense all the things they said about what he must and must not do. When he came back from the war he would have brandy openly; he would eat sucking pig. If they were not careful he would marry again. There were women who would marry him. Ja, they would marry Mooiplaas and his reputation. It would be something for one of them to be his widow: to bear his sons. He would take a young woman with juice still running in her, and breed sons from her: a new batch of sons, and see if he could do better this time.

The wind was lovely in his hair, blowing it back. Nearly a hundred, and a fine head of hair. No one ever told you things like that. No one ever complimented an old man. His beard was beaten flat; it lay like a board against his chest. This was a good horse. The ground was passing under him in great waves as he bounded forward. Stones were flying. Sparks there must be, too, if you could see them. How fine I must look, he thought, galloping on this red horse, my hair flying and my beard white against my chest!

The firing was louder. They are at the spruit, he thought. That is where they are fighting. Oh, much louder. Dropping his reins he took his gun from his shoulder—a charge of powder, the wad, the bullet; he rammed them home. That was good, he could still do it at a gallop. It was war. It was good.

There they were. He saw the red line of their coats. The verdomde Rooineks daring to fight on his farm. He would show them. "Damn them . . . damn the Rednecks . . . damn Kattie and Reuter!" He drove home his spurs and the red horse took to the air. His head surged up and down as he galloped in great plunges. If I wanted to stop him I could not, he thought. "Damn them all, damn everybody! Magtig, how happy I am!"

It was many years since he had been so happy. The last time had been when he was hunting elephants on the Elands River. There they were, he was nearly there now. He would fire and swing his horse away. He raised his gun. It was much heavier than it used to be, and the muzzle wavered. Still it was up. Now he would fire. He was near enough. He fired, a man fell, throwing up his hands. That was good. Old Philippus was the same man : still the hunter afraid of nothing.

He picked up the reins to swing the horse. Nothing happened. The horse did not answer to the rein on his neck. He pulled harder. Still nothing. Now he was getting too near. A bullet passed near him. One more pull. The horse galloped on. That was what came of riding other people's horses. When Bles got old he should have trained another for himself. Very well, then, if he would not turn he could go on. He would go through them. He drove his spurs in again and lay low over the horse's neck.

There they were, getting bigger every minute, every second. Rooibaadjies . . . Rooineks with red faces and red coats, with white helmets, white belts across their bellies, and long knives on their guns. Oh, it was something to be charging the Redcoats alone like this. Old Philippus the hunter charging the Redcoats! That would make Kattie take notice when she heard of it. He wished more of his friends were living so that they too could hear of it. No doubt they would look down from heaven and see him. No doubt his wives were leaning over the edge of the firmament smiling to see him. But there were plenty of others, a whole commando on the hillside was watching him. If he were killed, it would not be wasted. He was making history.

He let out a yell. What stupid red faces they had! As red as their coats, and their mouths gaped open. If only the gun was still loaded. One of them tried to stop him with the knife on his gun. Stop him? Stop Philippus the hunter? He swung the horse towards him. Yes, now he would swing—now. That was the worst of red horses, they had too much temperament—like red-headed women. He drove the muzzle of his gun into the soldier's open mouth. Jan van der Merwe had married a red-headed girl and a fine time he had had with her.

He was among them now. They were jumping about under his horse, all round him, jumping like big red grasshoppers, but they could not shoot for fear of hitting each other. The horse leaped a wounded man and took the bank. He was through. All by himself he had ridden through them, and he was nearly a hundred . . . for all practical purposes he was a hundred. If there were more men like me, he thought, it would soon be over.

Through them and nothing but the open veld in front of him. The horse's neck was black with sweat and speckled with white foam. Magtig, what a horse to get so hot for so little! He thought of the horses he had had . . . of the wives he had had . . . of the huntings, the battles, the dogs, the wagons, the cattle. . . . Before God, he would reload and ride through them again; he would go on riding through them. He was still immune to bullets. Hundreds of them and they could not hit me, he thought. He swung the horse in an arc. How sweetly he turned now. That was like a red-haired woman, to be wild and then tame and then wild again . . . woman was it? . . . horse, he meant.

He felt for his powder to cup it out in the palm of his hand. He could not hold it. His palm shook too much. "Almighty damn," he said, " I am old. I wonder how I have done what I have done. And I am tired. I would sleep now. Lena . . ." Where had she put that brandy? He would give her a piece of his mind. His own house . . . and not even good brandy at that . . . not French . . . just dop . . . dop . . . cape smoke . . . When he woke up, he would look again. . . . And that fool Reuter always complaining, always wanting something.

This was an extraordinary thing. He looked about him. To be out on the veld on a wild red horse. Why did no one take care of him? Did they not understand that he was nearly a hundred and should be pampered? Not put on a horse and sent galloping off alone. It was that Kattie. That girl wanted him dead. If he did not die of this, he would give it to her . . . he would take the skin from her back with a seacow sjambok . . . he would . . . if he did not die. But this looked like the end. He felt himself going through space. It was warm and wet and smelt of horses. Why should space smell like that? Did heaven smell of horses, and there were all those women in heaven. . . .

There it was, he heard music. . . . That was the heavenly trumpet sounding. Now he could not beat Kattie. . . . He could not go on that round of visits that he had been considering in secret . . . and it was not even French. . . . They were wrong about clouds. They were not soft, they were hard—like stones. . . . Helena . . . Helena, here I am." He had thought it would be more complicated to die than this, and less painful. Music . . . shots . . . the smell of horses and the shouting of the captains. . . .

CHAPTER XII

A CAGE OF BIRDS

I

THE soldiers had been gone some time. Lena was waiting for Tanta Martha to leave. They would go to her house first and then to Mooiplaas. She had her best dress done up in paper and her shoes were in their box beside her chair. The toe of the left one had got rubbed, but if she put a little butter on it to darken the leather it would hardly show.

They had nearly finished eating. She liked Mrs. Brenner's English cooking: roast meat, done much the way they did it at home, but with a kind of yellow bread served with it, and potatoes. At first she had thought she would not like the meat. It was not done through, being red and bloody in the middle, but she had liked it. That's where the meat juice is, Mrs. Brenner said. That's where the goodness lies. Mr. Brenner had eaten a lot—three helpings. They were all so happy. Seeing the soldiers, dancing with the officers, had reassured them. They were good, kindly men. There would be no war. And Charlie was so much better. He sat in his mother's lap, like a baby, eating bits from her fork. The purge had worked. Everybody was full of praise for Tanta Martha, who, smiling happily, complimented Mrs. Brenner on her cooking. It was absurd to think there could be war. There would be more discussions, there would be more talk. They were having the pudding now. "Bread and butter," Mrs. Brenner said it was, layers of buttered bread, with milk, sugar, and eggs, with layers of raisins and currants. It was browned in the oven till the crust was sharp and crackled under the spoon as it was cut. Mr. Brenner hummed: *Kiss me, darling . . . Kiss your darling daughter. . . .* Then he coughed and wiped his moustache. There was pudding on it. How that tune stayed in your mind! If I can remember it, I will teach it to Boetie, Lena thought.

Everything was very beautiful and homelike and Dirk would soon be back. It was nice sitting here drinking tea with the Brenners and Tanta Martha while she thought about Dirk's return. But she wished Tanta Martha would finish, she was anxious to get home. What a lot there would be to tell them! She wanted to tell Oupa about it—about the colour and the music and the wine that pricked you. She thought of his brandy. Poor Oupa, he would be angry with her, but how was she to have known that Tanta Martha would make her stay?

155

The tea had a slight flavour of coffee which improved it. That was the way things were. When someone came, Mrs. Brenner said : " Tea or coffee?" Whichever it was they got it, and each always had a slight flavour of the other. It was not the washing-up. It was just that if you used the same pot for both, you got the flavour of both.

Mrs. Brenner left them to put Charlie to bed again. " There is no danger for him now if he does not catch cold," Tanta Martha said.

Lena pushed the hair away from her forehead. It was silly to talk of catching cold in this heat unless there was a storm, and there was still no sign of that.

Her mind swung the other way again. Everything seemed to be going so well that something would go wrong. In spite of the heat she felt chilled; it is a premonition, she thought. There were no such things and you could not guess what would happen. Perhaps it was not her heart that was heavy, it might just be that she had eaten too much. It's just the food, she thought happily. Charlie was better, the soldiers had gone, and everything was going to be all right. She wanted to get back now. She could think of Dirk better at home. It was easier to think of him there, where everything reminded her of him—every tree and stone, every chair, every dish. And she wanted Oupa. She missed him. She was used to looking after him and no one else understood his ways or cared for him as she did. Reuter loved him, but a Zulu body-servant was not the same as a woman. When a man was very old, or very young, he needed a woman to care for him.

Thoughts of the soldiers had made her uneasy again. Having seen them like that made them real. But everything was going to be all right. What was the good of worrying when even the soldiers themselves said there would be no war? And if she was at home and stayed there, Dirk might come to see her. If they were near, he might find time to come—a few hours, a night. If he comes, she thought, if he comes, then . . . She was not clear in her mind what would happen if he came; at least she pretended she was not clear. She must get back. Dirk must come to her. There must be no war. They would get married. She moved on her chair uncomfortably.

" More tea, Lena?" Mrs. Brenner said.

" Yes, please." She liked tea for a change, and Tanta Martha said it was healthy.

She watched Mrs. Brenner fill her cup. What would she think if she knew what was going on in her mind? Lena felt herself blushing. But perhaps such thoughts came to all women. Perhaps Mrs. Brenner had had them once, and Tanta Martha, and Ouma. How could one know what went on in people's minds, or what thoughts they held hidden even from themselves by giving them other names. I want to get married, she thought, and I can say that to any one. It is all right to say that. But what does that really mean? It means that I want Dirk. That I want him to hold me, to touch me, to . . .

But you could not say those things, even if all women knew them and felt them in their hearts. It would be immodest. Therefore immodesty was what you said and not what you thought . . . not even what you did. Yes, did; for how could love-making be modest? That was what she had been half-thinking for so long, but only now had she dared to recognize it. It was the truth which stood at the back of everything, that made everything beautiful and natural, or spoilt everything. It was the recognition of it that made people like Oupa and Tanta Martha sweet as old wine, and others, like her grandmother, sour. Those who did not feel this way, who refused to face truth, were turned to vinegar.

Perhaps all people were like wine, as Oupa said. They either matured and became good, or failed, and turned into vinegar. And he was right about there being two people in each person. She was aware of it in herself and saw it in others. Certainly this was true of women. There was the modest one, the respectable one; and there was the other who was about as respectable as a heifer or a filly; and it was this one that ruled the other, compromising her, and getting her into all manner of trouble. It was the other one that was saying Dirk must come back . . . when Dirk comes back . . . It was this one that knew very well what would happen and laughed at the other's blushes and denials. Woman was a strange paradox of strength through weakness; of fulfilment through emptiness, through the children, new men and women, born of the earth woman whose existence convention denied.

She sat forward. Putting down her cup she started up. What's that? Tanta Martha pushed back her chair. "It's a horse galloping," she said. "And why would a horse gallop like that?"

There were shouts. They all ran out. From the bedroom she could hear Charlie calling : "What is it? What is it?"

An English soldier was galloping down the street; women were coming to the doors. She recognized the horse, it was the colonel's charger. He was the only white one. What could have happened? Splashed with mud, coated with dust, streaked black with sweat and . . . it could not be blood! . . . . it could not . . . it could not . . .

"That looks like blood on his shoulder," Tanta Martha said. She went into the middle of the road to meet the horse. The soldier pulled up. It was one of the little drummers. He had been leaning forward over the horse's neck. Now as he reached them he pushed his legs forward and lay back on the reins. The horse threw himself on his haunches as the heavy bit forced open his jaws. His lips were bleeding, and it was blood in big blotches on his neck and shoulders.

As the boy let go, Lena sprang to the horse's head, soothing him with her hands. The boy slid from the saddle.

"They got us," he said. "Christ Almighty, they got us, the whole bloody lot. . . ."

Mrs. Brenner was holding him. The horse stood with his legs spread out. His flanks were heaving, he was blowing great gusts from his dark nostrils, his legs were trembling. Without noticing what she was doing, Lena undid his cotton head-rope and made his fast. Then she offsaddled him. He must not have water yet, she thought. Then she was surprised at what she had done. She could not understand how it was that she should be tending the English colonel's horse. The boy was still gasping for breath and sobbing.

"Take him in," Tanta Martha said.

People were gathering round them. "What is it?" they asked. "What has happened?"

An old man touched the stain on the horse's shoulder in front of the black sweat mark of the saddle with his finger. He held it close to his face to see it better, then he smelt it. "That's blood," he said. He picked up the saddle. "More blood, and a bullet hole." He traced the furrow of the bullet.

"Get him in," Tanta Martha said again. "Give him brandy, then we will learn what has happened."

They got him in, holding him between them. Mrs. Brenner went for brandy. He took it and spluttered, but he seemed easier, he was gaining control of himself. He rubbed the tears from his eyes.

"The colonel sent me back," he told them. "He said: 'Take my horse, Timmy, and go to the Brenners, tell them what has happened and ask for help. We must have bandages . . . food . . . blankets.' My God! My God! they got us proper . . . and they are all there bleeding on the bloody road with nothing to tie 'em up." He struggled to his feet. "Are you coming?" he said.

"We will come," Mr. Brenner said. He had been at the back of the store. "But tell us what happened." He patted the boy's arm.

"We was marching along playing. Yes, I was playing on my drum, and then we saw some Boers, just a few. They was on horseback on the top of a hill. One of them came with a white flag. He said we must stop, but the colonel wouldn't stop. 'The Ninety-Fourth don't stop when they're marching.' It was about ten miles from here, by a little river. And then they began to shoot. There must have been hundreds of 'em all hidden, and before we could take extend they had most of us down; the transport bolted, and there we was. All my mates is there. . . . They're there," he shouted, "lying there in that bleeding sunshine! Christ, 'ow I 'ate that sunshine! It ain't proper . . . an' the whole road running with blood." Tears were flowing down his cheeks. "Are you coming?" he said.

Mr. Brenner was giving orders to Jacob. " Inspan the wagon, bring all the linen, blankets, food, bread, meat. . . ."

" Come, Lena," Tanta Martha said, " get the horses in, we must get back. How lucky it is that I have been making extra salves! We'll get there long before the wagon. Do you know where it is?" she asked.

" No," Lena said.

" It's on Mooiplaas, that's where it is. From what the boy says they must have caught them at the drift at the top end of the farm. Magtig, what fools the Rooibaadjies are to let themselves be caught like that!"

" Are you coming with me?" the boy said. " I'll show you, but come fast, hurry," he said. The colonel said to hurry. . . . ' Take my 'orse and ride like hell,' he said. Can't you understand?" the boy shouted. " My mates is bleeding. The bandages are out, we only had a few. We wasn't ready for war. Christ," he said, " O Christ. . . ."

Tanta Martha took him by the shoulder. " Listen, boy," she said. " You see those horses and that Cape cart?"

" Yes," he said. He was calmer now.

" These are my horses and cart, and we are coming. But first I must go to my house for the things we need—medicines, bandages. You will get on your horse and come with us."

He seemed dazed. " You mean you're not coming at once?"

" We are coming at once, but we must pick things up first. Of what good is it to come empty-handed?"

He put out his hand for more brandy. " Yes," he said, " I see that, but hurry. We must hurry."

The people round them were talking, shouting, arguing. Someone had resaddled the white horse. He shook himself so that the stirrups swung out on their leathers.

Lena was trying to understand what had happened. Her mind was repeating the sentences she heard. There had been a battle . . . this boy has brought news of it . . . the war has begun. . . . We are going to help the wounded . . . that is why we are here talking. It is all perfectly clear. And she could not understand why it was not clear when it was clear. . . . She heard what every one was saying, she heard people speak her name and talk to Tanta Martha, she heard her answers and Tanta Martha's, and understood them. But the comprehension was only super-ficial. Inside her these words and sights, this milling of women and children, these shouts were without effect. If they were going, why did they not go?

And then, without knowing how it was, she found herself in the cart beside Tanta Martha. They were driving to her house and the boy on the white horse was riding beside them. His head was hanging low. This she really understood. He does not wish to see people or look them in the

face. He is defeat—all defeat personified. All men who have been beaten
must look like this. . . .

The familiar houses they passed looked different. So did the people who
stared at them curiously. So did the trees, the blue gums, and the peaches
loaded under their fruit. It seemed wrong that they should be so opulent,
so unmoved and so productive.

They were there now. Lena got down, following Tanta Martha into the
house. The boy sat his horse at the gate. She looked back from the door
and saw him bareheaded, sagging in his saddle, the scarlet of his coat and
the white hide of his horse blazing in the sunshine. They are like a torn
and trampled flag, she thought. This morning they were brave and
beautiful in the breeze. Now they are tattered, dragged in the dust. That
is what they did to our flag. The Vierkleur had been dragged in the dust,
but that was just material, just bunting, and there were men and horses—
there are living. She closed the door to hide the boy and the horse from her
sight.

" Take this, and this, and this . . ."

Tanta Martha was precise and definite in her movements : unflustered.
She seemed slow, but she wasn't.

It was all incredible, impossible. It was only a few hours since she had
watched them march out with the band playing and the colonel's white
horse dancing under him. It could not have happened here in Brennersdorp . . . a battle at Mooiplaas within two miles of her home. . . . She
thought of those boys—young men, soldiers with their pockets stuffed
with peaches, their music, their gay red coats. She knew she should hate
them, but she could not. It was not their fault. What she hated was the
thing they represented, the grasping English hands that had used them.
And what chance had they against her people? Against men like Dirk and
his father or her brothers? It could not be true. But it was true.

Even as she was thinking it could not be true, Tanta Martha was handing
her more pots of ointment, bottles, bandages, and splints. She felt sick
at the thought of the sights she was going to see; and yet she was drawn
to them. She longed not to be going, but she wanted to go. Had any of
their own people been killed or wounded? Some must have, but not many.
It had been ambush. One of her people's regular manœuvres that they had
learnt at great price from the old wars with the Kaffirs. She saw it in her
mind—the red coats, the wagons, the Boers, tall and bearded, standing
beside their horses or lying down resting, smoking and talking with their
rifles by their sides while they looked at the wounded and the prisoners.
It was terrible to think of it. None of those men should be there—neither
the English soldiers nor the Boers.

Everything was packed now. Pots, basins, brandy, bandages, and
medicines were all piled into the cart and tied fast, and under them were

the things she had bought at the store, with her new dress and shoes. I should have taken them out, she thought, but how could one remember everything? Louisa had made them coffee. They drank it. The little drummer had dismounted. He was sitting on the steps of the stoep holding his horse's reins. He refused coffee. He kept saying: " I must get back . . . I must get back."

" Now we will go," Tanta Martha said. " We have everything we need and can make haste. But it is only the fools who make haste too fast." The cart heeled over on its springs as she got in.

2

What a drive it was! How extraordinary it was to be here beside Tanta Martha, in this cart that she knew so well, behind horses she knew, with a load of bandages, salves, and brandy; with the boy swaying on the colonel's horse beside them and calling to them!

" Come on . . . for Christ's sake, come on!" he kept shouting, and then falling over his horse's neck, grasping at its mane. Recovering . . . falling . . . recovering again.

And the road. How well she knew that, too. The war had come to Mooiplaas. Dirk . . . Louis . . . Stoffel . . . Where were they all? It was war. That it had come struck her down; she felt herself recoil under the knowledge.

" It is war, then, Tanta Martha," she said.

" Yes, my heart. What else?" She nodded at the boy. " With dead and wounded lying by the road. Before God," she said, " dead men and wounded. Men frightened and angry with the fears they will not show. Men licking their wounds like dogs. How much of it I have seen! But never white against white before."

" Those boys," Lena said.

" Ja, those boys with pink faces like babies' behinds," Tanta Martha said. " What could they do against men? Discipline, the colonel said. What has discipline to do with war on the open veld—with Boer fathers who fight for their homes? Did he think they would stand like sheep to be slaughtered?"

It had all been so gay. Lena thought of the men's faces . . . their greetings as she passed them. Even the little drummer boy, she remembered him quite well. This morning he had stood beside the big man in the tiger skin, nearly crying because he could not fill his pockets with peaches. What had he known of war? What had he to do with it? Why was he fighting? What was he doing here so far from his home? Why had his mother let him come? There he was, a little boy whose voice was only just breaking, riding in front of them on a blood-flecked horse and cursing at them, muttering every curse he had ever heard, shouting them. . . .

The cart rocked. It was badly balanced. With all that stuff on the tail-board they could not put the seat far enough back. Tanta Martha was heavy. Her weight bore down the pole, throwing the weight on to the horses' shoulders, so that one of them stumbled. Tanta Martha hit him and clapped her whip. They broke into a faster canter, banging along the road, swinging to the right and left as she called to them.

The boy kept looking back. "For Christ's sake . . . my mates! Make those bastards gallop. . . . Gallop, I say!" His voice rose to a shriek as he wheeled the colonel's horse, circling them. Then he sagged forward in his saddle again.

"He will fall," Lena said.

"He will not fall, Lena. When men are like that there is no end to their endurance. He could go all day. I know, for I have seen it."

What strange things Tanta Martha had seen! And would this never end? Would they drive all their lives behind a wound-drunk boy who cursed them? This was war . . . war . . . war. Where was Dirk? The sun beat down on them, it was getting hotter and hotter. Lena was soaked with sweat, everything stuck to her. Her head ached as though it would burst. The red tunic of the boy became double before her eyes. There were two boys—one boy, two boys on two white horses. One boy again. . . . Sometime it must end. Sometime they must get there . . . get to the battlefield.

Then it seemed as if they would never get there, as if they would go on like this for ever, with the road unwinding itself in front of the horses' ears and passing under their feet. . . . with the boy riding and turning back, nearly falling and riding on. And they were nearly on Mooiplaas now. It had happened at the spruit, at the top end of the farm, only about two miles from home. She had to keep repeating this to herself; and still, no matter how often she did it, it was not credible. The same spruit that lower down ran past the willows and the hammerkop's nest. I walked along it the other day with Dirk, she thought . . . that night when . . . the night he had gone. It was all so near, all part of her life. And now whenever she saw the stream she would think of the blood in it. Yet she had not seen it, nor the battle; she did not know if there would be blood in it, and she felt like this. Tanta Martha had said she was taking her back this afternoon, back to Mooiplaas. And she was going back, at a gallop, by the top road that they hardly ever used. They were on the farm now. In a minute they would be over the rise and dropping to the watercress drift. That was what they called it, for the watercress was good there.

They were over. They were dropping down, the horses lying back against the pole. There was the battleground. It was not what she had thought it would be. She had not known what she had expected, but not this. She put her hands in front of her eyes. There were men lying . . . men still crawling . . . wagons and carts were overturned, an ox was bellowing. Why did somebody not put a bullet through it?

Tanta Martha struck the horses so that they jumped forward at a gallop again, but faster than before, afraid that the cart would overrun them. The drummer boy had left them. She could see him standing by some men, he was pointing back at them. He is saying he has got help, she thought. There were the Boers : big men beside their little horses; some standing beside them and some mounted. That was the way she had pictured them.

Tanta Martha swung the horses on to the veld to avoid the broken wagons. Lena felt the cart jump up and down as the wheels rode over the tussocks and banged on the stones. The horses were wild and would not settle down after their gallop.

"They smell blood," Tanta Martha said. "Animals are wiser than men. They do not like it."

She calmed them with her voice and whistled to them to slow up. They steadied, but went up and down rattling their harness, cocking their ears, and stepping daintily in their fear.

"My beautiful ones," Tanta Martha said, "my beautiful black ones . . ." They turned their ears back to listen to her.

How untidy it was! That was Lena's impression of a battlefield—how untidy and dirty! Blood . . . there was blood drying in pools. Blood had run into the ruts and was thickening there as it turned black. Rifles were lying on the ground . . . red coats, white helmets, packs, pipe-clayed equipment, were scattered everywhere. Over there some rifles were standing upside down on their bayonets; they had been driven into the ground and helmets were set on their butts. That must be to mark the more distant dead. Already the vultures were circling, going round and round in wide, low rings. Nothing could die or be near to death without the assvoels knowing. They were always there : above the world, out of man's sight, but seeing man and waiting for him to die; to pick out his eyes, to draw out entrails . . . pulling and pulling, quarrelling and pecking at each other as they ate.

The cart had stopped. I must get down, she thought. I must get out on to the road. I must put my foot on the ground . . . perhaps there will be blood there. She thought of her shoes. Suppose she stepped into blood : that would be a bad sign. She thought of the new shoes she had danced in yesterday with the men who were dead to-day. Yesterday was a year ago. She looked down—there was no blood. Her eye caught the shining tyre of the wheel. There was blood on that, and more than blood—pieces of something. She knew what it was. It is bowels, she thought, but she would not let her mind think the word; she held it back. I will not think it, she thought, I will not. . . . She raised her eyes. The aasvoels still circled the heavens. They were tireless, they could wait. Dead man, dead horse, dead ox; it was the same to them. There was no comfort to be found looking upward. She looked towards the spruit. How quiet the Boers were! Was that . . . was it . . . ? She put up her hand to shade her eyes. It was Swartkie . . . It was Dirk.

" Tanta Martha, there is Dirk." She pointed.

Tanta Martha sat like stone. The horses were still at last, they stood with only their tails flicking. Men were coming towards them. They had only just got there, yet they seemed to have been sitting in the cart waiting like this for an hour.

" Look well, Lena," Tanta Martha said. " Look well on your first battle. Look well, and look at man's work. Is it for this we bear them? This is man's work," she said. " It has nothing to do with the Almighty God."

She spat over the side of the cart. " So, Frans, it has begun." It was the commandant, Joubert. He looked old and tired.

" It has begun, Tanta Martha. We prayed to stop it, we did all that men can do, but it was not enough. There are many dead," he said.

" Ours?"

" No, only one dead and five hit—of theirs; it was like fighting children."

" Are you going to get me down? Are you going to send men to help me or must I sit here for ever, Frans?"

The others who had joined him began to laugh. He took off his top hat to wipe his forehead with a blue handkerchief.

" What do we do to get you down, Tanta Martha?" someone said.

" What do you do, Gerrit?" Lena heard Tanta Martha say.

Yes, it was Dirk. And there was his father, and Louis and Stoffel. They were all safe.

" Are you not a married man, Gerrit?" Tanta Martha went on. " Can you not put your arms round a woman to lift her down?"

" I could do that with a woman, Tanta Martha," he said.

Everybody laughed.

" And what am I?" Tanta Martha asked. Dirk had seen them and was coming. " Am I an elephant?"

" You are a woman," Gerrit said, " a very fine one, but if my wife is a koppie, then you are a mountain, and I do not know what Anna would say if I hurt myself with you."

" I know what she would say, jong," Tanta Martha said. " She would say, if you must rupture yourself, you had best do it with me. . . Come, kerels, get me a box. With a box and someone to guide my foot when I turn, I can get down by myself."

Dirk was at her side. " Lena! Lena, my heart, what are you doing here?"

" I do not know, Dirk. I know nothing. I am only glad that you are safe."

He threw his leg over Swartkie's neck and slipped to the ground. "Come," he said.

He held out his arms to lift her down. His hands were on her waist. How good they felt!—the thumbs in her belly, the width of his fingers over her back. She was in his arms, her toes were twitching as they reached for the ground, but she hoped they would not find it. He could hold her in the air for ever if he wanted to. She felt the ground beneath her. He kissed her mouth. His hands were moving down her body, she felt herself trembling. Out of the corner of her eye she could see the Boers smiling. She did not care how they smiled. Swartkie pushed his nose between them.

"He is jealous, Dirk," a big black-bearded man shouted. "He wants to kiss her too."

"Come, Lena," Tanta Martha said, " we must attend to our business. There will be time for kissing and the rest after. Foei, would, you make love before all these men? Have you no modesty?"

I have none, Lena thought. "You will be here, Dirk?" she said. "I mean, you are not going away?"

"Where would I go, my heart? I am here till we ride."

She turned to Tanta Martha. She was undoing the riems that held her things. The horses had been taken out. The point of the disselboom, with its rings, lay in the road. Beside it was a dark patch. Lena looked away.

An officer stood beside her. She had danced with him yesterday, but hardly recognized him. His eyes were sunk into his head, his red coat was stained and torn. He had his left arm bandaged and slung.

"It was good of you to come," he said. "We are now the enemy."

Tanta Martha turned on him. "You are men, are you not? And where men are hurt you will find women."

Captain Langdon joined them, he had been hit too.

"I am glad you came," he said, "we have many wounded. And dead," he added. "It went too fast for us, we were not ready. You have got bandages, I hope," he said. "I had only a few."

"I have brought what I could," Tanta Martha said, "but Meneer Brenner is coming with more. He was inspanning his wagon when we left. What we can do will be done."

"Ja, it will be done, Captain," Joubert said. "We would hurt no one. You should have stopped, and then there would have been none of this."

They began to tear sheets into strips and roll them. How terrible it was—how slow! But how lucky Dirk was here! To have been thinking of him all the time and then to find him like this . . . It was wonderful. And Swartkie had known her.

"Set out the things," Tanta Martha said, " set them by the roadside. I have seen many wounds and cured them too."

The wounded were very quiet . . . uncomplaining . . . and the dead.

The Boers were like statues beside and on their horses. The prisoners sat wiping the sweat from their faces. Red necks . . . Rooineks. They were well named. Blue-eyed with red, peeling necks and faces. Their tight red tunics were undone, their belts loosened. One near her was writing, holding the paper on his knee. Lena wondered what it was he wrote. The transport oxen were outspanned and grazed nearby. A Boer was superintending the flaying and cutting up of the dead oxen. The wounded one that she had heard bellowing as they came had been killed. If there was peace before the storm, a quiet, then this was the peace after it, a quiet for its contemplation. For what had been done was irrevocable. Not only were the dead dead, the wounded wounded, but there were the implications of the action, the commitments.

The doctor had dressed as many of the wounded as he could, but many were still untouched. She saw him moving along the line bending over the fallen men.

" A bandage, Lena . . . a splint . . . a pad . . ."

How wonderful Tanta Martha was! How patient the men beneath her hands!—smiling while they sweated with pain, or waiting in line with their teeth clamped fast, the muscles of their jaws bulging below their ears.

" Water . . ."

" Yes, water," Tanta Martha said.

A Boer was going round with a bucket in one hand and a little beaker in the other. They drank thirstily. Some of the prisoners were washing in the spruit, others ate watercress and peaches. Those were the Brenners' peaches that they had picked this morning. There were peaches in the road. There was one lying in a pool of blood—that was an extraordinary thing to see. Two men passed her carrying a dead soldier sagging between them. His pockets bulged with peaches.

" A bandage, Lena, a big one. Now hold his arm . . . higher . . ."

She held the Englishman's arm higher. He stared past her, his eyes blank as the sky. He will show nothing, she thought. It was Mulligan, the transport sergeant, who had been cursing the oxen this morning.

When they had done with him, he said : " Thank you." Only his mouth moved. He still stared.

She heard the sound of a mallet beating on wood. More tents were going up. There was the sound of picks. The ground was stony here, it would be hard to dig so many graves. She saw the doctor moving among the men with his two assistants. Yesterday he had been looking at Charlie. She saw two women, they were helping, too. She had seen them this morning in Brennersdorp. They were soldiers' wives. Had their husbands been wounded? she wondered.

The aasvoels were much lower. As she looked, one fell with outstretched wings, landing with a little run near the offal that had been drawn from an ox. It sat hunched at the roadside. Another landed, another and another, but there were still as many in the burning skies.

The sweat was running down Lena's sides, it was running from her forehead into her eyes. She wiped it away with her hand. I expect my face is streaked with blood now, she thought. She did not care. How hot it was, how tired she was . . . But Dirk was here. Dirk was safe.

" Bandages, Lena. Get more from the cart."

They were running low now, but Brenner's wagon should soon be here. She was astonished that she felt so little. It must be because I am so tired, she thought. When would Dirk come back to her? When would it all be done—the last man tied up?

The worst wounded were those who had been near the wagons when the oxen had bolted, overriding and mangling them terribly. One woman, the sergeant-major's wife, they said, was hit. And a hundred and twenty men, of whom forty were dead. This morning they had been alive.

An Englishman came up to them. " The colonel wishes to see you."

" To see us?" Tanta Martha said. " What for?"

" To thank you, I think."

" Where is the colonel?"

" In a tent." He pointed. " He is wounded : badly," he added.

The colonel badly wounded and every officer but one hit. They must have picked them off first. What marksmen her people were! But even now when you were in the middle of it it was impossible to realize it. Only officers had been at the dance last night, and now all but one were dead or wounded. It was so short a time ago. They reached the tent. Joubert was there, his tall hat in his hand. He stands, Lena thought, as if he was in the presence of the dead.

The colonel was on his bed, a camp bed that they must have carried on their transport. It must open and close like a musical instrument—a concertina, she thought.

" Tanta Martha and Miss Lena du Toit," the colonel said. So he had recognized them, and had remembered their names.

" You know them, Colonel?" Joubert said.

" Yes, I know them. They are my good friends. Last night I danced with both of them in Brennersdorp."

" With both, Colonel Anstruther? Before God, you are a brave man." They all laughed.

" He will die," Tanta Martha whispered. " I can see it in his face."

It was strange that they should all be laughing round a wounded man. If we did not laugh, we should cry, Lena thought. But he was brave to face death like this, smiling and unafraid.

But Dirk was alive. He was out there with the others. And Swartkie had known her. That was remarkable after so long. Less than a month, really, but a lifetime. Ja, a lifetime to a girl in love, but a month to a horse. That was a funny thought. Men . . . horses . . . Dirk alive; the colonel dying; the peaches lying in the blood of the road . . . What was he saying? He was talking to an orderly.

" Get the wine from the mess cart. We will drink, Commandant," he said. A strange folk, these English.

The man came back with the bottle. It had a fat cork and was covered with gold.

" Shall I open it, sir?" he asked.

It opened with a pop. She felt herself jump. It was the same wine that they had had last night, the wine that was so pretty in the glass, yellow with small bubbles that rose upwards and then collected at the sides, but that tasted of nothing but needles pricking in your mouth. Another soldier brought in glasses. They were the same wide-topped; long-stemmed glasses. He brought also a cloth that he spread on a box. It was of fine linen : a fine linen cloth at a war! The first soldier had a napkin that he wrapped round the bottle; wiping off the mouth first, then he held it as a baby.

" Shall I pour it out, sir?"

" Yes, Stribling, pour it, please."

He filled the glasses. The bubbles rose as they had last night.

" You will drink with me, Commandant?" the colonel said.

" I will drink, Colonel."

" Then first to these two ladies, whom I thank from the bottom of my heart." He raised his glass.

" To the ladies," Joubert said and drank. He made a face as the needles hit him.

The orderly filled the glasses again.

" Another toast," the colonel said, " but one you will not drink. To Her Majesty the Queen, God bless her."

" No, Colonel. But I will drink to your queen in our fashion. Here's to Queen Victoria! May she live a long time and take her soldiers from our land."

There was someone at the entrance of the tent. Lena turned. It was Dirk.

" What do you want, Dirk?" she asked. " Do you want me?"

" Yes, I want you. It is Oupa."

" Oupa?"

" Yes." Dirk was scratching his head. " He has been in the battle. Reuter has just found him. We can do nothing with him. He wants to ride with us. He fell off his horse. It was Louis's chestnut that he rode."

" What is all this nonsense?" Tanta Martha said. " Oupa . . . you must be wrong."

" That is what I thought at first, Tanta Martha, when they told me.

Then I saw Reuter and the horse. Magtig, but how angry is that old man! He is calling for more brandy all the time."

" Is he badly hurt?" Lena asked.

" He is not hurt at all; just bruised. He is drinking for pleasure."

" The world has gone mad," Tanta Martha said. " Here we are drinking prickly wine with a man about to die, and your great-grandfather riding to the wars by himself and now drunk in front of the English. Watch over him, Dirk. We will come in a minute."

The doctor came in. His assistants were with him, they were carrying things that shone. Lena did not like to look at them.

He smiled at them and said : " You're having quite a reception, Colonel."

" Yes, aren't I?"

" But you shouldn't have done that." He pointed to the wine.

" You think not. After all, there are the laws of hospitality. And there was the Queen . . . once more to the Queen," he muttered.

" Perhaps we should go now, Lena," Tanta Martha said.

" It was good of you to come," the colonel said, " and thank you again in the name of the Ninety-Fourth."

Tanta Martha turned to Joubert. " Are you coming, Frans?" she asked.

" Ja, I am coming. Good-bye, Colonel," he said, " and good luck."

" Good-bye and good luck, Colonel," Tanta Martha said. " Good luck," Lena echoed softly. Good luck, indeed, she thought; he will need it, since they are going to take off his legs. That was what those things were for. Tools . . . saws and knives that shone in the sun as they were brought in, and rattled, clinking together. The commandant was out of the tent. Tanta Martha was sidling through it. Lena got ready to follow her. She could hear Oupa shouting outside. She had never known him to behave so badly.

As she went out, one of the men who had come in with the doctor closed the flap of the tent behind her, lacing it fast. She stood dazzled in the sun. Inside they were talking. She could hear those things being moved, and the colonel's voice.

" They did not get the colours, Doctor. We got them away," he said.

She wondered what he meant. She would ask someone later. Meanwhile there was Oupa. He had seen Joubert. He was shouting at him.

" Magtig, Frans," he shouted, " that is a fine thing that I make a cavalry charge by myself. No one has seen such a charge by any one of my age, and then you are too idle to pick me up when I am wounded. No, Frans,' he said, " it is not right that I should lie for days on the veld till I am found by my faithful servant. Before God, there I lay without food or water waiting to be picked up by a Kaffir while my own folk make merry."

" It was a great oversight on our part, Oom Philippus," Joubert said. " I sent two men to look for you, but they found nothing."

"Ja, that's what I say. A great oversight and a great loss to the nation if I had died lying out for days."

"It was not days," Lena said. "It is only a few hours since the fight began." She was angry with him for making a spectacle of himself and she wanted to go with Dirk.

"And what do you know of war, girl?" Oupa said. "And what are you doing here, a woman alone among so many men? It is not decent."

"Decent, you old fool," Tanta Martha said. "Do you think it decent to charge into a war where you are not wanted, when you are a hundred years old—and then to get drunk? And, besides, Lena is not alone. Am I not a woman? Is there any one more woman than I?"

"A woman you! A seacow—a murderess who nearly killed me once with her purges . . ."

"And will again," Tanta Martha shouted, her hands on her hips. "Ja, I will purge your bowels out, and your wickedness with them, as soon as I get you back. And if you will not take it, I will have you thrown and drench you like a horse. 'Seacow'!" she shouted. "And what are you, Adonis? Ja, that's what you are, an old bobbejaan of a man, an old baboon, a bag of skin and bones and wickedness and blasphemy, a disgrace to your nation, a drunkard among strangers."

"It was good brandy, Martha," Oupa said, "better than I get at home."

"Get my horses in," Tanta Martha said. The Boers were all laughing.

"Get them in, you skelms, and stick him in the back of the cart. Make him fast with riems. See to it, Dirk." His arm was round Lena.

So she was not even to have that. He moved from her.

"Come, Reuter," he said, "help me with your master."

They took Oupa by the arms.

"The Baas knows the Old Baas lied," Reuter said. "I am no Kaffir. I am a Zulu. It is easy to see. I am one of Moselekatse's men."

"Yes, you are a Zulu," Dirk said.

Lena followed him then.

"Get into the cart, Reuter, I'll hand him up." How strong Dirk was. "Now tie him." The old man was tied fast, his head was sunk on his chest. "You stay with him, Reuter."

"Ja, Baas, I will stay. But the horse? The red horse? That was how I knew, when the horse came home alone. I rode him back to find the Old Baas. To-day," he said, "I can do nothing with my master. Sometimes he has a devil in him. Baas," he said, "I am Zulu. Please make it clear to the others."

"I will make it clear. Now see he does not fall, and the horse can be tied behind the cart. Where's the red horse?" he shouted.

"I have him," Louis said. "He is my second horse and too young for war." He looked at his great-grandfather. "So he is drunk," he said. "And

I wanted to tell him that he had lamed my horse. Look at his leg filling up." He pointed to the chestnut's off fore.

"Come, Dirk." Lena dragged his hand. How strange men were! Did he not want to kiss her? Did he not want anything from her now that God had brought them together in this wonderful way? "Come, come," she said. She led him by the hand. Behind that overturned wagon would do. Anywhere would do where there were fewer men. That was funny: fewer . . . a few did not matter, but a lot did. She flung herself into his arms.

"My love . . . my heart," he said. He kissed her and held her to him. He kissed her mouth, her eyes, her neck, his hands were on her breasts. She thought of her best dress. If she had had it on, he would have seen it, but it would have been spoilt with the dust and blood . . . Blood . . .

"Is there blood on my face, Dirk?" she asked, remembering suddenly.

"Yes, there is blood on your face, and dirt," he said. "But you are beautiful to me. Dirty or clean, you are beautiful."

She felt someone at her back. Tanta Martha must have come to fetch her. Why could one not be alone—almost alone with one's lover for a moment? She turned. It was Swartkie, he was nuzzling her back. That verdomde horse had brought her back from another world . . . a world of love, of the warmth of Dirk's arms, of the feel of his hands on her, of his soft beard against her skin, of his smell. "The Dirk smell" she called it in her mind: part man, part clothes, part horse, part leather, part tobacco, part coffee. But she was out of it now. The horse had broken the spell. For an instant she wanted to slap his mousey nose. What business had a horse to interfere? What business had Oupa going to war and making them hurry to take him home? Brandy . . . She would never give him brandy again. She would empty the bottle over the veld and steal no more for him. How thin Dirk looked! Only a month, and he was so much older-looking, and thinner—that coat would not be too tight now. She would not have to change the button.

They were walking back. He said: "Go and see Boetie, give him our love, say you saw us and that he is the man on Doornkloof."

"I will go," she said. His arm was still round her, but it was different. Before, something had been coming. She had been waiting for his kisses . . . his hands. Now it was over. There was only the memory of them and that she could not have till she was alone again. You could only remember really well in the evening before the sun fell, when the world was still, as though it was waiting; and in the mornings, before you were quite awake, you could dream; and at night before you were quite asleep. But you had to wait for those times. Her meeting with Dirk was over, and they had said nothing. He had said she was beautiful and had touched her. She had said, you're safe; thank God, you're safe; and had touched him. She had hardly spoken to her brothers or his father.

There was the doctor's cart with its red cross painted on the tent. How was it she had not noticed that it was overturned before? Charlie's birdcage was broken, and the veld-birds were free. The veld-birds were free, and the men were dead, and the rose-red peaches were scattered on the bloody road.

Dirk kissed her, but she hardly felt it. Her mind was in the other kisses when they had been almost alone. He said he would come to-night if he could. But she knew he would not be able to come, that those were just words. She put her foot on the step of the cart.

She was going home . . . Dirk was going on to war . . . it was war. It had begun, and only the birds were free.

CHAPTER XIII

SO THIS WAS VICTORY

I

Dirk watched Lena get into the cart. He saw Tanta Martha raise her whip. The cart jerked forward as the horses plunged. Oom Philippus nearly fell; Reuter put out his hand to hold him. They were off, splashing through the drift. They were going up the hill. The cart was getting smaller and smaller. Lena was almost invisible now, the back of her head no more than a dot among the other dots that were Tanta Martha's head and Oom Philippus's and Reuter's. They were over the top.

What had been the good of saying he would be over to-night? It was only a couple of miles; ten minutes, at a gallop. But he would not be over. He would not go even if he could; he could not go even if he would. He had orders. The prisoners were to be taken to Heidelberg. He was part of the escort.

In going over the hill, Lena had gone out of his life, perhaps for ever. It was war, and in war you did not know. He patted Swartkie's neck. Stoffel rode up to him.

"Well, jong," he said, " we are taking them in, I hear. You, I, and some others."

"Yes, we are taking them, Stoffel."

It was not something he looked forward to. There was an indignity attached to it : both to the prisoners and the guards. Men herding other men like cattle; and the prisoners helpless as cattle, separated from their arms, unable to determine their fate, even to stop or start, to march or rest, eat or drink at will. There was something indecent in this. All concerned must be degraded by it.

"It will be good to drive the English swine," Stoffel said.

Dirk said nothing. What good was it to argue with one so set in his ways as Stoffel? Stoffel had proved himself as a fighter, but Dirk wondered what he would be like if things were not going so well.

"What do you think of that old fool Oupa?" Stoffel said. " What an exhibition!"

"An exhibition of courage, of a great heart set in a frail body. Philippus Jacobus is a man and a great one."

"A great fool, to my mind. But it will hasten his end," Stoffel laughed.

"It is a good farm, is it not?" Dirk said.

173

" Ja, it is a good farm. None better than Mooiplaas. But why that tone of voice, Dirk? Do you not get your share—the portion of our sister?"

Dirk felt the muscles on his back twitching. He turned from his horse to face Stoffel.

" Listen, cousin," he said. " That you are a cripple and soon to become my brother-in-law does not permit such things. Think what you like, but it is unwisdom to speak some of your thoughts. Something might happen." He stooped to pick up a stick at his feet and broke it between his hands. " Like that," he said.

" A threat?" Stoffel said.

" A threat? Who threatens? What have I said? I have broken a stick. But there are men I like and men that I do not, relations or no, cousins or no, brothers or no. Some words I like and some that I do not. And I do not like those who mock the aged or the helpless. To do so is to mock God, and God is not mocked."

" A predikant . . ."

" A burger like yourself."

" Anyway, we take them in and we will chase them fast along the road. Joubert saw my good work at the battle. He complimented me how well I shot. They fell like rooibok, to the right and the left." He stroked his rifle. When he swung his horse away, the feather was still upon his back. It seemed wonderful to Dirk that a man could go through a battle with a guinea fowl's feather on his back. What a number of accidents must take place for such a thing to happen—a tarentaal preening its plumage at a given spot; a Boer burger to lie and rest there upon his back so that the quill of the small spotted feather should become engaged in the cloth of his jacket; the English in another spot: the English and the Boers meeting in conflict in such a way that one of their number should go through the battle without displacing something as fragile and as contrary to war as a feather. There was no sense in anything. Such a thing as this denied probability and the accepted laws of chance.

He looked over the spruit at the hilltop again. How would all this seem in ten years' time? Perhaps it was unwise to think of this. But it would look different; some things would be forgotten and others changed in their actual order and proportion by the passage of time. Lena had gone out of his life—a small black speck in a small black cart. That was the way things were to-day. The pattern of his life was being woven like a Kaffir mat of reeds. Like a reed she had gone out of it; she was underneath it, invisible. Like a reed under the fingers of a Kaffir woman, she would reappear when the time was come.

He took off Swartkie's saddle and bridle and walked with his arm round his neck down to the water. Poor Swartkie. What had he to do with all this? The horse drank a few mouthfuls. He was not thirsty and seemed to drink only to please him. Then he splashed himself and rolled in the sand by the drift. When he had shaken himself, he stood nearby, nibbling at the grass, selecting a mouthful here and a mouthful there. Dirk munched watercress and picked a bunch to carry with him. It would be good on the dusty road.

Some Englishmen were filling a water cart. What equipment they had, those English! For a moment he was despondent of beating them. They had so much of everything. He thought of their wagons, their tents and gear. Then he saw it the other way. Because they had so much they would be beaten. They were tied to the roads. They were limited to the speed of oxen walking in the yoke, while the Boers could do fifty, seventy, and a hundred miles in a day. Their meat went on the hoof. Loose oxen could be driven over the veld, could be hidden; and could, if it was necessary and for short distances, be made to gallop as fast as a horse. He became less depressed.

But his was a difficult nature. It was best to see only one side of a question. To see more than one took away your certainty. He thought of his argument with Oupa about lions. Who could be certain whether they were born with their eyes open or shut? Whatever he had asserted, he was uncertain, being convinced that they might be born both ways. That was the trouble. When you came to think of it, every one was always right. There was a reason for everything. Even Stoffel was what he was because of certain things. He was a cripple. He had been badly brought up by his grandmother. That winter he had been left with her as a child; and his father, broken by his mother's death, had only paid attention to Lena, neglecting the boys. It was a terrible thing to have no mother.

He thought of his own mother and his baby sister. Boetie was the man of the family at Doornkloof now—the man, but blind. There were boys here no older than Boetie. You thought you had things. You thought you had a glimmering of the life pattern and then it was broken to pieces before your eyes. Why was Boetie blind? What sense was there in that? Whom had he harmed? Perhaps it was not a good thing to be as thoughtful as he was, but there was a reason for that too. He had got it from his father, and the war gave you time for reflection. There was so little else to do.

By now Lena would be home. He thought of her at home. It was no good thinking of her at home; he dragged his thoughts away from her. Mooiplaas. Why, this . . . he looked across the veld . . . was Mooiplaas. This was her farm of which Stoffel said he would obtain a share. He knew it, but it was hard to believe.

"Come, Swartkie." He whistled. To-day, and for all the coming days till it was over, he must live with his horse and his gun. Till it was over. One day it would be over. It would be best not to think of anything till then. He shook the water from the roots of the cress. It was only the other day he had walked along the spruit with Lena. He thought of the stick he had thrown out of her path.

2

Brenner's wagon had come and gone back loaded with wounded. The camp was broken up except for a few tents where those too bad to be moved lay waiting. It was said that the English colonel was going to die.

The prisoners were grouped under their guards. Dirk looked at them. Soon he would have to join them, but until they were ready to start he wanted to keep away. His father was not going. This was another parting. War was a series of partings—of breakings up . . . of comings together . . . of little bands swirling in on the current of events, of being broken up into their integral parts, and swirling out again to join other groups . . . always changing . . . always moving, always becoming smaller. Already they, the Boers, who had suffered nothing, nothing relatively that is, were fewer. Keiser was killed, and Coetzee so badly hit that they despaired his life. The English doctor had been very good, helping their wounded as well as his own; and Tanta Martha had done wonders. But the greatest wonder of the day had been the accident that had brought Lena to him.

Why must men be hurt before they could become brothers? Was their amity between them only when they lay dead? He looked at the blanket-covered body of Keiser. This morning he had been riding and laughing— a man. And now what was he? Food for the aasvoels and the jackals if they left him; for worms if he was buried. And he had a wife and child. Who had killed this man? The soldier who fired the shot? The English Queen? The English people? Only one English officer was left un-wounded, so Coetzee was well revenged. But would those dead boys com-pensate Hester Coetzee for her empty bed and her fatherless son?

The prisoners' guard was mounting. He took his father's hand. "This is good-bye, Pa," he said.

"No, my son, not good-bye. It is just tot siens . . . Till I see you, my son. We will pray each night for one another, for those at home, and for the victory of our people."

"Yes, we will pray. But do you not think that the English pray also to God for the safety of their sons and victory?"

Dirk plaited Swartkie's mane as he spoke—in, out, over . . . the long black hairs felt good in his hand—like Lena's hair, for hers was thick and strong, but as different from it as the horse was different from her. His hand was plaiting Swartkie's hair; his mind was plaiting Lena's.

"Yes, I think so," his father said. "I think they pray also."

"It is all very strange, Pa."

"So strange that it is beyond our understanding. But pray, Dirk; pray for all of us. I think the others are deluded and that God is with us, since we fight for our homes. We have nothing to gain but freedom!" He threw out his hand pointing to the horizon. "This is our Africa," he said. "Now ride, my son. My heart is with you."

Dirk's foot was in the stirrup. He was up. Swartkie was twitching under him, flicking his tail and cocking his ears, moving no foot, but ready to jump forward when he felt a tightening of the reins on his mouth or of the knees that held his barrel.

Dirk bent forward. "Kiss me, Pa," he said.

They kissed.

"Geluk, boy." His father's voice was gruff.

"Good luck, Pa."

His reins were up, held high, his knees tightened on the flaps of the saddle. Swartkie leapt forward. Everything was behind now— Lena, his father, this part of the country. No man could tell what lay in front. Death, certainly. That lay before all men; but in fifty years or in an hour, that was what no man who rode could tell—neither of himself nor of another.

How dejected the prisoners looked! It made him ashamed to see them. Stoffel raised his rifle in greeting. He seemed to have forgotten their disagreement, such was his elation. That was how war took men : some in one way, some in another. Dirk thought of his own excitement during the battle, once he had conquered his fear. He had felt no pity then. Herman Prinsloo was in charge. He was another bitter one, a real English-hater. Dirk looked at the others. There were two more, young Bok and Frederik Erasmus. None of them men he liked.

"Come," Erasmus said, "we will move."

The Englishmen who had been sitting at the roadside got up.

"March," Prinsloo said, riding his brown horse almost into them. "Trek, I say."

They adjusted their helmets and began to move. Not like soldiers, but to drift forward aimlessly. They did not know where they were going, how long they must march, or what would happen to them. They were still dazed by the battle. It had been so quick, so sudden. Since this morning when they had been at Brennersdorp their position was entirely changed.

"Take the rear, Dirk van der Berg," Prinsloo shouted.

"I will take it," Dirk said. He reined Swartkie to let them pass.

Prinsloo was in front, leading them on his brown horse. Then on the left was Stoffel on his roan, the half-brother to Louis's second horse that Old Philippus had ridden. Erasmus was on the other flank and Bok had ridden off. Prinsloo had sent him somewhere, no doubt to bring news of their coming.

At the rear Dirk got all the dust they kicked up with their dragging feet. He dropped farther back to allow it to settle in front of him. There was no reason why he should ride in it. His rifle lay across his knees. His reins were slack in his hand. He hung them over his wrist to light his pipe. They were riding south. Prinsloo's farm was not far from here. They might be going there. If there had been more of us, I might have been able to get over to Mooiplaas to-night, after all, he thought. But they were too few. There would have to be guards all night, though the Almighty only knew where the English would run if they did escape in the darkness. Wherever you looked there were other commandos riding : big ones that raised great clouds of red dust; and smaller parties of men scouting or on missions. The veld was alive with Boers. The nation was up. It was in the saddle and riding.

Some of the prisoners were very tired. Others helped them along with their arms round their waists. Two or three were slightly wounded and must have fever. One man fell and two of his comrades carried him between them, passing him from one to another as they tired. They were good men, these boys. But they had had no chance. We were ready for them, Dirk thought. We are fine shots and we had the range paced out to a yard. He thought of the battle again and of the feather on Stoffel's back. It was still there. He could not get that grey feather, spotted with white, out of his mind. And it was better to think of that than of men falling, than of the feel of the bolt sliding in your hand, the barrel hot in your fingers, or the smell of exploding cordite.

Stoffel had used some dum-dum bullets. He said so himself. That was not a good thing to use on men. Such wounds could be recognized and would bring discredit upon them. And he had made others. Dirk had watched him cutting off the copper tops of his bullets and nicking the soft lead of their cores. Nor was it good to see Boers who were honest men taking the watches and rings from the fingers of the dead and demanding their trinkets of the living. No, that was not good. Such things should go back to the wives, the mothers, and the sweethearts of those who had died.

Already right at the beginning there was so much that was deplorable. Why had Joubert not stopped it? he wondered. There was only one reason, for the commandant was a good and kindly man. He had not stopped them because he could not. There were so many like Stoffel who were too wild to be held. And the German Afrikaners like Hoffman—he had seen him loot the dead—were among the worst. It was hard to say that, since they owed so much to the Germans who had sent them rifles and some machine-guns they had captured in war from the French, and even cannons, it was said. His own rifle was a Mauser. Yes, they owed a lot to the Germans, but there was something he did not like about those he had met. He did not like the way they talked, or the way they treated the Kaffirs. Some Boers might be brutal, but they were not cruel.

The prisoners were getting more and more exhausted. They should be halted, he thought. They need rest and food and water. The weakest were dragging back so that he had to stop Swartkie to wait for them : the horse walked so much faster than they. Only the strongest could march; the others staggered, weakening at each step. They were strung out now, like a herd of cattle, according to their strength. In front the well and strong; at the rear the sick, the halt, and the lame. Still it was wonderful to see how they moved. And they had already marched from Brennersdorp this morning. We could not do it, he thought. We are a mounted people. We are lost on foot, and helpless.

There was Prinsloo's farm; he could see it among the trees to the left. They were wheeling, turning towards it. And there was Bok coming at a gallop to meet them. It had been as he thought. He had been sent on to make preparations. Now they would soon be in. It was as well. The prisoners could not have gone much farther. He stood up in his stirrups to ease his legs.

" Is that where we are going?" a soldier asked.

" I think so," he said.

" Thank God," the soldier said. " We're about beat."

You could recognize the different varieties of trees—the oaks, the poplars, the syringas. There were beasts about, and staring Kaffir servants. They were very near now. They were among the poultry. Dirk looked at a hen scratching for her chicks under a small mimosa thorn. That was a strange thing, the way poultry never went very far from a house, not much more than a hundred yards. A string of white ducks, about twenty of them, waddled past in single file.

" This way," Prinsloo shouted. He was leading them towards the cattle kraal. It had high stone walls. His wife stood watching him, her hands on her hips, from the doorway of the house. " This way—this way, kerels. We will kraal the English cattle like oxen," he shouted.

As they marched in, the flankers fell away to the sides of the gate. Dirk felt like a dog herding cattle as he drove them. The last one was in. The first were already sitting and lying in the powdered dung of the kraal.

" Shut the gate," Prinsloo said. " Stay on guard, Stoffel . . . and you others water your horses and come to the house to eat."

" What about them?" Dirk said. He pointed to the kraal. " They need water."

" Let them wait," Prinsloo said. He turned his horse. His wife was coming towards them. She was a stout, strong woman with eyes that looked two ways.

Dirk gave the prisoners a last look. By God, it is a shame not to give them water, he thought, and if I was a bolder man I would resist the order. He was ashamed of himself for not having answered Prinsloo. If there had been one other of my mind who would have backed me up, he thought . . . But in his heart he knew that this was no excuse. His father would have spoken his mind, alone against a hundred. He followed the others.

By the house he offsaddled, took off his bridle, felt Swartkie's legs. First the horse and then the man—that was the way he had been brought up. He knee-haltered him; he could water himself at the furrow that ran below the trees. The horse raised his head, holding his leg high as he did so, to look at his master's face. No mealies . . . no rusks? he seemed to ask. Always at home he got something when he was loosened for the night.

"There's nothing, Swartkie," Dirk said. "Nothing for man or beast. Till it is over we must forage for ourselves."

"Come in, jong," Prinsloo shouted. "Come in, meneer," his wife said. "There is food on the table. Good food for the victors of Bronkerspruit."

Dirk went in.

Herman Prinsloo had a good house. It was comfortable and well kept. His wife might be cross-eyed, but she kept things well, very clean and shining : he looked at the plates and beakers on the dresser. And from the smell of the food on the table, she could cook. And not the least of her virtues, from her husband's point of view, was that she had been an Erasmus of Six Mile Spruit—they owned half the world, and this farm had been her portion. This was well known and well denied by Prinsloo, who said he had bought it from her father because his darling loved it so. Ja, Dirk thought, he bought it by taking Magdalena off her father's hands. Frederik Erasmus, who was of their party, was her cousin. They spoke of Jan Erasmus, the blacksmith of Brennersdorp, who was their uncle.

But it was good to sit at a table again : to drink hot coffee with milk and sugar; to eat meat, and earth apples, and pumpkin and peas, good Boer bread with butter, and finish it up with mossbolletjies and watermelon konfyt.

It was not so good to listen to the talk, to the boasting and the threats, nor to hear Herman Prinsloo tell the tale of Makapan. He drank glass after glass of brandy and kept going back to it. "I was a young man then," he said, "a boy younger than you." He pointed to Bok. "But we taught the Kaffirs a lesson that day."

Every one knew the story, but Dirk had never met any one who had actually been there before. What these men did not seem to see was the cause. Would Potgieter have been captured by the Kaffirs and flayed alive while he was held pinned to the ground by their spears if he had not made repeated forays among them killing right and left while he sought their children to sell as slaves to the East Coast traders? First, slave raids, then revenge; and then a revenge of extermination for the revenge.

"We were five hundred," Prinsloo said, "men of Lydenburg and the Zoutpansberg. We had a hundred and sixteen wagons and two cannon. Makapan did not wait for us. No, he would not fight Boers. He ran to the mountains and fought there among the kranses. Then, when we had beaten him, he retired into some great caves in the Berg, and that was a problem. What do you think we did?" he asked.

They all knew, but no one answered. He must tell his tale. He must not be interrupted.

"First, we tried to blast them out with dynamite, but we could not. Then we tried to smoke them out, like honey bees, but that was no good either. The blasting did not work because the caves were in slate that would not blast. And the smoke did not work, for the caves were too big. They held hundreds," he said. "All Makapan's folk—men, women, and children— were hidden in them. They had prepared them with stocks of food and water.

"So there was nothing we could do but besiege them, shooting those who came out for food or water as their stores got short. They had stores in the caves against such a day," he said again, "but they were too few. Those of us who were not on guard went hunting. It was good there, and so there was much meat; but some of our men were killed, nevertheless, by those treacherous dogs. They would crawl out and stab the guards in the darkness.

"And then we made a great plan. We walled them in. Three weeks it took. And all the wagons loading stones, and ground for dagher. We built well, laying stone upon stone as if we built a house. But they kept coming out, pressed for food, and as they came we killed them. There were some small places we did not know. And in all, from beginning to end, we killed a thousand like that. But inside . . . Magtig," he said, "I often wonder what it was like inside. The smell of it came through those walls we had built so strongly that we had to move our camp. Inside those Kaffirs were dead and rotten. But how they stank! At last after a month we broke down our walls. Inside there was no sound, only a great smell. We did not go in. No man could have gone in, not even the most coarse and uneducated. It was over. We got our horses, inspanned the oxen to our wagons, and we left. But Makapan was done. His people were no more, and many brave Boers had died—among them young Potgieter, the nephew of the Potgieter whom they had skinned alive.

"It was done, a fine brave deed," he said. "For some days we rode together, a great triumphant company, and much entertained wherever we passed the farms, for now there was no more danger from Kaffirs. Then we broke up and went home, but it was done. I would that we could do as

much to the Rooineks . . . that we could starve them in caves till they
rotted. They bring it on themselves," he shouted, banging the table.
"Kaffirs, Rooineks . . . all who will not let us alone, who will not leave
us to live our lives and worship the Almighty after our fashion."

His face was purple with rage, his eyes bloodshot. Was it some defect in
him that he could not feel like this? Dirk wondered. Should a man be able
to love his land so much that he could see nothing else, neither right nor
wrong?

"I will read from the Book," Prinsloo said, and got up to fetch it from
the small side table where it lay with the hymnals. He put it down in front
of him and opened it at hazard. . . .

Now therefore hearken, O Israel, unto the statutes and unto the
judgments, which I teach you, for to do them, that ye may live, and go
in and possess the land which the Lord God of your fathers giveth you.

Ye shall not add unto the word which I command you, neither shall
ye diminish ought from it, that ye may keep the commandments of
the Lord your God which I command you.

Your eyes have seen what the Lord did because of Baal-peor : for all
the men that followed Baal-peor, the Lord thy God hath destroyed
them from among you.

But ye that did cleave unto the Lord your God are alive every one of
you this day.

Behold, I have taught you statutes and judgments, even as the Lord
my God commanded me, that ye should do so in the land whither ye
go to possess it.

Keep therefore and do them; for this is your wisdom and your
understanding in the sight of the nations, which shall hear all these
statutes, and say, Surely this great nation is a wise and understanding
people. . . .

Dirk did not listen. When it was over, it would be his turn on guard.
He would have to watch those miserable men shivering in the cold of the
night, lying close to each other on the dung for warmth. From where he
knelt he could see a picture of the Zulus' massacre of Piet Retief's party. It
hung to the right of the dresser. On the other wall were the guns, one
above the other lying alternately, butt to barrel, secure on pegs driven into
the soft brick wall : old guns, heavy muzzle-loading roers, elephant guns,
and lighter guns that even a girl could use. At the bottom there was a
modern rifle, twin to the one that Prinsloo carried. He wondered why a
man should have two guns of the same calibre and kind. Over a big chair
there was a lion skin that was showing wear. He looked at Tanta

Magdalena's hands as she held them up to her face. They were stubby and ingrained with dirt. The house was clean, but her hands were dirty.

Then it was over. Prinsloo closed the Book, and put it back in its place with the hymnals. He stretched himself, pulled his watch from the pocket of his vest.

" It's time for you to go, Dirk," he said. " Tell Stoffel to come to the house. There is coffee for him, and food, and he can sleep here if he wants to. Three hours," he said, " and then call Bok if he does not come. You have a watch?"

" I have a watch."

" Then watch well." Prinsloo laughed at his joke. " But if there is any nonsense," he said, " shoot and we will come."

Dirk took his rifle from the corner and went out. The night was still and dark, the sky sharp with stars. Night, and everything covered by it. All happiness, if there was happiness now, all sorrow. The stone walls of the kraal were a sharp black line against the dark blue night.

He went towards the gate. Near him Dirk could hear a horse cropping grass. He whistled. It was Swartkie. Swartkie would not go far.

" Halt, who goes?" Stoffel challenged him.

" It is I, Dirk. You are to go in now and get coffee."

" At last," Stoffel said. " You have eaten, I suppose?"

" Yes, we have eaten, but there is food for you, and a bed in the house."

" A bed will be good. Do you want to count them?" he asked: " the cattle I have been watching. They sleep," he said. " They sleep on the powdered mis. That is what they should sleep on—manure."

" No, I don't want to count them," Dirk said. " Have they had water?"

" Water? Why should they have it, and how could I have watered them alone? Let them wait. We can water them with the other beasts in the daylight. Then we can see to shoot them if they try to run. Water . . ." he said. " They are lucky not to be dead. If I . . ."

" If you what, Stoffel?"

" Nothing," he said. He was going now. " But they would be better dead. All Englishmen would be, and would be dead if I had my way. God damn them!"

Dirk watched him disappear. He waited to see the light from the door as it opened. Stoffel du Toit was in the house with his friends. No doubt Prinsloo would tell the story of Makapan again.

He put his hands into his pocket for tobacco. What was this? the watercress. He had forgotten to eat it. Fragments of tobacco were sticking to it so that even if he had wanted to eat it . . .

" Sir . . . Sir . . ."

An Englishman was speaking to him. He turned, his rifle held ready.

" Who is that?" he said. " What do you want?"

"Sergeant Hopkins of the Ninety-Fourth, sir."

Dirk saw him silhouetted against the sky.

"I heard what you said to the other guard. Water," he said. "Can't we get some for the boys that's hit?"

"How did you understand?" Dirk asked. "Do you talk the taal?"

"Ja, meneer. I understood what you said. I learnt it in the Lydenburg. I nearly married her," he added, "and would have but for the wife at home . . . Liverpool, that is . . . and the war. But could you let us have some water, meneer, even a little?"

"I have no water. And how can I get you any and leave you unguarded?"

"Yes," the sergeant said. "That's a bit difficult." He was silent.

They should have water. It was not right to have left them like this, the wounded as well as the others.

"Couldn't I stand guard while you went, meneer?" the sergeant said.

"How would I know you would not run away?"

"If I gave my promise I would not run or let the others . . ."

"I have no bucket," Dirk said. That was a way out. He wanted to give them water, but he was afraid. In his heart he knew this. You are afraid, Dirk van der Berg, he said to himself. Your father would not be afraid. All the time he was afraid now. Except that once when he had nearly struck Stoffel. But even they had been alone, man to man, and Stoffel was a cripple. It was that he did not like trouble. It was not that he was afraid. But a voice inside him kept saying: You are afraid . . . afraid . . . you are afraid. You are glad there is no vessel for water. His mind was evenly divided between wanting to get water for them and being afraid of getting it. It was much easier to be brave in battle. Then the decision was made for you. Besides, your fear—even if you conquered it—made you bold in self-defence.

Then the sergeant said: "There are milk buckets. I have found them."

So, when Bok had moved the cows to make room for the English, he had left the buckets.

"They were on the top of the wall," the Englishman said.

That was enough. The for and against had been evenly balanced before: his desire and his fear. Now here were the buckets thrown into the scale. It was the will of God: an indication. It would also prove that he was not afraid; and after all there was only the smallest chance of getting caught.

"You swear, in the name of the Almighty God," Dirk said.

"I swear . . ."

"Repeat it."

"I swear, in the name of the Almighty God, not to escape myself or allow any one else to escape," the sergeant said.

"Bring the buckets."

He was back in a minute. Slinging his rifle, Dirk took them. There was a fountain just below the kraal; the water ran strongly from the hillside into a small stream that Prinsloo had dammed to make swimming water for his ducks. It was funny that ducks could not breed without deep water in which to mate.

Dirk stood beside the water. It was black as velvet. It was like a dress of his mother's. And on the blackness there floated a star. He dipped the first bucket. As he held it under the star was in it. That was a good sign. He was catching a star in his bucket : a star for Lena. He smiled. One day, on a still night like this when they had their own home, he would take her out and say : " Come, Lena, get a bucket; we will catch a star as I did once in the war with the English." And Boetie. That was the kind of thing he would like to hear about, though he had never seen a star. He pulled the bucket out of the mud and put in the other one. A star in each. As he lifted them the stars escaped. Boetie . . . It was wonderful what that boy saw who was blind. Much more, he knew, than many who had eyes. It was really he who had put that idea of a world of night beasts and another of day beasts into his head. The water slopped as he carried it. It ran into his shoe, ice cold on his foot.

" Thank you, sir," the sergeant said, " thank you. That will do them good."

" If there is not enough for all," Dirk said, " I will go back."

" There is enough for the boys and them as is hit," the sergeant said. " The men can wait. Make soldiers of them," he said, ". . . and after to-day . . ." He took the buckets towards the men who were lying against the walls. " Here, Timmy," he heard him say, " here's water, Timmy." Dirk saw him going from one to another. His eyes were used to the dark now and he watched him dipping a beaker into the bucket and giving them water. He emptied both buckets, but took no mouthful himself. That is a man, Dirk thought. I wonder if I should have been able to do that?

The prisoners had settled down again. He stood leaning against the wall watching the stars. You never got tired of that. There was the Southern Cross . . . Orion's belt . . . You could be friends with the stars; even to think of them was good. It brought you peace.

He heard someone move. " Halt ! " he shouted. " Who goes ? "

" Friend . . . Bok come to relieve you."

How quickly the time had passed !

" Come, then," he said. " I am tired." He was very tired and sleepy. What a day it had been ! What a night ! Guarding men like cattle. That was not a thing that men should be set to do. There was no dignity in it.

He went towards the house. There was his saddle on end against the wall and his blanket drawn through the rafters where they overran the roof. He took them to the foot of a big sering tree. That would be a good place to sleep, better than the house. He lay down with his head on his saddle, his blanket rolled round him, his rifle leaning against the tree. He moved to brush some berries from under him, the seeds that fell from the tree after the sweet mauve flowers were gone. Nothing ate them, for they were poison, though sometimes a pig died from such berries, but generally they were safe enough. Beasts were wiser than men, knowing what was good or bad.

He thought of Lena sleeping at Mooiplaas. It was funny to think of people sleeping : of him being here under a big sering, of his father God knew where, of Lena at Mooiplaas, of Herman Prinsloo sleeping with his cross-eyed wife. It never seemed right to him that people no longer young should lie together, but they did. It was not beautiful as it would be . . . as it had been with Lena. It made him ill to think of her. But they did. To-morrow Magdalena Prinsloo would be complacent, her cross-eyes absent. She would be like a cow that had been served.

Swartkie had found him, he was standing nearby, sleeping on three legs. A good horse. A good friend. Now he must try to sleep.

In the morning Stoffel came out of the house, laughing.

"We have a fine plan, Dirk," he said. "You will laugh." He was doubled up. "The prisoners . . ." he said.

"What about them?" It was hard to think of anything funny about them.

"You will see, Dirk. You will see," Stoffel said.

Dirk stirred the fire under his coffee; he had not felt like going into the house, preferring to use his own slender store. When the time came he would know. If Stoffel thought it would be good, then it must be bad.

The prisoners were allowed to go down to the water. They drank in great gulps and washed. Some of them took off their coats and shirts to wash under their chests—they seemed to like it—and put their heads right under water to blow like seacows.

Prinsloo had found food for them. Some old sheep that a Kaffir would have refused to eat had been slaughtered. But even this he had resented, saying : "I know they are old sheep but they are still sheep, and who will pay me? It was a mistake to come to my own farm," he said. "We should have gone elsewhere."

"Elsewhere?" his wife said. "Was it not worth three old sheep to see me?" She looked at him coyly.

"No," he said. "It was not worth one sheep." He was in a temper. It's the drink, Dirk thought.

But the English had eaten. They had had water. He felt happier about them.

"Mount," Prinsloo said, "we will go."

"Now you will see, Dirk," Stoffel said. He looked at Prinsloo. "Don't forget the wagon, Herman."

"Go over there," Prinsloo shouted to the English. "Over to the wagon and pick up the yokes." They hesitated. "Any one who disobeys I will shoot," he shouted. He raised his rifle. They went to the wagon. "And you others, push . . . take the wheels . . . Now, trek, you skelms. . . ."

The wagon was empty; it had been lying near the house with the trek gear spread out in front of it, eight ox yokes and seven chains. The prisoners pulled at the yokes, four to each; others pushed behind it and laid on to the wheels to help them. Stoffel handed the reins of his horse to Bok and climbed on to the wagon-bed as it began to move. He nearly fell as his bad foot failed him. He recovered and shouted :

"Kom . . . Loop . . . trek . . . trek . . . We are off on the Great Trek of English to Heidelberg." He was laughing loudly. "This is the trek of the English out of our land : the first wagon of their trek."

He picked up the long bamboo whip that lay along the wagon rail and clapped it over the heads of the sweating men. The cracks came loud, following each other like rifle shots . . . between them Dirk could hear Tanta Magdalena's laughter. The wagon was moving faster, the men were almost trotting; the whip clapping harder; Stoffel, swaying on his good leg, was sweating as the long bamboo bent under the weight of its thong. Bok was almost off his horse with laughter.

It was not right. Nothing could justify this. Dirk stared at the English prisoners bent over the ox yokes. More indignity, more brutality out of which still further events would be born. He drew away. You could avert your eyes, but you could not stop your ears. He ought to do something—protest. I ought to act, he thought, but how? In other things he had always been adequate, rising to occasions as they came about : farming at home, hunting in Bushveld. But here was something different. It was not a personal matter, this dealing with other men. If only his father were here.

Then suddenly, when they had gone about a mile, Prinsloo shouted : "Enough . . . let go." In a lower voice he said : "We must get them in alive or there may be trouble."

"What about the wagon?" Bok asked. "Should they not drag it back?"

"The Kaffirs will fetch it. Now march, dogs. March to Heidelberg and you do not know how lucky you are to be alive."

After that it was just marching. Marching, resting, offsaddling and watering the horses; eating, sleeping, guarding the prisoners, marching while the road unwound in front of them.

Dirk spoke no word to any one except Sergeant Hopkins. After much hesitation he said :

"I am sorry that such a thing should happen, but I am alone."

The sergeant said : "I understand, sir."

But Dirk wondered if he did. He did not understand it himself. I should have done something, he thought. But what? It does not matter what, a voice inside him said. But you should have done something . . . anything. Boetie, your little blind brother, would not have stood it and you are less a man than he. What had happened was shameful. By your silence you condemned yourself as an accomplice. Not to protest against evil is to condone it.

The town, as the seat of the new government, was full of men, of rumours, of news. Each man had his own version of the war, each started new rumours as he contradicted the old.

The prisoners handed over, Dirk had his time to himself. He had never been in Heidelberg before. He rode through the town, glad to be alone, but looking for someone that he knew. Among so many there must be some from his part. He looked at the horses as much as the men, for often you recognized a horse before its rider. Wagons, tied horses, cannons, dogs, oxen, men on horseback and on foot, even loose horses with trailing head-ropes filled the streets. The town was full, but of strangers, it would seem. There were few women and children. That is, there were the normal number, all those who habitually lived here, but they were swamped by the tide of men—Boers, Kaffir servants, and Bastaard transport riders. In the outspan there might be someone. He rode through the lines of wagons slowly, peering into the tents. Only then did he acknowledge to himself how lonely he was for his father, his mother, for Lena, for Boetie, and his little sister. Before, he had pretended to himself that he was just riding round to see the town. But now he was looking for a friend : any friend. Almost he would have welcomed Stoffel of Mooiplaas, because of Mooiplaas. Someone shouted to him : " Dirk . . . Dirk . . . Dirk van der Berg." He turned his head.

" Why, Barend, who would have thought to see you here?" he said. It was Barend Klopper that he had met hunting once who was calling. Their wagons had lain wheel to wheel on the Koodoos Rand for a month three years ago.

He rode towards him. They were cooking coffee over a small fire.

" Sit, Dirk. Sit, man. It is good to see you. Pa," he said to an older man, " this is my friend Dirk van der Berg of whom I have often spoken."

" Good-day, meneer," Dirk said.

" Good-day, young man. Are you newly in?"

" To-day."

" They say some prisoners were brought in," Barend's father said. " Do you know if it's true?"

" Yes, it is true."

" How do you know? Magtig, this is not like being at home. In a town like this one's ears are more filled with lies than wax. Among one's friends one is content. At home you know the liars."

" I know because I brought them in."

" Then you do know. So at last we know one thing that is no lie. But do you know how the English treat our prisoners?" he asked.

"How do they treat them?" Dirk said. It seemed strange to him that the English would treat their prisoners badly. They seemed very civilized despite their godless habits, and he was not in a mood to discuss the treatment of prisoners.

" How do they treat them!" the old man shouted. "Terribly . . . terribly. They make them wash all over every day as if they were going to be married. Magtig," he said, " that is the only time a good man ever washes all over."

" Suppose he marries twice, Pa?" Barend said.

" Then he washes twice, but I will split no hairs with you. I say a man washes only once, in principle as it were."

" I do not wish to argue, Pa, but I say every man washes three times in his life even if he is only married once."

" Three times . . . That is a lie."

" It is the truth. I go further. I say that before you are in the ground you will wash three times, yourself, Pa."

" Me . . . Never!" his father shouted. " I washed for my wedding, and you should have seen the clothes I had : a new hat nearly a yard wide, a new coat, dark brown it was, of thick frieze with brass buttons, nearly new trousers, and a new saddle."

" To have seen it, Pa, which I would have much enjoyed, it would have been necessary to have been born out of wedlock some years before the ceremony, which seems improbable, having some knowledge of my mother's principles. Nevertheless, had it been possible I should have enjoyed it," Barend went on, " especially if I had been old enough to drink. You had drink, I suppose," he said. " Wine and brandy?"

" Of course we had it. They still talk in the Rustenburg of the feast we had."

" Then I am sorry I missed it."

" My son has no respect for me, Dirk," Klopper said. " We spoilt him as a child. He was so beautiful then. But you never know how they will turn out. Besides, he was the first, which is interesting."

" I still say three times, Pa."

" Three times what?"

" Wash."

" Wash what?" his father shouted.

" Men."

" Never. No good Boer."

"Yes."

"Then when? Tell me that if you can. Magtig, how I loved you before you could speak : a beautiful child!"

"When they are born," Barend said, "when they are married, and when they die."

"Then I have you." The old man jumped up. "Once and once only does a good Boer wash, and that is at his marriage. Those other times you speak of are nothing, since it is done against his will. Neither a baby nor a corpse can make effective protest : such a washing is null and void.

"What was I saying before Barend interrupted me?" he asked.

"Yes, the prisoners. That is not all. The other is worse. It is terrible. Disgusting. The English make them all go in one place. Our folk are free men who are used to the whole veld. Latrines they call them, holes in the ground. I tell you those English have no sense of decency. It is worse than animals. Only a rhinoceros goes in one place, and then each has his own." He spat. "Will you drink coffee?" he asked.

"I would like coffee," Dirk said. He got out his pipe. "Tobacco?" he asked.

"I would like tobacco." The old man took some from Dirk's hand. "I like to try my friends' tobacco," he said. "Then if it is good I ask for seed. It is your own, of course?"

"It is our own. Doornkloof is a good farm for tobacco. It is good for everything," he said. How good it seemed now!

"I have heard that." Old Klopper lit his pipe. "And I am glad to meet the son of Groot Dirk of Doornkloof. You are like him." He puffed the smoke slowly. "It is good," he said. "Will you give me seed?"

"Yes, I am Groot Dirk's son, and you shall have it when it is over. You will come and visit us? My father would be glad to see you again."

"When it is over, jong, then we will all go visiting. It will be like it was and the whole world ours once again."

Dirk got up.

"More coffee?"

"No more now, friends. I must get back for orders."

"Then tot siens."

"Tot siens."

They shook his hand. "And good luck."

"Good luck," he said. He mounted.

Hendrik Mostert might be here somewhere. He was sure he would be on Kruger's staff. It would be nice to see him again.

As he rode past the last wagon of the outspan, someone shouted : "There's one of them. One of the victors of Bronkerspruit."

He did not turn his head. He thought of the battle again, of the feather on Stoffel's back, of the marching prisoners . . . of the night while he stood guard over them, of the star he had caught in his bucket. He thought of Lena, a black spot going over a hilltop . . . of the wounded . . . of the buried . . . of the dead.

So this was victory.

CHAPTER XIV

THE GAME OF STONES

As THEY drove up the hill from the battle, Lena looked back. Between Oupa's sagging head and Reuter's she could see the flash of the spruit edged with bright green cress. Louis's chestnut horse was dragging at the riem that tied him to the side of the cart—the battlefield lay along his flank. It looked very small; the white tents were no bigger than the nail of your small finger. And there were red pin-points—dead English still lying unburied on the veld. A bigger red patch to the side of the road was the prisoners, and dark figures on foot, or mounted on miniature horses, were the Boers. One of them was Dirk.

Oh, this was something she would never forget. This battleground . . . the drive to it with Tanta Martha calling out to her horses, and the drummer boy cursing at them in English, using words she did not know, yet knew to be obscene : words that he must have picked up from the men. The wounded colonel . . . Dirk calling her name and coming towards her . . . and Swartkie . . the expression on Stoffel's face. He had hardly spoken to her. Oupa . . . That was a fine thing, to have disgraced them all with such glory. But in her heart she thought how wonderful he was : no more to be trusted than a baby : going off to the wars at his age. But it was funny. She laughed to herself; and it was something to have the blood of such a man in your veins. That is why I understand him so well, she thought. She felt anxiously for her parcel—the dress. It was on the seat beside her. She looked under the seat for the shoe box; it was still safe. She took a last look at the drift. It was hard to believe those spots were men; that one of them was Dirk.

They were over the top. The horses were trotting. That was the last she would see of it. When would she see Dirk again? What would Ouma say? Louis was right, Oupa had lamed his horse; he was not trotting even. Well, he would have plenty time to rest.

She looked at Tanta Martha's face. How she had hated to kiss it as a child! It was so bristly. But you got used to everything in the end, even to kissing bristles. There was one very long one, not really a bristle; it was more of a hair, since it was curly, that grew out of a dark brown mole on her chin. She watched it moving with the wind and the motion of the cart. She thought of the silky down on Dirk's face. The young man silky; the old woman harsh. Later he would have bristles too, a fine curling golden beard. But his lips would be shaven. How handsome he would be! How proud she was of him! He was going to be as big as his father.

She looked at Tanta Martha again, her hands this time : they were fat and wrinkled. There was still some blood on them at the bottom of the nails. She shivered. All this talk, all this wondering and trying to persuade oneself . . . And now it had come. She called it " it " in her mind. That was the best way. How much thinner Dirk was! How hard his arms had been when he held her! She wanted his arms.

She felt tears running down her cheeks. She was not weeping, just crying soft tears that ran down her face and tasted salty on her lips as she licked them. She did not want to touch her eyes. She did not want Tanta Martha to see. She felt a hand patting her leg. She looked down. It was black and gnarled. It was old Reuter, he had put his arm through the back of the seat to comfort her. He was good. He was like a good dog pushing his nose into her hand. He knew. But Tanta Martha's face was set. Her eyes had almost disappeared, as she held them narrowed, into her cheeks. They were black slits. Her jaw with the long trembling hair was thrust out.

There was the farm, the trees, the brown thatched roof of the house, the outbuildings. Lena saw people moving. How small they were! As small as those on the battlefield, but instead of getting smaller they grew bigger. Kaffirs working, leading water. One of them was carrying something into the big shed, another was inspanning one of the wagons. She wondered if they had the news yet. The battle they must know of, having heard the shots. But of the victory? Did they know that? And what would Ouma say about Oupa? There was no disguising the fact that he was drunk, very drunk indeed. She thanked God for Tanta Martha, and looked at the shoe box again. It had not moved. Tanta Martha was capable of dealing with any situation.

Lena saw one of the maids run into the house. It looked like Rosina. She has gone to say we are coming, she thought. But Ouma would never come out to look. She would just sit on the stoep sewing and waiting. She turned towards Tanta Martha again. Her face was unchanged : still set like a stone . . . if there could be a fat stone; set like dough that was turned into stone. With a movement of her strong hands she checked the horses as the cart came to furrow and then let them go again when they were over it, but her expression never altered. Perhaps she would stay the night? The horses were tired. She would never stay for herself, but she might for her horses.

As they passed the main kraal, Titus took off his hat to them and waved to them.

" The meisie is back," he said. " There has been a battle."

A peacock ran across the road, its long tail dragging. The dogs ran out barking. There was Ouma. Only now, as the cart stopped, did she look up. Had she been sitting there all the time? Would she sit there while the end of the world came, while men fought and died? Lena felt nothing would make her understand her grandmother. She wondered what had

H.O.D.

happened to make her like this . . . something must have, perhaps many things. Nothing seemed alive in her except her hatred of the English; and the tips of her fingers, which, no matter how still she sat, moved continually, rubbing against each other.

Titus came with a box for Tanta Martha; Willem appeared from somewhere and was at the horses' heads; Reuter was unloading Oupa. He fell into his arms as the riem about his middle was loosened. Titus came to help Reuter take him to his room.

Ouma turned her head to watch them. Then she spoke.

"The old fool, at his age. It may well be the death of him, but it is something that even the near dead rise from their beds to strike at the tyrants. So you have brought the girl back, Martha," she said.

"I have brought her back and would spend the night with you. My horses are tired." She paused. "We come from the war. There are many dead."

"How many English?" Ouma asked.

"Many," Tanta Martha said.

"That is good. And of ours?"

"Only one, but others are wounded."

"Did you see many people you knew? The Kaffirs say it was Frans Joubert's commando, is that true? And were my grandsons with him?"

"I saw Stoffel and Louis."

"That is good. Was either hit?"

"Neither is hit." Tanta Martha sat on a chair on the stoep. It sagged under her weight. Ouma had picked up her sewing again. She was satisfied.

Lena left Tanta Martha's side and went back to the cart to get her dress and shoes. She told Titus to get the other things and set them at the back. It was funny to think of them having been under those piles of medicines and bandages. What a lot had happened since they had been packed in Tanta Martha's cart at the store! Ouma was still silent. She had not asked her why she had stayed with Tanta Martha, and said nothing more about Oupa or the war. She need not have worried about Tanta Martha staying, for there was no talk or questions all the evening. Lena kept looking at her grandmother's face. It was as silent as her voice.

A person could have a silent face. It could be still, as a tomb is still: silent, as a stone is silent. Sometimes, if you broke a big stone or saw one that had been broken, there were shining crystals inside it. You wondered what had happened to make them, what had gone on inside the stone. Ouma's face was like that. Lena had never seen any light in it except the light of anger and hatred.

They talked, she and Tanta Martha, but about nothing, only people. Ouma asked how Tanta Aletta was, and Tanta Martha said she was well considering her age and the troubles she had seen. They were still asking of her when Lena went to bed.

The dress was put away, carefully folded in the chest near the window. The shoes were put away, wrapped separately in paper and packed heel to toe in their cardboard box. The brooch that Meneer Tryolla had given Tanta Martha and that Tanta Martha had given to her was on a little dish that stood on the table beside her brush and comb. She was worried about Oupa. He had not spoken and lay on his bed breathing heavily. Men did that when they were drunken. But was he only drunken? Such an adventure as he had had could not be beneficial, there must be bad effects which no one would know till he woke. She must go in to him again. She would not be able to rest until she had seen him. She went into his room.

" How is he, Reuter? " she asked.

" The same. Still drunk, and his ears are warm. As long as his ears are warm he is better." He got up and felt his master's ears. " Feel," he said. She felt his ear. It was warm, as Reuter said. " Hold the lamp higher, higher, higher," he said, " and let us look at his eyes."

Reuter pulled at his master's eyelids; they flinched away from his fingers. How thin and transparent they were!—like the eyelids of a hawk. " You see, it is good," Reuter said. " He crinkles them like a child when you try to open them. The old skelm does not like it. As long as his ears are not cold and I cannot pull open his lids, it is good. A dying horse, a dying cow, and a dying man are much the same. Their ears grow cold and their eyes come open."

" I have been so afraid, Reuter," Lena said. " I have . . ."

" Be not afraid. The Old Baas is drunken. Later he will wake and be angry. Then he will beat me, which will take the rancour out of him, then he will sleep again and wake up well. That is how it will be—you will see that it will be so."

" I do not see why he beats you so much," Lena said.

" Who else would he beat? " Reuter asked. " And how else would he show that he is the Groot Baas? "

" To whom does his beating of you show this? "

" To him. It makes him happy and does me no harm. He makes a great noise with much swearing. And I make a great noise, bellowing with pain, and then, when it is over, we go to sleep. Has the meisie ever seen a mark on me? " he asked.

" No," Lena said.

" There are no marks," he said. " Once, in the old days, when he was strong and the Baas was making a Christian of me, it was different. He also had to beat me to make me wear trousers which inconvenienced me and chafed my legs. It was easier," Reuter said, " to make me a Christian than to make me wear breeches, since I could see no necessity for them.

Except in war I have never been a naked Zulu, but always a modest man who wore a loincloth. Yes," he went on, " he still beats me and I should be sad if things changed. Does the honey bee hurt the flower it enters?" he asked. " Does the night wind hurt the leaves? That is what the Baas is to me—a night wind, and a honey bee."

She stood still watching the old man.

" Go to bed," Reuter said. " Sleep well, and leave me to watch my master."

" You are not afraid you will fall asleep?"

" Does the lion sleep as it watches its kill?" he asked. He answered his own question. " Ja, it sleeps, but have you ever known anything to happen to the kill? That is the way I sleep. The way I always have as I watched over the Old Baas. For the lifetime of a man I have slept beside him with my eyes open and my spears in my hand."

" Then I will go. If he needs me, you will call."

" Yet it might be good to have something for him if he woke," Reuter said. " A little brandy wine : just a mouthful. That is the best medicine for the Baas's sickness. For a man mauled by a lion you give him lion's flesh. It follows, therefore, that to a man mauled by brandy you give brandy."

Lena laughed. " And who would drink it," she asked, " you or he?"

" We would drink it," Reuter said. " Do you think I would leave none for my master? And did not the Old Baas teach me out of the Book that the women who masticate the Kaffir corn for beer should not be denied nourishment . . . or was it oxen?"

" You mean muzzle not the ox that treads out the corn?" Lena said.

" Ja, that is what he taught me. But women and oxen are one to me now, save that I prefer oxen. As you grow old the beauty of fat oxen grows as that of slim maidens wanes. No man has yet been betrayed by an ox."

" But what has this to do with brandy wine, Reuter?"

" It has this to do—that it says in the Holy Book that the servant who watches his master should not be denied a sopie when he asks for it."

" You will not drink it all?" Lena said again.

" The meisie has my word. I can say no more. My heart is sore that the words of Tabankulu, the induna, are not believed. But if the meisie has no brandy, then a little meat would be good. Some meat with fat on the edges?"

" I will get you some meat."

" Meat alone is for dogs," Reuter said. " I am my master's dog."

" . . . and some brandy," Lena said.

" Brandy is for men," Reuter said. " I am my master's man."

In the morning Tanta Martha got ready to go. She ate; she inspected

her horses; she demanded more mealies for them and had them fed under
her eyes; she had the wheels taken off her cart and the axles greased; she
looked over her harness. Then she called Titus and told Lena to come
with her.

"We are going to get some roots for medicine," she said. "Also branches
for infusions. In your father's time I came here often for such things. Now
I come seldom, so when I come I must have more. Then I will purge your
grandfather again before I go."

"You have seen Oupa?" Lena asked.

"Yes, I have seen him."

"How is he?"

"Still drunk, my heart, but he is strong. As it has not killed him, it may
do him good. Men are like that. The things they do either kill them or
make them more alive. It is on that principle that I administer my medicines to men, and most are very alive. He is very alive," she chuckled,
"but was still too drunk to resist me when I dosed him."

"What did you dose him with, Tanta Martha?"

"I dosed him with dynamite, Lena. I gave him strong medicine for his
liver; strong medicine for his bowels; strong medicine for his bladder;
and a special brew of leaves that is for the complaints of women and
remarkable for the lasting qualities of its bitter taste."

"Why did you give him that?" Lena asked.

"That was for calling me a seacow."

They were walking over the veld towards the koppie behind the house.
Tanta Martha was breathing heavily. Suddenly she pointed.

"There is one, Titus," she said; "dig it up and get more of the same
kind. Look, there is another; there are plenty here."

He began to dig up the bulbs. They were like onions, but had foliage
that opened in a big green fan.

"Women are different," said Tanta Martha. "Women have only one
sickness and that is men. It is the men who make them sick and the men
who make them well again. Look for the man when woman is sick. To
make a woman fat and happy, marry her. To make her thin and sick, take
her man away. Look at me," she said. "I have been very happy. I am
very well."

"But . . ." Lena said.

"Ja, you would say I have no husband. But I have had two: both good
men; men who sang bass—who loved me. No woman can be happy with
a tenor. They are never faithful to one woman; they go about singing like
courting birds. The women like to be sung to and go to bed with them. I
have seen much, but never a good husband who was a tenor. I have sometimes thought my husbands loved me so much that they died. That is a
pleasant memory to have of them. It keeps me warm at night; not as warm

as they did, but warm. And there has been much talk and scandal about me which was bad at the time, but is good now. It makes me laugh. Magtig, how I have been admired!

"Get that one over there, Titus," she shouted. "And do not take the kleinkies. The little ones must be allowed to grow.

"When you are married, Lena, I will tell you some of the things men have said to me. When you are married, we will have many talks of love and men. There are things I would tell you that are not seemly now. Men are strange—like animals, at once infuriating and beautiful and stupid. My God," she said, "only a woman can ever know the stupidity of men— not only of tenors, but of all men. It is unbelievable, but we get pleasure from them. Sometimes I think our only pleasure is to go to bed with a man." She looked at Lena. "Perhaps I should not have said that to you yet. Nevertheless, it is good all the same to sleep with a man. It is also good to eat, to sing, to drive good horses and make the sick well.

"That will do," she shouted to Titus; "put them in the sack and come to this tree." They went towards a small grey-leaved tree. "Cut off the branches, Titus," Tanta Martha said.

"Yes, my child, there are many good things in the world, and though I am not the kind of cook who praises her own cooking, I cannot help telling you how happy I have been. Nor can I help giving you such wisdom as has come to me. There are things you should know, my heart, and one of them is that a buck hanging by its legs from a tree is worth two that still run on them."

Tanta Martha was always like this with her sayings, her proverbs, her texts, her anecdotes, her gossip, and her wisdom. Lena remembered it from her childhood, never changing and always changing. She remembered in early days, when her father had taken her to see Tanta Martha, how Pa had laughed at her and with her. She had been just as fat then : just as happy. She had always seemed placid in an active fashion, quick to act in an emergency, but unperturbed as she acted. But now Lena saw that there was something underneath all those jokes and sayings. Pa had recognized it and now she recognized it herself.

Tanta Martha spoke brightly to her, said things to make her and others laugh, but she was a woman of great depths. Her smiles, her laughter, her jokes sometimes not in the best of taste, were the way she had of meeting a world which accepted her at her face value. Her jokes and stories of her husbands were a disguise for the way she missed them. Her ministering to the sick and the hurt, both in mind and body, was a way of using the vast mass of her affections, spreading them thinly over the whole world because there was no one on whom she could spread them thickly.

Perhaps there was even a similarity between Ouma and Tanta Martha. They had lived through the same times, seen the same things; and what they had seen and suffered had affected each according to her nature. If you looked at Tanta Martha when she thought herself unobserved, her face looked very different. Lena thought of the way her face had been set yesterday on the drive back from the battle. It was this that had been the bond between her and Pa. Both were gay because at heart they were more serious than others. Both were kind because, more than others, they saw the brutality of life in which one thing preyed continuously on another; where, though there was little happiness, there were always men ready to destroy that little out of jealousy. She remembered a story of her father's about a man who had killed his neighbour's dog because he had a better farm than he. They saw all this just as they saw more beauty in life than others. They simply saw more and cared more.

She was helping Tanta Martha strip the grey leaves from the branches Titus brought them. They were pulling them off and putting them in a muslin bag that Tanta Martha had brought out of the pocket of her petti-coat. She had found a rock to sit on. The rock was hot. You could feel it through your skirts. Tanta Martha said :

" It is good to sit on a hot rock. What the animals do is good for us too, Lena. The baboons sit on hot rocks, and the birds, and the lizards, and the snakes. There is virtue in it from the heat on your hinder end. But never sit on a cold wet rock or put a child on one. That is the first thing I learnt of children, and you will do well to remember it against the day you have yours. Never put a hot baby on a cold rock, Lena, and never listen to what others tell you of children. Feed them full, keep nits from their hair, worms from their bowels, and let them run on the veld. They they will grow up strong, good, and wise."

How suddenly I have learnt to understand things! Lena thought. It all came from the night of Dirk's going, when he had . . . when he loved me . . . she hesitated in formulating the words . . . and from the battle yesterday. For the first time she understood her Tanta Martha and the parables in which she talked, mixing foolishness with wisdom so that you had to scratch for it, as a fowl scratched for grain in the chaff of a threshing.

The bag was half full. Their fingers moved on the branches stripping off the leaves. Tanta Martha's fat ones, Titus's black ones—he was helping them now—and her own. Tanta sat up straight and put her hands on her knee, folding them the one over the other so that they looked like two little lumps of dough on her lap.

" This is a hard time for all, Lena, and you have only seen the beginning. It may come that we are separated by war, by circumstance, by illness, or even death," she said. " So listen to me. Life is not something to be avoided. It must be taken, and it is useless to fight against it as your grand-mother does. Nor is it good to try to change things or to endeavour to explain them. Invert not the appointed order of things, Lena, nor be curiously trifling; but suffer a man to be beautiful as a man; and a woman as a woman; a deformed man, to be deformed as a man. Therefore, curl not your locks nor pluck the hair from your legs. Leave such things, they have a natural course. Another hath care of such things." She looked up at the sky and paused.

What a strange woman she was! What did she mean by these words? Still looking up, but lower so that she looked out over the farm, Tanta Martha went on :

"Are all horses swift? All dogs sagacious? Neither is a bull, nor a gallant-spirited man formed all at once. A man," she said, "should be neat as a man; a woman as a woman; a child as a child. If not, let us pluck out the mane of a lion that he may not be slovenly. And the comb of a cock; for he ought to be neat too. Yes, he should be neat, but let it be as a cock; and a lion as a lion; and a hound as a hound. Anything but this is impious, an affront to the Almighty God who created all things. To change them is to deny their creator; to change them is to know better than God . . ."

"What is this, Tanta Martha, that you have just said? What does it mean?"

"I do not know fully, Lena. It is something I learnt from Meneer Tryolla. He made it into our language for me and I learned it. It seemed very beautiful to me, and very wise. I think of those words when I wish to change things, which is often, and it gives me comfort. That is why I tell it to you, that it may comfort you too, for these are days when we must wish all things changed . . . days when nothing seems good." She smiled. "And I will tell you something else before I go, Lena. You will have trouble with Oupa."

"You mean he will be ill?"

"Not for long. He is ill now. It is when he is well you will have trouble. It is in my heart that he will be like a hawk whose wings were cut that has suddenly found himself with new, strong pinions. From being an old man who could think of nothing but his great past, he has become a hero of the present, and therefore his mind will turn to the future. Having done so much he will wish to do more."

"But what can I do?" Oupa a hawk, when he had always seemed a baby . . .

"You can do nothing. If you thwart him, he will be ill. If you don't thwart him, he may kill himself, but he will be happy. And Reuter can take care of him. I have spoken to Reuter," she said. "I have also spoken to your grandmother. You can come and see me whenever you wish. You must have someone to speak to in these times. So come to me, and speak also to Boetie, Dirk's brother, for being blind he is passionless and his head is clear."

On the way back to the house, Tanta Martha stopped to pluck the tops from some weeds on the path.

" What are those?" Lena asked.

" The name I do not know," Tanta Martha said, " but they are just what I was looking for. I will make them up in a ball with fat and give them to Oupa before I go. They are a wonderful, slow-working purge that will keep him quiet for a week, since they will allow him no time to brood. Ja," she said, " it is an excellent plant and has only one objection—it does not keep and must be gathered fresh each time."

" He will not take it," Lena said.

" Yes, he will take it, Lena. If he will not, I will put a twitch on his ear and hold him like a horse . . . Seacow!" she said. " I will teach him about seacows."

Tanta Martha had gone two days ago. Oupa was still sick and more fractious than Lena had ever known him, but quiet, only grumbling instead of cursing and swearing. Tanta Martha's medicine was still working. Her grandmother would not speak to him, or of him, except to say that he had disgraced them. Even the peacocks, which generally gave Lena so much pleasure, failed to satisfy her now. They seemed stupid birds : vain and ridiculous. She had taken the new shoes out of their box several times to look at them. She had shaken out her new dress in the sunshine and folded it carefully in the chest again. There seemed to be nothing to do but wait. She was as busy as ever. There were many things to attend to—the making of butter, even the supervising of the boys on the lands and the dosing of sick cattle and sheep—but they failed to occupy her. They were things you knew so well that you did them with your body, your hands. Even your tongue spoke the right words at the right time, gave orders, as your ears heard things, reports from the fields and kraals that you answered while wondering how you could be so intelligent when your mind and heart were not there. You went through the days as a buck trots over the veld, passing through them, seeing them in front of you and leaving them behind.

There was little news. Pretoria was said to be besieged; there had been fighting at Potchefstroom; but there was no real news. News, to Lena, meant news of Dirk. She was at war with herself, for in her heart she said, I do not care if the whole world falls to pieces so that I get Dirk and he is safe; while her mind said : You are a Boer woman, and if it is necessary for the freedom of your people you must give your man as the others have given their fathers, sons, husbands, lovers. It is they who must fight for the unborn children of your unborn children, they who must fight that the nation may be free.

For Lena, the farm had died. She missed her brothers. She did not love Stoffel, but his chair and Louis's that were always against the wall now drove home the hole their going had made in her life. Louis, though he spoke so seldom, she loved. Having him there was like having a great reliable dog near you, very comforting; and above their absence and the silence it caused, and the space in her life that could not be filled, was the knowledge that Dirk was gone; that he would not come riding in on Swartkie when his work was done; that for the time being he was gone from her; that often she must, in the press of events upon his life, be out of his mind for hours together.

And always it was Dirk. Everything was Dirk, though she might pretend sometimes to herself that it was her brothers. And in a way it was her brothers. Their absence, their chairs against the wall, would not let her forget for an instant. If Dirk came back, her brothers need not. That was a terrible thought. But she would hate her brothers if they came back and Dirk was killed. Many are called and few are chosen, she thought. But he might be among the chosen. There would be many empty saddles before it was over. There would be horses led back to the farms by the friends of the dead men, by their brothers and fathers : tired horses trotting behind men, horses with heads outstretched, their stirrups crossed over the empty saddles.

In her room she had the stick Dirk had thrown. It was in water. It was growing. It had leaves coming on it, and little white roots, like hairs, were growing from its base. Soon she would plant it in a pot. That it was growing seemed to her a sign. It was wonderful, but at the same time terrible. Suppose it stopped growing. Suppose the leaves—they were so pale and fragile—began to wither and the roots to rot.

Oupa, who should have been a comfort to her, was petulant when she helped him to bed and sulky when she spoke to him. He argued, he complained about Tanta Martha's betrayal of him. He wanted brandy in his milk—not just once, but twice a day. He refused his pap unless it was laced; demanded meat, and then when she gave it to him he was sick, which made him angrier still.

But the days passed. Merging into each other without reality they moved in an endless, dull, and meaningless procession. One day it would end and she would be happy. But she wanted happiness now, much more than future freedom for her people; and yet again what was life without freedom? So she swayed back and forth in battle against herself as she went about her tasks. The fresh cream must be mixed with the old so that it would all be of one consistency when it was churned; bread must be made; there were five motherless lambs to be hand-reared; there were skins of dead beasts to be breyed; a furrow broken here; a roof to be mended there—and no one to advise. Oupa would talk of nothing but his charge, which he considered his finest exploit and the one by which he was most likely to be remembered; and the profound indignity of his purging that gave him no rest.

But what had these things to do with a girl who wanted her lover's arms about her? Who wanted the feel of his rough jacket against her, the smell that was so particularly his own in her nostrils; who wanted to see the sun glint on the golden down of his beard. Who wanted it now . . . now . . . at once. Just once more. If only I could see him once more, she thought, as she stirred the cream. Pale yellow and thick it clung to the long wooden spoon. She wiped the handle with her forefinger and licked it clean.

There were more pans of milk to be skimmed on the stone shelf beside her. The floor was wet with water and there was an opalescent milky puddle by her feet. She covered the big cream crock with muslin to keep out the flies and poured more water into the wooden churn. It had to be kept full when not in use. She wrinkled her nose at the sour-sweet smell of the dairy. Women were always smelling things. They lived in a world of special smells—of milk and cream, of cooking, of preserving, of washing and ironing, of wood smoke.

A woman knew every house smell: the smell of a baby, of a man, of cooking meat, of burning sugar, of dust, of bedrooms, of the tobacco smoke the men left behind them when they went out, of wet clothes drying, of dogs that came in from hunting, of newborn motherless lambs set beside the kitchen fire, of kittens and puppies in a box: the smell of things and the feel of things on their hands—of dough as you made bread, of butter as you forced it into the moulds, of raw meat, of children's hair and men's . . . In the gloom of the dairy Lena thought of so many things that she had never thought of before, saw many things that she had not seen before: the words of her dead father and Tanta Martha that had taken roots so many years ago were bearing flowers in her mind and heart.

She turned to see her grandmother at the door.

" You have been here a long time," she said.

" I have been stirring the cream," she said.

" Yes, you have been stirring cream. As a girl, I too stirred cream. There is no Boer woman who has not stirred it."

She put her hand on her arm. Lena could not remember such a thing happening before.

" You have been here long enough, Lena. They will come back," she said.

She turned away. Lena followed her. So Ouma knew. She also felt things, but could not say them.

When they were in the house, Ouma said: " Go and lie down. You need rest. One day I will tell you many things. It will be hard for me, for my heart has been frozen fast so long, but one day I will tell you." She gave her a push.

Everybody was going to tell things—Tanta Martha, Ouma, and Oupa; but they could not tell her the one thing she wanted to know. Where was Dirk? When would he come back?

She lay down and watched the flies on the ceiling. They circled and came to rest without reason or system. Yet she felt they had reason and system.

She thought of the flies at Tanta Martha's . . . of Netta and the way she had looked at her. In some way that coloured girl had known about Dirk—about what had happened under the blue gums that night.

Tanta Martha had said : Go and see Boetie, he has understanding. She would go soon : to-morrow. He had more than understanding. He was Dirk's brother. There was something in him of Dirk that pulled at her heart.

Katarina du Toit sat on the stoep, her fingers moved against each other in little circles. Why had she spoken as she had to Lena? What had come over her to promise that she would speak? Why undo the work of years? Why open old wounds again? I acted on impulse, she thought. Then she wondered how many years it was since she had done that. It was the war . . . always a war of one kind or another. Always the English. Never any peace, any rest . . . And how long would it go on?

In some obscure way she felt that by suffering discomfort herself she eased Stoffel's burdens on commando. She worked harder; she ate less. She had given up coffee, her only luxury, pretending suddenly to think that it was bad for her. Day after day went by without news, with nothing to hearten her but her prayers to God, and her hatred, now boiling, for the English, who, on top of all that they had done to her people, had now taken her grandsons from her side. My grandsons, she thought. If it had been possible I would have given my husband and my sons. But still she hated them for having taken her grandsons; more particularly her grandson Stoffel. Heaven must be filled with the men and women and children who had directly or indirectly been killed by the English.

As she moved about the house and outsheds, as she worked, as she sewed, they were all round her—a company of ghosts visible to her alone. A company that whispered strange things in her ears, that told strange stories, reviving memories that she thought dead : of the hanging at Slagtersnek; of the men hanged, who had come so often to her father's house, men on whose knees, horselike, she had ridden as a child; thoughts of her father, old Rudolf; of Kaspar, whom she had called uncle; of others—Hendrik ven der Berg, of Herman his son, Swart Piet du Plessis. Before God, the death of all these and many more lay at their door : Frederik Bezuidenhout, Jappie de Jong, more men and women than one could count on the fingers of one's two hands, and these only the ones that she had known intimately and well. Like dogs her people had been driven from their places ever farther into the wilds, but separately or in little family groups. Only now were they united and of one heart. Only now had they turned, driven to bay by the endless pursuit of a foreign nation.

Sometimes she thought that no one but she understood real hatred. What the others felt and spoke of was lukewarm, was like water to the acid of her hate. Indeed they spoke more of love than hate; spoke more of how much they cared for their privacy, their way of life, and their dislike of interference than of their hatred of oppressors. They did not see that hatred was stronger than love; that it was like steel, cold, sharp, and implacable. Yet there were some who, like her and her Stoffel, would go until the English were driven into the sea from which they had come. Then, then only, when they were gone and the land was free, would it be time enough to talk of the love one bore one's country, for then it would be proved.

Now one could not love it. One could not love a thing defiled. To-day Africa was a virgin raped; strange hands roamed over her secret places. Strange men, speaking a foreign tongue, came with gold to buy such favours as they could not snatch. They wanted her body and soul; to rule, to exploit, to use; and all that stood between them and their wish were the commandos in the field and the burning, bitter hearts of the women on the farms. A small people, Boers—farmers, but a race that believed in God and worshipped Him, not perfunctorily once a week, but daily, each time that they broke bread; upon waking, before they slept; and who praised His glories while they worked : a small, but chosen people, and mighty in their faith. She sewed savagely, as though each stitch was a bayonet thrust into an English heart.

How happy she had been as a little girl before the English had come to the Border and killed her Uncle Frederik! How happy on the Baviaans River with her dolls and toys and her great cock Paulus! How her mind kept going, now more than ever, back to the past! To her childhood; to Aletta whom she had loved, and to Stephanie whom she had hated. Aletta lived in Brennersdorp now, but she hardly ever saw her, but she had been glad when Tanta Martha told her she was well. To see her reminded her of too much. It was one thing to remember and another to be reminded. When you remembered, you chose what you would out of the past. Infinitely selective, your mind picked and chose among the days, taking this day and leaving that one.

One thing that had remained with her was her love of poultry. No one had such poultry as she; no one had such a variety. All her life she had collected strange hens. Whenever she found one that was different she bought it. She had one from the East; it was white with feathers that were like silk hair, and had bright blue wattles; she had two with long feathers on their legs that looked as if they wore trousers; she had some with a mop of feathers on their heads that almost covered their eyes, and some with lumps under their chins like goitres—but she had no cock that could compare with Paulus that had been killed the day that the English hanged those burgers of the Great Fish River at Slagtersnek.

She thought of the trek North with Tanta Letta and Kaspar van der Berg . . . of Old Oom Christiaan. How they had suffered up there in

the wilds from fever, Kaffirs, and wild beasts! Then Johannes du Toit
had come riding out of the South. He had been hunting elephants and
had stopped at the farm to pass the time of day. When he had left a week
later, she had gone with him, travelling at his side till they found a predikant
to marry them. Then the Great Trek. Johannes had been one of the men
that guided it. Paul Kruger . . . He was a leader now. She remembered
him well—a thick-set, strong-willed boy. She thought of Hendrik van der
Berg, a cousin of her stepfather Kaspar; of Sannie his wife—the one that
they called the Lily of the North : a harlot and a byword; of Jacoba, her
daughter, who was Lena's mother. She thought of the massacre at Canaan;
of the death of Sannie and her lover, Swart Piet the slave trader; of old
Tanta Anna de Jong, and Jappie, and Louisa, his concubine, that Anna
had passed on to Tanta Martha when she died; of Rinkals, the witch
doctor.

How long ago it was! How long ago, but even then she had hated
Philippus Jacobus, her father-in-law, hunter, braggart, and fornicator.
Some spoke ill of Hendrik van der Berg, but he had been a religious man
who, over-tempted and deceived by his wife, had fallen. But her father-in-
law had never waited to be tempted. He had married wife after wife, killed
them with his attentions, and left bastards in every kraal from the Limpopo
to the lowlands of Natal.

And all that time the English had been pressing upon them, sending
missionaries and traders among them as spies, sending officers up to hunt
in their lands and map them, fomenting trouble with the Kaffirs they had
subdued, and seducing such of their own folk as they could. Even to-day
there were Boer traitors, men who preferred the English rule, who saw
advantage in the new ways, who preferred the Mammon of the English to
the God of their fathers, who liked the English ways, English clothes,
English customs. Particularly was this so at the Cape, where the old
families had succumbed to them, even marrying them, and giving them
their daughters in marriage.

And now she had promised to tell Lena all this and more. To tell her the
story of her life, of the death of her sons and the persecutions of her race.
She wondered what had come over her to make such a promise. On the
other hand, the girl must be told. She was going to marry Dirk. She would
have children. The stories must be passed on. Hatred must not be permitted to die out. She must tell all—all, no matter how it hurt her : no
matter how her heart bled. The thread of that hatred must be passed on
by the women; it must get stronger, not weaker, as the years passed and
the people grew in numbers. Eventually, when there were enough of
them, men and boys imbued with hatred, they would drive the English
out and regain their land. They might do it now. They had had one
victory and there were rumours of others, but the spirit must be kept alive

in her people, lest they worm their way back after the war, and it must be done by the women. Tanta Martha had told Lena things, so had Oupa, and her father before he died. But what they had told her was not sharp enough. They had tempered the wind of their hatred, blunting its edge, turning it into a dislike, almost humorous in its toleration, for their strange godless ways.

She picked up her sewing again. Lena loved Dirk. Dirk would give her sons, but she, her grandmother, would give her the sacred spirit that must dedicate them. That is why I must speak, she thought, breaking the silence of these years. But not yet. The time is not yet come. She thought of how well she had succeeded with Stoffel and how ill with Louis. She must succeed with Lena, for in this women were more important than men. Hatred must be taught to the young while they were babies, while they clung to your skirts. If you did that, they never forgot. That was why she had failed with Louis and how she had brought Stoffel to her mind. He had been left with her one winter when he was four years old and too sick to go with his family to hunt in the Bushveld. She sighed. It might be hard with Lena, she had so much of her father in her, and he had been a weak, kindly man.

Tanta Martha was right to tell me to go to Doornkloof, Lena thought, as she drove up to the house. She looked up at the mountain. There were Boetie's goats. He must be up there, but Tanta Johanna would send a picannin up to fetch him. Dirk's mother was at the door to meet her. She was holding Klein Johanna in her arms.

Tanta Johanna waved her hand. The child waved a fat little hand, the dogs ran out barking. It was good to see Doornkloof again. It was Dirk's home, he had been brought up here. In a minute she would go inside and be among the things he had known all his life. To do that, to see the house, and his mother and sister, and the dogs, made him real, and the fact of his return certain. She must tell his mother how he had looked when she saw him. She tried to think how he had looked. She seemed hardly to have noticed anything about him except that he was thinner, his eyes harder and tired-looking. They had sunk deeper into his face and looked bigger, and their expression had changed. But could she tell his mother this? How would she put it into words, since she had never really thought it out to herself? It would be best just to say that he looked well, but was thinner. Men were bound to get thinner in war, and as to the rest, his mother would guess it without being told or she would not guess, and anyway she would see it when he returned.

Lena waved her whip. The baby was shouting: "Tanta Lena . . . Tanta Lena." That sounded funny to her. But it was so. Soon she would be Klein Johanna's aunt.

Johanna van der Berg was smiling. How tired she looked, and anxious!
" It was good of you to come, Lena," she said as the cart drew up. " You
will outspan?" she asked. " You can stay a while?"

" I will stay," Lena said.

Willem went to the horses' heads and led them to the side of the house.
When she sat down, Lena felt happier than she had for many days. Dirk
was with her here. He had sat on these chairs. He had eaten at this table.
She put out her hand to touch it. His mother came in with cups and the
coffee-pot. She brought spoonful milk and sugar, then she sat down and waited
We are both waiting for the other to begin, Lena thought. We are both
thinking of him; both tied to him by our womanhood, which is common
to him. She brought him forth and to me he has entered and I will bear his
sons. So that we are one. We are the women of two generations and he is
the man that links us. Because we know this, we are silent in the face of
such a mystery . . . the mystery of man and woman . . . male and female
as He created them.

" Take plenty of sugar," Tanta Johanna said. " We have a bag of it, so
there is no need to be careful."

Lena took an extra spoonful to please her. Dirk's mother brought rusks
to dip in the coffee. If you held them in it too long, they melted away and
sank to the bottom. The way to do it was just to dip them and eat them
half soft and half hard. When she had been young, she played a game
seeing how long she could hold one in without melting it.

Klein Johanna was playing with a doll made of rags. She held it up.

" My brother Dirk made it for me before he left to fight the English,"
she said. " Is it not beautiful?"

" It is beautiful," Lena said.

She put down her cup. " I saw him," she said to his mother.

" He is well?"

That meant, he is alive . . . he is not wounded? That was something
a woman would not ask, since by putting such a thought into words you
created danger. How well she understood things now! How suddenly it
had come! First Dirk had made her into a woman under the trees with the
star-pricked heaven above her. Then Tanta Martha had finished it, pressing home the truth on her mind as Dirk had pressed it on her body when
she gave it to him.

" I saw them both—Dirk and his father," she said. " They are well. But
Dirk is thinner." She would say nothing about his eyes or his mouth. " It
was after the battle," she said. " You heard of that? That it was on our
farm, at the top end by the spruit where the road crosses it?"

She was telling Tanta Johanna about her son and husband. She was
giving information that in some way no longer concerned her, since the
facts she gave were established. As she spoke, her mind was busy with
other things—with Dirk's love-making. Before he came to me on that

night, she thought, he sat in this room. When he was here he thought about me. She could feel it in the air of the room : the warmth of his thoughts concerning her and the ghostly shadow of his presence. Her mind was saying, Dirk . . . Dirk . . . over and over to itself. Her heart was aching for him. I want him now. I want him. She had difficulty in keeping still.

"I heard that," Tanta Johanna said, "but I am glad to have news of them . . . to hear that they are well."

She was silent again, her eyes were cloudy. She is thinking of her husband and her son, Lena thought : of how the one came to her; of how the other came forth from her womb; of how they both rode off together that morning, leaving her empty till their return.

"Let us pray for them, Lena," she said. They knelt side by side at the table.

As she prayed for Dirk, Lena kept thinking, This is the table he has eaten at all his life. Dear God, let him come back and continue eating at it . . . let things be as they were. In her heart she knew that things never could be as they were . . . not quite as they were, for already they were changed. Dirk was no longer a boy, but a man, as she had become a woman. The future might be beautiful, it would be, but they would never be a boy and girl together again. War and their making love had changed all that . . . they had eaten of the fruit. They must pay the price. Then she remembered to pray for Groot Dirk. Which did Dirk's mother pray for most, she wondered, the boy or the man . . . her husband or her son?

They got up. She felt better for having prayed, but ashamed that she had almost forgotten to pray for his father. It had been an afterthought when she had prayed all things possible for Dirk.

"I have sent for Boetie," Tanta Johanna said. "The boy I sent to fetch him can watch his goats and bring them down in the evening. He would be unhappy if he missed you, for he loves you greatly. He always wants to see you and likes to talk to you."

"Yes, I must see him," Lena said. That was the reason she had come. "I love him because he is Dirk's brother and he loves him, but I love him for himself also."

"He says you are beautiful, Lena."

"I am glad he thinks so," Lena said.

"And he is right. Without eyes he sees more than many who have them. Sometimes I am afraid for him, afraid he will come to harm."

She is thinking that if anything happened to the others she will still have Boetie. She is almost glad that he is blind and cannot be taken from her, Lena thought.

"And sometimes I am afraid of him," his mother went on. "He knows too much. He says things that I do not understand."

"His is a different world from ours," Lena said. "Though things are dark for him, it must be very beautiful. He sees only good, and it shows in his face."

"Only good, Lena. And what is to happen to a boy who sees only good?" Lena put her hand on her shoulder to comfort her. "Do not fear, daughter," Tanta Johanna said. "I am strong. I shall not weep, for I am wept dry. That is one of the things Boetie knows, though he has never seen or heard me. There is nothing left for us now but to pray and to hope and to wait. It is harder for you, for you have had nothing, and it is new to you. But I have waited through other wars for my man, but never for my son as well, before."

"It is for us they fight," Lena said. Her eyes were fixed on the wooden cradle in the corner of the room.

"Ja, for us. But if they die fighting, how will it help us? This is not a Kaffir war," she said, "where all must fight or all be slain. This is a political war that should have been fought with words. What have dead men, English or Boers, to do with this matter?"

"The English have stolen our land," Lena said. It did not sound very convincing to her as she said it. For they were still on Mooiplaas, and Doornkloof was as it had always been. Still, there was the Volksraad, there was the Vierkleur, the beloved flag, and the broken promises, but . . .

"Yes, the English are wrong, and it may be that we will drive them into the sea. But what then? Many will be dead. We shall have revenged old injustices by many new ones, and some of the English must be good men. There was one who stayed here for a night. He was riding a fine red horse and when he left, he gave Boetie a beautiful knife with a cork-screw, a sharp-pointed instrument, two blades, and a pick for getting stones out of horses' feet. He was kind and gentle. And besides, it is said that many in England are against this war."

"But what can we do?"

"Nothing. It has begun. Yet it is in my heart that women should do something to save men from their foolishness."

"Some are more bitter than the men," Lena said. She thought of Ouma.

"I have no answer for you, Lena. I am but a woman. I do not understand politics and freedoms and flags. I would live my life with my husband and my sons."

The dogs which had been lying on the floor got up with cocked ears. Lena heard music. The dogs ran out of the house.

"It is Boetie," she said, "he is coming."

That was the sound of his music, that always preceded him. You often heard the blind boy before you saw him. They went to the door together. Tanta Johanna put her arm round Lena's waist. Klein Johanna pushed her head out between their skirts grasping their legs with her hands. Then she squeezed past them and ran towards her brother. The dogs were with him already, jumping up at him. Round him, behind and before him as he marched, was a drifting tide of white, black, brown, and yellow goats. At his side walked a big white billy whose horns, twisted like a koodoo's, reached his shoulders. The music came louder and louder, as gay as a bright plume, rising and falling as he piped his flute. The boy who had been sent to fetch him walked behind the last goat. He carried a kid in his arms that its mother kept trying to reach with her nose. It must have just been born. Johanna was holding on his belt and trying to keep the dogs from knocking her down and the big goat from stepping on her bare feet.

As he drew level with them, Lena shouted: "I am glad to see you, Boetie."

He took his flute from his mouth, shook it, and said: "It is good to see you, Lena. I came at once when I heard that you were here."

"And the goats," his mother said; "I told Hezekiah to herd them till evening."

"That is what he said, Ma. But when I heard the news that Lena was here I had to play for gladness, and when I play the goats come. So we are all here. It will not hurt them to be kraaled early . . . And there is a new kid."

He laughed, put his pipe to his mouth and played again. The goats moved after him, their feet raising a dust as they rattled on the hard ground. They passed . . . Hezekiah passed, carrying the young kid; its mother passed, still nuzzling at him.

Lena turned back to the house with Tanta Johanna. There were tears in her eyes. She could not think why she should cry, but something had moved her deeply: the boy marching as straight as a soldier with his shoulders thrown back . . . the stream of goats coming homeward with the great dark mountain behind them . . . the child holding on to her brother's belt . . . the mother goat reaching towards her kid . . . and the music so gay that it hurt, so happy that it made you sad.

She helped Tanta Johanna put away the cups and wash them. More coffee was added to the coffee-pot and it was put on the back of the fire. The sugar bowl was covered with a muslin square hung with beads, to keep the flies out of it. The milk was poured into a bowl for the dogs. Chairs were straightened. Without knowing it, we are doing all those things that women do, Lena thought; moving things from one place to another, washing things that have been soiled. How ineffectual a woman's life was—a never-ending round of doing things, of washing things that would soon be soiled again. It was stupid, it was dull. Yet there was a strange comfort in it, and it did no one any harm. That seemed important now—to live so that you hurt no one.

The horses were being put in. It was time to go, and she had not seen Boetie.

" You'll find him at the kraal with Johanna," his mother said. " At least I think you will."

" Then I will look there. But I will say good-bye to you now."

" Good-bye, my daughter. It was good of you to come. Come often. His home is yours."

" Thank you, Tanta Johanna," Lena said. " His home is mine and his mother too." She flung her arms round her neck.

The dogs—they had come back after accompanying Boetie—crowded round them sympathetically, looking at them with soft brown eyes and slowly wagging tails. They know, Lena thought. That is why they stay so close. Their master is away and they watch. Tanta Johanna still held her and patted her. It was wonderful how one could think of many things at once . . . could do one thing, and think of another . . . speak of one thing, while you thought of another.

" It will end one day," Tanta Johanna said and kissed her. " And tell Boetie to bring in his sister when you see him."

Lena left her and went out. The horses were inspanned and tied to a tree half-way between the house and the kraal. She walked past them. They turned their heads towards her. They are getting tired and want to go home, she thought. But first she must see Boetie. He had come down from the mountain to see her.

She looked about. There he was. He was sitting with Johanna near the gate of the kraal. He was playing with her. She went towards them softly. Johanna saw her coming and she was sure Boetie heard her, but they took no notice. They were absorbed in their game. Between them was a small clear space of ground that they had swept clean with their hands, and on it were a number of round stones, polished from use, and of various colours. Sometimes Johanna moved one and sometimes Boetie, first feeling with his hands to find out what move she had made, would move another. Johanna seemed very happy, looking first at the stones, then at her brother, then back at the stones.

" What are you playing, Boetie?" Lena asked.

" We are playing the game of stones."

" How do you play it?" There seemed to be no marks on the ground or system about their moves.

" It is very complicated, Lena," Boetie said. " Only Johanna can play it."

" Only me," Johanna said. " They are Boetie's stones. He finds the ones that are beautiful and then we play the game of stones—just him and me."

" You are going now, Lena," Boetie said.

" Yes, I am going."

He got up. " I brought Johanna here so that you could be alone with Ma. It will be good for them to be alone, I thought. They are my brother's women, his mother and his wife."

"Not yet," Lena said. She must give him Dirk's message. "I saw him." she said.

"You saw Dirk?"

"Yes, and your father. That is what I came to tell your mother; that they are well." She thought again of Dirk's thinness and the look in his face. "He said : 'Give my love to Boetie and tell him not to forget he is the man on Doornkloof now.'"

"Who said it, my father or my brother?"

"Both said it," Lena said. But it had been only Dirk. She had hardly spoken to his father.

"Boetie is the man at Doornkloof now," Johanna said. "He takes care of us : him and the dogs. We are not frightened with Boetie and my father's dogs."

Boetie put out his hands. He ran them over her as he had done that other time when she told him she was going to marry Dirk. Over her face, her neck, her breasts, her waist, her hips and legs. His hands were round her ankles as he finished on his knees before her. He stared up at her with clear blue eyes. "You are thinner," he said; "still beautiful, but thinner. We miss them, do we not?" Then he said : "But I am glad you are thinner. If you were not you would not love him."

"I am going home now," Lena said.

"Kiss us," Boetie said, "and come back soon."

She kissed him. Johanna was jumping up and down to be kissed. Lena picked her up.

"I love you, Tanta Lena," she said.

"I love you too." How hard it was to talk like this, to finish and get away! She wanted to be alone and think of Dirk, but she wanted to remain because these were Dirk's family and she was one of them.

"Good-bye," she said. "I will soon be back."

"Come soon," they said.

"Soon," she said. She was walking to the horses. They raised their heads again; one of them whinnied. They were restless, moving their feet and switching their tails. She got into the cart. Willem climbed in beside her when she had the reins. The horses started forward, one before the other, shaking the cart, then they pulled together. She was on her way home again. All the way she would think of Dirk. Here was another road that belonged to someone. As the road from Mooiplaas to the dorp belonged to her father, this road from Doornkloof to Mooiplaas now belonged to Dirk. She thought of the table in the house where he ate and at which they had prayed. She had seen his bed through an open door. That's his bed where he sleeps, she thought. Then she thought of the sun on the soft, golden down of his beard . . . of his mother . . . of his sister . . . of the dogs and goats . . . of Boetie playing the game of stones with his sister while he waited for the war to end . . . of Boetie, the man of Doornkloof.

And she had been going to try to teach him the tune the English band had played. . . . *Kiss me, darling.* . . . *Kiss your darling daughter*. How stupid she had been to think she could even hum it to him once when her throat had been closed with tears!

CHAPTER XV

"I WILL PAY VISITS . . ."

I

OUPA sat on the stoep; except for the purges Tanta Martha had forced on him—they were much too powerful for so old a man, and the bitter taste the first one had left in his mouth had lasted for days—there was much to be said for this life. Even Kattie had been silenced, dumbfounded by his exploit. As a matter of fact, when he thought it over he was dumbfounded himself. I certainly owe a lot to that red horse of Louis's, he decided. He thought of van der Merwe's red-headed wife again—what a devil of a woman, hot as a poker; but he had owed her a lot, too, until she had killed him.

The thing to know with red horses and red women was when to get off. That was where he was so remarkable : his judgment; he always knew where to stop. And they gave him brandy now; good brandy. It was French, not dop. That was thanks to Martha, and made up, almost, for the purge which had been, he was forced to acknowledge to himself, excellent in its purpose, though destructive to his dignity. A man should not be purged like a child; he boiled with rage at the thought. Like a child, indeed! He had been drenched like a horse. He had had a bolus thrust down his throat like a dog. On the other hand, a child could not be given brandy like a man, so in the end things levelled up; and if in order to get brandy it was necessary to be purged, then he would have the purge, since it was, in his case at least, the reverse side of the brandy—the other side of the medal. The purge had been very bad, but the brandy very good. Such paradoxes proved that there were such things as Providence and justice. Also that whatever you obtained you had to pay for, either before or after.

But what a ride it had been! What a ride! And it took skill to fall from a galloping horse as he had without hurting himself. You had to have fallen many hundred times to do that. Any fool could ride, but to fall off took a horseman. But he wished more people could have seen him; after all, what was a commando of two hundred men? A thousand should have seen me, he thought.

He was much better now : much better than any one except Reuter knew. If they knew how well and strong I am, he thought, they might stop the brandy, or give me worse brandy. And he wanted to get stronger still. Before long, in a few days he would exercise his authority, but to do that he must be very well indeed. Meanwhile, there were the compensations of illness to be enjoyed. He was allowed to have his gun at his side as he sat on the stoep. It was there behind him leaning against the wall. They were giving him meat, special pieces cut very fine, and every half-hour someone came to ask how he felt and what he wanted. He always wanted things, even when he did not want them, and by evening he had a collection on the ground by his chair.

And there had been visitors, other very old men from farms who had heard what he had done; boys, women who brought him this and that: a shawl, a pot of konfyt, a fat chicken. And when the Kaffirs passed going about their work on the farm, they pointed to him with their thumbs. He knew what they were saying. "There sits the Old Baas . . . the Groot Baas . . . Aaii, what a man is the Old Baas!" They spoke of him again by his native name, "The Destroyer." That was what they had called him in the old days.

"The Destroyer, that's me," he said to Reuter.

"Ja, Baas. The Baas is an old devil, so all men say.'

"A devil, you skelm?"

"A devil to destroy, that's what the Baas is—he destroys everything : lions, elephants, buffalo, tigers, rhinoceros, kameels, countless buck of every species, Kaffirs in the wars beyond counting, and now, in his old age, white men. Ja, the Old Baas is a devil to destroy. He is well named."

"Do they say that in the kraals, Reuter?"

"That is what they say and more."

Reuter turned up his foot to examine the skin between his toes. He spent much time sitting on the ground by his master's chair looking at his feet. His assegai was leaning against the wall beside his master's gun. He put down his foot and took snuff from the brass cartridge case that hung from his neck by a string, pouring it into a little bone spoon and sniffing it up, holding first one nostril closed and then the other. He sneezed. Tears ran down his cheeks.

"It is good, Baas," he said. "It is good strong snuff."

"It is disgusting to take snuff, Reuter."

"Would the Baas have some of Reuter's snuff?" He looked round. "There is no one about."

"Give me the case."

Reuter passed it to him. Philippus put some on the palm of his hand and took a pinch and sniffed. He sneezed, choked, coughed, and spluttered. Tears ran down his cheeks.

"You are right, that is good snuff, Reuter," he said, "and a pleasant change from smoking. But it is a disgusting habit, nevertheless."

"I also like a change, Baas. To take snuff and to smoke is like having two wives. It makes a change. Yes, it is like that except that they never quarrel. Once I had six wives," he said. "Fancy that . . . I was very foolish and extravagant in the flower of my youth. But fancy paying sixty cows for six women—good cows for bad women, and it did no good. I never reaped the reward of my daughters. It was all for nothing. They would be old women now," he said, " but they were beautiful piccanins. I was lucky all six had girls. But it was for nothing," he said again. " I left them when I went to fight with Moselekatse. If I had returned, I would have been killed. Moselekatse himself spoke to us. He said : ' You must take your choice. I go to found a kingdom. Will you come with me or return to T'Chaka. If you go back, he will kill you.' I said I would stay; if I had not, Moselekatse would have let me go, loading me with gifts of captured oxen and then sent men after me to slay me. He was a very generous man to those he was about to slay. That was how the Matabele— ' those who hide behind their great shields '—came into being. They were Zulus like me and they bred with the captured women and prospered on the captured oxen.

"Aaii . . . I was a great man in those days, an induna and councillor to the King. He gave me a thousand cattle for myself. There I was Tabankulu, Captain of the Blue Horizon Regiment," he said, " Tabankulu meaning ' the great mountain.' And I had other names—Dukuduku, ' the beating heart that beats not with fear.' That was what the maidens going to water with pots upon their heads called me as they passed. How beautiful they were! Like tall, straight black bucks shining with oil in the sunshine . . . Lusikiski was another name—' the wind that whispers in the reeds.' So my enemies, those that feared me, called me, for like a wind in the reeds did I come upon them and destroy.

" I often think of those days before the Baas saved my life and made me a trousered Christian," he said. " A thousand head of cattle of my own, more captured maidens than even I could use. They made up for the six wives I had left in my kraal in Zululand, but I never counted them my wives. They were presents from the King—pretty, sleek, and gentle they were, and they tilled my fields well, but I never counted them wives, since I had got them free, a reward for my courage and services. It is in my heart a man only values a woman that he pays for. And I had paid a great price—a top price for six wives, and valued them accordingly . . . But the Baas has only had four wives."

Reuter began to count on his fingers.

" I am a Christian," Philippus said.

" Snuff and tobacco to smoke are like two good wives that are sisters. Two of my wives were sisters," Reuter said, staring out over the veld, " but I got them no cheaper, which I still consider an injustice."

" Here you are, then." Philippus gave him a handful of loose tobacco from his pocket. " And where did you get that snuff?" he asked.

" I took it, Baas. I thought the Baas would like it."

" From whom?"

"A dead Englishman on the day of the battle," Reuter said. "It was in a little paper package."

"You mean that when you were supposed to be looking for me, your master, who lay wounded on the veld, you paused to loot the dead! By God," he said, "what are you, a vulture? It comes hard to find that I have held an assvoel in my bosom for so long. . . ."

"I found very little, Baas, only the snuff. The white men had been over them first, and I did not go out of my way. I only looked in the pockets of those who lay directly in my path."

"You are bad, but it is too late to change you," Philippus said. "And now, listen well, I have a plan."

"A plan for us, Baas?"

"Yes. As soon as I am stronger we are going to show who is Baas here. Ja, we are going to leave this place and go visiting. I have been thinking of it for some time."

"Where are we going?"

"All over. We may go down into the low country. It will be good to travel again and see our friends."

"Who are our friends, Baas? Are they not all dead? Is not the Baas, like an old elephant, the last of the herd? And are not the men on the farms away?"

"That is nothing. With the men away we shall still be entertained."

"The Baas means we can get drunk?"

"I can get drunk. It is my privilege. I am white and I charged the English alone. It is only right. And as to our friends being dead, they have descendants, have they not? I am known, am I not? And I am curious to see these descendants. It may be that theirs are no better than mine. And that would be comfort to me."

"When do we start, Baas? And how are we going to escape? . . . they watch us now. Shall we fight our way out? We could kill the mevrou and take the klein meisie with us."

"No, you fool. That is what I am telling you. By this great act of mine I have regained status. That they give me good brandy proves it. I shall get up one day and say : ' I am taking a wagon, Kattie, and a couple of horses for myself and my achterryder . . . ' "

"You mean me?"

"Yes, you. I shall say : ' And I want two boys, and a driver. We are going visiting.' And then we will go with ribbons tied to our whipstick and the tent as if we were a wedding."

"And the English," Reuter asked. "What about them?"

"That is what the horses are for . . . we will charge them and put them to flight. Besides, we shall not meet any. I will inform myself first before I start. I do not like them."

"I do not like to charge," Reuter said. "We are too old for that sort of thing, and it is dangerous. Look what happened to the Baas. He fell off and is still sick of it."

"That is not so, Reuter. I cast myself from my horse when I found I could not turn him to charge again, so I that could shoot at them from behind a rock, but I had the misfortune to strike my head on a stone so that I was stunned for a moment. That is when you found me and spoilt everything, as is your habit."

"The Baas would have been dead if I had not found him. No one else would have bothered to seek him."

"And why did you bother? Only because without me you are lost—a masterless Kaffir, idle, useless, and heathen."

"The Baas has made me Christian and without me the Baas would be dead many times."

"And did I not save your life, Reuter."

"The Baas saved my life, but only once. He saved it first. That was a mere accident of chance as to who should save whose life first. And I am not known throughout the world as the Baas's servant. Many would be pleased to have me, for my mind is very devious with all the tricks my Baas has taught me. It can be said with truth that I am a snake in the grass and a credit to my teacher." He tapped his chest. "Who can lie like me, or steal like me? That I am old is nothing, for my head is full of knowledge." He looked at his master. "But when do we start, Baas? It would be good to travel once again."

"We start soon: as soon as I am stronger. Then I will get a little drunk and confront that woman with demands."

"Shall I get the Baas brandy now? Then we could go at once."

"Brandy? You can get brandy?"

"I can always get everything," Reuter said. "The Baas has taught me."

"Do you mean you have always been able to get it and have not done so? That you have watched me suffer for years? A snake in my bosom ... a viper, and an aasvoel! And to think I saved your life."

"The Baas means he wants brandy?"

"That is what I mean."

"The Baas shall have it. The Baas should have asked me before.

2

Reuter sat waiting for his master to wake up. He was a very annoying old man . . . unpredictable, an old devil and a sore trial to his servant and all who had anything to do with him.

The shadows were lengthening. Reuter watched the shadow of the blacksmith's shop reach out towards the big oak tree that stood near it; he watched the shadow of the oak reach out to the gums and the shadows of the gums throw a cloak over the green rounded trees of the orchard. He had done what he was commanded. And the Old Baas was an old devil and not to be trusted. That he brought brandy did not mean that it should all be drunk at once. Still, it was too late to change masters now, and if things were bad they might easily have been worse. One had one's memories of fights, and beer drinks, and women, and hunts; and one had other pleasant thoughts of the unpleasantnesses one had been able to avoid.

Suppose, for instance, the Old Baas had not saved his life. Not that that did not work two ways. Like everything else it cut on two sides like the blade of an assegai, for if his life had not been saved the Old Baas would not have got a good servant : none better, who had on other occasions saved his life many times. But if he had not been saved, then he would have been dead and missed a number of things. And if he had gone back to T'Chaka with the others . . . ? What had happened to them, to the defeated impi? Regiment after regiment had gone to its death springing into the void to make food for the royal vultures.

But the Baas was an old devil riding to war by himself like that. It took some forgiving, and there was much injustice in the fact that because you were black you could not participate in a white man's war. War should be for all. There should be no discrimination. "The old devil," he said to himself. "The old devil. I wonder if he will wake up soon. I want to talk to him." He kicked his master's foot. Philippus Jacobus moved. Reuter stopped kicking him. He moved again. Then he was awake : wide awake. He could still do that. He was still a hunter.

"I had a dream, Reuter," he said.

"Ja, Baas? The Baas has had a dream, that is remarkable."

"It was a remarkable dream. I dreamed I was hunting giraffe. A big dark bull, he was nearly black, and he kicked me." Philippus looked at Reuter. "I suppose you did not kick me?"

"Who—me, Baas? Would that be respectful? Is it right that the Baas should say such things to me after a lifetime of faithful service? Such service as he would have got from no one else. Aaii . . . aaii," he said, "this is gratitude. This is honour . . . this is justice."

"I asked, did you kick me?"

"No, Baas. I have sat like a dog at your feet watching you; like a lion lying in the long grass keeping the vultures from his kill; like a mother watching her child."

"Well, it is very strange. In my heart I think you kicked me. I have never known a kameel to kick. At least I have never known myself to get so near one as to let him."

"And the Baas has known his servant to kick him many times?"

"No, Reuter. If I had I should have beaten you. You are too slim to be caught. But I think you were tired sitting there. You wanted to talk to me. Ja, you are like a child. You want me to amuse you all the time. What is it you wanted to say?" he asked.

"Nothing, Baas. I am silenced for ever. I am ashamed . . . only . . ."

"Only what?"

"I will not say it. I will have my tongue torn out before I say another word. It can come out by the roots, and my ears and eyelids can be cut off. I can be smeared with honey and set in an antheap, and still I will speak no word. Reuter is silenced. He is now for ever dumb. But still . . ."

"Still what, you skelm, what is it?"

"Did I not perform my duty? Did I not steal brandy for the Baas so as to put courage into his heart?"

"You brought me brandy when I told you. And where is it now?" Philippus moved the karos on his knees and peered over the edge of the chair.

"It is done. I disposed of it for the Baas so that he would not be ashamed if caught with it."

"It was not done. There was some left."

"It was done."

"You drank it."

"I disposed of it for fear the Baas would be ashamed. Though his breath stinks—fui, how it stinks of spirits! The Baas smells more of brandy than a hyena of carrion."

"You call me a hyena! Get the sjambok and I will beat you."

"I said the Baas smelt of liquor. No more than that. But I am disappointed in my master. Meneer Philippus Jacobus du Toit the hunter, the fighter who betrays his servant."

"I betray no one."

"I am betrayed and silenced," Reuter said. "For ever. You have heard my last words. These are the last words of Tabankulu, who was Captain of the Blue Horizon Regiment in the time of T'Chaka. Tabankulu whom the white men call Reuter. He has been betrayed, not by women to which he is accustomed, but by his master in whom he had such faith; his master, who was a mountain under whose shelter he lived. His master who was a cow buffalo to him giving him milk and protection as to her calf, his master who was the sun and the moon and the stars to the orphaned exile. By him has Tabankulu, Captain of the Blue Horizon, been betrayed. But it is nothing, Baas," he said. "It is just the shock. I shall get over it in time, but it was like the charge of an elephant, very unexpected. By it I am struck dumb : no grave more silent, no heart more frozen, no tears more dry. Tabankulu is betrayed. He stole brandy for his master and what is his reward? He is told that he kicked his master; that he has drunk the brandy. Nothing is said of a theft which sits heavy on the soul of a Zulu captain. The Baas does not say he is sorry. He does not say : 'You stole brandy to give me courage to face that woman so that we could go free, and I disgraced you. I got drunk on it and slept the day away.' No, the Baas does not say these things. He makes his servant ashamed for his Baas."

"It is not easy to drink just right, Reuter. It is an art and I have lost practice. You must have just so much. Then comes the moment for action. It comes like a butterfly—one more drink and it is too much. But you have to recognize it as it flutters."

"Ja, that is so, Baas. It is in my heart we missed our butterfly. But we will try again."

"Ja, Reuter, we will try again."

"But it must be soon, Baas. We grow no younger. And it will be good to visit . . . And what is the Baas going to do about his breath that perfumes the evening wind so that the bucks on the veld become tipsy? The women will find out and then we will be back in the same kraal where we began."

"That is the problem that I am now considering. I will make a plan. But I think I could plan better with a mouthful of brandy—just a sopie. I suppose you have not got a sopie left, Reuter?"

"The Baas always verneuks me. My heart is soft for him," Reuter said, and handed him the bottle which he had between his legs.

Philippus drank and handed the bottle back.

Reuter held it to the light. "That was a sopie, Baas," he said. "Yes, it was a sopie. If elephants drank brandy and an elephant came along the road and said : 'Tabankulu, Captain of the Blue Horizon Regiment of Zulus in the time of T'Chaka, will you give me a sopie of brandy?' and I said : 'Meneer Elephant, I will certainly give you a sopie'—then if that were so, that is the kind of sopie, in my opinion, that the elephant would take." He put the bottle to his lips.

"I have a plan," he said as he finished it. "Baas, it is wonderful what brandy does. The Baas is right—a sopie of brandy is not only a comfort to the belly, but an inspiration to the intellect."

"It is only wonderful that you should think."

"The Baas has taught me," Reuter said. "I will take the Baas to his room . . ."

"Ja, you will take me to my room . . . ?"

"Then I will run to the meisie and ask for brandy. I will say : 'The Baas is sick, give me brandy.' She gives it to me. I bring it to the Baas."

"You bring it to me . . . ?"

"Yes, I bring it. I throw it over the Baas's head."

"First you kick me, then you throw brandy over me."

"It is for your own good, Baas. It is to save you shame and to enable us to escape."

"Ja, you throw it over me. Then you tell the meisie you have thrown brandy over me, and then things are much better . . . ?"

"On the contrary. I tell the meisie that I was so upset at your sickness that I spilt it. That will account for the way you smell."

"The meisie kisses me good-night. The Almighty knows why, but she does. She kisses me good-night and I like it."

"Then I did not spill it all, Baas, only some. The rest you drink."

"That is better, Reuter, more lifelike. That she will believe. And I had better beat you a little."

"Beat me, Baas . . . when I have thought of such a plan?"

"Ja, I will beat you. Get me the sjambok, the rhinoceros one that is bound with brass and copper wire. Naturally I must beat you to make it seem real. First for spilling the brandy, and then for having drunk so much. If you had not drunk you could never have thought of such a plan."

"Ja, Baas, I can see that now, but there is no justice. If I had seen it sooner, it would have been no use. Of what use would a plan be to explain the stink of the Baas if the Baas did not stink. And does it not say in the Christian Book that the poor man shall not be grudged the crumbs from the rich man's table? And is not the Baas a rich man owning land as far as the eye can see, and is not Reuter a poor man, his servant? And is not a sopie of brandy—that which is left over after the Baas has become drunken, which is never much—but a crumb? For if bread is the staff of life as the Baas has taught me, then brandy is the staff of the spirit, as I have found out for myself, of my own perspicacity watching the actions of the Baas and considering them at my leisure, which is why I say there is no justice nor right upon this earth, and am again struck silent as by a bolt of thunder at the ingratitude of men that becomes increasingly apparent to me.

"For forty years I have sought to find good in the Baas, going over his actions hair by hair as a baboon goes over his hide for vermin. But this is the final blow, the assegai in my throat—that the Baas I serve grudges his servant a crumb of brandy, having drunk nearly a bottle himself, and knowing full well that without his servant he would have had no brandy. Now is the sun finally sunk behind the mountains; now is the bird in my heart finally stilled; now is my tongue shrivelled between my gums.

Baas," he said, "come quickly." He picked up the gun. "Now is the moment. She is in the kitchen. I can hear her."

"You think it's safe?"

"Ja, it is safe. I will lead the Baas out of danger as I have always done. Hold me, Baas. Hold on to me. And do not paw the air like a stallion, there is but one step."

Oupa was glad to be lying on the bed again and to leave everything to Reuter. Things could be left in his hands with confidence, he had trained him well. But drunk . . . it was absurd to think he could get drunk on what he had had. His head was very clear, which proved beyond doubt his sobriety. It was only his feet that behaved in an unaccountable fashion, going this way and that. One's feet should go together, he thought, like a pair of good oxen in a yoke. If they went two ways you got nowhere. That was a profound thought.

He heard Reuter talking to Lena. He hoped he would get the brandy. There would be tears of sorrow in his eyes as he told of his anxiety, then he would get the brandy—at least, he hoped he would get it. He also hoped he would not drink it on the way. It was a good plan, but would have been unnecessary if Lena did not kiss him good-night. And after all, why did she? It was Dirk she wanted to kiss—a fine young man, though nothing compared to what he had been himself at that age. Why, even to-day, that was in his mind when he had first thought of those visits. He saw now why Kattie had made him an invalid and spread rumours of his weakness abroad so that the women no longer looked at him. But he would show her. Before God he would show that girl . . . he would come back with a fine young wife, if she was not careful—a fat sleek heifer of nineteen or twenty. That would teach her to meddle in his affairs.

Where was Reuter? Here he came. He was beside him. The glass was nearly full. He was a good boy, he had drunk no more than a mouthful. He felt his arm behind his head. That was a good smell—the mixed smell of brandy and Reuter. He was used to the smell of Reuter; he smelt like all Kaffirs, but a little different—of Kaffir flavoured with the slightly rancid mutton fat that he rubbed himself with and . . . The brandy was good. It burnt his throat as he swallowed. The glass was pulled from him; it was above him. Reuter was pouring it over his face and beard. It was cold, it stung his eyes.

"Magtig, you black bastard, you have spilt the dop!"

"Meisie . . . Meisie!" Reuter shouted. "The Baas has choked, come quickly . . . with more brandy. The Old Baas is choked, he has a spasm."

Philippus tried to get the brandy out of his eyes. Lena was bent over him. He could feel her hands and smell her. She smelt very clean and of woman. Yes, he would get married to a young girl like Lena—not so beautiful because beautiful women were a nuisance, and when you did not see very well, beauty did not matter—but soft to the touch, and one that smelt good.

"Oupa . . . Oupa, are you all right? What was it?" she asked. "Were you taken suddenly?"

"Ja, it was sudden, my heart."

"It was sudden," Reuter said. "He fell like an elephant shot below the eye with a ball that goes four to a pound. Like an elephant, the old devil," he said.

Kattie came in. Kattie would not be so easy. She came over and sniffed. "He is drunk. The old fool is drunk again. He is a disgrace to his name and race."

Oupa sat up. "A disgrace!" he shouted, "I, a disgrace? I am old, but once I was a man. And you, you old bag of bones, who talk to me in this fashion in front of a child and my servant! A woman . . . magtig, you were never even that; you are just a thing, a scorpion that my son must have found under a rock. He thought you were beautiful because he was a hunter and had seen no white women for a year. If a man has no cows, any cow seems good; if he is hungry, any meat is edible. Being without perception you fail to see that I am the pride of the Transvaal. I need care and tenderness, yet all I get in my home are insults. It is shameful, Kattie. You had better leave me before I strike you," he said. "I have always wanted to and to-day I am in the mood. And as for you, Reuter," he turned his head, "I shall certainly beat you when I am well for spilling brandy in my face."

He felt for his sjambok. Reuter should have put it down on the floor beside his bed.

"Now you have made him cry," Lena said. She sat beside him and took his head in her arms.

It was nice to have his head on her breast, and he certainly would get married. Then they would see, the lot of them. That would show them. It might be the death of him, but it would show them. His final exploit to die in the arms of a young, plump woman: his penultimate one, the charge. These things would round off his life, fulfilling it in no common fashion.

That affair of last night had gone off very well considering the difficulties of the situation, and Reuter's behaviour had been very creditable, a remarkable tribute to his teaching. But there was unquestionably a crisis coming . . . a new turn to events. He had sat idle for too long. It had been a mistake to give up his active life so soon and allow himself to be dominated by women. It was a dull business just annoying Kattie by not dying, and waiting for Lena's baby when she was not even married yet. She could not get married till the war was over and then he must wait for nine long months. No, it could not go on like this, the whole thing was negative and contrary to his character which was above all things positive—very positive. Very few men were as positive as he. That ride had done him good. It shook up my liver, he thought, and it was dull at home with a war on.

And then there was this matter of getting himself another wife. That would infuriate Kattie. Anything which indicated that you were not as dry and stiff and as devoid of juices as last year's biltong annoyed her. And Lena was no good now; she kissed him, but she did not put her heart into it. To-day she had no affection for her Oupa. She thought only of that boy, which was a sign of her ignorance. Of course there had never been a woman in his life that resembled Helena, or had taken her place in his heart, but he was exceptional, naturally monogamous and capable of only one great love. Helena had burnt him up. After her death there had been only embers in him—glow, but without a flame. With her he had been a leaping flame. But he had found out many things after her death—the fact that women were much the same, and that if you could not get one another would do. But would Lena listen to him when he told her this? When he said, if Dirk is killed you will marry another and have his children and be happy, she would not listen. No one listened to him to-day but Reuter, and even he argued and was never satisfied. Still, that had been a good plan of his and it had gone off well.

Something was moving in the potato creeper that climbed the stoep pole near his chair : a chameleon, a big one : Johnny-go-lightly, they called them : bright, unshining green. It walked very slowly, extending first one foot, then another. Along its side there was a yellow stripe, pale yellow like that of a sour lemon. Its tail was curled round the step of the creeper. As it moved, its tail became undone, sliding along with it. Never had he seen a finer chameleon. Sometimes you saw very little ones either alone or on the backs of their mothers, their tails curled round hers. That was a beautiful thing to see, he would like to see it again. The chameleon's eyes looked two ways, moving on pivots, one examined him while the other looked out over the orchard. They were cones covered with green skin that ended in the small dark eyes that were so quick to see a fly or spider. It came still nearer, walking with great precision, gripping the creeper with its two-toed feet as it advanced. He put out his hand and caught it. They were not like lizards. You could catch them easily if you were clever. In his hand it turned from green to black and blew itself up, hissing at him through its open mouth. Reuter had jumped away when he seized it. He laughed.

"You are frightened, Reuter," he said. "You, Tabankulu, Captain of the Blue Horizon, are fearful of so small a thing."

"I am not frightened, Baas. Fear I do not know : neither of men nor beasts. Nevertheless I do not like those things. They are so ugly that they offend me."

Not for anything would Reuter have touched it. Philippus smiled as it bit him. Its jaws were wide, toothless and strong. Inside that big mouth was its long sticky tongue that it could fling out like a spear. He put the chameleon back on the creeper. It ran among the leaves : it was hidden. Then he saw it again. It had changed from black to green, and was stalking another fly.

There are men like that, he thought, who change the colours of their coats—of their political jackets and their convictions as it suits them. Ja, there were chameleon men as there were men of all kinds. And men did not change in character : a Johnny-go-lightly man was always a Johnny-go-lightly man. Men do not change, he thought, no more do beasts. A greedy pup makes a greedy dog, and a bold bull calf makes a bold ox. The nature of men and beasts is clear before they are weaned, and as they are so do they remain all their lives long. This he had seen many times with both men and women, cattle, dogs, and horses. It had nothing to do with being good or bad. But it was strange that courage and generosity and gentleness were most commonly found among the biggest of their kind. It was the small dog that bit, the small bull that gored.

It was interesting to sit and think, and speculate about men and beasts and life when you were no longer young : interesting to think of the things you had done and the things you had missed. He had had a good life and it was not done yet : a life that had been both sweet and dangerous. A good life should be like that, like the opening of a bees' nest with an assegai and then licking the honey from the blade while the bees buzzed and stung you. Sweet, and dangerous, and as sharp as a spear. Sweet as honey in the tasting of it, and in retrospect when you looked back. Yes, sweet as honey on the tongue, that was what a man's life should be, but still sharp and pricked with spears.

He lit his pipe. Only now, with his experience behind him, could he fully savour his life or fully live it. Men died like trees, when their appointed season came. Some men lasted longer than others because of the goodness of their breed, or because they had been better nourished, or had put their roots down deeper into the soil of life, drawing nourishment from all things. Such a one was he.

Reuter was speaking again. You could never think for long with Reuter about ; he had to gossip like a woman.

" What is it now . . . what do you want? Am I never to have rest or peace?"

" I want nothing, Baas. I only want to know if I have been a good servant to the Baas?"

" You have been a good servant."

" Then there is something . . . Baas, I have waited for forty years for it."

" What have you waited forty years for, Reuter?"

" It is very personal. That is why I hesitate."

" Well, what is it? You irritate me, Reuter, with your hesitations."

" We are no longer young now, Baas."

" No, we are no longer young."

" Therefore, if I hesitate too long the Baas might die, then my protest would be too late."

" Or you might die, Reuter. This conversation is without profit. Our youth is past. No talk can bring it back."

" That is it : that is why I have waited. I said to myself : ' I will wait till the Baas is very old, on the verge of death.' "

" I am not on the verge of death."

" Nevertheless, the Baas is a hundred."

" I am not a hundred."

" The Baas is nearly a hundred. He boasts of it."

" That is different, and neither here nor there. But what is your complaint? Always complaining—that is a fine thing for a man to have to say of his servant, to have to say that he is never satisfied."

" No, I am not satisfied."

" About what? I have been a good master to you."

" The Baas has not been a bad master to me, but . . ."

" But what, Reuter? Magtig, but you send me mad! And to think I have been a mother to you."

" Ja, Baas, a father and a mother to me : that is just it. The Baas has taken advantage of me. The Baas never consulted me about the name he gave me . . . Reuter. I do not like Reuter."

" I called you that after my last servant, the Hottentot who was killed by an old elephant cow on the Elands River."

" Ja, Baas, that is it. It is not lucky to be called after a dead man. Look at the things that have happened to me with my new name. I was wounded twice by Kaffirs in the wars the Baas took me to. I was gored by a buffalo and again by a bush buck. I was bitten by a puff adder. I lost the hearing of my left ear from an abscess brought on by a tick. And no woman that I have had since I have served the Baas has remained faithful to me. All this I put upon the name the Baas gave me. It was bad luck, and now I would change it before it is too late. But I have hesitated. Ja, I have hesitated, to give the Baas pleasure, but now I must think of myself. My greatgrandson in Zululand has sent me a message. He says there is a woman there who thinks of me."

" Has she ever seen you?"

" No, but she thinks of me, he says. She has seen me in a dream. And he says also that she is young and fat. Of what use are cows to me now, Baas? Of what use the riches that the Baas has given?"

"Of what use is a woman now?"

"I could look at her, Baas, and I could think of the past. Besides, who knows? There are fine doctors in my country. It is the name that troubles me, a man with the name of a dead man begets no children. I have noticed that."

"How have you noticed it?"

"I have tried, Baas. I have tried very hard."

CHAPTER XVI

THE OUTSPAN

I

THERE were no orders for Dirk except that he was to wait for orders.

No, he was not to return to his commando. He was just to wait. A special duty was being assigned to him. "Meanwhile just wait, jong." His father was right : war was mostly waiting.

He went back to Barend and his father at the outspan. They were waiting, too. Their wagons were being used for transport, but at the moment there was nothing to move.

"So we wait, Dirk, and our oxen get thinner and thinner in this place where each day there are more oxen, and owing to their numbers, less grass for them to eat," the old man said. "But life is like that. And before God, nothing is as lifelike as war, since it shows up the absurdity of all our actions."

"I do not like to wait," Dirk said. "I want to finish the war and get married."

"You are too eager, young man. Do not forget that the time may come when you want to finish your marriage and go to war. Even I, who am a good husband and father, find a little war now and then a relief. A change of monotony is, after all, still a change; but you are too young to understand such things. Yes, you are too young, and Barend, my son, too foolish."

"There is a great deal to be said for heredity, Pa," Barend said. "A fast horse begets fast sons, and it is possible, or seems so to me, that a foolish old man might beget foolish son."

"Are you calling your father a fool?"

"Pa, I am confident of my own intelligence and believe in the marvel of heredity. It is you who puts such doubts into my mind. . . . You must be careful what you say to my father, Dirk; he is very vain and touchy."

"I am the very soul of understanding and forbearance," his father said, "but like Job I have been much plagued in my life, and if it were not that my oxen grow thinner daily I would be willing to stay here on the Heidelberg outspan till the war is done. It is very peaceful here. I have time to think and plenty of friends to talk to. There is much pleasure and little danger in conversation. But, come, let us eat."

"Yes, we will eat," Barend said. "Then we will drink coffee and have brandy. We will make merry. I do not believe in eking things out. Eat and drink what you have, I say, and the Lord will provide."

" The Lord provides manna and not dop," his father said.

" I have greater faith than you, Pa."

" Then, if we are to eat, let us eat."

Dirk sat between them. Swartkie was tied to the wagon wheel and was eating the two hatfuls of mealies that Dirk had been able to buy and had spread on a bag in front of him. It was pleasant to hear him while Oom Adriaan gave thanks to the Lord for what they were about to receive.

" Now we are going to eat well," Barend said. He pulled the pot from the fire and smelt it. " Is there anything better than rice cooked with herbs, spices, and the fat from a sheep's tail?" he asked.

" Yes, there are better things," his father said. " Seacow fat is better than sheep's fat—more pure. And the tongue of a kameel is better cured and smoked. Once," he went on, " when I was courting your mother I rode fifty miles with a giraffe's tongue tied to my saddle as a present for her. I sometimes think it is because of that tongue that you are my son, Barend—at least my son by your mother. She said I was a very thoughtful young man. It is one of my trials that by it I established a precedent. How was I to know that I was expected to be thoughtful for the rest of my life? It would account too for the way you talk and the interminable length of your conversations, and is thus a double judgment upon me." He began to chuckle. " But I might have a worse son. Ja, that is my comfort—that you might have been much worse."

The relationship of Barend and his father was new to Dirk. He had never seen anything like it before. It was entirely different from his own relationship with his father, which was much more serious. How these two loved each other! Whatever the old man did Barend watched to see that he came to no harm. And whatever Barend did his father thought was wonderful. Yet as they talked they never ceased to argue and insult each other. It was very strange and pleasant. It was even beautiful to see the old man and the young together.

" My mother loaded us up with food," Barend said, " and we are lucky to be engaged in the wagon train. We have all our comforts."

" Not all, but some," his father said. " I cannot be comfortable without your mother. I am very used to her. I miss her habit of complaint and her cooking. I have had a very happy life," he said. " May you young men have lives as good," he said.

Barend patted his father's shoulder. " We will soon be home, Pa," he said. " Now coffee, and then we will drink. You will be better with a little drink in your belly. It will warm your heart, Pa."

" We have good brandy, Dirk," he said. " Grape brandy, and peach brandy, and brandy made from the fruit of the kaalblad."

" I have never had brandy made from prickly pears," Dirk said.

" You shall try some to-night. Magtig, how I like to make merry! It is in my blood. My parents like to entertain. To drink and eat with your friends in your home, what is there better than that? And to have everything made on the place, to ply them with delicacies that your mother has made. That is good. Man, that is good." He filled his pipe and brought a bottle from under the kartel. "That's the place to keep liquor," he said. "Everything of value is under our bed."

2

The effect of drink was funny. Of course, I have never drunk very much, Dirk thought. But still it was funny. At first it had made him very happy. Then he had become sad. He had told Barend and his father the story of his life, told them about his father, his mother, about Boetie, about Doornkloof, and how lovely it was with the mountain behind it. Then he had told them about Lena and how he loved her. Barend and his father had been very sympathetic. They had told him about their lives and their home. But he could remember very little of what they had said, though it had been very interesting at the time. But his sadness, he could never remember having been so sad before.

He decided to go off by himself. "I will go a walk," he said.

"A walk is good," Barend said. "But you will come back? You are sleeping with us at the wagon?"

"I will come back," Dirk said. He got up and set off towards Headquarters. There may be orders, he thought.

Drunkenness was a sin. So were gluttony, avarice, adultery, murder, the bearing of false witness, the coveting of oxen, maidservants, and asses. So were . . . It seemed suddenly to him that he had committed every sin. He was remorseful about Lena. He had seduced her. It had been wonderfully pleasant, but that was what made it so wrong. All pleasant things were wrong. If it had not been pleasant he would not have wanted to seduce her again. That's why I want to go back, he thought. I want her. I want her all the time. I want to make love to her, which is a fornication and a sin. And it was said that you could commit fornication by eye alone. If that were so, he had done it every time he saw her. He had lusted and had given in to his lust. How nice it had been! It was impossible to think of his sin without thinking of its beauty, and its completely satisfactory consummation, which only proved its wickedness. And he had certainly coveted Stoffel's "match of span" oxen : a full colour span. How beautiful they were, dark red with long horns, as like each other as peas in a pod. And it was not that he had no matched span. He had a beautiful span, but whenever he saw Stoffel's he wanted that too. He began to cry a little. There was small comfort in the fact that he had never coveted any one's ass, since he did not like donkeys.

But how had all this begun? He was not drunk. If he had been, he would not have been able to think with lucidity. He rested his back against a wagon. Someone was asleep inside the tent. He could hear him snoring. The sound was beautifully rhythmic. It began with a slow intake of breath, rose to a high note, deepened, and ended harshly; then it began again. For a man to sleep like that he must be good. His own wickedness had been suddenly revealed. He wondered if he would ever sleep well again. He decided that he would not live long. There was now no question in his mind that he would soon be killed and that it would be right. The punishment of sin was death.

He found some difficulty in walking. It was not that he had forgotten where he was going. It was just that he found it strangely hard to hold his direction and was entranced at the difficulty. It was an obstacle to overcome. He was not drunk. His mind was perfectly lucid. He could think logically. He began to think logically, just to show that he could. Then he sang. The words were clear in his mind, but they did not come out quite as they should. Well, what of it? He would sing later.

The thing to do was to concentrate on his feet. It was by means of his feet that he would reach Headquarters. By my feet, he thought, and then laughed. How many know that? he wondered : that it was by their feet that they went anywhere. That just showed how clearly he was thinking, and now that the problem of his advance was simplified he would put it into practice. He must move his feet one after the other. " Left . . . right," he said in English. That was what the English sergeant shouted. Left . . . right. He would show them. He would show his feet. He would show Mr. Left and Mr. Right. " Left . . . Right," he shouted. Right struck a stone and he fell down. It was extraordinary how nice it felt lying down. It surprised him. He had never really appreciated it before. He rolled on to his back. There was a stone between his shoulders, he moved his hand towards it. Then he stopped moving his hand and lay still. It was ridiculous to bother about lying on a stone, to let a small thing like that disturb him. He began to think of drunkenness. Of course he was not drunk.

He looked at the sky above him. Surely it was over-full of stars? Perhaps after all he was a little drunk. He was thinking very clearly now. If he was drunk it would explain everything, it was only in this way that things could be explained. It would reconcile the wagons of the outspan swaying, moving as trees in the Bible did when they moved like men. It would explain why the stars were so restless to-night. It would explain their incredible size, brilliance, and their unprecedented numbers. But it was interesting to watch them swing majestically from side to side. They were like great candles hung on the end of a string. He noted the precision with which they moved. There was nothing erratic about them. He watched carefully for this, but there was none; you could not catch them out. But their very regularity was irregular and contrary to what he knew of the movements of heavenly bodies. They were making him dizzy and he turned his head to the side. Then he got up. He was on his way to Headquarters.

Only drunkenness would account for the strange way the surface of the outspan had changed from the flat ground he had ridden over this afternoon to waves. The outspan was like a great sea upon which the wagons rode at anchor, rising and falling, upon the invisible tide that rocked them, like ships—like cradles. He thought of the cradle at home. That would come to him when he was married. But he would never be married now, he was going to be killed quite soon. Tears flowed down his cheeks again. If people, all those sleeping in the wagons, knew, he thought, how sorry they would be for me. And how brave I was to-night showing nothing of my sorrow! He went on. Looking at the stars certainly made a man dizzy. He would give it up. Yes, the outspan was like a land newly ploughed with a tremedous plough into fantastic furrows. That was it. That's what they were—furrows.

Furrows . . . To cross furrows one had to lift one's feet high. For big furrows, such as these, he must lift them very high. Very high, indeed, so that his knees almost touched his nose. Also when going downhill, when he slid into these tremedous troughs, he must lean back; and conversely, as he climbed the opposite slope, lean forward. Going uphill one leaned forward and downhill back. Why had he not thought about that before? The whole trouble was that he had started too fast. He was too eager. Who had said : " You are too eager, Dirk "? All that had been necessary was this period of reflection. That was the trouble with most people. They did not think long enough before they acted.

He fell. He got on to his knees; got on to his feet. " Lean back," he said to himself, " lean back, you fool." He felt the ground slip away from in front of him again. It sloped steeply. It was steeper than anything he had ever known. He wished he were on a horse. It would be nothing if I was on a horse, he thought. He had reached the edge of the world. All Africa was a pit in front of him : the whole High Veld set vertically so that unaware he should fall into it. He sat down suddenly. It was the only thing to do. He had leaned back so far that he had sat down. He congratulated himself that the action had been premeditated. There was nothing fortuitous about it. He was very happy. Mind, on this occasion, had conquered matter. His intelligence had brought the pit digged beneath his feet to naught. All his sensations were pleasant. He felt a warm glow spread over him. It was no good arguing, I am drunk, he thought : and I like it. On the edge of the abyss he lay down and slept.

When he woke, Barend was standing over him with a cup of coffee in his hand.

He felt very ill. He felt so ill that he could not tell Barend how ill he felt. He put out his hand for the cup. The coffee was good. It burnt his throat. It washed some of the thick dryness from his mouth. And for a moment, as he swallowed, it cleared his head. But only for a moment.

"It was that prickly-pear brandy, Dirk," Barend said. "It is very strong."

"I do not know what it was, but I am sick. Last night I saw visions. I had a premonition of death. Perhaps this illness is the beginning of the end."

"Last night you were very drunk."

"I went to Headquarters for orders, but cannot remember if I got them." Last night certainly had been puzzling. He could remember so little about it. He sat up suddenly. "Swartkie," he said. "Has he been fed and watered?"

"I took care of him," Barend said.

"I thought something might have happened to him. She is fond of him," he said. She had ridden Swartkie. Somehow the horse was tied in his mind to Lena. Whenever he had been to see her it had been on Swartkie.

"I was drunk, you say?"

"Yes, you were drunk."

"I walked a great way and then I was lost."

"I followed you, Dirk. You went to the seventh line of wagons, that is where I found you. You were asleep."

"You mean I did not get to Headquarters?"

"You got to the seventh line of wagons."

"Does one always feel like this if one gets drunk? I have never been drunk before."

"One gets used to it, Dirk, and one can get a little drunk without much harm."

"It was a very pleasant feeling in the beginning," Dirk said, and it had been. "I felt very bold and free. But afterwards on my walk it was not so good. Nothing stayed in its place, neither the ground beneath my feet, nor the stars above, nor the wagons about me. It is very strange to stand still in a rocking world."

He thought of Oupa du Toit. Did he feel like this often? And if he did, why did he drink?

"If I did not get to Headquarters last night, I must go to-day," he said. He sat up. The sides of the wagon tent swung about in front of him, oscillated more slowly and finally came to rest. "I am better," he said.

Barend gave him more coffee. "It is a pity you did not vomit," he said.

"Is it good to vomit?"

"It is the best thing to do."

Dirk lowered himself from the wagon-bed on to the ground. Swartkie whinnied when he saw him.

"Shall I saddle him up for you?" Barend asked.

"I can do it."

Dirk put the bit into his horse's mouth, girthed the saddle, and slung his rifle over his shoulder. He mounted. He felt better on the horse with his saddle under him. He settled his feet in the stirrups.

"Barend," he said, "I have made a decision."

"What is it?"

"I have given up drink. From now on I will drink no more."

Barend laughed. "It will save you money," he said, "and time, but you will lose much pleasure. Good luck, jong, and don't fall off." He was still laughing as Dirk turned his horse.

This time there were orders. And they were not welcome. Stoffel and he were to accompany Captain Elliot, the only officer left unwounded in the battle at Bronkerspruit, and another officer, Captain Lambart of the Twenty-First Lancers, to Natal. They had been given their parole, undertaking not to take up arms again, and had to be escorted to the Border.

If you did not like a thing or a man, they seemed to be thrust upon you. He had hoped to be done with prisoners for good and to avoid further intimate contact with Stoffel. But there it was. In war your hopes had nothing to do with your orders. He rode back to the outspan slowly. They were to start to-morrow. The officers were driving an American spider with four horses, and once they had seen them safely away they were to return to their commando which, from what he could hear, had been in action again.

When he got back, Barend and his father were entertaining another man. He sat between them on a box of ammunition. Beside him with her head on his knees was an old pointer bitch. Dirk dismounted and tied his horse.

"This is Oom Frederik Jordaan," Barend said.

Dirk put out his hand. "I am Dirk van der Berg," he said.

"Where are you from?" Jordaan asked.

"I am from Doornkloof in the District of Brennersdorp."

"I come from the Waterberg," Jordaan said, "and I am to join the artillery. The Almighty only knows why, unless it is that once I was in the artillery in Holland. But I deserted; I did not like the noise. I do not like the idea at all," he said. "As one grows older, one likes noise less rather than more, and it does not seem right to me that, having deserted and come so far to avoid a thing, I should find myself back where I was as a young man."

"How did they know you were in the artillery?" Oom Adriaan asked.

"It was well known," Jordaan said. "I often spoke of it, saying how I hated it. But how was I to know there would be war, or that my own words, spoken among my friends, would be used against me? No, I do not like it," he said. "And apart from the noise it is dangerous. We have few guns and the Rooineks will try to capture them. They will charge at them with lances and sabres. When any one comes close, I like to get on a good horse and ride away, but with cannons you cannot do that. And there is my dog. She is too old for war, but also too used to me to be left alone. As a result, I am in a state of great despondency."

" When do you join your gun?"

" To-day, at once. That is why I am here trying to delay matters a little and to forget."

" But they may start without you."

" They cannot. Not one of them can lay a gun. That is what depresses me. I do not wish to hold a position of such importance. I have to teach them, and I am responsible for what occurs. I wish it was over," he went on. " I want to go home and grow some new tobacco. It is seed I got from abroad. It came in a letter from my cousin in Amsterdam who got it from another cousin in the East."

" You grow tobacco, too, then?" Barend's father said.

" I am a great grower of tobacco. It gives me much pleasure. But till now only snuff tobacco. This is special, and I do not know how long the seed will stay good."

" Will you give me some seed?" Oom Adriaan asked. " Meneer van der Berg is giving me seed. He has good smoking tobacco. Give him some to try, Dirk."

Dirk gave him a pipeful.

He lit it. " Yes, it is good," he said. " Now why must we fight when we could be happy growing good things? A land of tobacco is beautiful, with big green leaves and fragrant flowers. But no, I must come and teach men to fire guns. A gun is not a good thing to play with. Sometimes the breech blows out, and then where are you?" He looked at the sun. " I suppose I had better go now. But wish me luck, friends."

" Good luck and tot siens," they said.

" Good luck," he said. " Good-bye, and if you see Paul Kruger tell him I do not like it: that it is not what I expected of him. I tried to see him myself to-day, but he was engaged. He is my friend. Once he ate at our house when my wife was alive. He ate a whole chicken by himself, a big one; and is this what you would expect of a man who eats one of your big chickens by himself? It pains me to think of it," he said as he left them.

" And you, Dirk," Barend said, " have you got your orders?"

" Yes, I have them, and I don't like them. Stoffel du Toit and I are to conduct two officers to the Border."

" It will be a nice ride," Oom Adriaan said. " You will be able to visit on the way and there will be no danger. For my part I think you are lucky."

" I do not like to have to do with prisoners," Dirk said.

" Well, forget it, young man, till the time comes, and then remember nothing is as bad as you think it will be, and nothing as good either, for

that matter. We will pass a pleasant day smoking and talking and eating
and to-night we will have another party."

" It must be without drink," Dirk said. " I have given it up."

" Then we will drink," Barend said, " and you can watch us."

" What is there to eat?" his father asked. " I like to know early what
I am going to eat at night. It gives me something to look forward to."

" There is half a sheep," Barend said.

" Which half?"

" The hinder half, Pa."

" That is good. For a moment I was afraid you were going to give your
old father the front half. Kaffirs' meat that is : head and neck and chest
and shoulder. But it is a strange thing that all the good parts should lie
behind, the hump of an ox being the only exception. Even with women this
is so. The head for brains, yes, but the behind for beauty."

" It is as well that we are on the veld when you talk like this and that
Ma cannot hear you," Barend said.

" That is one of the compensations of war, Barend. But your mother
knows what I think. She is a fine woman to-day, but as a girl she was
beautiful : like a young cow in early summer. She wobbled when she
walked. I never tired of telling her how graceful she was—equally beautiful to observe from before or behind."

" Such conversation is indelicate, Pa, before two young men who are not
married and know nothing of such things." Barend winked at Dirk.

" Some might think so, my son, but from whom would it be better to
learn the true standards of beauty than your father, or the father of your
friend? Ours is a simple culture : simple and Biblical in its expression. It
is for this, our way of life, that we fight. Your mother weighed two
hundred pounds when we were married and she was only eighteen. For
a girl to be fat and sleek is a sign of both health and good nature. There is
no vice in a fat young woman. You would almost think they had no gall
bladders, and they are so friendly that it is sometimes embarrassing to a
shy young man. Your mother embarrassed me a great deal at first. It was
spring," he said, " and at that time I was less aware of the natural order
of things, or that the natural order was inclusive of all female things, even
young girls. But one lives and learns," he said. " Indeed, one has almost
done living by the time one has learnt those things which would have been
useful in the beginning. For with the skill that comes of use comes also
the exhaustion of age. Like a saddle or a gun or a wagon, a man wears
out. He begins to rattle, to come loose; his hair and teeth fall out, he loses
his powers. But sometimes I think of myself as a young man. It is good
to sit smoking and thinking of it, but I would not go back. Even to think
of it tires me."

" Yes, you are a poor old man, Pa, and near your end."

" Near my end! Who said I was near my end? I am not young any more, it is true, but I am matured. I am like an old violin, still capable of producing music. Ja, my son, it is not for nothing that they say the best music is played upon an old fiddle."

" But with a new bow, Pa; that is what worries me, Pa. Where is your new bow?"

" You have no respect for me, Barend. But cook that sheep well. Do not burn it and do not serve it raw. And I wish we had some onions," he said.

" We have them; I got some yesterday."

" Then I forgive you."

They began to laugh at each other. Barend poked his father in the ribs. He laughed so much he nearly fell off the box he was sitting on.

" You must not tickle me, Barend. Suppose someone saw, what would they think?"

" No one has seen," Barend said. " And when I was little did you not tickle me? Magtig, what a time I have had to wait to get my own back on you!"

How friendly it all was! Dirk thought. What a fine relationship men could have with each other if they were of the same temper! Barend and his father reminded him in a way of Oom Philippus and his servant Reuter. My father and I are too serious, he thought. We love each other, we like to work and hunt together, but sit solemnly side by side in silence when we are alone. Like begets like, as Barend said. Barend's father is gay and his son is gay. My father is serious and I am serious. All the same it is pleasant to watch. These are good friends to be with.

They were still playing together like two children when he lay down beside his horse to sleep. The old man was right. It was no good worrying about to-morrow till it came. But no more drink. It was a poison. Let those who wished to poison themselves do so, but no more for him. At least, no more till his wedding. Then he would have to drink. Not only would it look strange if he did not, but he would need the courage that drink gave. To-morrow he would be gone. He wondered when he would see Barend and his father again. He wondered about Jordaan the gunner. What good friends he had! How they would like Lena, though she would be too thin for Barend's father's taste! But she was to his own taste, very much to his taste. From under his hat, that was pulled over his face, he could see Swartkie's hind legs and the tip of his tail. It was black like Lena's hair. He thought of Lena's hair, of her eyes that were like brown wine, of her slim body. She was like a buck, as sleek, as slim, as beautiful.

The spider the British officers were driving was a good one, lightly and strongly built, the kind that was being imported from America; and he was glad to be able to examine one so closely. Their four horses were bays, well matched, each having a white star on the forehead.

Dirk thought over the last few hours. He could hardly believe he was here riding behind the spider, with Stoffel on his red schimmel beside him. Last night had passed pleasantly with roast mutton, onions, and potatoes; much coffee, smoking, good talk, and no brandy. He had slept well. He had watered and fed his horse, had said good-bye, and had picked up Stoffel and the prisoners at the courthouse. Evidently in war you got into a state of acceptance of all that occurred. To be doing this now seemed the most natural thing in the world. The veld was beautiful. Swartkie was fresh and full of strength as he trippled under him. That was a nice feeling—to have him moving like this, first both his near legs, then both his off. He was lucky to have such a good horse : so strong and willing. There was a herd of springbok in the distance. They were pronking, jumping high into the air, their white manes glinting in the sun. Earlier they had seen two herds of blesbok, almost purple in the bright light. They had stood still, staring at the cart, their white faces turned sideways following them as they moved. Then they had sprung forward and galloped away, their brown bodies glinting like metal in the sun.

When they came upon the second herd, Stoffel had shot one, though they had meat, from his horse's back. Then, as they broke, he had shot another running. His horse was well trained and stood like a rock as he fired. He was a fine shot, but too ready to shoot. Not that I do not like it, too, Dirk thought, but only in winter when I can make biltong would I shoot more than one buck. The Englishmen had been astonished at his skill, which was no doubt why he had shot. The first had been shot between the eyes, the second behind the shoulder. They loaded one on to the cart and the second they had left for the aasvoels after taking out the kidneys, liver, and tongue. All his life Stoffel had practised at shooting : not as most Boers, firing one shot each day, the sighting shot, at a mark each morning when they had eaten, but many shots from all positions, standing, walking, sitting with his elbows on his knees, even lying on his back with the barrel of his rifle resting on his feet. But particularly had he exercised himself in shooting from a horse and in training his horses to steadiness. When there were competitions, he always won them : so much so that many refused to compete if he was firing. That was his gift—marksmanship and the management and training of beasts—horses and oxen and dogs. Dirk wondered if there could be a relationship between these things and his deformity; wondered if a man who was less than a man in some ways might not strive to become more than a man in others. And Stoffel had changed since the battle, being more confident of himself and arrogant than ever.

The Englishmen were very silent. They had talked a little to each other, but even when the blesbok had been loaded on the back of the spider they had hardly said anything except that Stoffel's shooting was remarkable. They had never seen anything like it, they said.

They passed scattered farms and a party of Boers riding north, but too

far off to hail. But towards evening they decided to stop at the next farm
they came to. It was not long before they saw a house in a valley on their
left. At Stoffel's order the Englishmen turned the cart towards it. It
seemed deserted, though the stock was there; and if it was, there must be
people—Kaffirs at least. As Dirk was thinking this, an old Kaffir appeared.
He came out of the kraal with a bucket of milk in his hand.

" Is there no one home?" Stoffel asked.

" The mevrou is at home."

They rode closer to the house. " Who is there? Who comes?" someone
shouted. It was a woman's voice.

" We are Boers. We are taking prisoners to the Border. Are you sick?
Is there anything we can do?" Stoffel shouted back.

" I am not sick. Come in, come in. If you are not afraid of seeing a
woman in bed, it will be pleasant to have some conversation. My husband
has gone to the war and left me here."

" Then you are sick," Stoffel said. " Perhaps we should not disturb you."

" I am not ill, I tell you. Come in, man, and talk to me. I am getting
sick of this business, though. I liked it at first, but one gets tired of everything at last."

They tied their horses and went in. The big room was empty, but in the
bedroom that opened out of it a fat woman lay in a great double bed, almost
filling it. She seemed to Dirk almost as wide as she was long. They went in.

" I am Sarie Labuschagne," the woman said, " the wife of Hans
Labuschagne. Before we were here, we were the Swart Ruggens in the
Colony. Now tell me the news. I am hungry for it." She raised herself up
in the bed. " Do you know why I am here?" she asked, and then answered
her own question. " It is because Hans, who is from the Colony, loves
ostriches. He found a nest and brought the eggs home for me to hatch like
a hen. So I must lie in bed covered with heavy blankets for weeks,
surrounded by eggs that roll about as I move. That also is good for them,
he says. But it is not right to put a woman to bed with eggs and then to
leave her. I miss him greatly, though we could not sleep together, even if
he were here, in a bed full of eggs.

" Magtig," she went on, " it is good to talk to white men again. What
are you doing? Why have you a cart? I heard wheels. Are you alone?
What is the news of the war? Do you think there will be rain? We need
rain, but no storm. A big storm would kill my eggs. It kills chicks—all
chicks—as dogs kill rats."

Dick left the talking to Stoffel. He was too astonished at the woman : at
the mass of her body, which, beneath the covers, rose like a mountain from
the little hills of the eggs; by her volubility; by the fact that a man should
set his wife, like a hen, to hatch out eggs.

" We have prisoners with us," Stoffel said. " We are taking them . . ."

" English?" the woman said. " I want to see them. Bring them in. I have only seen one Englishman. He was a small man with red hair. He smelt strongly when he was hot. Are these small men with red hair?"

" We are taking them to the Border," Stoffel went on. " And the war is going well. We are winning. The Almighty God is with His people. He is in the heart of every man who rides."

" He is not in my husband's heart," the woman said. " If God was in his heart, would he leave me like this to fret my life away? I ask you that. I ask you if there is any companionship in an egg, in a great number of eggs? I ask what pleasure a woman can have with an egg? I am a young woman : a fine woman. And my husband leaves me a prey to any wandering stranger! I lie naked and helpless on the bed sacred to our union : the nuptial couch on which I lost my maidenhood; it came up with us on our wagon from the Colony. What could I do if I was attacked? How could I defend myself naked in a bed full of eggs without breaking them? I tell you that man would sooner I was seduced than I broke an egg. He thinks nothing of seduction, neither for himself nor any one else. Last time I was seduced : it was not eggs that time : I was sick. And afterwards, when he came to . . . afterwards, that is . . . he said : ' Sarie, what is all this? He was a nice man, wasn't he?' and I said yes. Then my husband said : ' And he took nothing from you, for you are the same. What then is this, how are you insulted, and what has been changed?' And that is the man you say God is inspiring. God has never inspired him. But I miss him. And will there be a storm? Magtig, I am so nervous in a storm. In a storm, meneer, I cling to my husband like a child. It has a tremendous effect upon me. The greater the storm the greater the effect, and in that case the eggs would die, anyway, and he would not be surprised . . . But make yourselves at home. Bring in the Englishmen, but protect me from them."

By this time she seemed to regard Stoffel as her protector, heaven-sent, and more than welcome whatever his mission or intentions. Her eyes followed him as he moved in the other room.

" There is food," she said, " in the cupboard, and coffee, and sugar. Klaas will bring milk from the kraal. You must have seen him," she said. " Klaas! Klaas!" she shouted. " Bring milk for the Baas. Make haste. Bring milk—bring milk." Her voice rose to a wail. " The verdomde skelm," she said. " He drinks the milk."

He did not drink it all, for a moment later he came with it. Dirk went to the door to take the bucket. Stoffel made up the fire. The Englishmen were outspanning their horses.

" There was a girl," the woman said. " She takes care of me, but she ran when she saw you coming, abandoning me to my fate. She fears men even more than I. Men are strong and women so weak that they are helpless before them."

Dirk looked at her arms. They were as thick as his thighs. The arms of the cotton nightdress she wore bulged with muscle. That woman with a broomstick or a wheel spoke could have routed a commando.

"Women are weak," she whimpered. "They have no chance in life, but can only take it as it comes. Men are like baboons," she said. "They have no respect for women. That is one reason we left the Colony. There were so many baboons there. That was why our farm was called Baviaans kloof, and they did not respect me. When my husband was away and I went on to the lands to chase them away, they took no notice. The big old man baboons laughed at me. That is a fine thing, meneer, when a baboon laughs at a white woman, and that made the Hottentots laugh at me too. Can you imagine it, meneer? That's why we left, I say, and because we owed so much. Magtig, my husband owed money as far as Grahamstown and beyond it. But we were sad to go and to give up our ostriches. My husband was the first man to tame them. They said he was mad. But my husband is not mad. He is a great judge of female beauty, which leads him astray. It is in my heart a man cannot care for beauty in women and leave them alone. Not that I complain for myself. I have no reason. He always says I am the most lovely woman he has ever seen. But I think he compares others with me and goes very far to see if they resemble me in his search, which is carrying a love of beauty too far. Now my father loved scenery. He said the mountains of our district were beautiful and the rivers. Meneer, he would contemplate a river for hours which prevented him working, but did my mother no harm. He could not betray her with a river."

Dirk brought in the blesbok from the cart.

"Blesbok, that is good," she said. "I like blesbok."

The Englishmen sat down on a bench outside the house. Captain Lambart was asking how badly Sergeant Mulligan had been hit. He had been a lancer and was only temporarily attached to the Ninety-Fourth.

"Badly, I think," Captain Elliot said.

Dirk asked them to come in. They decided against it. "We like to sit outside," they said.

The woman was now talking about ostriches again. "Do not think I do not care about ostriches," she said. "I do not care as much as my husband, but I care. They are beautiful. In the breeding season the cocks have red thighs and necks. They make love. They fight. They are beautiful; they are like people. A sick ostrich lies down with its neck stretched straight out in front of it; and an angry cock—that is something to see. Ja, a Quei ostrich is something when he sits down and flaps his wings and blows up his red neck. He throws back his head, beating it on his back with a loud noise. Ja, meneer, ostriches are both beautiful and intelligent. They dance in the mornings, though this is bad, since sometimes they fall and break their legs, which are very fragile. And to see a hen bring her chicks to her by rattling her quills! Did you know, meneer, that the hen, who is grey, sits on her nest by day, and the cock, that is black and white and thus invisible in the darkness, sits on it at night? Is that not intelligent? Is it not wonderful?"

She hid her head under the covers. She brought it out very red. She was breathing hard.

"Meneer, they are coming," she said. "I can hear them. Meneer has brought me good fortune." She looked at Stoffel with soft eyes. "Yes, you have brought me luck," she said. "Would meneer like to listen? You can hear them tapping."

Stoffel got up and went in to the bed.

Dirk decided to join the Englishmen. War was a strange business and beyond his understanding.

CHAPTER XVII

THERE WAS NO MURDER

I

When they left in the morning, Stoffel said : " That is a fine woman. She has a heart of gold."

" Yes," Dirk said, " she is a fine woman."

He was in no position to argue with Stoffel, nor was he in the mood to. He had spent the night camped with the Englishmen beside the spider. That he had liked them made the war still more incomprehensible. They had got on very well together. The Englishmen even had a fondness for his people and many happy memories of the country, having hunted over much of it. But the attitude of the professional soldier was a mystery to him. They had fought in India, but had nothing against the Indians. They liked India, too, having hunted there, killing tigers, leopards, and buck in the mountains and jungles of that country. " Gladstone does not want this war," Elliot had said. " He wants no further colonial expansion, but he is not in power now, so it goes on."

There was plenty to think about. Dirk rode with slack reins trying to formulate a principle which would explain the circumstances, not only of war but of life; of the relationships of men to each other; of men to women; of men to their lands and their concepts of right and wrong, and of good and evil. But the more he thought, the more complex everything became and the less he could understand. It was evident that Stoffel did not love the fine woman with whom he had passed the night. Why, then, had he slept with her? To give her pleasure? That seemed unlikely. To give himself pleasure? That seemed inconceivable.

There must be another answer. It must be that Stoffel was male and the woman female. That he had taken her as a bull would take a cow if he came upon one in heat. Yet this seemed over-simple; surely men were not like that. It partly covered the situation, but did not deal with it in its entirety. Stoffel's club foot might come into it. But how? He could not think of how it did, but still felt it must. Being a part of Stoffel, it influenced all his doings, though he pretended to ignore it.

And love . . . That was something beautiful. At least he saw it that way between himself and Lena. He would have liked to ask the Englishmen about these matters. They were educated men, but his English was not good enough for such a conversation and he was shy about beginning

it. Nevertheless, he felt he had missed an opportunity. And Fate . . .?
Why was Captain Elliot, the paymaster of the Ninety-Fourth, the only
officer left unwounded? Why had he been selected in this fashion? Saved
at the expense of others? What was the justice of this matter? What
indeed was justice?

Smoking, which usually clarified his mind, failed to help in this. He
felt himself and every one to be caught in a machine. He felt that they were
the wheels of some great vehicle that was being dragged in a given direction by some unknown force. All they could do was to revolve, to turn in
accordance with their natures. When you saw it this way, some order came
out of the chaos. Suppose you thought of every one as a wheel that turned—
his father, his mother, Boetie, Oupa, Stoffel, even Lena. All rolled on,
surmounting obstacles, crashing through them; or were held up, as a
wagon is held up, till they found a way round, and then, finally, all were
broken up by death. That was the road all travelled. In that a man or
woman resembled a wagon; eventually they were used up. It was something irrevocable that could not be stopped.

The war was changing him. Till now he had accepted what happened
without much thought. In ordinary life you were too busy to think. Also
you did not meet enough people or travel enough. You worked; you
hunted; you talked to men and women that you had known all your life.
But you did not have conversations with English officers, with men like
Barend and his father, or Jordaan, the artilleryman from Holland. Yes, war
broadened your mind and by its very monotony forced you back on to
yourself so that you must seek to come to conclusions hitherto evaded. This
accounted for the superior wisdom of the older men who had been on
many campaigns. With the danger of death ever present, you had also to
think of birth, its counterpart. You had to stand naked before yourself,
since at any moment you might stand naked before your God. You had
to think of your mother when you were parted from her; of your wife,
and your love when you left her; of the past when you had been born of
your mother, and of the future when you would have your own children
born of the woman you had chosen for yourself.

He thought of the star he had caught in the bucket. How easy it had
been to catch it! You had the illusion of holding it, but you could do no
more than that. You could hold, but you could not touch. He thought
of the dead Englishmen, of his elation in battle which was comparable to
his elation with Lena—and the peace beyond understanding that followed
both. Was it due to the making of life and the making of death and the
fact that you had made them without damage to yourself? He thought
of his fear when the bullets were striking round him; of his horror at
seeing men wounded. How fragile men were, emptying themselves of
blood like broken bottles and dying as they emptied!

He thought of the strange chance that had brought Lena to the spruit.

That was something beyond understanding or calculation. As strange in its way as the feather that had remained on Stoffel's back throughout the battle.

2

There seemed to be some confusion about which drift the Englishmen should take. According to them they had been told to cross the nearest one, but Stoffel, who said he knew this country, had ordered them to follow him. On the second day they refused to go farther, being convinced that they were being led astray. Captain Lambart knew the country, too, having been all over it buying horses for the army. This would account for his matched span. He had had the pick for himself.

"Very well, stay here then, and camp while we go on and find the drift," Stoffel said.

Dirk and he rode towards the Vaal, finally striking it where it was joined by the Klip. There was a boat there and they returned to fetch the Englishmen. But when they reached the river again, there was more argument, for, as Lambart pointed out, the boat was too small to take his cart or horses. He demanded to see Stoffel's orders.

Stoffel said this was the crossing they were to take, and that the boat was Pretorious's punt. Lambart said there was no mention of Pretorious in the orders. They said they must either be shown the proper drift or taken back to camp. The river was in flood. There must have been big rains in the mountains.

"All right, then, we will go back." Stoffel's mood was changing. The little vein in his forehead was beating and he was handling his horse hard, pressing him and holding him back at the same time. Suddenly he turned his head and said :

"Come, Dirk, we will leave them. Let them find their own way, since they know it so well."

Hardly an hour after they had left them, they met a party of Boers, who asked them for news of the English officers. "We have a message for them from the government," they said. "Ja, a message. They are to go at once or they will be shot."

"We have just left them," Stoffel said. "They will not cross. I took them to the river, but they are afraid of the flood."

"They were told to be over the Border in twenty-four hours."

"Whatever they have been told, they are still here."

The leader of the party, a big, black-bearded man on a flea-bitten grey, said : "Come back with us. We will put them across. You have been too gentle with them."

The Englishmen had not moved, but had camped and were cooking a meal when they got back.

Smit, the big dark man, ordered them to inspan at once. " I have orders to see you over the river," he said. " We are going to take you to Spencer's drift."

They put in their horses and, surrounded by the Boers, drove off again.

Since the situation had changed, Dirk had hardly spoken to them. He felt he should do something, but was at a loss to know what to do. Stoffel had been in command of the party till they met Smit; had become infuriated at losing his way; and still more infuriated to find that Lambart knew the country better than he. " A damned Englishman thinking he knows the veld better than one of us," he had said. To have said anything then would have precipitated a crisis. And now there was Smit. He was a Field-Kornet, one in authority, and of a nature even more sullen and bitter against the English than Stoffel. It was getting dark. The storm that had been threatening for two days looked as if it was really going to break. There were big banks of purple clouds that rode heavily over a reddish under-sky. Dirk wetted his finger and held it up. The wind was blowing towards the clouds. There would be rain if it held, for they were riding up against the wind—piling up in front of it and travelling towards them. He thought of the woman in bed with the ostrich eggs again. He hoped she would be frightened and that the eggs would die. It would serve her right. He thought also of how uncomfortable it was going to be camping that night : no wood. There were no trees here : no dry cow-dung : no shelter from the wind which would change with the rain and from the feel in the air there was the possibility of hail. The grass was coarse and sour, so even Swartkie would go hungry. And he did not like Smit's party. They were back-veld Boers, as savage as the animals they lived among. Stoffel seemed to be getting on with them, though, which only confirmed his feeling that all was not well.

Night fell and still they rode. There were flashes of lightning that showed up Smit's grey horse. The thunder rolled and clapped. The storm was getting much nearer, but instead of its getting cooler the night stayed hot and the air was still between the claps, charged with uneasiness. Sweat dripped from him. As he stroked Swartkie's mane, it crackled with sparks. There was going to be no rain : at least none yet. It was a dry storm.

Smit pulled up suddenly. He commanded them to halt and rode on alone. Dirk saw him in the flashes. He was turning towards the river. He stopped his horse on the top of a high bank and raised his hand to his eyes. Then he shouted : " Bring them up here. Here's the drift."

The spider moved on surrounded by Boers. They reached Smit and halted again. He cannot mean them to cross here, Dirk thought. The flooded river was roaring between high banks. There was a big splash, as part of the bank, undercut by the water, fell. In the light of a flash he saw that there was a road leading down to the water and ending there.

So there was a drift here, and Smit had found it in the dark. But it was impassable. There must have been a big storm in the mountains. Either they would have to camp and wait for the water to run down, or work up higher in the hope of finding a better crossing place, or a ferry capable of taking the spider. There was more lightning, the river showed small white-capped waves—a tree swirled past them.

No one spoke. The men, Englishmen and Boers alike, stared at the river. The horses backed uneasily away from it raising their heads and laying back their ears. Swartkie pulled at his bit to loosen the reins, lowered his head, and pawed at the ground. Dirk patted him again. Still silence. Still only the noise of the running water and the splash of more falling banks. What were they going to do?

Then Smit shouted : " What are you waiting for, Englishmen? There is the drift."

Lambart said : " Can we not camp and try in the morning? I do not know this drift."

He said nothing about the flood.

" Cross at once !" Smit shouted.

Lambart spoke gently to his horses and drove them to the water. The leaders hesitated on the edge of the drift. He struck them with his whip. They went in. The near leader stumbled and fell. He picked him up and they went on farther. The water was over the axles of the spider. The bays were very restive, backing and pulling alternately. The off leader swung round in spite of the whip and fell into a hole. The cart turned over.

Dirk heard someone shout; he could not tell if it was Elliot or Lambart. " Send us help to right the cart or we will come back." It was terrible to see. Those beautiful matched horses and the imported spider, and the two men—a moving blur in the turbulence of the black river. They were in danger. They should try to get back, he thought.

" If you turn we will shoot," Smit shouted, cupping his hands.

There was another flash, a very bright one. Dirk saw that all the Boers were unslinging their rifles. The Englishmen had taken off their jackets. They were going to abandon the cart. They dived, and only just in time. A big tree coming down the river struck the cart, sweeping it off the drift. The horses' heads appeared for a moment swimming, they were swept on and disappeared. They would have no chance in their harness. Dirk found himself at Stoffel's side. There were more flashes of lightning. He could see the Englishmen's heads were bobbing in the water. Stoffel raised his rifle. He was going to fire. Dirk jerked Swartkie's head and drove his spurs into him, swinging him up into a rear as he leaned forward to jerk Stoffel's arm. He had not been in time. Stoffel had fired. There was a cry : " Oh . . . Oh," from the river. One of the heads went under as

Stoffel's rifle fell to the ground. He was almost unseated. The two horses were savaging each other, squealing with anger.

"You fool, Dirk! What do you think you are doing?" Stoffel cried.

"I am doing nothing," Dirk said. "I tried to stay your hand. I tried to stop a murder."

"Murder!" Stoffel said. "There was no murder, and is it murder to shoot a dog of an Englishman? I was only putting a shot near them. If you had not jerked me, I should not have hit him. If harm has been done, it is your doing."

The horses were apart now, but still angry and fighting for their heads. Stoffel had dismounted to get his rifle and the roan was pulling away from him.

Dirk turned his horse. This was the end. Orders or no orders, he was leaving them. There were no orders for such things as this. Swartkie was ready to go. There was no more lightning. The storm seemed to have ended with Stoffel's shot. The night was black, almost solid, as they galloped through it, and much colder. He pulled up suddenly. He was going to be sick. Dismounting, he vomited, wiped his mouth, remounted and rode on at a walk. You could not gallop away from yourself.

At dawn he found himself back at the farm where the woman lay in bed with her ostrich eggs. He wondered if she had enticed someone else into her bed to keep her company. He bent forward to stroke his horse. What a horse he was! To find his way through a night like that to an old camp. He turned him away from the house and struck due north. He was bound to meet some Boers and could make inquiries for Joubert's commando. As soon as the sun was really up, he would camp and rest. Swartkie must graze and he must sleep if he could : if you could sleep when you had seen a murder. This time he had done something. He had acted, but he had not acted quickly enough. Which of them had been killed? he wondered. Would he ever know? Had either survived the flood?

3

That Joubert's commando was operating to the south he learnt from a dispatch rider that he halted : a man called Baruch, riding a very fine brown gelding that he said had been taken from the English. Things were going well, he said. Both Potchefstroom and Pretoria were besieged. But the English General Colley was approaching with a big army, and more troops were said to be on their way from India. "But we'll smash them first," he said. Then he knocked out his pipe and vaulted on to his brown horse. "These are for Oom Paul." He patted the bag he carried strapped on his back. "Tot siens, brother, tot siens and geluk." He waved his hands, drove his heels into the English brown, and was gone.

That had been an hour ago. Things were more settled in Dirk's mind now. Certain decisions had been made. He had parted with Stoffel for good. He could stomach no more of him, brother-in-law or not. He was rested and fed. Swartkie was rested and fed. He knew, if not the actual whereabouts, at least the direction of Joubert's commando.

The day was lovely, cooler from the rain that had fallen somewhere, and last night seemed like an evil dream. He had to persuade himself that he had really seen it. Later he would have to decide what he was going to do about it. For that he must see his father and get advice. It seemed to him that he must report what had happened—first as an explanation for his defection and next because such things should be reported. They were wrong and could do their cause no good. This was what Stoffel's pride in his marksmanship had brought him to. Still he was pleased with himself about having done something. It showed an improvement. Too late, but still he had made the effort for the first time in his life.

Now that he came to think of it, he had never been opposed to any one before the war. He had always been in agreement with whomever he was with. What it really amounted to was that what you did depended, not only on the circumstance, but also on the events that preceded it. Everything in your life went towards your life; you built it out of the past with the bricks of your previous actions, so that in the end you were like a wall, and the bricks were either good or bad.

This, too, was the explanation of Stoffel's action. He had trained himself to shoot better than any one, therefore, he must show every one how well he shot or there would be no point in it, and therefore, because of his training, when he fired he could not miss, he could not even if he wanted to. He might have wanted just to put a bullet near one of those heads in the water, but his skill had betrayed him.

You were what you were. The decision was not of the moment, but of all previous moments. That was why he had been so helpless in his inexperience. Now, having spoken up once in the face of oppression, he would be able to do it again. It was just that first time that was hard; and because he had seen no oppression, and had been, as he saw it now, almost unaware that men could do wrong, so rightly did his father and those with whom he habitually associated behave. He could not imagine his father being cruel or unjust, though he could imagine him very terrible and implacable in his justice, extorting eye for eye and tooth for tooth, but doing so without rancour.

He was avoiding any men he saw. He wanted to be alone with his thoughts and speak to no one of what he had done till he had seen his father. Towards dusk he found a small wood and decided to camp there. There was water for his horse and himself and he had meat and rusks and some coffee and sugar left.

Taking the small axe from his saddle, he felled a dead thorn. In the middle of the tree, in a little chamber near its centre, he found a small frog very beautifully formed, black and shining, marked with coral dapples. Once before he had found a similar frog in a similar position and had never ceased to wonder at it. How did it get there? As far as he could see there was no hole in the tree. What did it eat? How did it breathe? The little frog was a marvel, one more inexplicable bead in the necklace of God's creation. He watched it hop away from his hand, a small rose-pink and black speck on the bare red earth. It disappeared into the long grass and he lifted his axe again.

When he had cooked, he sat staring into the fire. There was company in a fire, in its crackle as he threw on fresh branches, in the quick flare-up of the twigs, in the hiss of the moisture from the wood and the slow dying down of the flames. He watched it till the logs lay, no more than glowing cores among the embers. A fire was alive. The shining ash collapsed into low heaps; it flew up on the breeze in little eddies; the burning wood and the stones round which it was piled reminded him of a thousand things—of houses, of snakes, of ranges of scarlet mountains. It seemed to him that the fire whispered to him as it died. A man with a fire was not really alone.

Dirk felt better now. The miracle of the little frog was set against the murder. In the balance of his mind it almost compensated it, proving God by its perfection; proving good as last night had proved evil.

These last days, riding along in search of his father, were like a dream, without reality. The riding away from home, the days in camp, the hours of hunting on the veld, Lena, the whole of the past, was cut like a string. Soon he would be with the others again, marching, their horses nickering and snapping at each other as they rode side by side. It was war. They were encysted, each privately and very alone—outside was their public action, within was their private core. Quite alone now, he realized how alone each man was even in the company of others. Only Stoffel seemed to be happy in war. And he had never liked Stoffel. It was not that he took exception to his club foot. God made men as He saw fit, but it was as if something in his mind was also clubbed—distorted. Events had proved this view justified. He was a hard young man, close in his mouth and his dealings. Not simply slim, delighting in a good deal even if some trickery were involved, but closer than that, a cheese-parer and humourless He was like a wild dog, always watching for the weakest buck and ready to pull him down.

Dirk thought of the way wild dogs hunted. Making the pace one after the other, always pushing the hunted beast to his fullest speed and falling back as they were expended, to allow another to take up the chase. Then, as the buck tired, they began to kill him, running at his side, leaping up at his flank, tearing at his stifle till they could pull out his entrails. Then they closed. Such men as Stoffel fattened in distress. Before God, he was honest enough, but like so many honest men, very hard in his dealings, interpreting always the letter and not the spirit of justice, and over-hard in his dealings with man and beast. His mind set a curb on his heart, and his heart was cold.

Sometimes, as he rode, Dirk's mind was empty, even of Lena. At others he thought continuously of her, of his brother and mother, of life as it had been before this, of his work on the farm; wondering if they had had rain, if he would be back in time to reap the mealies, if the stock was well, if the Kaffirs would choose this time to steal sheep and goats. He thought of how silent his father had been. He had hardly spoken since they had left home. He thought of the first day when they encamped, of how he had put his hand on his shoulder and said: "All will come right, Dirk. Do not fear. I have been thinking all day and it is in my heart that we must have no fear . . . It is for them that we fight."

His father had known all the time what was in his mind. It was wonderful that he had known, and yet perhaps it was not wonderful. What he thought must be in each man's mind. Thought of the home he had left, of the woman he had left, of his beasts and his cultivated lands. He rode past farms, and women carrying children with other children clinging to their skirts came out to wave to him. He waved back, but did not stop. There were no men in all the land. There were just commandos riding over the veld and women and children in the homes. No man had been allowed to stay. Even the lukewarm and half-hearted had been dragged in. Kruger had used the words of Our Lord Jesus Christ: "Those who are not with me are against me, and all men must declare their intentions. They must fight with the burgers or against them," he had said.

It was true that the English had brought some prosperity, had beaten Secocoeni in the North and the Zulus in the East, but the price of freedom was too great a price to pay for a prosperity that meant so little to his people. In that lay the fundamental difference of the two. The English thought of gold, of profit, whereas the Boers thought of their way of life. It was a special thing and had nothing to do with money. The Boers did not know what to do with money. He thought of some of them, his uncle, for instance, who had sold two farms for great sums and who only complained that he had been driven out. The money was useless to him. He needed nothing, and it remained in the bank or was buried under a tree. Old Joachim had sat with a gun in his hand for days shooting at prospectors. He knew there was gold on his farm, but was content to let it stay where it belonged, in the bowels of the earth. Then he had trekked to look for some place where he would be safe from disturbance, for a flat farm without any ridges or koppies where minerals could be discovered.

His father was right: things would come out, and if they did not it could not be helped. There was nothing that could be done. They must go on now till it was over. The plough was laid in the furrow. They must go forward. He patted Swartkie's neck. Lena liked his horse; that she had ridden him brought her near to him. When she thought of him, she must think of them together : think of Dirk and his black horse Swartkie. He wondered where she was, what she was doing. He wondered about her great-grandfather and when they would argue about lions again; and about her grandmother. He thought of the pretty frog; of old Joachim whose search for a farm where there was no gold must have been interrupted by the war.

In two or three days he would pick up Joubert. Then he would be with the others, but still alone : still enclosed in the box of his thoughts and memories. . . .

CHAPTER XVIII

HE WENT AS A BRIDE . . .

I

LENA was angry. This could not go on. If it did go on, Oupa could look after himself, or let Reuter look after him. What if he had charged a regiment by himself? What if he was almost a hundred? What if he had slain two hundred and eighty-four elephants, seventy-one lions, forty Kaffirs in the wars, according to his count, and two Englishmen last month? What if he . . . She stamped her foot.

" You will do as you are told, Oupa," she said.

" Ja, young miss, still wet from your birth, I will do as you tell me! I will eat the messes you bring me. I will sit where you put my chair. I will be sent to bed like a child. I will be shamed in front of my Kaffir and those who come to see me and hear my tales. And all this because you are like a little mare who misses her horse. Ja . . . Ja!" he shouted. " I will do these things. I will do them as surely as the Devil sits on a cloud in heaven picking his teeth with his three-pronged spear; just as surely will I do them. I am tired of it. No more brandy save what Reuter steals; no more sucking pig; no more chicken; no more beef; no more mutton; no buck; just pap because I have no teeth. Me, whose gums are harder than the teeth of others . . ."

Had he gone mad? How could he speak to her like this? Lena stepped back as he spluttered over her. Reuter grinned up at her from where he sat at Oupa's feet.

" The old lion turns," he said. " Magtig, it is as they say, the old lion becomes a man-eater when his teeth are gone."

" Silence, Kaffir!" Oupa shouted.

" Baas, I am a Zulu. I am Tabankulu of . . ."

" Of the Blue Horizon. Good God, do you think you have not told me a thousand times? But when I am angry, you are a Kaffir, a black dog like those others that I have shot; but one that I saved, to my detriment, that he might plague me in my old age. Silence, then, Zulu, silence. Close your ugly pink mouth and listen to my words with respect and attention. You, too, girl, go and fetch that woman; the time has come."

" Aaii . . . the time has come," Reuter said. He wriggled his toes with pleasure.

" Silence again, I say, and more silence. Bring the woman that my son Johannes married out of his abstinence. Because he would not sleep with

255

Kaffir maids when he was hunting, his rut betrayed him with that stick who masquerades as a white female. Bring her, I say, bring her here, for the hour has struck."

"Who . . . what?" Lena said.

"Who? What? Are there two such women in the world? Bring Kattie, your father's dam, in whose womb my seed was ruined."

"Baas, Baas," Reuter said, "save yourself for the charge. Save your strength. It is the old cow we must pull down."

"Silence, I say. But you are right, nevertheless. We must not exhaust ourselves." He grew calmer. "Bring your grandmother to me, Lena. I would see her."

"I am here, Philippus, if you want me."

"For the first time in your life, as far as I am concerned, woman, your coming is opportune," Philippus said. "I have reached a decision. I am going from here."

Lena had fallen back behind her grandmother. Going? Where was he going?

"I am taking my servant," he went on, "and we are going from here. We are going on visits. We are going to make the rounds. I am tired of this place. I am like a bull in a kraal, with an old dry cow and a heifer calf; neither of them interests me : neither is able to understand my qualities. I want the big wagon inspanned with the best span of red matched oxen. I want two boys and a voorloper. I want two horses, I want bedding, cook-pots, food, and if it is not ready to-morrow morning I will take the hide off your back. Now go, the pair of you, go and leave me. I would think of other and more pleasant things which is impossible while you stand there to remind me of my son's mistakes."

Lena was surprised when Ouma left him without a word. Her silence astonished her no less than Oupa's sudden fury.

When they were in the house, she had followed her grandmother and was trembling like a frightened horse.

Ouma said : "We will let him go : the old fool. We shall be well rid of him. He will eat and drink himself to death. Get out the things he will need. I will tell the boys to be ready. He can go, and then we will have peace. Perhaps he will be shot by the English. He seems to have forgotten that there is a war."

Lena went to get blankets and pillows for the kartel of the wagon, to sort out cook-pots, beakers, plates, pans, water-pots, buckets, tools. She heard her grandmother speaking to Titus, instructing him to prepare the wagon, to get out the trek-gear, riems, and spare gear—and set up the tent and bed in the back.

"But the war," Titus said. "I would sooner stay at home till it is over."

" The Old Baas will take care of you," Ouma said. " Is he not a great captain? Besides, this war is a white war. It is not against Kaffirs."

" Nevertheless, my heart is sore," Titus said. " Those English do not shoot as the Boers shoot. They shoot very wide, and in shooting at the Old Baas a bullet might easily strike Titus."

" Prepare the wagon and do as you are told," Ouma said.

Lena took a frying-pan from the nail where it hung. He would need a frying-pan and they had another one which was quite good, though the handle was a little loose.

But how funny it would be without Oupa! Bad as he was sometimes, he was human. He was wise. He understood her even when he said things to her that made her cry: a little mare, indeed. Tears ran down her cheeks. Oh, he made her so angry—he was so right.

2

" Baas, that was well done."

" Everything I do is well done, Reuter."

" Still it remains that it was well done, and I am entitled to say so. That is no criticism of the Baas. It is merely an observation. It is permitted for a servant to make observations. And this time it was just right. Which is owing to me. Too little, and the Baas would not have done it. His heart would have been too cold. Too much, and the Baas would have slept. No," he went on, " much is owing to Tabankulu, once Captain of the Blue Horizon Regiment of Moselekatse's impi in the time of T'Chaka. For a month now I have tried measuring it out in various quantities till I got it right. Aaii . . . aaii, to-day we have set our hands upon the butterfly. To-day we have caught the fleeting moment as it flew. To-day we have caught it with much skill, holding its painted wing between our fingers. This is a further observation, and worthy neither of compliment nor reply. Nevertheless, it remains a creditable action and as such will be registered in the great book that the Baas says is kept by his God up in the skies." Reuter raised his eyes to heaven. " There it will be written that Tabankulu made his Baas just drunk enough to face a woman in anger. Truly men and lions have much in common, both are man-eaters when they are old, as I stated previously. Both may be admired in youth, but both need only be feared in age when their teeth are gone . . ."

" You talk too much. I get no peace with your talk."

" Does the Baas imagine that I would dare to speak to him without being first spoken to? That is a great injustice that the Baas does to his servant. On the contrary, Tabankulu, not daring to speak to his Baas, being for ever silenced by his terror of his master, is driven to speaking to him as a child does. Only Tabankulu understands Tabankulu. Only Tabankulu will listen to Tabankulu. The Baas would be surprised at some of the conversation he has had with himself. Not that he would ever say anything against the Baas. He would never say: 'Tabankulu, your master is a drunken old fool.' Should he say something like that, Tabankulu would smite Tabankulu upon the mouth. No, no, Baas. The Baas must not think of such things. Tabankulu says to Tabankulu: 'What a wonderful master you have! He is like a bull. He is an elephant, he is the dust devil that raises the leaves spirally before the storm, he is the eagle, the hawk, the wild cat; he is the personification of beauty, of courage, of virtue and virility.' These are the things he talks about when he is forced to talk to himself because his master's mind is occupied with greater things."

"Have you done, Reuter?" Philippus asked.

"I am done, Baas. I am silent. Like a kameel there is no sound in me. I am incapable of speech. I can neither cry, groan, nor speak."

"Then let us sleep a little, Reuter. We have had victory."

"Aaii, and what a victory it was, O master!"

3

For once everything went according to plan; there were no setbacks. The wagon was ready with a full red span; the two boys, Titus and Job, were ready. The voorloper sat below the horns of the leading oxen with the lead riems in his hands. The two saddle horses were fast to the wagon-rail at the back. The tent was spread, the boxes, barrels, and oddments, including his own chair that Oupa insisted on taking, were lashed down. The wagon pack hung from its hook below the bed balanced on the other side by a spare water barrel.

Lena could not take her eyes off Oupa as he walked round his equipage, poking at everything, examining everything. You would have thought he was going away for ever. He had his guns, his powder barrel, his lead, and his bullet moulds. He is back in the past, she thought, in the days when he trekked for months hunting and trading in the wilds. He looked younger. He stood erect and walked briskly cursing every one while Ouma sat on the stoep sewing and not even raising her eyes when he spoke.

Reuter came out with a wooden box fastened with a padlock in which he kept his personal possessions. The boys' rolls of blankets were stowed. Everything was ready and they all stood watching Reuter as he drew from the pocket of his trousers some pieces of soiled ribbon—white, red, blue, green, and yellow. He tied them to the wagon whip and on to the tent. He produced an ostrich feather, dyed red, from somewhere, and made it fast to the yoke of the leading oxen.

"This is to make it gay," he said.

"Hurry!" Oupa shouted. "Make ready to trek, we are going to move."

He came up on to the stoep and folded Lena in his arms. "Good-bye, my child," he said. He kissed her. His breath smelt only of tobacco; there was no brandy on it, which surprised her. "Do not fear," he said. "One day he will return. But if he does not, others will come to you for your honey. The rumours of a woman's beauty go forth flying over the veld. They are like a honey-bird twittering to men hungry for such things. So fear not, my heart. Your fulfilment is certain and only the means of it in doubt."

To Ouma he said: "I go, woman. Driven forth from my own home by blows and inhospitality, by promiscuous purges, by neglect, by lack of nourishment—the meat and brandy which as a master are my due. Be shamed, therefore, I go," he said. "I go without farewells, since I am driven out at a hundred years of age to seek my fortune like a boy among strangers who, nevertheless, having heard of my exploits, will treat me better than my kin." He turned from her, went to the wagon, and climbed on to the seat above the disselboom. "Trek!" he shouted. "Come, trek."

The voorloper sprang up. Titus clapped the long beribboned whip. Job made loose the brake.

They were off. Oupa had gone from them. He had gone in a wagon decked out for a bride. He went as a bride, Lena thought. What a strange world it was and what changes there were! Someone else had gone. Now, indeed, it was a place of women. She stood watching the wagon till it was out of sight. Ouma neither spoke nor moved.

Before he had been gone an hour, Lena knew the hole he had left in her life. He had been so old—yet so alive. She even longed for his complaints. Sitting in his chair, motionless, he had still dominated the farm by his presence, and now even his chair was gone. If he had died, there would still be his chair, she thought, and his things—his old muzzle-loading guns that he would not give up for anything as new-fangled as a breech-loading weapon. To be safe, a gun should shoot out of one end, he said, and the other should be enclosed. To fire a gun that opened at both ends was to tempt Providence. There would have been his guns, his red kat karos, his plate and beaker. There would have been his hat hanging from the big ox horns in the passage.

For him to have died would have been explicable. It was even something she had long expected. But for him to go out of her life with all his possessions and his room swept bare was an event for which she had made no preparation.

But she did not have long to brood. She had hardly done supervising the cleaning of his room when there was a shout from outside.

"Lena . . . Lena!" She ran to the window.

It was Tanta Martha, Tanta Aletta van der Berg who so rarely visited, and another woman almost as fat as Tanta Martha: a stranger in a country where there were no strangers. Who could it be? As she went out, she wondered how the two of them had got into the cart and how they would ever get out. Tanta Aletta sat alone behind them.

Ouma was standing on the stoep.

"It is my little Kattie," the fat woman cried, flinging out her arms so that she struck Tanta Martha's breast. "My Klein Kattie."

"I am Katarina du Toit," Ouma said, "but who are you?"

The woman laughed till the cart shook.

"That is good! Magtig, that is good! I am Stephanie, your sister. I am back. I have returned to my land, and what a time I have had!" She began to wriggle her thighs clear of Tanta Martha's.

"A box," Tanta Martha cried, "a box for us to get down. Was it not good of me to bring your sister, Kattie?" she asked. "She has just come. She went first to Letta's and then said we must all come here to see you. And we passed Oom Philippus on the road," she said. "He was clapping his whip and singing."

"Yes," Stephanie said, "you lose one person and gain another. You lose a father-in-law and gain a sister."

By this time she was down. It had not been easy. She ran to Ouma, her small feet twinkling under her bulk. She enveloped Ouma, sweeping over her as a flood sweeps over an obstruction. For a moment Lena could not see her grandmother. Then she reappeared, only to disappear again. It was said that a drowning man came up three times. Lena waited. Ouma came up again and fought herself loose.

"Stephanie!" she said. "Yes, this is certainly a surprise. And your husband, where is Meneer van Zyl?"

"My poor husband," Stephanie said, "poor man! He is dead. Later, when we have eaten, I will tell you how he died. Poor man! Now I am a widow again for a second time."

"Again?" Ouma said.

"Yes, again. I have had great misfortunes. They have left me money and property, but what is that?" She began to cry. "If you knew how I longed for my country through those terrible years. I have seen everything in the world. I have done everything—eating and drinking and dancing with red slippers on my feet, with burgomasters and councillors. But I have longed for my folk, for Letta and my little sister—Kattie." She fell on Ouma again.

The horses were being outspanned. A box was taken from the back of the cart.

Tanta Stephanie had come from Holland to stay with her baby sister. That was funny, to hear this fat woman calling Ouma her little sister. Tanta Stephanie was back. Lena tried to remember what she had heard of her. She could remember very little except that Ouma hated her and that she had left the country in the old troubled days when Ouma was a baby to marry a rich Hollander.

4

It was strange to see Stephanie again. Tanta Katarina looked at her face. No, there was nothing in it that she could recognize. It was the face of a stranger, not that of a sister. You could not be expected to remember someone you had last seen when you were three. But you should have feelings about your sister. There should, it seemed to her, be some inward perception of your common blood. There was none. She had no feeling for this fat blowzy woman who was overdressed in the foreign fashion that she disliked so much.

" You can have Oupa's room, Stephanie," she said.

I should have given her a better welcome, she thought, but I have got out of the habit of welcome, and besides I do not like her. I never did and I have not changed. It was surprising how little she had changed, but her coldness passed unnoticed. Stephanie and Tanta Martha were talking to Lena. Ouma looked at Letta. They smiled at each other.

It was sixty-four years since Stephanie had left home to marry van Zyl and go back with him to Holland : van Zyl the traitor, van Zyl the weasel. But all that she had learnt later from Letta. Sixty-four years—a lifetime in which they had both lived out their lives. Stephanie had been a girl then and Kattie had been a baby. And between those years—the year she and Stephanie had parted and to-day—they had grown up, blossomed, fruited, and died. When you had nothing more to live for you were dead, whatever any one said. Stephanie had married, had become a widow; had married again, and become a widow again; no doubt she had borne children; had travelled over the seas; and now she was back. And yet it seemed only yesterday that her great cock Paulus had been killed and the martyrs of her nation had been twice hanged. She saw it all : saw April, her father's servant, kill her pet cock; saw Kaspar on his horse; saw the English dragoons in their blue coats mounted on short-tailed horses that were maddened by the flies as they surrounded the great gallows. She saw her father, Rudolf, sick from his spear wound; she saw van Ek, old Oom Christiaan. She saw the great wagon rolling off to the north; she saw herself held between Letta's knees peering back to see the last of the Baviaans River and her home. She looked at Letta again, How different she was from Stephanie, but, of course, they were not sisters, only foster sisters; but where Stephanie had been blown out by time like a fat pink rose, Letta had been shrivelled by age like an apple. Her skin, folding into a thousand wrinkles, made a network that covered her face and neck. Their eyes met again. Letta smiled at her and said : " She has not changed. Stephanie is still the same."

They all went into the house. Rosina brought coffee, Ouma got out bread, biscuits, Boer-rusks, and preserves.

A world of women, Lena thought, as she watched them : a world of women whose lives lie backwards; and each one different from the other. But it was good to see Tanta Martha again and Tanta Letta whom she saw but seldom. She kept herself to herself—pleased to have visitors when they came, but she encouraged none of them and never went out. Usually silent, she now talked quickly, raising her hands with quick little birdlike movements and turning her head from one to the other. Lena was silent. She had nothing to say nor had they words for her. Their talk was of the past, of the time before she was born, or even thought of. Stephanie talked of her adventures, of Holland, of England, where her husband had taken her later. She had even seen the English Queen driving in her carriage behind eight cream stallions that were ridden by men in red-and-gold coats and small black velvet caps. She talked about her second husband, who had been a councillor. She spoke of her children. " My eldest son is sixty-three," she said.

" Mine would have been sixty-two," Letta said. " Ja, he would have been sixty-two on the sixth of May. And fancy, Jacobus van Zyl only dying five years ago. It was forty years since Kaspar had died."

" My second husband, the councillor, only lived three years," Stephanie said, " but he was a fine, full-blooded man : a great reader : like my Jacobus. I have always been attracted to educated men. There is something about them that is different." She went on to speak of Kaspar.

That was Tanta Letta's husband, who had reared Ouma in the Northern Bushveld. But it was strange to hear one woman talk of another woman's husband, and to think of all that had happened in the old days. They could not have loved as I do, Lena thought. She could not believe that they had, but as they talked it would seem that she was wrong. They used words that were in her own mind.

" I loved Kaspar van der Berg," Stephanie said. " Magtig, he was a beautiful man—if only he had been more educated : so big, so strong, so brave. But he treated me badly, which was due to lack of culture. He did not understand a young girl's feelings which are very delicate and easily bruised." She spoke of his words, his gestures, the bright gold hairs on his arms. He must have been like Dirk, Lena thought, and listened harder. As Stephanie went on about the way his hair grew in a peak on his forehead, Tanta Martha was silent. She just sat breathing heavily, with her hands like lumps of dough on her knee, looking from Stephanie to Letta. Ouma sat, too, not talking, but stiff, her fingers moving against each other, her eyes charged with malevolence, darting glances at Stephanie's face. If she were going to stay long, there would be trouble, Lena thought. More trouble—as if there were not enough already. These old loves worried her. If they were once like us, then one day we shall be like them, she thought. And Tanta Aletta was not taking to this talk of Kaspar kindly either. But there was no stopping Tanta Stephanie, she was like something wound up that must go on till it runs down.

5

Aletta listened to Stephanie: asked questions, answered them; but she had not got used to having Stephanie back again. She wondered if she ever would. And how was it that Stephanie remembered Kaspar so well? Stephanie, whom he had never loved, seemed to know him better than she, who had been his wife for twenty years. As Stephanie spoke, she remembered things about him that she had forgotten. Had I really forgotten them? she wondered, or were those memories put away, like keepsakes with rose leaves and fragrant herbs in a chest? Or perhaps Stephanie had thought more of him, whereas she, living with him, had simply lived and not thought overmuch. It had been enough to live with him, to share with him, to bear his children, and to love him. Then after his death she had set up his memory in a little shrine in her heart, sealing it with her tears, and then leaving it, knowing that she was buried there beside him. Not thinking any more of her Kaspar, but conscious of him and certain that he was still near her.

Stephanie's talk upset her. She did not wish to think of Kaspar in this way. It was indecent. Yet that was the way Stephanie had always thought of men and spoken of them—as if they were horses or bulls. She tried to turn her thoughts for fear that Stephanie would see what was in her mind. She tried to speak of other things, of her grandchildren, and great-grandchildren, but she could not. Stephanie kept bringing the conversation back to Kaspar, and asked how he died.

Aletta wanted to refuse to answer. Instead she said: " Kaspar was killed by an ox, Stephanie: a tame ox that swung his head to reach a fly when Kaspar was near him, and his horn pierced his eye, entering his brain. Ja, it was a strange thing that a man who had hunted elephants and lions, who had fought Kaffirs and Englishmen all his life, should die from the poke of a tame pole-ox's horn."

All this had been pent up in her. Never before had she spoken of the irony of his death. It had only hovered on the edge of her mind. Now irony was piled on irony—that of her being alive and here with Stephanie; that they should both be alive, the one dried up like a leaf and the other bloated, while strong men died about them. Truly the race was not to the swift nor the battle to the strong. But it was lonely. Dear God, how lonely it was! Stephanie's coming had made her much lonelier, reviving all these things, raising the dead men from their graves so that they walked. Her talk desecrated the dead.

How lonely it was to be old! Aletta looked at Lena. It was lonely to be

a young girl too. That was a strange thing to think of—the loneliness
of age and youth; but youth had the future, which would not be lonely, to
look forward to, while age had only the past, which had not been lonely,
to look back upon. Letta thought of her own youth and Stephanie's by
the Great Fish River, and of Kattie, a baby playing with cock and dolls.
When a girl became a woman, her blood flowed, her breasts swelled,
and then later she flowered, as her belly grew great, quickened by the life
her man had put into her. Then she was no longer lonely and grew to
full ripeness, with continued swellings and burgeonings, grew fat with love
and milk, growing in weight and solidity till she was a mature woman,
round and thick and soft with the rich fat of her life and its contentment.
Then the time came when she could bear no more children, when as a
giver of life her life was ended, and she grew fatter still and more quiet.
That was what the years had done to Martha Kleinhouse and Stephanie.
Others dried up. I dried up, she thought, from the inside when my sap
ceased to flow. Kattie was like neither the one nor the other. She had
always been thin and never over-rounded. Letta put thoughts of others
from her. She wished to think of herself. Only yesterday she had looked
at herself, wondering where the beauty that Kaspar had loved had gone.
The skin on her belly that had been soft and smoothly rounded now hung
in loose folds, her breasts were flat like empty purses with chewed ends.
That was age. We are very old, she thought, Stephanie and I. To be old
was to be respected by your descendants because they were descendants,
but you were not loved nor could you love; you were too far removed from
life, from the present, though you were in it. Love and respect went but
rarely hand in hand. And Stephanie could scarcely be respected : no more
to-day than in the old days. How little people changed the form of their
character! Man-mad as a girl she was still man-mad. Vain as a girl and
still vain. She watched her toying with a string of crystal beads that hung
from her neck to her waist.

" They come from the Indies," Stephanie said. " My second son Jappie
brought them to me. He is a sea captain owning a part share of his ship.
He always brings me things—silks, ivories, perfumes . . ."

Before God, Letta thought again, she has not changed. A fury possessed
her suddenly. Stephanie had tried to seduce Kaspar and take him from
her—so long ago, so long ago, her mind said. It is all over . . . long, long
ago. But her heart could not see it as long ago. It was yesterday, and then,
when she had failed to get him to lie with her behind a bush, she had tried
to betray him. To betray her Kaspar, with a price on his head, to the
English.

She wrinkled her nose in disgust. " Perfume ! " she said.

" Smell," Stephanie said.

" Me smell you ? " Letta drew up her eyebrows. " At your age you
should have more sense," she said. " Who is going to smell you now ? "

She sniffed again. " Or since you use so much, who is going to help smelling you? Magtig, Stephanie," she said, " you smell of mice."

" It is musk," Stephanie said. " A rare and delicate perfume that comes from a deer."

" I have heard of it," Letta said. " It comes in a bag with other things in the hinder part of a male buck."

" It is rare," Stephanie said. " Great ladies use it."

" Great ladies may like to smell like the hinder part of a buck, but for you to smell like one will not make you into a great lady. You are a Boer woman, the daughter of Rudolf of Baviaans River, and it seems to me that you have changed very little to still be whoring at eighty."

" How dare you speak to me like that," Stephanie said, " when I have come so far to be at home! How dare you!" She tried to get up, pushing her ringed fingers against the table, but the chair was drawn too close and she subsided.

" Do not be angry, Stephanie," Letta said. " It is just that you make me laugh. Once I hated you, but now you make me laugh."

Ouma filled all the cups with coffee, but took none herself; she said it was bad for her.

Tanta Martha was chuckling. " It is like the old times," she said, " when we were all young, with lovers and husbands and children, when we were loving and quarrelling and being brought to bed."

" And it is good to have you back, Stephanie, no matter how badly you smell," Aletta said. Her lips quivered; she put down her cup. Her anger had gone.

What was all this? Why were they here? It was a mockery. Why were there no men, no guns hanging on the walls? Every one was dead, and the country at war again. Too much had happened recently. When you were old, you did not want things to happen. The drive to Mooiplaas had upset her. So had passing Philippus on the road. She had hoped to talk to him. He had loved Kaspar, they had been close friends. And Stephanie coming suddenly like this . . .

" It is time we went back, Martha ," she said. It would be better to get back. In one's own house one could compose oneself. There were things there had helped you, objects that you could touch : things of Kaspar's. She longed to be home so that she could touch something of his again; his clothes that she still kept folded in a box; his guns; his silver jackal karos that had no hair on it now.

Tanta Martha got up and called for her horses. Stephanie sat at the table still, drinking coffee and eating preserves.

" Soon," she said, " I will look out for a little place, a house in the dorp where I can see my friends; but it is no use now till this is all over and the men are back."

" Men!" Letta said. " Is there nothing in the world but men?"

"Men are interesting," Tanta Martha said. She pinched Lena's cheek. "Are they not, my heart?"

"It is my nature to like men," Stephanie said. "And many men, not boys naturally, still think me a fine woman. There was a man on the boat, a Hollander, who wanted me to go to Java with him. He has a great farm there where he grows rice in the swamps and spices on the mountains. I miss him," she said. "And he said: 'Do not forget, if you change your mind, Stephanie, I shall be there.' It was hard to leave him, but what could I do being so recently widowed? It would not have been right to marry him. One must wait. But we are going to correspond. He wrote me a poem and gave me a lock of his hair."

Letta bent over her to kiss her. "Come and see us before you go to the Indies," she said.

"I should be able to see Jappie there," Stephanie said, "which is another advantage, since his ship is in the Eastern trade. You may laugh, but I miss that man; ja, I miss him."

They said good-bye to Ouma and Lena.

It had been an extraordinary day. Oupa gone, Tanta Stephanie here, and from the look of it rain was coming at last. A big storm was riding up on the wind. Lena wondered if they would get to Brennersdorp before it broke. She wished it would come soon; a storm before it came always made her nervous, restless, and unable to settle down.

But it did not break till late. It came when she was in bed—suddenly with a great crash of thunder, as if the heavens were being burst asunder. The lightning and thunder came simultaneously; the storm was right on top of them, right over the koppie. The lightning flashes came in under the eaves and lit up the timbers that held the roof. They were so continuous that she could count them. How funny it was to lie here counting the roof-poles in the lightning. Now that it had come she felt at ease, the tension was gone.

If only I was in Dirk's arms, she though, and then she was angry with herself for thinking of such a thing. Where was her modesty? Yet she knew she had thought of it many times. Not only of Dirk, but before she loved him, she had thought of lying in the arms of a husband while the rain poured down in torrents and the outside world was torn by storms. For it seemed to her that this was the way a woman must always see herself—held by a man in security, with the man, the husband, the father of her children, stretched out, a protecting shadow between herself and a hostile world. Turning, she put an arm over the pillow. If only it was his shoulder, if only she could have buried her head in his chest! To-night she did not want sleep, she wanted to remain balanced, poised on the storm, aware, and think of Dirk, pretending his body lay at her side.

Dirk . . . she thought. Where was he in this storm? Her pleasure in it was destroyed by the knowledge that he might be out in it. The events of the day passed through her mind again, coming as pictures—Oupa's going, his wagon fluttering with ribbons; the coming of Stephanie . . . She thought of Dirk again; of his father; of her brother Louis; of Stoffel. She thought of Ouma and her love for Stoffel. He was, in her eyes, all that a young man should be, she could not do enough for him. It seemed to Lena that her grandmother behaved as if she owed Stoffel something, as if his misfortune was in some way her fault. She did not behave as though she was sorry for him; on the contrary, where he was concerned she acted with a fierce pride, acted as though his deformity was a banner, something creditable to be displayed. But why? For whom or against whom Lena could never imagine. She was, and always had been, sorry for Stoffel; a little ashamed, perhaps, certainly not proud, and on account of her shame tried to be more gentle with him and tolerant of his savage moods whose cause she thought she understood.

Yet she did not love him; but only when he boasted of his riding and shooting did she hate him. The rest of the time she was sad for him. That's what I feel for Stoffel, she thought : sorrow always and hatred sometimes for this strange moody man who was her eldest brother. Also, though she would scarcely acknowledge it, she feared him. He was, about his beliefs, fanatical to the point of madness. Stoffel, she felt, would kill ruthlessly for his principles, and she was not sure that his principles were right.

There were so many patterns. She had not known them before. The pattern of Ouma's hate, of Oupa's peacocks, of Tanta Martha's medicines, of Reuter's devotion, of Stoffel's warping, of Louis's solidity, of Groot Dirk's solemn love of his family and home-place, the pattern of her own love for Dirk. That strange talk with Tanta Martha, when they were getting roots and leaves, had thrown all the various pieces, the strange tangles of character and motive and design, into a great pattern that not only included all these things, but a much vaster and all-embracing thing, that reached from the depths of the earth beneath her feet into the tremendous flashing bowl of the sky above her head.

The storm still roared. There was no end to it, no understanding of it; it was infinite, and though visible completely inexplicable in its relation to her love, which was part of all love, not only of man and woman, or woman and child, but of beast and flower and tree, and in some way the storm was part of it. She turned over in bed and pulled up a blanket. It had got much colder suddenly. There would be hail.

And Dirk had done this for her. By loving her he had welded the world into a single whole of which she was a part : a little wheel spinning with the greatness of her love for him : a little wheel among a thousand other little wheels. She thought of Timmy, the drummer boy, on the colonel's big white horse, who had come to fetch them to the battle : that had been the pattern of defeat that all defeated men must follow. She thought of Boetie's blindness : that was the pattern of the blind to which all the blind must conform.

She thought of herself. My love pattern, the pattern common to all women who loved. Yet it had never happened to any one before—not exactly. No one had ever felt quite as she did. But it had also happened since the beginning of time and would go on till the end of time. That was why they had talked as they did this afternoon. All women, even Ouma, from whom she was descended, had felt as she did once—the exact resemblance depending on their personalities; but within the limit of their individuality they had all felt as she did; and all those who would come from her, in the limitless future, would feel as she did now. Knowing nothing of her, perhaps not even her name, they would feel thus because they were women, just as she felt what those others, who had preceded her, had felt, because she was a woman. That was the wonder of it. That was what hurt you and made you glad : this endless recurrence : this endless repetition in which nothing was ever repeated, and everything that occurred was different from everything else that ever would or could occur. A bird flew through the air, but the same bird could never fly through the same air again. The endless waiting days must pass, dragging their broken wings, but no matter how slowly they passed, not one of them could be recaptured.

She thought back to her afternoon at Doornkloof, to Tanta Johanna, Klein Johanna, Boetie, and his game of stones; to the goats, to Groot Dirk's dogs of which he thought so much, to the house in which Dirk had lived, the home in which he had been brought up. She had played with Dirk ever since she could remember. Were they not cousins? But why had it never entered her head in those days, when they were little, that she would love him? Yes, she had loved him then, but as a cousin, as a playmate, when she had not hated him as a cousin and a playmate. That was when he had pulled her hair or put cockleburs in it so that it tangled in knots that must be cut out and left her hair looking like the bedraggled tail of a cow. She had hated him then. Now he said her hair was beautiful, black and sleek as the black leopard he had shot once. A black tiger was very rare; only once in many years was one killed. Oupa had killed one too. Dirk must always have been interested in my hair, she thought : only he did not know it, nor did I. That was why he could not leave it alone. She must tell him that when she saw him again.

When would she see him again? Where had he been to-night? How far had the storm gone? But when I do see him, she thought, I shall forget to speak of it. Then I do not want to speak : I only want to be near, to be held, to have his hands upon me. She thought of those early days when they were both children and Boetie a baby in the wooden cradle. His father had lain in it, and Dirk, and then later Johanna. Perhaps, she thought, our children will lie in it one day. It was very old, having come from Holland in 1652 with the first van der Berg; and that he had brought it showed that it was old and valued even then.

Everything in the house at Doornkloof was the same as it had been when she was little. Even some of the dogs, grey about the muzzle now, had been dark-faced pups then. But last time, as she had prayed with his mother, it had all been different. It was as if she had seen it for the first time in her life instead of the hundredth. That was what love did to you. It made you see and feel. It made you think and know, but not through your mind. You felt things through your skin, your hands, through the pain in your breasts that seemed heavy with knowledge, as if it were a foretaste of the milk that would dilate them later. You knew so much without learning. Or perhaps you had always known it and only by love did it become conscious knowledge . . . a cupboard suddenly flung open and found full of treasures stored one by one in your life, but never seen together in their full glory till that instant. She thought of Boetie again. If Boetie should suddenly see all the things he knew by touch and smell and hearing, that would be like love : a thousand half-understood mysteries becoming one glorious mystery, one all-enveloping desire, one hope of fulfilment that dwarfed all other hopes, thoughts, and desires.

The pain in her heart increased, the ache of her emptiness swept over her. She was a woman now, all woman, and for this pain there was only one solace, only one answer. Because she was woman the answer was man. Because she was Lena the answer was Dirk. Nothing else would do. Till he held her again she lived, but was not alive. To lie in his arms was her destiny. Only there was to be found the fullness that could make her whole. With him she felt herself opening like a flower; even at the thought of him, and away from him she closed up again like a bud at dusk.

She thought of his home once again, of Groot Dirk his father, of his mother, of Boetie who was so beautiful with his wheaten hair and dark blue sightless eyes, so trusting that it made you want to cry. What had the storm done to her that she thought in circles, first of one thing and then of another and another and then going back to the first? It seemed to her that by these thoughts she could bring Dirk near to her; that by her sleepless nights she could give him sleep; that by tearing herself to pieces with her imaginings she could cradle his head on her breasts and could give him rest. Surely by suffering yourself you could ease the suffering of others; surely by paying endlessly you could bring others profit. Or was it for nothing? She put the thought from her. Sometimes Dirk was so near her. She knew at those times he was thinking of her as she thought of him; that no matter what the distance between them was, they were together, the skein of her love thoughts tangled with his.

She moved restlessly. How many nights were there to be like this? How often must she lie awake listening to the night sounds?—to the crow of a cock in the moonlight?—to the laughing cry of a hunting jackal. the bark of a dog, or the hoot of an owl?—veld sounds, night sounds . . . to how many storms? And Dirk was out there in the night. But where? She never knew in which direction to send her thoughts—north, south, east, or west. Perhaps thought went in circles so that it did not matter which way you faced. What mattered, what must matter was the intensity of your thought and the suffering that it caused you. It was this that sent them palpitating into the void till they were caught up by his answering thoughts. She hardly dared to stop thinking of him now in case their thoughts should miss each other on the way; any more than she dared to go far from the house for fear of missing him if he came.

She sat up in bed and shook out her hair. She pushed it back from her forehead. She ran her hands through it. It was the hair that Dirk had pulled when they were little; it was the hair he had kissed, burying his head in it now that they were lovers. They were one. That was a comfort to her since it was fact, and had been. He had taken her under the blue gums. The leaves had been a black lace veil over the night-blue sky. There had been stars, bright jewels, the only witnesses of that consummation: the bright stars, the trees, and the nightjar that had passed them in its moth hunt, covering them with its swift, cutting wings. And I made him, she thought. That is the woman's power that I have. I made him take me. I can make him come to me because I am a woman. She lay back and ran her hands over her body: her ribs, her smooth belly, her hips, her thighs. But it was his hands she wanted.

CHAPTER XIX

A WOMAN'S LIFE

OUMA put down her sewing. The time had come. Not only had she told Lena that she would talk to her, but the presence of Tanta Stephanie in the house, the visit of Tanta Martha and Tanta Letta yesterday, and the going of Oupa, had all conspired to revive the past. It was afternoon. Tanta Stephanie was sleeping. She seemed to spend much time resting; and Lena had just come from putting the bread into the big oven that stood in the yard behind the house.

" Come here, Lena," she called.

" You want me, Ouma?" she said.

" Yes, I want you. Sit down. The time has come for me to speak to you. You have heard much," she said, " I know that. You have been told stories by your great-grandfather, you have heard them from Tanta Martha and from others. Some are lies, some are the truth. The story you have never heard is my story. I tell it to you so that you may tell it to others, passing it on, for it is thus that our history lives within our hearts. It is not something out of books, for with us there is only one.

" Yes," she said, " there is but one Book, the one that governs our lives. Tanta Letta you have known all your life. You have known that she brought me up, thus repaying her debt to my Uncle Frederik Bezuidenhout whom the English slew, and to my father, Rudolf de Wet, who took her in after Oom Frederik had found her a captive among the Kaffirs. That you have not seen more of Tanta Letta is that she has kept herself to herself since Kaspar died. And though she and I love each other, when we are together the past comes too close to us. I think we would forget those old days and the hardships we suffered if we could. We are not like some others."

Lena knew she was thinking of Oupa and Tanta Martha, who boasted continually of the past.

" The past was not good," she went on. " It was bitterly hard, what with English oppression, the Kaffirs and the Bushmen, the wild beasts, and the sicknesses." She paused.

" I saw the hangings at Slagtersnek," she said. " That is something you must tell your children when they come, that their great-grandmother saw the hangings. That broke up our lives upon the Great Fish River. It was beautiful there. I wonder sometimes if the great fig where my father's anvil stood is still there. I used to play under it with my dolls."

It was funny to think of Ouma as a child with dolls.

" And I had a tame cock called Paulus that Tanta Letta made April kill to make broth because I was sick. She did not understand the regard in which I held that cock. That was on the day of the hanging or the day before it : I forget which." This explained Ouma's love for poultry. " And just after it, my father was wounded by a Kaffir who lay for him on his farm, and then we trekked. Tanta Stephanie had gone off with a Hollander, a traitor in the pay of the English; and Kaspar van der Berg, a cousin of Groot Dirk's father, was being hunted for his life. He was with Coenraad de Buys the outlaw, having joined his band. It was to them we went later, and then from there on into the North after Tanta Aletta had been married to Kaspar. How we lived I do not know—by hunting and trading, by fighting sometimes : Tanta Letta fighting at his side, with me and the other children fighting too, loading and firing guns if we could. Then there came a great drought, but that was much later, and all the cattle died. It was terrible to see them.

" We had been forced into the bad country just before it began, by the English. Kaspar had come too near the Border, and we trekked west with the King's dragoons after us. Kaspar knew that country and thought we could come through it and that the English would not be able to follow us. Years before, a boy, he had been in a war against the Bushmen there with Coenraad.

" We did come through, but empty, broken, leaving our wagons and beasts dead behind us. We trekked from empty water-hole to empty water-hole. The sun was hotter than I have ever known it. The ground was shining brass that burned through our veldschoen. The oxen died in the yokes, the leaves on the thorn trees were shrivelled and brittle. There was no game; even the gemsbok which can live without water were gone. There were no wild melons; they, too, had failed to mature or were shrivelled. There was no water even to be sucked through reeds in the dry riverbeds. It was bad everywhere we heard afterwards, but at that time we did not know it and had chosen this moment to venture into the desert.

" The working oxen died in their yokes," she went on. " We abandoned everything we could to lighten the wagon, just leaving it on the veld; and even empty, the wagon still sank into the loose sand which hid the felloes and came half-way up the spokes. The loose cattle kept licking the iron tyres of the wheels in the evening to cool their tongues and stood round us bellowing, looking at us with bursting eyeballs and swollen tongues. The dumb beasts called to us, and when you live like that they are your friends. It is terrible. Each ox and cow and calf is known to you. Others had been before us on that trek-path and some of the pans were full of dead oxen that had died and rotted there. We managed ourselves with water from the barrels slung under the wagon, eking it out a cupful at a time, and the beasts just lived on such rotten water as was left.

"But at last we could go no farther. Six working oxen lay dead in the yoke; the others, the loose cattle and horses, staggered as they walked and lay down beside us to die. In a few hours they were fly-blown and stank. The flies covered them like black mats. They were piled thick, one on top of the other, on the carcasses, and the trees round us were filled with vultures waiting for us to die. They were like great fruits on those trees. There was no shade anywhere except under the wagon which we could not use for the stink of the dead beasts; and as soon as we moved from it, the aasvoels fell on the dead oxen and tore them so that when we returned for a cup of water, the ground was strewn with entrails and flapping birds that would run a few steps and then begin to tear at another beast, first taking out its eyes and then working into the soft parts of the body from between their legs, sometimes becoming entirely hidden in the cavities of the beast, even getting stuck there within the ribs. We should have died if it had not been for Kaspar's Bushman Adam, who then, when all seemed lost, said he would try to find some of his people. He had been taken from those parts. It was a great risk, for the wild Bushmen hate the tame, and kill them if they catch them, with many tortures. But he went and returned with two wild Bushmen almost as the last cup of water was done.

"They had agreed to lead us to water if Kaspar would hunt for them. They wanted seacows that they could not kill with their poisoned arrows. They were mad for fat, which was absent even round the kidneys of those beasts that they could kill in the drought. We went with them, drinking foul water from the ostrich eggs stoppered with wax that they had buried under the ground in various places over the veld. We were with them a year. Everything was gone, wagons, working oxen, cows, horses—nothing was left. We children lived through it running half naked and wild with the Bushmen. When Kaspar left them, the drought had broken, and they showed us a place known to none before where there were many dead elephants. Here we got much ivory and were able to re-establish ourselves.

"That was a strange place, Lena," she said. "Many have spoken of it, but few have seen it : a great swamp where all elephants return to die. There is nothing like it in all the world. There were hundreds, thousands, of great skeletons, all with big tusks, some yellow and almost black with age. There were old elephants standing up to their knees in mud swaying their trunks while they waited for death. They made no movement against us. For them we were not there. Nor was there any need to shoot. The tusks were there; all we had to do was to chop them out of the skulls that lay everywhere. You never saw so many vultures, so many hyenas, so many jackals—all tame, all so fat they could scarcely move. Maribou storks, eagles—a carrion world; a charnel house set in a great green vlei that was pink with flying flamingoes!"

She was silent as if she was seeing it all again.

"We got porters," she said, "and carried away much ivory which we sold to the Portuguese. We were re-established and safe from the English. Anything, even the worst that could happen, was better than being captured by the English. Kaspar, my foster father, was always afraid of them and never dared to go back after that. He never saw his father and mother again. They were rich, having big wine and sheep farms in the Colony, but they could do nothing for him.

"Then, when I was seventeen, Johannes du Toit, son of Philippus Jacobus, came North hunting. He had been looking for the swamp to which all elephants return when they are ready to die. He never found it, but was convinced of its existence. Swart Piet du Plessis had told him he thought he had been near it once with Rinkals, the old witch doctor, who accompanied him everywhere. They were going to seek it together later, but then came the scandal with your grandmother Sannie, wife of Hendrik van der Berg, and Swart Piet was killed with her at Canaan, so no more came of it. None of us spoke of what we had seen. We had sworn an oath to Kaspar to say nothing of the place of elephants. To-day is the first time I have spoken of it. It was a place of ill omen. Though I was married to Johannes, I said nothing. It was the only thing I kept from him.

"My husband, your grandfather, was one of the guides on the Great Trek. He knew that country. He knew it all. He told me then that Hendrik was deluded in settling in the valley they called Canaan. He said it was a bad place, beautiful but unhealthy, and that he should have pressed on beyond the Lebombo Mountains into the rich lands that lie between them and the coast. I was with him on the Trek," she said, "and knew them all—Uys, Potgieter, Piet Retief, who later was killed by the Zulus, Paul Pieters. Ja, I remember them all," she said.

"We went in little companies and laagered every night. I saw Paul Kruger then. He was just a boy and now he is the father of our people. Our Oom Paul, and our hope. Where was I?" she said. "Oh, yes, the Trek. After that we stayed in Lemansdorp for a while. Johannes was still hunting and trading. Sometimes I went with him, sometimes I did not.

"Tanta Martha was there, married to Gert Kleinhouse, the grandson of Old Tanta Anna de Jong. How they hated each other, those two, at first. Martha's first husband Coetzee was related to us on my mother's side, his grandmother having been a Bezuidenhout. Then, after that, after we had been in Lemansdorp some years, Johannes took up some land to the south by the Nyl River Vlei in the Waterberg. That was a fine farm with wonderful veld and plenty of water. Magtig, we never forgot that drought and would not be caught again. I had seven children then, and another coming, when it happened . . ." She stopped talking and stared out of the window. "Get the book, Lena," she said suddenly; "it is all in there."

Lena went for the Bible, carrying it back in two hands, and put it on the table.

Ouma opened it. "Here it is," she said. "You have seen it all before,

Lena, for I have seen you looking at it, but it meant little to you. You did not know that those names were the story of a woman's life."

She turned the pages.

"It meant nothing to you," she said. "What are they but names, some in my hand, some in my husband's—names, names," she said. "The name of my father, Rudolf de Wet, married to Maria Bezuidenhout in 1790. Stephanie, born March 3, 1800. Katarina Hendrika—that is me—born June 20, 1813, and here, married to Johannes Philippus du Toit on the 11th of December, 1830. Names," she said again, "dates . . . And those, look well at those, Lena; those are the names of my sons. Your six great-uncles, who died before your birth, and that of your father. All boys," she said. "Seven boys that were my pride."

Lena read :

Johannes Hendrik	February 1st 1832	Murdered
Rudolf Carl	June 7th 1834	with their
Adriaan Johan	April 20th 1835	father by the
Christiaan Piet	April 10th 1836	Zulus at the farm
Kaspar Stoffel	December 8th 1839	Rietfontein on
Emile Philippus	December 25th 1840	the Nyl River
Pretorious Jacobus	September 1st 1845	March 10 1847

She waited to hear what her grandmother had to say. But Ouma was staring out of the window. Lena, turned back the pages. How many names there were! The Bible was more than two hundred years old. She was descended from all those people—from those names. That was all they were to her—just names. She looked at the first entry . . . made by Joachim Abraham du Toit :

Landed to-day, Tuesday the sixth day of March in the sixteen hundred and fifty-third year of Our Lord at the Cape of Storms . . .

That was when the first of them had landed at the Cape, bringing this Bible with him. Lena thought of those old people, coming over the sea from Holland—one bringing a cradle, another a Bible; all bringing those things that were most dear to them—things to be seen to this day treasured in the homes of descendants : a china cup or plate; a glass; a pair of candlesticks; a sword, or a silver-mounted pistol.

". . . Your grandfather was at home," Ouma said. "He was not hunting then, and we were happy on the farm. The times were quiet. . . . At that time," she said suddenly, "I had a little white dog with short hair. A very beautiful small dog it was, all white with a pink stomach that was marked with small black spots. She also had one brown eye and one dark one, and never left me. A small dog was rare in those days. Every one had big Boer-hounds such as we have now, and Dirk has; but little dogs were scarce, so scarce that I could not find a husband for her. I called her Bolletjie, for she was beautiful, like a white bouncing ball . . ." Ouma stared out of the window again.

" I was out on the veld a mile or so from the house," she went on, " searching for medicinal herbs on a little rankie of rocks. The farm was mostly vlei and the roots I wanted only grew here. I had your father with me; the other children were at the house with my husband. He was mending the afterclap of the wagon, stitching it up where it was torn, and they were helping him and playing about him. He was good with the children. He was good with every one : a good man : a good father and husband : a man who feared nothing . . .

" I was bent down getting up a root when I heard a shot, but thought nothing of it. What is a shot on the veld? Then suddenly one of our boys came running. His name was Samuel. He had been with us many years.

" ' Hide,' he said, ' hide, they have come! The master is dead. Aaii . . . the Baas is dead, and the young masters '—tears were running down his cheeks—' and the other boys are killed,' he said.

" I could understand nothing. I started up to go back. Your father was crying and hiding in my skirt. Samuel pulled me down. I struck him— a Kaffir putting his hand on me! But he would not let me go. Then I heard shouting and saw flames and smoke from the direction of the house. So it was that—the Kaffirs were up again. They had surprised us. My husband and sons were dead, my home burning. It had happened to me, too, as it had happened to others in the past.

" ' The Kaffirs,' I said.

" ' Not Kaffirs,' Samuel said. ' They have killed many Kaffirs. They are naked Zulus, an impi that is eating up the world on its way home.'

" They would not pause. I knew this of them. Sent forth by their king naked without even a loincloth, they ravaged the land killing everything. Moving so fast that none heard of their coming, they preceded the news of the depredations coming like a storm to destroy, and passing on. Samuel was right. We must hide.

" There was a cleft between two rocks that was screened by a bush. We crept into it, holding your father between us. The little dog was on my knee. Then I saw them through the branches. They were running through the high grass, naked but for their plumes and ornaments. They jumped high, like hunting dogs that seek game, leaping with stiff legs and hissing between their teeth. They had short stabbing spears, big oxhide shields, and kerries in their hands. Some of them beat their shields with their spears, rattling them against each other. They were beating the veld for us. The hard ground of the rankie would not show our spoor. These were Zulus, not Bushmen. They were killers of men, not hunters who could trace the movement of a buck on solid rock. But they came very close. Bolletjie began to growl. In a minute she would bark. I put my hands round her throat and choked her. Ja, Lena, with your father trembling beside me and Samuel nearly white with fear, I strangled my little dog. We stayed there till next day and then Samuel crawled out to see if they were gone.

"When he came back, he said there was no sign of them and that a commando was at the house. They wanted to see me before they went in pursuit. I went out leading your father by the hand and carrying my dead dog in my arms. Your father was hungry, he was crying for food. My house was ashes. My husband and my sons were laid out in a row. They were arranged according to their size. First my husband and little Emile at the end of the row. Having nothing to cover them with, the Boers had spread reeds over them. But they were much mutilated, each speared in many places. Emile's skull had been crushed by a kerrie blow.

"An uncle of Paul Kruger's was in command. I could not weep. I stood beside them while they buried them in one long grave. Before it was covered, I put my little dog in Emile's arms. They had loved each other.

"When it was done, I went to neighbours and then joined my father-in-law. Since then I have remained in Mooiplaas. On that day I died. Only your father was left. Then he died. And then there were only his children. Only Stoffel and Louis and you . . .

"That is my story," she said. "That is something for you to tell your children . . . and tell them the cause of it. There is only one cause : that is the English who drove us before them into the wilds; who have always destroyed all that we have tried to construct. Now we are at war with them again. Now it must be ended one way or the other, and at the end there must be no English in Africa, or no Boers. For that I would give my grandsons as I would have given my sons and my husband had they been spared to fight. For we fight Mammon, Lena; we fight unrighteousness. And God is with us who fight for our homes and heritage."

She was silent. Then she said : "Leave me, Lena. It has been hard to speak of these things." And she had not been able to tell of her eighth son—stillborn, after the massacre, before his time . . .

Ouma wondered what good had she done? She was alone now. Lena had left her, but what had she told Lena that was new? What could you make a young girl understand? She had not known her full story—few did. But what did it amount to when it was told? How did it differ from other stories equally unhappy? In every family there were such things; every family in the North, that is. Only in the Colony, and only there, at a distance from the Border, had life been secure.

But then what was security bought at the price of living in close relations with the English? Danger was better than that, and death. Liberty or death was the issue to-day, and for that issue were her people in the field. For that and that alone she prayed. For liberty . . . our folk, our flag, our land, our God, our way of life founded upon that of the patriarchs. She had meant it when she said she would give her husband and her sons. They had gone too soon, but she was giving Stoffel, who was the apple of her eye. Had she not trained him to this? Was it not she who, seeing his disability, had taught him how to compensate for it, gaining respect by horsemanship and his skill at shooting, to this one end.

She thought of her burnt home again, and the big grave. She had forgotten to tell Lena how she had gone back two days later and had found in that desolation one living thing. Killing everything—cattle, horses, dogs, cats and poultry—the Zulus had forgotten the tame meerkat. And it was there perched up on the blackened embers of the fallen roof-tree to greet her. It still had its collar on and came to her when she called. It had belonged to Christiaan. He had brought it in and tamed it. It was quite fearless of the dogs, playing with them and sleeping curled among their paws. She thought of how they had often tied it to the leg of the table; of how you could not stop it from stealing; of how it would sit up on its hind legs and drink milk from a spoon; of how it had loved the sunshine, lying flat on the stoep as if it had been poured out like a liquid. She had taken its collar off and left it. There was no place in her heart now for tame animals.

Her husband had been a great one for pets, bringing home many young things for the children—young buck, tortoises, chameleons . . . There had been an otter once, a young wild pig another time, a zebra foal . . . lion and tiger cubs. A secretary bird they had had a long time. Once it had eaten a kitten alive and there had been the problem of what to do, for they could hear it crying inside its stomach. In the end they left it there. They had many cats and only one secretary bird. She remembered seeing it kill a snake quite near the house, striking at it with its wings. Pigs were good for snakes too. They simply ate them paying no attention to their bites. She wondered how that was. The Bushmen had remedies for snake-bite that no white man knew. So did the Swazis. She had never heard of a Bushman or a Swazi being killed or even seriously hurt by a snake-bite. How muddled her mind was! How it all came back! . . .

Now that the pain of speaking was over, it was pleasant to let her mind drift over the past, picking out a scene here and another there. She wondered how many thousands of miles she had travelled, at how many camps she had slept, how many meals she had cooked. She thought of the change in the times; of the ever-increasing number of Uitlanders who came to Africa in search of gold and diamonds. They had brought their wantons with them.

These were the things they were fighting against, not merely the Uitlanders, but the ways and customs that they had brought with them and sought to introduce. It was this that had brought her into conflict with Oupa. He tolerated the foreigners, the English as much as the others. He was incapable of real integrity or real hate. His exploit had been something, since he seemed to have killed or at least wounded two of them. But it had been done for the wrong reason. He had done it as an exploit to aggrandize himself, not to destroy Englishmen; and in no small part to annoy her.

And that Zulu of his, she thought, Reuter. It was terrible to have to live with a Zulu who in his youth had been a warrior. She saw the Zulus again, plumed and leaping; she heard them hiss in their teeth, and the rattle of their spears. She covered her face with her hands. Then she pulled herself together. She had got over all this long ago. She must stick to her maxim that by meeting trouble half-way you foiled trouble by being prepared for it.

Trouble was like an enemy for whom, by this means, you were ready; and the element of surprise that might lead to disaster was missing. By refusing happiness you avoided the unhappiness which followed it. Thus deviously was Fate disarmed and a static unhappy peace obtained which was a solid basis, since being unhappy you had nothing more to lose, even worse unhappiness, being merely the old, and differing from it only in degree. She had been very happy at times in her life. But each time the price had been too high.

It was best to turn your mind the other way and to expect the worst. Then anything better than the worst was good, was better than that which you had expected. There was no joy that was not barbed with hook of potential misery. If you gave nothing, you could lose nothing. If you accepted nothing—neither kindness nor love nor affection—you could lose nothing, nor were you under any obligation. In this way you could live alone, isolated from life, living it, but enclosed within the safety of expected disappointment. Since you cared for nothing, nothing mattered very much; indeed, as time passed, nothing mattered at all.

Yet, in refusing to love, inevitably you abandoned yourself to hatred. Sometimes she thought the great love she had borne for her sons and her husband—the great past love of her youth—was the same as her present hatred of the English who had caused her desolation. She felt it with the same intensity. It tore at vitals, twisting her insides as her love had done. Though it was hard, as one reflected about the matters, to see how such things could be the same, yet in her heart she knew this paradox to be the truth. At least to-day she was prepared for anything. You could prepare yourself for disaster, but not for joy. You could build yourself an armour for unhappiness, though sometimes it was over-heavy.

But the reward would come later. It would come in heaven where a virtuous life of abstention and continence was paid for with untold bliss. It would even come in this life by the defeat of her enemies, by their utter annihilation. But now at this moment she faced an issue. She must put on the armour again that she had taken off to talk to Lena. She found herself

trembling at the intensity of her feelings. How could she have told Lena?
How could one person explain their feelings to others? How could you
make them see things in the light you saw them? How could you represent
events exactly? What could a young woman, thinking only of pleasure in
the future, understand of the words of an old woman who thought only in
terms of misery in the past? What had the young budding breasts, with
upswept nipples, to do with old dugs that hung like dry bags on your
belly?

Only later would Lena understand : only after she had suffered and
paid. Only when the days of her happiness were passed and blurred
would she understand that which had been told to-day.

CHAPTER XX

PATROL

I

THE war days passed slowly for Boetie. The days of his life were the same. He still took his father's goats on to the mountain, piping them up in the morning and piping them down at dusk, playing the tunes he had devised and listening to their echoes among the rocks and kloofs. There were certain places where the echoes were very fine, where he would halt in his playing and wait, between the notes, for their return. Fifty-one days had gone by. He knew this, for he had them notched on a stick that he kept on the wall of the kraal just by the gate on the right-hand side. There it was out of the way where his sister could not get hold of it to play with and to lose.

The nights of the war were different. The mountain was the same because no one had ever been up there with him, but at night the house was empty. Each night when he came in he notched his stick, counting the old cuts and making a new one. A little cut up, a little one down, and then he pulled out the chip with the nail of his thumb.

The great storm had frightened him. And next day the mountain had been filled with the sound of running water. It was beautiful to hear it running and splashing. It was good to feel the wet ground under his feet. If he stood still and then moved them up and down in one place there was a pleasant sucking feel and a little noise like the squeezing of a lemon. Coming home that night, he thought, I must wash the mud from my feet in the spruit to make it easier for my mother. She washed his feet each night, but he liked to get the worst off for himself. There had once been talk of making him wear shoes. He had tried it to please them, but he had got lost in shoes. I cannot see in shoes, he said. I do not know where I am. They had not understood this till he explained. There were so many things he had to explain to them. My eyes are in my feet, he said. You tell me that you see with the eyes in your head and thus know where you are. With me I know by the feel. I know the touch of the different grasses, the coolness of the vlei, the rough gravel of the drift, and the feel òf different bushes and rocks. I know things by their feel and by smell, by my feet and my hands, my ears and my nose. If I must I will wear shoes, but it makes it hard for me. They had taken away his shoes and there had been no more talk of them.

He still thought of the storm, though it was days past, and wondered about his brother and his father. Had they been under cover? Had they got wet? Had they had to sleep out? It must have been terrible for them, but, on the other hand, they would have been pleased; for the rain, if they had had it, would make the grass grow well for their horses. He thought of Swartkie. Dirk was his father's son, and Swartkie was the son of Galant, his father's horse.

There was so much to think of. New tunes that came to him. He listened to the singing of the birds, to the little rustlings in the grass at his side. He felt the shadows that passed over him as an eagle or a vulture came between him and the sun for an instant. It would be wonderful to see a bird flying, he thought. If I could see, that is what I would like most—to see a bird fly. He had no great desire to see people, since he knew them by touch and smell. But a flying bird was something that could not be understood if you were blind.

There was no news of the war save that of the battle that had taken place at Mooiplaas which Lena had brought. There were rumours—there had been fighting in Natal . . . victories. The war was said to be sweeping this way again. It came and went and it was hard to understand what happened. And what was war? Why was war? What was this thing that had taken Pa and Dirk from their home and left his mother to cry out her loneliness. She did not know that he knew how she cried. He did not know how he knew, except perhaps that when he kissed her she tasted salt. No matter how much she washed, she could not wash the salt of her tears from her skin.

They had made what preparations they could at Doornkloof. Two horses were kept in the kraal each day, changing them about so four always ran on the veld while two stood ready to hand. Ma had baked great quantities of rusks; there was meal done up in small bags, and there were biltong and spare ammunition and bandages and two blankets and a coat. They had done what they could as every Boer must, so that if men came hard-pressed they could change horses, get food and ammunition quickly, and ride on. Only in this fashion, by picking up what they needed from the farms and capturing supplies, could their men be supplied in the field. But it was not enough. He wondered what more he could do.

There was war, but still the birds sang. The crickets chirped and the cicadas cut the heat of the day with their shrilling. War, and the trees blossomed perfuming the air. This made it all the more inexplicable, for with war surely the world should stand still, surely the sun should stand fast in one place till it was ended. And until it ended he was responsible for Doornkloof. He was the master here : the only man. This made him hold his head high and blow out his chest, but inside him his heart fluttered with anxiety and fear. Also he was shamed that he was not there with the others. There were boys younger than he fighting at their fathers' sides and old men like Oom Philippus were fighting too. He thought of Oom Philippus's charge against the English. If he had been able to see, he would have liked to do a great thing like that.

If only he could do one fine thing, just one, before he died, so that men would not say that he had been useless, a burden on his family and his nation. A man, he felt, should justify his existence by exploit; a single one would have satisfied him. Till the coming of the war and the going of the men, to be alive and herding goats and making music had been enough. Now it was insufficient. But what was there he could do? What point of contact was there between a blind boy and a war?

2

It was dusk on the fifty-second day. The notch was cut, the stick replaced; the goats safely kraaled. Johanna was fed and asleep in bed when Boetie went out on to the veld again. He was restless and uneasy. He had felt he must go out. He was not tired. He had slept in the mountain under a wild olive. He could smell its sweet scent still, and the evening was cool, soft as a woman's cheek.

It was in his heart to go and sit by a rock and listen for the coming of the night sounds. The wild cry of the nightjars, the squeaking of the bats, and the hoot of the owls. The hunting jackals would soon be crying and the night world come into being. Sometimes he felt that it was more his world than that of the day, though he was not clear about the difference between darkness and light. For me it is always light, he thought, only at one time it is hot from the sun and at another cool without it.

He found the rock he sought. It was still hot from the sun. He sat on the east side of the great stone which was nice and cool. He was at peace. In a world at war I am at peace, he thought. Pulling out his flute he played it softly : little hesitant notes. A melody was coming. This was how they came, by bars, hesitantly on halting steps. He heard them in his mind. Then he played them, comparing what he heard in his ear with what he had heard in his mind, played on and on very softly till they coincided. Once he had them, they were his for ever. This would be a lovely tune—an air at once both sad and gay. He had no words for it, but he saw Lena and Dirk as he made it. It was for them. He saw their coming together, their parting, and then—here the music became very bright and pretty—it was for Dirk's return.

To make music you had to think of things, to build them up in your mind. That might be what people called pictures, but his were not pictures, at least not visible ones. Yet they were composed of visual feeling. You could, even if you were blind, see love and joy, sorrow and beauty. You know some places were good and others bad. There was a bad place on his mountain that he always avoided and his father had told him when he asked about it that a man had been killed there twenty years ago by wild Kaffirs. There were good places, too, ones sanctified by love. The ground and the trees and the rocks absorbed goodness and badness, sorrow and joy, and then afterwards and for ever gave them back to those who passed those places if they were ready to listen.

Yes, this tune was going to be beautiful. He longed for Dirk's return to play it to him. And one day they said he was going to be given a real flute. That would be wonderful. To have an instrument that he could really play well and loudly, that had stops and keys. He had never had one in his hand, but he had heard of them. People who had heard him play had spoken of them and said Boetie should have a real flute.

He sat up straight. Something was happening. He cupped his hand to his ear. Horses were coming, slowly—many horses. They were coming this way. He flattened himself against the rock and waited. The tune kept running through his head. He went on repeating it in his mind so that he should not lose it.

They were close. Boers . . . he could hear them talking. He could hear the creak of leather and the shuffling steps of the horses. They were tired and the men smelt sweat-odour. A commando, he thought, that is nearly exhausted; and tired or not they must go on. He thought of Dirk and his father. This was war. No matter how you felt you had to go on. No matter if your horse was weak. If it died you abandoned it, continued on foot if there were no spares. He stood clear of the rock and hailed them.

" Have you seen my father or my brother?" he asked.

" Who are you?"

" I am Boetie van der Berg and I am blind. I am the son of Groot Dirk of Doornkloof. He is with Frans Joubert's commando."

" We have not seen him, but we are joining Joubert. We will tell him that we have seen you. Tot siens, jong."

With that " good-bye till we see you, young man," they had left him, their noise growing less and less. He sat still till he could hear them no longer and then followed them by smelling the dust that rose over the veld behind them, and feeling for the grasses broken by their horses, stiff beneath his feet. They were joining Pa's commando. They had been fighting. No one had told him this, but he knew it. They were going on and he must return home. He was useless. People were gentle to him, but he was useless, a burden and a charge to his family.

He turned back and took out his flute to continue his tune. He had not forgotten it, but he never put the pipe to his mouth. There were more horses coming and these were different. They were not the horses of his people. They were heavier and were handled differently. They were in hand and not being ridden with loose reins. He stood waiting. They were much nearer. For the Boers he had waited hidden because he was ashamed; for the English he stood in the road. It pleased him that he could be able to do this. He could hear the rattle of their horses' head-chains, of accoutrements and the rattle of shod hoofs on the stones as they struck them. They were coming straight at him at a trot. He would not move. Curb-chains were jingling, there was the strike of metal upon metal, of sword scabbards. Words in English. For a moment he thought they would ride him down, but they pulled up right at his feet. He could feel the breath of the leading horse on his face and was splattered by foam as it shook its head. The horses were excited and fresh. They plunged and bucketed, annoyed at the delay. There was a light following wind and the dust they made blew on to him as he stood waiting. He would not move. Nothing will make me, he thought. They must go round or over me. These men must be pursuing the Boers who had passed earlier. He must delay them if he could

"Have you seen any men, boy? Did you see a commando pass?"

It was the man on the horse near him. The horse must be tall, for the voice came from high above him. He raised his head. As the horse fidgeted and passaged in front of him, he followed it with his eyes. They must not guess. No doubt it was the officer who was speaking to him. He sounded young and was breathing hard with excitement.

"I have seen nothing," Boetie said. And that was not a lie.

"How long have you been here?"

"A long time."

"You'll get nothing out of the boy, sir," someone said. "But they came this way all right. They're making for the hills and their horses are tired."

Before God, the man was right. Their horses had been tired. But it was strange that these men could not see where they had gone when, without eyes, he had followed them so far reading their spoor with his feet. Why, even the dung of their horses was still moist and dustless.

"Come on, then," the officer said, "they can't be far. We must be close on their heels. Come on or they'll give us the slip."

The troop swirled past him. More dust, the clatter of steel scabbards, of stirrups, of chains, of iron-tipped heelrope pegs, the creak of leather, the smell of man and horse-sweat. But their sweat smelt different. It was sweet, not sour; both men and horses were fresh. One horse was forging. These big horses were full-fed, corn-fed. The men were fresh and well armed.

After they had gone, he still had in his ears the rattle of their sabres, the jingle of spurs and chains, and the sound of their carbines creaking in their saddle buckets. He still heard their grumbling curses and the sound of shod hoofs on the veld long after they had gone. He would never forget it. There were about thirty of them, he thought, but there might have been led horses or pack-horses. He could only count horses. He could not tell what they carried.

The evening was warm, but he was cold with fear. He wanted to go home to his mother, but was unable to move. He was waiting. He must wait until he knew. He strained his ears. He knew what he was waiting for. It would come soon. If only he had been able to hold them a little longer—for a quarter of an hour instead of a few minutes.

Then it came : a single shot : two more, singly. Those were his people. They were in contact. The English did not shoot like that. He wondered how he knew how the English shot. Perhaps it was the sound of the rifles, but he knew that those were aimed Boer shots. He knew that they had emptied saddles. Tears came into his eyes. If only I were with them. If only I were not useless.

Now came the answering fire, much faster, the rattle of shots from the English carbines. The English would have dismounted. They had to have horse holders, one man to three or four horses. They could not shoot from the saddle; and when dismounted their horses would not stand. That meant that one in four at least was occupied holding the horses of the others, whereas all the Boers could shoot on horseback or on foot. He breathed a sigh of relief. He had been afraid of the English being able to get into them with their sabres. If his folk had made them dismount, they were safe. They would be able to fight them off as they retreated towards Joubert.

There was a jackal crying, the night was coming fast. Thank God for the night. His father and Dirk were with Joubert. If they were near they would ride out to help them. Perhaps they would be able to lead them into a trap. The officer had seemed very young from his voice. Perhaps he was inexperienced. If the Boers stood and ran as was their custom, they might lead them into an ambush. He was happier now that he had thought of this possibility. He would wait a little till he was calm and then go home. His mother would have heard the shots and be uneasy. He was the man of Doornkloof. He must be able to comfort her, but before he could do that he must first comfort himself. He must seek strength from God. He must think awhile, and listen for those sounds that he had come out to hear : for cries of the birds and beasts, for in them he heard the voice of God.

The wars which had been distant was now near. If there was one troop of English cavalry there would be more. The English did not fight independently in small commandos like the Boers.

He began to be afraid for Dirk and his father. There were still shots but they came faintly. They were fighting a running action. It was the way the Boers preferred to fight. They were fighting their way back from koppie to koppie towards the hills. But it was not the troop that worried him. It was the fact that it might be only one of many converging on a given point according to some strategical plan. He did not know how many men Joubert had; or if they had food, ammunition and water; or how fresh their horses were. Even if the rain had been general, the grass would not yet have had time to grow and their horses might be poor. He thought his father and Dirk tired with fighting, facing fresh, well-mounted troops. The English could do nothing against his people if they had fresh horses, food and ammunition, and room to manœuvre. They were fighting on their own farms; and in every commando, no matter where they were, there were men who knew the country: men who owned it, or who had been there hunting or visiting relatives and friends.

He felt better now. There were no more shots. Another jackal was hunting. Two bats were squeaking shrilly about him and a night hawk called. Full night had come and with it peace. He would go back. He could face Ma now. He got out his flute and stood up.

He walked slowly. He was thinking of the battle as he made his music. The theme had not escaped him. It was, as he had thought it would be, a beautiful little melody, but how had he held on to it when so much had happened? He played it over, and over again. It was his, transfixed with the spear of his memory. But still it was funny that he had been able to hold on to it. It was this that made him one with the singing birds. They, too, sang without thought. Song, he said to himself, is the gift of God. Such things come to you, to some men even if they are blind, and to some birds. For there were songless men and silent birds.

But perhaps you had to be blind to understand. He often had thought this, dismissed it as absurd, and then for some reason came back to his original conclusion. It worked this way, he decided; if you lost in one way you gained in other ways. And God must have said: " To this little one who is blind I will give other gifts. I will gift him music that he can hear in his heart, and I will give him fingers that can play it. I will make him one with another world, that of the dumb beasts that others think to be without understanding. I will make him so that all are kind to him, and his life such that he will be loved and know no roughness." But God had not known of the war or that his heart would be broken by his uselessness. No, the Good Lord had not known that. War had nothing to do with God.

He could smell his home now. There was the sweet scent of the wood smoke from his mother's fire and the smell of goat and cattle kraals. He could hear the bleating and the lowing of the beasts. One of the dogs was barking. It was Dassie—a pup. She might be barking at anything. A beetle was enough to start her. If there had been anything serious, the others would have joined her. Nothing could survive his father's dogs. The ten great Boer-hounds, descendants of other hounds that had made the Great Trek and had lived before that on the Border of the Colony helping their masters hunt and defending the homes of the farmers against Bushmen, Kaffirs, and wild beasts. They would face a tiger, and many a thieving Bushman had been pulled down and torn to pieces by them before they could be beaten off. He loved the feel of their rough shaggy coats, of their cold wet noses pushing against him, and the warm soft flews of their lips. How few understand dogs, he thought. It was said that they had no souls and were unable to think, but this was a grave error and due to lack of thought and observation. Dogs dreamed, did they not? Just as men did. Without memory or thought, how could they dream, since a dream was, if not the result of reflection, at least a mental process? He thought of how after hunting they cried and twitched in their sleep; of how once Donker, the biggest of his father's hounds, had sprung up, straight out of his sleep, pawing at the wall, growling and worrying, and had knocked some plates from the dresser.

His mother was waiting for him. She had Johanna in her arms, she must have woken her up. He must be calm. He must remember Dirk's message to him : the man of Doornkloof.

" You heard the shots, Boetie?"

" I heard them."

" I was afraid," his mother said.

" There is nothing to fear, Ma. They would not hurt a woman alone."

" But you were out, my Boetie. I feared for you. Suppose they had come upon you."

" They did."

" You saw them?"

" I saw them all. First our folk and then the English. I spoke to them, but could not hold them for more than a minute. Still, a minute is something, and I was not afraid," he said. And he had not been. All he had felt was anger that he was blind and could not be with the others. Perhaps anger was the answer to fear. If you were angry you could not be afraid.

" You saw them," his mother repeated after him, " and spoke to them."

" Ja, I saw and spoke to them." He knew what his mother meant when she said, " you saw." For him it was seeing—she knew that. Only he saw in other ways.

" And the firing?" his mother said.

" Yes, there was firing, but I think they got away, though their horses were tired. They were joining Joubert and Pa and Dirk." He pointed to the south. " They were going that way."

" I wish we had news," his mother said. " It is very hard to live without news."

" Ja, Ma, it is hard to live without news. It is hard also to be a man and to be here. Magtig, to-day I was ashamed : first to face our folk and then to face the English. I told our people and sent messages to my father and brother. But I did not tell the English. They do not know that I cannot see and must wonder what I was doing at home. Oh, Ma," he said, "I am ashamed." He clung to her. He was a man. He was fourteen years old and too old to cry. But his father and brother were fighting and he was doing nothing to help them. Johanna began to wail.

"They have made my brother cry. The English have made him cry. I hate them. I want my Pa."

"Is there nothing I can do?" Boetie asked. "Is there nothing, Ma?"

"There is nothing, Boetie. We can do no more than have things ready for our people should they be in need. We have done that. It is not your fault. And is to comfort me and watch over Doornkloof as your father and brother told you, nothing?" She held him to her.

"I know it is not my fault," Boetie said. "But it twists my heart inside me. Every one has gone," he said : "boys younger than I and old men like Oom Philippus. I am alone in all the land. I am left like a woman or a Kaffir and I am no use here."

CHAPTER XXI

THE LITTLE TREK

JONANNA VAN DER BERG could not get Boetie's encounter out of her mind. The war had put its fingers on her last son. For a time he had been under its hands, and it was just chance, the fact that the English had been pursuing greater game, which had prevented the fist from closing on him. What was he to them, alone on the veld? A Boer boy, possibly a spy, an enemy. And what could she do? What had happened once might happen again. It was no use talking to him. He would face them, ashamed either to take precautions or acknowledge his blindness. It would be a judgment of God upon her if something happened to him, since she had been congratulating herself upon the blindness that made him safe. No one was safe. It had been wrong of her. For years, since his birth, when it had first become apparent, she had in her heart blamed God for this thing; then with the war she had thanked Him and seen the wisdom of His work. It had seemed to her, in her bad moments, that neither her husband nor eldest son would return and that God, knowing this, had given her a second son, born blind, to be a comfort to her. But now . . . now she wondered . . .

He was on the mountain again with his goats. Suppose she confined him to the mountain, would he obey her? Since his father's and brother's message that Lena had brought, he had changed towards her. He was a man now, suddenly. He had become one with the going of his father and his brother: the master and only man on Doornkloof. It brought tears to her eyes to think of him, of his courage in his affliction, of his pride, of his gentleness with his sister and the beasts with whom he lived.

She sat on the stoep staring towards the mountain. Little Johanna played at her feet. The dogs were lying round her. The puppy, Dassie, was digging in the hard ground and bending to snuffle in the hole. Brindle, black, yellow, yellow and white, as big as small calves, her husband's hounds guarded his family and house.

" What is the matter, Ma?" Johanna said.

" Nothing, my heart."

" It is something," the child said. " You look funny and stare at the mountain. Is it Boetie?"

" Boetie? Why should it be Boetie?"

In the afternoon a boy came from Mooiplaas wtih the young cock in a basket that Tanta Kattie had promised her a year ago. His coming at that moment with a breeding cockerel made up her mind for her. It must have been meant.

She put the bird down. "Wait," she said. "I have a message." She got a pencil and paper from the drawer. It was funny she had not thought of this before. It was funny that she had forgotten all about the cockerel she had asked for and that it should come at this precise moment as an answer to her prayer.

She sat down at the table. Writing was not easy to her. She tore a sheet from an exercise book and smoothed it. There were marks on it where the accounts her husband had written had passed through the paper. His writing, so ghostly white, upset her. Perhaps that, too, was a sign. I must not be stupid, she thought, I must not imagine things.

Dear Kattie, she wrote, *things are bad here. Yesterday Boetie was out and was stopped by English soldiers. I am afraid for him. Could we come to you, bringing the stock with us? A hundred head of cattle, six horses, and two hundred goats. It is not that I am afraid for myself, but for Boetie. Here by the mountain we are in the path of war.*

She signed it and folded it over.

"Take this back," she said.

Now there was nothing to do but wait for an answer. She wondered what Groot Dirk would say when he heard of her decision. It depended, of course, on Tanta Kattie, but there was little doubt in her mind about the answer. It was war and in war neighbours were bound to each other. Dirk would know that she had not been afraid for herself. There was no danger of his misunderstanding her motives or intentions.

Wait. How long women waited! They waited to get married; for children to come; for men to return from war. She went in to get her knitting. Men could smoke, but women could only sew or knit. Still, with her hands busy a woman could manage. That was because she lived more by her hands than a man. For him, his muscles leaning against a dam scop or on the handles of a plough were a satisfaction; as he worked he occupied his mind with thought. Women did not think much. They did not have to. They knew. And a woman worked more directly with her hands, a woman used few tools. They used needles, pots and pans, but more often their hands were directly in contact with their work, more often in dough, in bread-making, than a man's with the actual earth. A man needed tools and weapons: a woman only hands. It was with her hands she tended a child.

She watched her fingers as they worked. It was astonishing how methodically they moved. In her mind she saw her son Boetie, her son Dirk, her baby daughter, and her husband. She saw them as one thing— my family, my life. It was impossible to think of life without them or as being separate from them. I am they, and they are me, she thought : the man who came to me, and the children that came from me, because of him. The woman was in essence the link with reality. She was reality itself. She had felt that with Lena the other day. Though they said nothing, she knew that they had both felt it. Men had to speak. They had to persuade each other, inflame each other. Sometimes she wondered about speech. Often it undid the intention that had produced it. This thinking and making of decisions exhausted her. But if I don't, who will? she thought. And there was Boetie. Whatever she thought she came back to him. Her men had gone, but her children were still with her. But what would she tell Boetie? She was half afraid of him now. He had cried on her breast like a child, but he was changed. His voice had broken last year; that had frightened her. It meant other things. When your son's voice changed, you had almost lost him. He was a man with a man's needs. That they were not yet urgent was nothing. Being a woman who knew a man. Her Boetie was a man. It had begun last year, it was finished now. And she knew it. A man with all the implications of manhood and its necessities. A woman . . . a girl. Where was there one who would take a blind man? Would he never know the joy of woman? This was her new worry. She wanted his happiness, but was at a loss to know how it would be achieved. There could be none for a man alone. Soon he would stretch out his arms. Soon a woman's voice would call to him with golden bells. And what would happen?

But that was in the future. The crisis was to-day. Boetie must be saved from himself. She wondered how she would do it : how he would take it.

On the mountain Boetie was thinking of yesterday. Last night he had not been able to sleep. He had lain down and tried to, but sleep would not come. He had kept thinking of those others out there. It seemed to him that by not sleeping he could help them. He had tried to build up a battle in his mind. To think what it would be like. But he could not. To do this a man must be able to see and visualize. He could only think in terms of shape, smell, and sound. What I think is a battle is the way a battle would appear to me, since it is thus, that if I were in one, I must feel it. But it is not the way it really is. Nothing is the way I feel it is, he thought. All my world is different from theirs, which is as bright to them with shapes moving, and colours, as mine is to me with sounds, smells, and feeling. They say the neck of a sweating horse is black and creamed with foam. To me it is hot and sticky. Sticky, yet slippery at the same time, and the foam on it is loose, like soap froth, and

pebbled with grains of dirt. And it smells good, of the outside and movement. Each hair is sleeked down to the next, and as you press it hard,
water comes in front of your hand as you pull it along.

Again now, outside, he tried to think of a battle. It might be easier
here, but it wasn't. It came to him suddenly that he did not know what
a horse was really like, or what anything was really like. Yet to him
each thing had reality, form if you touched it, a feel, a smell, and a sound
of its own. Even stones, the round ones from the river, seemed to have
life. And there was a big shell at the house, that had been given to him
by a traveller who had been to the sea, that roared in your ear as you held
it up. It would be wonderful to listen to the sea. He thought again his
old thought of a bird in flight. That is the only thing I would really
like to see, he thought. How fast their wings must move to make that
whistling sound. He thought of the doves on the mountain going to
water, of the nightjars in the evening, shattering the silence with a hard
rush of wings as they turned and darted.

But the battle again. There would be shots, naturally. The smell of
bursting cordite, powder, of hot oil from the guns. He knew that, and
the feel of a gun hot and oily in your hand. There would be the feel
and smell of sweat, your own, that of your horse, that of other men and
other horses, and the feel of your horse's arching, muscled neck. The
reins would be slippery with sweat and his mane hairs would be stiff under
your knuckles. The men would smell like those who had passed yesterday, acrid and bitter, with their juices drying out on coated dust. They
would smell of rough food, hurriedly eaten, spilt and soured in the sun;
of strong tobacco and stale dirt. There would be shouts, the cries of
the wounded, the crack of enemy bullets; the smooth click of slipping
metal as bolts opened and closed, the glass tinkle of the expended
cartridges falling on the stones, the hammer of galloping hoofs; the whip-
crack of high bullets, the bee-sting of the low.

This was the only way that he could think of a battle; by bringing
together all those noises, scents, and feelings that he knew—the sound
of hoofs, the rattle of accountrements and chains, the shots, groans, and
curses that he could imagine and make them into a solid perception.
To others, he felt, what he saw would be like a battle in the dark, save
that even there they could see the flashes of the guns.

Yes, if I was in one, that is the way I would see it, he thought again.
If I . . . But what was the good? He would never be nearer than he
had been yesterday. He was useless, a herder of his father's goats and
of less value than a Kaffir. He would go back now with his goats. This
was his life, climbing the mountain and going back again while about
him the history of his people was being made. He would go home and
try to forget.

But there was something wrong with Ma. When he got in he felt it at once. It had nothing to do with her words or manners. He pretended to notice nothing.

"What was it like on the mountain?" she asked.

"It was good up there," he said, "quiet and peaceful. It was as it always is—the mountain changes not."

There was something wrong. Later he would find out what it was. He was never mistaken about such things. The words might not change, nor the manner, nor the voice, but something was different in all three, some subtlety, or perhaps it was the smell. You could smell if people were happy or unhappy, or if they were afraid. He could not decide; it was very hard to separate one sense from another. All he knew was the result of what he felt. And something was wrong with Ma. She was waiting for something. When it happened he would know, but for some time now things had not been as they once had been with her. Even before the war and the going of Dirk and his father, he had been coming closer to Dirk and was farther from his mother. He was no longer quite a child. He wanted to be a child and find his safety in her, but he wanted also to be a man and find his life in the outside world. It was not that he loved her less or that she loved him less. If anything, he thought, they loved each other more; but the love was changed. He was protective towards her, and now, with the war, more masterful, doing as he willed, convinced that he knew best what was good for him and convinced that she knew it, too, and watched it from afar.

He was becoming a man. There was evidence of it, which took him from her and drew him to other men. Later he knew that had he not been blind it would take him, as it had taken Dirk, into the life of another woman. From one woman, a mother, into the arms of another woman, a wife; and as a boy, no longer a child, he stood on the threshold of the path that led from one woman to the other. That he could not see made no difference to his feelings. It merely changed the results of those feelings, since he knew that, thought there was already a flowering within him, there could be no fruit. A blind man lived alone with some member of his family. That was even arranged. He was to live with Dirk and Lena. He would hold their children on his knee. But if he had not been blind . . . If I had been able to see, he thought, then I should have been out with the others and then later I should have married and lived as other men.

But Ma was very still. She was not even knitting. He sat on the floor and began to go over the dogs for ticks, feeling in the little flap of their ears, in their ears, under their arms, between their legs, along their backs and shoulders, and between the pads of their feet. That was something he could do for his father. The dogs stood round him as he felt them, licking his face and neck, banging him with their tails or pawing at his thighs with urgent feet.

Dogs, if you treated them rightly, were people. They were as different as people—courageous, cowardly, generous, mean, jealous; there was no human characteristic that was not shared by dogs, and a man's dogs were often a reflection of himself. His father's dogs were like his father, Groot Dirk: brave, gentle, and quiet; friendly to their friends, but unforgiving and fearless of their enemies.

His mother's foot was tapping the floor—gently, it was barely moving up and down, but loudly to his ears. She was strung up and worried about something. He rolled the dog in front of him on to his back and began to search his belly.

The evening passed and nothing happened. They ate. There was still the feeling of waiting: his mother's for some event of which she did not speak: his, for the words that the event would bring forth. It was time to go to bed and still nothing. He kissed her good-night. It was no use asking questions. It would only embarrass her. Things that were in your mind should not be dragged out by others. They should be allowed to ripen and be born in their full time. If she did not tell him to-day, then she would to-morrow, or the day after . . . or never. How could you know what was in the minds of others—even that of your mother? There must be much in her mind and heart which was no concern of his. A whole existence that concerned only her and his father. There were other parts of her mind, too, that concerned his brother and her; his sister and her. There was only one part—that which dealt directly with him—that he could consider without impertinence. It was the same with him. His love for his family and home-place and beasts was a great general all-enveloping love, but it was divided into segments, like the parts of a sweet lemon that were separated from each other, though only by taking them together, in combination, could one conceive the whole. Every one's mind must be like this, since, blind or not, men's minds and hearts were similar in their operation: not exactly the same, but much alike, moving by the same principles along similar lines.

He undressed slowly. Dassie licked his legs as he took off his leather trousers and then lay down on the sheepskin beside his bed. He kept Dassie in the house at night because he was young, foolish, and likely to bark at nothing. If the others were uneasy, then there was good cause. Dogs were like men, experienced or inexperienced. In a way, he thought, I am like Dassie—a puppy; young, troubled, and without much understanding. As the pup counted on the older dogs for a lead, so had he counted on his father and brother. But they had left him as you might leave a young dog, saying: " Stand guard till we return." So help him God, he would, but he was troubled and afraid.

Day had come. Boetie was out on the mountain again. His mother was knitting while she waited; every now and then she looked up at the tiny spots moving on the heights. You could always tell where he was from the goats.

She had been silly to expect an answer last night. Kattie would want to think things over, and ten miles was ten miles, especially at night with the boys so afraid of spooks.

She would hear to-day. Any time now the message might come, and then, if the answer was yes, she would have to break it to Boetie. He had never been away from Doornkloof except on a visit, to nagmaal, or on a hunting trip with his father and brother. He would be upset, but would do it for her sake. What he must not know, she thought, is that I am doing it for him. If he thought that, he would be ashamed and refuse to move. The obstinacy of men, if they were afraid, had never ceased to astonish her. Women had none of this, but life was simpler for women. Their issues were cleaner-cut, more definite, and without fine shades of meaning since they dealt with such realities as men, children, food, comfort, and safety. She had forgotten to tell Kattie how handsome the little cock was and to thank her. But she would understand.

But it was not till late afternoon that the message came, brought by the same boy. She took it and sent him to get food from the cooking-place. There was always something left in the pot and sour milk in the gourds. He was to come back when he had done.

When he had gone, she opened the note. It was short. Kattie had written simply: *Come*.

Kattie, the silent and bitter, was like all others of her people. There was never any question about such things among them. To write and ask had been to state—merely the exchange of a civility. It was war. In war people stood together. When the boy came back, she would tell him when they were coming. Only that remained to be decided.

The sun was beginning to sink when he came.

" You have eaten," she asked, " and rested?"

" I have eaten and rested," he said.

" Then tell the mevrou that we will come to-morrow."

She went into the house and came out with some tobacco for him, an inch cut from a tight sausage roll.

He held out his cupped hands, clapping them together in thanks. He stowed it in his pocket and raised his hand.

" The mevrou will be told," he said, " it is to-morrow."

" That is right, to-morrow."

He turned and walked away. In a few minutes she could not see him. He was beyond recall. The decision was made; now she must tell Boetie and give the orders for stock. She would drive four horses, two could be ridden by the herders. Old Jan would stay here with the dogs to guard the place. She would leave some old sheep to be killed—their food and his; the poultry could remain. And he must watch for his master or other Boers so that they would know where to find them if they were sought. It was nothing of a trek. They would take no household gear or wagon : just some clothes and blankets.

It was no use postponing it. When Boetie came in, she said : " Come here."

" Yes, Ma," he said. " What is the matter?"

" Many things. I am worried."

" It is hard to wait," he said, " but what else can we do?"

" We are going to trek, my Boetie. We are going to Oom Philippus and Tanta Kattie till it is over. It will be better there."

" We are going to trek because of the war. We are going to trek from here. Why are we? What do we fear?"

" It will be better there and we will be with Lena. You will like that."

" I will like that, but it will be dark for me there. I do not know the veld. And how shall I graze my father's goats in a strange place where it is dark? There," he said, " I will be blind as you say I am."

" I am going to give the orders now," Johanna said, " so watch your sister. Stay with Boetie, Johanna," she said.

" We will stay together," Johanna said. " But where are we going? Why are we going, Boetie? Is it because of the English? Are we going to find our father and brother? Are we?"

She heard no more. There were many orders to give, things to see to. Boetie had taken it well. She had forgotten that in a strange place he would be lost. If she had thought of it, she might have waited . . . or had she considered this? Was it not because of it, that he would be safe at her side and unable to stray . . .

In the morning the horses were inspanned to the Cape cart. A small wooden wagon-box was lashed on the back. The cattle were collected and the herd of goats ready to move behind them. The dogs were shut up. It was time to go.

The little trek, in no way comparable to the great one of her people in '36, was about to begin. But it was not easy to leave your home, even if you knew you would soon return to it. And would Dirk think she had done right? Now that there was no going back, Johanna wished that she had not made up her mind so fast. But it was too late to think of that. She became impatient to be off, to get started. The beasts would follow slowly. Old Hans would take care of things and the dogs protect the home. Hans, who worked round the kraals and house, could handle them. There was nothing more to wait for. She put her foot on the step of the cart. Her left hand, that held the reins, grasped the dashboard.

"Come, Boetie," she said. "Come, we are ready."

He was sitting on the ground with his back against the wall of the house. He had kept moving his head to listen to the different sounds made by the cattle, the goats, and the cart; to listen to the dogs howling and barking in the shed. At the sound of her voice he felt under him and got up with a long package wrapped in sacking. Johanna wondered what he was taking with him. She had not seen him prepare anything. Hans lifted Klein Johanna on to the cart and her mother gripped her with her knees. When she looked back, Boetie was beside them. He was holding up his package.

"Take it, Ma," he said.

"What is it that you have brought?"

"I am bringing my brother's other rifle," he said. "Be careful, I have loaded it."

She began to say something and then stopped. He knew what it was that had been on her tongue. She had been going to ask what a blind boy would do with a rifle. But she had not said it. Often he knew what people were going to say, and that they bit off their words before they hurt him.

"Take it, Ma," he said again, holding it towards her. He held it high, waving it a little till he felt her hand on it.

"Listen," he said. "It is my brother's rifle. He may want it or I may. Those who look at me do not know that I am blind. They say my eyes are clear and blue. Therefore, it is in my heart that if anything happened, you could stand me right, with the gun in my hand, and none would know. Before God," he said, "all they would know would be that a boy confronted them with a gun in his hands. All they would wonder would be why he was there and not out on the veld with the others."

He got up beside her. His feet were pushed against the dashboard, his back braced against the seat. They moved off with a lurch. He put out his hand to touch the reins his mother held.

"That is Meisie on the near side," he said, "and Bloom on the off. Is it not so?" he asked. Now he must be more alert than ever.

"Yes, Boetie, I have got Bloom and Meisie as wheelers," his mother said, "but how did you know?" They were not generally used as wheelers in the Cape cart.

"I do not know how I know," he said, "but I know; and for leaders you have the two new horses my father bought from the Free State. I know that also." He was silent. Then he said: "Now I am nothing, Ma. Now I am going to a strange place that my feet do not know, and I am nothing."

As the wheels turned, he knew this more than ever, but he strained all that was in him to feel and listen.

"We are going uphill," he said. "The ground is more stony here." Somehow he must learn the changes in the ground. He could tell much by the sound of the iron tyres. They came to a bank of oaklip, he could feel how easily they ran; then to some other kind of ground, it was covered with small hard stones that slipped away from the wheels or passed under them without being crushed. The horses' hoofs sounded different too. It was funny, he had driven over to Mooiplaas many times before, but had never thought of the road like this. Those had been visits. This was a trek. "Tell me what you can see from here, Ma," he said. "Can you see the mountain?"

"Which mountain, Boetie?"

"Our mountain where I graze our goats."

He felt his mother turn. "Ja, I can see it well and you can see it from the stoep of Mooiplaas too. We are not going far, my Boetie. Mooiplaas is near."

"Near," Boetie said; "yes, it is near, but another world to me."

CHAPTER XXII

"MY BROTHER'S HORSE . . ."

I

MOOIPLAAS was even worse than Boetie had thought it would be. Though it was good to be with Lena, Old Oom Philippus and Reuter, to whom he liked to listen, had gone from the farm. His charge had not been enough, he must go adventuring still farther. And there was a newly come old woman, Tanta Stephanie, who smelt strangely and mixed the High Dutch of Holland with the taal when she spoke. She said that she had known the old days on the wild border. But this was hard to believe. Her talk was all of clothes and men.

And he was lost here. Dear God, how lost! Even in the house he had to move carefully and get Klein Johanna to lead him. He was almost a man. He had been the man on Doornkloof and charged with it. Now his trust was betrayed and he must be led by a child. Fourteen and useless: blind and useless. There was nothing for him to do here but wait, and he was afraid.

The days that followed did not make him less afraid. It was new. It stayed new; he was always getting lost. The feel of the farm was strange to his feet. His nose was unaccustomed to the smells, his ears strange to the sounds. His father's goats were mixed with the Mooiplaas goats in the big kraal. Witbooi had a battle with the leader of the herd in which neither had been victorious and both had been hurt. There were new scars on his curled horns and a gash on his head above his eye. They had charged each other, their lowered heads meeting with tremendous force. Then they had retreated and charged again and again. Neither being able to obtain mastery, they had abandoned the struggle, but at any time it might begin again, he could do nothing to stop it. He missed his father's dogs and wished that they had brought at least one of them. Dassie being young would not have fought with Wolf and Bismarck.

Each day he went out with the goats, allowing himself to be led like a dog at the end of a line by the picannin who herded them. But some days he would go on alone with Witbooi, holding him by the collar, his hand on the bell beneath his neck. He had put the bell on the big billy so that he could tell where he was, and when they were together like this, if the wind was right, it seemed to him that he could smell his

300

mountain. Then he would stand with his hat off, his hair blowing, and smile into the wind. Only at these times was he happy.

There was no days and nights for him. There was only time, which was divided into that part which was warm and that part which was cool; into the sounds of what they called day and night and which were associated with the heat or cold. That was what they called the night. And there was a time when it was warm—hot. Then it was the day. But often as he had done at home he slept in the heat and walked by night.

But at last and by slow degrees he had begun to learn his way about the home-place. He knew the kraals and often went into them. Not only the goat kraal, but the others. He would run his hand over the horses, feeling them alive beneath his fingers. They stood for him, not even getting up if they were lying. The oxen and cows he knew, too, touching them and scratching them between the horns and behind the ears, even milking the tamer cows into his mouth as he knelt under them. It was wrong to steal milk, but a mouthful now and then did little harm and tasted good—hot, with a pleasant taste of cow.

Sometimes in the moonlight—they told him it was moonlight, but he had known without being told—he felt so different and restless, he would go out to play his pipe softly, so as not to wake his mother, but loud enough for his goats to hear so that when he came to the kraal his father's goats had separated themselves from the others and were clustered round the gate to meet him. Then he would sit on the ground among them and play to them while they greeted him with nibbling lips and Witbooi clashed his bell. They would stay round him, putting their feet on his shoulders and licking the salt from his face.

He got to know different places and liked some better than others. Below the house there were some big blue gums and that was a good place. He liked to sit there at night and listen to the rustling leaves. He loved the smell of eucalyptus that came from them if he crushed one in his hand. He loved the feeling of the great smooth trunks in his arms. It was a happy place.

Day after day passed. Each was the same. You could get used to a place without accepting it. This was not home. In all the world there was no place like Doornkloof, his home. And always he listened for the sound of a passing horse, a mounted horse. There might be news. And if it came it would come this way. If it was a friend, he could tell who it was when he was far off. There had been several friends. Only once had he been wrong. He had called to Martinus du Plessis.

"Is there news, Martinus?" he had shouted. "Have you seen my father and my brother? They are with Joubert."

"I am not Martinus," he had answered. "I am Jannie Fourie. But I have seen your father and brother. I was with Joubert two weeks ago. They were well."

" You are on Martin's horse," he had said.

" Yes, he lent me his horse. Mine has been shot from under me."

But that had been his only mistake and had not been one. He had been right about the horse and wrong about the rider. There was no mistaking horses. It was for horses that he listened.

Tanta Kattie spoke to him seldom, but then she did not speak much. He liked to be with her because of her silence. She smelt faintly of herbs. Her clothes were stiff and rustled. Also there was the sound of her rubbing fingers if you were near her or the wrinkling of material and the long pull of thread as it followed her needle as she sewed. Lena and he talked much of Dirk. What they thought was different from what they said. But he knew something of what went on in her heart and her desire for his brother. They could speak of other things, of anything together, it did not matter, for they understood each other.

Tanta Stephanie was still a noisy perfume. But life was no longer beautiful, it was too difficult, too strange, and he missed his days alone upon the mountain. He was with Lena and his sister most of the time. Klein Johanna had become inseparable from him and still insisted on leading him by the hand from place to place. With Lena it was easy to be silent, each of them concerned with their thoughts, and each aware of the other's mind. When would it end? Where was Dirk?

Sometimes he took her hand and sat holding it. It was she who had first taken him to sit under the blue gums.

" This is a good place, Lena," he had said.

" Ja, it is a happy place, Boetie, but sad too."

" That is why it is happy, Lena. Without sadness there can be no joy. A bird sings as if its heart would break with joy. I wish I could see a bird," he said. " It must be wonderful to see a bird." He had never said that to any one before.

They had funny talks together. He wondered what Tanta Stephanie would have thought of them. Old Oom Philippus would have understood, and Tanta Martha and Dirk, perhaps, but no one else. They were together now, walking up the spruit towards the willows where the hammerkop nested. He knew she was thinking of his brother. Nearby a woodpecker was driving little hammer-blows into the trunk of a tree. Of all other things he had formed his own conception. Even the galloping of a horse you could understand without seeing it, but birds . . .

" What is happiness, Lena?" he asked. " I did not know there was such a thing till I lost it with the going of my father and my brother. That is strange to me, that I did not know, and only conceived it when it had gone. It is like a bird that you hear singing and which as you approach it flies away on silent wings."

" For me it is like a garden, Boetie, with a high white wall. In the wall is a green gate, and the garden is more beautiful than can be imagined,

filled with great shade trees, with flowers, and wide grass swards. There
are pools with leaping fish and bright-coloured singing birds and butterflies. The air is warm and moist, soft, filled with hum of honey bees.
It is fragrant with the scent of flowers. I know this, for I have been there."
"With my brother?"
"Yes, Boetie, we were together there for a short time once. We went
through the little door. Then . . . then we came out again, but it was
unforgettable. It was the end to which we had been born."
"And me, Lena, why was I born? I often wonder. I never did
before, but now I wonder."
"One day you will know, Boetie. Perhaps it was to comfort others
as you do me: perhaps to inspire them by your courage."
"I have no courage," he said. "You must not tell any one, but I am
always afraid. I was very afraid of those Englishmen on their big horses.
Only Dirk knows how frightened I am of things, though it is better at
home where I can understand what goes on about me."
"We will all be happy again one day," Lena said. "But we must
wait."
"It is not easy to wait, if you are a man." He turned his head to stare
over the veld and raised his hand. "That is where I should be: out
there."
"It is not easy if you are a woman who loves," Lena said.
"That is it. We would each go our ways. The way we were meant
to go when we were born: you to the man you love, and I to the war
that is for our land. I am glad it is my brother, Lena," he said suddenly.
"We must go home now," Lena said. "Do you pray for him?"
"I pray for him and my father, and for all our people."
"That is all we can do. We must wait and pray."
"Tell me what you see before we go. I have never been up the
spruit so far."
"I see the spruit. It is running well."
"I can hear it."
"Then to the left are the white poplars and we are near the big willows
now. Their branches dip into the water. They are hung with fink nests:
they are like pears swaying in the wind. And I can just see the hammer-
kops' nest: a big platform of sticks and rubbish. The ground rolls up
from us into two rankies, one on each side of the stream, and behind
us are the house, the kraals, the orchard, and the lands."
"Thank you, sister. I can see it now," he said. "And thank you
for taking me out like this. I have enjoyed it greatly. Sometimes I
am very alone, even among people. But to be with you is good. It is
nice to go out, the two of us together, and think of Dirk. For to think
of him is to pray for him. In my heart I think he knows our thoughts
and they help him."

" I think that, too, Boetie, and I feel he is near : nearer than we know."

They were walking more quickly, following the spruit towards the house.

"I know where I am now," Boetie said. He stopped her. "The dam is over there and the horse kraal is there and that is the house." He pointed to each thing.

"Yes, you know," Lena said. "It is wonderful."

"And I think I could find my way back to the place where we turned and you told me what you saw. It is five hundred and ten paces from here. I counted them. It is thus that I have always learned my way. It is not that I really mind being lost, but I do not like to be a nuisance to people. Even Johanna cannot play her games as she will, since she feels she has to lead me."

"You are getting about better and better. Soon you will know Mooiplaas as well as Doornkloof, which is good, since this is my home and I am to marry Dirk. You will be here a lot. Do you know what I thought of the other day?"

"What did you think?"

"I thought I would give you a horse from here. Then you could ride him from Doornkloof; he would bring you here, and lead one of your own horses to ride home. Each would go easily to his home; all you would have to do would be to change the saddle from the one to the other."

"Will you do that, Lena? Will you give me a horse? Then when we go back I can visit you till you are married without troubling any one."

"Yes, I will do it, Boetie . . . When Oupa comes back I will speak to him. There is a grey mare, the mother of Stoffel's roan and Louis' second horse, that I think you can have. She is very tame."

"You are very good to me, and I know the mare."

"You are Dirk's brother and I love you. Because of Dirk you are my brother too."

2

Boetie had woken up twice. Why could he not sleep to-night? Why was he uneasy? He wanted to get up, but he had promised his mother not to. He had been out all last night and the night before. If he went out too much, she made him promise to stay in for a day or two. Then she would let him go again. He would ask her to-morrow. If he could not sleep, it was better to be out. He turned over on his bed and closed his eyes.

A moment later he sat up. What was that, had he been dreaming? He ran to the window. It was not a dream. There was a horse gallop-ing. He recognized the hoofbeats; they were what he had been listening for. He ran to the door.

"Ma . . . Ma!" he shouted. "It is my brother's horse and he is going hard." He pushed open the door of her room. He felt her sitting up in bed. "It is Swartkie . . . the gun," he said. "Get me the gun."

"I can hear nothing, Boetie, my heart," his mother said.

"It is my brother, I can hear him. Give me the gun."

She jumped up. "I can hear now," she said. "It is a horse galloping."

"It's Swarkie, I tell you. He is running hard. It is my brother, he is pursued."

His mother pushed the rifle into his hands. He opened the bolt and closed it. The cartridge slid into the breech. He half-opened the bolt to feel it and closed it again. How cold the gun felt in his hand! Even the walnut butt felt cold. He went into the front room, stumbled against the table, found the door, and opened it. The horse had not slowed down.

Tanta Kattie joined his mother. He could hear her behind him. "What a night to ride like that," she said. "It's as black as pitch."

Tanta Stephanie was shouting from her room. "What is it . . . what is it? Magtig, it is the English, none of us will be safe—no woman is safe with them."

Lena was beside Boetie, but stood quietly. She smelt good, warm from her bed; she smelt like fresh bread. He was very afraid. It was comforting to have her near.

"Light up the lamp, Ma. Light it quick so that I can be seen against the light."

He heard her strike a match. She was slow. He heard her hand tremble as she fitted on the glass.

"Is it alight?" he asked. "Is it on the table behind me?"

"It is on the table, Boetie."

"Then saddle up a fresh horse, Ma. There is a good one in the kraal. His tail is rubbed a little near the root."

"What colour is he?" his mother asked.

" Colour?" Boetie said. "I do not know. He's a big horse, a stallion. You can't mistake him. He is the only one with a rubbed tail."

"He's a bay horse with a star," Lena said. "We call him Starretjie. I will get him, Boetie."

"Run, then, Lena. Saddle him and hold him ready at the back."

By raising his right elbow, Boetie could feel the door frame. He was in the middle of the doorway. His bare feet gripped the flat stone that was let into the threshold. How cold it was, colder than the gun which had got warm in his hands. He felt a corrugation in it with his big toe of his right foot and rubbed it back and forth. His rifle was held across him, ready to raise.

The horse was very close. Above the sound of his hoofs he could hear his gasps for breath. Swartkie was almost done. But the horse Lena was saddling up was a good one. He knew that from having felt him over. He was sound, young, well-muscled, with fine strong quarters that would drive him over the ground. He was easily the best horse there: much better than the six they had brought from Doornkloof or Louis' red horse that Oom Philippus had lamed. He was well now and no longer favoured his near foreleg, but he was too hot for work like this, too wild, and he might break down again. Once his brother was off on the new horse, he would go outside and let them shoot towards the light. The women must go to the back and hide. Lena could take Swartkie, who must be saved. Then from the yard and the kraals he would fire towards the sounds. If he shot fast and often, moving continually, they would not know he was alone and would be delayed from following Dirk.

It was all clear in his mind: his duty much clearer than his fear—mastering it. Dirk must escape. But how could he have thought of so much so fast, of so many things at once, all in an instant? It could not have been more than five minutes since he had first heard the horse and called his mother. It is because I planned it out before, he thought. Without knowing what I did, I must have thought of it all. That was why I brought the rifle; why I went over the horses so carefully to find the best one. Starretjie was much better than any of their own horses that had come with them.

Swartkie was up to them now. He raised the rifle to his shoulder and lowered his cheek on to the butt. "Stop or I shoot," he shouted.

It might not be Dirk. It was Swartkie, but there might be someone else on his back. He thought of his mistake with Jannie Fourie.

"Boetie . . . Boetie, what are you doing?"

It was Dirk. Swartkie pulled up, his hoofs scraping along the ground.

"The new horse is ready, Dirk," he shouted. "Run to the back; Lena has him saddled and ready at the back. Ride on, brother, I will hold them."

"What is it, Boetie . . . What is the matter?"

"Are you all right, Dirk? I thought you were being pursued and that Swartkie could do no more. I have never known you to ride like that. I was afraid. It was in my heart that they were behind you."

"I am not being followed." Dirk had dismounted. Swartkie was breathing in great gasps, blowing the air out of his nostrils and sucking it in again. "But I need a new horse. I came for you. I want you to come with me."

"Why so fast? What is it, Dirk? Why do you want Boetie? You took a chance riding so hard on such a night," his mother said.

"Will you come with me, Boetie?" Dirk asked.

"I am ready," Boetie said.

"Get your coat on, then, and your hat. Make haste."

He went for them as Lena brought the bay horse to the front. Dirk took her in his arms so suddenly that the bay went up into a rear with fright. He pulled him down and spoke to his mother.

"Ja, Ma. We take chances and must take more. There is such need for haste that I have no time to explain. I must have Boetie. I wasted time riding first to Doornkloof, only to find you were all here. Joubert needs him." Dirk had mounted.

"You are not taking Boetie to the war? What can he do?"

"Ja, what can I do, brother?"

"I'll tell you on the way. Come here."

Boetie went towards the horse and felt for his brother's leg. His hands went down behind it, for the leather. It would be hanging loose and ready for him. He held the iron with his left hand, put in his foot, gave his left hand to his brother, grasped the cantle with his right, and swung up.

"Hold fast, we are going to ride."

The horse was up in a plunging turn. "Good-bye!" Dirk shouted.

"Good-bye!" Boetie's voice sounded weak to him as he cried out.

There were voices from the house. He could just hear them above the sound of the horse's hoofs.

"Good-luck, good-bye. Come back . . . Good-bye. . . ."

He was holding on to his brother's waist. The saddle was pressing into him. If he was not careful he would be galled. Under him the horse's quarters were moving strongly. He was carrying them both easily, the great haunches moved without effort gathering themselves and striking downwards at the ground. It began to rain almost at once, even before they were off the boundary of the farm. Dirk's back sheltered him from it, but he felt it on his hands. The front of his legs were soaked.

Where were they going? What did Joubert want him to do? What use could he be to him? He was going to the war with his brother. He would see Pa. Blind as he was, he was going. His prayer had been

answered. He tried to ask Dirk, but he did not answer. They were
riding too hard for him to hear him. The noise of the rain and the
splashing slip of the horse's hoofs drowned everything. Once the horse
almost fell. He sprawled, slipping sideways, but Dirk gathered him
again, and held him. What a fine rider Dirk was! He was bent forward along the horse's neck to ease him and to shelter his own eyes from
the rain. Boetie lay over, too, burying his face in his brother's back.
He could feel the muscles running over his coat.

The ground was getting rougher. There were the loose stones. He
remembered them slipping from under the cart wheels. He sat up
straight. The rain stung his face. He breathed deeply. Yes, he was
right. He could smell it, there was no mistake. It was the smell of his
mountain. They were getting nearer and nearer home. The certainty
increased. He wondered where the camp was. Were they laagered?
Had they wagons with them?

He felt the horse swing under him. Dirk was turning. "We are
nearly there!" Dirk shouted over his shoulder. "There are the fires."
Boetie wondered how they had kept them burning in such rain. The
horse was slowing up. Dirk leant back in the saddle. They had stopped.
There was only the rain coming down. Dirk's chest was moving quickly
as he breathed. . The horse was blowing.

Then Dirk shouted, "I am back, kerels. I have got him. Where is
Joubert? Tell the commandant I have got my brother."

Men were running from all around.

Dirk dismounted by throwing his leg over his horse's neck. "Come,
Boetie," he said.

He felt Dirk's arm round his waist. He lifted him down. His legs
would hardly hold him. I am weak with excitement, he thought. It
had been a long ride, over ten miles at a gallop without a saddle. It had
stopped raining.

"You have got him, Dirk?" someone said.

"Is Boetie there?" It was his father's voice.

"I am here, Pa. Dirk has brought me; I am here beside him."

"Can he do it, Dirk?" his father asked.

"I have not asked him, but I know he can."

"Do what?" Boetie asked. "Is there anything I can do?"

"Do not hurry him," Dirk said. "He must not be shouted at, give
him time. Where is the commandant—let Joubert tell him. Get back!"
Dirk shouted to the men around him. "You will bewilder him. I got
him out of bed to bring him here, and he is blind. Are the men ready?"
he asked. "The commandant said he would hold them ready, for we
have little time."

"Magtig, it is too dark," a man said: "dark like the inside of a beast."

"That is why I fetched my brother," Dirk said, "and foundered my horse to do it."

"Where's the boy? Has Dirk brought him?" It was Joubert. "Is this Boetie van der Berg?"

"I am Boetie." He took a step forward. A man took his hand. The hand felt good; it was that of an old man, hard, worn, and veined. But it was warm and confident.

"Now listen, Boetie, to what I tell you," Joubert said. "We are here with two hundred men. We are at the drift. The English are in the North and a big commando is driving them this way. Our part in the plan is to hold them here and not allow them to cross. They are retreating towards the drift we are holding and do not know we are here. Do you understand this, Boetie?" He spoke very quietly and patiently.

"I understand," Boetie said. "You hold the drift. They will not be able to cross and the big commando will have them, they will not be able to pass before two fires—one before and one behind."

"Ja," Joubert said, "that is it. But something has gone wrong with our plan. A small force of English has got to the top of the mountain. We command the drift, but they command us. They got there before we did. We were going to get them out to-night. We were going to attack, but there is only one track path up from this side."

"Yes, there is but one. It is the one I use to climb the mountain with my father's goats."

"That is what your brother told me. When I said it was no good and that we would have to abandon the position, he said, 'I will ride for my little brother, he will help us.'" He paused. "Will you help us, Boetie?"

"Me help? Commandant, how can I help?" Boetie's lips were trembling. "Did my brother not tell you that I cannot see?"

"That is why he fetched you. To-night the Transvaal needs a blind boy."

"But what for? What can I do?"

"You can lead Joubert's commando."

"Lead?"

"Listen. It has been raining, and even before it rained the night was so dark that we could do nothing. It is not a road. It is a goat track. Can you lead us up it in the dark?"

"It is never dark for me. Put me on the bottom of the track. I am bewildered and it would take me time to find it. Put me there and I will lead you."

Of course he knew the path. Did he not take it every day of his life? Blind, and suddenly his blindness was a help and not a hindrance. Without him two hundred men could do nothing and the English would be able to pass.

"Get ready, men. We are going up the mountain," Joubert shouted.

"I will go next to him," Dirk said. "Then our father will come."

"I will follow Groot Dirk," Joubert said. "Come, Boetie." He led him through the water which was running high. It was above his knees.

"Here is the path, jong," he said.

Boetie paused and cast about a little, feeling the ground with his feet. He put out his right hand—there should be a bush here. He found it. He moved a pace or two tentatively: felt the ground again with his toes.

"I know where I am," he said. "I am ready to climb."

"Take the riem, then," Dirk said.

"What riem?"

"The riem you are to lead us with." He put the rawhide riem into his hand. "Wrap it round your waist. All the others are fast to it."

So that was how they were going to do it. Two hundred riems all fastened together in a long rawhide snake, a man to each riem. It was a good plan. Two hundred, all following him : all following me, he thought : blind Boetie leading Joubert's commando! What a responsibility! Suppose he led them wrong. But why should he? Still he was suddenly afraid.

"Lead on, Boetie," Dirk said. "You know the path, there is nothing to fear."

"No, there is nothing to fear." His brother's voice and hand on his shoulder reassured him. He stepped forward. His feet found the path easily. They knew each stone and root, each bend, each rock. He recognized the scents of the mountain herbs. He recognized the little breezes, the small eddies that came from the kloofs or swept upward from the kranses. Here it was warmer : here it was always colder : here a breeze hit your left cheek : here one hit your right. He knew them all. The rain kept off, but it had been hard. He could hear the water running down the mountain, pouring down the kloofs and running over the cliffs in cascades that roared into the void beneath. Parts of the track were slippery with water. Showers of water fell from the stunted trees as he brushed them, soaking him again.

"Magtig, Boetie," his father said as they halted to rest, "this is a path for goats and baboons. I never knew you came this way. If I had, I would never have let you come. Why, if you had slipped . . ."

"I never slip, Pa. It is my mountain."

It was his mountain, and how good it was to be on it again. He laughed to himself. How happy he was! How strange it was to be blind and to be at home here among these crags and cliffs and yet lost in a strange house! Did they think he did not know about the cliffs and precipices? Why, he often threw stones from the path and listened to them bounding down. Perhaps it was as well the night was so dark.

Perhaps if there had been more light the burgers would not have climbed. Among them all, because he was blind, only he, Boetie van der Berg, could see. Dirk and his father would be proud of him. And the others would be ashamed not to follow where a blind boy led.

He stopped again.

"We are nearly there, Pa," he said.

A few yards more, and he came to the face of a low cliff. A baboon barked. There was the crying of a young baboon, then another bark of the baby's scream. Mother baboons beat their babies when they scream. The first baboon barked again. That was the old man, the leader giving warning. If the English knew anything of the veld, they would know something was happening. But they were not likely to know, and it was too late now.

"Here you must climb, Dirk," he said, "but it is the last krans. After that you are on the top."

He felt for a finger-hold in the wet rock. He found it. He pulled himself up. He found another. His feet sought the rock-face, gripped it, and he pushed up again; once more, and he lay flat on his belly. He was up. Dirk was breathing heavily beside him. Then came his father. Their rifle barrels clinked as they moved near to each other. More men came up—more and more, blowing like spent horses, cursing under their breath, "Magtig, what a climb! Nothing for a boy, perhaps, but for married men with guns on their backs and a hundred rounds of ammunition in their bandoliers."

More men . . . all the men . . .

"I am the last," someone said. And still no challenge. The English are sleeping. Joubert was whispering instructions. The men were spreading out. Boetie could feel them fanning out on either hand. His father pushed him down behind a big stone.

"Stay there, Boetie, and wait. We will come back for you."

He must wait now. They had done with him. He felt very cold and alone, very frightened. The rain had seeped into him. He could feel the men leaving him, creeping forward. He knew just how they would be crouching. Joubert had told them not to show themselves against the skyline. Now they had gone. He could not hear a sound except the slow drip of water when the wind shook a tree beside him. They were creeping towards a camp of sleeping men. They would surprise them . . .

He waited. His heart was hammering against his chest . . . waiting. It must come in a minute, it must . . . it must. He thought of the English cavalry and how he had waited then. This was the same thing, only worse. Now his father and Dirk were here with guns in their hands. They were going to fight. He knew they had fought already, but this was different. It was immediate, urgent. It was . . . It was on his mountain as he had dreamed it.

There was a shot . . . a shout. A fusillade of shots, more shouts. A bugle call and the blowing whistles. Then everyone was shouting and shooting. Bullets cracked over his head. One smacked into the rock beside him. Something hit his arm; it was like the sting of a whip. He put his other hand on the wound. The blood ran hot over his wrist. I wonder how bad it is, he thought. It did not hurt. It could not have hit a bone, but it was funny to sit like this in a battle, wounded, and not to know how bad it was or what it looked like. There were cries from the wounded, groans and curses. More shots, more and more. He could smell the cordite drifting in on the morning wind. They had only just got there in time. Joubert was shouting; he heard his voice clearly above the noise. He was roaring like a bull. " They are running!" he shouted.

He heard his father's voice shout to Dirk. " Shoot low and don't hurry." For a moment he thought it must all be a dream. He had dreamed of the war before and had thought of it continually. But you did not bleed in a dream. It was all as he had imagined it would be when he had sat on the mountain and tried to think of a battle. It was so like it that he felt no surprise. But he was frightened. That fear he had been unable to think of, since till to-night real fear had been unknown to him. He was trembling like a hunting dog. Great shivers started at his head and ran down to his feet. His teeth chattered with fright and cold. The blood that had run hotly was now cold on him like water. A bird began to sing. It must be dawn. There was a terrific burst of fire. The birds were still singing, more of them now. The fighters must have wakened them. Then a single shot, and his father called to him.

" Boetie, Boetie, are you there?"

For a moment he could not answer. His mouth was dry. Then he said : " I am here, Pa."

" Are you all right?"

" I am all right, Pa." He could hear him coming towards him. " Is Dirk all right?" he asked.

" I am fine, Boetie. But what is it?" They were both running towards him. " You are hurt, my heart."

" It is nothing. I bleed, but it does not hurt me."

They were beside him.

" What is that blood on your face?" Dirk said. " Are you hit in the head?"

" In the arm," he said. " It must be from my hand : the blood on my face, I mean."

Dirk held his arm while his father washed out the wound with a rag and water from his flask. " It has only gone through the flesh, I think," his father said. " Move your hand, Boetie, move the wrist round and round."

Boetie moved it.

"It has not touched a muscle then," Dirk said. "We will tie it up and can dress it later."

They made a sling with a neckcloth. His father wiped the blood from his face and kissed him, holding him fast against his chest.

"Where's the boy?" It was Joubert again. He took his good hand. "You are hit, jong," he said.

"It is nothing, Commandant."

"He is hit," his father said, "but the bullet went through his arm. It has cut no muscles and looks a good clean wound."

Joubert still held his hand and was shaking it. "I want to thank you," he said. "Without you I do not think it could have been done. And had it been a fair night we could not have done it. We are burgers, not baboons. The English came the other way, from the back side of the Berg."

"I know that way, too, but it is very far," Boetie said.

"Well, that's the way we are going back, my boy, no matter how far it is," Joubert laughed. "Again I thank you, Boetie van der Berg," he said, "and in the name of my commando and our land. The President shall hear of it."

Men were crowding in from all round now.

"Not just the President," someone said. "Everyone shall hear of it." . . . "They will make songs of this," an old man said. "The song of Boetie's climb." . . . "It was the will of God that he should lead us," another said. They were pressing against him, man after man taking his good hand and shaking it.

"It is as the Lord Jesus said . . . 'A little child shall lead them.' . . . It is a miracle, it is a sign . . ."

Boetie could not understand it. As they came to congratulate him, they had tears in their throats. Dirk was crying and his father kept patting his shoulder. "If it had not been for you, Boetie . . ." they said.

Yes, if it had not been for him, there might have been many dead, and Boer homes desolate. This he knew. The English would have got through and the fighting have been hard. But why this talk? He had done what he had been asked to do; what each one of them would have done in his place; and now that it was over it seemed to him that he had never done it; that it was not he who had led them—that these men were talking past him, talking of a stranger. I did it, he thought, I did it, but it was not me. All the time as they climbed this had been in his mind— that it was another who did it. I could not do this; I could not lead a commando, he had thought as he did it. And he was exhausted now. He wanted to sleep. He felt the men and smelt them near him. They pushed up to him to pat his shoulder, to ask if his arm hurt . . . but he felt a long way off from them all. He had known, when Joubert explained what he wanted, that this thing could not be done—that a blind goatherd could not lead troops. Yet it had been done and it was he that had done it. Still more men kept coming to him—the whole two hundred must be shaking his hand, ever more men who said, " If it had not been for you . . . It was the will of God . . . the hand of God . . . " They spoke of David.

Ja, it must have been the will of God that had guided his feet and hands in unaccustomed places, for he had never been to the very top before. His goats had been up. He knew that, and had felt for their footholds in the rock. But he had never climbed that last krans. He had never dared.

CHAPTER XXIII

THE FATTED PIG

OUPA sat on the wagon-box. He was wondering why he had not gone
visiting before. It was pleasant to sit here looking at the backs of the
oxen and watching the world pass slowly by. It was the most dignified
and comfortable way to travel.

Reuter touched his arm.

"Baas, something has happened," he said.

"Something always happens. What is it now?"

Philippus was in a good temper. The round of visits had been a success.
They had been well entertained at Wonderfontein, at Winterveld, at
Klipgat, at Kromkuil, at Elandsfontein, and they were now on their
way to Botha's place, Sterkwater, that lay a little to the west of Kranskop.
How well he knew this country and how little it had changed! Except
that there was less game, it was almost the same as he always remembered
it—a few more houses, fewer trees, but the mountains still stood where
they had when he was a boy. He had crossed the same rivers and the
same drifts. It had all been wonderfully pleasant.

He had met some beautiful maidens who had listened wide-eyed, their
pretty mouths sagging open, at the stories he had told them. There was
no dearth of maids and widows in the land. It was just a matter of making up one's mind, but that was not so easy. How long would one of
them listen to you like that, open-mouthed, if you married her? It was
hard to remain a hero to a woman with whom one had intimate connec-
tion, and even this aspect presented some embarrassment to a man of his
age. It was all very well for him and Reuter to console each other on this
score, even though it was done obliquely as was necessary between a black
man and a white; but was it practical after all? At best it would be tiring
to have to make love again, and something of an anticlimax to his past
loves . . . it must all be considered carefully—weighed up. It was no use
going too far and inconveniencing oneself too much just to annoy somebody else. It might be less trouble to die in such a way as to create a
scandal. If he was to die, he would certainly do this. Marriage and
begetting a child was one way, and such a death the other. It was a hard
choice, and when he came to think of it he had little stomach for either.

The best thing was just to go on. It did no harm to look at the girls
and pinch them a little so that they giggled and squirmed; that committed no one and was pleasant relaxation. Again one's dignity had to

be considered. He had never failed at anything. Throughout his life he had held his head high. Suppose you married and a year passed without a child? There would have been all that work for nothing; there would be bitterness in the home, and the danger of becoming a laughing-stock if the woman was indiscreet and a gossip. There was no counting on what a woman would say if she was not content. She might take to another man and then he would have to fight him. That would be very annoying to have to shoot someone at his age. It was one thing to shoot an Englishman or two, and another to shoot a friend for committing a sin of which he had every sympathy.

There seemed to be endless possibilities for trouble; endless complications, situations, and combinations of situations which could do his reputation but little credit. And it was absurd to spend a hundred years building up a reputation to risk it like this at the last minute for a whim. Anybody could have a child. It was a matter of age, not of skill or subtlety. Put a young man and a woman in bed together, leave them an hour— half an hour would do—and there was a baby. It really was not worthy of him to attempt something which was more of an indiscretion than a feat even if it were successful. But it was pleasant to ride around just thinking about it and picturing to himself what he would have done to those girls eighty years ago. Magtig, how full of fire he had been then. After all, a man was spiritual. He was not an animal. He lived in his mind, and you could go to bed with a maid in your mind.

Reuter was still trying to tell him something. It was extraordinary how that boy gave you no time to think. Abstract thought should not be interfered with. And a man of his intellectual capacity should not be continually disturbed by trivial questions when his mind was occupied with greater things. He wished now he had asked Maria Bokman how she had cooked that sucking pig. It was roasted. When they asked him what he liked best, he always said sucking pig, and he had eaten six already; but what had she put in it? That was the question. There was a flavour he could not recognize. It was wonderful to live well again and well worth the pains it gave him. Living as he had for so long on pap, and bread milk, and broth had given him back his palate. Real food tasted good when you had hardly tasted it for twenty years. What he had at Mooiplaas was not food.

But what could it have been? . . . Onion, sage, parsley, mint, taragon . . . all those he had recognized; but there was something else, or was it the blending of the materials in the stuffing? A woman like that would make a man a fine wife. She could cook. His mouth filled with water as he thought of her food, and she had the haunches of a prime ox. When that woman moved, slowly and gracefully, wobbling all over, it was beautiful to see. He had always had a weakness for full-fleshed women and he had not changed. They still excited him It was wonderful to watch one moving about the house, floating along like a goose on water, her flesh swaying to her movements, rippling and rolling, soft ellipse converging on soft ellipse, rounded part on rounded part, curve upon swelling curve, and the whole structure of the woman held up by strong legs set like pillars beneath her. He was delighted with the quality of his thought . . . A hunter and a poet, he thought. There was something in him of both Nimrod and Solomon.

He thought of the Song of Solomon . . .

For, lo, the winter is past, the rain is over and gone;
The flowers appear on the earth; the time of the singing of birds is come, and the voice of the turtle is heard in our land;
The fig tree putteth forth her green figs, and the vines with the tender grape give a good smell. Arise, my love, my fair one, and come away . . .

" Arise my love, my fair one," he repeated again. And there were some fine pieces after that about ripe lips and thighs and bellies like brass and breasts like little hills. That had always been his favourite part of the Holy Book. He often thought of it. It made you realize how beautiful life was. And then there was a good description of an ostrich in the Book of Job, and of a war horse and an eagle. But the things he thought of for himself were fine, too, beautiful and subtle without blatancy or flamboyance, they got to the heart of any matter, presenting it like a fragrant flower set in a vase of clear glass. There was so much to think of—women, sucking pigs, French brandy, and the wonderful feeling when you lit your first pipe of strong tobacco in the morning and felt it grip you.

But Reuter was certainly a plague. To be his master was to be an Egyptian, cursed with seven times seven plagues and annoyances. But it was no use putting things off. He might as well listen now and get it over. Then he could go back to his thoughts again.

" Is there something you want, Reuter?" he asked.

" Master, I had it from the boys, so I do not know if it is a lie or the truth. Probably they lie, having no master to instruct them in religion; but among them it is said, though again, what I say is not of my own knowledge, with my eyes I have seen nothing and therefore briefly, and asking the Baas respectfully to understand that what I repeat is hearsay only, and that I state what I hear without prejudice, and shall feel deeply hurt if the Baas beats me upon finding certain inaccuracies, but . . ."

" What is it? What are you trying to say? Before God, I have not so many years, must I waste them listening to you?"

" Baas, I waste no one's time. I am brief to the point of bluntness. It is merely out of respect and politeness that I cover the spear point of my tongue with the karos of good usage. Naturally, as the Baas knows, I am a knob kerrie for directness, the flight of an assegai for accuracy, and without either subterfuge, double meaning, or hesitation either in my words or acts. Again briefly, if the Baas will give me a moment to tell him ... It is said among the Kaffirs that a battle has taken place on the mountain near Doornkloof, the one that is called the Hill of Doves. It is in my heart that the Baas should know this, though as I said it is merely hearsay and ... "

"Turn the wagon!" Philippus shouted. "Turn the oxen, Titus, we are going back.

"Before God I shall beat you, Reuter," he said. "Another battle at home, within ten miles of my house, and you tell me nothing. Are we men or pigs to go round from swill tub to swill tub when there is war at our back door? Ja, magtig, you shall lose the skin from your back for thinking your master a pig. Calling me a pig, you Kaffir! And this time I will not ride that red horse that goes lame if you canter him over a few yards of veld. I shall ride the bay stallion and you can follow well behind in case of accidents. I do not wish to lie with a broken leg on the veld again for days.

"Drive faster, Titus!" he shouted. "Faster, you skelms, there is a war at home."

As they neared home, Reuter said: "The Baas is troubled?"

"I am never troubled."

"Nevertheless, it is in my heart that the Baas is troubled. Perhaps he regrets the name he gave me which has caused me such ill-fortune and searches his mind for a new one. Or perhaps he cannot make up his mind about all those women we have seen. It is a hard thing for the Baas that, being rich, he cannot buy them all because of his religious convictions. Aaii ... Such a religion must press very hard on a man's mind and loins, since they tend to see things differently."

"You are a Christian, too. Do not forget that after the trouble I have taken with your conversion."

"Baas, I could not forget, but I can think back to how good it was before, can I not?—to the time when I was an induna with six wives, each in her own hut, each as comfortable as a worm wrapped in its own cocoon? Magtig, the Baas should have known me in my glory, with my wives, my children, my cattle, and my regiment. The Baas should have seen me dance, leaping high into the air, shouting and slapping my thighs. Then I was Tabankulu, Captain of the Blue Horizon; then I was a man, a Zulu induna. I had great honour in the land and much respect was accorded to me. When I walked with my ornaments on my legs and feathers in my hair and my little cloak of feathers about my shoulders, even the cattle turned their heads to see who it was that came with such beauty and magnificence.

"And my wives—how they respected me, even when they betrayed me! And the men who had them took them less for themselves than because they were my wives. For them it was like eating the heart of a lion which all men know gives the lion's courage to the eater. By lying with my women they gained a measure of my potency and magnificence. But now if I get that new wife my great-grandson speaks of—the one who has seen me in a dream—I will have to beat her. Ja, Baas, and the thought depresses me. If I get her, Baas, I will have to beat her much to make her respect me, which is hard, since once that respect came naturally."

"It is a mistake to beat women, Reuter, except for amusement, and then only if they like it. It is a strange thing, but some like it. It is after all an attention. It shows you think of them and it cannot be done in an absent-minded manner."

"That is my opinion, Baas, and I am glad the Baas agrees with me. For men of our age the beating of women is good. It is good for two reasons. As the Baas says, it shows we think of them and thus makes up for other things, since we are not the men we were. Aaii, what men we were! And secondly, even if we wished, we cannot beat them over-hard, which makes them think themselves lucky, so that they say in their hearts, 'My husband is old, but suppose he were not . . . suppose it were a young, strong man who beat me?' Then also it keeps them from brooding. Women are great brooders. They sit upon their wrongs like hens and hatch them into devilry."

"There is much in what you say, Reuter. It is an interesting subject for discussion and it is pleasant to talk of women now that we are no longer bothered with them. But beating is still dangerous, for they will bring up the fact of having been beaten upon occasions which are in-auspicious. Some talk of the memory of animals, but I have hunted and worked with beasts since I could walk, and I consider the memory of women, about things which should be forgotten, remarkable. Ja, Reuter"
—he paused—"I should say women were the most intelligent and dangerous of beasts and that it would be well for us to walk softly and not leap from the frying-pan of our loneliness into the fire of further matrimony. Fire should be met with fire and our fires are nearly out."

"Yes, Baas, sometimes I regret my youth," Reuter said. "I was much admired then and it is good to be admired."

"I am admired now. My charge against the English is the talk of all the world."

"Ja, that is so. But did the Baas let me participate in his glory? No, the Baas was selfish, he must have all the glory himself. Having been in a hundred battles with his servant, he rides to the hundred and first alone. My heart has been very sore since then. It is that which has made me turn my mind to women again. A man must be loved. He cannot stand alone . . . He said she dreamed of me."

"It would have nothing to do with sleeping alone, Reuter?"

"No, Baas. I do not mind sleeping alone except in the winter."

"Then we are different, Reuter. For when I think of a fine, fat young wife, it is in my mind to sleep with her."

"And the Baas thinks he can?"

"I do not know. But I think back to my first elephant. I was only twelve. My father said: 'To-day you will shoot an elephant,' and I said: 'Do you think I can?' And he said: 'Try and see.' I shot it. That incident has had a great bearing on my career. It influenced me profoundly. Since then I have hesitated at nothing. And to fail with a woman is not as bad as failing with an elephant."

"That is so, Baas. A woman has no tusks or trunk. She cannot kneel on you and smear you over the veld. The words of the Baas are a comfort to me."

"And now be silent, Reuter. I am tired of advising you. Is there nothing in the world but women?"

"Baas, there are many things—there are brandy and beer, tobacco, music, and there are sleep and warmth and war. There are also the hunting of great game and the eating of meat, particularly of meat with fat upon it. Meat with fat on it is like a woman—hard and soft at once. And there are women who would like to eat, sleek young maids."

"Reuter, you disgust me. For forty years I have explained what is right or wrong. It is right to marry one wife. That is a holy sacrament."

"It is as the Baas says, but would not to marry two women be two sacraments? Once I had six beautiful young sacraments to till my fields. But then I was young and strong, a thing of fire, of dancing beauty. Aaii . . . I was a roaring bull, a neighing stallion. I was a man! And now we are going home to that woman. She will not be kind to us. That is a terrible thing to be unkindly treated at home and to have no redress. If the Baas had not been so good, he would have let me spear her long ago. There are great defects in the Baas' religion. If I had known them sooner, I am not certain that I would have been converted, no matter how much the Baas chose to beat me. Nor am I sure that there was justice in it. Other men merely beat their servants, but they do not interfere with their souls. My soul was a fine thing when I was young. It was hot in my breast. It reared up like a lion when it saw a maid, and then the Baas trapped it and put it in a cage. Ja, when I think back I know what a fine wild soul I had."

"Silence, Reuter. You never give me time to think. At my age I have much to consider and little time in which to do it."

"What is the Baas going to think of—of brandy, of food, or women?"

"I am going to think great thoughts. I am a philosopher and a poet. Also I have plans to make. We must knee-halter that woman."

"It would be better to spear her. Let me spear her, Baas. It could be an accident. My spear could slip into her belly one day. Then I would give it a little twist. I have often thought of it. It is a small thing to ask the Baas and would give me pleasure."

"No, I tell you. You cannot do that. But I am still puzzled about how you got that brandy so easily."

"The brandy, Baas? That was easy."

"It is not easy, for I have tried. The door is locked and the window is too small."

"Baas, it is easy. There is a long stick with a loop on the end. It is in your hand. There is the bottle," Reuter pointed over the veld, "there is the loop. Look, it is falling over the neck. It is fast. Now, slowly . . . slowly, so as not to disturb its brothers . . . Slowly, slowly, you raise it, you draw it in. Is it there in your hand."

"That is stealing, Reuter. I have told you not to steal."

"The Baas also told me to get brandy. If the Baas had only told me sooner, he would have had more. I have been doing it for many years. Not enough to be noticed, but just a bottle now and then when my heart was sore."

"It was stealing, Reuter."

"To take brandy is different, Baas. To take brandy is not quite stealing, since they should give it to us. It is the Baas' farm and we are old. Our bowels are cold within us."

"We must not get caught, Reuter."

"When have we been caught?"

"Never yet, but we must plan carefully."

"Ja, Baas, we will plan. Let us plan. But I should like to spear her."

A coming back was very different to a riding out; there was a sense of accomplishment in the return if you had done what you had set out to do. But it was over. It had been and could not be again. Even were it done again, it would be different, even if you visited the same people, said the same things, ate the same food from the same plates, it would be different. You could not kill the same elephant twice. You could not even love the same woman again or eat the same sucking pig; each time was final both in its implication and the circumstance of its beginning. Water ran down a spruit. It was as it has always been, but at no time was it the same— only the principle of the running water was the same; it was constant, and as such resembled lust for woman, or the desire to hunt and kill. But there was no getting away from the fact that the water was always differerent from minute to minute, from instant to instant—it only looked the same.

How appearance deceived me! That was something you did not understand in youth. Things were not what they appeared. And

H.O.D.

happiness : what was that but a state? It had no visible cause like unhappiness. There was always a circumstance for unhappiness. You thought you wanted this . . . if you had it you would be happy; or if this circumstance or that one could be changed, you would be happy. That was foolishness; happiness was a multiple thing and infinitely variable in quality. A young man was happy on a good horse, with a good hunting dog, a new rifle, to which were added the open veld, plenty of game, a full belly, and the glory of his bodily strength. He was happy with a maiden lying with him under a canopy of trees, with the earth to which they belonged beneath them. A man was happy with his first child on his knee, and his first grandchild. After the first of each the other children counted less.

I have lost count of the children I have held, Philippus thought. They were of my blood, but not of my spirit, and it was his spirit a man sought in the stock he got. Only Lena was left. She was his last hope, and with Dirk she should breed something good. He would be able to recognize it at once if he held it, even before its eyes were open. That was one of his jokes and made young mothers angry. But they were fools. The blank eyes of their babies were not open. They only opened when the spirit entered them; at three months, four months, it began, and came almost fully with their teeth.

A baby was nothing; it was only in its potentialities that it was interesting. Who would want a baby if it stayed a baby? But you looked at them when they began to run and thought of their lives that lay in front of them. There was a sadness in that which was very moving. That soft little girl's body would be broken open by the fruit of its love. Somewhere, while you watched her playing, there was a boy growing up to that destiny. By him, through him, she would be broken and divided. By her, and through her, his unformed seed would be thrust out, amid her cries, into the world to beget more seed or to bear it.

It was not that there was anything beautiful in maternity that moved you. On the contrary, for it was concerned with blood and pain, with milk and excrement. Nor was a woman's love for her child wonderful. It was no different from the love of a cow for her calf, or a mare for her foal. It was a direct and natural event, a part of a sequence, as unavoidable as death and perhaps of less significance. Desire was followed by pregnancy, and pregnancy by birth. Before God, did men think that a cow thought of a calf when she sought out a bull? Was the bull a father when he mounted her and she bowed beneath his bulk? It was not so. That was not the answer. The urge was the answer, and that the answer itself was a question meant little, for was it not in the heart of man or beast to procreate?—rather was it their burden, and to their detriment that it happened. It was the consequence of the act to which their urge had driven them. A man loved his children when they came. But before that? Could one love what was not there? He himself had never felt this and doubted it, save for such practical purposes as the breeding of sons that would bear guns and hunt and work. If a man was to stay always young, would he desire children? No, he would not. And it was not this that made birth and desire and love wonderful. It was the fact of its universality, the fact that all living things were driven by the same force to the same end, that their desire was not only identical, but that it had gone on for ever in an endless sequence—that each man, each beast, was a living link in a chain that stretched back into the infinite past. . . .

I shoot a lion, he thought. Perhaps my father shot its father, perhaps my son will shoot its son. As we bred and grew, so did they breed and grow. While we were living in one place they were living in another. A lion's life was much like a man's, and they lived thirty or forty years. That is to say, they lived fully as a man did, but knew no old age, being cut off from life as their powers waned. No beast knew old age. He thought of the Englishmen he had killed. How strange that they should have been born to die so far away from home beneath his bullets! How strange, how inexplicable!

The great wheels rolled, rumbling on their axles. How many hours had he travelled by wagon? How often would he travel again? Perhaps never. This might be his last return. And there had been another battle. That was an extraordinary thing that in youth you should leave your home to seek adventure, and that in age, when you thought everything was over, it should come to your chair. It was bad luck to have missed this second battle. But who would have thought such a thing possible? You should have been safe in assuming that a battle was like lightning and would not strike in the same place twice. Though this was not entirely true—there was places where it struck continually, but those were well known: Koppies filled with iron that called the lightning down. Perhaps Mooiplaas and Doornkloof were like that too—attracting war. If so all he need do was to sit and wait for it to come again. Pleasures when you were old were few and far between and time of little importance. Still it was a pity to have missed it—a great pity.

Facts were facts and there was no gainsaying them, nor striving to avoid their consequence. So were men weighed by diverse measures and balanced by diverse weights. When death came he wondered what would be flung into the scales of judgment against him. He wondered who would speak for him and who against. With age he had become less clear about the accepted standards of virtue. He had thought much of Ooom Christiaan van Ek's philosophy and found little wrong with it. It was principle that mattered, not detail. Many men were like calves, always licking their coats and the coats of others, always prying into the small, unimportant things. A calf that licked too much could

die with hairballs in its belly. Once, on opening up a dead calf, he had
found sixteen, each bigger than bullets that went four to the pound. And
there were men who sucked themselves like cows, drawing out their own
virtue and consuming it, as a cow did her own milk when she got the
trick of it. When he had had a cow like that, he had sold her. You
could not cure them, they taught others, and even stole their milk.

How like animals men were! Whatever a man did there was always
a parallel in the life of a beast. There were men who were like hyenas
and baboons that when they ran away stopped to look back over their
shoulders. They were like Lot's wife and were destroyed like her. There
were men as obvious as seacows. But who knew the real life of a hippopotamus that conceived, gave birth, and suck in the depths of the river?
What did you ever know of the secret life of man, especially those who
lived so openly that this openness itself could be a part of their deception
—the seacow and the whited sepulchre?

Young hippos came up for air and went down for milk. There were
men like that and you could not get away from it. But he had never
been like that. What he had done, good, bad, and indifferent, was
known to all the world. He had not lived privately. He had hamstrung
life as a Massai warrior hamstrung an elephant, fearlessly and without
disguise. He thought of the wonders he had seen; of the beauties. How
beautiful it was to see a baby hippo, grey pink, riding on its mother's
back; to catch it like that in the red light of dawn, its wet back shining;
to see it fat and happy as a baby which indeed it was. He thought of a
hen ostrich squatting in season while the cock, black, scarlet, and white,
with hot blood danced before her; of puff adders that brought forth
their young alive and were said to die in so doing, though he doubted
this; of egg-eating snakes that had teeth set like a saw in their throats
which cut the egg in two as they swallowed it; of mambas as fast as a
horse. That was something to see—a mamba twelve foot long and no
thicker than your thumb, run over the tops of the bushes like the drawn
lash of a whip, and so fast that you must be a good shot to hit it.

He thought of the forest in Zululand, where the women walked with
flat stones on their heads to protect them from the green mambas that
struck down upon them from the trees. He thought of that time—it
was very long ago now—when he had seen a string of women go down
to a river and each pick up a great stone from a heap, set it on her head,
and then continue down the bank and into the water. As they came out,
still in single file, each had put down her stone on another heap. That
had accounted for those heaps on each side of a river that was too deep
to ford. With stones on their heads they had just walked across the
sandy bottom.

He thought of how a waterbuck was safe among crocodiles. They

would always let one pass safely through a river, not because they did
not like to eat buck, but because wild dogs were particularly fond of
this variety and would follow it; and above all things crocodiles liked
dogs, wild or tame. They had that in common with tigers. Before
God, no small dog was safe from a leopard. They would take one from
a wagon where it slept upon its master's bed. He thought of that time
he had been hunting with dogs; they had been fine ones, big Boer-hounds,
and they had been holding something at bay in a thick bush. He had
been young and reckless then and had ridden up to see what it was. A
leopard had sprung out, landing with its paws on his shoulders. Yes,
he had been strong then, and had flung it off among the dogs who had
finished it. It was a pity they had spoilt the skin, and two of them had
been killed.

Dogs, horses, cattle, farms, battles, men, women, children, wild beasts
—how many he had known, how many had he loved, had he killed!
And nothing had been mean or private or secret; all men knew of him,
and what he had done to his friends and enemies had been open. This
at least would be held in his favour. He had done what he had had to
do, fearlessly, and hurt as few as he might. And some, like Reuter, he
had saved from death, though now when it was too late he sometimes
pondered on his wisdom in saving Reuter. That boy had been a great
trouble to him, a great trial.

Movement . . . the slow movement of the wagon was conducive to
thought. This had not been the least part of his pleasure. The entertainment that he had enjoyed had been punctuated by long periods of
constructive thought, due, he was convinced, to the excellence of the
food that he had been given. It was years since he had thought so well
or constructively. It was also years since he had had decent food. It
became crystal clear that a man's mind was dependent upon the state of
his belly. Bread and milk could not produce strong thought. If he
was to continue this intellectual pleasure, he must also have the meat
and brandy which were its foundation. This thought exercised him.
He would soon be home now. Without doubt they would kill the fatted
calf for him, though in this case he hoped it would be a little pig. But
after that, would they continue to feed him properly? Was he strong
enough to insist upon it? That was something that would be decided
later. Meanwhile it was pleasant to doze and dream about his welcome-
feast. As to his pains—brandy was the antidote to indigestion. Its warm
fire burnt up the pain.

Two more days and he would be home.

One more day now, but yesterday had been a bad one—very bad. It
even seemed possible that those who said he should not do so much were

right. He must be more careful and conserve his strength : especially
now that he was so near home. They must not see that his visiting had
done him harm, for that would be to put ammunition in their guns.
He must appear very well and gay, as he arrived at least. After that
he could give in a little. After all, a journey might tire any one; but
he had had another of those spells. They did not frighten him—they
were even rather pleasant; but if those women saw them they might
refuse him the comforts for which he had regained a taste. Brandy was
a necessity which should be denied no man, no matter what his age.
And he needed meat. Not only did he like to eat it, it did him good,
especially sucking pig, ox tongues, and kidneys. This was an important
point that he must not lose sight of. It was for this, as well as to look
over the girls, that he had left home. If you were going to do something
new and were uncertain of the result, it was best to do it among strangers.
The results had surpassed his hopes. His digestion had stood every test.
There was no question that he had a wonderful stomach and these spells
had nothing to do with what he had eaten. There must be no mistake
about this, and Reuter talked nonsense when he pointed out that they
always followed a heavy meal. That was accident and coincidence and
only a fool or a Kaffir would be deceived by it.

He thought of women again. Since it did not seem much use looking
forward on this subject, he looked back. Except for Helena, and she
was in a class by herself, all women were much the same, except in
colouring, and there they were not variable as were cattle, dogs, or horses.
A woman was dark or fair or intermediate between the two. She had
dark eyes or blue eyes or intermediate eyes. Of course there were red-
headed ones. But they were not for sensible men. He thought of van der
Merwe again. It was a pity women could not be beautifully marked
like animals—cream with black points; chestnut with white legs; spotted
black and white. That was the tragedy. It was not whom a man married,
but the fact that any other might do equally well that made it so sad.
This was what you knew when you reached an age of discretion. Any
man, even of seventy, would agree with him.

But very young men were different. With them it was not so. No,
a young man must have this woman or that one. And it was little use
for an older man who had known many women trying to explain. To
such a man—himself, for instance—any good-looking woman who was
plump, with wide hips and a pleasant nature, was enough. If added to
this she had a light hand with pastry and came with a good farm and
cattle from her father or a dead husband, it was even better. It was said
that many books had been written on the subject of love—philosophy
they called it. But why books only the Almighty knew. No man could
learn about love from reading. Why read when it was all as simple as
the meat in an egg? Break the shell of any egg and you would find

the meat. Break the shell and you will find the meat in all men, and all women too, though sometimes it might be stale and stink.

It was this that the predikants never understood when they talked of sin. Original sin! magtig, why not speak of an original yolk in an egg? Take what they called the sin out of a man and what had you? A shell and some slippery white. The sin was the yolk, the kernel, the basis of the whole business. And how was it that the predikants imagined they understood these things? Either they did not understand them at all, or if they did, they should not. With this as with everything else it was a matter of practice, and if this was so, what could a good man know of women? What could he know? How could he learn if he persisted in his virtue? That was the strange thing—that a bad man could make any woman happy and keep her happy, whereas a good man must be rich, indeed, even to hold her content.

And there were things he must tell Lena. He must explain life to her so that she would understand it. He must try to help her. He began to compose his speech to her in his mind. It would go this way: he would say:

"I believe in many things, Lena, but I can think of nothing that I believe which I should be willing to modify or discard. I am not consistent. Men say"—he touched his forehead—"that I am mad. But I am not mad. It is only that I know too much; that I can see the plot and the counterplot; that I know things are not what they seem. Listen," he would say, "some men can hear the cry of a flittermouse, others cannot. To a small creature the grass among which it lives is a forest and it can have no knowledge of a tree or a mountain; therefore, since this is so, it is in my heart that there are many things unperceived by men and no less real for that. No, my heart, knowledge is a trick whereby our experiences are made to bear some relation to the thing that we call life. Because I can think, I am better than a beast, or perhaps not better, but different. Because I think too well, men have said that I was mad and have attempted to destroy me; but I do not know the meaning of their distinctions of good and bad, of high and low, or whether they have, in the great scheme that I perceive dimly, any real meaning—sometimes I doubt it.

"And yet for men—and being men, we think as such—there is, for most things, a good way and one less good, and beyond this we need not go. Even if there be no such thing as freewill, it is best to believe that it exists, for by it more can be achieved. But remember that men think like men; bucks like bucks; dogs like dogs; all living in different worlds, each isolated from the other.

"And what has man to do with the universe, or the path of a star in the skies? What do we know, Lena," he would ask, "even of so simple a thing as an egg? An egg is a great mystery, and when you see it as such and do not accept it as an ordinary thing, then you have gone far along the road of wisdom and can laugh at the fools who think to explain the world with the words of their mouths. There are secrets that are beyond all comprehension. Go about, my child. Look, stare, watch, and listen, and you will see that what I say is true : that there is no such God as the predikants describe him, but a greater one. Ja, a very great God of which you and I and all living things are a part."

This was his wisdom that he must pass on. But he must tell her soon. He was strong, but he was old, and could not live for ever. He thought of food once more—bobotee; breede, made of mutton ribs; cucumber sambal, sassaties, fricandel of minced mutton, kabobs, and roast sucking pig the best of all. Yes, he must talk to Lena as soon as he got back. But whatever any one said there was nothing to compare with roast sucking pig. His mind dwelt on the sows at Mooiplaas. There was one that should have farrowed. By now the little pigs should be ready, if she had not lain on them or eaten them. That was the worst of pigs, they were unpredictable. When you came to think of it, that was the only thing the matter with pigs—their unpredictability. It was also part of their charm. It was not only that there might be little pigs that would be ready for roasting, but the fact that there might be no little pigs. This gave his return some spice, some uncertainty, some interest. It was hard to live without excitement of any kind. To-morrow they would be back. To-morrow he would know. He chuckled. The fatted calf . . . no, not the calf, the sucking pig. That was a good joke.

Both jokes and uncertainty had returned to his life. Adventure and happiness. There was no doubt about it. He was looking forward to getting home again, though he would acknowledge it to no one when he got there. He had wanted to go. Now he wanted to return. Life was like that. The best things in it were going forth to adventure and returning from it to tell the tale of your doings. He had thought of bringing a wife back, but to speak of the women he had seen would be as good. He could hold them as a threat over that woman's head, and tantalize her with the possibilities latent in a fifth marriage and another child. The idea of it would do as well as the fact, and was much more manageable.

It was wonderful how he thought things out in such details, how he still planned with such precision. You will give me sucking pig, or . . . brandy, or . . . there were unlimited possibilities. His desire to be home became more urgent. He wanted to put his plans into practice; also he wanted to rest comfortably. This was his last trek. He was reconciled to that now. After all, what point was there in trekking about the land, since he knew it all and there had been no improvements. On the contrary, nothing was as fine as it had been; and apart from that, there had

been the danger of running into the English who doubtless would wish
ot revenge themselves upon him for his charge which had put one of
their whole regiments to flight. One man against a thousand. It was
fitting that it should be he. Philippus Jacobus, who had been chosen
to be that man.

Now he was going home, returning from his last trek, and would
await the end with his customary fortitude, restraint, and patience. It
struck him again how remarkable he was, combining so many apparently
opposite virtues. No man could be braver or hotter than he in action,
no man more patient and restrained in peace. Yes, he thought, I have
been fortunate in my disposition as in my bodily strength, being far above
the ordinary in both.

He thought suddenly of courage and how cheap it was. All young
men were brave if they were frightened or being watched by a woman.
He thought of his own courage in youth, of his exploits. They were
great, he thought, because I was so nervous and got frightened so easily.
Then out of my fear came anger, and out of anger came courage. It
was something a young man could not help—a rush of blood! it was
comparable to tumescence, to desire. It was the effect of a cause—a
result that produced further results. Fear of death produced the death
of your opponent. How different was his present bravery, such as he
had exhibited in his charge against the English by himself. That had
been cold, calculated; the result of a skilled weighing of dangers . . . a
computation only possible to one of great age, and very creditable where
it was achieved.

But it would be good sitting at Mooiplaas, thinking, drinking brandy,
eating well and smoking his pipe, while he waited his hundredth birthday, Lena's marriage to Dirk van der Berg, and the birth of her first
son. After that he would be at liberty to go. He would have done
everything and seen everything. Death might even be very pleasant. No
one knew anything about it. All any one knew about was dying, and
not about death. The act itself was not pleasant, but then neither was
it pleasant to jump into cold water, whereas afterwards, once you were
in it, it was very nice to swim about and feel yourself master of the
element. Flying as an angel might be like that too, though of course it
might not be as easy to learn to fly as it was to swim. Not that he could
remember ever learning. Perhaps it had come naturally to him just as
riding and shooting had. In this case he might take to flying, and there
would be his wives to advise him. He could hear them already. Helena
saying, "Kick harder, Philippus. Kick and flap your arms," while the
others watched him smiling.

He felt ill again. His pain came and went. That it should come now
was proof that it was not due to heavy food, since he had eaten little on

the trek. Rather did it prove the reverse, that it was through lack of
rich food. Time would prove this contention, but he must be careful.

He thought of Mooiplaas . . . of his home. He thought of it lovingly:
of the trees, of the house, the outsheds and the kraals, of his peacocks,
and Kattie's poultry. He saw it all. He saw them standing on the stoep
to welcome him. A triumphal entry. The Old Baas is back, the Groot
Baas, the master. That was what a homecoming should be. There had
been so many and this was the last. He was back to stay. As the wagon
rocked and rolled, crashed over stones and stumps, slid with brake-locked
wheels down the slopes, lurched upward over steep, sharp rises, he saw
this homecoming as wonderful—the last return of an old man to his
resting-place, the house that he had made. The home with its flocks and
herds, its horses, cattle, sheep, and goats; its orchard, its garden, its lands
and fields; its trees, streams, dams, and weirs; its fences and gates; all
bred, grown, planted and made under his direction; all products of his
mind and hands. He thought of the little graveyard at the foot of the
koppie behind the house where his wives and many of his children lay
—where soon, when his mission was accomplished, he would lie himself.
He was ready. He was even eager. He wanted to see this child of
Lena's—the last of his line that he would see—and to be a hundred. Then
he would be at liberty to have his last joke—the scandalous death that
would brand that girl. Only these delayed him, but they were important,
since they would round off a life that must, because of its perfection,
become a legend in his land. He would have lived a hundred years.

For more than a hundred years after his death he would be spoken
of and held up as an example. There would never be any one like him
again. There were not even any like him to-day. He was the last of
them: the last of a kind that, with his going, would have vanished from
the face of the earth. Men!—he spat over the wagon-rail—there were
no men to-day. Who was there that in any way resembled the friends
of his youth: Old Frederik Bezuidenhout, Hendrik van der Berg, Christiaan van Ek, Kaspar van der Berg, Paul Pieters, Coenraad de Buys,
and the others he had known. But it would be good to see them again.
He sighed. Well, he was near them. Very near to-day—only a few
days, months, or years away. Time and distance were one thing. I am
coming, friends, he thought; I am trekking towards you. The wagon
of my life is rolling fast; the oxen of my spirit are straining against the
yoke of my years. I come, my friends. I come to join my friends and
my fathers . . . I come, comrades . . . I feel near you in my heart.

He watched the plodding red oxen. With that distinction they drew
their load! Every one had complimented him on his match span—as
like as peas—sixteen oxen that no one but their owner could tell apart.
And he had bred them, and their fathers too, and their grandfathers.
The evening sun caught the wide white spread of their horns. It shone

on their black points. Its light was thrown up from their chestnut hides.
Beautiful . . . how beautiful was such perfection! It brought tears to
his eyes to look at their long, wide backs. In all the Transvaal there
was no finer span. In all Africa nothing that could equal them for beauty,
courage, or docility.

They were carrying him home: to his house; to his grave, to his
friends . . . to a fatted sucking pig.

CHAPTER XXIV

MY SON, MY SON . . .

ALL DAY Johanna waited for Boetie's return.

Dirk had taken him away. He would bring him back. She kept going out of the house to look down the road, but the road remained empty. And a battle was going on. That was the extraordinary thing. To be here living in a house, eating, sleeping, sewing, trying to do all the things she had always done while something else, not far away, a battle was in progress. She fetched a jug of water for the pot plants on the stoep. There was pink begonia in flower, there were geraniums and ferns. As she poured the water on the earth, filling the pots carefully, she thought of the battle. She was pouring water while men were pouring out blood.

She had got used to her husband and Dirk being at the war. Groot Dirk had been to other wars; and as he grew to manhood she had known that if the occasion arose, her son would have to go with his father. But Boetie, her blind baby. She stopped to think of him as a baby—of that terrible day when she and her husband, after weeks of hoping it was not true, of pretending that if it was it would pass, had decided that he was really blind, that he would never see. That the beautiful world in which they lived would never belong to their child; that nothing they could do would help him; that even their suffering and their prayers could not lift him out of his darkness. It was the will of God. With rebellion in her heart she had knelt by her husband. Side by side they had prayed for him.

Klein Johanna was dragging at her skirts. "Boetie," she sobbed. "I want my brother Boetie. I want to play the game of stones." She had the little skin bag in hand.

"He will soon be back," Johanna said. "Sit on my knee and we will wait for him together."

The day was endless. Evening came. Then night. Klein Johanna was put to bed, still crying for her brother.

"He will come to-night," her mother said. "Dirk took him last night. He will bring him back to-night. In war they have to move in darkness, it is safer."

"Then why did you wait all day looking up the road?" Johanna asked.

Why, indeed. The argument that had seemed plausible and good enough for a child had failed.

"Just in case, Johanna, my heart," she said. "Now sleep."

" When he comes you will bring him in? You will wake me?"

" When he comes I will wake you."

" You promise?"

" I promise."

" Then I will be good."

Her mother bent to kiss her. She was all that was left her. A little girl who might one day suffer as she suffered now. You loved, you married, and then, to pay for your joy, you suffered.

Where was Boetie? What had happened? Perhaps he had been hurt. And Dirk? Surely he would come for Swartkie if he was all right. Yes, that was it. And there was a battle going on; he was busy with it. That was a strange thought, but a true one—busy with war. He would bring his brother back when he came for his horse. He wanted to give him a full day to rest before he fetched him. Her son and his horse were inseparable. She thought of his father, her husband, Groot Dirk of Doornkloof, as men called him : big, slow, honest Dirk whose simplicity and directness had won her heart so long ago. How lucky she had been! How happy! Was he all right?

Johanna slept curled, her lips parted in a smile, her little hands half-clenched above the blanket. There, in that little sleeping body that lay so still, with hair spread out over the pillow, was all that she had left. She had lived to do just this—to bring one small girl into the world. Thirty-eight years ago, she thought, I was a small girl like that. I was the " Klein Johanna " of my father's house. How then is anything bettered that I have lived just to duplicate myself?"

A great despondency crept over her. Hope that she had held by fighting for it all day, grasping at straws, fell back and left her alone, defenceless against despair. Her men were gone—even Boetie. She would never see them again. They were dead. She was left with her daughter and her dead son's horse. She knelt at the bedside and prayed for courage.

Miraculously, when she got up, it was restored. To-morrow there would be news. God, who had helped them in every adversity, would not desert them now. With renewed confidence she undressed and got to bed beside her child. She wanted to press her to her breasts, and hold her, but she resisted. If she held her, she would hold her too tight and she would be frightened. Her own fears would communicate themselves to Johanna. And to be afraid was to create cause for fear. Nothing had gone wrong. She must keep saying that to herself. Dirk and Boetie were only delayed. But what could have delayed them? What could have? She tried to think and renewed her fears.

Then she stopped and fixed her mind on Lena. What must Lena be feeling about Dirk? How brave she had been last night, not trying to hold him when he said he could not stay. A true Boer girl who would make him a good Boer wife. They would marry when it was over. Lena

would bear his children and she would hold them on her knee. She
thought of Dirk, her firstborn, as a baby. How beautiful he had been,
how perfect, how strong! Now that strength that she had brought forth
and held, first within her womb and then against her breasts, would
bring forth more strength—sons of her son, bone of her bone, and blood
of her blood. Her heart went out to Lena who would bear them. She
was crying now for Lena and Lena's children. Unborn, they were born
to suffering and sorrow, but also to joy and gladness, to love and faith and
beauty.

Still she cried at the thought of joy and beauty. But softly and happily.
God had sent her comfort in these thoughts of her unborn grandchildren.
They would play round her, they would grow, they would have farms
and wives and children—while she and Groot Dirk sat by and watched
. . . . Pain, yes, there were pain and sorrow and suffering in the world,
but there was also joy, and a great glory. There was the veld that was
their own, there was all Africa, their promised land, spread out before
them. There were wide lands to be broken to their ploughs, wild beasts
to be killed for their hides and meat. There was the blue sky above them
and the hard red earth beneath. There was Africa . . . one's land . . .

And soon there would be news. She put her arm over Johanna. To-
morrow would bring Boetie back.

It was a Boer from Joutbert's commando who brought news of the battle
to Mooiplaas. He came at midday, riding a black horse with a blaze.
Lena saw him first and ran out.

"I have a letter," he said, taking off his hat. "This is Mooiplaas, is
it not?"

"This is Mooiplaas." Lena held out her hand.

"Tanta Johanna . . . Ouma!" she shouted. "A letter—there is a letter,
come quickly." She turned it over in her hand.

Tanta Johanna came out, rubbing her hands on her apron.

"It is for you," Lena said.

Ouma came out, walking slowly. Tanta Stephanie ran down the
steps, her curls bobbing. They were still in screws of rag.

"It is from my husband," Tanta Johanna said. Her fingers trembled
as she opened it. Lena watched her read it. She held the letter in front
of her, her lips moving as she read. Then she put it down, holding it
against her thigh, and stared out over the orchard.

It's bad news, Lena thought. Something has happened. Is it Dirk?
O God, is it Dirk?

Tanta Johanna's mouth was set. She raised the letter again, looked at
it, and then handed it to Lena. "They have taken him," she said. "It
was all for nothing. Not even his blindness could save my Boetie. They
have taken my baby—my son . . . my son!" Tears were streaming from

her eyes. She made no effort to wipe them away. They ran down her cheeks and dripped from her chin on to her dress. " The war has taken my last son," she said again. " And God, who made him blind, permitted it."

It was not Dirk. Anything was better than Dirk. Even Boetie dead was better than Dirk—even defeat, even anything. She looked at the letter. It was in pencil.

> *Johanna, my heart,* she read, *Boetie is coming with us. That we won last night is due to him. He led us up the mountain. He is acclaimed a hero. Joubert asked him what he could give him as a reward. " Let me ride with my father and brother," he said. " I have brought you luck. If I ride I shall not be ashamed and I can stay with horses when you leave them standing. No matter what happens I can calm them with my music. Let me come, let me ride, Oom Frans." Then the men all shouted: " Let him come . . . we will be lucky with him. We want Boetie van der Berg to ride among us." We are well, my heart, both I, and your sons. It will soon be over, they say, and it is for the Republic. I am glad you are at Mooiplaas. It is better for you there. Tot siens, and God be with you. Always I am your loving husband, Dirk.*
>
> *I am sending this with the friend who comes for Swartkie. Joubert is keeping the bay Dirk borrowed. We will bring him back at the end and perhaps some English horses as well. I would like to get some mares.*

So Boetie was with the commando and riding on with them. He, too, had gone out of her life. First Dirk, his father, and her brothers; then Oupa, and now Boetie. Lena looked at Ouma; she was speaking.

" Tell me about the action," she said to the messenger. " Were many killed ? "

" Many English were killed," he said. " But we only lost four men killed and six wounded. I saw them and worked on their graves. They were hard to dig," he said. " The ground up there is stony."

" Do you know their names ? " Ouma's voice was calm, but her thumbs were rubbing against her fingers, they were going round and round.

" Mevrou, I knew none of them. I am not from these parts. I am from the Cape. Down there everyone knows Jan Bothma. I came up to help my brothers in the Transvaal," he said.

" What were they like—the dead ? "

" There was a blond man, he was very big and heavy to move. He was shot through the head. Someone said his name was Johan."

" That might be Johan Marais," Ouma said; " go on."

" There were two small, dark men that looked like brothers, and a

mouse-haired man with a twisted foot." Bothma turned his foot inwards.
"He was shot between the eyes."

"How big was he?" Ouma asked. Her voice was still calm, but her
fingers moved faster.

"He was neither large nor small, and his eyes were blue. He was of
medium size. They said he was from round here, and called . . . I cannot remember what they said he was called." He twisted his hat in his
hand. "Would there be anyone from about here called Stoffel something?" he asked. "I think it was Stoffel."

"It would not be Stoffel du Toit?"

The hat was being turned more rapidly. "Mevrou, it might have
been. But I do not know. I am not from these parts. I am from the
Cape and was told to fetch a horse. The one Dirk van der Berg left
here the night before last."

Ouma turned to Tanta Johanna. "Your son and my son. The son
of my son who was a son to me . . . O Absalom, my son Absalom," she
said. Her hands were still now. They hung from the ends of her arms
like dead things.

"You must eat," she said to Bothma. "Lena, give Meneer Bothma
food and send for the horse." With that she walked away from them,
her eyes fixed upon the sky. She went straight through the orchard
gate and was lost behind the trees.

"This is terrible . . . terrible," Tanta Stephanie said, uncurling the
rags from her hair. "Magtig, war is terrible, and does she feel nothing?
To walk off like that—no tears, no cries. Truly a hard woman."

How suddenly the blow had fallen! Lena thought. The thing you
thought could never happen . . . Stoffel dead and Boetie gone. You
thought of such things. Yes, she had thought of Dirk's death . . . of his
being wounded; but had never believed that it could happen.

She was alone with Tanta Johanna and the burger who had brought
the message. Ouma had gone to be alone with her sorrow among the
trees. You took your joy and your sorrow to the trees. But Dirk was
well. She wanted to dance and sing. "Dirk is well, Ma," she said to
Tanta Johanna.

"Yes, daughter, he is well, and my husband is well, but for how
long? And Boetie is gone. It is judgment upon me. Always till the
war, and their going, I questioned God's wisdom in making him blind,
and then with war I thanked Him for it. Now I see that it is wrong to
blame God. It may even be wrong to thank Him. His ways are not our
ways, His methods are inscrutable to us. And to think that my blind
boy should lead Joubert's commando. What could be stranger than
that? And what more lonely than my heart . . . My baby a man, and
riding. My poor blind baby . . ."

Yes, Lena thought, what could be more strange? Not even Oupa's charge against the English, not even his leaving home after so many years, not even her joy at Dirk's coming out unscathed or her lack of feeling at Stoffel's death. Tanta Johanna was right, the ways of God were inscrutable.

"Come, meneer," she said, "you must be hungry."

"I am hungry," he said.

She set food before him and got coffee from the fire.

"It was wonderful," he said when she came back to pour it, "the way that blind boy led us. Looking back along the path in the daylight I could not believe that we had climbed it."

"Why did Dirk not come for his own horse?" Lena asked.

She was not interested in the battle. Dirk had come through it safely. That was enough.

"He was on duty," Bothma said.

"We are going to be married, meneer, when it is all over."

"You and Dirk van der Berg?" he said. He seemed surprised.

She wondered, now that she had had time to recover from the shock of Boet's going and Stoffel's death, that Dirk had not seized this chance of seeing her.

"Could he not have got someone else to his duty?" she asked. "Could you not have done it? Then he could have seen me."

"He did not ask me. If he had, I certainly would have taken it. But he is a conscientious man, I think. One of those who sees only his duty."

"And me," Lena said. "Does a man owe nothing to his betrothed? Has he no duty to her?"

"I am from the Cape," Bothma said as if it was an answer.

Lena gave him more coffee. A Kaffir stood at the door holding Swartkie by the bridle.

"Is that the horse I am to take back?" Bothma asked. "He looks a good one and very like my own. They would make a good pair."

"He is a good one, meneer."

"Then I had better be going." Jan Bothma got up, stuffed a last piece of bread into his mouth, and took the reins from the boy.

When he had gone, Lena went towards the blue gums. Boetie had said it was a happy place. It was happy with memories that cut you like whips, but there was a peace to be found in their scourging; and that was not the least wonder, that you found happiness of a sort, and peace, in misery.

It is not Dirk . . . It is not Dirk, she told the trees. For weeks she knew now she had thought of his being killed, of a world without him; tried to think of the unthinkable, but not consciously. The thoughts had never come out into the open till the relief of his living and Stoffel's death had forced them upon her. They had merely accompanied her everywhere—formless shadows that had clouded every issue; that had destroyed all beauty. It is not Dirk, she thought, it's Stoffel. She had never loved her brother; it was hard to think of him dead, but the sun still shone.

She twisted the Zulu bracelet Dirk had given her on her birthday two years ago, pushing it up till it bit into the skin of her forearm. From what Bothma said it seemed as if the war would end soon; as if the English were nearly defeated. They had had no real success anywhere. She thought of war, of the dead men, of the wounded she had seen at the battle that day. It seemed so long ago, thrown back by Dirk's present safety into the distant past. I was a girl then. I was a girl when I went with Tanta Martha to the scene of the battle. That battle . . . The dead lying where they fell, grotesquely twisted; the wounded crawling like maimed beasts to the side of the road. She thought suddenly of the look on the face of the man who had been crushed by the wagon wheels. He had looked so surprised as he put down his hands to feel his flattened thighs. He had looked astonished that where his legs had been strong and round, they were now mashed flat. She thought of the smile on the colonel's face as he waited to have his legs cut off. She heard the cries, the shots, and curses in her mind. She had not heard them then, having come when it was over, but she heard them now. She saw the young officers with whom she had danced running forward with drawn swords, shouting: "Come on! . . . Come on!" That was what the drummer boy on the colonel's white horse had called to them: "Come on . . . for Christ's sake, come on!" What had happened to Timmy?

Her mind went back to Dirk; to his kisses when he had held her by the wrecked transport wagons; to Charlie Brenner's broken cage of birds in the doctor's cart; and all the while she thought of these things there were bells ringing in her head; they said: "Dirk is safe. Dirk is well and safe. When it is over we shall be married." Marriage to Dirk was an end in itself. Life would go on after that. No, that was not it: till then there could be no life. Stoffel was dead and she could give no thought to him. She had come here to rejoice among the trees. Dirk lived, in her joy there was no room for mourning. She thought of Ouma walking off to the orchard alone. She had gone to mourn Stoffel, not to rejoice over Dirk. Dirk was nothing to Ouma. Stoffel, my brother, she thought, is nothing to me—nothing. It was as frightening to find you cared nothing for your brother, whom you should love, as to find you cared so much for another man and that the whole world could be destroyed provided he were left unhurt. Love was a destroyer: a destroyer of everything but love.

To marry Dirk was to begin her life. How eager she was to begin! To do things for him; to move the button on his best coat; to cook his food; to carry his children under her heart; to—to do everything, and to dwell at his side sharing all things with him, good and bad alike. These were no young girl's dreams. She was no longer a maid, but a woman with knowledge of man. It had happened here—twice. Under these trees that stood beneath the star-pierced sky. When she had opened her eyes, she had seen the stars above her, beyond Dirk's head and the column of his neck.

It was good to sit under the trees in the exact place. Afterwards, before they left, she had looked to mark it well. Two were in alignment with each other, and if you lay on your back, a branch from either tree, near your right shoulder, drove straight out pointing its broken end straight to the north. Boetie had been right. This was a happy place: the happiest in all the world.

2

Katarina du Toit stood among the orchard trees. She was waiting for the messenger to ride back with Dirk's horse. The road passed the corner of the orchard and she would call to him. There were more questions she would ask. She must know more. She could never know enough. But she must see him alone. She thought of what she had said in the past: I would have given my husband and my sons and their sons. It is for our Land. It is for Africa, for the Republic and the Flag. It is for our way of life, and the Bible which is our law. I said I would give them, she thought, and the Lord has taken me at my word.

In a way Stoffel was more to her than his father had been. He was akin to her. They had understood each other. And she had been so proud of him—too proud, perhaps. How well he had shot; what a horseman he was, what a farmer. Lame or no, there were few who could compare with her grandson . . . and he was dead. It was hard to think of him dead. She saw him again as a baby that winter when he had been left with her by his parents. It was then that they had come together. "You must hate them," she had said, speaking of the English. "Ja, Ouma, I will hate them. When I am a man I will drive them out." His hands had been clenched round her skirt. "But I am lame," he said. "I am not strong and fast like the other boys." Oh, it was like yesterday. She thought of his courage, of the way his heart had risen at the tales she told; of his sorrow at his handicap which would stand between him and his ambition. "One day I will be a burger," he had said, "but what will I be able to do since I am not whole?"

It was then she had planted the seed that had made him what he was. "Listen, Stoffel," she had said. "Can a horse move faster than a man?"

"Yes, Ouma, a horse can move faster."

"It can move faster even than a man who is not lame, can it not?"

"It can move faster, Ouma."

"And a rifle bullet can strike more quickly than a man?"

"That is so," he said.

"Then on a good horse with a rifle in his hand a man, lame or not, would be as good as another man. Do you believe that?"

"I believe it."

"Then make yourself master of horse and gun. Think of nothing else. Do this and none will think of your twisted foot."

"I will do it," he said. And he had done it. Every time there was a competition he won it. Till at last no man would shoot against him. And there was no horse he could not ride. And none he could not train to fire. That was what she had done. She alone, and because of it he had died. It is for the Republic, she thought again. I said I would give all I had for that, to drive them out. But now that she had given Stoffel, she was less sure: less certain that, had she been able, she would not have changed the past.

But could you change things? She thought of Johanna's Boetie. A blind boy . . . surely she should have been able to count on keeping him, and thank God for him, without shame even, seeing His hand in it. But he had gone too.

She began to pace between the lines of trees. Down, and up again. Her feet beat a little path in the harrowed soil. That was Stoffel's idea to keep the ground clean and harrowed between the trees. So many ideas were Stoffel's . . . When would he come? How could a man sit and eat at a time like this? That is my heart, she thought. In my mind I know very well how he can. It's months perhaps since he had real, house-cooked food and coffee. He will eat full. Then he will slacken his belt and pass the time with Lena if she is there, or gossip with Stephanie. Her curls will be in order now and no doubt she will have changed her clothes since a man has come. Yes, he would sit there smoking and talking of his part in the war. Boasting, as men did. Then he would saddle up slowly, mount his horse, and ride off leading Swartkie. That was the way things were. She must just wait. He would come in time. Everything came if you waited long enough.

She went on walking her little path, never deviating from it: up towards the house till she came level with the big Chinese peach—how good its flat fruits were—and back again towards the water land, till she came to the quince hedge. He must come soon. He could not stay all day. Till he came she must walk. How Stoffel liked baked quinces! how . . . But what was the good . . . If only that man would come!

She stopped to look at a jack-hanger's larder. That was a strange thing, a wonder that a bird should impale beetles, locusts, mice and even small birds on thorns and then return to eat them at its leisure.

Everything was strange to-day. Nothing stranger than Stoffel's death, for though in war men were killed you never expected your own to fall. Not even when it had happened before. You felt protected by past tragedy, as if because you had suffered so much a debt was owing to you and you could count on safety. That was what you thought. But it was not the way things happened. *To him that hath shall be given; to him that hath not . . . shall be taken away . . .* There was Louis still, but he struck no chord in her heart: a good stolid boy without fire. And Lena, a woman, but tolerant and forgiving. Incapable of understanding national wrongs, anxious only for marriage and a personal life. So few were uncompromising, so few understood. Still she walked. What good peaches those were! How he had liked baked quinces! . . .

There he was. He was coming now. She went to the wall and waited. She could see him coming round the bend. He was walking his horse, smoking, and leading Swartkie. She stood still waiting till he was near. Then she stepped forward.

"Meneer," she called.

He pulled up his horse. Swartkie advanced a pace so that the two horses stood, their heads level, looking at her. It was funny how you noticed things like that.

"Mevrou du Toit," he said. He had taken his pipe out of his mouth and held it in his left hand, with his reins and Swartkie's rein. "What is it?" he asked. "Is there a message I can take?"

"There is no message, meneer. But I have thought of some things I would like to ask you—more things," she said. More, she thought. She must know how he died; where exactly he had fallen; where he was buried. There had been things she had not been able to think of then, when he had brought the news. It had come as a shock.

"Where was it exactly?" she asked.

"Where? You mean the battle? Mevrou, you know the place well. You can see it from your house. It is the mountain at the back of Doornkloof that they call the Hill of Doves."

Of course she knew it. She had known it when he told them. But she must know more. She could never know enough. By her knowledge her hatred, her one secure possession, would be branded more deeply into her heart. There was comfort in hatred. The Hill of Doves—that was why Dirk had come to fetch Boetie. He knew that mountain, having spent most of his days upon it. What had he said? No, it was not he . . . it was in the letter from Groot Dirk, and then he had confirmed it. Boetie had led the commando up the mountain. Then if it had not been for him . . . She hated Boetie suddenly. That blind boy had killed him. This was not true and there were many English dead. It was what she had prayed for. We are winning, she thought, but Stoffel is dead. He lay dead on the Hill of Doves with a bullet between his eyes.

"O Absalom, my son Absalom," she said softly. Then raising her eyes, she said: "He was hit in the forehead, you said?"

"I think so. I think it was he who was hit in the forehead, but I did not pay much attention."

She could not understand that. To him it was just another dead burger, it was not Stoffel.

Bothma looked away from her. Grief he could understand. He had seen much grief and weeping in his life, much gnashing of teeth and tearing of hair, but this old woman's grief was different. There was something here he did not understand. She was too old, much older than he was, and must have seen as much or more than he. The sorrow of a wife or a bride he could understand. They were clear. They ran their course. But this woman was only the dead man's grandmother, and he was not even sure that he was the man. Why then, did she heap coals of fire upon her head? What could he say to comfort her? It was a very embarrasing position in which to find himself. He had thought this would be a pleasant ride with the certainty of a good meal at the end of it, and he had let himself in for this. Why in God's name had not Dirk come for his own horse? He understood the reason very well in his heart now. He had been afraid to face his mother, since it was he who was responsible for taking her boy away. That was why he had asked him to ride over in his place and bring his father's letter. But this . . . She had said ' Absalom.'

"Absalom, the son of David," he said, " was killed in the forest of Ephraim, caught in the branches of an oak tree by his hair and there slain by Joab in spite of the king's orders to deal gently with his son . . . Second Book of Samuel, chapter eighteen, verses nine to fifteen." He was proud of that. Not every one would have remembered, not only the quotation, but the reference. He put his pipe back into his mouth, sucked at it, and eased himself in his saddle.

Absalom, killed as he hung by his hair from a tree. It had always gone on. Young men dead, killed as they hung in trees, killed as they rode, as they stood fighting, young men dead as they strove for their home-lands, dead on the thresholds of their homes—young men dead . . . young men dead. And he quoted the Bible at her. What had he to do with her? A strange man on a strange horse with a pipe in his mouth. How was it he was here? What was the relationship between one thing and another? It was all due to the English. Everything, every evil that had come upon her, and upon her people, was because of them. She flung back her head.

" As the bird by wandering, as the swallow by flying, so shall my curse follow those who killed him, about the earth. To-day is nothing. There are days to come, many days, years. I see them humiliated. I see them dead, in piles, in foreign lands. I see their very homes besieged. So do I, a Boer woman, place my solemn curse upon the English. For what have they not done? Have they not chased us like buck from our homes

into the wilds? Have they not cut down our young men like trees? Have
they not removed our ancient landmarks? Have they not, in their
worship of Mammon, ravished the bowels of our land to search for gold
and precious stones with which to bedeck their harlots?"

"I have brought you evil news, mevrou," Bothma said. "But Stoffel
died for his country, for the freedom of our land. He died casting the
blood of his life upon the waters of our freedom."

It was this she could not bear : the idea of Stoffel's blood running out
upon the veld among the mountains : her Stoffel dead upon the mountain, dead upon the Hill of Doves.

"You buried him up there?" she asked.

"Yes, we buried him with the others. There are many dead there of
the English, and those four of ours. We buried them near-by to the
English, but in separate graves."

Many dead of the English. It was poor consolation, but apparently
the best he had to offer.

"Six of the English were officers—one a colonel," he said.

Why did he not go instead of trying to comfort her with words? What
was the good of setting dead officers against her dead grandson as if the
space dead men left in the lives of women could be measured in a
balance? When you were old there were so many empty spaces in your
life, and this was another of them, perhaps the bitterest, for she had
thought herself schooled to meet it—and I was not. Before God, I was
not ready for this thing. At her age you had ceased to live directly, and
saw life only vicariously through the young lives round you. Dry yourself, used up, you saw it through the seed-bearers you had borne; through
the sowers, the sown, and those about to sow. You saw the world as a
field, a land filled with the seed of your race, the seed of your womb—
and of those who were left, it must be Stoffel who was cut down. The
only one whose hatred she had been able to trust.

She looked at Bothma again. Not that she had to move her head; she
had been staring at him, but past him, while she thought. This surprised her. It was in her mind that she had done this, looking through
him, back at the farm that had been her grandson's home, behind him.
To see him she had only changed the focus of her eyes.

"Geluk . . . good luck," she said. "Ride on, meneer, and thank you
for bringing us the news of victory."

"Tot siens, mevrou, and thank you for your hospitality. Sad news it
was, but he died for our land." He raised his hand in greeting, touched
his black horse with his heels and pulled on Swartkie's rein.

Katarina stood frozen. For an instant she saw the man—the two black
horses. For a moment she thought how well matched they were,
astonished at the coincidence that a man should come on one black horse

to fetch another. Then she no longer saw the man and the horses. She saw nothing.

From near the house came shouts and the sound of a clapping whip. Clap after clap, like rifle shots . . . It was a rifle shot that had taken him : a shot between his eyes, and he was buried on the Hill of Doves, where she had fallen.

She sat down upon the ground.

She had thought herself unbreakable; thought that now no blow could fell her, no pain bend her, no disaster overwhelm her. She moved her hands in the soft, warm, harrowed earth, lifting it up and letting it filter through her fingers. Dust . . . ashes . . . out of the earth . . . back to it.

It came very hard to her. Not only Stoffel's death : that was the cause, but the effect was as irrevocable as death. Her resistance was broken, her armour pierced. The epoch that had begun with the death of her husband and children beneath those Zulu spears, to-day was ended. That day she had killed herself and her feelings. To-day she had come alive again and it hurt her—O God, how it hurt her!

CHAPTER XXV

A MAN AMONG MEN

BOETIE was happy.

God had answered his prayers. He had been of use to his country. He was with his father's commando. He was a man among men. He could feel them all round him. It was good to smell men, and hear them again. He did not know how much he had missed the smell, the sound, and the feeling of men. He had been the man of Doornkloof and then the man of Mooiplaas, but the responsibility had been almost too much for him. That was the implication of the smell of women, of their rustlings, of their high voices : that you were a man, and that they looked to you. Even the sweet smell of his mother and the new warm bread smell of Lena had lately begun to weigh upon him. But now he was with men. By degrees he would get to know some of them, recognizing their voices and steps. It was no use even trying to remember a name till you knew these. A name was an empty thing that was important only when filled in with the solidity of sound and touch and scent. Then a name became something whole and living.

How good it was to sit here and feel this activity about him! True, the men were resting, at ease, after the battle. There had been fighting all day. The English had been stopped at the drift. The fight on the hill had been but the beginning. The continuation of the battle had been bigger and more complex than that of the mountain. Since he had stayed in the laager Boetie had been unable to follow it. But the English had been beaten and many prisoners, much ammunition, and other matériel taken. There had been some Boers killed and wounded, but he did not know how many. Dirk and his father were safe. Stoffel, they said, had been hit this morning. He had not heard him since they had climbed the kop last night.

He stretched himself out on the grass. It was strange that, with men sleeping all round you, you still felt their activity. Doing nothing, they were more active than the women on the farm, who never ceased moving about on their affairs. That had been movement undirected, and therefore without real activity, a mere bustling about, a rustling of skirts and garments, an opening and shutting of ineffectual doors. But this peace after battle was active with past movement and the possibility of future battle. It was like the pause in the gait of a strong horse, where one movement ceased, for an instant, before the next began. It was the pause in that sweep of strength, drawn out and stretched to its final intensity, that he felt. It was a silence between the roar of battles; the moment that must exist between two lion springs. Its duration had nothing to do with relaxation or peace. Its quiet was a threat . . . and he was a part of it.

He pulled his little flute from his pocket. He thought of last night when he had run back to get it with his coat and hat from his room when Dirk had fetched him. It went through the battle in my pocket, he thought. And suddenly it meant much to him—more than it ever had before, since they had shared this experience together. Twice now it had faced the English. He stroked the smooth wood. "Little flute," he said, " did we ever think when we made you, old Reuter and I, that we should see all this?"

He put it to his lips and began to play. He played sweetly, and low. Then gaily, for his heart was gay. He had achieved his heart's desire. How many did that, he wondered. How many who were well and whole? How many of those who could see what was before them and did not have to be told everything? God indeed was good. Taking with one hand, perhaps, but giving generously with the other.

He played on, ceasing only when he heard someone coming towards him.

"You are Boetie van der Berg?" the man asked. "I am Carl Burgers."

Boetie stood up and raised his hand towards the stranger.

"I am Boetie," he said.

"You play on the flute," Burgers said. "You play well."

"I play," Boetie said. "I play much."

"I was among those you led last night. I am proud to shake your hand again." He paused as if embarrassed. "I have come to give you a present."

"A present," Boetie said. "Why should you do that?"

He wondered what it could be. What could a stranger have for him, and why should he give it? The man was fumbling with something.

"Put out your hand," he said.

Boetie put out his hand.

"What is it?" Burgers asked. He was laughing to himself.

"I do not know," Boetie said. "It feels . . . it feels like a big flute . . . a fife."

"A fife it is," Burgers said. "I was at the battle of the spruit. I took it from an English musician, for it was in my heart that I would teach myself to play. But it was too hard. I have music in my head," he said, "but my ear is no good. The sounds I make disturb me. So, when I heard them say that you played a flute, I thought you would like to have it. I said to myself, 'Carl, what is the good of carrying that thing about? You will never play it; you have even thought of throwing it away. Give it to the boy. He will make use of it.' So there it is."

Now it had come. Everything had come. This was the last of his dreams fulfilled. Above all, ever since he began to play he had wanted a good instrument, but had not dared to ask. Such a thing, he thought, must cost the price of a good ox.

"I do not know how to thank you, meneer," he said.

"Do not thank me, jong. Play it . . . it was no use to me." He turned away.

Play it, he had said. Yes, he would play it. But it would take time to learn, and his arm was stiff from his wound. How lucky he was that it had not been worse! It would have been terrible to have a new fife and not be able to play it for weeks. In a few days he would be well; even now he was only stiff and bruised.

He blew a note. It had stops that moved on little levers. There were finger grips, like that on a gun. He moved on, he blew again. What music! What clear, lovely notes! How loud and clear the sound! By the time he got home at the end of the war, he would have mastered it. How astonished Witbooi and the other goats would be! How they would dance and play to his new music! How pleased Ma and Johanna would be! It was too much. Now he had everything.

He thought of Johanna dancing, jumping up and down on her fat little legs to sounds so loud and beautiful. He was blind, but here put into his hands by God Himself was a means of giving joy to others.

Dirk had stood aside watching Burgers give Boetie the fife. He had asked him if he thought his brother would like it. He was waiting for Burgers when he came back. He was smiling.

"Magtig, Dirk," he said, "how he likes it! It is good to make some-one happy; it gives you a warm feeling in the stomach. And it was no good to me. It was just an idea that I had," he said sadly. "But when he can play it I will listen to him. I like to hear good music and to sing old songs."

"He will play to you," Dirk said. "He loves to play for those who ask. I am going to look at the horses. I am waiting for my own to be brought back. I had to leave him when I fetched my brother."

"I will come with you." They went towards the grazing herd.

"What is this business of Stoffel du Toit?" Burgers asked. "It is said that they seek him for an inquiry and that you know something of the matter."

"Who seeks him?"

"I do not know, but I think the English have complained to the com-mandant general and demand that he be tried for murder—the murder of an Englishman, an officer, on the Vaal River."

This was not something Dirk wished to discuss. When he had re-joined the commando, his father had known all about it. He had even known that it was Captain Elliot who had been killed and that Lambart had escaped to carry the news to the English. They had sent an official remonstrance and were demanding an inquiry, but the witnesses, Field-Kornet Smit and his party, were not to be found.

"So forget about it, Dirk," his father said, "till they call upon you, if they do; and then do not worry. Tell them the truth. Say what you saw, no more and no less, and meanwhile say nothing. To speak of it can do no good."

"Well, I do not know how they will find him. He was hit last night, you know."

"He was not killed, then? I heard that he was killed."

"He was hit in the leg and has gone off to rest till it is cured."

"If he has gone home, they will find him."

"Perhaps he has not gone home," Dirk said. He had an idea of where Stoffel would hide.

"I thought he was dead," Burgers said again. "I do not see how such a mistake could have been made. He had a disfigurement and those who were of the burying party said it was he."

"There was another man with a club foot. He came from the Free State alone. There was talk of Stoffel's wound. The burial party must have heard his name and they saw the body of a man with such a foot They had not served with us, coming late, as you know, of their free will from the Colony, and undertook the work because they thought it would be less painful to them than to us. That is how this talk of his death must have begun. But it might be better for Stoffel if it was believed for a while . . . if the English were told that he was dead."

"They will find out."

"Yes, they will find out, but later. Much can happen between now and then," Dirk said.

Dirk was of two minds. It was right that Stoffel should be punished . . . murder, they said. Well, it might be; at least it was near murder. Yet in a way Stoffel was mad and not responsible: mad with his marksmanship. But Dirk did not want Lena's brother shot. If he was caught and found guilty, that was what would happen. And there had been several things like that. It was not just Stoffel. There were other men among them who were also mad. What kind of name would such things, if they got publicity, give the world about the Boers. There were representatives of foreign newspapers with the forces of both sides. An Englishman, fully accredited, had joined them only a few days ago. When he had a chance, he would talk to him. He was not like some Boers refusing to see anything good among the English. In addition, it seemed right to him to examine both sides of any question. Victory they must have, but compromise and friendship must follow it, or there could be no lasting peace. That, too, was his father's view, and his father was always right.

They had reached the horses. Some ran free, others were knee-haltered. Beyond them, the working oxen that drew the wagons and guns were grazing; and beyond them again were the slaughter oxen. Burgers looked at his own horse and left Dirk to wait Bothma's return.

Here again he had failed. Not only had he failed Lena, who would have expected him to come for his horse, but his mother, whom he should have gone to, to comfort and explain what was in Boetie's heart; and above all he had failed himself because he had not dared to do that which he knew to be right. Instead he had persuaded his father to write to his mother, had persuaded Joubert to give him an important duty, that of checking the slaughter oxen; and, then having obtained it, he had persuaded Bothma, one of the volunteers from the Cape who had just joined them, to take the letter and fetch the horse. He had even betrayed his horse, who would have expected him.

The improvement he had thought to detect in himself had proved a very slight thing, quite unlasting, and was evidently only a product of the moment. His self-congratulation had been too soon. It could be said that Boetie had pleaded to stay and it was his own responsibility. Was a man his brother's keeper? He knew very well that he was his brother's keeper. And that he had feared to face his mother, having deprived her of Boetie, more than he had feared any battle he had been in, or any that was to come. His disillusionment with himself was complete. He had betrayed every one. That his intentions were good was of no importance. Integrity went beyond intention; it was itself the core of all morality. To betray was to bear false witness. To send a proxy into a situation you feared, even though the proxy stood in no danger, was the act of a coward.

But Boetie was happy. He could hear him testing his new English fife. He was a hero, and that he was was due to him—to his inspiration to fetch him; but even that had, in a sense, been wrong, since it was the prostitution of his disability.

His eyes remained fixed on the Mooiplaas road. He looked for a mounted man leading a horse. Bothma should come any time. Suppose Swartkie was sick? Suppose he had foundered him? That his legs had not been equal to the strain he had put upon them on their night ride? What could have delayed Bothma? He must have eaten. That, of course, would take time. Bothma was a full-blooded man who would not have a taste for hurried eating. And then there was Lena. To talk to her was enough to delay any man.

He was suddenly jealous of Bothma. Not of what might happen—Lena was not like that—but of the time he would have been able to spend in her company. And I might have done it, he thought, if I had not been afraid of Ma. And also, if I had not been afraid of Lena. He was always afraid of seeing her, because he kept thinking of the time he must part from her which tied his tongue and twisted his stomach while he was with her. He wanted Lena. But he wanted to stay at her side : to have her always with him. And for this reason he hesitated to see her; went even further, avoided seeing her, since, owing to the war, there could be no finality in their communion.

There was Bothma at last. It must be he. A man and two horses were coming from the direction of Mooiplaas. He got up and went down to meet him.

" Well, jong, that was a fine job you gave me," Bothma shouted. " A fine business, and I am glad it is over."

Dirk looked at his horse. Swartkie was neighing and dragging at the riem that Bothma held.

" Let him go."

Bothma dropped the riem and Swartkie came to him, putting his head on his shoulder and rubbing his nose against his neck.

" What was it?" Dirk said. " What was the trouble?"

" What was it, indeed? It was everything. Everybody in tears. The whole farm in an uproar at the loss of Boetie whom they see already dead, and at the death of the club-footed one—that Stoffel. No, not even the good food and an hour passed with the pretty Lena are enough to compensate for such a thing. That old woman is mad. She cursed the English and I was afraid she would curse me for bringing her the news."

" Stoffel?" Dirk said. " Stoffel is not dead. Who says he is?"

" I do. I buried him, did I not? A man with a club foot. If you bury a man, then he is dead."

Dirk began to laugh. What a muddle it all was! " You buried another man with a club foot," he said. " There were two of them with us. He was from the Free State."

" But I heard men talk of Stoffel du Toit."

" Yes, they were talking of him. He was wounded and has ridden off to be nursed well. You heard talk, because of an inquiry that is being made about him. The English have lodged a complaint."

First Burgers and now Bothma—that was how false news got about.

" You mean I have made a mistake? That I went through all that for nothing?"

" Yes, it is a mistake. I saw Stoffel ride off."

" That is an extraordinary thing," Bothma said, " that there should be two club-footed men in a commando, both of medium height, with blue eyes and hair the colour of rope."

They were back in camp now.

" We must send her a message, Dirk. We must relieve her mind," Bothma said. " The old woman is in despair."

" Yes, we must do that. I will think of a way."

" Why do you not ride over to-night? Your mother will be glad to see you. And Lena was upset, it seemed to me, that I had come in your place, though I did my best to entertain her."

Bothma dismounted and lit his pipe.

"Well, thank God it's over," he said. "A good meal is no compensation for such a day. And now I am going to sleep." He lay down.

Alone again Dirk thought of Lena and himself. They were like two twigs on the tide of circumstance, of war. Twisting and turning on the flood they travelled separately towards a light that shone faintly, in the future; towards a sea they did not know; towards an end so ill-defined that it was blurred, a misty island where they might find peace, or failing peace find misery, or happiness; towards the flowering of their lives that must include pain, since it was a part of life. Separated, they moved in the isolated pattern of their circumstance, bound together by their hopes and thoughts. Coming together, parting, coming together again as the web of their lives was tightened.

He thought again of the feather on Stoffel's back; of the murder on the river; of the strange chance that had saved Elliot at the battle only to kill him later; of his father's friendship for Adriaan Klopper and his pleasure at their meeting. Last night after the battle he had had a dream. Or was it a vision. Exhaustion made it hard to think clearly, but this had been very clear. After a long and tiresome journey, one which had lasted many years, he had come to a small stream that flowed very peacefully, very fully, onwards through wide, flower-strewn fields. It had in its course flowed under many bridges, and gained rather than lost by its experience, mellowing and sweetening as it went along. Having drunk of it he was grateful, for he had come upon it by hazard, in his necessity. He had found it when he was near to the end of his endurance, when his face was a mask that failed to hide despair, and his body a thing that twitched, gnawing like an animal at his soul.

Gratitude was an idle word, but above all things that men sought stood affection . . . friendship . . . love, which was not the taking of anything, but joy of finding someone who was willing to receive. That had been his dream or vision, and Lena was the stream which flowed peacefully where he, driven by forces he did not understand, could pause to think and rest.

Everything is so simple now, Dirk thought. This struck him as a curious thing about war—its simplicity. It was much more simple than farming when you got used to it. This dream had been so simple, too, so beautiful; and it was born of war. He knew that in peace he could not have dreamed it.

In wars you just went on thinking as you rode. Lena was always in his mind, always near him—sometimes so close that it seemed as if by stretching out his hand he could touch her and pull her into his arms.

He had thought of death a great deal; of life, of birth; of his love for his father and Boetie. He had thought of his mother, his home, and his baby sister. But he felt awkward about his mother. He did not know how he would face her if anything happened to Boetie. It was I who thought of it. It was I who fetched him from her arms. It would not matter to her if he told her how happy Boetie was, or what a fuss was made of him. He would get the best of everything and be a real help with the horses. He would be able to hold them together by his presence among them, and, by his music, keep them calm even if an English shell exploded near them. And the men believed he had brought them luck.

But what was he going to say to Ma? For now it was clear he must go to Mooiplaas to-night to clear up the misunderstanding about Stoffel. It was his own fault. If only he had gone in the first place, he thought. And now he must go, and in addition to other difficulties he would have to explain why he had not done so in the first place. He was a bad liar and would become confused and contradict himself.

He could not stop thinking of what might have happened if he had gone back for Swartkie himself. He would have seen Lena. Even to think of seeing her made him feel ill, but still he thought of her. It would have been something just to see her among the others, and then there might have been more than that. They might have been able to steal away together. If he had done that, by now it would be over, and he would be thinking of what they had done—of her kisses; of what she had said; of how she had looked. Now he was thinking of what he would say when he went to-night. There might be some misunderstanding. He wished it was over.

Burgers interrupted his thoughts.

"Where is your horse?" Burgers asked. "I heard he had had a hard time, and I have some medicine for his legs if they are strained."

"He is over there," Dirk said. "But his legs are well."

"Is he wild? Can you get up on him? We could put on my medicine just in case."

"He is tame," Dirk said. "I will call him." He whistled.

Swartkie raised his head and swung round. His ears were cocked. Dirk whistled again. "Now he sees us." Swartkie began to trot towards them."

"That is a pretty thing to see," Burgers said. "How did you teach him?"

"I had him young. He is the son of my father's horse, and always I have fed him when he came to me. He follows like a dog."

"It is a pretty thing," Burgers said again, "and you have a good horse." He looked him over.

Dirk petted Swartkie while Burgers rubbed his legs with ointment. The horse was pushing his head against him. His coat was sleek. He did not seem to have suffered in any way. His eyes were as full and bright as ever; his ears as lively as he turned them this way and that. His tail was high with its twist to the right that showed his Arab blood. Yes, Burgers was right, he was a good horse. And it was good of him to have brought the medicine. But he was glad of the bay; a second horse was a good thing to have. If we had known it would be war, we would have brought two horses each when we started out, he thought. He went on stroking Swartkie's neck and shoulder. The horse whinnied with pleasure and blew air from his nostrils.

"Come, let us go back now, Dirk," Burgers said. "I am glad he is so well. I was worried about him, knowing how much you think of him."

"You are right," Dirk said. "To us a horse is our life."

"Yes," Burgers said. "Companion, servant, friend—that is a horse. And that we are winning we owe to our horses and our women: our horses that carry us so well and swiftly; our women who are not afraid to be alone and who care for our farms and stock while we are away."

"Our horses and our women," Dirk thought. Lena and Swartkie. Burgers was right.

But he must see that journalist. Meneer Newman, his name was. "Go back, Swartkie," he said. The horse had followed them. "Go back." He took off his hat and slapped him softly with it. "Go back." The horse turned and trotted back to the herd. From there he stood watching his master.

They were in camp again. This was their moving home, their home on wheels. They fought without it, on their horses alone, but at the back of their minds was the knowledge that their camp was following them in safety, fifty or sixty miles behind the screen of their movement. That was where they would rally when it was over, to rest and refit; where they would draw new ammunition, new slaughter oxen, spare horses to replace those killed, new rifles for those that were lost or damaged. Besides these the great tented wagons were a reminder of that other life— the real life of his people. The life of the farms, each with its wagon standing in the shade of a tree ready for use. In his wagon a man went hunting, and travelled to visit friends. Wife, horse, wagon, farm, rifle, Bible—these were the things that made up their lives; it was for these that they fought.

Before the war, Dirk had never thought of this at all. I just accepted things as they were, he thought, and imagined them unchangeable and fixed. But things are not like that. You had to strip them down in your mind, take them to pieces as you might a wagon or a rifle, and see of what they were made: see what had to be discarded; what had to be kept and what must be replaced. Life was to some extent what you made it, but you were also what life made you. It seemed to him, even now, terrible to kill men, but if those men were going to kill your

H.O.D.

way of life, kill all that you believed in and leave you only the empty shell of existence, then you must fight and win, or fight and die. It was better to lie dead but undefeated on the open veld for the vultures and the jackals than live under the dominion of those who understood none of your beliefs and hopes.

He wondered why he had never thought of this before. I was too busy, he thought. Now there is nothing to do but think. We ride, we camp, we manœuvre from place to place, and upon occasion we fight. But the fights are short: just intervals, between long periods when there is nothing to do but think. We ride, we sit, and we talk and smoke.

Another thing was the number of men you met. Before the war perhaps he had known thirty or forty men by name, perhaps less. Now he knew more than a hundred, and they came from all over the Transvaal—some even from the Cape and the Free State. They had new ideas. They had seen strange sights and had nothing to do but speak of them. Some men lied, but you got to know them.

But there were things that puzzled him. There was, for instance, Hendrik Neethling, who claimed that the world was round. It was said that he had told Paul Kruger that he was on his way round the world. "Round it?" Kruger had said. "You mean a voyage in the world." "No, round it," Neethling said. "If I start in one place and go west far enough I will find myself back where I began." He had reached Africa on his voyage when war broke out and had joined them for the adventure. But after this conversation Paul Kruger, who had wished to hear his views on what the world was thinking about the war, expressed no further interest in him. He said he was a liar.

But it was an interesting lie all the same. It made one think. Suppose the world was round as he said—like an orange. Why did one not fall off it? The same Neethling had said that in the Southern Seas islands were made by little goggas . . . insects. He said insects made islands of coral. He said they were still making them.

This was a strange thing. If it was true, it meant that the whole world was not created, as it said in the Bible. A thing could not have been created in six days if the creation was still in progress, if it was still being made. To believe this would shatter all belief. It was certainly a lie, and therefore, since this was not the truth, it would follow that the world was not round and Oom Paul was right—Neethling was a liar, though an interesting one. He wondered how these ideas had begun. Where did they come from? Certainly such ideas had never been heard in Africa before.

Now he must see Joubert and get permission to ride to Mooiplaas. Five hours would be enough, and he would ride the bay to save Swartkie. But as he got up, someone shouted:

"Get ready, kerels; we trek. We move to-night.'

They were to move. Now Ouma would not know. She would think Stoffel dead. He thought about the charge against him. If he were taken and shot later, it might be better for her not to know. That would be too hard. To have mourned him; to hear that he was only wounded; and then to be informed that he had been condemned to death for murder.

There was nothing for him to do but wait for the order to saddle up. He could not stay here with his mind in a turmoil. Picking up his rifle he went to the small spring that he had found a few days ago. It was near enough for him to see what was going on in camp and far enough away for him to be safe from interruption. As he sat by the water Dirk was possessed by a sadness. Time was time no longer. Hours, days, weeks, ceased to signify. Time, man-made, had died in the face of God; was obliterated in man, as for the birds of the air, the beasts of the field, and the insects that crawled upon their bellies. They knew not time, but only seasons. We live like beasts, he thought. Eating, sleeping, fighting, lusting . . .

He had to acknowledge his want of Lena. Now that he could not go to Mooiplaas, he wondered why he had hesitated in the first place; wondered what he had feared. Want . . . love, he thought. What is it but lust? What but an all-consuming longing to hold, to touch, to feel, possess, and then possess again. It was more than that, much more, but that was the pain of it. That was the ache, the sickness, the insatiable gnawing at his loins that demanded fruition, that cried for the flower of her womanhood since only by her could their power be fulfilled. He was like a man amputated. He had left a hand behind him and the wound ached, throbbing in the night. Men had told him of that; had told him how an arm or leg that had been cut off could hurt them. Not the stump —that could be healed; but that they felt pain in the limb—in the empty space that had once held a leg or arm. His heart was like a flower that had been trampled by cattle as it began to bloom, and he had to tend it, watering it with the thoughts of his mind so that one day it would bloom again.

It was beautiful here by the fountain. He looked at the great rocks that shadowed it; at the trees that bent over it; at the ferns, frilled green tongues that arched over the water. Everything was curved and rounded, bent in arcs, softly, greenly, voluptuous. There was something womanly and beautiful about a spring, something life-giving. The bubbling source of water was a fundament, a mystery, a beginning of other life, a symbol of undreamt fertility.

Out of his love and war had come new knowledge. It seemed to him that neither love nor war would have been enough alone, or isolated from each other. It was that they had come together. It was not the thunder of war, or the lightning of love; you could hear distant thunder and see nothing; you could see lightning in the night and hear nothing—these left you unmoved. The majesty and terror of the storm came in its combination, in the impact of the thunderclap so close upon the lightning that you heard it crackle and saw, while your ears were deafened, the world illuminated blue-white for a trembling instant that seemed eternal. It was then, in that instant, that you understood God.

And so it was when love and war came together, when life and death struck a simultaneous blow, and made you reel in the light of your new knowledge. Proud that you should know so much, but equally appalled at the ignorance that your knowledge had revealed to you. He had held beauty in his hand : held it a captive like a trembling bird. It had escaped him. Beauty was elusive, but you found it again in odd places. He had found it here. It was an escaped bird, but once you had had it, you held some of its feathers in your hand and tried to match them. All your life you must do this; all your life you must seek beauty, and see, in its diversity, the similarity of its essence. That was all a man could ever learn.

He bent over the water to drink. A full knowledge of himself he could never have, neither he nor any man. He raised his hand to take off his hat. It was his right hand, but in the water it was his left. That was the most a man could know of himself and his motives. He could never see himself save as a reflection. When he thought he raised his left hand, it was his right.

He heard shouts. It was time to go. But much had been revealed to him.

CHAPTER XXVI

THE SPRINGBOK COME

I

Oupa was home.

They were turning—now, in a minute, he would see the house. In a minute.

"Clap your whip, Titus . . . Clap it good."

The whip clapped. It clapped again and again. The koppie behind the house echoed and re-echoed to the cracks of the great sixteen-foot thong. The whip stick bent beneath its weight. The house. Now he could see it. He clung to the frame of the tent to stare at it. What had happened? Why was no one there? Where was Lena? Where was Kattie? They must have heard him coming.

And who was this that came wobbling out on to the stoep? A strange welcome to be met by an old woman dressed in purple silk, her dyed hair hanging in greasy ringlets about her bulging neck. She was running towards him. She was at his side.

"Why, Philippus Jacobus, do you not know me?" she cried. "I have come back after all those years. I am back for good."

"I do not know you," he said.

"And once you thought I was beautiful." She bridled, arching her neck like a horse. "You said so," she went on. "It was on the banks of the Baviaan's River."

"On the banks of the Monkey River," he said. "All rivers are one to me now. All women are one. I have come home to die."

It made his head ache to be asked to remember like this. Where was Lena? Where was his little heart?

"But I am Stephanie."

"Stephanie," he said. "There was a Stephanie once who was enamoured of my friend Coenraad." He paused to remember. How hard it was! How long ago! Coenraad with his great laugh, his chestnut horse. There had been a race and Kaspar's horse had been savaged. It had been in a vlei. How green the vleis had been those days! There had been a great blue heron flying, and his friend Christiaan on his little dun horse. Coenraad . . . who had married a Kaffir queen : the mother of Gaika. He had it . . . He snatched at the memory as you would catch a passing ball.

357

"You are Rudolf's daughter," he said. "The one who went off with that Hollander—a traitor who had the face and manners of a meerkat. Sharp, he was, and you nearly sold young Kaspar to him."

He looked her up and down. "And you have not changed. You are old and fat now, but still vain—vainer than my peacocks and with much less cause. You still lust after men and try to seduce them with bobbing curls."

"This is not what I expected from you, Philippus," Stephanie said. "This is not good manners nor chivalry."

"I am too old for manners and my belly aches. Where is my little Lena who understands me and my wants? Where is that Kattie? Before God, am I only to be welcomed by my dogs and a strange whore from foreign parts?"

He climbed down from the wagon.

"Outspan, Titus," he shouted. "We are back. This is our welcome."

I was fool, he thought, to expect so much. A man should expect nothing. In the end there was nothing: only illusion, and safety lay in the dead past; only there was security and comfort. Your dead friends you could still love. Your dead enemies you could afford to forget, since they no longer endangered you.

But where was Lena? He went to his room. Before God, they had dared to put her in here, to stall the harlot in his chamber. It stank. He began throwing things out of the window. Pots of unguent, a bottle of perfume. He wiped his hands on his trousers . . . A hare's foot covered with red powder—so that was how she pinked up her raddled cheeks. Clothes, underclothes, petticoats, frippers, fans, gewgaws, all followed each other.

"Come, Reuter!" he shouted. "Come here, you black bastard."

"I am here, Baas. Shall I help you?"

Oupa raised his hand and held his nose with his fingers.

"Get the dogs, Reuter. Bring them in. I would have a natural smell in my room. Get them in!" he shouted. "And get in my things from the wagon; get yours, and sit across the door with your spears. She must not come in. I remember her well now. No man is safe from her."

"Can I use my spears, Baas?" Reuter was hissing between his teeth, his feet were tapping the ground. "Aaii, they are hungry; my little spear is thirsting for blood . . . Baas, is it an order? Can I kill? Can I kill them all but the meisie?"

Stephanie, who was standing in the yard picking up the things he had thrown out, began to scream.

"We are going to be killed . . . Murder, murder!" She lifted her skirts in both hands, started to run, but tripped on a scarlet petticoat she was trailing, and fell. She lay on the ground screaming and sobbing. "Spare me . . . oh, spare me. I am an old woman, I have done nothing."

Oupa sat on his bed and wept. It was wrong that he should be threatened at his age. Wrong that he should have no peace. Where was Lena? She would protect him and get him brandy. He was home, but what a homecoming it had been; what a welcome! And his insides hurt him, but he must bear it or they would send for Tanta Martha. He had thought everything settled. And now here were a new set of problems—new worries, new troubles. Never had he thought he would find someone whom he disliked more than Kattie, and then here she was, just when he had hoped for rest and peace. He listened to her screams.

"Shall I find the meisie?" Reuter asked. He had become calm again.

"She will come," Oupa said, "and I must not be left alone." He was going to be ill, really ill. He was twitching all over. His teeth were chattering. He fell from the bed on to the floor.

2

Tanta Martha had come and gone many times since Oupa's stroke. She was here again. Sometimes when she dosed him he did not notice, but took her medicine like a child; at others he cursed her in no common fashion: in a way that made Lena stuff her fingers into her ears and then pull them out a little so as not to miss too much.

"It is age," Tanta Martha said, "his great age that is pressing upon him. The weight of his experiences confuses him so that he sees them all, but not clearly, nor can he place them in the order of their happening."

"Can we do nothing for him?" Lena asked. "It makes me sad." She was crying.

"There is nothing to do. But there is no necessity for sorrow. It is in my heart that he is happier with his dead friends than with those living about him. We are all, even Ouma, Tanta Letta, Stephanie, and I, children to him. We serve no purpose but to remind him of the past. Seeing us means nothing. We mean only those great events and men that he associates with our earliest days."

"It is terrible," Lena said.

"No, child. It is nothing. It hurts you to hear him call for his wife, Helena, who was already dead before your mother's birth; for Coenraad; for Christiaan van Ek and Hendrik van der Berg. But do not let it hurt you. Soon he will be with them and already he sees them. He sees them much more clearly than he sees us."

"But sometimes he seems almost well and talks sense," Lena said. "That is what I do not understand."

"Nor do I understand it," Tanta Martha said. "But I think it is like this—that being so old, so near to death, he passes from the kraal of the distant past into that of the near future where he will rejoin his past. But in passing between them he is for moments of varying length in this present world of ours, and it is then that he, as we put it, " talks sense "—though it seems possible to me that for him that is the only time that he talks nonsense. Then, his soul is like a bird that pauses in its flight to rest for a moment as it goes from one place to another. What is of importance to the bird—its winged journey or its momentary pause? With us he pauses, Lena. His soul is voyaging. We are witnessing a great thing," she said : " the passing of a soul."

2

" Yes, Oupa," Lena said. " Yes."

What was it he was trying to tell her? He was like this most of the time now—very muddled in his mind; starting to say something and losing the thread of his talk in the wild multitude of his memories.

But this was a special thing that he had begun several times. It had to do with his religion, his beliefs. And she could not make head or tail of it. Good and evil . . . for all his thought and talk, he seemed less clear about them than she was herself. What did he mean by saying that there was meat both in an egg and a man which made them much the same : by saying, men are like men . . . bucks like bucks . . . dogs like dogs—each living in its own world and each isolated from the other. How did he say, at his age, dare to say there was no God, and then talk of God continually, and speak of meeting his wife Helena on the other side. The name of his friend Christiaan van Ek came up all the time. God . . . no God. No such thing as sin. Or that sin was simply the other side of virtue and that without sin there could be no such thing as virtue . . . Right only existing in comparison to wrong . . . Poor old Oupa! How he had loved beauty, confusing it with God; denying God and then pointing to a spread of a peacock and crying, There is God—there in each eye of that bird's tail.

" You understand, Lena," he kept saying, " you must understand, because I have not much time. I should have spoken of these things before."

" I understand, Oupa."

She understood none of it except that he was a good old man despite what was said of him, and that he was trying to explain the miracle of life and love to her. Not understanding, she still understood, not the words but the sense. It was what her father had also tried to tell her. It had in it much of what Tanta Martha had spoken of, though it went beyond them both. He was so near his end, and by it, so far from her.

She held his hand in hers and said, " Yes, Oupa," again. " Yes, I understand."

"And you believe?"

"I believe," she said. She pulled the karos up higher over his legs. His eyes were closing. She looked at Reuter and put her fingers to her lips.

"Yes, he will sleep now," Reuter said softly. "The Old Baas will sleep now that he has said what was in his mind."

Perhaps he would be better when he had slept. Lena smoothed out the karos. When he woke again for an hour or two his mind would be almost clear. That was the strange thing about him. Perhaps, as Tanta Martha said, all the very old were like this—fluctuating between reality and a state of mind that was like a dream; one in which everything was disordered, misplaced, and nothing impossible.

His words had left her very thoughtful. He had lived so long and was now trying to hand on some of his wisdom. She could feel how he was trying to give her something and was unable to do so out of his very urgency. If only he did not try so hard, she thought. It is that that does it. He is like a child trying to run too fast and falling upon his face. But there he was, feeling his time near and trying to put all that he had learned of life in a hundred years into an hour so that it would help her. It made her very sad. What would they do when he died? There was no doubt that his end was near. The battle, and then his round of visits, had hastened it. There was great comfort in Oupa. No matter what happened he had seen it happen before and remembered how it had been dealt with. No matter how bad it was, he was likely to have seen worse and come through it.

There seemed to be an amazing duplication of circumstance, of disaster, if one had lived long enough to observe it. A man was killed: to Oupa it was not a man—it was just another man and he had seen so many. Stoffel's death had meant nothing to him. He had never forgiven Stoffel for having the birds that destroyed the orchard fruit killed. He had not even noticed the change his death made in Ouma: that she was more gentle, even more silent, and sat quite still now with nothing in her hands. He took it as his own doing. He thought he had put her in her place. He thought he was master once again.

Lena sat on beside him with Reuter at her feet, immersed in a sadness of her own that she would not give up. She clasped it round her, holding it with the hands of her mind like a cloak to cover her nakedness. Oupa's illness was mixed up with her love for Dirk. Being sad gave her a knowledge of her happiness. It was this aftermath, this after-taste; this opslag, this second growth of the cut crop, that proved that the crop had been.

Without unhappiness there could have been no happiness, Oupa said. It was the one thing she had understood. It was at once the price and the reward. It was the dark shadow that surrounded the flower of past days throwing them up in brilliant relief. There would be more of it, but always between the happiness of yesterday and that of to-morrow there must be the unhappiness of to-day. It was this that gave it reality.

Above all now she needed reality. That was why she looked at her dress and shoes so often. That was why she tended the stick, that Dirk had thrown, so carefully. It had two little branches and six leaves. It was on her window-sill. She watered it every third day and moved it round when it bent too far towards the light. Everything, even a plant, reached for light, for happiness. But as long as it stayed well and continued growing, she felt safe. The whole of her life seemed suddenly to be wrapped up in this small plant. Her memories, that now were so much more real than her life—her hopes, her security—were rooted in the cutting, as it was rooted in its little blikkie. As it grew so did her love.

She ran out to stop a picannin from whistling at the turkey cock. It was funny how furious it got, sinking its head into its back, blowing up its wattles, redding them and spreading its tail with rage. But things should not be teased; nothing should be hurt in times like these.

How she wanted to be beautiful! She stared at herself in the glass and wondered what more there was that she could do. She did all the things she had ever heard of now. She never washed except in lukewarm water on which floated a drop of yellow lily oil. This would keep her cheeks soft and pink. Each night she laid out her towel on the grass and rubbed herself with the dew it had collected. She wished she knew more things she could do. She wished she could ask other girls what they did. Some of them at the dance had been so lovely. She was envious of Hester Marais who was so blonde and big, whose cheeks were rose-red and who had lips like wet cherries. There was never any question about Hester. If only I was as beautiful as she is, Lena thought.

And yet Dirk loved her as she was. Still, if she could become prettier, perhaps he would love her more. There was so little a girl could do really but wash well and brush her hair a lot. She was still puzzled at Dirk's not coming back for his horse and wished she could ask someone about that too. Tanta Martha. Yes, Tanta Martha, perhaps, when she saw her again, if she dared. It was a hard subject to discuss. But Tanta Martha understood men and might give her a reason. Surely it would have been worth coming even if he had only seen her for an instant. I would have done it for him, she thought. And she must ask Tanta Martha for more lily oil, she always got it from her; and that would be a good chance. She could lead up to it that way. She was going to dorp again to-morrow and would do it then. She went more often now. Ouma never tried to stop her, because if there was news it would first be known there.

4

"For stomach-ache," Tanta Martha said, "roast flour, stir it into hot milk, and give it quickly. It must be drunk hot and fast. For earache, if hot turnip does no good, go out and dig for a worm, char it in a porcelain saucer, mix the ashes with good brandy, and pour it into the sore ear a drop at a time. Willow leaves for lameness and pomegranate roots for worms," she said. "For baldness a dried cock's gizzard rubbed into dust and then mixed with goosefat into a paste; and old tea leaves for a burn. These things are important, Lena," she said. "I have tried them all with much success, they are the accepted remedies of our people. All are natural things for natural ailments." Lena looked at the pots, jars, and bottles on Tanta Martha's shelves. Now was the moment.

"Have you some lily oil, Tanta Martha? I have nearly finished what you gave me."

"You must use a lot," Tanta Martha said.

"I use it every day."

"You must use a lot. One drop is enough, and besides you do not need it."

"But I want to be beautiful for Dirk when he comes back," Lena said.

"You will be beautiful, you cannot help it. And you will be more beautiful still when you are married. Till she marries a woman is a bud. Then she flowers. Magtig, how I flowered!" Tanta Martha said.

She smoothed the front of her dress and reached for a bottle.

"I will give you some more to make you happy," she said.

"And . . ." Lena began.

"And what?" Tanta Martha said.

"Is there nothing else I can do?"

"Yes," Tanta Martha said. "You can take the purge I will give you, and . . ."

"What is it? I will do anything."

"You can think about him. There is nothing as good as that."

"I think about him all the time," Lena said. Now was the moment, she must not let it slip. "But there is something I do not understand. Why did he not come to see me when he was near? He said he was coming after the battle by the spruit, but he never came, and then he sent a stranger to fetch Swartkie. And even when the commando lay near-by he did not come. Surely he should have come, even for an instant, just to see me," she said. "If I had been him I would have come."

"Ja, you would have done so," Tanta Martha said. "That is because you are a woman. He did not come because he is a man. Men are afraid of coming for a short time. They are afraid of the parting. All the time he was with you he would have thought of the moment he would have to leave you.   They are like that."   She shrugged her shoulders.   "Very foolish, but they cannot help it.   They avoid all unpleasantness even if it is pleasant.   And Swartkie," she said.   "Do you not see why he did not come back for him?"

"No. I expected him. I waited."

"Before God, a young maid in love is a fool," Tanta Martha said. "Was not Tanta Johanna also waiting?"

"She was with me," Lena said. "We waited together and spoke of him and Boetie."

"And still you do not see?"

"No."

"He was afraid of his mother. Since Boetie had decided to stay, Dirk was afraid. Not only of you and parting from you, but of explaining to his mother; since he had fetched Boetie she would have held him responsible. Men do not like to explain, it makes them ill. A man will ride a hundred miles to avoid the simplest explanation. A man who will hunt lions on foot will be afraid of telling a woman why he puts on a clean shirt, or turned to the right instead of the left. For some reason, known only to God, such things embarrass him."

"I am not like that," Lena said. "I like to explain."

"You are a woman. All women like to explain. They like to talk—to say, if I had not done this then that might have happened. Then they go on thinking what would have happened if that had happened. They can think and talk like that for hours. Men and women are different, not only in the formation of their bodies, but in their minds. Now take your oil, my child, and here"—she handed Lena a bottle—"is more medicine for Oupa. It is very strong and must only be given if he gets too excited. He could die that way very quickly in the midst of an excitement. And this is for you—open your mouth." She thrust a spoon into it. "It may be bitter, but it will do you good, purge you and clear your spots."

Lena swallowed. "But I have no spots, Tanta Martha."

"If you have none, it will keep them away. A girl parted from her lover gets spotty very easily. And here is some news you can give Oupa," she went on. "I have heard that the springbok are moving. Being a hunter, that will interest him, for it is a great marvel."

"A trek of the bok is something I have never seen," Lena said.

"Let us hope you never do, for it can bring desolation. But tell him, it will occupy his mind. And in two days I will drive over."

As an afterthought she gave Lena another small bottle. "This is perfume," she said: "very faint and delicate, and, therefore, not contrary to the laws of God. Save it for when Dirk comes. Then put a little behind your ears and between your breasts." She laughed as Lena blushed. "Though you need no roses nor perfumes. You are man-ripe, my heart, naturally perfumed and embellished. Now, good-bye, and do not let the old man excite himself. Tell him of the bok, that they approach, but do not say you heard it from me or that you saw me, for he fears that I will purge him again, which I will, in two days when I come. Tot siens, child. It does me good to see you, and how we will dance at your wedding!"

5

Oupa did not like Lena's going to the dorp. He missed her as he lay on his karos under a tree with Reuter and Bismarck, one of the dogs that was old and savage and had never reconciled himself to Stephanie's presence—or was it to her smell, Oupa wondered—beside him. Only thus was he safe from her conversation.

He was waiting for the return of the cart. He did not like her going, for though she always brought him a present—tobacco or sweetmeats—it was in the dorp that she concocted her conspiracies with Tanta Martha to purge him. Before God, that woman was nothing but a witch doctor with her purges and her black draughts. A woman who got her pleasure in abusing the young, the old, and the sick. A woman who delighted in cruelty, disguising it as help. A mountainous whited sepulchre . . . a tiger disguised as a sheep . . . a . . . but what was the good? He thought so often of all the beautiful things he could call her, and then, when she came, he forgot them.

His memory annoyed him. It did not work willingly any more. It was like a bad dog that wished to hunt on his own and refused to come at his whistle. He left Tanta Martha to sweat in her own fat. An old cow . . . a witch doctor . . . a devil whose sting was in her purges; and thought of some of the wonders he had seen; a hyena drinking at a pan, kneeling like a man; a great black vulture's nest on a flat-topped thorn; of the fish that could live in hard dry mud during a drought and were revived as soon as the rains came once more. He thought of the questions to which there was no answer: Why should mules attack and kill a horse or donkey foal, setting upon it and chopping it down? Did puff adders suck the milk from cows or did they not? Wonder upon wonder, miracle piled on miracle, and all unsolved: all inexplicable unless in death, that was so near, he would find the answers he had sought all his life. That was an exciting thought.

He thought of the animals he had seen courting and making love—lions, wild dogs, bucks, snakes, and birds. Each in its act having the precision, the perfection of male and female—cattle, horses, donkeys, peacocks, ducks. He had never seen elephants mate and now he never would. But van der Merwe had seen it. He said that they had stood beneath a great tree and that the bull had fondled the cow with his trunk, passing it all over her. Then they had stood side by side, he said, with their trunks entwined and put the tips into each other's mouths. That was how their love-making had begun. What a hunter van der Merwe had been! What an observer of the beauties and wonders of creation! And why did the period of gestation vary as it did? Why should it take eleven months to make a horse foal, and more than a year to make a donkey? Two hundred and eighty days for a calf, and sixty-two for a dog? These were things no man would ever know, and because of it they were the very things that interested man profoundly.

To grow something, to breed something; to kill something, either slaughtering it with domestic panoply or killing it in the field, meant that an important event had occurred, a mystery had taken place, an act of fulfilment. A man only gained as he sweated. In labour, by the water he lost from his body his mind gained peace. The ache of his muscles brought satisfaction in his soul. When things went wrong, you armoured your heart against disaster and went on. A dam broke; you built another. A beast escaped you; you went on hunting. A crop was ruined, you replanted it. There was no end to anything, there were only new beginnings. Even death was not an end, but a new beginning. That you were afraid was simply because you must start once more in a strange land of which you knew nothing. To a young man it was terrible, for he would be alone in it and friendless. But for one such as he it was nothing, having a greater acquaintance among the dead than among the quick.

Only when you had seen all that there was to be seen on earth, only when you had savoured every pleasure and every sorrow, were you ready. Then you were tired of life and ready to begin death, even eager to meet the friends of your youth again. Nothing existed now. No reality. There was no present; even the past was going. He dreamed of the past, but so much of it had dissolved in the acid of the intervening years. Remembering things, he could still see that they were not quite as he remembered them. There had been other factors that were forgotten or misplaced.

And the future? He thought little of that, since there was so little of it: just his ambition to be a hundred before he died, and to hold Lena's child upon his knee. The future he considered was that of death, when the past would live again. He thought of money—this new thing that had come to Africa. He thought of its defects. This was something that many did not understand. They could not see that there were things, moments, that could not be bought for money. That was the failure of the Uitlanders. That was why they would never understand or really conquer this land.

Africa was like a woman. You could enjoy her, but you must serve her. You could not possess or take away from her. Not a jot or tittle could you take. What happened to the leafy branch, dew-jewelled, if you cut it down? Could you carry it away in its perfection? Or the miracle of a bird's nest woven in the reeds; or the spread tail of a peacock in the sun? All you could get was the shadow of these things with money. Diamonds shone like dewdrops, but they were not dewdrops; there was no virtue in them. The tail of a peacock could be plucked out and mounted in a fan, but there was no life in it. A harlot could be hired and the act of love duplicated with her; but it was not love. There was no peace to be found in the arms of any daughter of the horseleech . . .

And Lena—how much had he been able to explain to her? It had all been so clear in the wagon as he rode home. But his welcome—he spat—had destroyed it. It was not his charge; it was not his over-eating or his drinking; it was this sudden discovery that he had outgrown the love of his descendants that had broken him. In their hearts, all of them, not just Kattie, thought that he had lived too long.

6

When Lena got in, Oupa was in bed. Reuter had undressed him.

"He is sick," he reproached her, "because you left him, and then she came—the smelling one that is hung with bells. That was too much for my master, who is accustomed only to consort with the great and is now alone, having survived them all. The old elephant should be allowed to die in peace and not be chased from beneath the shade tree where he rests by such a woman—one whom even the most savage of our dogs scorns to bite lest he defile his yellowing teeth."

He took snuff from his little spoon. "When is she going?" he asked. "How can I find peace for my lord while she is here, when he will not let me find the answer in my spears? Aaii . . . my meisie," he said. "It would be nothing for me; my spears are eager, they rattle together with desire." He took more snuff. "But to-day I frightened her well. I gave her a good skrik, hissing at her beween my teeth and leaping into the air with my short spear gleaming."

Lena looked at his short stabbing assegai with its long wide blade. It was strange to think of Reuter as the warrior that he really was: a Zulu, one of the terrible ones of T'Chaka: her Oupa's servant, but a warrior. A strange pair—the old white man and the old black.

"You fed him?" She looked at the sleeping man. How fragile he looked, how transparent! How thinly his hot blood ran now; how faintly his bold heart beat!

"He is well fed," Reuter said. "I gave him pap and soup and coffee and then a sopie of brandy and some of the snuff that I got from the dead Englishman. I do not let him smoke in bed now since he set himself on fire."

It must have been a good sopie, Lena thought, to put him into such a sound sleep. She smiled down at him. So old, that to a woman he was a baby again. After nearly a hundred years he was back where he had begun, his fires burnt out, and only the ultimate simplicity of his humanity remained—that, and the tremendous accumulated wisdom of all those years which now, having passed the time of its usefulness and practical application, had curdled within his shrunken skull.

" You will call me if . . . " There was no need to finish the sentence.

" I will call the meisie," Reuter said.

She got herself bread and coffee and went to her room. There was so much to think about: Oupa . . . Reuter . . . the bottle of lily oil and the perfume that she was to put behind her ears and between her breasts : of the strangeness of men. She thought of what Tanta Martha had said about their fear of explanations. She thought of Boetie and the way, while he had been at Mooiplaas, his personality had permeated the whole farm. She brushed her hair, counting the strokes—a hundred each night and morning : two hundred strokes a day. How many thousand before he came back? How many before she could use her little bottle of perfume?

What had Tanta Martha meant by saying she had her own perfume, her own embellishment? If only I was beautiful, like my mother, or my grandmother whom they called the Lily of the North : Sannie, my grandmother, she thought. If only I was blonde, golden like Hester Marais, instead of dark. If only I had blue eyes instead of brown. There was so little one could do. Tanta Martha had said so. Thinking was the best, she said. If that was so, then she must in course of time become incomparably beautiful, for she never stopped thinking of Dirk. She was still thinking of him when she put down her brush and got into her bed to dream of him. Here in the morning and evening in the half sleep that preceded actual sleep, he came to her. She could bring him when she willed it. Then, no matter where he was, he was with her. She got up to move her plant from the window to the table. She was afraid the night air would hurt it.

She dreamt of Boetie. She dreamt of his goats; of him piping them in; of Klein Johanna and the dogs of Doornkloof leaping beside him. As she dreamt, she knew it was a dream. That happened sometimes. You said, I am dreaming; this is a dream. Soon I will wake up; it is a dream. She moved on to her side. A dream . . . but was it a dream? There was no music, it was true, but there was the sound of hoofs—a pattering; a series of little snuffling snorts that were half a whistle. What was it Tanta Martha had said? The buck . . . She had been told to tell Oupa, but he had been asleep.

She sprang up and ran to the window. Dawn was breaking; pearl-grey, streaked with pink. But the world was utterly changed. The yard was changed. Nothing was to be seen but a sea of slowly moving backs—the buck had come.

She did not know what to say, what to think. She was struck dumb and silent by the spectacle. They did not run; they walked slowly. They streamed like water over the walls of the kraals and orchard, they swept round the wagon—a white swirl of buck round a blue painted rock. She heard the dogs growling and the ringing of the bell on Witbooi's neck. She went out. There stood the big billy clashing his bell against his chest. There were the dogs driven to bay; their jaws dripped with blood from their killing. They were breaking up a small buck that they had dragged up with them, but they were exhausted, terrified to find their killing ineffectual, to see that there was no end to it.

They looked up at her, wagging their tails, waiting for orders. Their blood-streaked jaws were open. They would go on killing if they got the order, but alone they could do no more. It is too much for them, she thought. Wolf, a red dog, sprang up and put his bloody paws on her shoulders, staining her nightdress with dirt and offal. His breath was hot and foul in her face. Bismarck, the fierce one that was Oupa's favourite, sprang off the stoep into the thick of the moving herd and slashed a big ewe in the throat, severing her jugular with one cut of his heavy jaws. For an instant he stood over the twitching body, growling, and then fell back. He could not understand the buck being unafraid.

Witbooi came up to her. She scratched him between his horns. The goats . . . Why was he alone? Then she remembered what she had heard. Sweeping into the kraal they had carried them away with them—Boetie's goats and their own were gone, scattered all over the world and unable to turn back. Only Witbooi, the leader, had been able to fight his way back, helped perhaps by the dogs with whom he had formed an alliance soon after he had come from Doornkloof. But why was she alone? Surely the others must have heard. She turned round to find Reuter beside her. His spears dripped blood. He was covered with it from head to foot. He was hissing to himself.

"Aaii . . . my meisie," he said. "What a killing! After so many years of peace to be free to kill is something, if it is only buck. Aaii, my spears have drunk blood. All night we have fought them—I and the dogs beside me. Look "—he pointed to the goat kraal—" you can see the heaps of dead."

There was indeed a heap; the oncoming buck leapt it as they came, gathering themselves like horses and leaping with the white plumes of their backs erect, and falling in a froth of foam.

"I could stop them," Reuter said, "but it was good to feel my spears bite meat again and to smell blood . . . much blood. But there should have been fire and cries; there should have been the smell of smoke, the hissing of my comrades, the shouting of the wounded and the clash of spear on spear. Once before it was thus," he said. "Aaii, once when I led the Blue Horizon we came upon a trek of bokke. The king had said, Go through, slay all that you see; and we halted not for the buck nor deflected from our path. The king had thrown his spear. We followed its course and cut our way through. We lost men, killed, crushed beneath the little feet of the multitude, but they did not stay us; there was a wide swath behind us of dead buck that lay for many years and told, with the ruined and burnt kraals, of our passing."

He paused.

"But to-day I, Tabankulu, Captain of the Blue Horizon in the time of T'Chaka, fought alone with the dogs at my side." He scraped some dry blood from his arm with the edge of his spear. "It was good," he said. "My little ones were thirsty.

"But once they nearly had me," he went on. "Once I was down, and if it had not been for the dogs it might have been the end. A fine end for me, a Captain," he said, "crushed beneath a thousand hoofs. That would have made my master laugh. Aaii, how he would have laughed!"

"And your master . . . I told you not to leave him. Suppose he was taken worse."

"He is my master," Reuter said. "I take no other's orders. And why should he want me when he sleeps the sleep of the just and drunken? This was an occasion, one that he would understand. It lies between him and me, both warriors and hunters. Both men who understand the precise art of killing . . . that of other men and beasts. Aaii, we be men, he and I. The old white one and the old black. There are none left like us to-day. We are elephants.

"And when he went on his charge, did he not leave me?" Reuter asked. "Not even making me drunk before he went, as a consolation."

So Oupa was drunk; and Tanta Stephanie always slept like the dead, and since her long residence abroad, was immune of sounds of a farm and unable to estimate their value or their order. If you lived on a farm and were accustomed to it, you were aware of its rhythm and responsive to any irregularity. And Ouma . . . Lately Ouma had cared about nothing. Her world had fallen with Stoffel on the Hill of Doves.

It was therefore ended, and the destruction caused by this multitude of buck could do no more. A thing ended was ended: a thing broken beyond repair was irreparably broken. Still it was strange to be alone with a Zulu who had reverted to his savagery, in a world suddenly controlled by beasts.

It was light; the sun was up. She still could not believe that what she saw was true. It was still a dream. She had heard about it, every one knew that the springbok trekked sometimes from the North driven by drought. It was not a regular happening, but one which occurred every ten years or twenty years, there was no rule—only the precedent of their trek, and the tales told that she had always thought to be exaggerated, hunters' stories : the stories of those who wished to be important because of something they had witnessed.

But she had never believed it could be like this. There were thousands of them, hundreds of thousands. As far as the distant hills the veld was white with slowly moving buck; the world was blanketed with them. Some were so near that she could almost touch them. They ignored her; ignored Reuter and the dogs. They walked past with their lyre horns raised, their golden eyes unseeing, a mass of white backs and pale brown flanks streaked with a chestnut bar. Already the ground was cut up by them. The smooth, goose-grazed grass in front of the house torn, as if it had been harrowed. The grass was gone and the small bushes gone or hanging loose from their roots. Another astonishing thing was that there were big buck with them—blesbok, kudu, even a zebra foal. That was a strange thing to see in your front yard. Caught up in the stream they were unable to turn back. She wondered where the zebra had come from, there were none near-by.

There were always some springbok about—houbokke, they called them, that lived in these parts; but these were from the distant North, they were the trekbokke. No one knew whence they came or why they came—though it was assumed to be drought that drove them—or where they went. She had heard somewhere that they went as far as the distant sea, and, drinking the salt water, died there along the strand in great banks that, rotting, smelled so strong that people living there were driven from their homes.

She heard shouts from the house. It was Oupa. He had been roused by Reuter. He was cursing and calling for his guns. A minute later he was out, clad only in his shirt, with his hunting belt buckled round him. "Get my chair," he said. "Bring the powder and bullets."

Reuter was serving him. The dogs crowded about him. He was their master, the hunter, and they knew the guns.

His chair was set up near a stoep pole and he began to fire methodically : firing, lowering his gun, and handing it to Reuter, who gave him another. The barrel of powder had been rolled out and was beside his chair. Oupa was smoking. A spark would have blown them all up, but he seemed happy. He was in action again. Yesterday he had been a baby; to-day he was a man again, had become one suddenly, stimulated by this circumstance, living again perhaps as Reuter had in some distant past, duplicating again some tremendous scene that he had lived through; young and strong because in the pressure of the moment age was forgotten in the suddenly present past. He was muttering and swearing. He was smiling and spitting through the gap in his teeth over the rail, as he fired.

Tanta Stephanie had peered round the door, awakened by the firing, and had run back to lock herself in her room. Springbok or English, war or disaster, she had before going complained to Lena of her immodesty in staying with Oupa. First she had said: "So it's not the English. I thought they had come." Then seeing Oupa she had told Lena to go in. "It is not decent for you to stand here, since you are unmarried. in the presence of a naked man."

Poor Oupa. For the first time Lena became aware of his bare legs, his shrivelled thighs. Every day putting him to bed she had seen them, but there in his room they had looked different. There he was an invalid. Here, confronting this spectacle, his weakness was apparent, underlined by the power of the moment.

"Get back, woman!" Oupa shouted, "this is no place for you. It is my place, and the place of my women who have my blood."

"It is not seemly," Tanta Stephanie screamed between shots as she ran in, "and that Zulu . . . O God, that murderer!"

Lena heard her bank the door of her room and bolt it. Klein Johanna ran out and was pulled back into the house by her mother.

And still the buck pressed on, slowly, strongly, irrepressibly, weighted by their thousands. Oupa's bullets cut through them bringing down several sometimes with a single shot. But it made no difference. At last Oupa put down his guns.

"It is enough," he said. "Get the boys, Reuter, they can get through and let them begin to flay. If we have lost much, at least we have some skins."

Lena came to stand beside him. Awed by the magnitude of the spectacle she could not speak. Ouma had joined them, but had said nothing.

It was Biblical—like one of the plagues sent upon the Egyptians. The world was white with moving bodies; the horizon obscure with red dust through which, as it parted, only more buck were to be seen.

"How long will it go on, Oupa?" she asked at last.

"I do not know," he said. "It is only a little trek. When I was young they really moved. Then they were so thick that their bodies touched each other. I am tired now," he said.

He sagged in his chair. Reuter held him up.

"He must rest," he said.

Lena thought of the medicine Tanta Martha had given her. He must not get excited, she had said; it might be the end of him. She wondered if anything could have been more calculated to excite him.

"It has been bad for him, Reuter," she said.

"Aaii," he said, "bad, yes. But good, too. Bad for him to us, but good to him. Am I not his servant? All night I had pleasure killing in the moonlight. Would I not share my joy with my master? Aaii, the last kill to the old lion is good. It is a kill."

He put his arm under his master to raise him.

7

The day passed, and the night, and there were still no fewer buck; more were killed by the boys with kerries and sticks, by Reuter with his spears; and still they came. All night she listened to the muffled thunder of their tiny hoofs; clouds of dust hung colourless in the moonlight, suspended in the dew-damp air. There was no ending to their whistling calls; no end to the white bodies and black, inward-twisted horns. The dogs, utterly cowed, stayed in the house where every one fell over them. There was no real sleep for any one. The animals were confined waterless in the kraals—the cattle and horses; the small stock, the sheep and goats, were gone. Much of the poultry was gone too, trampled down; but some remained perched on the roof of the house and in the trees. The geese, led by the old voortrekker goose, were safe, and sailed in white circles on the water of the dam. The peacocks had taken wing and not one was to be seen. Lena knew that somewhere in the distance the rear and flanks of the herd were being harried by wild dogs, lions, leopards, and jackals : knew that all the predatory beasts were taking their toll; but that it was as nothing—that their attacks were like a man striving to empty a dam with a spoon.

Next day was the same. Still the buck came, a wide blanket of moving backs being drawn from the North into the distant South. The flood showed no signs of ending. But it must end : there must come an end of everything. Lena's eyes were sore, inflamed with dust. Her head ached. Oupa was bad again, much weaker, and kept crying for his guns. Tanta Stephanie sulked and still blamed her for the discomfort caused by the buck, talked of her immodesty, and spiced her conversation with obscenities that she considered the pleasures of a virtuous marriage; while Ouma, somewhat recovered, had begun to sew again and stitched without looking up or casting a glance through the window; and Tanta Johanna tried to amuse her child and keep her in the house.

But at last, on the third day, the buck thinned down. These were the laggards and weakly ones that came. They got thinner and thinner. A wild dog came right past the house. Lena had never seen one so close before and wondered why he was alone. How ugly he was with his black, yellow, and grey blotched hide, black muzzle and big pricked ears! The house dogs flung themselves upon him. At last there was something they could understand.

Lena ran out with a rifle and Reuter came with his spears, but nothing could be done with that mass of snarling, rolling bodies. There was only dust with the sound of snarling. Hound and wild dog were indistinguishable till it was over. There they stood, she and Reuter, waiting for a chance to help the hounds, while a solitary buck limped past. He was the last. The trek was over. It had gone by. The dogs had finished, too. They left the wild dog and came to Lena. Bismarck was badly bitten and Wolf had lost part of an ear.

The buck had gone, but they had left desolation. No green thing stood. There was not a buck to be seen, only in the distance a dust cloud to the south showed the path that they had taken. There were only the dead buck mangled by the hoofs of the multitude that had passed over them; the flayed bodies of those that the boys had skinned; and the sky filled with the circling vultures that followed the herd to eat the sick and fallen, and to clear up what was left them by the killers. Grass and bush were gone, and the smaller trees were hung with white hairs rubbed from the buck as they passed under them. The air was heavy with the smell of rotting bodies.

War had come to them. Now had come disaster. A world empty of grass to a folk who lived by it. How wide a swath had they cut? Veld must be found somewhere for the cattle.

And Boetie's goats were gone: all but Witbooi. How would she tell him when he came back?

Lena began to cry. It was too much. It was all to much for a girl who wanted only peace and marriage.

THE only thing that had broken for Dirk the monotony of the commando's march to the Natal Border had been his meeting the gunner Jordaan on the second day of the trek. He was alone, going in the wrong direction, and had stopped when Dirk hailed him.

"Yes," he said. "I am on my way back."

He asked him why he was returning home and Jordaan said he was seeking his dog. "When I find her I will return. I always knew no good would come of this. You have not seen her, I suppose? You remember her—a liver-and-white pointer very beautifully marked, but no longer young."

Dirk had laughed. There was something funny in this; in the old man abandoning his gun to look for his dog. But Jordaan had been hurt by his laughter.

"This is no laughing matter," he said. "And I have permission from the Field-Kornet. At first it was not so bad. They gave me a little ship's-gun that was made of brass and bucked like a horse when you fired it. It was unmanageable, you understand, being a sea-gun and unaccustomed to the land. But then they gave me a big one and that is what caused the trouble.

"It happened this way. We got into action over there "—he pointed back, over his shoulder. "I laid my gun and fired. A wonderful shot it was. I had lost none of my skill. My dog stood at my heels. She trembled at the great noise of the gun, for neither she nor I like noise, but she stood. We reloaded and fired again. That was too much for her; as I told you, she is very nervous and highly strung and is no longer young. She ran, Dirk van der Berg. Magtig, I have never seen a dog so run—much faster than a buck. I called to her, but she did not heed me. Her nervous system was no doubt shattered.

"So what was there to do? There was only one thing. I went to the Field-Kornet, a very sensible man from my parts who understands the relationship that exists between me and my dog. He has one of her pups at home. And in my heart I think it is he who is responsible for it all—my being called up as a gunner, I mean—so perhaps he was ashamed. His name is Grundling, Field-Kornet Jappie Grundling of Sterkwater;

and I said to him : ' Jappie, my dog has run away from the battle. Please to excuse me while I find her.' He said : ' Yes, I will excuse you.' Then, to make it better for me and not to hurt my feelings, he said : ' You are good here without your dog.' So I said : ' You will excuse me in writing; you will give me a letter saying I may go; for then, if I am picked up, I shall not be called a deserter, which, apart from the danger of getting myself shot, would be offensive to my pride, since it would be my second desertion and men would point their fingers at me."

" To desert once is nothing, Dirk," he went on, " and requires no authority; it is in fact the only sensible thing to do; but twice is different. Jappie understood." Jordaan pulled a paper from his pocket. " And here it is. This is my excuse signed by Field-Kornet Grundling. You are sure you have not seen her?" he asked again.

Dirk had assured him that he had not.

" Then she has gone home. But two hundred miles is a long walk for an old dog. I only hope the neighbours feed her. It is in my heart that she will go to Swart Piet's; she likes his wife and they also have a pup of hers, one of her last litter. And it is near my house—only eight miles if she crosses the mountains. But that worries me, too, for there are tigers in the mountain and she might come to harm."

He had taken Dirk's hand. " Good-bye, young man, and good luck. I always knew no good could come of all this. Good luck," he said again, " and wish me luck in my search."

" Good luck," Dirk said.

And they had parted, Dirk riding after the commando in the contrary direction.

This had been just another incomprehensible incident. Another added to the collection that went round and round in his head. He looked at the camp they were approaching.

The march down had been fast, for a major engagement seemed to be about to take place. Both sides were forcing the issue.

This was the biggest camp he had seen. In the distance beyond it rose the jagged peaks of the Drakensberg—black dragons' teeth biting into the blue, bright sky. It lay on the flat top of a nek. The wagons were arranged in a great square surrounding an open space where the staff tents, from which fluttered the little flags of the commandants and the field-kornets, were set in lines. Near them, lying side by side, were some captured English artillery limbers. They had been taken at Inogo with other matériel. The camp was empty except for a few coloured servants and the general's secretary, who was in a bad mood at not being allowed to go to the front with the others Still he greeted Joubert, saying how pleased he was that he had come.

" The general was expecting you," he said.

" Did he leave orders?" Joubert asked. " What are we to do?"

"Offsaddle and send your horses out to graze. There is nothing for you to do to-day. To-night the general will be back and he will decide."

Joubert turned in his saddle.

"Dismount," he said, "and get rest and food, but be ready in case we are wanted." He spoke to the secretary again. "You will tell him that we have arrived."

"I have already sent a message." He picked up his quill again and bent over some papers.

So we are here at last, Dirk thought, with the main forces in Natal. He wondered what friends he would find here. Would Barend and his father be among them? He would like to see them again. He gave Swartkie a slap and sent him off to join the other horses. Then taking Boetie's arm he followed his father to the cooking place. There were great pieces of newly slaughtered oxen hanging on a cross-bar between two poles. Every one was cutting what he wanted. He cut for the three of them while his father set about making a fire. Near-by there were big kettles of tea and coffee and biscuits in bags—a very hard kind of biscuit that the man in charge of the rations said had been captured from the English.

Having eaten they lay down to rest. Groot Dirk slept with Boetie lying at his side. But Dirk could not sleep. He did not feel tired. A new excitement possessed him. Things were nearing a conclusion of some sort. He wondered what a big battle would be like. Very like other smaller actions probably, except that you would have the feeling of participating in a national effort instead of a local one. You would be fighting with all the men of your nation instead of the men of your district.

From the south there came the sound of some scattered shots. He got on to his elbow and felt for his rifle; then he lay back. It was nothing. To-day they were to rest. He looked at Boetie. In his sleep he had crept nearer to his father and lay with his head pillowed in his arms. What a change the last weeks had made in him! He was no longer a child. He was a man. A blind young man beloved by all. And he had grown. Despite the hard life and fare, he was stronger and heavier than he had ever been. He thought of the miles Boetie had ridden on the little grey mare that he had drawn for him from the spare herd. How good and quiet she was, never pulling on the riem as he led her. There had only been one trouble—the time she had come into season. During that time Boetie had ridden the Mooiplaas bay, and now the mare was in foal to Swartkie. When it was over, they would buy her out for Boetie.

It was nice to think of things like that : his horse the son of his father's, and Boetie's horse the wife of Swartkie. That had been a pleasant interlude to every one concerned—to see a foal conceived in the middle of a war. That was reality. That was a part of their lives. That was farming. Such things must go on as they always had, and gave promise of the future. He wondered what colour the foal would be—blue roan, perhaps; with a black sire and a grey dam it seemed likely.

All round him men were resting; they lay sleeping or sat smoking and talking. A few still cooked meat, holding it over their dying fires on the ramrods of their guns. He knew them all; they were a band of brothers. Joubert, the commandant, was walking about talking first to one and then another. How lucky they were in him!

He thought of the last action they had been in : of how clever Joubert had been. He had used the old ruse of oxen dragging trees to create a dust that would give the English the impression of a large force moving. He had done this knowing that they would not be fooled and would detach a squadron to capture the oxen. But then, before he sent the oxen, he had taken his whole commando and hidden it, behind the screen of dust. Galloping up to surround the cattle the English had found themselves surprised in an ambush. How Joubert had laughed! It was a trick inside a trick, he said; a new trick inside an old one.

, Dirk recognized a disconsolate figure—a man walking alone in a dejected fashion, and wondered who he could be. He knew his shape, but could not place him.

It was Meneer Tryolla.

Dirk went up to him. " What are you doing here?" he asked.

" That's what I want to know. I have been here a week."

" I do not understand why you are here," Dirk said.

" Who does? There I am up in the mountains "—Tryolla pointed to the berg—" with my two donkeys. You remember Romulus and Remus?" he asked.

" I remember them," Dirk said.

Every one who knew Tryolla knew his donkeys, almost white with age they had carried his tools and equipment over every range in the country.

" Well, there I am with them," Tryolla went on. " I have found colour in a stream and I am panning my way up to its eye. I am very happy. There are fish in the water and plenty of pheasants and partridges in the hills, also buck that could be got with no trouble. The donkeys are fat, happy; everything in the world is good—and then they came." He spat.

" Who came?"

" A couple of Takhaars. Two backvelders who said I was a spy and took me prisoner. It was nothing that I spoke the taal better than they; nothing that I knew their land better than they. I was English, they said.

" They asked me that first when they came upon me. They said, " Who are you?" and I said, " Tom Tryolla." They said, " Then you are a Uitlander, with that strange name. You are an Englishman."

" Magtig, that made me mad. Me an Englishman! ' I am a Cornishman,' I said."

" ' Where is that?' they asked. ' Is it not in England?' ' No.' I said,

'England is attached to Cornwall in east and north. England is, as it were, a piece of Cornwall, which is a duchy.'

" ' It is in England then,' the big one said. ' Did I tell you there was one big one and a little one like a barrel?' he asked. " ' If England is in Cornwall, then it follows that Cornwall is in England.' ' Ja,' the little one said, ' England is the foal of Cornwall. They are attached evidently, and the one is inside the other.'

" ' What did you say your name was?' the big one asked again. ' Tryolla,' I said. I spelt it out: " T-R-Y-O-L-L-A.' ' That's a funny name,' he said, ' and we will take you with us.'

" Damn them!" Tryolla shouted. "A funny name. It was my father's name and his father's, and what's funny about that? In Cornwall there are plenty of them; they are as full of meat as pasties, and as filled with spice. But they brought me here, and here I wait with Romulus and Remus getting thinner every day. They miss me, those donkeys; we are used to each other, and they will not let me sleep beside them in case I escape. When I was examined here by the general and his secretary, they asked what I was doing. I said I was doing what I had always done—I was looking for gold.

" ' In a war?' they said. ' What war?' I said. How was I to know there was a war? I had been away five months and those fools—the big one and the little one—had said nothing of war or I should not have resisted them. At least from what they said I thought it was some Kaffir trouble, which made me angry, since it is an insult to think I would spy for Kaffirs. Besides I was busy. You do not know what it is to hunt for gold in the mountains, Dirk," he said. His eyes became dreamy. "You go on and on, always hoping; always finding a little—but you know one day you will hit it. Gold!" he said. "Think of what you can buy with it. I mean real gold, not what they think they have found on the Witwaters Rand." He spat again. "I mean gold in nuggets, in veins that you can scrape out with a knife, in chunks. That is what we prospectors dream of. If I found real gold I'd buy a farm, get married, and settle down."

Dirk laughed. "It is said that when you were younger half the girls in the country were after you, each with a good farm. It is said that you ran away into the mountains because you were afraid."

"When I was young it was different," Tryolla said. "Then I was shy."

"You would never settle down. The mountains would call to you."

"Yes, they would call, but I would not go. I have seen them all, and besides my feet get sore climbing now. I have got corns that worry me. But I am very angry, Dirk," he said again. "Here I am a prisoner, at least nearly a prisoner, and I am bored; I do not like it. There are too many people about," he said. "Every man in Africa is here, including three men to whom I owe money. They are in different commandos so that if I get away from one I get near another. Now they have met and are combined against me. And they had thought I was dead.

"If I could find gold I would marry," he said. "I need a woman to protect me. But it is good to see you, Dirk. Very good to see a friend instead of a creditor."

"You have many friends," Dirk said.

"Yes, I have," Tryolla said, "but I owe most of them something and that comes between us."

"I thought there were only three."

"There are only three big ones, but the little ones are many. How was I to know that a war would bring them all together and throw me into their midst?"

"It is hard," Dirk said.

"Yes, it is hard, and my tobacco has been stolen. Those two took it. They smoked it all the way back, hardly stopping to spit." He sat down against a wagon wheel. "But it is good to see you. Perhaps I could move my blankets over to your lines?"

"I can see nothing against it." Dirk gave him tobacco. "Our men all know you."

"That's the worst of it. Every new commando that comes in brings more men to whom I owe. What memories men have! What memories!" He sighed. "But see what you can do. I do not think I ever touched your father for anything."

He went off to see to his donkeys, and Dirk rejoined his father and Boetie at the commando.

"I have news," Groot Dirk said.

"What is it?"

"We have arrived at the right moment. We attack at dawn, so get what rest you can."

"Tryolla is here," Dirk said, "a prisoner. He wants to lie with us; will any one mind? He is a good old man who thinks only of stones."

"Why should any one mind? If they do, he is my friend and that will be enough. Let him come."

"Is there going to be a battle?" Boetie asked.

"Yes."

"And what will I do?"

"Stay here in the camp," Dirk said, "and wait for us to return."

"I do not like to stay in camp."

"Well, you must leave something to Joubert," his father said. "You cannot lead in every battle."

They laughed, and lay down to sleep, if they could.

At dusk the general came back from the line and called the command and the older burgers of Joubert's commando.

"We attack at dawn," he said. "The English are on the Spitzkop"
—he pointed to the sugar-loaf hill—"three miles away. Your commando"—he spoke to his cousin Frans—"will take the east, which is
the best side if you time your attack so as to reach the crest when the sun
is coming up and behind you. They cannot shoot into our bright sun,"
he said, "so I am counting on you to push your attack home. As soon
as you are engaged, the other commandos, Fourie's and Retief's, will
attack from the west and north. You will be supported by picked sharpshooters who are already in position. Is that clear, brothers?" he asked.

"It is clear."

"Has any one anything to say?"

No one spoke.

"You had better take your horses to the foot of the kop; riding in
the dark they will be safe and in dead ground by the time it is light."

"The plan is good," Groot Dirk said.

"Ja, it is good," every one said.

"Then go, get rest; and good-luck, friends. Pray to the Almighty
God," he said, "for this is a decisive action."

Boetie plucked at Dirk's arm. "I shall not stay in camp. I am going
with the horses. I shall stay with swartkie under the kop."

Frans Joubert shook hands with the commandant general. "God
helping us we will do our duty," he said. They broke up, going back
to their lines.

2

Dirk thought of the course of the war so far. The main operations
with which Joubert's commando had not been concerned had all been
here in this area, on the frontier line between Natal, the Orange Free
State, and the Transvaal, centering on the road to Pretoria where it crossed
the Drakensberg. It was here that the English would have had to cross
the berg to relieve the garrison besieged in the Transvaal. A body of
Boers had been thrown forward to Meekis and behind them were
assembled the reserves. General Colley's first headquarters had been at
Pietermaritzburg. From there he had advanced to Newcastle and had
attacked the Boers at Langsnek, where he had been defeated and forced
to fall back on Mount Prospect. Another action had followed at Schuins
Hooghte on the Inogo River, and now the English had entrenched themselves while waiting for reinforcements from England and India. The
Boer plan was to force the issue and defeat them before they could arrive.

Dirk looked at the sugar-loaf hill they were going to attack to-morrow;
it was called Amajuba by the Kaffirs, rose out of a nek that connected
it with a spur of the Verzamel-Berg and was joined by Allemansnek and

Langsnek to the main range. The English held a strong position, but Dirk felt no doubt of success. Doubt only came to him as they saddled up in the dark. All round him the men were talking to each other, soothing or cursing their mounts, and only the greys, like Boetie's little mare, stood out like ghost horses in the night. He put Boetie up and held the mare's riem in his hand. He should have insisted on his staying at the wagon lines. I should have made Pa tell him, he thought. But if they had, he knew Boetie would still have come on his own, going towards the noise of the fire alone after they had left.

"You will not move when we set you down?" he said.

"I will not move, Dirk. I will stay with the horses. Already many of them know me and stay near my music," Boetie said. "They are like my goats, only bigger." He laughed with happiness. "It is good, Dirk, to take care of the horses of my comrades."

"We trek, friends . . ." Those who were not mounted got on to their horses. They bunched together, stirrup striking stirrup, and then fed themselves out in single file, like a string that was being unrolled into the night. There was no more talking, no smoking; only the sound of the horses' hoofs and the creak of saddles and gear.

Dirk pulled Boetie near to him and patted his thigh. "Do not be afraid," he said. He found himself very much afraid and his voice sounded queer. He hoped his brother would not notice it. The bulk of the kop was mounting, looming up in front of them, menacing them. How big and high it looked in the night, blocking out the stars that frilled it! A gigantic black cone of rock. By the time the sun is high, Dirk thought, we shall be on the top or lie dead upon the slopes. He wondered how many were thinking the same thoughts as he.

Men were beginning to dismount. He lifted Boetie down, knee-haltered the grey, and slacked her girths a little. He slacked his own girths two holes, and took the bit out of Swartkie's mouth, making it fast to the bridle on one side. The reins he left trailing. The two would stay together and Galant would not go far from them. A grey mare was a fine thing to hold horses or mules together.

Boetie had taken his hand; he squeezed it, unable to speak. His father was beside him. They pushed past the horses that were already opening out a little as they began to graze. Besides Boetie, two other men were staying with them. Their duty was to see that the herd stayed in the dead ground under the berg where they could not be seen or fired upon. They were safe from a flank attack, being covered, by the supports that were behind them, but not from shell fire if they moved out too far.

Joubert was speaking. "Is every one ready?" he asked. "Are all here? Then get together. Find your friends at whose side you would fight, for we are going to move."

There were the voices of men calling softly through the darkness—a boy here looking for his father; two brothers seeking each other; friends, men from neighbouring farms. In a few minutes the movement and grouping of men was over.

"We are ready," they said. "We are ready, Oom Frans."

"Then kneel and let us pray."

They all knelt on the dew-wet grass. They began to get up, first one and then another, and unslung their rifles. Dirk heard whispered talk and the click of cartridges and the soft rattle of bolts and magazines.

"We are going," someone said. Dirk bent to kiss Boetie; he had followed them. He heard his father kiss him. None of them said anything; but, as they went slowly, feeling their way, he heard Boetie playing his little flute, the one he had played to his goats very softly. He is playing to cheer us, Dirk thought, to show that he is unafraid. His brother's courage embarrassed him. How could Boetie find the breath and spit to play when neither he nor his father had trusted themselves to speak? How could he be so brave alone, with a herd of horses that might be stampeded by a shell at any time, in a strange place set directly below a battleground? How thin that little sound was now, almost muffled by the shuffling rustle of the climbing men!

His father was on his right, Louis du Toit on his left. He thought of Duifkop, the Hill of Doves; once again they were climbing in the night. Once more the terrifying moment must come when they would appear against the skyline. This was always the moment of greatest danger. In other directions other commandos were climbing, and the sharpshooters were waiting for dawn as they lay fingering their rifles in the wet grass. The reserves were no doubt standing-to beside their saddled horses waiting for orders and ready to come in if there was a movement of British cavalry on the plain they had just left.

He fell and hurt his hand. He got up again. He thought of Boetie down there playing his flute. Despite the climb he was cold. It must be nearly dawn, he thought. This was the cold hour that preceded it. It got lighter; the sky was a dark grey, the colour of a gun barrel, and the plains and valleys below them white, carpeted with mist. They were alone in the world, a commando suspended on a black menacing world above the clouds. At any moment there might be a rattle of shots. He stared upwards expecting the dark bulk of the mountains to burst open with stabbing flames of fire.

But nothing happened. Still they climbed. Now they were on the very lip of the first crest: poised beneath it. Here they halted, without an order or a word, each man stopping the one beside him by putting his hand upon his shoulder. It was good to feel your father's hand upon your arm. They lay down side by side. Pa was breathing hard. Dirk wondered what was going on in his mind. His own was blank, except the thoughts of Lena and his mother, but he could not even really think of them . He could only repeat their names over and over in his head. Lena . . . Ma . . . Lena . . .

It was light now. A spattering fire came from the Boer sharpshooters. Dirk heard the bullets crack as they passed over his head. It made him feel much safer. There was no danger of being shot from behind by their own men. At three hundred yards a Boer would put a bullet into the ground away from you, just to attract your attention, if it was too far to shout.

Below them, the mist illuminated by the rising sun was a glowing pale rose-pink blanket. In a minute the world would come. He never heard it. I must have got up with the others, he thought, as he found himself running forward; climbing and running forward. They were on a small flat ridge. It was this that they had been told to take. Joubert had picked the moment. The sun was directly behind them and dazzled the English.

He knelt to fire and stayed kneeling, not lowering his rifle from his shoulder to load. It was terrible to see the effect of their fire. It was over in a few minutes and they went on running over the dead and wounded. There was more firing from all round. They had lost no one. They had reached the true top. Here they halted again, just below it. "We stay here till the others are up," Joubert passed the word down. They waited. The sun rose higher and higher. The rocks got hot, but still there was no word to move. And then suddenly it came . . . Attack.

With a shout they were over. There were the English, already driven from some position, trying to defend the little stone walls they had thrown up. More Boers were advancing, running forward, and flinging themselves down to fire. Dirk passed an old burger who had made himself comfortable against a rick and was shooting as coolly as if he were in a competition, firing, checking his shot, and firing again.

Dirk felt no fear now. I am mad, he thought. I am like a dog that is set on. There were the Redcoats : that was all that mattered : to get at them, to shoot, to kill, to fire as you could. He heard a Gatling go into action. They must be getting artillery support from somewhere, he thought. Then some bigger guns fired; the shells passed overhead, but they were driving the English back. Another party of Boers was enfilading them; they were being driven out of their defences. Magtig, they were standing up shoulder to shoulder, a red line firing volleys at Boers they could hardly see. He heard someone shout in English for ammunition. They seemed to be running short. They began, a few at a time, to fix bayonets. "Give 'em the steel!" an officer shouted, and sprang forward sword in hand. He fell, jumping in the air as a bullet took him in the throat, but his men went on and were dropped like muck as they charged. They came on like a stream of thin red water—that creeps forward, covering the ground as it advances, and finally stops. The last one he stopped himself—a young boy that he shot through the chest at point-blank range. Before God, he thought, that was too near. A bayonet before your eyes was unpleasant.

There were only a few left now. They had rallied round an officer. A moment later they were down and someone shouted, "They have killed the general! Colley is dead. They have shot Colley." Some English stragglers flung themselves over the edge of the kop trying to escape down a krans, clinging to the bushes and stones. As he watched them many fell, shot by the sharpshooters. They fell like fruits from a tree. One minute they were there, the next they had fallen to be crushed on the great rocks below. There was no more firing. It was over.

He stood up. Where was Pa?

"Pa!" he shouted.

"I am here with Louis."

They came together and stood silent holding their rifles by their barrels, resting their butts on the ground.

Joubert, soaked with sweat and black with dirt, was mopping his face. "Who was the officer they closed round at the end?" he asked. "Does any one know his name?"

He pointed to a fallen man. His white helmet had been pulled over his face by someone.

A wounded English officer went up and lifted it. "It is Colley," he said.

Then it was true the general had been killed.

Joubert turned to him. "You are sure?" he asked.

"I give you my word of honour," he said, "that is General Sir George Pomeroy Colley." He put the helmet back over the dead man's face. "The general has been shot in the forehead. You have killed the bravest gentleman on this field," he said.

"Yes," Joubert said, "he fought well."

A man beside Joubert said: "He was a very nice gentleman. He dined in my house whenever he came to Pretoria."

Looking out over the veld—the mist had cleared—Dirk saw a big commando galloping round the kop to cut off the retreat of some kilted Highlanders. The battle was over.

"We can go back now, kerels," Joubert said. "General Smit is going to hold the kop; his men are fresh."

They went back to the horses, climbing down by the same route that they had attacked over a few hours before. God had, indeed, been with them. They had suffered few casualties and had inflicted a third and most severe defeat upon the English.

When they got near the horses, Dirk shouted. Boetie was beside Swartkie. He picked up the reins, climbed on to his back, and came towards them at a gallop.

H.O.D.

"You are all safe?"

"We are safe, son," his father said, "and are on our way back to camp now. It is in my heart that the war is nearly over. That was the battle of Amajuba. Do you know what that means in Zulu, Boetie?" he asked.

"No, Pa."

"It means the Hill of Doves. I have just remembered," he said. "Spitzkop to us, but the Hill of Doves to them. The dove is for peace; and two battles upon their hills."

His father was right, Dirk thought. It was a strange coincidence. Not that hills should be named after doves in Dutch or Zulu, for there were many such duplications—many sugar-loaf hills, many hang-lips, strong fountains, table hills, as there must be, since place-names were descriptive. But that these battlefields should be named after doves . . . the birds of peace . . . It was ironic and difficult to understand. It was a dove that had come back to the Ark bringing Noah the olive branch in its beak. Or was it not ironic? Might it not be a sign that peace was near? That it must come soon?

3

Some of the men were angry when they heard from a commando of Free State burgers that negotiations were going on between President Brand and the English. Though they were not yet at war with the English, these men had ridden in to help them in the event of the negotiations failing. The death of Colley had been a great blow to the English, as had their losses in officers, men and matériel.

It was said that to the English there was something astonishing about the way the Boers had conducted the war. They refused to call them soldiers because they would not fight their way, according to rules of which they had never heard. But the heart of the matter really lay in their respective employment of their arms. Dirk went over to look at the rifles captured a few days ago at Majuba. The sights of many taken when the heights were stormed were set at two hundred, three hundred, and even five hundred yards. He picked up a Martini-Henry and put it down. How could men shoot at almost point-blank range with their sights set so high?

The journalist Newman joined him. He had recognized him and said, "We were together with Joubert's commando, were we not?"

"We were," Dirk said. He put out his hand. "My name is Dirk van der Berg."

Newman had left them a fortnight ago to attach himself to Kruger and his staff.

"Mine is Newman," the journalist said.

"I know your name, meneer." They continued to look at the rifles.

"That is why we lost the war," Newman said, as he slipped one of the sights down. "That and poor generalship, overconfidence, and the short training of our men. Men!" he said; "they were only boys."

"You think we have won, then? That it is over?"

"The negotiations are going on and an armistice is expected to-day or to-morrow."

"I will be glad when it is over, meneer. I do not like war."

"There are many in England who do not like it either." Newman took out a pocketbook. "You can read English?" he asked.

"I can read it," Dirk said.

"Then read these—they are Gladstone's speeches. It was only the Conservatives who wanted this," he said.

Dirk took the clippings from him.

The Conservatives [Mr. Gladstone said] have annexed in Africa the Transvaal territory, inhabited by a free European Christian Republican community, which they have thought proper to bring within the limits of a Monarchy, although out of 8000 persons in that Republic qualified to vote on the subject we are told, and I have never seen the statement officially contradicted, that 6500 protested against it. These are the circumstances under which we undertake to transform Republicans into subjects of a Monarchy.

In the next one, dated November 20, 1879, Mr. Gladstone again declared that:

There is no strength to be added to your country by governing the Transvaal. The Transvaal is a country where we have chosen, most unwisely, I am tempted to say insanely, to place ourselves in the strange predicament of the free subjects of a monarchy going to coerce the free subjects of a republic, and to compel them to accept a citzenship which they decline and refuse. But if that is to be done it must be done by force.

In the third he said:

We have undertaken to govern despotically a body of human beings who were never under our despotic power before. We have gone into the Transvaal territory, where it appears—the statement has not been contradicted—that there were 8000 persons in a condition of self-government, under a Republican form. Lord Carnarvon announced, as Secretary of State, that he was desirous of annexing their own territory if they were willing. They replied by signing to the number of 6500 out of 8000 a protest against the assumption of sovereignty over them. We have what you call "annexed" that territory. I need not tell you there are and can be no free institutions in such a country as that. The utmost, I suppose, that could be done was to name three or four or half a dozen persons to assist the Governor. But how are they chosen? I apprehend not out of the 6500, but they are chosen out of the small minority who were not opposed to being annexed. Is it not wonderful to those who are freemen, and whose fathers had been freemen, and who hope that their children will be freemen, and who consider that freedom is an essential condition of civil life, and that without it you can have nothing great and nothing noble in political society, that we are led by an Administration, and led, I admit, by Parliament, to find our-selves in this position, that we are to march upon another body of freemen, and against their will to subject them to despotic government?

In the last one he said:

Lord Beaconsfield omitted to speak of Africa, and did not say the Radicals had created any difficulties for him there. But there he has contrived, without, so far as I am able to judge, the smallest necessity or excuse, to spend five millions of your money in invading the Zulus who had done him no wrong; and now he is obliged to spend more of your money in establishing the supremacy of the Queen over a community Protestant in religion, Hollanders in origin, vigorous, obstinate, and tenacious in character, even as we are our-selves—namely, the Dutchmen of the Transvaal.

"He said that last March," Newman said. "At that time the elections were turning against the Conservatives and his return to power likely. So you see, all Englishmen are not bad. No, by God," he said. "Not the common Englishmen like the boys you've shot. But it's the rich who rule the country. They are ready to give their own sons and everyone else's as well, to protect their money."

"Are these true?" Dirk asked.

"I wrote them," Newman said. "I heard the speeches and reported them."

"And you are here to write about the war—about the things you see?"

"Yes, that is my job."

"It is a strange one," Dirk said. "Ja, it is strange to me. And I have heard that you are not alone; that there are others who write too—others with us and with the English."

"That is so. We are war correspondents; we write reports for the papers. I have reported three wars," he said. "The American Civil War in '61 and the Franco-German War in '70. Those were terrible wars. Americans fighting each other and devastating their own land. And the swift fall of France . . . I was in Paris and saw the Germans march in."

"I never heard of the American war before," Dirk said, "though of course it was before my time. Perhaps my father knows of it. The German war I know of. The Germans are our friends, for their country is near to Holland, lying beside it.

"It is all very strange, meneer," he continued. He handed the clippings back. "And beyond my understanding. This Meneer Gladstone seems to understand our people and to be in sympathy with our ends, which are so simple that it is hard to believe that any could misunderstand them. Our desire is only to live out our lives in freedom according to the laws of God."

"My friends and I understand," Newman said, "and so do many others. From the beginning I have been with your commandos—with Joubert's, with Cronje's, and with the staff of the Commandant General Jacobus Joubert. I have lived with you, seen you fight, and eaten your food. So much so that I have been reprimanded by the paper I represent for being pro-Boer." He laughed. "When it is over and I get back I shall write a book about this war to show its injustices and foolishness."

"Ja, it is foolishness," Dirk said. "When it is over I am going to get married. That is very serious, much more serious than war, for there you make, you do not destroy. Are you married, meneer?" he asked.

"No, I am a bachelor."

"I am sorry," Dirk said. "I should not have asked."

4

The days dragged. Messages were exchanged between the British and Boer generals, between their governments, between the English forces and their government at home. General Wood had replaced the dead Colley, and President Brand was still mediating.

Joubert, the commandant general, had sent a telegram saying that he agreed no more blood should be shed, but that it was alone in the power of the English Ministry to check it, since the Boers were doing no more than to defend themselves. "We are ready to accept every offer of peace," he said, "in so far as it is not in direct opposition to our liberty."

But in the Boer camps wherever Dirk rode he found much unease and dissatisfaction. There was always a crowd round Paul Kruger's tent at the main laager where the vice-president sat beneath a tall pole that carried the Vierkleur. How beautiful it was to see it floating again against the sky of Africa, with its green stripe straight up and down against the pole and the long stripes of red, white, and blue extended in the breeze.

"He is fooling us, Oom Paul," they said. "That General Wood is verneuking us and playing for time while he awaits more men and guns." They pointed out that some reinforcements had already arrived, and said: "We should go on now. Let us finish it and drive them into the sea. Let us finish what we began and then go home to our farms."

But Paul Kruger just sat and smoked his pipe.

On the fifth of March a meeting took place between General Wood and the Boer leaders. They met midway between the lines of the two camps. They agreed to a cessation of all hostilities between noon on the sixth and midnight on the fourteenth. Neither party was to make any move forward, but each was to retain liberty of movement within their own lines. General Wood was at liberty to send food, but no ammunition, to the besieged garrisons in the Transvaal, and Joubert undertook to send word of the armistice to the commandants who were investing the besieged towns of Potchefstroom, Standerton, Wakkerstroom, Rustenberg, Lydenberg, and Marabastadt.

The Boer leaders, Joubert, Uys, and Fouchée, were explicit about their own demands. Complete amnesty for all leaders and entire freedom of the Transvaal from the British Government except for its suzerainty, which they were ready to acknowledge. Dirk got all this news very fully from Newman, who had attended the meeting.

Meanwhile, in the slow days of waiting more and more Free-Staters came in; and the rain, which had been intermittent, came down for days in solid sheets, washing away the road between Mount Pleasant and Newcastle. Many men and horses caught colds, and coughs and sneezes were mixed with the curses of the waiting men. Owing to the weather, which delayed the coming of Paul Kruger, who had gone back to Heidelberg, the armistice was extended till the sixteenth, when another meeting took place in which nothing was achieved and no settlement arrived at. Before going to it, the commandant general made a speech to the assembled burgers.

"I go to speak for you; to represent our nation. We have only one demand, and on that we have taken our stand, and will keep that stand to the end. That demand is that we get our freedom back again. Nothing else will satisfy us; we must have that before we do anything else. The Transvaal must be given back to us, and until we get it nothing but war must prevail. Peace is out of the question. Give us our independence, recall Shepstone's annexation proclamation, allow us to manage our own affairs as we desire, then we shall be prepared to act in friendly accord with Britain for the interest of British people in South Africa.

"But independence must come first. We took up arms when everything else had failed, when we had exhausted all arguments, and we will not lay them down at the bidding of English politicians, and trust to them doing what is requisite. We have had enough of the promises of such people. They promise, but they do not fulfil, and we cannot any longer put faith in their promises; they are not carried out. We are determined to know exactly what is to be done, and what is intended before we make any final arrangements. We will on no account trust to the fine promises of English politicians, because our experience of the past makes us have no confidence in them.

"With regard to the alleged appointment of a Royal Commission in England, I am willing to agree to a further armistice if the English people will do as we will, and stop all movements of troops. If they won't do that, it is evident they only want an armistice to suit their own ends—to let them get a large body of men together; and we will never consent to that; we will fight to the end. We have believed in the righteousness of the British Government. We sent a deputation to the Queen of England to lay our case clearly before her, but all to no purpose. I want to know why Mr. Gladstone, now Prime Minister of England, had not carried out his promise to return the Transvaal to its rightful owners, seeing that he considered the annexation a disgraceful act? When we read his words we relied upon the great English statesman doing us justice. He has not done so. We desire to know why? With regard to the death of General Colley, we are all very sorry indeed at his death. He was a man I knew well, and all of us were grieved when, after the fight, news was brought that he was dead. We believed him to be an honourable, straightforward English gentleman, but he was deceived by the reports of his subordinates. They wilfully did all they could to deceive him, and, acting upon these reports, he, in his turn, unwittingly misrepresented our case to the people of England. Instead of being rejoiced at his death, we are very sorry. I wish to contradict the statement that he was shot twice—the last time at close quarters. That is utterly untrue. None of our men aimed intentionally at him, and the bullet which killed him struck the top of his forehead, and came out at the back of his head. It has caused me great pain to hear that in some newspapers it was reported that we had wilfully killed a man whom we all held in great esteem. Such statements are deliberate insults to us, and do more than you would imagine to stir up hatred between the Dutch and the English. And where there is hatred there can be no peace."

There was a further extension of the armistice, and more and heavier rain. A new meeting was arranged for the eighteenth. Kruger had caught a chill and was too ill to attend; Doctor Jorissen was also unable to be there; so the commandant general went alone with his brother to meet General Wood and Colonel Buller at the farm of an Irishman called O'Neill. There was still no settlement.

With late summer rains like this the Boers were all uneasy for their horses. At any time an epidemic of horse-sickness might break out. Swartkie had a bad cold and the medicine burgers made for him seemed to do little to alleviate his cough. Dirk kept him covered with his own blanket and slept with Boetie, but a blanket did little good if it was never dry.

With Kruger away, the men were getting out of hand and demanded either war or a complete end so that they could go home, before their horses died, to reap their crops.

"If we get no satisfaction soon," Joubert said at last, "we will fight again. Stand by each night, and the first morning there is a mist we will attack Mount Pleasant."

After that the men became more quiet and before dawn every commando was saddled and ready. But each day was clear, and then at last, on the twenty-third of March, a settlement was reached; Kruger, Joubert, and Pretorious signing for the Boers and Major-General Wood for the English.

The young Boers were not satisfied with the terms, but the older put their trust in President Brand, who had acted as intermediary, and in General Wood. It was not all they had hoped for; it might not even be lasting. But it was peace and they wanted to get home.

The wagons were inspanned. The great whips clapped. The commandos mounted, and the assembly, that had come together at Paardekraal, for discussion, and had continued from there to war, was broken up.

CHAPTER XXVIII

WE RIDE HOME, BROTHERS . . .

As the commandos had come in from their farms—running in like the spokes of a wheel towards the hub—so now did they run out again to their farms, like the spokes of a wheel, away from the hub of their victory; broken up, dispersed, by their accomplishment of the issue which had brought them together.

First, along the single road that led to the north went the stream of wagons, men, and driven herds; then away from the great road, into the little roads that led this way and that—to the west and east, to the northeast. The men who had come in from all over the land were returning to their places in Ermelo, in Carolina, in Vryheid; to the Waterberg, the Zoutpansberk, to the Lydenburg. Each going towards a solitary farm set in the mountains, in the plains or the bushveld; each little farm, to the returning burger, a jewel mounted in the setting he had chosen.

Whole commandos would swing away from the moving army of farmers, making their horses dance under them, raising their wide hats and firing their rifles into the air in a manner most beautiful to see.

It was a fine thing to be party to such a movement of men and beasts; to see them distributed over the veld as they rode home; to know that you were riding home yourself: to know that it was over and that there would be no more dead. Singly and in parties men kept breaking away from the commando. As they reached the roads that led to their homes, they would ride up to Joubert to say good-bye; and then, having shaken the hands of their friends, would turn off, wheeling their horses to stand facing their comrades as they rode past. Then they would set off at a gallop, or a walk, according to the difference in their natures.

Men were as different as horses and dogs. That made Dirk laugh. Before this, he thought, I knew much more of dogs and horses than of men. I thought of all men as being like my father and myself. And women? He had not thought of them at all except for Lena. His mother he did not think of as a woman, but as his mother. Yet women must be as different as men—as different as dogs and horses, with natures that were hot or cold; passionate or sluggish. It was this difference in men that made some ride away fast, setting their spurs into their mounts; while others rode slowly and reflectively. That was why some stood waiting with stern, set faces; while others wept, why some waited till they had all gone past, and others scarcely looked back as they rode. Yes,

men were very different from each other. Only one thing had they all
in common at this moment—all were going home.

"It's a pity we missed Langsnek, Dirk," Bok said. He had just ridden
to his side.

"You mean the battle?"

"What else? It would have been good to be there."

Dirk could not see how it would have been good to have wounded or
killed more Englishmen, and perhaps to have been wounded or killed
oneself.

"Yes," he said, "it would have been good."

Not to have agreed would have been to acknowledge his fear. Having
spoken, he regretted it. Even now, after all this, he was still unable to
take his own line and contradict any to their faces.

It was Louis who took up the argument.

"I am against all war," he said. "I am against all fighting."

"That is wrong," Bok said. "Suppose everyone thought that? What
would happen then? There would be no war."

"That is just what I think," Louis said. "If no one wanted to fight
there would be no war—there could be none. It has taken me three
months to reach this conclusion," he said slowly, "but it is reached and
my mind is made up on the subject."

"But you fought," Bok said.

"Yes, I fought, but without pleasure. It is against my nature. I hold
that if it was against every one's nature there could be no war."

"Then you would have let the English do as they liked and offered no
resistance."

"No," Louis said. "I said every one, and I meant every one. This
would include the English who, in my heart, I think dislike fighting as
much as I. It is not good to fight," he said. "It is good to farm, to eat,
and drink, and make love. It is good to be happy, to build, and not to
destroy."

"You are mad," Bok said.

"I am sane. How is it mad to harbour no hatred? How mad, to believe in the words of our Lord Jesus Christ, unless our Lord Jesus were
also mad? I can go no farther," he said, "since it has taken me the
whole war to come thus far; but my mind is clear. It is made up."

He lit his pipe and was silent. He had no more to say.

How little one knew of what went on in the heads of other people,
Dirk thought. He could find no fault in Louis's argument. And it had
never occurred to him that Louis thought at all. He had considered him
stupid, as a beast is stupid, simple and honest. But he had had the
courage to refute Bok. He had had an answer ready for him. Louis
had been thinking in terms of fundamentals while he had dreamed of

Lena's long dark hair. But that, too, was a fundamental. He got some comfort from the thought.

He thought of Bok again and the others like him. Stoffel would agree with him. True, the peace terms had not been all that they could have hoped for, but by them their wrongs were righted, and to hope to defeat such a nation as the English was, in the long run, probably impossible if they chose to employ their full strength. And besides—he looked at Boetie and his father—we are all safe. We are riding home. That was perhaps the finest thing in all the world—to be riding home to your sweetheart. Even their horses were safe; and Swartkie's cold was well, thanks to Carl Burges's medicine, which at last seemed to have taken effect.

How differently victory took men! Many were angry that their victory had been too inconclusive and the terms obtained insufficient to give them full satisfaction. The Republic, though free, was to remain under the suzerainty of Britain. They wanted no more of Britain, nor of the English. They had left their farms to make an end and they wanted an end made, even if they must die to achieve that end. But Dirk had no heart to listen to their grumbling, especially since some of the greatest grumblers had not been overconspicuous for their courage in battle.

It was enough for him that it was over: that he was riding home to Lena in the company of his father and brother, with Louis du Toit and old Tryolla, beside him. They had all come through alive and unhurt save for Boetie's wound, which had healed well and quickly. Their horses, which were a part of themselves, had come through. They were riding home to their mothers and wives and sweethearts; to their small sisters and brothers; to the places that they had ridden out from to defend. Their duty had been accomplished. The war was won. It was peace. He thought of the wisdom of Joubert's proclamation . . .

I earnestly implore each one of you to let us hear no more after this day of Boer, or Englishman, or Hollander, or of Kaffir. Let us bury the dead completely, or only remember them for our good. No one party in the State can get on alone, and if we each go our own way we shall fall to the ground. We must therefore go hand-in-hand, and if we do so we must prosper. Extend, then, the hand of friendship to every citizen of the State, or any stranger who wishes to remain such, or whatever country he may be. We may all have felt aggrieved at the action of individuals, and especially those who have misled the British Government, and have misrepresented us; but these are not the British nation, which has now done us justice; but when you look at an Englishman in the future, I do not wish you to regard him as one of that nation, and so also with all other Europeans. We all come of one stock, and so should live in the land as brothers.

If men would stand by it there was no reason why this peace so cheaply, he saw it as that now, bought should not last for ever. The cloud had lifted. The sun was shining again. He was riding to Lena. Each pace that Swartkie took brought him nearer to her. Each camp at night was nearer. All were nearer to their hearts' desire. Days passed slowly, but still they passed. No longer living disassociated from reality, in the vacuum of war, time had come back and was once more calculable. The realm of improbability, of chance, so vastly increased by war, was reduced to its normal proportion. Before, since he had left Lena, he had hardly dared to think of his marriage. Now he thought of nothing else. Before, though Lena had been continually in his mind, he had held her back by main force, by the power of his will, being afraid of where his thoughts would lead him. Now he was no longer afraid. He let his thoughts run like hounds over the days of the future; even the consummation of his hopes and of his desires; over her beauties of mind and body; over the life they would lead, the house they would have, the children they would raise. This riding-in was a dream, as the riding-out had been, but one of a very different quality, for where the first had been charged with fear and doubt, the second was filled with the joy of certainty.

It was good to sit loosely in the saddle with slack reins, while Boetie, his mare tied to Swartkie's saddle, played on his new English fife. The horses danced to the music, keeping time with it, stepping to it, and cocking their ears in unison. And the veld was more than beautiful— this wide, free, rolling country was their own: their land: their Africa, that once again had been bought and paid for with Boer blood and tears.

As they approached Brennerdorp, the commando was weakening almost hourly; soon only men from his own district, those who were riding farther north, would be left. Then it would be less like a commando than a hunting party.

Home . . . they were all going home. To me that means Lena, he thought, and to each of these others something else, some other woman. He looked at his father's face. It showed no gladness. It was firmly set, yet he knew him to be glad and anxious to get back. He wondered what he could be thinking about as he rode. His farm and crops, the responsibility of a place, a family, perhaps?

This familiar country had its own special beauty to Dirk as he looked round. That it was familiar made it beautiful. To-morrow they would be in Brennersdorp. To-morrow, Brennersdorp . . . to-morrow night, Mooiplaas . . . Mooiplaas and Lena. His heart rose fluttering like a bird in his chest. He began to sing to Boetie's music.

When they off-saddled for the night, he thought: This is the last night on commando. Now only did it seem to be really over. Now only was it really ended, and he was able to see the war as just a piece cut out of his life. It was like a section of cord that was bad. His business now was to splice the two ends and endeavour to forget it.

He thought again of what the commandant general had said . . . *Let us bury the dead completely, or only remember them for our good* . . .

That was right. That was the way that things must be. It was Christian, and more than that, it was good sense. But how was hatred to be obliterated from the hearts of many who had sucked it up with their mothers' milk? How was not only this new past, but the old past, to be wiped clean for this new beginning? Slagtersnek and the Great Trek were not things that could be undone. Nor could the fallen of this war be restored to life. These were the problems that must be faced, for while this generation lived, they would recur continually, subject for further discussion, for argument and dissension, that might, if it were fanned by foolish action, lead to further war. That was why Jacobus Joubert was right when he said the dead must bury their dead . . . That, respectfully remembered as heroes, the cause of their death must be forgotten. But was it possible?

Boetie put his arm about his neck. They had been sitting side by side, but, lost in his thoughts, he had forgotten.

"It is over, Dirk," Boetie said.

"Yes, it is over."

"Things will be the same when we get settled home again. The house will be there, and the goats and dogs, and Ma, and little Johanna. Everything will be the same, but because of this all will be different . . . You will be married."

"That will make no difference, Boetie. You will come to live with us. You will visit Ma and Pa. You will play your new fife. We will go to dances and festivities, to nagmaals, together as we have always done."

"That is the way you see it, Dirk. But you are a real man, whole, with sight in your eyes. I who am blind see things in another fashion, and therefore think in another. When I left, when you fetched me, I was a child—a boy. You had thought to comfort me with your message—'You are the man on Doornkloof now.' But you knew, and I knew, that I was just a boy. But to-day I am changed. I am a man. Never having left my homeplace before, I knew nothing of the world or other men. Now I have learned to wander. I like it. And I find with my new flute I can give men pleasure. Strangers listen to me, men who do not know that I am blind and therefore under no obligation to give praise."

"That is true, Boetie, you are a man now. You can decide for yourself; no one will gainsay you."

"No, they will not because they could not, but things are much changed. I can no longer herd my father's goats upon the mountain. And there is nothing for me to do in my father's place nor in yours and Lena's. You will have children, Dirk. They would be sorry for me. I could not have that; it would hurt me too much."

"What is it in your mind to do?"

"A strange thing, Dirk. I am going to find a servant and I am going to wander over the face of the land, making songs and music for the people. I have talked to men and many say they will welcome me at their homes. I may even be able to teach others to play and sing. And Dirk, did you know that in ancient times, in other lands, there were such men as this? Men who lived travelling—singing, playing and, telling tales. It is such a man that I would become. I would bring peace and joy that is in my heart to others. Able to do nothing," he said, "I can still serve. It has become very clear to me that this is the path of my life."

"If you have decided, then it is so," Dirk said. "That also is the fashion of our people, to think for themselves and to decide. It was for this right we fought."

He took his brother's hand. "I understand," he said, "but all that I have said stands. My house is your house, my possessions your possessions. Let that be a compact between us."

"I am glad you undertand, Dirk. I was afraid you would be against me, but it would have been useless, for my mind is made up."

They were riding through a mealie land. The cobs were formed, the lower leaves yellowing, and the weeds high. Dirk thought of the crop at Doornkloof; soon they would be reaping, and when the harvest was over they would turn the cattle into the stalks.

That Boetie, too, as well as Louis, had been thinking, had reached conclusions of his own, surprised him. Then he was surprised at his surprise, for after all each man and woman, each child, must be thinking of something all the time. It was only that he had never thought of it in this way before. He wondered if each person went about as he did, in a world of his own detached from that of all others. Did Lena? What did he know of her mind? He only knew of her heart which wanted him as his wanted her. They came together in their desire, but their minds were separate and must remain so, for it seemed to him that there could be no full communication of the mind.

No one could have been closer to any one than he had been to Boetie, yet he had known nothing of what was going on in his head. He had been completely unaware of the change that had taken place in him nor had he even foreseen such a possibility.

And his father? What did he think about? Had he changed? He spoke so little that it was hard to tell. But what could one do with words? How did words help, since they could never express what you felt or really thought? He thought of how tongue-tied he was with Lena. That was not because his mind or heart was empty, but rather because they were overfull, and what filled them inexpressible, except by a look or the touch of a hand.

What would it be like to be a man like his father and be riding home after a war to his wife and small child, accompanied by his sons? This was something of which, since he had none of these things, neither wife nor sons nor child, he could have no comprehension. It was all much less simple than it had seemed when you thought of the world in terms of yourself alone and thought of everything else in its relation to you . . . when you only considered other people in relation to yourself. You did not see, when you thought like that, that this was universal and that the others thought of you differently . . . of you only in relation to themselves —all men and women with themselves as the centre and core of their particular universe. Yet that was the way it must be, each man and woman a centre, and yet none of them centres; all living in a private world that no one, not even they themselves, could understand. He wondered if he had changed. It seemed to him that he had not; that he was as he had always been. He had thought he had gained in courage and under-standing, but Louis's argument with Bok and Boetie's decision had proved him wrong again.

As they reached the outskirts of the dorp, they drew together, into a short column, riding four abreast. Dirk rode with his father on his right, Boetie on his left, and Louis on the outside. They all sat erect in their saddles and tightened their hands on the reins, bringing up their horses' heads and forcing their hocks in under them. A feeling of pride came over Dirk. He was part of his nation, one of a commando that, having performed its duty in war, was riding home.

They began to pass the first houses. Women and children, friends, came to the doors and ran out on to the road. Men stooped from their horses to lift children on to their saddles. A girl—Minnie Fourie—ran up to Louis, who swept her up on to his horse, which made every one laugh.

Jan Marias shouted from the back. " You court quickly, Louis. Before God, at the sight of you maidens leap upon your horse."

" I court slowly," Louis said. " For six years I have courted Minnie."

So that was it. That was how no one had known in a dorp where nothing was secret.

There were more shouts of greeting, more kisses, and then they in-creased their pace. There was no order given, but the horses shook their heads with excitement and fought for their heads. They knew they were home and neighed shrilly. All entires, they were going back to the wait-ing mares. Then men had their rifles loose in their hands. By the time they reached the outspan, the commando was cantering. Then suddenly they galloped, opening out and sweeping across it in a wide line, shout-ing and firing their guns. Minnie, in Louis's arms, was screaming with fright. As they reached Hutting's Hotel, they pulled up, drawing their horses back on to their haunches so that their long tails lay along the ground.

Then they dismounted. It was the end. Only Joubert and a few others were going on from here. They were surrounded by women and children and old men, who shook hands with every one; who shouted: "Our commando is home . . . the men are back!" Kaffirs ran forward, hat in hand, to hold the horses, to greet their masters and their masters' friends. Dogs, long separated from the men they loved, jumped up at them. Small children, shoulder carried, both among those welcomed and the welcomers, were crying.

By a led horse, her head resting on the empty saddle, her arms about his neck, a woman wept. Dirk turned away from her to pat Swartkie. He could not bear to see her or listen to her sobs. It was Hester Coetzee, the widow of the first of their men killed in the war. Who had fired the shot—what Englishman? And who had fired the first Boer round? That was Stoffel; and was there a woman weeping in England for the man he had brought down? Dirk thought of Lady Colley, who had come to visit her husband's grave a few days after he had been killed. With every commando there must be similar sights—other led horses who came back with their stirrup leather crossed over their empty saddles.

Tryolla came up to them. He had not joined in the charge across the outspan, and was dishevelled, his arms torn out, he said, with the battle he had had between his borrowed horse that had wanted to join in the gallop and his two donkeys which had refused to be hurried beyond their usual pace. They had gone together to say good-bye to Joubert. He had shaken hands with them all. They had wished each other luck. Joubert had again complimented Boetie on his exploit.

Tryolla said: "Am I free now?"

Joubert asked him what he wished to do. Was he going back to look for gold in the berg?

"No," Tryolla said, "now that I am free I am going to see my friend Tanta Martha Kleinhouse and see if she has a remedy for corns. I have given her many recipes that will cure illness and it is time she did something for me."

Joubert and his companions had remounted. Someone shouted to Dirk from the stoep of the hotel. It was Jordaan the gunner. He had a pointer tied to a string that he held in his hand.

"What are you doing here?" Dirk asked.

"I am on my way to rejoin my gun."

"But the war is over."

That is nothing to me. I obtained leave to fetch my dog. I have her and I return to my duty with the commando of Grundling. A gun is a special thing," he said. "It is like a woman and cannot be lightly left.

I learned my duty in Holland where I was once a famous gunner. But come in," he shouted, "come in with your friends and drink with me, and I will tell you about the handling of ordnance. It is a fine reunion."

"No, thank you," Dirk said. "I have given up drink, but it is good to see you and I am glad you have found your dog."

Jordaan went back into the saloon.

"Now we will go home, Pa," Dirk said. "Now we can go."

"We will off-saddle first, son, and water our horses. It is ten miles from here to Mooiplaas and that we are glad gives us no excuse to abuse the horses that have carried us so well."

"Yes, Pa," Dirk said, and loosened his girths.

A strange man, his father. One whose patience was beyond his understanding, but he was right. They had no business to forget their beasts.

He wondered when Louis would marry his Minnie. He had not seen him since they had pulled up at the hotel. How frightened she had been at the charge and the firing of the guns!

It was only ten miles from Brennersdorp to Mooiplaas, an hour's ride, or less: to-day it would be less. He wondered if they expected them. It would be good to surprise them . . . to surprise Lena. But, on the other hand, if she did not know he was coming, she might be out. His hands trembled as he lifted off the saddle. Perhaps she was going to have a baby. Suppose she was. That was the real reason he had not wanted to go back to her. But till this moment he had not acknowledged it. Till now he had pretended other causes—good reasons, but not the right one. Suppose I had been killed, he thought. He looked at Hester Coetzee as she passed him, leading her husband's horse. Her little son sat bravely on the horse's back, holding the mane. For them it was not the end of a war—but the end of a life.

CHAPTER XXIX

WELCOME

I

GROOT DIRK saddled his horse slowly. Dirk had gone at a gallop. He smiled as he thought of his son riding to his love. Even Swartkie had seemed to know his urgency. He would draw no rein, uphill and down he would gallop, splashing through the spruits. A young man in love was like an arrow loosened: a young man kept waiting, an arrow from a bow drawn to its extremity. But I, he thought, would savour my joy more slowly. When he gets there, Dirk will tell Johanna that I am on my way with Boetie. She will know that we are coming. He put the saddle on Boetie's grey.

"Mount, son," he said, "we are riding home to your mother and the baby."

"Yes, we are riding home," Boetie said. "I never thought it would be like this when you and Dirk rode out. Never thought that I should be with you on your return."

He thought of the sound of their going: of the sharp clatter of Swartkie's hoofs; of the rattle of accoutrements; of the bandolier pressed into his chest as his father kissed him. He bent forward to pat his horse's neck.

"We are going slowly, Pa," he said, "and I am glad, for I would think. It is in my heart to make a tune of this."

"Yes, we are going slowly, Boetie, for I am a slow man, and solemn, some say." His father laughed. "But I was not always so. Once I rode as hard as Dirk. Once I loved your mother as Dirk loves Lena, but now our love has grown into a greater thing. Where it was urgent, it is now strong. There is no urgency where two are welded into one, for there can be no separation. Once your mother knows we come, her heart will be at peace. She will wait quietly."

"Johanna will jump up and down," Boetie said. "If she has eaten, she will make herself sick with jumping." He laughed at the thought of Klein Johanna and at his joy at seeing her so soon.

But life was funny. Here they were riding home; here was his brother gone like a flash of lightning on his black mare; here was Louis, who should have been with them, staying in the dorp with his betrothed. Here was he, the blind boy of Doornkloof, returning with his father from commando, walking and cantering slowly along the road that would bring them home—that would bring his father to his mother; that would bring him to his mother. He thought of her softness, of her smell so good and clean . . . of Lena's hot new-bread smell . . . of Klein Johanna's smell of soap and milk and dog. It was impossible to keep her away from dogs.

Life was very beautiful and the song was coming. He screwed his fife together and began to play. Then he put it back in his pocket.

"Dirk told you my plans, Pa?" he asked.

"Yes, he told me."

"And what do you think?"

"I think, Boetie, that your life is your own. Being a special person, owing to your blindness, it is for you to act specially if you feel so called upon. The Almighty saw fit to put no sight in your eyes, but music in your heart in its stead; therefore, what you decide to do must be according to the Almighty's plan and not one in which either I or your mother can interfere. Your home is yours to come to and go from as you wish. A boy—you have made a name in the land. We are proud of you, since, though still a boy in years, you are a man in reputation."

"Thank you, Pa," Boetie said. "But I am sorry about the goats; they may think I have betrayed them." He sniffed the air. "Where are we now, Pa? We must be near, for I think I can smell the mountain as we ride into the wind."

"We are coming to the second drift. We are on Mooiplaas, and the mountain is beyond us; I can see it against the sky. And to-night we will be home. To-night all of us, united once more, will sleep at Doornkloof beneath the shadow of the hill. Dirk took my message to your mother; she will be prepared to move."

2

At Mooiplaas and elsewhere they had known that the negotiations had been drawn to a conclusion and that the war was over. They had known, too—more recently—that the men were riding home. The news of both had come as it always came in Africa, as rumour, as a word passed from Kaffir to Kaffir across the vast width of the veld. Rumour—yes, but such rumours were invariably confirmed. In that most wide and secret land, nothing was secret. As things happened, they were known almost on the instant.

Now on every farm the women and children were waiting. The impatience of the last months had concentrated into an intolerable restless urgency that gave no one peace; that drew all to the doors and windows of their houses; that dragged them down the roads to meet those whom they knew to be upon them, in the hope of meeting them sooner. If you went up the road for half an hour, then you met them half an hour sooner. After months of uncertainty and waiting, thus were half-hours to be gained. And because the time was short now, each instant dragged, each hour became a day.

Lena kept going out and coming in, only to go out again. Tanta Stephanie kept dressing up in her best clothes and curling her hair. Tanta Johanna remained seated on the stoep waiting for her husband and her sons. Only Ouma—and Oupa, sunk in the lethargy of his dreams—remained unchanged.

The war being won would be considered by some a compensation for those who had lost their sons; for the empty beds of those who had lost their husbands. Compensation. Ouma hated the word. She hated the eagerness with which Lena stared down the farm road. Before, she could have stood anything unmoved, and it was a strange thing that Stoffel's death, for which she would have needed his capacity to withstand the blows of fate, had destroyed this power to withstand that she had so slowly and painfully built up. That was irony itself, the ultimate blow, that Fate could deal her, leaving her now, in her old age, naked where she had been clothed in armour. There was no compensation . . . no justice. How did the Lord compensate? Had He compensated Stoffel for his deformity? Yes, by his ability to ride and shoot, in which she had been God's instrument, and by which he had been destroyed. And how had she been compensated for the death of her husband and sons beneath those Zulu spears at Rietfontein on the Nyl River? There was no compensation.

The war was won, but by a compromise. The English were not swept into the sea; the Republic was subject, in the sense of England's suzerainty, to England. The English were still an infection on the land. Their railways would continue to creep northward; their fences continue to cut up the veld that God had left open to her people. Their hated language would still be heard. Compensation . . . the word kept recurring to her. What was it but the substitution of the second best for the best? What was it but a palliative? Tears rolled down her cheeks and fell on to her folded hands. It was over, and there was no compensation. Once and for all her heart was emptied. She could only wait now until she died for comfort, died and found her loved ones again. She was suddenly envious of Philippus Jacobus—he was so near his end while she had long to wait. She had her spells, a momentary dizziness every now and then, but they passed. They were nothing. What was there left in life? The Boers had won, but their ancient landmarks were gone. There was a lion in the way—a lion in the streets who, like the daughters of the horseleech, cried: Give . . . give . . . *A generation passeth away, another cometh . . .*

Victory, and still the English would remain walking with stretched-forth necks and wanton eyes, walking and mincing as they went. Victory, but victory by compromise, by negotiation. Their leaders had touched

pitch and were defiled. Stoffel was dead. Surely it would have been
better if all had died and finality once utterly achieved, fulfilment in complete victory or death, which being death could know nothing of the
indignity of defeat. Ended, they said. But in her heart she knew it was
not ended. The Republic had been regained . . . the flag . . . the Volksraad; but they were not free. It was like a horse that thought himself
free because he was not knee-haltered and could walk with some measure
of ease; but to that horse's leg was tied a long riem that would throw him
if he tried to run.

3

A man was coming down the road, at a gallop. Lena could not see the
horse's colour. He raised a cloud of dust. She put her hand up to her
hair. Was it tidy? Was it Dirk? If it was not Dirk, it did not matter
how she looked. She shaded her eyes. The rider was leaning over his
horse's neck; he had a rifle over his shoulder. It was a returning burger,
and who but Dirk would ride so fast? The horse was black! It was
Swartkie! It was Dirk! Her hand went back to her hair. It went down
over her dress to smooth it. If only she had put on the pink instead of the
blue, but she had worn the pink yesterday.

Each day, and many times a day, she came to the road to stare; each
time knowing that it was unlikely she would meet him, but each time
certain, as she came back, that the next time he would be there. To-
morrow . . . she had said to herself each night; and now that to-morrow
had come at last.

The rider was waving his hat in his hand and shouting to his horse.
She could see his face and Swartkie's. He was still galloping and only a
few yards away. For an instant she was frightened of being overridden,
and then, in a whirl of long forelock, mane, and tail, Swartkie went up
pawing the air, and sank back till his hocks nearly touched the road as
Dirk sprang from him. One moment Dirk had been high above her,
his horse's hoofs pawing the air in front of her. The next she was in his
arms. He was kissing her: holding her till she could not breathe. How
strong he was! And why had she not used that scent Tanta Martha
had given her—just a little behind your ears and between your breasts,
Tanta Martha had said.

She pushed closer to him. Could she ever get close enough? Dirk
had returnd. Dirk, her lover, her husband, was back; the war was really
ended now . . . but she still thought of the scent as she kissed him. In
that instant, as they kissed, the world was changed—all time stood still.
There was nothing in the world but Dirk. She had no feeling of her

own existence. She had merged into him. The months of waiting were gone.

It was as if he had been with her all the time, as if they were still together beneath the blue gums; as though, in full daylight, it was that night again. She smelt the earth once more and saw the trees through her closed eyes, black against the night-blue sky. She felt herself trembling, like a leaf in a wind, she thought. . . . And he has never seen the dress I made to wear for him. She thought of how she had been going to make it secretly, and come in, the stiff taffeta rustling about her knees . . . and my new store shoes.

She saw everything as he held her: the day of the battle—that was the last time he had kissed her; she saw him throw the stick that was now growing in her room, as they had walked down the stream; she saw the past and future, and still her eyes were closed. She saw their children about them; she saw herself old with Dirk. She saw herself young with him, when he had pulled the hair he was stroking now. She felt herself one with him—one and inseparable—and was astonished. I am not Lena any more, she thought. I am ill. I feel faint. It would be terrible to faint; he would think her stupid. But her legs did not give way.

His lips were on her mouth and neck, his hands were on her. In a bush nearby a bird sang. Sang ever a bird so sweetly? And a cicada shrilled, while Swartkie cropped the grass beside them. She could hear his teeth cutting and his bit rattle against the curb as he snatched at it. Then it was over. Dirk had let her go. It was day again: a day of glory. He picked up the reins. Turning from him, she straightened her dress and hair. He must not see her now. He must not see her eyes. She was crying with happiness, but there was more in them than tears. She gasped for breath. The blood pounded in her ears. It makes a noise like a waterfall, she thought. The bird had stopped singing, but the cicadas still shrilled with redoubled vigour—more had joined the first one. In the sky above them a small hawk hovered.

4

Tanta Johanna had seen Dirk come. She had watched his meeting with Lena. But where was Boetie? Where was her husband? Where was Louis? Why had Dirk come alone?

They must be all right or he could not have been so gay. She watched them walk back, his arm round Lena. But why had the others not come if all was well?

Klein Johanna was dragging her forward. "It's Dirk! It is my brother Dirk who comes back from the war. Come, Ma . . . come. I want my

Pa . . . I want Boetie. They should have all come together. Why did they not come together? Tell me why. Why . . . Why?

She let go of her mother's hand and ran forward to her brother. "Dirk! Dirk!" she cried. He picked her up. Lena and he were laughing; nothing could be wrong or they would not laugh; but where were the others; what had delayed them? Tanta Johanna thought of the last time she and Klein Johanna had watched the road with Lena—the day after Dirk had taken Boetie, as they waited for him to bring him back . . . Where was Boetie? Where was her husband?

Dirk saw the anxiety in his mother's face. "They come, Ma," he shouted. "My father and Boetie are on the road. He said you are to get things ready, for we return to our house to-night."

"They are safe?"

"They are safe and well. Boetie had a wound in the arm, but is recovered."

Boetie wounded . . . her baby hurt! It was only yesterday she had held him in her arms, and he was hurt. Dirk spoke of it as if it was nothing. He was smiling down at her. He bent to kiss her.

"We are back, Mother," he said. "The war is over."

"They are coming, you say?"

"Boetie is coming with Pa!" Johanna shouted. "Boetie is coming! He will be here soon."

"They will be here in an hour," Dirk said.

It was wonderful. In an hour her family would again be united. And to-night they would all go home to Doornkloof. My husband and my sons, she thought.

They were almost back at the house now, Dirk walking on one side of her and Lena on the other, while Johanna danced in front of them and Swartkie followed. It was over. She could think of nothing else. It is over, she thought again and again. Dirk is here with me. My husband and Boetie are coming. They are on their way, she thought. She was content to wait for them. She would leave Dirk and Lena, they had no need of her, and walk back down the road to meet them. She would wait as Lena had waited for her lover: as she had waited when she was a girl for Groot Dirk . . . as Lena might, one day in the future, go to wait for young Dirk, her husband, the father of her sons.

As she waited, she thought of the situations of women . . . how alike they were, how similar their actions and feelings. The feelings of all girls in love must be much the same; they must feel much the same as they were made love to and abandoned themselves in its consummation. They must feel the same when they were with child; suffer the same pangs when they gave birth; feel the same pain in the swollen breasts and the same delicious ease when they were emptied by the pulling little mouths that clung like leeches to their nipples.

She thought of the partings of women with their men; of their reunions; of the infinite variety of the circumstances of both the partings and meetings, and the infinite resemblance of the emotions—the smiles and tears that must accompany them. Nothing was ever new; nothing ever different; and yet nothing was ever the same. A peaceful glow spread over her. I am so happy, she thought. I could wait for ever. But she knew she would not have to; that she could only think that she could because it was not for ever; and that at any minute she might see those two figures riding along the road towards her.

She was possessed by the wonder of her life—at the extraordinary fact that she was a woman, a wife, and a mother of men; at the whole subtle beauty of her life that was now, in this moment of waiting, revealed in her. Except for Boetie's blindness there had been nothing but goodness and beauty in her life; nothing but love and gentleness and the infinite understanding of her husband, who had stood between her and all hardship, interposing his great body and his slow, careful mind, between her and anything that must have hurt her. To that end since her marriage he seemed to have lived—to temper the winds of a hard life for her, and to encourage and support in those few cases where he had not been able to interpose. It was he who had saved her from despair at Boetie's blindness; it was he who had done everything to make their life at Doornkloof the thing of beauty that it had been. Once he had said so. Once he had said, " It is to this end I live . . . "

And here he was coming back to her. He was on his way. To-night they would be home. There were few arrangements to be made. The stock was already back on Doornkloof. It had been sent there with the Mooiplaas cattle after the veld had been devastated by the springbok. What luck that had been, that apparently covering the world they had not touched their home. Mooiplaas had not been in the centre of their trek, but on the flank.

Dirk was already here; Boetie was coming. Her heart was full. Boetie was a hero, they said; but to her it was still her baby that had been wounded: his wound outweighing his exploit a thousand times. . . .

At last they were coming : a figure, a small one, and a spare led horse. She got up. Her husband was riding his own horse and was leading Boetie on a little grey. The third horse was Starretjie, the bay that Dirk had ridden when he took Boetie from her. Boetie was playing a new flute as he rode. He could not have been doing that if he was sick. Groot Dirk waved his hat. The notes of Boetie's music came to her thinly. Boetie took his flute from his mouth as his father spoke to him. They began to canter, getting bigger and bigger. They pulled up and dismounted.

She was in her husband's arms, Boetie was patting her back as she kissed him. Another meeting had taken place on the Mooiplaas road.

Thousands of such meetings must be taking place all over the land, on the roads and outside the houses. Thousands of women must in these days be meeting men and seeing the pain of their waiting months wiped out by such returns.

Her husband and Boetie was talking to her as she thought of this. They were saying: We are back; it is over. Groot Dirk was asking about the farm; about his dogs. Boetie spoke of his goats . . . she would tell him about them later. Just now she could say nothing but, Yes . . . yes, you are back . . . how good it is to have you back! . . .

Boetie could not wait to show her his wound. It looked terrible, a livid scar; but both he and his father said it was nothing. " And it did not hurt much, Ma." That was foolishness. It was a terrible wound. Boetie told her of the friends he had made; of how he had been given the English fife; of how he loved Paarl, his little grey mare. And then he stopped them to feel Klein Johanna, to see how fat she was. He tickled her; she fell on her back laughing and rolling like a puppy.

" Yes . . . Yes," Tanta Johanna said to everything. They were back— to-night they would go home to Doornkloof. She saw her husband standing like a rock surrounded by the hounds that jumped up at him . . . Boetie sitting on the ground playing the game of stones with his sister . . . Dirk saddling his horse to go courting his Lena, while she cooked them food. " Yes . . . yes," she said. " It is wonderful, and you are back. Thank God, you are back safely."

And then she saw her husband's hat; he still held it in his hand. She looked into his eyes.

" Yes, Johanna, it was near," he said. " But God meant me to return."

CHAPTER XXX

I

IT WAS not till the second day after his return, on his third visit to Mooi-plaas, that Ouma gave anything more than a greeting to Dirk.

Then, as he came in, she said: "Where is his horse? I should have liked his red-roan horse; was he killed too?"

Horse . . . red-roan . . . Stoffel . . . Did she still think he was dead? He had not spoken of him because, with the charge of murder against him, the subject was awkward. And how was it that she had not heard? He had been coming over the night they had moved to Natal, but surely someone should have given her the information. Perhaps having given him up, she had not asked. Perhaps the others had thought, as he did, that the less said about Stoffel the better, since such a subject was painful to all concerned.

"He is on his horse, Tanta Kattie," he said. "I saw him ride off."

"How could he ride off? How can dead men ride?"

"It was a mistake," he said. "He was wounded, not killed, and may come in any day. He was hit in the leg: his bad one."

"That man, the one who came for your horse, said he had buried him on the top of Duifkop. Yes, he lies buried on the Hill of Doves. He described him very exactly, there can be no error—club foot, hair neither dark nor fair, and eyes of the brightest blue."

"That was another man, Ouma: a stranger with a club foot who had come to help us."

"Then he lives," Lena said.

She had been watching them both. It was all most remarkable. But she saw how the mistake could have occurred.

"Yes, he lives. Unless he has died of his leg wound, which seems unlikely. He went to a friend to get nursed."

"Why should he go to friends when he has a home?" Ouma asked. She stood up. "I do not believe it. If he were living and wounded, he would have come to me."

"There were reasons," Dirk said.

Now it would all come out.

"There could be no such reason. It is a lie."

How stubbornly she refused to give up her belief in his death!

"There was a good reason," Dirk said.

410

"Then give it. I demand the reason."

"Very well, if you demand you shall receive," Dirk said. "He is wanted for murder. The murder of an Englishman named Elliot, a captain of the Ninety-Fourth Regiment of Foot, whom he shot as he swam the Vaal. Stoffel feared he would be taken if he returned to his home."

"Another lie, Dirk van der berg."

"It is no lie. When he comes, he will tell you himself, and I was witness, though not party to it."

The night came back to Dirk. The plunging team of bays, the men stripped of their coats ready to plunge—small, white-shirted figures alone in the lightning and road of the storm. He saw the white-capped waters, the great tree come crashing into the spider. He heard the cry, Oh . . . Oh, as Stoffel fired.

"It is true," he said, "but I will say no more."

"Then why did you say nothing before?"

"Because I thought you must have known by now that he lived. And murder is not a pleasant subject for conversation. It is something I wish to forget if I can. Come, Lena," he said, "we will go out."

When they were outside, Lena said: "Tell me, Dirk."

"I would sooner not speak of it. In time you will know. It was a terrible thing to see."

She took his arm. "I understand," she said. "But what you told Ouma is true? He is alive?"

"Yes, I think he is alive."

"And where did he go?"

"I do not know, but to a woman he met in the war, I think."

"She will nurse him?"

"Yes," Dirk said.

And no doubt she would, among other things, and until her husband's return. The thought of that mountain of fat hatching eggs in a dirty bed revolted him.

"Come," he said, "let us walk."

The walk ended beneath the blue gums. They had made a circle away from them, but their feet had brought them circling back.

2

Stoffel rade back slowly. The war was over. His wound was healed, and how lucky it was that he had been hit in his bad leg and not his good one. It made little difference to him—always lame, he was now lamer, but he was used to it. Sarie had nursed him well. She had a heart of gold. She had wept when he left her standing on the stoep while ten little ostrich chicks, prickly as small porcupines, ran about her feet. The storm had not killed the eggs as she had thought it might, and her husband would be pleased. One day he might go and see her again: a good woman with a heart of gold.

Now he was riding home. His duty was done and no man had acquitted himself better than he. At last he had come into his own; acknowledged, not only as the equal of other men, but as superior to them. That was what war did. That was why he had rejoiced in war. With a rifle all men were equal in their power to take life—the dumb, the deaf, the halt, and the lame. Even the blind; he thought of Boetie. Lame . . . before God, why had he been cursed like this? He thought of the marching soldiers, the rooibaajies, the redcoats. How well they had marched! How straight they had stood!

He thought of how he had settled himself comfortably, his rifle barrel resting across his left hand. In a minute he would raise it. In a minute, when they were nearer, the silky, sun-warmed stock of the Mauser would be against his cheek. In his mind he was back at the battle. Then he had begun to shoot, as only he among the Boers could shoot—his bolt moving, opening, and closing as he reloaded: the empty cartridge cases spinning through the air; and each time a man had fallen. Straight young men brought down in heaps by one who was crooked: by one whom, if there had been no war, they would have despised as a weakling; by one that they would have been sorry for.

His sights had been set at three hundred. When they reached that bush, he would shoot. He had paced out the distance. He saw the bush. Their band was playing. Somehow it had pleased him that the band should be playing. They were much nearer now, a thick scarlet line marching down the dusty road. They must be sweating, their faces smeared with dust; their ears, eyebrows, and nostrils clogged with it. He had opened his bolt a little so that the brass cartridge in the chamber was pulled out an inch; he had closed it slowly again. His hand had tightened on the small of the stock. He gripped the reins harder. The officers were mounted. They would go first; then the non-commissioned officers, sergeants, colour-sergeants, and corporals. They would be easy to pick out as they rallied the men.

Then it had come The head of the column reached the bush he was marking, his finger had taken the first pressure on the trigger. It had gone on squeezing; he had fired. The first shot of the war. And the first Englishman had fallen. His roan horse sprang forward as he spurred it.

The accusation of murder meant little to him. As soon as he got back, he would declare his presence to the authorities and claim that he had only just heard of the charge against him. The war was over. If he was tried, it would be by a Boer judge and jury. It had been an accident.

Smit would testify to that. And there had been order to shoot if they tried to come back to the Transvaal or to stay there. He had done no more than put a shot near them. It had been too near, that was all. His real mistake had been not to shoot them both. It was his tender heart that had betrayed him. With both dead there would have been no one to carry complaints to the Government. Nor did he fear Dirk's testimony. It would be Dirk's word against his own; and, besides, if he was going to marry Lena, he would not attempt to clarify the issue too much. No, there was nothing to fear. It had been an accident, and if Dirk had not jerked his arm it would not have happened.

He would soon be home. He wondered if the boys had finished training the new oxen he had bought. Dingaan and T'Chaka should make a good pair. And there were the other two still to be branded. A Kaffir could never brand properly, they had not got the touch.

3

At Doornkloof, Boetie was listening to the boys collecting the Mooi-plaas cattle. They were going back. There had been good rains and the grass the buck had eaten was now up again.

That would have been a wonderful thing to see—a trek of springbok. Lena had told him about it and explained the loss of his goats. They had been carried away like sticks in a flood, she said. But he was glad Witbooi was safe; the others he had not regretted much. In a way he was even relieved, for he had been afraid of leaving them, since it had seemed to him a form of betrayal.

How swiftly things had moved in the last weeks since their return! Dirk's new house was half done. He was building it by the drift at the foot of the mountain. Boetie thought of the return from Mooiplaas. His father and brother had ridden on each side of him. Klein Johanna had been in the cart with Ma and behind the cart had trotted the white mare that Lena had given to him. He had felt his father's excitement as they approached the house. It was almost the first time he had known him moved. Handing over the leading riem to Dirk, he had gone up to ride beside his wife and daughter.

Then had come old Hans' welcome, and his report that all was well. But before that had come the dogs; they had recognized the cart and horses. They had come towards them, a pack in full cry, barking and whimpering with joy; they had nearly bolted the horses as they sprang up to greet them. "My dogs," Pa had said, "my good dogs."

Then there had been the excitement of outspanning and the opening of the house—a great banging of doors and shutters. And Ma's state of horror when she found herself covered with the fleas that had bred within it during her absence.

"I am black with fleas," she had cried. "Oh, Dirk, my skirt is black with them."

"We are all black," Pa had said, laughing, "but it is good to be covered with Doornkloof fleas instead of strange ones."

There had been much laughter and a great brushing of clothes, and Hans had run to the stad to get the women. Before dark the fleas had gone, washed out with soap and water, scrubbed out with brushes, brushed out with brooms; and new dagher had been smeared upon the stoep. Boys had come with wood, milk had been brought, chickens had been killed, eggs collected, and preserves opened. Johanna, who had fallen into a pail of mud and cow dung that one of the girls was spreading, had been washed, and the dogs no longer beat their tails against everything as they followed his father about.

It had been a fine thing to be home. To walk round and round, recognizing each place, each sfell, though some of these were missing since the goat kraal was empty. But they would buy Witbooi some wives, and the flock would begin again. He had heard his mother talking to Pa about the Mooiplaas cockerel.

"That is the one that Tanta Katti sent over just before we left; is it not beautiful?"

"He is beautiful," Pa had answered.

And then in the evening Dirk had got on to Swartkie and had ridden back to Mooiplaas. Every night since then he had ridden over, and during the day he built the house where he and Lena would live. It was set by the drift at the foot of the mountain, and already the walls were as high as one could reach. They were not going to wait till it was finished to marry, because they had already waited overlong. They would stay at Doornkloof till it was done and ready for them.

All that had happened, and more. Those were the big events, but round each was a collection of lesser events, of subtleties and implications. The darkness of war was over. This was the dawn for his brother and Lena, and the day would come in its full glory when they were married, and that was only one day away. Only to-morrow separated them, since the day after they would be united. Already people were riding in from all over the world to celebrate; and for Boetie, it meant that he had only one more day to perfect the tune he was going to play. It was arranged with Dirk that he was to play it by himself without accompaniment and that the guests were to be told that it was his present to the bride and groom—a composition for them alone.

He had said to Dirk, "Being blind, I have nothing to give—no lion skins that I have shot; no money from my work with which to buy something; nothing that I have made with my hands which could give you pleasure. Therefore, I have constructed a tune that I wish to play before all the people."

Now that it was decided, he was afraid. Perhaps he had been overbold and would not be able to play it . . . perhaps it was no good. But Dirk had heard pieces of it and liked them. And if it was good—he had words for it, too, though they were not completed yet—it might be that of all the presents Dirk and Lena received his might be the most lasting. For you could not break a tune or use it up, and if it was good it would not be forgotten. Thus, long after they were all dead—he himself, and Dirk and Lena, all of them—the tune might still go on, sung and played over the land, its origin forgotten, but the music still alive . . . still capable of giving pleasure when it was heard. It would be new the day after to-morrow, but one day men might say, "That is a good old tune . . . I think it was made by a blind musician in the early days."

His mother was calling him.

"Boetie . . . Reuter has come to see you, Boetie."

"Reuter, Ma?" What could he want? Boetie went to the back door. "Reuter?" he said.

"Ja, Bass, it is I."

"You have a message?"

"I have a private message for the Bassie: a communication of some import."

"Come then," Boetie said.

He went towards the empty goat kraal. This was the place where so much of his life had been spent, where he had considered his problems and hidden from the dangers that seemed to threaten him.

"Let us sit," he said.

"I sit, Baas," Reuter said.

"And what is your message?"

"That is a hard thing to say, Baas: a very hard thing. It is a matter upon which I need advice."

"Why do you come to me?" Boetie asked. "It would have been better to go to my father or my brother who are wise, or to your own master."

"They would not understand that which is in my heart," Reuter said. "Indeed, the question refers to my master and to another matter." He paused. "It is the question of my marriage which exercises me. I have after much consideration reached the conclusion that, though there is much to be said for marriage, it would perhaps be a mistake in my case and detrimental both to my reputation and my honour, for who in Zulu-land remembers me to-day? Aaii, who remembers Tabankulu, the eagle? But I seek an alternative and for that purpose I come to you. Listen well, Baasie. Baasie. I am an old man who was once very great, once the terror of the land. I am very old, but still a man and afraid of being alone. It was for this reason that I contemplated marriage with a maid who dreamed of me among the hills of Zululand. But now I doubt my capacity to survive either the ceremonies preceding it or the consummation that must follow it—and that is where the young Baas comes like an elephant out of the forest into the horizon of my desire. Only the young Baas can save me."

"Only I, Reuter? What can I do?"

"It is like this, Baas. Soon I will be alone and masterless. My master is near to his end. He prepares himself. That I know in my heart. He is getting ready, and then where will I be? I will tell you, Baas. I will be alone with none to serve or to love. Now the young Baas is blind, and once he gets off his own veld as helpless as rock rabbit in the open. Now it has come to my ears, as all things come to them, that the Baas is thinking of travelling over the land to make music for the people. In order to do this he will need a servant and a counsellor. Baas, I am come. Baas, behold your servant."

Boetie felt him get up.

"Baas," Reuter said, "I salute you." He sat down again. "I am glad that it is arranged," he said, "that the compact is signed between us, and that henceforth, that is, once my master has gone to his place in hell, I will serve you."

"In hell, Reuter? You should not say that."

"Ja, Baas, it makes me sad to think of it, but my Old Baas has converted me. It happened many years ago, but always since then he has said that hell is where I will go because of my wickedness. I have considered this many times and with much care, and find that the wickedness of my Baas exceeds my own, as is only right, he being white and my superior in every way, even in that of wickedness. Therefore I say when he precedes me to that hot place I will come to the Baas and be his servant and his eyes. The Baas will be safe with me and have the advantage of my great wisdom and experience in the ways of men. Also, since I, too, am old and must before long rejoin my lord, I will find and train for the Baas another servant who will take my place." He clapped his hands together. "It is good to have things settled. And does the Baas think that if I went to the house I would be given brandy? Just a sopie— I have come far and my stomach is cold within me. Aaii, my heart is glad but my belly restless."

"I will think of your words," Boetie said.

"Bass, why think? Why exhaust yourself with speculation about a matter that is finally arranged? Unless I die I shall come to you mounted, and with my spears in my hand. For when the Old Baas dies, I am going to ask for his horse. It is old and of no use to any one, but I like it, and an old horse is better than none.

"Farewell, young master," he said, but he did not move. "I say, farewell, young lord," he said again. "It is time I returned but my belly is too cold to move. It is frozen within me."

"Come," Boetie said, "I will get you a sopie."

At the house his mother gave him brandy for Reuter.

"That is good, Baas. It makes a young man of me, restoring hope and courage. A fine thing has happened for both of us to-day," he said. "The Baas has a servant who is without rival, and I, Tabankulu, whom men previously called Reuter, am saved from a marriage which could only have ended in disaster.

"And there is justice in it," he went on. "It was I who made the Baas his little pipe when he was a child. Now the Baas will play his new one and I will accompany him upon my drum."

He paused and went on:

"The wedding festival will be in two days. I will be there assisting and directing the operations of the servants and ministering to my master," Reuter said. "Till then, when I will see the Baas, I give him greeting. The days to come are in the hands of the Almighty white man's God, and hidden, as a calf is hidden in the womb of a cow elephant that is with young. Truly, young lord, each day, as we live it, is pregnant of to-morrow. Each day is born of the previous night. I see you, Bass . . . I give you greeting once again at our parting . . . greeting till we meet. Baas, I salute you."

"Till I see you," Boetie said.

He stood listening to Reuter's departure and wondering at the queer way things turned out, at the strange pattern of events. How had Reuter learned of his plans, since so few knew them, and was Oom Philippus really so near his end? But Reuter was right; each day that came was the result of the days and the events that had preceded it and was itself the bearer of to-morrow.

4

It was the wedding day. Boetie put on his best clothes that his mother had laid out for him : new leather trousers to replace those he had worn so hard at the war, a blue shirt, a red silk neckcloth, and a fine green hat. His mother had described each thing to him. Dirk was dressing in his best at the same time. This was the last day they would dress together in this room or sleep in it. From now on it would be Lena who shared his brother's life.

"It is your wedding day, Dirk," he said.

"Yes, Boetie, it is my wedding day."

"Then here is my gift to you," Boetie said. He put the knife the

Englishman had given him into his hand. "It is still new," he said, "for I thought it too good to use."

"Thank you, brother," Dirk said. "I will treasure it."

They were going to ride over to Mooiplaas together, and when they went Boetie had a parcel tied to the saddle.

"It is for Lena," he told Dirk. "Thus I will have given each of you a small gift, and for the two of you together there is my song. You do not think it foolish?" he asked. "You do not think it will make the people laugh?"

"They will not laugh, Boetie," Dirk said.

Boetie had often wondered what a wedding was like to someone who could see. He had been to other weddings with Dirk. But they had been nothing. Dirk had not been getting married then. There were great numbers of people, more than he had ever seen at a wedding before. Many of Joubert's men—almost all were here with their wives and children. They kept bringing their wives to him, saying, "This is Boetie van der Berg who led us at Duifkop. Yes," they said, "it was he who is blind who led us up the Hill of Doves in the darkness." Then they all shook hands with him.

The world of Mooiplaas that had become familiar since his stay there was strange with unknown voices and the smell of strange people. The sweat of the backvelders smelt different, perhaps because of what they ate. There was a great smell of women—he was only used to the women he knew; and the smell of many children—milky and sweet. But now suddenly it was silent. There was only the strange composite smell of the people, the shuffling of feet, and the nasal voice of the predikant, Pastor Johan Kruger, a relation of the President.

Boetie listened to Dirk's responses; to Lena's. What a beautiful voice she had—soft and rounded like her body. A voice, too, could sound the way warm bread smelt.

And then it was over. They were man and wife. Now they would be together all the time. Now they were one. Now Dirk need no longer ride over each day, returning as the first cock crowed. Now Swartkie would grow fat again. He had been doing forty miles and sixty miles a day for the last month, being ridden over on some days three times in twenty-four hours. Now Dirk's urgency would be replaced by peace. And now there was nothing to do till evening when the feast would take place and Boetie would play his tune. Till then he would hide. There was so much to think about; and the tune to be perfect must be played over and over. That was best done on the veld. He would go up the spruit where Lena had taken him that day and play it softly beneath the willows where the hammerkop was nesting. By now its young ones must have flown.

They were all outside—a great concourse of people, of men, women, and children. They were firing their guns in the air, the wedding shots. It was the marriage festival of his brother.

Boetie thought of the future. To-day was the end of the present. He had been a child when the war began. He was a man now, and free. He thought of what he had said to Lena : " I do not wish to be a nuisance. And what is a man blind loose about the house and farm? No, Lena. God Almighty chose to make me blind, but He gave me a triumph over those that see, for none can take away my glory . . . It was I who led Joubert's commando. But also He gave me a gift—that of song, of music like unto that of the birds who are also His creation. So I will ride out to make music for my people . . . to make music at their dances and festivals and in their homes. For this they will feed me. A blind man is not a man fully. A blind man with music in his heart is a bird . . . a bird, Lena, thought I shall never see one."

He was going because it was not in his heart to stay.

5

Had such a thing ever been seen before? Tanta Martha wondered. Had a war ever ended with such a marriage feast; had a marriage ever begun with such a war? Had it ever been witnessed by an ancient man who was all but a hundred years of age so that the festivity of the wedding was, in part at least, a festival in honour of his great age and unequalled exploits? For all the world was here, collected at Mooiplaas, Doornkloof, and on other neighbouring farms.

And there were three heroes : the bridegroom; the old one of a thousand battles; and the young blind one—Boetie, the brother of the 'groom, who had led Frans Joubert's commando to victory upon the Hill of Doves. For that reason almost the whole commando was here, two hundred men with few exceptions, together with their wives, children and dependants. The bride and 'groom were almost a secondary consideration, the excuse, as it were, for the rejoicing of a nation in its heroes, in its victory, in its freedom, and its regained flag.

But how many knew this? she wondered. How many understood the significance of their participation in this triple event? How many saw the glorious but obsolescent past tottering to its end, represented only by old Philippus Jacobus, the great man who had outlived the memories of his greatness in the minds of men; or the promise of new generations, in the coming together of Dirk van der Berg and Lena? How many really understood the implication of the flag that waved again? Very few, it seemed to her. Very few who could see the hand of God in Boetie's blindness. Very few who understood anything at all . . . very few who did not see this thing as a pleasure, as a legitimate debauch, as an opportunity for drunkenness and furtive fornications.

Great events took place for little personal reasons . . . the magnificent effect of a thousand small human causes.

Never—and she was an expert in marriages and deaths and births, and the feasts that accompanied them—had there been such a killing of all manner of beasts and fowls, both wild and domestic; never such a bringing of gifts of every kind—things to eat, preserves and dainties; of household goods, linens, furniture, cutlery, and china; never such a variety of livestock as presents to a young bride and her man; for here again was there a dual significance. It was an offering to God for peace. It was a festival of the births that would come about, symbolic of all new births that would compensate for the dead of their people—for those who had died and lay in their scattered graves.

Never had there been such a firing of guns—at least, not since the old days when the world was young, for never since then had so many armed men been gathered together on a private occasion. There were shooting matches. Tanta Martha paused in her work to listen to the shots, by the men who a few weeks ago had been shooting at a living human mark. There were horse races. There had even been a communion, for the predikant had seized his opportunity to declaim a sermon of thanks to the Almighty God and had passed the time, since his arrival in a fine spider drawn by four grey horses, in baptizing those children born in the vicinity since the war had begun.

There was anything here to-day: everything of her people: love-making, trading, the exchange of presents, of promises, even of blows, for in drink men were prone to argument and fighting. And there was drink—wine in barrels from the Cape; brandy of all kinds, grape brandy, peach brandy, prickly pear brandy; Holland's gin, van der hum—for how could a wedding or a victory be celebrated in full sobriety? The living toasted each other and the dead. The tented wagons covered the farm, the veld between them was black with grazing beasts, with draught oxen and riding horses saddle-galled by war. There was a small herd of captured English mares that Groot Dirk had collected by purchase from their captors as a present for his son. There were dogs and dog fights; bitches with pups trailing after them; and children trailing after the fat puppies, who kept picking them up and squeezing them till they yelped, and then putting them down. There were Kaffir servants, Hottentots, and coloured servants, both male and female.

It was a manifestation . . . a swarming of her people, a final clustering of the men, with their families, who had been together in war and were forever joined by the sufferings that had mutually endured.

She had come to Mooiplaas to help with the work of entertainment, and had brought with her half a wagonload of simples, for with so many gathered in one place there were bound to be many sick. They came to her in the mornings and she ministered to them. Men with headaches from their drinking, with bruises from fighting, both white men and black. Women, with those ills peculiar to women; young girls, old crones, sleek wives with fat babies cradled against their breasts. For ten days this multitude had been collecting.

Never had she been more content. Never had she seen such beauty. For here only was full beauty to be perceived, in the fruitfulness and communion of a people united by blood, by race, by language, belief, and creed.

And among the many who were here was the Cornishman, Tom Tryolla . . . She smiled as she thought of his corns. They were better now, but would always trouble him, having been too long neglected. She laughed. A man with corns was like a cat with buttered feet—likely to stay at home.

Nothing was the fault of any one. Everything worked itself out according to ends that were inscrutable. A fine day and something would not have happened . . . or a wet one. As the white ants flew after a storm and lost their wings in frail piled heaps against the doors and windows, so did things happen. Tanta Martha as she worked thought of men and women and their strange relationships: of man's foolishness. Because a woman had lain with him he assumed her surrender, not seeing that it was his. What fools men were in thinking that they chose the moment! Like birds they came to the net of the fowler . . . the thighs of a woman the limed twigs set to catch their vanity. Trick by trick they had so few to set against a woman. And it was all wonderful: all love, all hate . . . and those who were bound by either were bound for life. They would return to each other, to the ones they hated, as much as to the ones they loved. To the enemies as much as to the friends, enmity being more permanent than love. And out of this came their search for happiness, for what Meneer Tryolla called the golden fleece, though she had never heard of a golden sheep, only the golden calf did she know; but he was wise and must be right.

Happiness, she thought. How vague it was, how it changed with age! For a woman, in youth, it was a man. Then it was children; and later, if you lived widely, it was all men, all children, and out of that great love for all human things, all living things, came real happiness, with tolerance and the greatest of all virtues—a capacity for gentleness.

Her thoughts brought tears to her eyes. It was wonderful, this strange mixture of feelings, hopes, and fears that made humanity; wonderful to see it operating, as a yeast worked in bread, among the many assembled here. To see it in Dirk's love for Lena, in the high hopes of their beginnings; to see it in old Philippus Jacobus's resignation, in his happiness at the near completion of the task of living. Wonderful to see it in the open, smiling faces of children, as trustful as puppies; in the wide, seeking eyes of the girls who stepped like buck, aware, and waiting for the love that must come to them from one side or another . . . turning their heads, as they sniffed for the wind of appreciation. Wonderful, in the young mothers, cushion-soft and gentle, with their milk.

It was all here: everything; and she was a part of it. There could be no more than this. There could only be variations of it, in any place, in any land, at any time.

She turned to her work again—the baking of great pies, of pastries, the roasting of meat, the setting-out of food, the cooking of innumerable vegetables and fruits. She smiled as she thought of the feast to-night, at the great eating there would be and at the great purging that must follow it. She smiled because she had so well prepared. Five hundred, they said. She had purges for a thousand.

She thought of Tom Tryolla again, of how he had come to her when the commando had ridden in. He had come to her house with his two donkeys and his borrowed horse. He had stayed at her house despite the scandal that his visit had caused, while she attended to his feet; and then had come the wonderful evening that might yet change her life.

She had asked him if he sang.

"Do you sing, Meneer Tryolla?" she had asked.

"I sing seldom," he said.

"But do you?"

"Why have you never asked me before, Tanta Martha?" he said, and she had answered:

"It never occurred to me to ask you before. I never thought of you that way. It has come upon me suddenly. It is all this talk of weddings."

"I sing," he said. "Once I sang a great deal—when I was young."

"When I was young I sang much too. I sang like a bird in a tree," she had said, and had gone on to ask about his voice. "What is your voice, meneer? It is not tenor, is it?"

"I sing bass."

"I was afraid you might be a tenor. No woman can be happy with a tenor. A baritone is fair, but for a real man give me bass. Bass," she repeated dreamily as she stirred a pot. "I could be happy with another man who sang bass." Yes, that was what she had said.

"Would he have to sing continually?" he had asked.

"He need not sing at all," she had told him. "It is just the idea of the thing: the knowledge that if he sang it would be bass."

Life was beautiful as it rose about her, fomenting like wine. The people, the noise, the beasts, the cooking, the coming and going, were intoxicating.

Tanta Kattie was working beside her. They stopped to have coffee.

"How good it tastes!" Tanta Kattie said. "For a while I gave it up. I thought it was bad for me."

Stoffel came into the kitchen for a glass of cordial. Tanta Stephanie, her face swollen with tears, was eating great mouthfuls of cake while she re-read the letter her friend in Java had written to her; it had just come. He had married another woman, a girl of eighteen, which Stephanie said was not only deceitful but indecent—an old man like him lusting after such young flesh. "He wrote me a poem before we parted," she kept repeating, "and gave me a lock of his hair." Then she cut more cake and twisted her curlers tighter. No, Stephanie was no help at all, but she was funny to watch.

Everything was nearly ready now. Joubert was going to make a speech and then they would feast and dance. Long ago—how long it seemed!—Tanta Martha had told Lena she would dance at her wedding. Now she was going to dance with Tryolla. He asked her to: which just showed how your good acts were rewarded. If I had not almost cured his corns, she thought, he could not have danced. And he would be surprised at her agility. A big woman was often very light upon her feet— there were few bigger than she, and none so light. To-night she would dance like a fairy; to-night her happiness would put wings upon her heels.

6

They were shouting for Lena. It was nearly dark. Lena van der Berg! ... Lena! ... Lena! Come, Lena! Everybody seemed to be calling. Lena went towards the big shed. What could it be? Why did they want her? It was too soon for the great feast; that of midday was scarcely digested yet.

When she went in they all shouted : "Here she is! Here is the bride!"

Dirk came to her and took her hand. Boetie was alone on the musicians' platform.

Frans Joubert stood up and went towards him. When he reached him, he put his hand upon Boetie's shoulder.

"Friends," he said, "kerels, women and maids of this district, I have the honour to present my friend Boetie van der Berg, the blind hero of Duifkop, whom you all know. He has asked me to say a few words and express those sentiments which he finds himself unable to voice. This is the occasion of the wedding of his brother and comrade, Dirk van der Berg, to Lena du Toit. He wishes me to say that, being blind and without either possessions or the capacity to earn money with which to buy presents, he has made a tune for the bride and bridegroom. He says this is his gift, and the only thing he can give which is truly his own. He asks you to remain quiet while he plays it. And I, who had the honour to command Boetie van der Berg in the field, take this chance of announcing the fact that he has been pronounced a full burger of the Republic with all rights and privileges, despite his age of fourteen, by the Volksraad for his services in the war; and that any one who does not pay full attention to his tune, who coughts, spits, shuffles his feet, or scratches himself, will have the men of Joubert's commando to contend with when it is over."

He patted Boetie's shoulder. "Play, brother," he said. "It is fitting that you should play to-night—a burger of the Transvaal and the brother of the 'groom."

There were tears in the commandant's eyes when he got down. The burgers, burnt black and still heavily bearded from the war, glared round at any one who moved. They dared their own children, held by their wives, to cry or fidget. Certainly Beotie was beloved. Certainly no boy before in the history of the land had received such honour or was held in such respect.

Lena sat with her hand in Dirk's. Both were afraid for Boetie. "I hope he does not lose his spit," Dirk whispered.

Boetie had been trembling, but suddenly he stopped. He seemed to grow bigger as he raised his long black fife.

"He has not lost it," Dirk said softly. "I can see."

The music came softly, so softly at first that you hardly heard it. First you thought you heard music, at first you were unsure if you heard it. Then you knew he was playing. The music was coming from Boetie— beautifully. His fingers moved along the stops, flickering like butterflies, pausing, leaping as the music rose louder and louder, and then it fell again. You saw the march of men . . . you heard the drag of tired hoofs; you saw the battle, crisp and sharp, and heard the cry of wounded men. Then came the triumph, the march back. Here was great beauty: all beauty, it seemed to Lena. His little tune made her feel Dirk's kisses on her lips, made her see the dart of a kingfisher, orange and blue, into the dark water of a pool. How tenderly he played! She saw children now playing in the shade, running and shouting with laughter. And then he stopped. It was over.

Boetie had played his tune. She had received her present: the greatest gift of all: greater even than Groot Dirk's gift of English mares. Every-one was cheering and shouting.

Tanta Martha looked from Lena to the others. She looked at the old ones and the young. At Oupa, who had been brought in on his chair by Reuter. How far back into the past the lives of some here stretched! Oupa had been born in seventeen-eighty-five—ninety-five years ago. She herself and Stephanie and Aletta were the next generation; Ouma Katarina du Toit the next. And after her, skipping one, since none of it were left, came Lena and her brothers: Lena, now eighteen in eighteen-eighty. In nineteen hundred she would still not be old, only thirty-eight—she would not be old till forty years later. In nineteen hundred and forty she would be old; then she would be eighty-eight—an old woman waiting her end, if she had lived so long, but able to look back to this day of her marriage where her memories would touch on Oupa, she being one of the last alive who would have seen him. And she would have children and grand-children and great-grandchildren, some of whom would live to the year two thousand if the world did not come to an end before it.

This wedding and the feast was a junction place, as all places were in a lesser degree, of the past and the future. It was a time to be remem-bered and one that would be spoken of in years to come—a memorable occasion. There would be births and deaths, there would be great changes and more wars, but the blood would go on. The blood that was here, trickling through Oupa's veins and coursing through Lena's, would go on without fail. There was no end to life, or to living, for as one fell dead another came to life. She looked at a dog that had just come to seek its master. The riem with which it had been tied was bitten through and hung from its neck. It was a big grey Boer hound, a descendant of those dogs that had defended the homes of her people since they had come from Holland in sixteen-fifty-two. There would still be such dogs in the year two thousand. His blood would go on with the blood of the men and women—his life, that stretched back like theirs into the past, would go on into the future. The dog, as much as the man, was a symbol of God, of life.

It brought tears to her eyes to think of the magnificence of God's plan of its illimitable beauty, of its scope, of His great love for all living things, and the powers He gave to men of love, of courage in adversity, of charity. I am one of those who have seen His wonders, she thought. I am like Tanta Anna de Jong who taught me. We have seen much death, closing the eyes of many, covering them with copper coins to hold them to; but we have stared into them first, and we have delivered many women of their children and stared into those small eyes too. It is there, in the new born and the new dead, that the wonder lies, for their eyes are blank, dazzled by God, from whom they have come, or to whom they return when their time is done . . . And in the eyes of young lovers, young men and women, their eyes starlike with the passion of their desire, their breasts heaving with the life that God gave them to spend upon each other, and not to hoard. To those who looked, the world, with its people, its beasts and trees and flowers and mountains, was beautiful beyond compare, for in all things there was life, in all things was God and His will apparent—even in Stephanie.

7

What a day it had been! Lena thought. My wedding day. What an event! What a week of people coming, of congratulations and presents of all kinds! She thought of Boetie's song and his coming to-day riding the old grey Mooiplaas mare, leading Meisie, one of his father's horses, that would take him safely home. He had come to bring his present to her—the big shell that if you held it to your ear made a sound of rushing waters. It was one of his most treasured possessions, but he had apologized for it, since he said it had cost him nothing. But he had said he had something else for her as well. It was a secret; only Dirk knew about it. That had been his tune. And to Dirk he had given his knife with the many blades and the corkscrew and the instrument for picking a stone from the hoof of a horse when it got stuck in the frog.

She thought of the other things she had been given : the dishes and plates, cups, saucers, beakers, pots, pans; cocks and hens, cattle, sheep, horses and goats. The Doornkloof cradle, that was to stand waiting in their house as soon as it was finished, had been sent over by Tanta Johanna. Perhaps it would not have to wait overlong. She smiled. Dirk had been back a month. It had taken that time to prepare for so great a festival, to send out the invitations, to cook, slaughter, and pre-pare. She thought of the joke Joachim, Dirk's uncle, had made at the feast about a christening he had once attended. Someone had said the baby was wonderful for such a short-time child . . . "Ja, very fine and well formed for one who had come so early, making his appearance after only seven months of marriage. 'Early indeed,' the proud father cried. 'The baby is not early, it is a full-time child; it is just that the wedding was a little late.' And who do you think the father was?" he had shouted to the whole company as his wife tried to pull him down. "I was the father."

Then Adriaan Klopper had brought his present, a big packing case to be opened. "It is a strange delicacy," he said, "that was captured from the English and that we saved, Barend and I, for the first feast we should attend. An officer, a prisoner, told me how delicate and rich they are, thought I have never seen the contents of the box. He told me to keep them carefully, as such things have never been seen in Africa before." The box was pried open. It was full of cans. He opened a can and tipped out the contents on a plate; he smelt it. "Magtig," he said, "what is it? a klein voel pentz . . . Before God, what are the English who think the stomachs of little birds that stink of fish good eating? And to think that we have carried them hundreds of miles under our bed. To think of that."

"Let me see," someone said. He was the guest of a guest, a Hollander and part of the administration, much respected for his knowledge of the world and education. He poked the plate with his finger and began to laugh. "Those are not little birds' bellies," he said. "The officer was right. They are oysters, canned oysters, and rare."

"You can have them, meneer," Klopper said, "though I brought them for the bride. You may be right about them, too, but to us simple men they are the bellies of little birds which it is not our custom to consume."

Having said this, he left the plate on the table and turned to Baruch to ask him if he grew tobacco and what varieties he found the best. It had been very funny: very wonderful: the greatest day of her life.

The wedding was over: and the feast, though she could hardly believe it. And now she was dancing with Dirk, her husband. How beautiful it all had been!—like a dream. To be in Dirk's arms was like a dream too. She had dreamed of it so often. And she had been right about the plant; it had gone on growing and had ten leaves now and two little branches. Suppose I had not tended it so well, she thought. One day soon, when they had their house, she would plant it out, and then again one day, when many days had passed, they would sit in the shadow of that tree, sit there in the evening of their lives when they had grown old together.

She thought of Dirk's coat, the one he had worn to come courting her. Now she would be able to move the button forward; it was her right . . . And her dress. Every one said how beautiful it was. It swirled out away from her as Dirk swung her. She thought of the last time she had worn it, which was also the first time, at Brennersdorp on the eve of the battle. She thought of the many times she had looked at it, taking it out and folding it away again. And of her shoes of bronze leather. No one had seen that one of them was scuffed.

But it was as she had thought it would be: Dick had not noticed the dress. He had said she was lovely, that she was his heart. He had told her of the star he had tried to get her in a bucket. Dirk . . . how she loved him; how happy they would be! His ring was on her finger, his arm about her waist. She was his wife.

How hot it was! Her clothes were sticking to her body. She could hardly see the other dancers for the dust that rose from the floor. Only when they came near could she recognize them. There was Hester Marais now with a strange man, one of Joubert's commando. How good every one had been! What presents and gifts they had received; what congratulations!

They were passing the raised platform that held the musicians. And there on the right, playing his fife, was her dear brother Boetie, his blind blue eyes staring straight into her own. She pressed Dirk's hand.

"It is good to see Boetie. And how beautifully he played his tune for us!" she said.

The horse from Mooiplaas that she had given him made him indepen-
dent in his going and coming from Doornkloof. Everything was wonderful; everything was good.

She thought of the nights she had spent with Dirk under the tree: the
happy place, as Boetie called it. She was glad it had first happened there
under the stars. It was both right and beautiful. Perhaps not right, she
thought, since they had not been married then, but it had been beautiful,
and now they were married. She thought of the stars, the leaves and the
limb of the tree that pointed to the north. Nothing could make it really
wrong.

And Dirk had tried to get her a star in his bucket. It was for this she
had been born—to love Dirk and be loved by him. Everything was good
and beautiful to-night. Even Stoffel was back, recovered of his wound
and contemptuous of the charges against him which he said, now that
the war was over, would not be pressed home; and Ouma was happy.
Only Oupa worried her. She must leave Dirk and go to him again in a
minute. In the last weeks he had changed for the worse.

"I must go to Oupa now, Dirk," she said. "I promised to go and
see him."

CHAPTER XXXI

THE RUSTLE OF WINGS

I

LENA stood with her hand on the door of his room looking at her great-grandfather. He did not see her. His eyes were blank with the weak innocence of age which, having seen all things, has forgotten all things. He was beyond anger now; a faint querulousness was his nearest approach to it, and this only over small matters, for the great no longer concerned him—if his pap was too hot or too cold; his palate had gone and flavour was nothing to him; if the flies worried him, it was a disaster for true disaster now passed him by. He was beyond it.

He was almost immune to pain, since he now suffered it continuously, and even his memory had failed him. Lena had sometimes thought recently that it must have been his memory that had supported him. He could no longer tell her tales of his youth or of his loves, his hates, his hunting of beasts, his killings of men, were now suddenly confused. For many years he had lived on in this world of memory, reliving his life; and now, at last, these, too, had failed him, had faded, getting thinner and thinner, more misty and tenuous; the faces and the facts more elusive and harder to arrange. Chronology defeated him. Women long dead gave birth to the men who had been their lovers. Fact and fiction became sheer fantasy, and slowly, in the last weeks, as none listened to him, he had lapsed into a drooling silence.

No longer a man, but a gaunt frame of bones, hung with thin flesh and draped in a wrinkled hide : something that she and Reuter moved into the sun when it was cold or into the shade when it was hot—if they remembered, and sometimes they did not. It was hard to think that once he had been great, a name on the Border, the friend of heroes and the father of a multitude.

There were wounds on his skin—bullet wounds, the scars of spears, the wounds and the marks of hurts taken from wild beasts. Not once but a hundred times had he escaped death. But even his wounds, though he tried to show them, he had forgotten, and was no longer clear as to how he had come by them, though his skin was as mottled with scars as a lion cub with spots.

None lived who remembered him as he had been. Time had flowed past him, as a river flows past a rock in its bed. Had he died sooner his reputation would have lived longer. Shrouded in mystery songs would have been made of his deeds, but living he had stolen his own thunder, and only to Reuter was he still great. To him, this old wreck of a man, this living, brainless skeleton, was still the Groot Baas, the mountain under whose shadow he had lived so long.

True, there was his charge. But the story had got out of how his horse had bolted—of his drunkenness on English brandy. And the world preferred a young hero to an old one. Why waste respect and love on one so nearly dead? Philippus Jacobus du Toit, hunter, fighter, voortrekker, was displaced by Boetie van der Berg, the blind burger, musician, and leader of Joubert's commando at the battle of Duifkop. Perhaps it was right that the young must replace the old, but it was sad.

He saw her suddenly. It was as if, being dead, he had come to life. His eyes flickered with recognition as he turned his head.

" I will put you to bed now, Oupa," she said.

" Ja, put me to bed." She took off his shoes.

" To-night you will be a wife, my Lena," he said.

" I am a wife now, Oupa. You saw me married."

" I have seen so many people married," he said, " and I have been married so often. But I did not say that. I said to-night you would be a wife. To be married is not to be a wife. You will like it," he said. " You come of hot blood. The van der Berg blood is good, and your children will have it on two sides. Cousins," he said; " magtig, that nonsense about its being bad. If the blood is good, then the stock is good, even if it is mother to son or father to daughter or brother to sister."

" That is wrong, Oupa. Such things are not permitted."

" I speak of cattle and horses, Lena. Though if it is good with them, it should be good for men too. And I have seen it with men. There was Potgieter. He lived with his three daughters and had sons by all of them. I knew them all. They were my friends."

" That was in the old days, Oupa." It was weeks since he had spoken so clearly.

" Ja, in the good old days. But it is no good talking of them to women. Bring me my bottle," he said.

" Your dop, Oupa? You know you can't have that. You have had your sopie."

" Magtig, girl, it is a wedding, or have you forgotten? You are going to sleep with Dirk, and you deny your great-grandfather his bottle. I get much happiness out of it. Dop is sugar to the vinegar of my life with Kattie and that Stephanie."

They stopped talking to listen to the music of the dance that came in through the window, both turning their heads towards it.

" Before God, I sometimes think my son Johannes must have died happy. What is a Kaffir spear to her tongue? Only their fish spears are barbed. Now bring me the bottle and a glass and leave me, Lena. I wish to think."

She brought it.

"And you are not to smoke your pipe, Oupa," she said. "Because you may sleep and set yourself alight again."

"Send Reuter to me. I would have my servant with me. I wish to speak with him. And kiss me, Lena. Kiss your Oupa well and believe that he wishes you luck—all the luck in the world. Now dance, Lena, dance; be happy, and call your first son Philippus."

"He will be Philippus Jacobus," Lena said. "Ja, he will be named for you."

She wanted to leave him, he had asked her to go. He wanted to be alone. But she did not know how to go. I ought to stay, she felt; I ought not to leave him.

She ran to his bed, kneeling beside it. "Good-night, Oupa." She kissed him again. He stroked her hair. His fingers were so wrinkled that they caught in it as he passed them over her head. To-morrow, she thought, I must cut his nails. He hated to have them cut with scissors; he liked to pare them with his hunting knife, but could no longer do it.

"Good-night, my little heart," he said, "my beautiful. You will breed fine sons, new sons to our race. Now call my servant."

She went to call Reuter; he was never far away. But Oupa stopped her.

"Do not go for a minute, Lena," he said. "Do not go, for I would look at you. You are a mooi meisie. One day you may be beautiful if you get more fat on your flanks and croup. But all women are less fine to-day."

She kissed him again, but as she went back to the barn she was uneasy. There had been something strange about Oupa to-night. His mind had been too clear—there had been no confusion in his words. She thought of his expression when she had gone into his room, before he had seen her. What had he been thinking as he stared at the wall with blank eyes? What was he preparing to do? And he had kissed her, that old look had been back on his face . . . the old hunter's look, the peacock look, the look of an ancient mischievous child; and there had been a little smile on his lips. Was he going to get himself drunk again? Had Reuter been stealing rich food for him?

And now that she was leaving Mooiplaas, who would take care of him? Who would tuck him in his bed, undress him, give him his dop? To whom would he talk? She had said she must cut his nails to-morrow, but to-morrow she would be gone. It was her wedding day—that was why there was music and dancing.

Poor old Oupa . . . Name your first son for me, he said. Her first son . . . theirs . . . Would he, too, one day be old like the man he was named for? Had Oupa ever been young, a baby at his mother's breast? It was hard to think of that—of him sucking at his mother, nearly a century ago; of him a young man, a husband, a father begetting himself sons. surviving them and many of their children, living on when all were dead, a legend and an ancestor.

Her feet were tapping the ground as she walked. How gay the music sounded!—the fiddles, the concertinas, and the high note of Boetie's fife. Surely he must get tired blowing and blowing.

Dirk was at the door to meet her.

" He is all right?" he asked. " You were so long."

" He is all right," Lena said. But was he? she wondered. He seemed almost too well. " He wants our first son named for him, Dirk," she said.

" He could be named after no greater man."

They began to dance.

2

As soon as the door was shut, Philippus lit his pipe and filled his glass. Well, it had come. He would not live to be a hundred. He would not outlive that girl. He would not hold another little Philippus Jacobus on his knee. What a number of them there had been, and none of that name but him alive. Perhaps Reuter was right, and names were unlucky. But luck changed if you played boldly—and this one, this new Philippus Jacobus, would be great. He felt it in his heart. He would be conceived to-night while he . . . unless he was already on the way, which would be better—more fitting than the one should overlap the other who with a margin of a month or so.

And there were signs that this had happened. His little Lena had that sleek look that he had seen so often. The wide curiosity of the maiden was gone. Her eyes were no longer quick with desire. They were soft with dreams . . . satisfied with knowledge. She had not started like a a buck when he had said : "To-night you will sleep with Dirk." No, there were no more surprises for her.

And what could be more natural? Before God, such things were the most natural in the world—that men and women, male and female, so fashioned, should act according to their special ends. A young man, straight back, strong and hard from war; a waiting maiden, and the warm nights of Africa. Could circumstance be more neatly contrived, more delicately adjusted? And they were going to name the first child for him. He was suddenly comforted. He was not going to be able to have him on his knee, but they had met—the old Philippus Jacobus and the young one. He had been in the room to-night lying curled beneath his little Lena's belt. His waiting had not been in vain.

He smiled. How beautiful she was, like a young mare that soon would have a foal at foot. And it was good of her to help him on her wedding night. A good girl, but too tidy. Still she did not know what he knew—that this was the last time she would kiss him. He had known it suddenly when she was in his room. That was why he had said, " Do not go for a minute. Do not go, for I would look at you." As he stared at her he had seen his wives before him—all fine women, but none strong enough to live with him.

Reuter shuffled in rubbing the sleep from his eyes and dragging his sheepskin karos behind him.

" The Baas wanted me?" he said.

" Yes, I want you, Reuter."

" What is it that the Baas wants? I was asleep."

" I want you to dress me when I have smoked my pipe and had my dop."

" Dress you? But it is late. Where are we going?"

" You are going to dress me, Reuter. You are going to give me my old roer and my powder-horn and my bullets."

" Ja, Baas, and then what do we do?"

" We are old, Reuter. It is in my heart we are old enough. We are going to go out to die."

" Then I can die with the Baas? The Baas would not mind?"

" Ja, you can die with me, Reuter, as you have lived with me, and I have left a letter. I have written that we are to be buried together side by side. I wish my wives and you beside me on the veld on the other side of the graveyard fence, since you are black and cannot lie with white men."

" Baas, can I do one thing before we begin?"

" What is it, Reuter? Magtig, you are never satisfied. Never once since I took you has anything been enough. First my wives, and then you. All my life I have been plagued by someone."

" It is a small thing," Reuter said.

" What is it you want? I will not give you any dop. I will not die with a drunken Kaffir. I want to die drunk by myself. I have given this matter much thought."

" I would not drink the Baas's dop. But if the Baas is to die in his war clothes I would prepare too. I would get my spears and my shield. I would get my plumes and the ornaments on my legs. I have carried them for many years in my locked box."

" Ja, that is good, Reuter. Get them and then come back to dress me. That is the way it should be. We will die on the veld with our weapons. We will die as men with such dignity as to create a scandal."

" And Reuter," Philippus went on, " what of the maid in Zululand who dreamed about you? Why did you tell me such a great lie?"

" It was no lie, Baas, and why should a young maid not dream of me?

She would not be the first, and someone must be the last, though I have put her trom my mind."

"Then you were not lying, Reuter?"

"Baas, I was not lying."

"Magtig, Reuter, you make me angry with your inconsistencies. First you lie and then you do not lie. How am I to know what to believe? I am accustomed to believing you a liar, and then you do this."

"The Baas is right. That is what I have found out. To lie all the time is as bad as to tell the truth all the time. It is pointless. Then men knowing the habit of your mind can calculate your actions and base their conclusions on your veracity or lack of it. But to really verneuk people one must tell great truths and great lies alternately. This is an art that I have acquired, though only somewhat late in life."

"You mean you would have gone on doing it?"

"Ja, Baas. I have acquired the habit and it works."

"Now go, Reuter. You make me glad to die. Before God, you have forced it upon me before my time with the irritations you cause me."

What luck it was that it should come to-night! That death should pick so opportune a moment! Not only was a great concourse of people gathered here, unknowingly, to be witness to his end, but being occupied with festivities they would allow him to complete his plan in peace. Yes, it was all most convenient . . . providential as everything else in his life had been. It would save them trouble, too, being gathered here for Lena's wedding. They would just stay on to bury him instead of having to come back later. He had never liked to give people trouble and his death would be as consistent as his life: as well and as dramatically planned: a fitting end and a scandal that would never be forgotten.

When Reuter came back, he was nearly naked. In the light of the lamp his body shone with oil. He was wearing a head-dress of black ostrich plumes, a little mantle of black ostrich plumes covered his shoulders and a kilt of wildcat tails hung about his loins. In his hand he carried a black-and-white ox-hide shield, as tall as himself, two long assegais, a short stabbing spear, and a kerrie. He raised his right hand.

"Bayete," he said. "Bayete inkos, we go forth to die."

"Ja, Reuter. It is like the old days when I took you, to see you like that. I did not know you still had your war-clothes."

"Baas, I have kept them always and replenished them." He put his hand to his kilt. "But the moths have got into my rooikat tails." He picked it up. "See, Baas, the way they have damaged it? Those are the best ones, and now I have to wear them behind." He began to shuffle his feet and clash his spears against his shield. He was chanting. He gave a little leap into the air. "Look at that, Baas," he said. "And to think that once I could leap as high as a man."

"That is the uniform of the Blue Horizon, Reuter?"

" Ja, Baas. It is the uniform of my regiment. The Blue Horizon . . . the drinkers of blood, the eaters-up of men. My spears are hungry. Aaii . . . aaii, my spears are hungry. They call to me."

" Get me up, Reuter, I am drunk. I do not know why it is so long since I was really drunk. This is the first time since we went visiting."

" It was the women, inkos—the women who stood between you and the bottle, as they stand between men and all pleasures. For women there is only one reasonable pleasure, only one that they can understand, and that is women. Though that is nice, too, when one is young."

He leaned his spears and shield against the wall and pulled his master up.

" My shoes, Reuter. My coat. Now get my belt, the heavy one, and my long knife. My bullet-pouch and my silver-mounted powder-horn. Now get down the biggest gun and give me my hat." Philippus stood straight, swaying a little on his heels. " It is good, Reuter," he said. " Magtig, we have been fools to let them manage us so long."

" But this time they cannot manage us. This time we go forth to die. This time go forth to kill," Reuter chanted. " We go for blood . . . for women . . ."

" Stop, you fool. Do you want them to come in? Magtig, Reuter, if they came they would send me back to bed. It would be shameful. Come, let us go; and do not forget my saddle."

" Let us go, Baas. Can the Baas walk alone?" Reuter picked up the saddle.

" All my life I have walked alone."

They went to the door. Reuter stooped down to pick something else up from the floor.

" What is that?"

" It is my karos. I am taking it with me. Shall I take a blanket from the Baas's bed? Shall I bring the Baas's best karos, the one of silver jackal skins, or the rooikat?"

" I need no karos. Come, Reuter."

" It will be cold, Baas. Our blood is thin and we shall be cold out there."

" Come, I say. Blow out the lamp and come."

They went out slowly. Philippus was a little puzzled. Where would they go? That was the question. They could not go far. It was strange how heavy the gun seemed; yet he had carried it hundreds of miles in his hand and slung over his shoulder. Now the gun was heavier than a dead buck.

They would go to the blue gums. No one would find them there. He thought of the day he had planted them.

The light filtered down upon them through the trees. It struck the barrel of his gun; it shone on Reuter's spears. It was good to be on the veld again at night. Up there—he looked at the north—was the bush-veld that he loved. Up there lions were roaring as they hunted; seacows were sliding down their runways into the water, zebras were snorting; up there wild beasts were running with switching tails.

He felt very near to them. This would do. There was a nice bank here.

" We will stop here, Reuter."

" Ja, Baas. Shall I make the Baas a fire?"

" Do you want every one to come and see why there is a fire?"

" No, Baas, but it will be cold. Before dawn it will be very cold. I will make a little one."

" Do you understand what we are coming out to do, Reuter?"

" Baas, we are come out to die. But why must we die cold?"

" Arrange the saddle for my head and then lie down and keep still."

" Ja, Baas."

Philippus lay down. Reuter, rolled in his karos, lay beside him. A nightjar passed over them. It was good to be out here among the birds and beasts again. To be out of the house. Before God, he was sick of houses.

He was not going to outlive Kattie. But his death like this would make a fine scandal. They would say: "An old man like that should have been watched—should have been taken care of . . . " It would be something she would never be able to live down. He sighed with satis-faction. He thought of Lena again. Dirk van der Berg was a fine young man. He would see that Lena was not verneuked by her brothers when they shared the stock. They would pick them alternately, drawing a card for the first choice; then they would go on picking till everything was divided. And the boy's blood was good. The grandnephew of Hendrik the voortrekker. A bad man, they said now, but a great leader and a bold one.

He thought of the blood lines of the child that would be conceived to-night as he died, if it was not already on the way. And if not to-night, then soon. The little Philippus Jacobus. There was his own blood, and none was better than that; and the van der Berg blood; and the van Reenan blood through Sannie van Reenan and her daughter Jacoba, who was Lena's mother. It was a pity that there was none of Swart Piet's. But perhaps Jacoba was his child after all; there had been talk of it at the time. That would be a good strain, a fine addition.

He thought of his own wives—of Helena. Of Gertruida—had she been tall and dark, or was she fair, and had Elizabeth been dark? . . . of Whilhelmina. Of their children, of the lives he had lived with them. With each woman a man lived a different life. But only Helena had he loved. Helena had been his darling. He would soon see them now . . . and their children. Of all those children nothing was left but Lena, the rest was rubbish. Stoffel was no good. He could not understand being an ancestor of Stoffel's. He had thrown back to some other no-good breed. , Philippus began to worry. What would he say to Helena about those other women he had married? What would he do if they all claimed him?—their claims were legal. No marriage or giving in marriage . . . The Book said that, but with women you could never be sure. Still, he would not be alone. There would be precedents; there were other men dead who had married again, though few as often as he. In this as in so many other things he was special, a law unto himself. It was a pity he had not lived to be a hundred. If I had been more careful I could have done it, he thought.

It had been a mistake to go to war again. But then how could you help it if the war came on to your farm—if, sitting on the stoep, you heard the sound of guns? Must a man forgo all pleasures? A man was like the warhorse in the Book of Job. He ran when he heard the shouting of the captains.

Helena had known Gertruida, but Elizabeth had been a child when she died, and Wilhelmina not yet born. It would all take some explaining. But it would be good to see his friends again : Paul Pieters, Hendrik van der Berg, Swart Piet, Coenraad Buys, Christiaan van Ek, and the others. They would say : " Good-day, Philippus, we have waited a long time for you to come." Then they would rattle the quills of their wings with pleasure. How would you carry a gun on your back if you had wings?

Music was coming from the big shed. Why was there music? Ah, yes, little Lena was being married. How could she be married when she was only a baby? He must get up and stop it. But the music was beautiful . . . it was good to listen to it out here under the trees.

Reuter was moving. What did he want? Why must he always disturb him?

" What is the matter, Reuter? Why can you not stay still?"

" My feet are cold, Bass."

" Magtig, we are here to die, what does the cold matter?"

" I am not sure, Baas, about this dying. You see, I do not know about being buried."

" You are never satisfied. Forty years of it and you must still complain. It is as I said in the beginning, you have discontented nature. Have I not made plans for you to be buried beside me? What more can you want?"

" I am not sure I want to be buried, Baas. I have been thinking about it. If I am buried, who will open my belly to let out my spirit?"

" Open your belly, Reuter? No one will. You will be buried like a Christian. Have I not converted you many times? You are a Christian, I tell you."

" Ja, Baas, but I am not quite so much a Christian as I thought. My back is very Christian. Ja, Baas, you certainly beat Christianity into my back. It understands all about the Inkos Jesus and the great chief, his father, who ate up the world with a great flood when his impis failed him. Ja, he was a great and terrible chief. The kind I would delight to serve. But my belly is not Christian at all. It wants to be opened up with a spear as is our Zulu custom, and lie out on the veld so that it is consumed by the beasts and the great birds, so that my spirit may go free."

"We are here to die, Reuter. You should have thought of all this sooner."

"Ja, Baas, I am sorry. But the Baas decided very suddenly and my feet are cold. Is the Baas sure we could not make a fire? Just a little one like we used to? Then we could lie with our feet to it and die in comfort?"

"There will be no fire. And I do not wish to talk. What we do is important. I would think. This is the last thing we will do."

"I wish we had died in war, Baas."

"Well, we did not, and it is no use complaining all the time. We have had a fine life together."

"Ja, it was fine, we have killed many men. That is what I am saying to the Baas. I would kill some more and die with reddened spears."

"Silence, dog. I am tired of your whining. I am getting ready."

But Reuter was right. Perhaps they had waited too long. And what had he made of his life? Nothing at all. A great waste of time and effort. He should have stayed in the North and founded a Kaffir kingdom. He should have married a black queen as Coenraad had. But that certainly would have been something to explain to Helena.

Actually there was only Helena. How clear that was now in the bright light of coming death! A man might marry ten wives, but he had only one—his first. He might love her as he had Helena. He might grow to hate her as he had seen happen with other men. There were even men who had killed their wives. But they did this only when they hated them, from frustration, from the loss they had suffered at their hands. They killed them in anger for what they had taken from them, for their shattered and irreplaceable dreams. A man could marry a shrew, a slut, a harlot. He could be warned against her and call those who warned liars, for though they spoke the truth, to him it was not the truth. He was blind with love and it was this blindness, this betrayal of his life, that he blamed upon the woman if she were bad.

It was blindingly clear now. A man married only once. The others were women lived with, in wedlock or out of it, women in whom he sought his lost love. They were the waters in which he sought at once to drown his sorrow and find the fountain of the youth that he had lost. Now that the end was coming there was only Helena: only Helena. He had loved the others with a great tenderness. He would be glad to see them again, but they were not Helena. There was no woman like her. She was his woman. His marriages, even his fornications, and this was the extraordinary thing, had been his tribute to her, and to what he had lost when she had died. How many sides to every question there were! There was love; there was lust, the crying of unused loins; there was the pride of man in his possession of woman—all facets of a single stone : all part of man : all divided, the one from the other, but still all one.

This was the ultimate beauty. It was this that he saw in Lena, in her love for Dirk and his love for her. It was this that had made him so sad at their wedding. What was in store for them? What joy, what sorrow? What events would control their destiny? In them he saw himself and Helena again : saw all young men and maids; saw all life spread in a tremendous panorama before him : the future a duplication, in its essentials, of the past. To-night Dirk would create life. Lena, A new beginning. To-night he would be with Helena again. To-night he, Philippus Jacobus, would die. That was an end, also, and because of Helena, a new beginning.

It was coming now. Magtig, it was easy to die! He folded his hands on his breast. That is the way they will find me, with my hands folded, my head on my saddle, and my roer beside me. That is the way old Oom Philippus Jacobson du Toit the hunter should die—out on the veld. There will be talk and scandal of it for years. They will say she should have watched so old a man . . . they will say . . . Were those wings he heard? Was it a night bird . . . a heron flying? Were they angels' wings? It was the angels coming for him. He could see Helena, she was smiling at him; Gertrude, Elizabeth, and Wilhelmina were with her. They were all smiling. What a relief! He had been afraid of trouble. Van Ek was smiling, and Coenraad with his black queen beside him. Before God, it was easy, and Heaven would be good if all things arranged themselves with such facility. But it was strange that Coenraad's wife should have black wings to match her body—they were black and shone like oiled gun barrels.

It was Helena . . . It was his darling, and the music was loud . . . a jig. No one had told him they danced in Heaven . . . soon he would be dancing with his darling. And it was Gertruida who had been fair. Elizabeth was the dark one.

Once before, when he had fallen from his horse, in his charge against the English, he had thought himself dying; but that had been an error and this was not. This was death. He heard the rustle of Death's wings . . . Death's cool breath upon his face. In a minute now . . . in a minute . . . it was coming . . .

He flung up his arms. He sat up.

"Helena . . . Helena, my heart, I am come."

3

Reuter arranged his master's head on the saddle. His mouth he could not close. It would not stay shut. He pulled in his hands and folded them upon his chest. He spread his own karos over his legs and laid the elephant gun beside him ready to his dead hands. The Baas was dead. The Old Baas was gone. He raised his spears and shield in salutation. "A warrior is dead," he said. "A great warrior has passed from among us."

Then he smoothed his kilt, took off his head-dress, and put it on again in case it was disarranged. Picking up his spears and shield he went towards the dance-shed.

At the door he halted. Standing in the middle of it, the light shone upon him : a Zulu warrior armed for war. A woman screamed, others followed her example, some Boers ran for their guns. "The Zulus are here!" they shouted. The music stopped. Only Boetie, his new young Baas, who could see nothing, went on playing. Then they recognized him.

"It's Reuter," someone said. "What are you doing to give us a skrik like this? It is a joke. It is Reuter."

Then seeing his face they knew it was no jest, and a silence came upon them. Boetie had put down his fife. Lena, the young meisie, was running to him.

"What is it, Reuter?" she said. "What has happened?"

This was his moment. He raised his spear.

"You say it is Reuter," he said, "and I say it is not Reuter. It is he who was once called Reuter, but who is again named Tabankulu—the great mountain—who was once, in the time of T'Chaka, Captain of the Blue Horizon till he went with Moselekatse to found a nation—till, wounded in battle, a great chief picked him and saved him from death." He paused. "That chief, O people, is dead. My master lies dead beneath the trees upon the veld. Listen," he said. Again he raised his spears. "His hounds have found him."

It was true. They were howling.

When Reuter turned, all followed him. Lena and Dirk were the first to reach the body. Philippus Jacobus lay beneath the blue gums, on the bank; his face was dappled with the moonlight that came through the branches above him. Wolf lay beside him, but Bismarck sat by his shoulders, his nose pointed to the moon as he howled.

When two men bent to pick the old man up, he sprang at them growling. Lena had to hold him.

This was what it had been then. This was what he had had upon his mind. He had known he was about to die. This was why he had wished to look upon her.

They all went to the house, following those who bore him. Women were crying. Lena was crying, though she felt no great sorrow. It was right that he should die like this, a death of his choosing, under the stars. But it was sad. Oupa dying on the veld alone with his Zulu, first mourned by the hounds that he had bred.

4

It was over. Oupa's death had ended it. They were going home now, back to Doornkloof. The horses were ready.

" Come," Dirk said.

Hundreds of people seemed to surround her, all kissed her; strange, heavily bearded men that she had never seen before took her in their arms. Tanta Martha engulfed her.

" Do not grieve for Oupa," she said. " He lived to see you married. It was enough."

Ouma kissed her. Her brothers held her against their chests. She was going. Oupa was dead. Reuter in his war plumes and spears was crying out to her. And Boetie was playing his fife; he played, " Kiss me, darling, Kiss your darling daughter." She had taught it to him.

Lena never knew how it began. One minute she was in Dirk's arms, the next she had her legs across Starreijie's saddle. There was a shout, a volley of rifle shots, as Joubert's men sprang into the saddle, and they were off—galloping across the veld to Doornkloof. A thunder of hoofs, of tossing manes and waving tails, of rifle shots, of drunken burgers falling from their horses amid shouts of laughter. All in the warm moonlight; all with the knowledge of Dirk galloping beside her on Swartkie. A hundred men, two hundred or more, she would never know—as far as you could see on either side there were men riding, and from behind came the thunder of hoofs. Dirk van der Berg was married, and Joubert's commando was seeing to the style of his consummation, accompanying him and his bride to their home. Galloping beside him, shouting and shooting off their rifles into the air, though the shots of the most drunken came lower than they should.

And she was in her best dress. It was rumpled, raised up over her thighs, and her pretty new shoes were driven hard into the irons. But she did not care. I do not care at all, she thought, as her loosened hair blew out behind her. How Oupa would have loved this ride in the night! . . .

At last they were there. Tanta Johanna was waiting. Klein Johanna was beside her, jumping up and down. The burgers were all round them, their horses steaming in the cool of the night. As she went in with Dirk, she heard them say that they were camping about the house and would want coffee in the morning. Someone said: " What about our wives?" And a voice answered: " What can happen to our wives? Who can seduce them since we are all here?" This seemed unanswerable—at least there was no answer.

Tanta Johanna took them into the bridal chamber. It was Dirk's own room: the bed the one Lena had seen that day when she had driven over. Boetie was staying at Mooiplaas, in her room.

Boetie in her room; Oupa dead beneath the blue gums where Dirk had first taken her; and Tanta Martha going to marry Meneer Tryolla . . .

The door closed. Dirk took her into his arms. Outside the Boers still shouted on in ribald humour.

" We are staying, Dirk, to see that you do your duty . . . See that it is a burger, another boy . . . another van der Berg to ride with our sons to war."

Their fires were twinkling all round the house.

Joubert's commando had come to do them honour. It was peace; the war was over. The old life done, and the new begun.

THE END

GLOSSARY

Aardvark: anteater; earth pig
Aasvoel: vulture
Afrikaner: African
Agter ryder: mounted servant
Alle wereld: exclamation; all the world
Alles sal reg kom: everything will come right

Bastaard: Griquas
Baviaan's ooren: name of a root shaped like a baboon's ears
Bobbejaan: baboon
Bobotee: a dish of meat with curry and rice
Boet: brother
Boetie: little brother
Brak: salty; alkaline
Brei: to tan or cure leather
Breyed: hand-dressed
Bronkors: watercress
Bult: outcrop of rock
Bushveld: wild, thorn-covered country

Dagher: clay mortar
Dassie: rock rabbit
Disselboom: pole of cart or wagon
Dom: foolish
Dorp: village
Drift: ford
Duiwel: devil

Earth Apples: potatoes

Foei: exclamation; fie
French: imported French brandy, superior to local make

Geluk: good luck
Genesblaren: a healing leaf
Gogga: insect
Groot: big

Heidelberg: town
Hok: pen; small enclosure

443

Isandwhlana: a battle where the British were defeated by the Zulus

Jong: boy, young man

Kaalblad: cactus
Kappie: sunbonnet
Karree boom: variety of tree that generally grows near water
Karos: rug of sewn skins
Kerels: fellows
Klein: small
Kleinkie: little one
Klompie: bunch or group
Kloof: deep valley or cleft
Konfyt: preserve
Kop: hill; head
Koppie: small hill
Korhaan: a variety of bustard
Krans: cliff
Kweekgras: couch grass

Lappie: a rag, cloth
Loop: go
Lydenburg: district in the Transvaal

Maak los: let go
Magalaqueen: tributary of the Crocodile River
Magtig: abbreviation of Allemagtig: Almighty
Mebos: apricots preserved with sugar and salt
Meisie: young lady
Mis: manure
Mooiplaas: pretty, nice place
Morgen: measure of land, about two acres
Moselekatse: Zulu chief
Mossbolletjie: a roll or bun made with grapejuice flavoured with anise seed

Nagmaal: communion
Nee: no

Oom: uncle
Opsıt: courting custom
Opslag: second growth; aftermath
Ouma: grandmother
Oupa: grandfather
Outspan: unharness; or place where unharnessing takes place; market
place; square in every town

Pan: small lake that may be empty
Pap: soft food, mealie meal
Peetante: godmother
Peetkind: godchild
Poort: pass in the mountains
Predikant: preacher

Randjie: small ridge
Riem: rawhide thong
Rinkals: ringnek; cobra
Roer: muzzle-loading gun
Rooibaadjies: redcoats, British soldiers
Rooibekkie: small finches with red beaks
Rooineks: red necks; English whose necks burn red instead of tanning

Sarie Mare: old Boer love song
Sassaties: small pieces of spiced meat cooked on a skewer over a clear fire
Seacow: hippopotamus
Secocoeni: Kaffir chief
Sitkamer: sitting-room
Sjambok: whip cut from thick rawhide
Skelm: rascal
Skimmel: roan
Skrik: fright
Slim: cunning, clever; not derogatory
Sluit: ditch; washout
Sopie: mouthful
Spoor: footprints or tracks
Springhaas: spring hare
Spruit: stream
Stad: village, town, or collection of native huts
Steenbok: small antelope
Swart: black

Taal: Dutch dialect, now obsolete
Tarentaal: guinea fowl
Tiger: leopard
Tot siens: Till I see you; good-bye
Trek gear: ox yokes, harness, chains, etc.
Trek-tous: traces of twisted rawhide used to fasten the ox-yokes to each other
Trichardt: Louis Trichardt, famous voortrekker, pioneer
Tripple: pace, move both near and both off legs alternately

Uitlander: stranger, outlander

Vangstok: catching stick
Veld kost: food used on the veld
Velskoen: hand-made field shoes
Verdomde: damned
Verneuk: deceive, fool
Vierkleur: four-colour, Transvaal flag
Vlei: marsh
Volksraad: legislative assembly
Voorloper: boy who leads oxen
Voortrekker: pioneer; one who went in front
Vragtag: truly
Vrot: rotten
Vrou: married woman, mevrou

Winkel: store, shop
Witbooi: white boy, favourite name for a dog or horse

Zoutpansberg: salt pan mountains; district in the Transvaal

PORTWAY & NEW PORTWAY

NON-FICTION

Anderson, Verily	Beware of children
Anderson, Verily	Daughters of divinity
Armstrong, Martin	Lady Hester Stanhope
Arnothy, Christine	It's not so easy to live
Asquith, Margot	The autobiography of Margot Asquith
Barke, James	The green hills far away
Bentley, Phyllis	The Pennine weaver
Bishop, W.A.	Winged warfare
Blain, William	Home is the sailor
Brittain, Vera	Testament of experience
Brittain, Vera	Testament of friendship
Brittain, Vera	Testament of youth
Buchan, John	The clearing house
Cobbett, William	Cottage economy
Crozier, F.P.	Ireland for ever
Day, J. Wentworth	Ghosts and witches
Dunnett, Alastair M.	It's too late in the year
Edmonds, Charles	A subaltern's war
Evans, A.J.	The escaping club
Falk, Bernard	Old Q's daughter
Fields, Gracie	Sing as we go
Firbank, Thomas	A country of memorable honour
Gandy, Ida	A Wiltshire childhood
Gary, Romain	Promise at dawn
Gibbons, Floyd	Red knight of Germany
Gibbs, Philip	Realities of war
Gough, General Sir Hubert	The fifth army
Grant, I.F.	Economic history of Scotland
Hart, B.H. Liddell	Great captains unveiled
Hart, B.H. Liddell	A history of the world war 1914—18
Hart, B.H. Liddell	The letters of private Wheeler
Hart, B.H. Liddell	The other side of the hill
Hecht, Hans	Robert Burns: the man and his work
Holtby, Winifred	Letters to a friend
Huggett, Renee & Berry, Paul	Daughters of Cain
Jones, Ira	King of air fighters
Jones, Jack	Give me back my heart
Jones, Jack	Me and mine

Jones, Jack	Unfinished journey
Kennedy, John F.	Why England slept
Kennedy Shaw, W.B.	Long range desert group
Keyes, Frances Parkinson	St. Teresa of Lisieux
Keyhoe, Donald	The flying saucers are real
Lawrence, W.J.	No. 5 bomber group
Lethbridge, Mabel	Against the tide
Lethbridge, Mabel	Fortune grass
Masefield, John	The battle of the Somme
Neumann, Major Georg Paul	The German air-force in the great war
O'Mara, P.	The autobiography of a Liverpool Irish slummy
Pound, Reginald	Arnold Bennett
Price, Harry	The end of Borley rectory
Price, Harry	The most haunted house in England
Raymond, Ernest	In the steps of the Brontës
Raymond, Ernest	In the steps of St. Francis
Stoker, Bram	Famous imposters
Tangye, Derek	Time was mine
Tanner, J.R.	Tudor consitutional documents (1485–1603)
Vigilant	Richthofen – red knight of the air
Von Richthofen	The red air fighter
Whipple, Dorothy	The other day

PORTWAY & NEW PORTWAY

FICTION

Albert, Edward	Herrin' Jennie
Aldington, Richard	All men are enemies
Aldington, Richard	Death of a hero
Anand, Mulk Raj	Seven summers
Andersch, Alfred	Flight to afar
Anderson, Verily	Our square
Anderson, Verily	Spam tomorrow
Anthony, Evelyn	Imperial highness
Anthony, Evelyn	Victoria
Arlen, Michael	Men dislike women
Arnim, Elizabeth von	Elizabeth and her German garden
Arnim, Elizabeth von	Mr. Skeffington
Ashton, Helen	Doctor Serocold
Ashton, Helen	Family cruise
Ashton, Helen	Footman in powder
Ashton, Helen	The half-crown house
Ashton, Helen	Letty Landon
Ashton, Helen	Swan of Usk
Barke, James	Bonnie Jean
Barke, James	The land of the leal
Barke, James	Major operation
Barke, James	The song of the green thorn tree
Barke, James	The well of the silent harp
Basso, Hamilton	Pompey's head
Bates, H.E.	The purple plain
Baum, Vicki	Berlin hotel
Benson, R.H.	Come rack come rope
Benson, R.H.	Lord of the world
Bentley, Phyllis	Love and money
Bentley, Phyllis	A modern tragedy
Bentley, Phyllis	The partnership
Bentley, Phyllis	Sleep in peace
Bentley, Phyllis	Take courage
Bentley, Phyllis	Trio
Birmingham, George A.	General John Regan
Birmingham, George A.	The inviolable sanctuary
Blackmore, R.D.	Mary Anerley
Blain, William	Witch's blood

Blaker, Richard	The needle watcher
Bottome, Phyllis	Murder in the bud
Bromfield, Louis	Early autumn
Bromfield, Louis	A good woman
Bromfield, Louis	The green bay tree
Bromfield, Louis	The rains came
Bromfield, Louis	Wild is the river
Brophy, John	Gentleman of Stratford
Brophy, John	Rocky road
Brophy, John	Waterfront
Broster, D.K.	Child royal
Broster, D.K.	A fire of driftwood
Broster, D.K.	Sea without a haven
Broster, D.K.	Ships in the bay
Broster, D.K. & Taylor, G.W.	Chantemerle
Broster, D.K. & Forester, G.	World under snow
Buchan, John	Grey weather
Buchan, John	The Runagates club
Buck, Pearl S. *(Trans.)*	All men are brothers (2 vols.)
Buck, Pearl S.	Fighting angel
Buck, Pearl S.	The hidden flower
Buck, Pearl S.	A house divided
Buck, Pearl S.	Imperial woman
Caldwell, Erskine	Place called Estherville
Caldwell, Taylor	The arm and the darkness
Caldwell, Taylor	The beautiful is vanished
Caldwell, Taylor	The final hour
Caldwell, Taylor	Let love come last
Caldwell, Taylor	Melissa
Caldwell, Taylor	Tender victory
Callow, Philip	Common people
Chandos, Dane	Abbie
Chapman, Hester W.	To be a king
Church, Richard	The dangerous years
Collins, Wilkie	Armadale
Collins, Wilkie	The dead secret
Collins, Wilkie	The haunted hotel
Collins, Wilkie	Poor miss Finch
Common, Jack	Kiddar's luck
Comyns, Barbara	Our spoons came from Woolworths
Cookson, Catherine	Maggie Rowan
Cookson, Catherine	Mary Ann's angels

O'Brien, Kate	The flower of May
O'Brien, Kate	The land of spices
O'Brien, Kate	Mary Lavelle
O'Brien, Kate	Pray for the wanderer
O'Brien, Kate	Without my cloak
O'Flaherty, Liam	The assassin
Oliver, Jane	Crown for a prisoner
Oliver, Jane	Isle of glory
Oliver, Jane	The lion and the rose
Oliver, Jane	Queen of tears
Oliver, Jane	Sing morning star
Oliver, Jane	Sunset at noon
Onstott, Kyle	Drum
Onstott, Kyle	Mandingo
Ouida	Moths
Page, Gertrude	Paddy-the-next-best-thing
Pain, Barry	The exiles of Faloo
Pargeter, Edith	The assize of the dying
Pargeter, Edith	The city lies four-square
Pargeter, Edith	The eighth champion of Christendom
Pargeter, Edith	Holiday with violence
Pargeter, Edith	A means of grace
Pargeter, Edith	Most loving mere folly
Pargeter, Edith	Ordinary people
Pargeter, Edith	Reluctant odyssey
Pargeter, Edith	The scarlet seed
Pargeter, Edith	The soldier at the door
Park, Ruth	The harp in the south
Prior, James	Forest folk
Porter, Jeanette Stratton	Freckles comes home
Proctor, Maurice	No proud chivalry
Prouty, Olive Higgins	Now voyager
Pym, Barbara	Jane and Prudence
Pym, Barbara	Less than angels
Raymond, Ernest	Child of Norman's End
Raymond, Ernest	Daphne Bruno
Raymond, Ernest	The five sons of le Faber
Raymond, Ernest	The fulfilment of Daphne Bruno
Raymond, Ernest	For them that trespass
Raymond, Ernest	A song of the tide
Renault, Mary	The friendly young ladies
Riley, William	Jerry and Ben

Riley, William	Laycock of Lonedale
Roberts, Kenneth	Arundel
Roberts, Kenneth	Oliver Wiswell
Roche, Mazo de la	Delight
Roche, Mazo de la	Growth of a man
Roche, Mazo de la	The two saplings
Sandstrom, Flora	The midwife of Pont Clery
Sandstrom, Flora	The virtuous women of Pont Clery
Seton, Anya	The mistletoe and sword
Seymour, Beatrice K.	Maids and mistresses
Shellabarger, Samuel	Captain from Castile
Sherriff, R.C.	The Hopkins manuscript
Shiel, M.P.	Prince Zaleski
Sienkiewicz, Henryk	The deluge (2 vols.)
Sienkiewicz, Henryk	With fire and sword
Sinclair, Upton	Boston
Sinclair, Upton	The flivver king
Sinclair, Upton	The jungle
Sinclair, Upton	Oil!
Sinclair, Upton	They call me carpenter

WORLD'S END SERIES

Sinclair, Upton	World's end
Sinclair, Upton	Between two worlds
Sinclair, Upton	Dragon's teeth
Sinclair, Upton	Wide is the gate
Sinclair, Upton	Presidential agent
Sinclair, Upton	Dragon harvest
Sinclair, Upton	A world to win
Sinclair, Upton	Presidential mission
Sinclair, Upton	One clear call
Sinclair, Upton	O shepherds speak
Sinclair, Upton	The return of Lanny Budd
Smith, Betty	A tree grows in Brooklyn
Smith, Eleanor	Caravan
Smith, Sheila Kaye-	The children's summer
Stone, Irving	Love is eternal
Stone, Irving	Lust for life
Sue, Eugene	The wandering Jew (2 vols.)

PORTWAY JUNIOR

Armstrong, Martin	Said the cat to the dog
Armstrong, Martin	Said the dog to the cat
Atkinson, M.E.	August adventure
Atkinson, M.E.	Going gangster
Atkinson, M.E.	The compass points north
Aymé, Marcel	The wonderful farm
Bacon, Peggy	The good American witch
Baker, Margaret J.	A castle and sixpence
Blackwood, Algernon	Dudley and Gilderoy
Coatsworth, Elizabeth	Cricket and the emperor's son
Edwards, Monica	Killer dog
Edwards, Monica	Operation seabird
Fenner, Phyllis R.	Fun, fun, fun
Haldane, J.B.S.	My friend mr. Leakey
Hill, Lorna	A dream of Sadler's Wells
Hoke, Helen	Jokes, jokes, jokes
Hoke, Helen	Love, love, love
Hoke, Helen	More jokes, jokes, jokes
Hoke, Helen & Randolph, Boris	Puns, puns, puns
Hourihane, Ursula	Christina and the apple woman
Lemming, Joseph	Riddles, riddles, riddles
Lyon, Elinor	Run away home
Parker, Richard	The sword of Ganelon
Pudney, John	Friday adventure
Pullein-Thompson, Christine	Ride by night
Pullein-Thompson, Diana	The secret dog
Pullein-Thompson, Josephine	Janet must ride
Pullein-Thompson, Josephine	One day event
Pullein-Thompson, Josephine	Show jumping secret
Manning-Sanders, Ruth	Children by the sea
Manning-Sanders, Ruth	Elephant
Saville, Malcolm	All summer through
Saville, Malcolm	Christmas at Nettleford
Severn, David	Burglars and bandicoots
Severn, David	Dream gold
Severn, David	The future took us
Sperry, Armstrong	Frozen fire
Sperry, Armstrong	Hull-down for action
Sperry, Armstrong	Thunder country
Stucley, Elizabeth	Springfield home

PORTWAY EDUCATIONAL & ACADEMIC

Abbott, W.C.	Colonel Thomas Blood
Abrams, Mark	The condition of the British people 1911—45
Adams, Francis	History of the elementary school contest in England
Andrews, Kevin	The flight of Ikaros
Balzac, Honoré de	The curé de Tours
Bazeley, E.T.	Homer Lane and the little common-wealth
Bowen, H.C.	Froebel and education by self-activity
Braithwaite, William J.	Lloyd George's ambulance wagon
Brittain, Vera & Taylor, G. Handley	Selected letters of Winifred Holtby and Vera Brittain
Cameron, A.	Chemistry in relation to fire risk and extinction
Clarke, Fred	Education and the social change
Clarke, Fred	Freedom in the educative society
Caldwell-Cook, H.	Play way (1 map, 14 illustrations)
Crozier, F.P.	A brass hat in no man's land
Crozier, F.P.	Angels on horseback
Crozier, F.P.	The men I killed
Dewey, John	Educational essays
Dewey, John	Interest and effort in education
Duncan, John	The education of the ordinary child
Fearnsides, W.G. & Bulman, O.M.B.	Geology in the service of man
Ferrier, Susan	Destiny (2 vols.)
Galt, John	The provost
Gates, H.L.	The auction of souls
Gilbert, Edmund W.	Brighton old ocean's bauble
Glass, David V.	The town — and a changing civilization
Gronlund, Norman E.	Sociometry in the classroom
Geological survey	The geology of Manchester and the south-east Lancashire coalfield (H.M.S.O.)
Hadow report 1933	Report of the consultative committee on infant and nursery schools (H.M.S.O.)
Harrison, G.B.	The life & death of Robert Devereux Earl of Essex

Smith, Norman Kemp	A commentary to Kant's "critique of pure reason"
Smith, P.W., L. Broke	The history of early British military aeronautics
Smollett, Tobias	The adventures of Sir Launcelot Greaves
Stocks, Mary	The workers' educational association—the first fifty years
Strutt, Joseph	Sports and pastimes of the people of England
University of London Institute of Educ.	The bearing of recent advances in psychology on educational problems
Wall, W.D.	Child of our times
Watson, Francis	The life and times of Catherine de Medici
Watson, Francis	Wallenstein — soldier under Saturn
Wells, H.G.	Crux ansata
Yoxall, Ailsa	A history of the teaching of domestic economy